GALILEO'S DREAM

Kim Stanley Robinson was born in 1952 and, after travelling and working around the world, has now settled in his beloved California. He is widely regarded as the finest science fiction writer working today, noted as much for the verisimilitude of his characters as the meticulously researched hard science basis of his work. He has won just about every major sf award there is to win and is the author of the massively successful and lavishly praised *Mars* series.

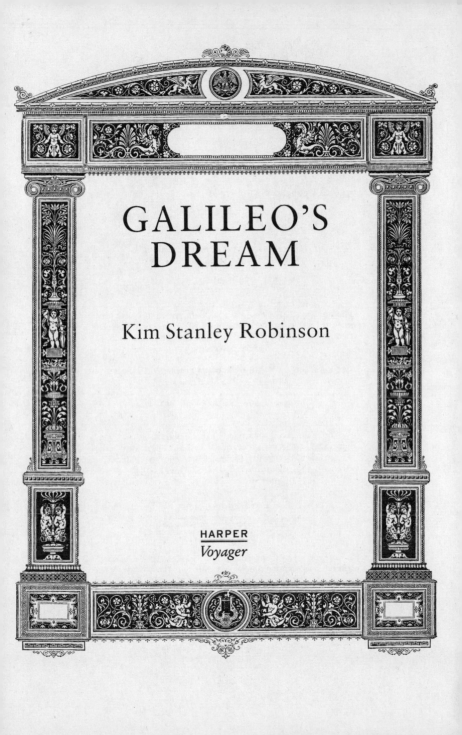

GALILEO'S DREAM

Kim Stanley Robinson

HARPER
Voyager

Harper*Voyager*
An imprint of HarperCollins*Publishers*
77–85 Fulham Palace Road,
Hammersmith, London W6 8JB

www.harpercollins.co.uk

This paperback edition 2010
1

First published in Great Britain by
Harper*Voyager* 2009

A catalogue record for this book is
available from the British Library

ISBN: 978-0-00-726032-4

Set in Sabon by Palimpsest Book Production Limited,
Grangemouth, Stirlingshire

Printed and bound in Great Britain

Mixed Sources
Product group from well-managed
forests and other controlled sources
www.fsc.org Cert no. SW-COC-001806
FSC © 1996 Forest Stewardship Council

FSC is a non-profit international organisation established
to promote the responsible management of the world's forests.
Products carrying the FSC label are independently certified
to assure consumers that they come from forests that are managed
to meet the social, economic and ecological needs
of present and future generations.

Find out more about HarperCollins and the environment at
www.harpercollins.co.uk/green

The Muses love alternatives.
—VIRGIL, *Eclogues, Book III*

Chapter One   The Stranger

All of a sudden Galileo felt that this moment had happened before – that he had been standing in the artisans' Friday market outside Venice's Arsenale and felt someone's gaze on him, and looked up to see a man staring at him, a tall stranger with a beaky narrow face. As before (but what before?) the stranger acknowledged Galileo's gaze with a lift of the chin, then walked toward him through the market, threading through the crowded blankets and tables and stalls spread all over the Campiello del Malvasia. The sense of repetition was strong enough to make Galileo a little dizzy, although a part of his mind was also detached enough to wonder how it might be that you could sense someone's gaze resting on you.

The stranger came up to Galileo, stopped and bowed stiffly, held out his right hand. Galileo bowed in return, took the offered hand and squeezed; it was narrow and long, like the man's face.

In guttural Latin, very strangely accented, the stranger croaked, 'Are you Domino Signor Galileo Galilei, professor of mathematics at the University of Padua?'

'I am. Who are you?'

The man let go of his hand. 'I am a colleague of Johannes Kepler. He and I recently examined one of your very useful military compasses.'

'I am glad to hear it,' Galileo said, surprised. 'I have corresponded with Signor Kepler, as he probably told you, but he did

1

not write to me about this. When and where did you meet him?'

'Last year, in Prague.'

Galileo nodded. Kepler's places of residence had shifted through the years in ways Galileo had not tried to keep track of. In fact he had not answered Kepler's last letter, having failed to get through the book that had accompanied it. 'And where are you from?'

'Northern Europe.'

Alta Europa. The man's Latin was really strange, unlike other transalpine versions Galileo had heard. He examined the man more closely, noted his extreme height and thinness, his stoop, his intent close-set eyes. He would have had a heavy beard, but he was very finely shaved. His expensive dark jacket and cloak were so clean they looked new. The hoarse voice, beaky nose, narrow face, and black hair made the man seem like a crow turned into a man. Again Galileo felt the uncanny sensation that this meeting had happened before. A crow talking to a bear –

'What city, what country?' Galileo persisted.

'Echion Linea. Near Morvran.'

'I don't know those towns.'

'I travel extensively.' The man's gaze was fixed on Galileo as if on his first meal in a week. 'Most recently I was in the Netherlands, and there I saw an instrument that made me think of you, because of your compass, which, as I said, Kepler showed me. This Dutch device was a kind of looking glass.'

'A mirror?'

'No. A glass to look through. Or rather, a tube you look through, with a glass lens at each end. It makes things look bigger.'

'Like a jeweller's lens?'

'Yes.'

'Those only work for things that are close.'

'This one worked for things that were far away.'

'How could that be?'

The man shrugged.

2

This was interesting. 'Perhaps it was because there were two lenses,' Galileo said. 'Were they convex or concave?'

The man almost spoke, hesitated, then shrugged again. His stare went almost cross-eyed. His brown eyes were flecked with green and yellow splashes, like Venice's canals near sunset. Finally he said, 'I don't know.'

Galileo found this unimpressive. 'Do you have one of these tubes with you?'

'Not with me.'

'But you have one?'

'Not of that type. But yes. But not with me.'

'And so you thought to tell me about it.'

'Yes. Because of your compass. We saw that among its other applications, you could use it to calculate certain distances.'

'Of course.' One of the compass's main functions was to range cannon shots. Despite which very few artillery services or officers had ever purchased one. Three hundred and seven of them, to be precise, over a period of twelve years.

The stranger said, 'Such calculations would be easier if you could see things further away.'

'Many things would be easier.'

'Yes. And now it can be done.'

'Interesting,' Galileo said. 'What is your name again, signor?'

The man looked away uneasily. 'I see the artisans are packing to depart. I am keeping you from them, and I must meet a man from Ragusa. We will see each other again.'

With a quick bow he turned and walked along the tall brick side wall of the campiello, hurrying in the direction of the Arsenale, so that Galileo saw him under the emblem of the winged lion of St Mark which stretched in bas relief over the lintel of the great fortress's entryway. For a second it looked as if one bird-beast were flying over another. Then the man turned the corner and disappeared.

*   *   *

3

Galileo turned his attention back to the artisans' market. Some of them were indeed leaving, in the afternoon shadows folding up their blankets and putting their wares into boxes and baskets. During the fifteen or twenty years he had been advising various groups in the Arsenale, he had often dropped by the Friday market to see what might be on display in the way of new tools or devices, machine parts and so on. Now he wandered around through the familiar faces, moving by habit. But he was distracted. It would be a good thing to be able to see distant objects as if they were close by. Several obvious uses sprang to mind immediately. Obvious military advantages, in fact.

He made his way to one of the lensmakers' tables, humming a little tune of his father's that came to him whenever he was on the hunt. There would be better lenses in Murano or Florence; here he found nothing but the usual magnifying glasses. He picked up two, held them in the air before his right eye. St Mark's lion couchant became a flying ivory blur. It was a poorly done bas relief, he saw again with his other eye, very primitive compared to the worn Roman statues under it on either side of the gate.

Galileo put the lenses back on their table and walked down to the Riva San Biagio, where one of the Padua ferries docked. The splendour of the Serenissima gleamed in the last part of the day. On the riva he sat on his usual post, thinking it over. Most of the people there knew to leave him alone when he was in thought; he could get furious if disturbed. People still reminded him of the time he had shoved a bargeman into the canal for interrupting his solitude.

A magnifying glass was convex on both sides. It made things look larger, but only when they were a few fingers from the glass, as Galileo knew very well. His eyes, often painful to him, had in recent years been losing their sharpness for nearby things. He was getting old: a hairy round old man, with failing eyesight. A lens was a help, especially if ground well.

It was easy to imagine a lens grinder in the course of his work holding up two lenses, one in front of the other, to see what would happen. He was surprised he hadn't done it himself. Although, as he had just discovered, it didn't do much. He could not immediately say why. But he could investigate the phenomena in his usual manner. At the very least, for a start, he could look through different kinds of lenses in various combinations, and simply see what he saw.

There was no wind today. The ferry's crew rowed slowly along the Canale della Giudecca and onto the open lagoon, headed for the fondamente at Porta Maghere. The captain's ritual cursing of the oarsmen cut through the cries of the trailing seagulls, sounding like lines from Ruzante: you girls, you rag dolls, my mother rows better than you do – 'Mine definitely does,' Galileo pitched in absently, as he always did. The old bitch still had arms like a stevedore. She had been beating the shit out of Marina until he had intervened, that time the two had fought; and Galileo knew full well that Marina was no slouch when it came to landing a punch. Holding them apart, everyone screaming . . .

From his spot in the ferry's bow he faced the setting sun. There had been many years when he would have spent the night in town, usually at Sagredo's pink palazzo, 'The Ark', with its menagerie of wild creatures and its riotous parties; but now Sagredo was in Aleppo on a diplomatic assignment, and Paolo Sarpi lived in a stone monk's cell, despite his exalted office, and all the rest of Galileo's partners in mischief had moved away or changed their night habits. No, those years were gone. They had been good years, even though he had been broke (as he still was). Work all day in Padua, party all night in Venice. Thus his rides home had usually been on a dawn barge, standing in the bow buzzing with the afterglow of wine and sex, laughter and sleeplessness. On those mornings the sun would pop over the Lido behind them and pour over his shoulders, illuminating the sky and the mirror surface of the lagoon, a space as simple and clear as a good proof: everything washed clean, etched on the eye, glowing with the promise of a day that could bring anything.

Whereas coming home on the day's last barge, as now, was always a return to the home fire of his life's endlessly tangled problems. The more the western sky blazed in his face, the more likely his mood was to plummet. His temperament was volatile, shifting rapidly among the humours, and every histrionic sunset threatened to make it crash like a diving pelican into the lagoon.

On this evening, however, the air was clear, and Venus hung high in a lapis lazuli dusk, gleaming like some kind of emblem. And he was still thinking about the stranger and his strange news. Could it be true? If so, why had no one noticed before?

On the long dock up the estuary he debarked, and walked over to the line of carts starting out on their night journeys. He hopped on the back of one of the regulars that went to Padua, greeting the driver and lying on his back to watch the stars bounce overhead. By the time the cart rolled past Via Vignali, near the centre of Padua, it was the fourth hour of the night, and the stars were obscured by cloud.

With a sigh he opened the gate that led into his garden, a large space inside the L the big old house made. Vegetables, vine trellises, fruit trees: he took a deep breath to absorb the smells of the part of the house he liked best, then steeled himself and slipped into the pandemonium that always existed inside. La Piera had not yet entered his life, and no one before her could ever keep order.

'Maestro!' one of the littlest artisans shrieked as Galileo entered the big kitchen, 'Mazzoleni beat me!'

Galileo smacked him on the head as if driving a tomato stake into the ground. 'You deserved it, I'm sure,' he said.

'Not at all, maestro!' The undeterred boy got back to his feet and launched into his complaint, but did not get far before a gaggle of Galileo's students had surrounded him, begging help with a problem they were to be tested on next day in the fortifications course at the university. Galileo waded through them to the kitchen. We don't understand, they wailed contrapuntally, though it appeared to be a simple problem. 'Unequal weights

6

weigh equally when suspended from unequal distances having inversely the same ratio as the weights,' he intoned, something he had tried to teach them just the previous week. But before he could sit down and decipher their professor Mazzoni's odd notation, Virginia threw herself in his arms to recount in officious detail how her younger sister Livia had misbehaved that day. 'Give me half an hour,' he told the students, picking up Virginia and carrying her to the long table. 'I'm starving for supper, and Virginia is starving for me.'

But they were more afraid of Mazzoni than they were of him, and he ended up reviewing the relevant equations for them, and insisting they work out the solution for themselves, while eating the leftovers from their dinner, all the while bouncing Virginia on his knee. She was light as a bird. He had banned Marina from the house five years before, a relief in many ways, but now it was up to him and the servants to raise the girls and find them a way in the world. Inquiries at the nearby convents, asking for pre-novitiate admissions, had not been well-received. So there were some years yet to go. Two more mouths, lost among all the rest. Among thirty-two mouths, to be exact. It was like a hostel in Boccacio, three storeys of rooms all over-occupied, and every person there dependent on Galileo and his salary of five hundred and twenty florins a year. Of course the nineteen students boarding in house paid a tuition fee plus room and board, but they were so ravenous he almost always fed them at a loss. Worse, they cost time. He had priced his military compasses at five scudi each, with twenty more charged for a two-month instructional period in house on the Via Vagnali, but considering the time it took from him, it had become clear that he made each sale at a loss. Really the compasses had not turned out as he had hoped.

One of the house boys brought him a small stack of letters a courier had brought, which he read as he ate, and tutored, and played with Virginia. First up was another letter from his sponge of a brother, begging money to help support him and his large family in Munich, where he was trying to make a living as a musician. Their father's failure in that same endeavour, and the old dragon's constant excoriation of him for it, had somehow failed to teach his brother Michelangelo the obvious lesson that it couldn't be done, even if you did have a musical genius, which his brother did not. He dropped the letter on the floor without finishing it.

The next one was worse: from his sister's unspeakable husband Galetti, demanding again the remainder of her dowry, which in fact was Michelangelo's share, but Galetti had seen that the only chance for payment was from Galileo, and it was a family obligation. If Galileo did not pay it, Galetti promised to sue Galileo yet again; he hoped Galileo would remember the last time, when Galileo had been forced to stay away from Florence for a year to avoid arrest.

That letter too Galileo dropped on the floor. He focused on a half-eaten chicken, then looked in the pot of soup hanging over the fire, fishing around for the hunk of smoked pork that ballasted it. His poor father had been driven to an early grave by letters just like these, and by his Xantippe ferreting them out and reading them aloud fortissimo. Five children, and nothing left even to his eldest son, except a lute. A very good lute, it was true, one that Galileo treasured and often played, but it was no help when it came to supporting all his younger siblings. And mathematics was like music in this, alas: it would never make enough money. 520 florins a year for teaching the most practical science at the university, while Cremonini was paid a thousand for elaborating Aristotle's every throat-clearing.

But he could not think of that, or his digestion would be ruined. The students were still badgering him. Hostel Galileo rang with voices, crazy as a convent and running at a loss. If he did not invent something a little more lucrative than the military compass, he would never escape his debts.

This caused him to remember the stranger. He put Virginia down and rose to his feet. The students' faces turned up to him like baby birds jammed in a nest.

'Go,' he said with an imperious wave of the hand. 'Leave me.'

Sometimes, when he got really angry, not just exploding like gunpowder but shaking like an earthquake, he would roar in such a way that everyone in the house knew to run. At those times he would stride cursing through the emptied rooms, knocking over furniture and calling for people to stay and be beaten as they deserved. All the servants and most of the students knew him well enough to hear the leading edge of that kind of anger, contained in a particular flat disgusted tone, at which point they would slip away before it came on in full. Now they hesitated, hearing not that tone, but rather the sound of the maestro on the hunt. In that mood there would be nothing to fear.

He took a bottle of wine from the table, polished it off, kicked one of the boys in order to tip the balance of their judgement toward flight. 'Mazzoleni!' he bellowed. 'MAT! ZO! LEN! EEEEEEEEEE!'

Well, no earthquake tonight; this was one of the good sounds of the house, like the cock crowing at dawn. The old artisan, asleep on the bench by the oven, pushed his whiskery face off the wood. 'Maestro?'

Galileo stood over him. 'We have a new problem.'

'Ah.' Mazzoleni shook his head like a dog coming out of a pond, looked around for a wine bottle. 'We do?'

'We do. We need lenses. As many as you can find.'

'Lenses?'

'Someone told me today that if you look through a tube that holds two of them, you can see things at a distance as if they were nearby.'

'How would that work?'

'That's what we have to find out.'

Mazzoleni nodded. With arthritic care he levered himself off the bench. 'There's a box of them in the workshop.'

*   *   *

9

Galileo stood jiggling the box back and forth, watching the lamps' light bounce on the shifting glasses. 'A lens surface is either convex, concave, or flat.'

'If it isn't defective.'

'Yes yes. Two lenses means four surfaces; so there are how many possible combinations?'

'Sounds like twelve, maestro.'

'Yes. But some are obviously not going to work.'

'You're sure?'

'Flat surfaces on all four sides are not going to work.'

'Granted.'

'And convex surfaces on all four sides would be like stacking two magnifying lenses. We already know that doesn't work.'

Mazzoleni drew himself up: 'I concede nothing. Everything should be tried in the usual way.'

'Yes yes.'

This was Mazzoleni's stock phrase for such situations. Galileo nodded absently, putting the box down on the workshop's biggest table. He reached up to dust off the folios lying aslant on the shelf over it; they looked like guards who had died on watch. While Mazzoleni gathered lenses scattered in pigeonholes around the workshop, Galileo lifted down the current working folio, a big volume nearly filled with notes and sketches. He opened it to the first empty pages, ignoring the rest of the volumes above, the hundreds of pages, the twenty years of his life mouldering away, never to be written up and given to the world, the great work as lost as if it were the scribblings of some poor mad alchemist. When he thought of the glorious hours they had spent working with the inclined planes they had built, a pain stuck him like a needle to the heart.

He opened an ink bottle and dipped a quill in it, and began to sketch his thoughts about this device the stranger had described, figuring out as he did how to proceed. This was how he always worked when thinking over problems of motion or balance or the force of percussion; but light was peculiar. He did not sketch any pattern that looked immediately promising. Well, they would simply try every combination, as Mazzoleni had said, and see what they found.

Quickly the ancient artisan knocked together some little wooden frames they could clamp different lenses into. These could then be attached to the ends of a lead tube Mazzoleni found in a box of odds and ends. While he did that Galileo laid out their collection of lenses by type, fingering each, holding up two at a time and peering through them. Some he gave to Mazzoleni to attach to the ends of the tube.

They only had the lamplit workshop to look at, and the area of the garden and arbour illuminated by the house windows; but it was enough to check for possibilities. Galileo looked at the lenses in the box, held them in the air. Inward, outward: the images blurred, went absent, grew diffuse, even made things smaller than what one saw with the eye alone. Although an effect the reverse of what one wanted was always suggestive.

He wrote down their results on the open page of the work book. Two particular convex lenses gave the image upside down. That cried out for a geometrical explanation, and he noted it with a question mark. The inverted image was enlarged, and sharp. He had to admit to himself that he did not understand light, or what it was doing between the lenses in the tube. He had only ventured to give classes on optics twice in seventeen years, and had been unhappy both times.

Then: hold up two lenses, look: and the potted citron at the edge of the garden appeared distinctly larger in the glass closest to his eye. Green leaf lit from the side by lantern light, big and sharp –

'Hey!' Galileo said. 'Try this pair,' he told Mazzoleni. 'Concave near the eye, convex at the far end of the tube.'

Mazzoleni slotted the lenses into the frames and gave the tube to Galileo, who took it and pointed it at the first tree branch in the arbour, illuminated by the lit windows of the house. Only a small part of the branch appeared in the tube, but it was definitely

enlarged: the leaves big and distinct, the bark minutely cor-
rugated. The image was slightly blurred at the bottom, and he
shifted the outside frame to tilt the glass, then rotated it, then
moved it further out on the tube. The image became sharper still.

'By God it works! This is strange!'

He waved at the old man. 'Go to the house and stand in the
doorway, in the lamp light.' He himself walked through the
garden out into the arbour. He trained the tube on Mazzoleni
in the doorway. 'Mother of God.' There in the middle of the
glass swam the old man's wrinkled face, half-bright and half-
shadowed, as close as if Galileo could touch him; and they were
fifty feet apart or more. The image burned into Galileo's mind,
the artisan's familiar gap-toothed grin shimmery and flat, but
big and clear – the very emblem of their many happy days in the
workshop, trying new things.

'My God!' he shouted, deeply surprised. 'It works!'

Mazzoleni hurried out to give it a try. He rotated the frames,
looked through it backwards, tipped the frames, moved them
back and forth on the tube. 'There are blurry patches,' he noted.

'We need better lenses.'

'You could order a batch from Murano.'

'From Florence. The best optical glass is Florentine. Murano
glass is for coloured trinkets.'

'If you say so. I have friends who would contest that.'

'Friends from Murano?'

'Yes.'

Galileo's real laugh was a low *huh huh huh huh huh*. 'We'll
grind our own lenses if we have to. We can buy blanks from
Florence. I wonder what would happen if we had a longer tube.'

'This one is about as long as we've got. I guess we could make
some longer sheets of lead and roll them up, but we would have
to make the moulds.'

'Any kind of tube will do.' Here Galileo was as good as
Mazzoleni or any artisan – good at seeing what mattered,
quick to imagine different ways of getting it. 'It doesn't have to

be lead. We could try a tube of cloth or leather, reinforced to keep it straight. Glue a long tube of leather to slats. Or just use cardboard.'

Mazzoleni frowned, hefting a lens in his hand. It was about the same size as a Venetian florin, say three fingers wide. 'Would it stay straight enough?'

'I think so.'

'Would the inside surface be smooth?'

'Does it need to be?'

'I don't know, does it?'

They stared at each other. Mazzoleni grinned again, his weathered face an entire topography of wrinkles, delta on delta, the white burn mark on his left temple raising that eyebrow in an impish expression. Galileo tousled the man's hair as he would a child's. This work they did together was unlike any other human bond he knew, unlike that with mistress or child, colleague or student, friend or confessor – unlike anyone – because they made new things together, they learned new things. Now once again they were on the hunt.

Galileo said, 'It looks like we'll want to be able to move one lens back and forth.'

'You could fix one glass to the tube, and set the other one in a slightly smaller tube that fitted inside the main one, so you could move that one back and forth but keep it aligned vertically. You could rotate it too, if you wanted.'

'That's good.' Galileo would have come to some such arrangement eventually, but Mazzoleni was especially quick concerning things he could see and touch. 'Can you bang something like that together? By tomorrow morning?'

Mazzoleni cackled. By now it was the middle of the night, the town was quiet. 'Simple stuff, compared to your damned compass.'

'Watch what you say. That thing has paid your salary for years.'

'Yours too!'

Galileo swatted at him. The compass had become a pain, there was no denying it. 'You have the materials you need?'

'No. I think we'll need more lead tubes, and thinner staves than what we've got around, and longer, if you want leather tubes. More cardboard too. And you'll want more lenses.'

'I'll send an order to Florence. Meanwhile let's work with what we've got.'

In the days that followed, every moment was given over to the new project. Galileo neglected his collegial obligations, made his boarding students teach each other, ate his meals in the workshop while he worked: nothing mattered but the project. At times like these it became obvious that the workshop was the centre of the house. The maestro was about as irritable as always, but with his attention elsewhere it got a bit easier for the servants.

While the various efforts of manufacture and assemblage and testing went on, Galileo also took time to write his Venetian friends and allies to set the stage for a presentation of the device. Here was where his career up until this point finally helped him in something. Known mostly as an eccentric if ingenious professor of mathematics, broke and frustrated at forty-five, he had also spent twenty years working and playing with many of the leading intellectuals of Venice, including, crucially, his great friend and mentor Fra Paolo Sarpi. Sarpi was not currently running Venice for the Doge, as he was still recovering from wounds suffered in an assault two years before, but he continued to advise both the Doge and the Senate, especially on technical and philosophical matters. He could not have been better positioned to help Galileo now.

So Galileo wrote to him about what he was working on. What he read in Sarpi's reply startled him, even frightened him. Apparently the stranger from the artisans' market had gone to others as well. And his news of a successful spyglass, Sarpi wrote, was apparently already widespread in northern Europe.

Sarpi himself had heard a rumour of such a thing nine months before, but had not considered it significant enough to tell Galileo about it.

Galileo cursed as he read this. 'Not significant, my God!' It was hard to believe; it was so lame it suggested that his old friend had been mentally damaged by the knives that had been stuck in his head during the assault.

Nothing to be done about that now. People in northern Europe, especially the Flemish and Dutch, were already producing little spyglasses. This Dutch stranger, Sarpi wrote, had contacted the Venetian Senate, offering to sell them such a glass for a thousand florins. Sarpi had advised the Senate against the purchase, certain that Galileo could do as well or better in manufacturing any such object.

'I could if you would have mentioned it to me,' Galileo muttered.

But he hadn't, and now news of the device was in the air. It was a phenomenon Galileo had noticed before; improvements at the artisanal level passed from workshop to workshop without scholars or princes knowing anything about them, and so it often happened that suddenly workshops everywhere could all make a smaller gear, or a stronger steel. This time it was a little spyglass. The claim going around was that they enlarged things by about three times.

Quickly Galileo wrote back to Sarpi, asking him to convene a meeting with the Doge and his senators in order to examine a new and improved spyglass that Galileo was inventing. He also asked him to ask the Doge to refuse to entertain any other such offers during that time. Sarpi replied the next day with a note saying he had done as asked, and the requested meeting was set for 21st August. It was now 5th August. Two weeks to make a better glass.

The action in the workshop intensified. Galileo told his frantic students they were on their own, even Count Alessandro Montalban, who had recently moved in to the house to study for his doctoral exams, and was not pleased at being neglected. But

15

Galileo had tutored many sons of the nobility by now, and brusquely he told the young man to study with the others, to lead them, that it would be good for him. Galileo then moved out into the workshop, where he examined very closely the devices they had made already, trying to figure out how to better them.

Understanding what was going on with the doubled lenses was no easy thing. For Galileo, everything physical came down to matters of geometry, and clearly this bending of the light was a geometrical action; but he lacked any laws of refraction, and could not discover them merely by substituting lenses one after the next. There were tangible variables involved, however, that they could subject to the workshop techniques they had already honed in previous pursuits.

So the workshop's artisans met in the hour after sunrise, some of them servants of the house, others local ancients retired from arsenals, or lads from the neighbourhood; still rubbing the sleep from their eyes, squeezing the bellows to get the fires in the furnaces going, picking up the work they had laid down the night before. They followed Galileo's routines: they measured things twice, wrote everything down. They worked while breaking their fast. Watched the rainstorms out of the open side of the shed, waiting for the light to get better so they could get back to work. The brick furnace was a bulwark just outside the roof, and they could stand near the back of it and stay warm while the rain came down, although as it was summer the afternoon thunderstorms weren't so cold. The large central area of the shop was earthen-floored and held several long tables, one of them under the back wall devoted to all their tools. In the dim rain-light they could clean or sharpen tools, put things in order, pick away at the goose carcass from the night before. When the sun came out they returned to the work.

They made so many alterations in every new spyglass, Galileo was not quite sure what change was having what effect; but it was too interesting to slow down and isolate the variables to make sure of things, except when pursuing a crucial point. The epistemology of the hunt was to follow one thing after another, without much of an overall plan. They found that tubes made of cardboard, sometimes reinforced by slats or covered with leather, worked perfectly well; the interiors did not have to be perfectly smooth, although one saw a clearer image if they were painted black. Most important were the lenses. The one next to the eye they called the eyepiece, the one at the far end, the objective. Both concave and convex lens surfaces, if properly ground, constituted sections of spheres, bulging either in or out. Spheres of differing radii gave different curvatures. The radius of the complete sphere that was implied by a lens, Galileo called its focal length, following the lensmakers' usage. Fairly soon their repeated trials with different lenses revealed that larger magnifications resulted from a long focal length for the convex lens at the far end of the tube, combined with a short focal length for the concave lens of the eyepiece. Grinding the convex lenses was easy enough, although it was important to eliminate small irregularities if possible, as these made for blurred patches. Grinding truly smooth curved depressions into the much smaller concave lenses, however, was harder to do. A small ball set in a rotating steel-milling mechanism that they screwed to one of the work tables served as their grinding tool. To see better they wore spectacles made of lenses ground earlier in the effort.

While this was going on Mazzoleni was also making cardboard tubes that would snug into his main tubes of leather and staves, giving them the ability to adjust the distance between the lenses and thus sharpen the image. The eyepieces were smaller, so they put the drawtube at that end, and fitted it with felt shims.

To find out what degrees of magnification they were getting, Galileo affixed a gridwork to a whitewashed part of the garden wall. This enabled him to measure accurately the difference between the enlarged image of the grid and the image he saw through the other eye at the same time.

*　　*　　*

On the afternoon of the seventeenth of August, Galileo examined their three best performers. All were about the same length, which was just over a braccio, as measured by their in-house yardstick. Studying the notes, Galileo compared all their dimensions, scribbling more notes as he did so.

All at once he laughed out loud. One of his special moments had come again, a flash of sudden insight at the end of a period of investigation, giving him a jolt and a shiver, as if he were a bell and the clapper had just tapped him. He shouted, 'MAT ZO LEN EEEEEEE!'

The old man appeared, more dishevelled and whiskery than ever, red-eyed with lack of sleep. 'Look!' Galileo commanded. 'You take the focal length of the objective – for this one, a hundred minims – and you divide that by the focal length of the eyepiece – in this case eleven minims – and you get a number which *identifies* the power of magnification of the device, thus here about nine times! *It's a ratio!* It's a ratio, it's geometry again –' He seized the old man by the shoulder: 'Not only that, but look! Subtract the eyepiece focal length from the objective focal length, and you get the distance apart that the lenses are when the thing is focused properly! In this case, just short of one braccio. It's a simple piece of subtraction!'

At this realization he grew somewhat glorious, as he often did when he was able to say new things of that sort. He congratulated everyone in the household, called for wine, threw crazia and other small coins at the servants and students who poured out into the courtyard to join the celebration, hugged them one by one while he was giving thanks to God and also indulging his most boastful humour, which was something to witness. He praised his genius for coming through for him again, he danced, he laughed, he grabbed Mazzoleni by the ears and shouted in his face:

'I'm the smartest man in the world!'

'Probably so, maestro.'

'The smartest man in history!'

18

'That's how much trouble we're in, maestro.'

This kind of poke in these moments of glory would only make him laugh and toss Mazzoleni aside, to be able to continue his jig. 'Florins and ducats, crowns and scudi, I'll buy Rachel and I'll buy Trudi!'

No one in the household understood quite why he believed the glass was going to make him rich. The servant girls thought he meant to use it to watch them doing the laundry down at the river, which he did already from what he thought was a discreet distance.

Eventually everyone went back to work. Mazzoleni was left holding the glass, shaking his head at it. 'Why should there be such proportions?' he asked.

'Don't ask why.' Galileo snatched up the glass. 'Why is what our philosophers ask, and that's why they're so full of shit. Because we don't know *why*. Only God knows *why*. If He does.'

'All right, I know. Just ask what, just ask how. Still. You can't help but wonder, can you.' Waving at the new page of Galileo's folio, filled with diagrams and numbers. 'It seems so . . .'

'So *neat*? Yes. Quite a coincidence, for sure. Quite the what-have-you. But it's just more proof of what we already knew. God is a mathematician.'

As a mathematician himself, Galileo found saying this sentence immensely satisfying; often it was enough to bring tears to his eyes. *God is a mathematician.* He would emphasize the thought by taking a hammer to their anvil. And indeed the thought rang him like a bell. He would bring his hands together as if in prayer, and take a deep breath and expel it tremulously. To read God like a book; to solve him like an equation; it was the best sort of prayer. Ever since that time when he was a boy, he would explain, when he had looked up in church and seen a lamp swinging on its chain, and realized by timing it to his pulse that it took the same time to make its sweep back and forth no matter how far it was swinging, he had felt the direct touch of God in all these things. There was a method to His madness, clearly, and that method was mathematics. This was a comfort when the madness seemed all, as when he was sick, or in pain, or struck down by melancholy; or witnessing the effects of the plague; or contemplating the immense realm of human wickedness. Then his only comfort was the world's inherent geom-etries.

The day for his Venetian demonstration approached, and their best tube showed things nine times larger than the eye saw it. Galileo wanted better, and thought he knew how to get it, but time had run out. For now, nine times bigger would have to do.

He had Mazzoleni's crew cover the exterior of the best tube with red leather, embossed with decorative patterns in gold fili-gree. Mazzoleni also adapted a tripod stand that they sold as an accessory to the military compass, so that they would have something to hold the spyglass steady. A joint on top of the tripod was made of a metal ball held captive in a hemispherical cup, with one screw through the cup to tension the ball, which was screwed on top into a brass sleeve wrapping the spyglass. Using the tripod one did not have to hold the glass steady while looking through it, something no one could do for more than a second or two. It vastly improved the view through the glass.

The resulting arrangement was a handsome thing, standing there gleaming in the sunlight, strange but purposeful, immediately intriguing, pleasing to both eye and mind. A month earlier there had been no such thing in the world.

On 21st August, 1609, he ferried in to Venice on the morning barge, the looking glass and its stand in a long leather case slung from a strap over his shoulder. Its shape was suggestive of a pair of swords, and he saw the glances of people looking at it and thought, Yes, I'm going in to cut the Gordian knot. I'm going in to cut the world in two.

Venice stood on the lagoon, its usual grubby midday self. Magnificence at low tide. Galileo got off the ferry at the molo at San Marco, and was greeted there by Fra Paolo. The great friar looked gaunt in his best robes, his face still a wreck, as it always would be; but his crooked smile remained kindly, his look still penetrating.

Galileo kissed his hand. Sarpi patted the case gently: 'So this is your new occhialino?'

'Yes.'

'Very good. Your audience is assembled in the Anticollegio. It's everyone who matters, you'll be happy to know.'

An honour guard assembled in response to Sarpi's nod, and escorted them into the Signoria, up the Golden Staircase into the Anticollegio, which was the anteroom to the Signoria's bigger halls. It was a tall chamber, sumptuously decorated overhead in the usual Venetian style, its octagonal ceiling covered with gilt-framed paintings allegorizing the origin myth of Venice, while the floor underfoot was painted like the pebbled bed of a mountain stream. Galileo had always found it a strange space, in which he had trouble focusing his eyes.

Now it was stuffed with dignitaries. Better yet, as Galileo soon learned, the Doge himself, Leonardo Dona, was waiting in the Sala del Collegio, the larger assembly hall next door that was the most sumptuous room in the Signoria. As he entered the room he saw Dona and the Savi, his six closest advisors, along

21

with the Grand Chancellor and other state officials, all gathered under the long painting of the battle of Lepanto. Sarpi had outdone himself.

Now the great Servite led Galileo to the Doge, and after a cordial greeting Dona led the entire group into the Sala delle Quattro Porte, then to the Sala del Senato, where many more senators stood in their purple around tables loaded with food. Under the intricacy of crowded paintings and gilt trim that covered every wall and ceiling, Galileo pulled the two parts of his device from their case, and screwed the spyglass on top of the tripod. His hands moved without a quiver; twenty years of lecturing to audiences large and small had burned all possibility of stage fright out of him, and it was also true that it was never that difficult to speak to a crowd to which you felt innately superior. So even though all his hundreds of lectures were now only the prelude to this culmination, he was calm and at ease as he described the work done to make the device, indicating its various features as he pointed it at Tintoretto's 'Triumph of Venice' on the ceiling at the far end of the room, fixing the image in the glass so that it revealed the tiny face of an angel enlarged to the point that it stood out even more vividly than Mazzoleni's had on that first night of work.

With a sweep of his hand he invited the Doge to have a look. The Doge looked; pulled away to gaze at Galileo, his eyebrows shot high onto his forehead; looked again. The two big clocks on the long side wall marked ten minutes' passage as he bumped the glass from one view to another. Ten more minutes passed as one purple-robed man after another took a look through the glass. Galileo answered every question they had about how it was made, although failing to bring up the ratios he had discovered, which they did not even know to ask about. He volunteered often that the process being now clear to him, future improvements were certain to follow, and also (trying to hide a growing impatience) that it was not the kind of device that could best be demonstrated in a room, even a room as big and magnificent as the Sala del Senato. Finally the Doge himself echoed this point, and Sarpi was quick to suggest that they take the device to the top of the campanile of San Marco to give it a thorough airing. Dona agreed to this, and suddenly the whole assembly was following him out of the building and across the Piazzetta between the Signoria and the campanile, then inside the great bell tower, winding up the tight iron staircases to the open observation floor under the bells. Here Galileo reassembled the device.

The floor of the viewing chamber stood a hundred braccia above the Piazza. It was a place all of them had been up to many times; from here one could overlook the whole of Venice and the lagoon, and spot the passageway through the Lido at San Niccolo, the only navigable channel into the Adriatic. Also visible to the west was a long stretch of the mainland's marshy shore, and on clear days one could even see the Alps to the north. A better place to display the powers of the new spyglass could not have been found, and to aim it Galileo looked through the device with as much interest as anyone else, or even more; he had not yet had an opportunity like this, and what could be seen through the glass was as new to him as the next man. He told them as much as he worked, and they liked that. They were part of the experiment. He stabilized and sighted the glass very carefully, feeling that a little delay at this moment was not a bad thing, in theatrical terms. As always, the image in the eyepiece shimmered a little, as if it were something conjured in a crystal ball by a magician – not an effect he wanted, but there was nothing he had been able to do about it. Feeling a sharp curiosity, he tried to spot Padua itself; on earlier visits to the campanile he had marked the vague tower of smoke coming from the town, and knew precisely where it lay.

When he got Padua's tower of San Giustina centred in the glass, as clear as if he were on Padua's city wall staring at it, he suppressed any shout, any smile, and merely bowed to the Doge and moved aside, so Dona and then the others could have a look. A little touch of the mage's silent majesty was not inappropriate at this point, he judged.

For the view was in fact astonishing. 'Ho!' the Doge exclaimed when he saw San Giustina. 'Look at that!' After a minute or two he gave over the glass to his people, and after that the rush was on. Exclamations, cries, incredulous laughter: it sounded like Carnivale. Galileo stood proudly by the tube, readjusting it when it was bumped. After everyone had had a first look, he spotted terra ferma towns even more distant than Padua, which itself was twenty-five miles away: Chioggia to the south, Treviso to the west, even Conegliano, nestled in the foothills more than fifty miles away.

Moving to the northern arches, he trained the glass on various parts of the lagoon. These views made it clear that many of the senators were even more amazed to see people brought close than they had been buildings; perhaps their minds had leaped as quickly as Galileo's servants to the uses of such an ability. They gazed at worshippers entering the church of San Giacomo in Murano, or getting into gondolas at the mouth of the Rio de' Verieri, just west of Murano. Once one of them even recognized a woman he knew.

After that round of viewing Galileo lifted the device, helped now by as many hands as could touch the tripod, and the whole assembly shifted together to the easternmost arch on the southern side of the campanile, where the glass could be directed over the Lido and the fuzzy blue Adriatic. For a long time Galileo tapped the tube gently from side to side, searching the horizon. Then happily he spotted the sails of a little fleet of galleys, making their final approach to the Serenissima.

'Look to sea,' he instructed them as he straightened and made room for the Doge. He had to restrain himself to remain serious, to hide his euphoria. 'See how using one's plain sight, one sees nothing out there. But using the glass . . .'

'A fleet!' the Doge exclaimed. He straightened and looked at the crowd, his face red. 'A fleet is approaching, well out from San Niccolo.'

The Sages of the Order crowded to the front of the line to see for themselves. Every Venetian holding in the eastern Mediterranean was subject to attack by Turks and Levantine pirates: individual ships, fleets, coastal towers, even fortress towns as formidable as Ragusa had suffered surprise assaults. Thus the rulers of Venice, all of them with naval experience of one sort or another, were now nodding to each other meaningfully, and circulating into the crowd surrounding Galileo to shake his hand, slap him on the back, ask for future meetings. Fra Micanzio and General del Monte in particular had worked with him at the Arsenale on various engineering projects, and their congratulations were especially hearty. They had first met him twenty years before, when they had brought him in to consider if there were ways the oars of their galleys could be reconfigured to give them more power, and Galileo had immediately sketched out analyses of the oars' movement that considered their fulcrum to be not the oarlocks, but the water surface; and this surprising new perspective on the problem had in fact led to improvements in oarlock placement. So they knew what he was capable of; but this time del Monte was shaking his hand endlessly, and Micanzio was grinning, with eyebrows raised as if to say: Finally one of your tricks will really matter!

And at this moment Galileo could afford to laugh with him. Galileo suggested to him that they time the interval between this observation of the fleet through the glass, and the moment when ordinary lookouts saw the ships with their unaided vision. The Doge overheard this and required that it be done.

After that Galileo had only to stand by the device and accept more congratulations, and point the thing to resight it if someone requested it. He drank their praise and he drank wine from a tall gold cup, feeling expansive and generous, the colourful throng around him with its impressive percentage of purple sparking more memories of Carnivale, memories that gave every festive evening in Venice an aura of splendour and sex. Combined with the height of the campanile, and the beauty of the watery city below them, it felt like they stood on Olympus.

*　　*　　*

On the winding way back down the campanile stairs, Galileo was joined on one dark landing by the stranger, who then clomped down the iron stairs beside him. Galileo's heart leaped in his chest like an animal trying to escape: the man was dressed in black, and must have lurked in waiting for Galileo, like a thief or an assassin.

'Congratulations on this success,' the man said in his hoarse Latin.

'What brings you here?' Galileo asked.

'It seems you listened to what I told you before.'

'Yes, I did.'

'I was sure you would be interested. You of all people. Now I will return to northern Europe.' Again: *Alta Europa*. 'When I come back to your country, I will bring a spyglass of my own, which I will invite you to look through. Indeed I invite you now.' Then, when Galileo did not reply (they were nearing the bottom of the stairs and the door to the Piazzetta), he said, 'I invited you.'

'It would be my pleasure,' Galileo said.

The man touched the case Galileo carried from his shoulder. 'Have you used it to look at the moon?'

'No – not yet.'

The man shook his head. As his face was a blade, his nose was its sharpened edge, long and curved, tilted off to the right. His big eyes gleamed in the stairwell's dim light. 'When you achieve a power of magnification of twenty or thirty times, you will find it really interesting. After that I will visit you again.'

Then they reached the ground floor of the campanile, and walked together out onto the Piazzetta, where they were interrupted by the Doge himself, there waiting to escort Galileo back to the Signoria: 'Really my dear Signor Galileo, you must do us the honour of returning with us to the Sala del Senato to celebrate the incredible success of your extraordinary demonstration. We have arranged a small meal, some wine –'

'Of course, Your Beneficent Serenity,' Galileo said. 'I am yours to command, as you know.'

In the midst of this exchange the stranger had slipped away and disappeared.

Unsettled, distracted by the memory of the stranger's narrow face, his black clothing, his odd words, Galileo ate and drank with as much cheer as he could muster. A chance meeting with a colleague of Kepler's was one thing, a second encounter deliberately made, something else – he wasn't sure what.

Well, there was nothing to be done now but to eat, to drink more wine, and to enjoy the very genuine and fulsome accolades of Venice's rulers. Two full hours of the celebration of his accomplishment were marked by the giant clocks on the sala's walls before the lookouts on the campanile sent word down that they had spotted a fleet approaching San Niccolo. The room erupted in a spontaneous cheer. Galileo turned to the Doge and bowed, then bowed again to all of them: left, right, centre, then again to the Doge. Finally he had invented something that would make money.

Chapter Two *I Primi Al Mondo*

Having come to this pass, I appealed out of my innocent soul to
the high and omnipotent gods and my own good genius,
beseeching them of their eternal goodness to take notice of my
wretched state. And behold! I began to descry a faint light.
　 － FRANCESCO COLONNA, *Hypnerotomachia Poliphili*
　　　　　　　 The Strife of Love in a Dream of Poliphili

The next night, back in Padua, Galileo went out into his garden
and aimed his best occhialino at the moon. He left Mazzoleni
sleeping by the kitchen fire, woke none of the servants; the house
was asleep. This was his hour, as on so many nights when his
insomnia took hold of him.

Now his mind was filled with the stranger's blade of a face, his
intense gaze: have you looked at the moon? The moon tonight was
near its first quarter, the bright part almost exactly half the whole,
the dark part easily visible against the night sky. An obvious
sphere. Galileo sat on a low stool, held his breath, brought his
right eye to the eyepiece. The little black circle of glass was marked
on its left side by a luminous white patch. He focused on it.

At first he saw nothing but a chiaroscuro flecking of greyish
black and brilliant white, the tremble of the white seeming to
flow over the dark spots. Ah: hills. A landscape. A world seen
from above.

A view from world to world.

He loosened the screw on the tripod head and tapped the tube, trying to capture in the glass the tip of the moon's upper crescent. He tightened the screw, looked again. Brilliant white horn: a dark grey in the curve of the horn, a blackness just slightly washed with white. Again he saw an arc of hills. There, at the border of light and dark, was a flat dark patch, like a lake in shadow. The sunlight was obviously shining horizontally over the landscape, as it would be of course, as he was looking at the area experiencing dawn. He was looking at a sunrise on the moon, twenty-eight times slower than a sunrise on Earth.

There was a little round valley; there another one. Any number of circles and arcs, in fact, as if God had been fooling around up there with a compass. But the strongest impression remained the range of hills, there on the border of black and white.

The moon was a world, the Earth was a world. Well, of course. He had always known this.

As for the assertions the Aristotelians made about the moon, that because it was in the heavens it was therefore a perfect sphere, made of some unearthly crystal that was of unchanging purity – well, its ordinary appearance had always rendered that a very suspicious statement. Now it was clearer than ever that Aristotle had been wrong. This was no great surprise – when indeed had he been right, in the natural sciences? He should have stuck to his strength, which was rhetoric. He had had no mathematics.

Galileo got up and went in to the workshop to get his current folio, and a quill and inkpot. He wondered if he should wake Mazzoleni, then decided against it. There would be other nights. This one was his. He could feel his blood pounding in his head; his neck muscles were sore. It was his night. No one had ever seen these things. Well, perhaps the stranger had. But Galileo suppressed that thought in order to glory in his own moment. All the years, all the centuries and their millions come and gone, the stars rotating above them night after night, and only now had someone seen the hills of the moon.

The moon must rotate on its axis at the same speed it circled the Earth, to keep the same side always facing it; this was odd, but no odder than many other phenomena, such as the fact that the moon and the sun were the same size in the sky. These things were either caused, or accidental; it was hard to tell. But it was a rotating sphere, that was clear. And so was the Earth also a rotating sphere? Galileo wondered if Copernicus's advocacy of this old Pythagorean notion could be right.

He looked through the glass again, relocated the white hills. The dark part west of them was extremely interesting. Land in shadow, obviously. Perhaps there were lakes and seas too, though he could see no sign one way or the other. But it was not as black as a cave or a dark room at night. One could make out dim large features, because the area was very slightly illuminated. That could not be direct sunlight, obviously. But just as the moonlight illuminating his garden at this moment was really sunlight bouncing off the moon to him, he was no doubt also seeing the dark part of the moon illuminated by sunlight that had bounced off the Earth and struck it – and then bounced back yet again, of course, to get to his eyes. From sun to Earth to moon and then back to him – which would explain the successive diminutions in brightness. As sunlight was to moonlight, moonlight was to the dark side of the moon.

The next morning he said to Mazzoleni, 'I want a stronger magnification, something like twenty or thirty times.'

'So you say, maestro.'

They manufactured a lot of spyglasses. Making the objective lenses bigger and smoother, while keeping the eyepiece lenses at their original size and grinding them both deeper and smoother, led to very satisfactory jumps in magnifying power. In a matter of weeks they had glasses that showed things twenty – twenty-five –

thirty – finally thirty-two times closer than the unaided eye saw them. There they hit their limit; the lenses could not be made bigger or smoother, and the tubes were twice as long as when they had begun. Also, as magnifying power grew, what one actually saw through the glass contracted down to a very small field of view. One could move one's eye around the eyepiece a bit to broaden the view, but not by very much. Accurate aiming was important, and Galileo got better at this by attaching an empty spotting tube to the side of the strongest glass. They also had to deal with a white glare that invaded the sides of the larger images, where the irregularities in the lenses also tended to cluster, so that the outer circumference of the image was often nearly useless. Here Galileo put to use a solution he had discovered to deal with the rainbow rings that plagued his own vision, especially of things seen at night. This unhappy phenomenon he tended to attribute to the strange incident of his near-death experience in the cellar of the Villa Costozza, which he also believed had caused his rheumatism, bad digestion, headaches, seizures, melancholia, hypochondria, and so on. Vision problems were only one more remnant of that ancient disaster, and he had long since discovered that if he looked at something through his fist, the aurora of coloured light surrounding the thing would be blocked from view. Now he tried the same remedy with the new spyglasses, fashioning with Mazzoleni's help a cardboard sleeve that could be fitted over the objective. The most effective one left an oval opening over the lens that blocked most of the outer third of its area. Why an oval worked better than a circle he had no idea, but it did; the glare was eliminated, and the image that remained was about as large as before, and very much sharper.

As the spyglasses got stronger, things in the sky were becoming visible that had not been visible before. One night, after a long inspection of the moon, he swung the glass across the sky toward the Pleiades, just risen above the house. He looked into the glass.

'My God,' he said, and felt his body ringing. Around the Seven Sisters were scores of stars. The familiar seven stars of the gorgeous little constellation were brighter than the rest, but surrounding them were thickets of lesser stars, granulated almost to white dust in places. The sense of enormous depth in the little black circle was palpable, almost vertiginous; he swayed a little on his stool, mouth hanging open. Even the spectacle of the mountainous moon had not prepared him for such a thing. No one else in the history of the world had ever seen these stars, until this very night, this very moment. It was the oddest feeling in the world. He sketched a quick map of the newly crowded group, making the familiar sisters little six-pointed stars like a child would draw, with the new stars tiny crosses – the drawing done almost unconsciously, a kind of nervous habit, deeply engrained after so many years of exercising it. Until he sketched something down his hand would itch with the urge.

He looked until his eyes hurt, and the points of light swam in the eyepiece like gnats in the sun. He was cold, almost shivering, his bad back like a rusty hinge inside him. He felt that he would sleep the moment he lay down: a luscious feeling for a lifelong insomniac, he bathed in it as he stumbled off to bed.

His empty bed. No Marina. He had kicked her out, and life was ever so much more peaceful. Nevertheless he felt a quick stab of regret as he dived into the deep pool of sleep. It would have been nice to have someone to tell. Well – he would tell the world. The thought almost woke him.

Only six days after his demonstration to the Venetian Senate, his reward came, in the form of a new contract offer. Procurator Antonio Prioli, one of the heads of the university in Padua, came out of the Sala delle Senato to take Galileo by the hand. 'The Senate, knowing the way you have served Venice for seventeen years, and sensible of your courtesy in offering your occhialino as a present to the Republic, has ordered your election to the Professorship for life, if you are willing, with a salary of a thousand florins a year.' He raised his other hand: 'They are aware that there remains a year on your current contract, and yet want the increase in salary to begin this very day.'

'Please convey to His Serenity and all the *pregadi* my deepest thanks for this most kind and generous offer, Your Honour,' Galileo said. 'I kiss their hands, and accept with the utmost gratitude.'

'Shit,' he said the moment he was out of earshot. And back home he started cursing in a way that emptied the rooms well before he stormed through them. 'Shit shit *shit*. Those pricks! Those cheap bastards, those *soddomitecci!*'

He remembered as he always did that Cremonini, an old duffer Galileo had enjoyed sparring with through the years, already made a thousand florins a year from the Venetian Senate. That was the difference between the standing of philosophy and mathematics in this world, an inverse ratio to justice, as so often happened: the worst philosopher had been paid twice the best mathematician.

Then also, a salary fixed in perpetuity meant there would never be another raise, and Galileo already knew to the last *quattrini* his expenses, which were such that this raise would only just cover them, leaving him still unable to pay off his sister's dowry and his other outstanding debts.

Also, the salary was a salary, paid for his teaching, as before – meaning there would be no time to write up his experiments, or make new ones. All that work in the notebooks in the workshop would continue to lie there mouldering.

So this was not exactly the most exciting result one could have imagined, given the extraordinary power of his new device, and its strategic importance, obvious to everyone who had witnessed the demonstration. The triumph of that day had had Galileo imagining a lifetime sinecure, all his debts and expenses paid, and afterward free from all work except research and consultation, which he would have applied most faithfully to the good fortune of La Serenissima. They would have benefited greatly; and in any duchy or principality or kingdom this kind of patronage would not have been unusual. But Venice was a republic, and courtly patronage as it was practised in Florence or Rome, or almost anywhere else in Europe, did not exist here. Gentlemen of the Republic worked for the Republic, and were paid accordingly. It was an admirable thing, if you could afford it.

'Shit,' he repeated weakly, staring at his workshop table. 'Those cheap bastards.' But a part of his mind was already calculating what the thousand florins a year would do to meet expenses and knock off debts.

Then he heard in a letter from Sarpi that some of the Senators had complained to the body at large that the spyglass was a commonplace in Holland and elsewhere in northern Europe, so that it had not really been Galileo's achievement, and he had presented his device under false pretences.

'I never said I invented the idea!' Galileo protested. 'I only said I made it much better, which I did! Tell those cheap bastards to find a spyglass as good as mine somewhere else if they think they can!' He ripped off a long letter that he sent to Sarpi to give to the senators:

News arrived at Venice, where I happened to be at the moment, that a Dutchman had a glass looking through which one could see distant things as clearly as if they were near. With this simple fact I returned to Padua, and pondering on the problem, I found the solution on the first night home, and the next day I made an instrument and reported the fact to my friends at Venice. I made a more perfect instrument, with which I returned to Venice, and showed it to the wonder and astonishment of the illustrati of the Republic – a task which caused me no small fatigue.

But perhaps it may be said that no great credit is due for the making of an instrument, when one is told beforehand that the instrument exists. To this I reply, the help which the information gave me consisted of exciting my thoughts in that particular direction, and without that, of course it is possible they may never have gone that way; but that the simple information itself made the act of invention easier to me I deny, and say more – to find the solution to a definite problem requires a greater effort of genius than to resolve one not specified; for in the latter case accident, mere chance, may play the greater part, while in the former all follows from the work of the reasoning and intelligent mind. Thus, we are quite sure that the Dutchman was a simple spectacle-maker, who, handling by chance different forms of glasses, looked also by chance through two of them, and saw and noted the surprising result, and thus found the instrument. Whereas I, at the mere news of the effect obtained, discovered the same instrument, not by chance, but by way of pure reasoning! I was not assisted in any way by the knowledge that the conclusion at which I aimed already existed. Some people may believe that the certainty of the result aimed at affords great help in attaining it: let them read history, and they will find that Archites made a dove that could fly, and that Archimedes made a mirror that burned objects at great distances. Now by reasoning on these things such people will doubtless be able, with very little trouble and with great honour and advantage, to tell us how they were constructed. No? If they do not succeed, they will then be able to testify to their own satisfaction that the ease of fabrication which they had promised themselves from the foreknowledge of the result is very much less than what they had imagined –

'Idiots that they are!' Galileo shouted but did not add to the end of the letter, signing it conventionally and sending it off.

Naturally Sarpi did not forward this letter to the Senate, but rather came out to Padua to assuage his angry friend. 'I know,' he said apologetically, putting his hand to Galileo's freckled cheek, now as red as his hair as he recounted the reasons for his fury. 'It isn't fair.'

And it was even less fair than Galileo thought; for Sarpi now told him that the Senate had decided that the stipulated raise in

Galileo's salary was not to go into effect immediately after all, but would begin the following January.

At this Galileo blew up again. And after Sarpi left he immediately took action to deal with the insults, working in two directions. In Venice, he returned to the city with a much more powerful spyglass, the best his artisans had made so far, and gave it to the Doge as a present, indicating again how useful it would be to the protection of the Republic, how grateful he was for the new contract, how much the splendiferousness of the Doge illuminated not just the Serenissima but the entire watershed of the Po, et cetera. Dona would take note of this generosity, perhaps, in the face of what could be seen as a very tepid response from his Senate, even a rebuff; and then maybe he would act to revise the raise accordingly. It was not the likeliest response, but it could happen.

Then, on the Florentine front, always a part of his life, even in these last seventeen years in Padua working for Venice, Galileo wrote to young Grand Duke Cosimo's secretary Belisario Vinta, telling him about the spyglass, offering to give the prince one of them and to instruct him in its use. A few of the closing phrases of this letter began the process of asking for patronage at the Medici court.

There were some difficulties to be negotiated here. Galileo had been tutor to young Cosimo when his father Ferdinando was the Grand Duke, and that was good. But he had also been asked to work up a horoscope for Ferdinando the previous year, and had done so, and found that the stars predicted a long and healthy life for the Grand Duke, in the usual way; but then shortly thereafter Ferdinando had died. That was bad. In the tumult of the funeral and the succession no one had said anything, nor even seemed to remember the horoscope, except for a single penetrating glance from Vinta the next time they met. So perhaps in the end it had not mattered; and Galileo had taught Cosimo his mathematics, and treated him very kindly, of course, so that they had grown fond of one another. Cosimo was a bright young man, and Cosimo's mother, the Grand

Duchess Christina, was a very intelligent woman, and fond of Galileo – indeed, his true first patron at that court. And as Cosimo was so young, and new to his rule, she was a regent-like power. So the possibilities there were very real. And when all was said and done, Galileo was a Florentine, it was his home. His family was still there, which was bad, but unavoidable.

So, still very angry at the Venetians for their ingratitude, he neglected his classes at Padua, wrote great flurries of letters to influential friends, and began to lay plans to move.

Despite the discord and chaos of the tumble of days, he spent every cloudless night out in the garden, looking through the best glass they had on hand. One night he woke Mazzoleni and took him out to look at the moon. The old man peered up through the tube and then pulled his head back, grinning, shaking his head in amazement. 'What does it mean?'

'It's a world, like this one.'

'Are there people there?'

'How should I know?'

When the moon was up, and not too full, he looked at it. Long ago he had taken drawing lessons from his Florentine friend Ostilio Ricci, the better to be able to sketch his mechanical ideas. One of the exercises in Ricci's treatise on perspectival drawing had been to draw spheres studded with geometrical figures, like raised pyramids or cubes, each one of which had to be drawn slightly differently to indicate where they stood on the hidden surface of the sphere underneath them. This was a meticulous and painstaking form of practice, very *polito*, at which Ricci had conceded Galileo eventually became the superior. Now Galileo found that it had given him the necessary skills, not just to draw the things the glass showed on the moon, but even to see them in the first place.

It was particularly revealing to draw the moon's terminator, where light and shadow mixed in patterns that changed from night to night. As he wrote in his workbook, *With the moon in various aspects to the Sun, some peaks within the dark part of the moon appear drenched in light, although very far from the boundary line of the light and darkness. Comparing their distance from that boundary line to the entire lunar diameter, I found that this interval sometimes exceeds the twentieth part of the diameter.* The moon's diameter had been proposed since antiquity to be about two thousand miles; thus he had enough to complete a simple geometrical calculation of the height of these lunar mountains. He drew the moon as a circle, then on it drew a triangle with one side the radius at the terminator, another a radius running up to the tip of the lit mountain in the dark zone, and the third line following the beam of sunlight from the terminator to the mountain top. The two sides meeting at the terminator would be at right angles, and he had distances for both, based on the assumed diameter, and thus he could use the Pythagorean theorem to calculate the length of the hypotenuse. Subtracting the moon's radius from that hypotenuse, one was left with about four miles of difference – which was the height of the mountain above the surface.

But on Earth, he wrote, *no mountains exist that reach even to a perpendicular height of one mile.* The mountains on the moon were taller than the Alps!

He spotted a perfectly round shape right in the middle of the terminator, and very near the equator. He drew it a bit bigger than he saw it, to emphasize how prominent it was to the eye, and how clearly it stood out from its surroundings. A good astronomical drawing, he decided, had to evoke the sight that subsequent viewers would look for, rather than represent it to perfect scale, which in the diminution of the drawing simply made it *too* small. Paying attention was itself a kind of magnification.

Drawing the constellations with their new host of companion stars was a different kind of problem, easier in some ways, as being mostly a schematic, but much harder too, in that there was no chance of representing what the view through the glass actually looked like. He altered sizes far beyond what he saw, to give an impression of the different brightnesses; but using black on white to represent white on black would never be satisfactory. White marks on black, as in an etching, would be better.

He drew till his fingers got too cold. He made fair copies in the mornings, exaggerating to make the impressions bolder than ever. He made ink washes, very delicate; also bold schematics that would serve as guides to an engraver, because already he had plans for a book to accompany the spyglasses, just as an instruction manual had accompanied his military compass. Although here it really came down to seeing for oneself. The Milky Way, for instance; he could see that it was composed of a vast number of stars granulated together, a truly astonishing finding; but there was no way at all to draw that. People would have to see for themselves.

He fell deeply into his new routine. He had always been an insomniac, and now there was a useful way to spend those sleepless hours. He simply did not go to bed, but stayed out on the terrace by the occhialino, looking through it and jotting down notes, comfortable in the solitary silence of the sleeping town. He had not known how much he enjoyed being alone. He wrote up what he had observed at dawn, and then slept through many a bright cool morning, wrapped in a blanket against a sunny wall in the corner, under the gnomon of the house's big L.

With the shorter days of November came winter, and clouds. On those nights he read, or caught up on his sleep, if he could; but on many a night he woke every hour or two, his brain full of stars, and went out to check the sky. If it had cleared he would stir the coals of the kitchen fire and put a pot of mulled wine on the grate, add a few sticks and go out to set up the glass, feeling that swirl of dust in the blood that he loved so much. He was on the hunt all right! And never had he had such a quarry! Nothing could keep him from looking when the night was clear. If his work in the daytime had to suffer – and it did – so be it. Those bastard *pregadi* didn't deserve his work anyway.

He had ordered one of the work tables moved onto the terrace, placed under a table umbrella, next to a couch. He had a lantern that could be shuttered, and workbooks, inkpots, quills; and three spyglasses on tripods, each with different powers and occlusions. Lastly, blankets to throw over his shoulders. Mazzoleni and the cook kept the household running in the mornings while he slept, and stocked the supplies for his nighttime needs; both were the kind of person who falls asleep at sunset, so they didn't see him at work unless he forced them to. After a while, he never did; he liked being by himself through the frosty nights, looking at first one thing and then another.

On the night of 7th January, 1610, he was out looking at the planets. As he had written in a letter he was composing for young Antonio Medici, *The planets are seen very rotund, like little full moons, and of a roundness bounded and without rays. But the fixed stars do not appear so; rather they are seen fulgurous and trembling, much more with the glass than without, and so irradiated that what shape they possess is not revealed.*

So the planets, being obvious little disks, were interesting. And Jupiter was now in the west after sunset. It was the biggest of the planets in the glass, no surprise to anyone used to the way it dominated the night sky whenever it was visible.

Galileo got it in the middle of the eyepiece, and then saw that there were three bright stars to left and right of it, aligned with it in the plane of the ecliptic. He marked their positions on a new sheet of his letter to Antonio, and looked at them for a long time. They did not twinkle like the stars, but gleamed steadily. They were almost perfectly in a line with each other. They were almost as bright as Jupiter, or even brighter, although smaller. Jupiter itself was a very distinct disc.

The next night he looked at Jupiter again, and was shocked to find that the three stars were still there, but this time all to the west of the great planet, whereas on the previous night two of them had been to its east. He wondered if the ephemerides was wrong about Jupiter's current movement.

On 9th January it was cloudy, and nothing could be seen. But the night of the tenth was clear again.

This time only two of the bright stars were there, both to the east of Jupiter. One was slightly less bright than the other, though on the previous nights they had all been the same.

Mystified, intrigued to the point of obsession, Galileo started a new sheet in his workbook, and copied there the diagrams he had already written in at the end of the letter to Antonio. The letter itself he put aside, as being premature.

In his new desire for night, the days themselves passed slowly, and he did the necessary work without paying the slightest attention to it, as if dreaming on his feet. This was a sign, well-recognized by the household: he was on the hunt. And just as they never woke sleepwalkers for fear of damaging their sanity, they left him alone at these times, and kept the boys quiet and the students at bay, and put food in him almost as if spoon-feeding a baby. Of course it was true he would beat them if they distracted him, but they enjoyed the craft of it too.

On the night of 12th January, Galileo trained the glass on Jupiter in the last moments of twilight. At first he could see again only two of the little bright stars; but an hour later when it was fully dark he checked again, and one more had become visible, very close to Jupiter's eastern side.

He drew arrows trying to clarify to himself how they were moving, shifting his attention between the view through the glass and his sketches on the page. Suddenly it became clear, there in the reiterated sketches: the four stars were moving around Jupiter, orbiting it in the same way the moon orbited the Earth. He was seeing circular orbits edge-on; they lay nearly in a single plane, which was also very close to the plane of the ecliptic, in which the planets themselves moved.

He felt the ringing in him. He straightened up, blinking away the tears in his eyes that always came from looking too long, and that this time came also from the sudden surge of an emotion he couldn't give a name to, a kind of joy that was also shot with fear. 'Ah,' he said. A touch of the sacred, right on the back of his neck: God had tapped him. He was ringing.

No one had ever seen this before. People had seen the moon, had seen the stars; they had *never* seen this. *I primi al mondo*! The first man to see Jupiter's four moons, which had been circling it since the creation.

Everything he had seen over the last week fell into place. He stood, staggering a little under the impact of the idea, and circled the work table as if imitating a moon. When there had been only two dots, the others could have been behind the big planet – or before it. And he saw also that the orbiting moon now outermost could perhaps have moved so far away from Jupiter as to be outside his eyepiece's little circle. The shifts in position suggested they were moving fairly quickly. Earth's moon took only twenty-eight and a half days for its orbit. These four seemed faster still, and perhaps could be moving at differing speeds, just as the planets moved at differing speeds in the sky.

If he was right, then he could expect to see several more things. Seeing the orbits side-on, the moons would appear to slow down as they approached their maximum distance from Jupiter, and be fastest when right next to it. They would also disappear when behind it (or before it) in a regular pattern, and always reappear on the other side, never on the same side. Repeated observations should make it possible to sort out which moon was which, and determine which orbited closest to Jupiter and which farthest away. Knowing that would help him to calculate each orbital period, and that would allow him to keep steady track of them, and even predict where they would be, in a Jovian ephemerides of his own devise.

'My God,' he said, overwhelmed at these thoughts, suddenly weeping, feeling he should fall to his knees to say a prayer in thanks to God, only his knees were too stiff, he was too cold. Anyway it was looking through the glass that was the prayer. 'I'm the first in the world!'

Which – when he recovered from the awe of it – really should be something he could turn to advantage. A truly new thing in the world – how could it not be useful? He had to hop about in the frigid night air to express his happiness. Mazzoleni and the rest would have laughed to see it, as they had laughed all the times they had seen it, after one good discovery or another: but none so good as this! He chortled, he shuffled around the terrace in a dance with the spyglass as his partner. He felt an urge to ring the workshop bell; he even began to walk toward the workshop, to wake Mazzoleni and the rest, and share the news with somebody. But he was the bell he wanted to ring, and if he woke the others, Mazzoleni would just nod and grin his gap-toothed grin, and be pleased that the new instrument was working better than the previous one. What went on in the sky did not matter to him.

Galileo stopped in his tracks and returned to the terrace. He recommenced his little contradance around the tripod and work table, singing nonsense words to himself under his breath. An old man dancing at midnight. Tomorrow he would write up his news, and publish it as soon as possible after that, to share it with the world. Everyone would know, everyone would look and see. But only he would be first, first always, first forever. This night was his. Feeling warm in his cloak, he settled on the stool under the tripod to look some more.

Then there came a knock at the garden gate. And he knew who it was.

Chapter Three Entangled

Galileo walked stiffly toward the gate, feeling his heart pound. The knock came again, a steady *tap tap tap*. He reached the gate and pulled up the crossbar, feeling a sweat of trepidation.

It was indeed the stranger, tall and gaunt in a black cloak. Behind him hunched a short gnarled old man, carrying a leather satchel over one shoulder.

The stranger bowed. 'You said you would enjoy to look through a spyglass of my own.'

'Yes, I remember – but that was months ago! Where have you been?'

'Now I am here.'

'I've seen some amazing things!' Galileo could not help saying.

'You still wish to look through what I have?'

'Yes, of course.'

He let the stranger and his servant in the gate, his unease written all over his face. 'Come out to the terrace. I was there when you knocked, looking at Jupiter. Jupiter has four stars orbiting it, did you know that?'

'Four moons. Yes.'

Galileo looked disappointed, also disturbed; how had the stranger been able to see them?

The stranger said, 'Perhaps you would enjoy to see them through my instrument.'

'Yes, of course. What is its power of magnification?'

'It varies.' He gestured at his servant. 'Let me show you.'

The man's ancient servant looked familiar. He wheezed unhappily under his load. On the terrace Galileo reached out to help him lower the satchel, briefly holding him above the elbow and against the back; under his coat the man felt like nothing but skin and bone. He slipped out from under the strap of the long bag carelessly, before Galileo had quite gotten hold of it, and it hit the tiles with a thump.

'It's heavy!' Galileo said.

The two visitors pulled a massive tripod from the satchel, and arranged it next to Galileo's instrument; then they drew a big spyglass out of the case. Its tube was made of a dull grey metal, like pewter, and they held it by both ends to lift it. It was about twice the length of Galileo's tube, and three times the diameter, and clicked onto the top of its tripod with a distinct snap.

'Where did you get that thing?' Galileo asked.

The stranger shrugged. He glanced at Galileo's tube, then spun his on its tripod with a light flick of the wrist. It stopped moving when it came to much the same angle as Galileo's, and with a small smile the stranger gestured at the instrument.

'Be my guest, please. Have a look.'

'You don't want to sight it?'

'It is aimed at Jupiter. At the moon that you will call Number Two.'

Galileo stared at him, confused and a little afraid. Was the thing supposed to be self-sighting? The man's claim made no sense.

'Take a look and see,' the stranger suggested.

There was no reply to that: it was what he had been saying himself, to Cremonini and everyone. Just look! Galileo moved his stool over to the new device, sat down, leaned forward. He looked into the eyepiece.

The thing's field of vision was packed with stars, and seemed large, perhaps twenty or thirty times what Galileo saw through his glass. At its centre what he took to be one of the moons of Jupiter gleamed like a round white ball, marked by faint lines. It was bigger than Jupiter itself was in Galileo's glass. The harder Galileo looked, the more obviously spheroid the white moon became, and its striations more visible. It stood out like a snowball against the stars, which burned in their various intensities against a depth of velvet black.

It appeared that the white ball, clearer than ever to his sight, had faintly darker areas, somewhat like Earth's moon; but more prominent by far was its broken network of intersecting lines, like the craquelure on an old painting, or the ice on the Venetian lagoon in cold winters after several tides had cracked it. Galileo's fingers reached for a quill that was not there, wanting to draw what he saw. In some places the lines appeared in parallel clusters, in others they rayed out like fireworks, and these two patterns overlapped and shattered each other repeatedly.

One crackle pattern clarified for him, gleamed in exquisite detail. Focusing on it appeared to increase the enlargement accordingly, until it filled the lens of the eyepiece. A wave of dizziness passed through his whole body; it felt like he was falling up toward the white moon. He lost his balance. He felt himself pitch forward, head first into the device.

Things fall in parabolic arcs: but he wasn't falling. He flew, up and forward – outward – head tilted back to see where he was going. The plain of shattered white ice bloomed right before his eyes. Or below him – maybe he was falling. His stomach flip-flopped as his sense of up and down reversed itself.

He didn't know where he was.

He gasped for air. He was drifting downward, now; he was upright again; his sense of balance returned just as distinctly as sight returned when you closed and then opened your eyes – something definitive. It was an immense relief, the most precious thing in the world, just that simple sense of up and down.

He stood on ice. The ice was an opaque white, much tinted by oranges and yellows; sunset colours, autumn colours. He looked up –

A giant banded orange moon loomed in a black starry sky. It was many times bigger than the moon in Earth's sky, and its horizontal bands were various pale oranges and yellows, umbers and creams. The borders of the bands curled over and into each other. On the moon's lower quarter a brick red oval swirl marred the border of a terra cotta band and a cream band. The opaque plain of ice he stood on was picking up these colours. He put his fist up with his thumb stuck out: at home his thumb covered the moon; this one was seven or eight times that wide. Suddenly he understood it was Jupiter itself up there. He was standing on the surface of the moon he had been looking at.

Behind him someone politely cleared his throat. Galileo turned; it was the stranger, standing beside a spyglass like the one he had invited Galileo to look through. Perhaps it was the same one. The air was cool and thin – bracing somehow, like a wine or even a brandy. Galileo's balance was uncertain, and he felt oddly light on his feet.

The stranger was looking curiously at Galileo. Beyond him on the nearby horizon stood a cluster of tall slender white towers, like a collection of campaniles. They looked to be made of the same ice as the moon's surface.

'Where are we?' Galileo demanded.

'We are on the second moon of Jupiter, which we call Europa.'

'How came we here?'

'What I told you was my spyglass is actually a kind of portal system. A transference device.'

Galileo's thoughts darted about in rushes faster than he could register. Bruno's idea that all the stars were inhabited – the steel machinery in the Arsenale –

'Why?' he said, trying to conceal his fear.

The stranger swallowed; his Adam's apple, like another great nose he had ingested, bobbed under the shaved skin of his neck. 'I am acting for a group here that would like you to speak to the council of moons. A group like the Venetian Senate, you might say. *Pregadi*, you call those senators. Invitees. Here you are a *pregadi*. My group, which was originally from Ganymede, would like to meet you, and they would like you to speak to the general council of Jovian moons. We feel it is important enough that we were willing to disturb you like this. I offered to be your escort.'

'My Virgil,' Galileo said. He could feel his heart pounding in him.

The stranger did not seem to catch the reference. 'I am sorry to startle you in this manner. I did not feel that I could explain it to you in Italy. I hope you will forgive me the impertinence of snatching you away like this. And the shock of it. You are looking rather amazed.'

Galileo shut his mouth, which had in fact been hanging open. He felt his dry tongue stick to the dry roof of his mouth. His feet and hands were cold. He recalled suddenly that in his dreams his feet were often cold, even to the point that sometimes he stumped about in boots of ice, and woke to find his blankets had ridden up. Now he looked at his feet, shuddering. They were still in their ordinary leather shoes, looking incongruous on the tinted ice of this world. He pinched the skin between his thumb and forefinger, bit the inside of his lip: he certainly seemed awake. And usually the thought that he might be dreaming was enough to wake him, if dreaming he was. But here he stood, in crisp thin air, breathing fast, heart thumping as it rarely did any more – as it used to when he was young, and frightened by something. Now he did not feel the fear, exactly, but only his body's response to it. His mind perhaps did not quite believe all this, but his body had to. Maybe he had died and this was heaven, or purgatory. Maybe purgatory orbited Jupiter. He recalled his facetious lecture on the geography of Dante, in which he had calculated the size of Hell by the ratio of Lucifer's arm to the height of Virgil –

'But this is too strange!' he said.

'Yes. I'm sorry for the shock it must have caused you. It was felt that your recent observations through your spyglass would help you to understand and accept this experience. It was felt that you might be the first human capable of understanding the experience.'

'But I don't understand it,' Galileo had to admit, pleased though he was to be considered first at anything.

The stranger regarded him. 'A lack of understanding must be a feeling you are used to,' he suggested, 'given the state of your research into physical forces.'

'That's different,' Galileo said.

But it was a little bit true, when he thought about it: not understanding was a familiar sensation. At home he never had any trouble admitting it, no matter what people said to the contrary. In fact he was the only one bold enough to admit how little he understood! He had insisted on it!

But here there was no need to insist. He was flummoxed. He looked up again at Jupiter, wondered how far away they were from it. There were too many unknowns to be able to figure it out. Its dark part, a thin crescent, was very dark. The gibbous part, well-lit by the distant sun, was strongly marked by its fat horizontal bands. The borders looked like viscous pours of oil paint, curling and overlapping but never quite mixing. It almost seemed he could see the colours move.

In the sky over his right shoulder gleamed what he took to be the sun – a chip of the utmost brilliance, like fifty stars clumped together into a space not much bigger than the other stars. As on Earth, one could not look at it for long. The sight of it so small made it evident that all the stars could be suns, maybe each with its own set of planets, just as the misfortunate Bruno had claimed. World upon world, each with its own people, like the stranger here, a Jovian it seemed. It was an astounding thought. The memory of Bruno, on the other hand, gave everything he saw a faint undercurrent of terror. He did not want to know these things.

'Is the Earth visible from here?' he asked, scanning the stars around the sun, looking for something like a blue Venus, or perhaps from out here it would be more like a blue Mercury, small and very near the sun . . . Many of the stars overhead, however, were tinted red or blue, sometimes yellow, even green; what might have been Mars could have been Arcturus – no, there was Arcturus, beyond the curve of the Big Dipper. The constellations, he noted, were all the same from this vantage, as they would be only if the stars were very much further away than the planets.

The stranger was also scanning the sky; but then he shrugged. 'Maybe there,' he said, pointing at a bright white star. 'I am not sure. The sky here changes fast, as you know.'

'How long is the day here?'

'The rotation is eighty-eight hours, the same as its orbital time around Jupiter, which you are on the verge of determining. Like Earth's moon, it is tidally locked.'

'Tides?'

'Gravitational tides. There is a – a tidal force exerted by every mass. A bending of space, rather. It is difficult to explain. It would go better if other things were explained to you first.'

'No doubt,' Galileo said shortly. He was struggling to keep his mind empty of fear by focusing on these questions, because underneath his studied (or stunned) calm, there swelled something very like terror. Perhaps it was only the memory of Bruno.

'You appear to be cold,' the stranger noted. 'You are shivering. Perhaps I can lead you to the city?' Pointing at the white towers.

'I will be missed at home.' Perhaps. It sounded feeble.

'When you return, only a short time will have passed. It will look like what you call a syncope, or a catalepsy. Cartophilus will take care of that end. Don't worry about that now. Since I have disturbed you by bringing you this far, we might as well accomplish what was intended, and bring you to the council.'

This too would serve as a distraction from his fear, no doubt; and the calm part of him was curious. So Galileo said, 'Yes, whatever you like.' It felt like grasping at a branch from out of a whirlpool. 'Lead on.'

Despite the effort to stay calm, his emotions blew through him like gusts in a storm. Fear, suspense – the terror underneath everything – but also a sharp exhilaration. *The first man who could have understood this experience*. Which was a voyage among the stars. *I primi al mondo*.

They approached the white towers, which still appeared to be made of ice. He and the stranger had walked for perhaps an hour, and the bottoms of the towers had appeared to him in half an hour, so Moon II was probably not as big as the Earth, perhaps more the size of the moon. The horizon looked very close by. The ice they crossed had been minutely pitted every-where, also streaked by lighter or darker rays, and occasionally marked by very low circular hills. It seemed basically white, and only tinted yellow by the light of Jupiter.

To one side of the white towers an arc of pale aquamarine appeared across the whiteness. The stranger led him to this arc, which proved to be a broad rampway cut into the ice, dropping at a very slight angle, down to where it cut under an arch or doorway into a long wide chamber.

They descended; the chamber under the ice roof had broad white doors, like city gates. At the bottom of the ramp they waited before these. Then the gates went transparent, and a group of people dressed in blouses and pantaloons of Jovian hues stood before them, in what seemed a kind of vestibule. The stranger touched Galileo lightly on the back of the arm, led him into this antechamber. They passed under another arch. The group fell in behind them without a word. Their faces appeared old but young. The space of the room made a gentle curve to the left, and beyond that they came to a kind of overlook, with broad steps descending before them. From here they could see an entire cavern city stretching to the near horizon, all of it tinted a greenish blue, under a high ceiling of opaque ice of the same colour. The light was subdued, but more than enough to see by; it was quite a bit brighter than the light of the full moon on Earth. A hum or distant roar filled his ears.

'Blue light goes furthest,' Galileo ventured, thinking of the distant Alps on a clear day.

'No,' the stranger said. 'The different colours are waves of different lengths, red longer, blue shorter. The shorter the wavelength, the more light tends to bounce off things, even ice or water, or air.'

'A pretty colour.'

'I suppose it is. Some spaces in here are illuminated with artificial light sources, to make things brighter and give them the full spectrum.' He indicated a building that glowed like a yellow lantern in the distance. 'But mostly they leave it like this.'

'It makes you look like angels.'

'We are only people, as I'm afraid you will soon learn.'

The stranger led him to an amphitheatre, sunk into the surface of the city floor so that it was not visible until they came to the curved rim of the highest seats. Looking down into it, Galileo saw resemblances to Roman theatres he had seen. The bottom dozen rows of seats were occupied, and in front of them other people were standing on a round stage. They all wore loose blouses and pantaloons that were blue, pale yellow, or the Jovian tones of Galileo's group. At the centre of the stage stood a white glowing sphere on a pedestal. Faint black lines crisscrossing it gave Galileo the impression that it might be a globe representing the moon they stood on.

'The council?' Galileo asked.

'Yes.'

'What would you have me say?'

'Speak as the first scientist. Tell them not to kill what they study. Nor to kill themselves by studying it.'

The stranger led Galileo down steps into the amphitheatre, now firmly holding him by the upper arm. Galileo felt again the strange lack of his proper weight; he bounced as he would have if standing neck-deep in a lake.

The stranger stopped several steps above the group and made a loud announcement in a language Galileo did not recognize. Only slightly delayed, he also heard the man's voice say in Latin, 'I present to you Galileo Galilei, the first scientist.'

Everyone looked up at him. For a moment they were motionless, and many of them looked startled, even disapproving.

'They look surprised to see us,' Galileo noted. 'Perhaps a bit baffled, or abashed.'

The stranger nodded. 'They want to be sheep, and so should be sheepish. Come on.'

As they descended further, some of the ones dressed in orange and yellow bowed. Galileo bowed in return, as he would have before the Venetian Senate, which this group somewhat resembled, in that they appeared elderly, and somehow used to authority. Many of them were women, however, or Galileo assumed so: they were dressed in the same kind of blouses and pantaloons as the men. If a monastery and convent had merged their populations, and could only express their wealth in the fine cloth of their simple habits, they might look like this.

Despite the scattering of respectful bows, several among the group were now objecting to the stranger's interruption. One woman, wearing yellow, spoke in the language Galileo didn't recognize, and again he heard a Latin translation in his ears – Latin in a man's voice, accented like the stranger's. It said, 'This is another illegal incursion. You have no right to interrupt the council's session, and such a dangerous prolepsis as this will not be allowed to change the debate. In fact it is a criminal action, as you know very well. Call the guards!'

The stranger continued to guide Galileo down the steps and onto the circular stage, until they were among the people standing there. Almost all of them were considerably taller than Galileo, and he looked up at them, amazed at their faces, so thin and pale – beautifully healthy, but manifesting signs of both youth and age in mixtures very strange to his eye.

Galileo's guide loomed over the protesting woman, and he spoke down to her, but addressed the entire group, in their language, so that again Galileo heard a slightly delayed translation in his ear: 'Who gets to speak is only contested by cowards. My people come from Ganymede, and we assert the right to speak for it, to help determine what people do in the Jovian system.'

'You no longer represent Ganymede,' the woman said.

'I am the Ganymede, as my people will attest. I will speak. The prohibition against descending into the Europan ocean was made for very important reasons, and the Europans' current push to rescind that prohibition ignores several different kinds of immense danger. We will not allow it to happen!'

'Are you and your group part of the Jovian council or not?' the woman shot back.

'We are, of course.'

'But the matter has been discussed and decided, and your position has lost to that of the majority.'

'No!' others around them cried.

Many there then spoke up at once, and the debate grew general, and quickly became a shouting match. People jostled around, contracting into knots like rival gangs in a piazza, growing red-faced with expostulation. The Latin in Galileo's ear broke up into overlapping shouts: 'Decided already – We asked him to speak! – We will have you removed! – Cowards! Anarchists! – We want the Galileo to speak to this matter!'

Galileo raised his hand like a student in a class. 'What matter do you discuss?' he said loudly. 'Why have you brought me here?'

In the pause that followed, one of the Ganymedeans addressed him. 'Most illustrious Galileo,' the Latin in his ear exclaimed, as the man bowed to him respectfully. He continued in his own tongue, which was translated in Galileo's ear as: '– first scientist, father of physics, we here among the moons of Jupiter have encountered a scientific problem so fundamental and important that some of us feel the need of a truly original mind, someone unprejudiced by all that has happened since your time, someone with your supreme intelligence and wisdom, to help us decide how to deal with it.'

'Ah well,' Galileo said. 'There you have it then.'

One woman laughed at this. She was big and statuesque, dressed in yellow. In the midst of all the arguing, she looked partly irritated, partly amused. The others began their raucous debate again, many becoming vehement, and in the din of all the squabbling she circled around to his left side, opposite the stranger. She leaned down toward him (she stood almost a foot taller than he), and spoke rapidly in his ear, in her own language; but what he heard in his ear was Tuscan Italian, somewhat old-fashioned, like that of Machiavelli, or even Dante.

'You don't believe any of that shit, do you?'

'Why should I not?' Galileo replied *sotto voce*, in Tuscan.

'Don't be so sure your companion has your best interests in mind here, no matter that you are the great martyr to science.'

Galileo, not liking the sound of that, said quickly, 'What do you think my interests here are?'

'The same as anywhere,' she said with a sly smile. 'Your own advancement, right?'

In the midst of a fierce harangue at his foes, the stranger looked over and noticed the woman and Galileo in conversation. He stopped arguing with the others and wagged a finger at her. 'Hera,' he warned her, 'leave him alone.'

She raised an eyebrow. 'You are not the one to be telling people to leave Signor Galileo alone, it seems to me.' This was still translated to Galileo in Tuscan.

The stranger frowned heavily, shook his head. 'You have nothing at stake here. Leave us alone.' He returned to addressing the entire group, which was now quieting to hear what was going on.

'This is the one who began it all,' the stranger boomed, while in his other ear Galileo heard the woman's voice in Tuscan, saying, 'He means, this is the one I chose to begin it all.'

The stranger continued without further *sotto voce* commentary from the woman he had called Hera: 'This is the man who began the investigation of nature by means of experiment and mathematical analysis. From his time to ours, using this method, science has made us what we are. When we have ignored scientific methods and findings, when the archaic structures of fear and control have re-exerted themselves, stark disaster has followed. To abandon science now and risk a hasty destruction of the object of study would be stupid. And the result could be much worse than that – much worse than you imagine!'

'You have already made this argument, and lost it,' a red-faced man said firmly. 'The Europan interior can be investigated using an improved clean protocol, and we will learn what we have wanted to learn for many years. Your view is antiquated, your fears unfounded. What you did on Ganymede has deranged your understanding.'

The stranger shook his head vehemently. 'You don't know what you're talking about.'

'I am only affirming what the scientific committee assigned to the problem has already said. Who's being unscientific now, them or you?'

A general debate erupted again, and under its noise Galileo said to the tall woman, 'What is it that my patron and his allies want to forbid?'

She leaned into him to reply, in Italian again: 'They don't want anyone to dive into the ocean under the ice here. They fear what might be encountered there, if I understand the Ganymede correctly.'

Then a group of men dressed in the blue shade of clothing came bouncing down the steps on the other side of the amphitheatre. A senator dressed in the same colour gestured at them and cried at the stranger, 'Your objection has already been overruled! And you are breaking the law with this incursion. It's time to put a stop to it.' He shouted up at the newcomers, 'Eject these people!'

The stranger grabbed Galileo by the arm and hustled him in the other direction. His allies closed behind them, and they raced up the steps two at a time. Galileo almost tripped, then felt himself being lifted by the people on each side of him. They held him under the elbows and carried him.

At the top of the steps, out of the hole of the amphitheatre, they could suddenly see across the expanse of the blue city again, looking cold under its green-blue ceiling, the people on its broad strada so distant they were the size of mice. 'To the ships,' the stranger declared, and took Galileo by the arm. As he hustled Galileo away, he said to him, 'It's time to return you to your home, before they do something we will all regret. I'm sorry they would not listen to you, as I think if you had been able to judge the situation you would have sided with us and made our point clear. I'll call on you again when I am more sure you will be listened to. You are not done here!'

They came to the broad ramp rising out of the city, through its gates and onto the yellowy surface. People dressed in blue stood in their way, and with a roar the stranger and his group rushed at them. A brisk fight ensued. Galileo, staggering in the absence of his proper weight, dodged around little knots of brawlers.

57

If he had been dreaming he would have happily started throwing punches himself, for in his dreams he was much more audacious and violent than in life; so it was a measure of how real it was, how different from a dream, that he held back. He wasn't even sure which side he should have been supporting. So he skidded through the fray as if on the frozen Arno, waving his arms as needed to restore his balance. Suddenly in his gyrations the stranger and another man snatched him up by the arms and hustled him away.

Some distance from the mêlée the stranger's companions had set up the big spyglass, and were making final adjustments to it. It was either the same one that had stood on Galileo's terrace, or one just like it.

'Stand next to it, please,' the stranger said. 'Look into the eyepiece, please. Quickly. But before that – breathe this first –'

And he held a small censer up and sprayed a cold mist into Galileo's face.

Chapter Four   The Phases of Venus

*In order not to burden too much the transmigrating souls, Fate
interposes the drinking from the Lethean river in the midst of
the mutations, so that through oblivion they may be protected
in their affections and eager to preserve themselves in their
new state.*
> – GIORDANO BRUNO, *Lo spaccio della bestia trionfante,*
> *The Expulsion of the Triumphant Beast*

He woke lying on the ground next to his spyglass, the stool
tipped over beside him. The night sky was lightening in the east,
and Mazzoleni was tugging at his shoulder.

'Maestro, you should go to bed.'

'What?'

'You were in some kind of a trance. I came out before, but I
couldn't wake you.'

'I – I had a dream, I think.'

'It seemed more like a trance. One of your syncopes.'

'Maybe so.'

On the long list of Galileo's mysterious maladies, one of the
most mysterious was a tendency to fall insensible for intervals
that ranged from minutes to three or four hours, his muscles rigid
the entire time. His physician friend, the famous Fabrizio
d'Aquapendente, had been unable to treat these syncopes, which

in most people were accompanied by fits or racking seizures. Only a few sufferers like Galileo became simply paralysed.

'I feel strange,' Galileo said now.

'You're probably sore.'

'I had a dream, I think. I can't quite remember! It was blue. I was talking with blue people. It was important somehow.'

'Maybe you spotted angels through your glass.'

'Maybe so.'

Galileo accepted the artisan's hand, hauled himself up. He surveyed the house, the workshop, the garden, all turning blue in the dawn light. It was like something . . .

'Marc'antonio, do you think it's possible that we could be doing something important?'

Mazzoleni looked doubtful. 'Nobody else does what you do,' he admitted. 'But of course it may just be that you're crazy.'

Galileo said, 'In my dream it was important.'

He stumped over to the couch under the portico and threw himself down on it, pulled a blanket over him. 'I have to sleep.'

'Sure, maestro. Those syncopes must be real tiring.'

'Leave me instantly.'

'Sure.'

Mazzoleni left and he drifted off to sleep. When he woke again it was the cool of early morning, sunlight hitting the top of the garden wall. The morning glory was a well-named flower. The blue of the sky had pale sheets of red and white pulsing inside it.

The stranger's old servant stood there before him, holding out a cup of coffee.

Galileo jerked back. On his face one could see the fear. 'What are you doing here?' He began to remember the stranger's appearance the night before. There had been a big heavy spyglass, that he had sat on his stool to look through . . . 'I thought you were part of the dream!'

'I brought you some coffee,' the ancient one said, looking down and to the side, as if to efface himself. 'I heard you had a long night.'

60

'But who are you?'

The old man shoved the cup even closer to Galileo's face. 'I serve people.'

'You serve that man from Kepler! You came to me last night!'

The old one glanced at him, lifted the cup again.

Galileo took it, slurped down hot coffee. 'What happened?'

'I can't say. You were struck by a syncope for an hour or two in the night.'

'But only after I looked through your master's spyglass?'

'I can't say.'

Galileo regarded him. 'And your master, where is he?'

'I don't know. He's gone.'

'Will he return?'

'I can't say. I think he will.'

'And you? Why are you here?'

'I can serve you. Your housekeeper will hire me, if you tell her to.'

Galileo observed him closely, thinking it over. Something strange had happened the night before, he knew that for sure. Possibly this old geezer could help him remember. Or help him in whatever might come of it. Already it began to seem as if the ancient one had always been there.

'All right. I'll tell her. What's your name?'

'Cartophilus.'

'Lover of maps?'

'Yes.'

'And do you love maps?'

'No. Nor was I ever a shoemaker.'

Galileo nodded, frowned, waved him away. 'I'll speak to her.'

And so Cartophilus came into the service of Galileo, intending (as always, and always with the same failure) to efface himself as much as possible.

*　　*　　*

In the days that followed Galileo slept in short snatches at dawn and after dinner, and every night stayed up to look through his spyglass at Jupiter and the little stars circling it, his typical intense curiosity now tweaked by an odd feeling in the pit of his stomach. He marked the four moons' positions each night using the notation I, II, III, and IV, with I being the closest in the orbits he was now untangling, IV the farthest away. Tracking and timing their movements gave him an increasingly confident sense of how long each took to circle Jupiter. All the expected signs of circular motion seen edge-on had manifested themselves. It was getting clearer what was going on up there.

Obviously he needed to publish these discoveries, to establish his precedence as discoverer. By now Mazzoleni and the artisans had made about a hundred spyglasses, and only ten of them were capable of seeing the new little planets; they became visible only through occhialini with magnifications of thirty times, sometimes twenty-five when the grinding was lucky. (What else had been twenty-five or thirty times larger?) The difficulties in making a device this powerful reassured him; it was unlikely someone else would see the Jovian stars and publish the news before him. Still, it was best not to be slow about it. There was no time to lose.

'I'm going to make those bastard Venetians really regret their skinflint offer!' he declared happily. He was still furious at the senators for questioning his honesty in representing the spyglass as his invention; he took pride in his honesty, a virtue he wielded so vigorously as to make it a fault. He also hated them for delaying their measly raise until the new year. And really, through all the years in Padua, eighteen now, he had kept in the back of his mind the possibility of a return to Florence. He had spent many recent summers back in his home city, some of them tutoring the young prince Cosimo, so he had laid the groundwork for a return.

Now it was time to build on that foundation. Ignoring the little awkwardness that had developed the year before with

Belisario Vinta, he wrote another of his florid notes. It was to accompany the finest spyglass he had: a gift to his most beloved student ever, now the grandissimo Grand Duke Cosimo. The red leather was embossed in gold with typical Florentine and Medici figures; even the transport case was beautiful. In the letter Galileo described his new Jovian discoveries, and asked if it would be permissible to name his newly discovered little Jovian stars after Cosimo; and if so, if the Grand Duke would prefer him to name them the Cosmian Stars, which would merge Cosimo and Cosmic; or perhaps to apply to the four stars the names of Cosimo and his three brothers; or if they should together be named the Medicean Stars.

Vinta wrote back thanking him for the spyglass and informing him that the Grand Duke preferred the name Medicean Stars, as best honouring the family and the city it ruled.

'He accepted the dedication!' Galileo shouted to the household. This was a stupendous coup; Galileo hooted triumphantly as he charged around, rousing everyone and ordering that a fiasco of wine be opened to celebrate. He tossed a ceramic platter high in the air and enjoyed its shattering on the terrace, and the way it made the boys jump.

The best way to announce this dedication to the world was to insert it into the book he was finishing about all the discoveries he had made. He pressed hard to finish; the combination of work by both day and night left him irritable, but it had to be done. He had the spirit for it and more. At night, working by himself, he felt enormously enlarged by all that lay ahead. Sometimes he had to take a break and walk around in the garden to deal with the thoughts crowding his head, the various great futures looming ahead of him like visions. It was only during the day that he flagged, slept at odd hours, snarled at the household and all that it represented. Scribbled at great speed on his pages.

He wrote in Latin so that the book, titled *Sidereus Nuncius*, 'The Starry Messenger', would be immediately comprehensible across all the courts and universities of Europe. In it he described his astronomical findings in more or less chronological order, making it into a narrative of his discoveries. The longest and best passages were on the moon, which he augmented with fine etchings made from his drawings. Of the stars and the four moons of Jupiter he wrote briefly, only announcing his discoveries, which were startling enough not to need embellishment.

He told the story of his introduction to the idea of the occhialino with some circumspection: *About ten months ago a rumour came to our ears that a spyglass had been made by a certain Dutchman by means of which visible objects, although far removed from the eye of the observer, were distinctly seen, as though nearby. This caused me to apply myself totally to investigating the principles and figuring out the means by which I might arrive at the invention of a similar instrument, and I achieved that result shortly afterward on the basis of the science of refraction.*

A few strategic opacities there, but that was all right. He arranged with a Venetian printer, Tomaso Baglioni, for an edition of five hundred and fifty copies. The first page, an illustrated frontispiece, said in Latin:

THE STARRY MESSENGER
Revealing great, unusual, and remarkable spectacles,
opening these to the consideration of every man,
and especially of philosophers and astronomers;
AS OBSERVED BY GALILEO GALILEI
Gentleman of Florence
Professor of Mathematics in the University of Padua,
WITH THE AID OF A PERSPICILLUM
lately invented by him,
In the surface of the moon,
in innumerable Fixed Stars,
in Nebulae, and above all
in FOUR PLANETS

swiftly revolving about Jupiter at differing distance
known to no one before the Author recently percei
that they should be name
THE MEDICEAN STARS
Venice 1610

The first four pages following this great proem of a title
were filled by a dedication to Cosimo Medici that was exceptionally florid, even for Galileo. Jupiter had been in the ascendant at Cosimo's birth, it pointed out, *pouring out with all his*
splendour and grandeur into the most pure air, so that with its
first breath Your tender little body and Your soul, already deco-
rated by God with noble ornaments, could drink in this univer-
sal power . . . Your incredible clemency and kindness . . . Most
Serene Cosimo, Great Hero . . . when you have surpassed Your
peers You will still contend with Yourself, which self and great-
ness You are daily surpassing, Most Merciful Prince . . . from
Your Highness's most loyal servant, Galileo Galilei.

The book was published in March of 1610. The first printing
sold out within the month. Copies circulated throughout
Europe. Indeed its fame was worldwide: within five years word
came that it was being discussed at the Chinese court.

Despite this literary and scientific success, the Galilean household was still running at a loss, with the master's time also massively over-committed. He wrote to his friend Sagredo, *I'm*
always at the service of this or that person. I have to eat up many
hours of the day – often the best ones – in the service of others. I
need a Prince.

On 7th May of 1610 he wrote again to Vinta. He did not
beat around the bush, but made it an explicit letter of application, a real piece of rhetoric. He requested a salary of a thousand florins a year, and sufficient free time to bring to
completion certain works he had in progress. Glancing up at

usty workbooks on the shelf to make sure he forgot
ing, he made a list of what he hoped to publish if he were
ven the time:

Two books on the system and constitution of the universe, an
overarching conception full of philosophy, astronomy, and
geometry; three books on local motion, an entirely new science,
as no one else ancient or modern has discovered the many
amazing properties that I demonstrate to exist in natural and
forced motions, which is why I may call this a new science dis-
covered by me from its first principles; three books on mechan-
ics, two pertaining to principles and foundations, one on its
problems – and though others have written on this same mater-
ial, what has been written to date is not one-quarter of what I
will write, either in quantity or otherwise. I have also various
little works on physical subjects, such as On Sound and Voice,
On Vision and Colours, On the Tides, On the Composition of
the Continuum, On the Motion of Animals, and still more. I will
also write on military science, giving not only a model of what a
soldier ought to be, but also mathematical treatises on fortifica-
tion, the movement of troops, sieges, surveying, estimating
distances and artillery power, and a fuller description of my
military compass,

– which is in fact my greatest invention, a single device that
allows one to make all of the military calculations I have
already mentioned plus also the division of lines, the solution
of the Rule of Three, the equalization of money, the calculation
of interest, proportional reduction of figures and solids,
extraction of square and cube roots, identification of the mean
proportionals, transformation of parallelepipeds into cubes,
determination of proportional weights of metals and other
substances, description of polygons and division of circumfer-
ences into equal parts, squaring of the circle or any other
regular figures, taking the batter of scarps on walls – in short,
an omni-calculator, able to make any computation you could
want, despite which hardly anyone has noticed its existence,

66

and even fewer bought one, so stupid is the common run of humanity!

– he did not add, and so moved on to his conclusion:

Finally, as to the title and the scope of my duties, I wish in addition to the name of Mathematician that His Highness adjoin that of Philosopher. Whether I can and should have this title I shall be able to show Their Highnesses whenever it is their pleasure to give me a chance to deal with this in their presence with the most esteemed men of that profession,

– such as they are, being for the most part grossly overpaid Peripatetic idiots!

– he did not add.

Reading over the final flourishes, it seemed to him that the opportunities being offered to any potential patron were too brilliant to decline. What a great application! What prince could say no to such a thing?

And, in fact, on 24th May, 1610, a reply from Vinta came to the house behind the church of Santa Giustina, the house on Via Vignali where they had all lived and worked together for eighteen years. *Grand Duke Cosimo*, Vinta wrote, *accepts your services.*

Galileo wrote to accept the acceptance on 28th May. On 5th June Vinta wrote back, confirming that his title would be 'Chief Mathematician of the University of Pisa and Philosopher to the Grand Duke'.

Galileo wrote back in turn, asking that his title be revised to 'Mathematician and Philosopher to the Grand Duke'.

He also requested that he be absolved of any further obligation to his two brothers-in-law arising from defaults on dowry payments for his sisters. That would allow him to go home without the inconvenience of embarrassing lawsuits from those disgusting chisellers, or the possibility of arrest. He would go up to them in the streets and say to them, 'I am mathematician and philosopher to the Grand Duke, go fuck yourselves.'

And all this was agreed to in his formal appointment of 10th July of 1610. The new service to Cosimo was to begin in October. It was understood to be a lifetime appointment.

He had a prince.

With the prospect of Galileo's move to Florence, what had never been more than controlled chaos at Hostel Galileo now fell apart into utter chaos. Aside from the practical tasks, Galileo had to deal with a lot of hard feelings in Padua and Venice. Many of the Venetian *pregadi* were outraged to hear he was walking out on his acceptance of their recent offer, calling it gross ingratitude and worse. The procurator Antonio Priuli was particularly bitter: 'I hope I never lay eyes on that ingrate again in my life!' he was said to have shouted, and of course this was quickly reported to Galileo. And it wasn't just Priuli; the anger was widespread. It was obvious Venice would never offer him employment again.

Galileo gritted his teeth and forged on with the chores of the move. This reaction was to be expected, it was just part of the price he had to pay to get patronage. It was a sign that the Venetians had valued him and yet taken advantage of him, and knew it and felt guilty about it, and as people would always rather feel angry than guilty, the transmutation of the one to the other had been easy. It had to be his fault.

He focused on practical matters. Merely boxing up the contents of the big house took weeks, and just at a time when his astronomical work was at a crucial point. Happily that was night work, so that no matter the loud and dusty tumble of days, he could always wake up after an evening meal and a nap, settle down on his stool, and make his observations through the long cool nights. This meant foregoing sleep, but as he had never been much of a sleeper anyway, often existing for months at a time on mere snatches, it did not really matter. And it was all too interesting to stop. 'What must be done can be done,' he would say hoarsely to Mazzoleni as he flogged them through the after-noons. 'We can sleep when we're dead.' In the meantime he slept whenever it was cloudy.

The household therefore avoided him in the morning, when he was often abusive, and even at the best of times a bit befud-dled and melancholy. He would throw things at anyone foolish enough to bother him in the couple of hours it took to pull himself together, and out of what looked like deep sleep he could kick with vicious accuracy.

Once up, groaning and yawning on his bed, he broke his fast on leftovers, then took a walk in his garden. Pulled a few weeds, plucked a lemon or a cluster of grapes, then went back in to face the day: the move, the correspondence, the students, the accounts, eating as he worked, wolfing down sugared ravioli or pork pies, washing it down with wine and cinnamon. At night everyone else would collapse into bed, while he went out to the terrazzo alone and made his observations, using spyglasses they had constructed back in the spring; there would be no more improvements made in them until he was settled in Florence.

And of course there was Marina to attend to. Ever since she had gotten pregnant, Galileo had provided her with the funds to rent and keep a little house on the Ponte Corvo, around the corner from his place, so that he could sometimes drop off the girls on the way to his lectures at Il Bo. Now Virginia was ten, Livia nine, and Vincenzio four. They had spent their whole lives between the two houses, the girls mostly in Galileo's big place, being taken care of by the servants. Now decisions had to be made.

Galileo stumped down to the Ponte Corvo unhappily, ready-ing himself for the inevitable tongue-lashing. He was a barrel of a man with a red beard and wild hair, but now he looked small. At moments like these he could not help remembering his poor father. Vincenzio Galilei had been the most hen-pecked pussy-whipped pancake of a husband in the history of mankind; he had felt the lash daily, Galileo had seen it with his own eyes. Marina was nothing compared to the old dragon, who was an educated woman and knew just where to stick the knives. Indeed Giulia was even now a more fearful presence to Galileo than Marina, no matter Marina's black gaze, her cobalt-edged tongue and thick right arm. He had heard so many harangues in his life that they simply bounced off him; he was an expert in them, a connoisseur, and there was no doubt in his mind that the old rolling pin was champion of the world. He recalled his father's hung head, the tightness at the corners of his mouth – the way he would pick up his lute and hit its strings, playing double time and fortissimo, even though this only served as accompaniment to Giulia's dread arias, which were louder by far than the lute – these scenes were all too clear in Galileo's mind, if he did not avoid them.

And yet here he had gone and done the same thing as his dad: coupled with a younger woman; no doubt it led to some fundamental imbalance, or just the natural contempt of youth for age. In any case here was another Galilei about to get thrashed by a strong-armed woman, hesitating to knock at the door. Fearful to knock.

He knocked. She answered with a shout, knowing by the rap who it was.

He entered. She kept the place clean, there was no doubt of that. Perhaps she did it to emphasize the paucity of furniture, or the confusion and squalor of his place. She stood in the kitchen doorway wiping her hands, as beautiful as ever, even though the years had been hard on her. Black hair, black eyes, a face that still caught Galileo's breath; the body he loved, her hand on her hip, washcloth flung over her shoulder.

'I heard,' she told him.

'I figured you would.'

'So – what now?'

She watched him, expecting nothing. It wasn't like the time he had explained what their arrangement would be, sitting on the fondamenta in Venice with her five months pregnant. That had been hard. This was merely awkward and tedious. They hadn't been in love for many years. She was seeing a man out near the docks on the canal, a butcher he thought it was. He had what he wanted. Still, that look, that time in Venice – it shot through into this time too, it was still there between them. He had a particular sensitivity to looks, no doubt the result of growing up with Medusa for a mother.

'The girls will come with me,' he said. 'Vincenzio is too young, he still needs you.'

'They all need me.'

'I'm taking the girls to Florence.'

'Livia won't like it. She hates your place. It's too loud for her, there are too many people.'

Galileo sighed. 'It will be a bigger place. And I won't be taking in students any more.'

'So now you're a court creature.'

'I am the prince's philosopher.'

She laughed. 'No more compasses.'

'That's right.'

They both went silent, thinking perhaps about how his compass had been an ongoing joke between them.

'All right then,' she said. 'We'll be in touch.'

'Yes, of course. I'll keep paying for this place. And I'll need to see Vincenzio. In a few years he'll need to move to Florence too. Maybe you can move to Florence then too, if you want.'

She stared at him. She could still flay him with a look; but the tightness at the corners of her mouth reminded him of his father, and he felt a stab of remorse, thinking that maybe now he was the Giulia. A horrible thought; but there was nothing for it but to nod and take his leave, the back of his neck crawling under the heat of that fiery gaze.

All during this time he continued to make his nightly observations, and to spread the word concerning the usefulness of his glass. Occhialino, visorio, perspicullum – different people

71

called it different things, and he did too. He sent excellent glasses to the Duke of Bavaria, the Elector of Cologne, and Cardinal del Monte, among other nobles of court and church. He was now in the service of the Medicis, of course, but the Medici would want the capabilities of his glass advertised to as many of the powers in Europe as possible. And it was important to establish the legitimacy of what Galileo had reported in his book by having it confirmed in other places by influential figures. He had heard there were people like Cremonini refusing to look through a glass, and others claiming his new discoveries were merely optical illusions, artifacts of the instrument itself. Indeed he had suffered an unfortunate demonstration in Bologna, when he had tried to show the famous astronomer Giovanni Magini the Medicean stars, and only been able to see one himself; which may have been because three were behind Jupiter, but it was a hard case to make, especially with the odious Bohemian climber Martin Horky there smirking at every word, obviously delighted that things weren't going as planned. Afterward he heard that Horky had written to Kepler telling him that the visorio was a fraud, useless for astronomy.

Kepler was experienced enough to ignore backstabbing by such a loathsome toad, but his characteristically long and incoherent letter in support of Galileo's discoveries, published as a book for the world to read under the title *Dissertatio cum Nuncio Sidereo*, was in some ways as bad as the Horky nonsense. Confusions from Kepler were nothing new, although up until this point they had always made Galileo laugh. One time for the entertainment of his artisans he had translated into Tuscan Kepler's claim that the music of the spheres was a literal sound made by the planets, a six-note chord which moved from major to minor depending on whether Mars was at perihelia or aphelia. This idea made Galileo laugh so hard he could barely read. He wiped tears from his eyes as he went on: 'The chapter's title is "Which Planet Sings Soprano, Which Alto, Which Tenor, and Which Bass!" I swear to God! The greatest astronomer of our time! He admits he has no basis for this stuff except his own desire for it, and then concludes that Jupiter and Saturn must sing bass, Mars tenor, Earth and Venus alto, and Mercury soprano.'

'But of course!' The workshop gang then sang in their usual four-part harmony one of their rudest love songs, replacing all the usual girls' names with 'Venus'.

That was Kepler: a good source for jokes. Now, reading Kepler's defence of his discoveries, Galileo felt an uneasiness that sharpened the further he read. Lots of people would read this book, but much of Kepler's praise was so harebrained it cut both ways:

I may perhaps seem rash in accepting your claims so readily with no support from my own experience. But why should I not believe a most learned mathematician, whose very style attests to the soundness of his judgement? He has no intention of practising deception in a bid for vulgar publicity, nor does he pretend to have seen what he has not seen. Because he loves the truth, he does not hesitate to oppose even the most familiar opinions, and to bear the jeers of the crowd with equanimity.

What jeers of the crowd? For one thing there hadn't been that many, and for another, Galileo did *not* bear them with equanimity: he wanted to kill every critic he had. He liked fights in the same way bulls are attracted to red – not because it looks like blood, or so they say, but because it has the colour of the pulsing parts of cows in heat. Galileo loved to fight like that. And so far he had never lost one. So equanimity had nothing to do with it.

Then further on in Kepler's fatuous endorsement he asked what Galileo saw through his perspicillum when he looked at 'the left corner of the face of the Man in the Moon,' because it turned out that Kepler had a theory about that region, which he now propounded to the world – that a certain mark there was the work of intelligent beings who lived on the Moon, who must therefore have to endure days the equal of fourteen days on Earth. Kepler wrote,

Therefore they feel insufferable heat. Perhaps they lack stone for erecting shelters against the sun. On the other hand, maybe they have a soil as sticky as clay. Their usual building plan, accordingly, is as follows. Digging up huge fields, they carry out the earth and heap it in a circle, perhaps for the purpose of drawing out the moisture down below. In this way they may hide in the deep shade behind their excavated mounds and, in keeping with the sun's motion, shift about inside, clinging to the shadow. They have, as it were, a sort of underground city. They make their homes in numerous caves hewn out of that circular embankment. They place their fields and pastures in the middle, to avoid being forced to go too far away from their farms in their flight from the sun.

Galileo's jaw dropped as he read this. He was growing to dread the appearance of the word *accordingly* in Kepler's work, a tic which always marked precisely the point where sequential logic was being tossed aside.

A few pages later—Galileo groaned aloud—worse yet: Kepler spoke of the difference Galileo had noted through his spyglass between the light of the planets and that of the fixed stars: *What other conclusion shall we draw from this difference, Galileo, than that the fixed stars generate their light from within, whereas the planets, being opaque, are illuminated from without; that is, to use Bruno's terms, the former are suns, the latter, moons or earths?*

Just the sight of Bruno's name in the same sentence as his own was enough to churn his stomach.

Then he came to a passage that made him go chill and hot at the same time. He didn't know whether to laugh or cry:

The conclusion is quite clear. Our moon exists for us on the earth, not for the other globes. Those four little moons exist for Jupiter, not for us. Each planet in turn, together with its occupants, is served by its own satellites. From this line of reason we

deduce with the highest degree of probability that Jupiter is inhabited.

Galileo threw this pretzel craziness to the floor with a curse and stalked out into his garden, wondering why his hilarity had so quickly turned to dread. 'Kepler is some kind of idiot!' he shouted at Mazzoleni. 'His reasoning is completely deranged! Inhabitants of Jupiter? Where the hell did *that* come from?'

And why was it so disturbing to read it?

The stranger . . . the man who had told him about the occhialino, that afternoon in Venice . . . who had appeared after the great demonstration to the Venetian Senate, and suggested he take a look at the moon – had he not said something about coming from Kepler? Quick flashes of something more – a blue like twilight – Had the stranger not come knocking at the gate one night some time ago? Had Cartophilus not joined the household soon after?

Galileo was not used to having a vague memory for anything. Normally he would have said that he remembered basically everything that had ever happened to him, or that he had read or thought; that, in fact, he remembered too much, as quite a bit of what he recalled stuck in his brain like splinters of glass, stealing his sleep. He kept his thoughts busy partly in order not to be stuck by anything too sharp. But in this matter that clarity did not exist. There were blurs, as if he had been sick.

Cartophilus appeared and picked up Kepler's book from the floor of the arcade, dusted it off, looked at it curiously. He glanced at Galileo, who glared at him as if he could drag the truth from the old man by look alone. A nameless fear pierced Galileo: 'What does this mean!' he shouted at the wizened old man, striding toward him as if to beat him. 'What's going on?'

Cartophilus shrugged furtively, almost sullenly, and put the book on a side table, closed so that the page Galileo had been reading was lost. Inhabitants of Jupiter! He said, 'I'm supposed to be packing the pots.' And he left the arcade and went inside, as if Galileo were not his master and had not just asked a question of him.

Galileo's return to Florence was now being called a breach of contract by the outspoken Priuli, as well as a personal betrayal: the Doge should ask Galileo for some of his salary to be returned.

With the mood turning so hard against him, it was a great comfort to Galileo to know that Fra Paolo Sarpi was a steadfast friend and supporter, as he had always been. Having Sarpi on his side was important.

The great Servite visited the Via Vignali when he was passing through Padua, to give support to Galileo, and to see how his combustible friend was doing. He brought with him a letter to Galileo from their mutual friend Sagredo, who was returning from Syria and had found out by mail about Galileo's decision to move to Florence. Sagredo, concerned, had written, *Who can invent a visorio which can tell the crazy person from the sane, the good neighbour from the bad?*

Sarpi, it quickly became clear, felt much the same. Galileo sat with him on the terrace overlooking the garden, fruit and some jugs of new wine on a table beside them. Relaxing in this little hole in the city under its stucco walls was something they had done many times before, for Sarpi was no ordinary priestly mentor. Like Galileo, he was a philosopher, and in the same years Galileo had worked on mechanics he had made investigations of his own, discovering such things as the little valves inside human veins, and the oscillations of the pupil of the eye, and the polar attraction of magnets. Galileo had helped him with this last, and Sarpi had helped Galileo with his military compass, and even with the laws of motion.

Now the great Fra Paolo drank deeply, put his feet up, and sighed. 'I'm very sorry to see you go,' he said. 'Things won't be the same around here, and that's the truth. I'll hope for the best, but like Francesco, I'm concerned about your long-term welfare. In Venice you would have always been protected from Rome.'

Galileo shrugged. 'I have to be able to do my work,' he insisted.

Sarpi's point made him uneasy, nevertheless. No one had better reason to worry about protection from Rome than Sarpi; the evidence of that was right there in Sarpi's horribly scarred face, his disfigured smile. 'You know my joke,' he reminded Galileo, putting his hand to his wounds. 'I recognize the curial style' – *style* meaning also a kind of stiletto.

It was all part of the ongoing war between Venice and the Vatican, which was partly a public war of words, a matter of curses and imprecations so angry that at one point Pope Paul V had excommunicated the entire population of the Serenissima; but at the same time it was a silent nighttime war, a vicious thing of knives and drownings. Leonardo Dona had been elected doge precisely because he was a notorious anti-Romanist, and Dona had appointed Sarpi to be his principal counsellor. When Sarpi had announced to the world his intention to write a full history of the Council of Trent, using as source material the secret files of the Venetian representatives to the Council, Paul was alarmed as well as angered. The files were certain to contain many ugly revelations about the Vatican's desperate campaign in the previous century to stem the tide of Protestantism. It would be an exposé, in short. Assassins were authorized by the Pope to go to Venice to murder Sarpi; but the Venetian government had many spies in Rome, and they heard of the plan in advance, with some of the assassins even identified by name. The Venetian authorities had arrested them on their appearance on the docks, and thrown them in prison.

After that Sarpi had accepted a bodyguard, a man who was to stay with him at all times and sleep on his doorstep.

Some of those involved in the matter were not convinced that a single bodyguard would be enough.

*   *   *

The attack took place on the night of 7th October, 1607. A fire broke out near San Maria Formosa, the big church just north of San Marco; whether the fire was set for this purpose or not, Sarpi's fool of a bodyguard left his post at the Signoria to go have a look at it. When Sarpi was done with his business, he waited a while for the man, then left for the Servite monastery accompanied only by an elderly servant and a Venetian senator, also elderly. He took his usual route home, which anyone could have determined by watching him for even a week: north on the Merceria, past the Rialto and Sagredo's palazzo to the Campo di Santa Fosca. Then north over the Ponte della Pugna, the Bridge of Wrestlers, a narrow stepped bridge over the Rio de' Servi, near the Servite monastery, where Sarpi slept in a simple monk's cell.

They jumped him on the north side of the bridge, five of them, stabbing his companions first and then chasing Sarpi down the Calle Zancani. When they caught him they smashed him to the ground and stabbed him and ran – later we counted fifteen wounds, but it took only a couple of seconds and they were off into the night.

Trailing at a discreet distance as we had been, we could only shriek and race over the bridge and kneel by the old man, applying pressure to the cuts as we found them in the flickering torch-light. A stiletto had been left in his right temple, apparently bent on his upper jawbone, re-emerging from his right cheek. That wound by itself looked fatal.

But for the moment he was still alive, his breath rapid and shallow, failing fast. Women were screaming from the windows overlooking the bridge, shouting directions for the pursuit of the cutthroats. Very soon we would be joined by others; already people were on the bridge calling out. But it was very dark despite the torches, so we shot him up with antibiotics and glued shut a slashed vein in the groin that was sure to kill him. When others arrived beside us, all we could do was help to lift him up, help to carry him as gently as possible to his monastery.

There in his bare stone room he lay hovering on the edge of death, not just that night but for the next three weeks. Acquapendente came over from Padua and watched over him night and day; we could only apply antibiotics when the great doctor slept. The doctor worried that the stiletto had been poisoned, and tried to determine whether it had been by having it stuck into a chicken and then a dog. The animals survived; and Sarpi survived too.

So now Sarpi could sit with Galileo, and warn him, with an ironic smile given an extra twist by his scars: 'Rome can be dangerous.'

'Yes yes.' Galileo nodded unhappily. He had visited Sarpi often as he hovered between life and death, he had even helped Acquapendente to extract the stiletto from his poor face. The pink scars were still livid. That Pope Paul had given the assailants a pension to reward them, even though they had been unsuccessful, both Galileo and Sarpi had found funny. Of course what Sarpi was pointing out now was true: Florence was under the thumb of Rome in a way Venice never had been. If Galileo ever offended the Church, as seemed quite possible, Sarpi reminded him, given his new astronomical discoveries and some priestly objections to them, not to mention Kepler's ravings – then Florence might not be far enough away from the long reach of the Dogs of God.

'I know,' Galileo said. But he was already committed to the move; and Sarpi's example cut both ways, so to speak: Florence was an ally of Rome's, Venice a fierce opponent, excommunicated en masse. Moving to Florence might give him some cover.

Sarpi seemed to read these thoughts on his face. 'A patron is never as secure as a contract with the Senate,' he said. 'You know what always happens to a patron's favoured ones: they fall. Sooner or later it always happens.'

'Yes yes.' They had both read their Machiavelli and

79

Castiglione, and the fall of the favourite was a standard trope in poetry and song. It was one of the ways that patrons showed their power, and stirred the pot, and kept those on the rise hopeful.

'So that's another way you will not be as safe.'

'I know. But I have to be able to do my work. I have to be able to make ends meet. Neither has been possible for me in Padua. The Senate could have made it possible, but they didn't. They paid me poorly, and worked me like a donkey. And they were never going to pay me just to do my own work.'

'No.' Sarpi smiled at him affectionately. 'You need a patron to be able to get money without working for it.'

'I work hard!'

'I know you do.'

'And it will be useful work, to Cosimo and to everyone!'

'I know it will. I want you to do your work, you know that. May God bless you for it, I'm sure He will. But you will have to take care what you say.'

'I know.'

Galileo did not want to agree. He never wanted to agree; agreeing was something other people did, with him, after they had disagreed. People were always giving in to his superior logic and his intense style of disputation. In debate he was boastful and sarcastic, funny and smart – really smart, in that he was not just quick, though he was that, but penetrating. No one liked arguing with Galileo.

But with Sarpi it was not like that. For many years Sarpi had been a kind of patron to him, but also much more: a mentor, a confessor, a fellow scientist, a father figure; and above all, a close friend, even now when Galileo was leaving Sarpi's beloved Venice. His scarred face, ruined by the Pope's murderous functionaries, held now an expression of grave concern, and of love and indulgent affection – *amorevolezza*. He did not agree with Galileo, but he was proud of him. It was the look you wanted your father to have when he looked at you. It could not be gainsaid. Galileo could only bow his head and dash the tears from his eyes. For he had to go.

So, after months of preparations, Galileo moved to Florence, leaving behind not only Marina and little Vincenzio, but also all his private students, and most of the servants and artisans as well, even Mazzoleni and his family. 'I won't be needing a workshop anymore,' Galileo explained brusquely. 'I'm a philosopher now.' This sounded so ridiculous that he added, 'The grand duke's mechanicians will be available to me if I need anything.'

No more compasses, in other words. No more Padua. He was saying good-bye to all of it, and didn't want any part coming with him. 'You can keep making the compasses here,' he told Mazzoleni, then turned his back and left the workshop. The compasses were what Mazzoleni had been hired to manufacture in the first place. Of course they wouldn't sell very well without the course Galileo gave in their use, but there were some instruction manuals left, and it was better than nothing. Besides there was artisanal work all over Padua.

The big house on Via Vignoli was emptied, its people dispersed. One day in the fall it was handed back over to the landlord, and that whole little world was gone.

In Florence Galileo had hastily rented a house that was a bit too near the Arno, but it had a little roof terrace for his night viewing, what the Venetians called an *altana*, and he figured he could find a more suitable establishment later. And a new acquaintance, a beautiful young Florentine nobleman named Filippo Salviati, assured him that during the year of his lease he could spend as much time as he liked at Salviati's palazzo in town and at his villa, the Villa delle Selve, in the hills west of Florence. Galileo was pleased; he found the river vapours in Florence unpleasant, also the nearby presence of his mother. Since his father's death he had kept the old washtub in a house in a poor part of the city, but he never visited her, and didn't want to now. Better to spend his time out at Salviati's, writing books and discussing philosophical matters with his new friend and his friend's circle of acquaintances, men of high quality. When Cosimo wanted him, he could ride into the city quickly; and there would be no need to fear running into his mother by accident. Fra Sarpi, who knew of this fear, had suggested that Galileo try to effect a reconciliation with her, but he didn't know the half of it; indeed, he didn't know the hundredth part of it. Galileo had recently received a letter from her welcoming him back to 'his home town', and asking him to drop by and visit her, who was so lonely for him. Galileo snorted as he read this; along with everything else stuck in his memory, in his pin cushion of a brain, there was something new to add: in their departure from Via Vignali the cook had found a letter left behind by a servant she had fired, one Alessandro Piersanti, who had earlier worked in Florence for the old firedog. Giulia had written to him,

Since your master is so ungrateful to you and to everyone, and as he has so many lenses, you could very easily take three or four and put them at the bottom of a small box, and fill it up with d'A'quapendente's pills, and then send it to me. Then, she went on, she would sell them and share the proceeds with him.

'Jesus Christ!' Galileo had shouted. 'Thief on the cross!' He had thrown the letter down in disgust. Then he picked it up and saved it in his files, just in case it might be useful someday. It was dated 9th January of that year – which meant that the very week that Galileo was discovering the Medicean Stars and changing the skies forever, his own mother was conspiring to steal his spyglass lenses out of his house and sell them for her own profit. 'Jesus son of Mary. Why not just steal the eyes out of my head.'

That was his mother for you. Giulia Galilei, suborner of servants, thief of the heart of his work. He would reside out at Salviati's villa as much as he could.

*   *   *

Florentine nights were at first smokier than in Padua, but as the fall of his *anno mirabilis* moved toward winter, they turned cold enough to clarify the air, and keeping track of Jupiter's four moons became easier. In December one of his former students, Benedetto Castelli, now a priest, wrote to suggest that if the Copernican explanation were indeed correct, then Venus was orbiting the Sun also, in an orbit closer to the Sun than Earth's, so that one might therefore be able through an occhialino to see it go through phases like the moon's, as one would be seeing either the side facing the sun or the dark side, or in between.

This thought had already occurred to Galileo, and he was irritated that he had forgotten to write it down in the *Sidereus Nuncius*. Then he remembered: Venus had been behind the sun the previous winter when he was writing the book, so he had been unable to check to see if the idea was right, and had thought it better to keep the notion to himself.

Now he turned his best occhialino toward Venus as it appeared in the sky after sunset. In the first days of viewing it was low, a small full disc; then as the weeks passed it rose higher and became larger, but was misshapen – possibly gibbous. Finally it was revealed in the glass to have the shape of a little half-moon, and Galileo wrote Castelli to tell him so. Eventually, when it began to sink again toward the horizon at its first twilight appearance, it was clearly horned. Galileo's latest spyglass had a very fine objective lens that he had ground himself, and in the eyepiece the image of Venus gleamed, distinctly crescent, a miniature of the new moon that had set just an hour before.

Standing up straight, looking at the brilliant white point, feeling the moon just under the horizon and still shedding its light into the night air, suddenly it all fell into place for him. Copernicus was right; the ball of Venus and the ball of the Earth both rolled around the sun; the ball of the moon rolled around the Earth; the balls of Jupiter's four moons circled the ball of Jupiter, which slowly circled the sun. Saturn was further out and slower, Mercury quickest of all, there inside Venus, where it was difficult to spot. Perhaps a good enough glass would see its horns as well, for certainly it too would go through phases. So close to the sun, when visible at all it would have to be pretty near quarter phase. Farther out from Earth, Mars rolled between Earth and Jupiter, close enough to Earth to explain the strange back-and-forth aspects of its movement, a shift of perspective created by the two orbits.

The whole system was a matter of circles going around other circles. Copernicus had been right. His system had called for Venus to have phases, and there they were; while the Ptolemaic theory, advocated by the Peripatetics, would specifically reject these phases, as Venus was supposed to be going around the Earth, like the sun and everything else in the sky. Venus's phases were a kind of proof, or at least a very suggestive piece of evidence. Tycho Brahe's weird and unwieldy formulation, which had the planets circling the sun but the sun circling the Earth, would also save these particular appearances, but it was a ridiculous explanation in all other respects, in particular simple parsimony. No, these phases of Venus were best explained by Copernicus. They were the strongest indication Galileo had seen – not exactly proof, but powerfully suggestive. All those years in Padua he had taught both Aristotle and Copernicus, and even Tycho, thinking that all of them merely saved the appearances without in any sense explaining what was going on. The Copernican explanation required that the Earth be moving, after all, which seemed wrong – an idea only, not a sensible reality. And the foremost advocate of Copernicanism, Kepler, had been so long-winded and incomprehensible that no one could be convinced by him. And yet here it was, the truth of the situation – the cosmos revealed in a single stroke as being one way rather than another. The Earth was spinning under his feet, also rolling around the sun. Circles in circles.

Again he rang like a bell. His flesh buzzed like struck bronze, his hair stood on end. How things worked; it had to be; and he rang. He danced. He circled his occhialino like the Earth circling the sun, spinning in a slow four-step as he made his little orbit on the altana, arms swinging, fingers directing the music of the spheres, which despite Kepler's craziness seemed suddenly plausible; indeed an audible chord was now ringing silently in his ears.

Then came a knock on the door below. He halted his dance with a jerk, looked down the staircase on the outside of the house.

Cartophilus was there inside the gate, holding a shuttered lantern, looking up at him. Galileo rushed down the stairs and raised a fist as if to strike him. 'What is this?' he exclaimed in a low furious voice. 'Is he here again?'

Cartophilus nodded. 'He's here.'

Chapter Five The Other

When she saw that it was not that I would not speak, but that, dumbstruck, I could not, she gently laid her hand on my breast and said, 'It is nothing serious, only a touch of amnesia, the common disease of deluded minds. He has forgotten for a while who he is, but he will soon remember once he has recognized me. To make it easier for him I will wipe a little of the blinding cloud of the world from his eyes.'

– BOETHIUS, The Consolation of Philosophy

Galileo strode to the gate and hauled it open just as another knock pounded it. The tall stranger stood there looking down at him, his massive perspicillum case in a heap at his feet. He looked flushed, and his eyes were like black fire.

Galileo felt his blood pound in his head. 'Already you have found me.'

'Yes,' the man said.

'Did this servant you foisted on me tell you where I was?' Galileo demanded, jerking a thumb toward the hangdog Cartophilus.

'I knew where you were. Are you willing to make another night journey?'

Galileo's mouth was dry. He struggled to remember more than that flicker of blue. Blue people – 'Yes,' he said, before knowing he would.

The stranger nodded dourly and glanced over at Cartophilus, who trudged out the gate and hauled the case over the paving stones into the courtyard. Jupiter lay low in the sky above Scorpio, still tangled with the trees.

The man's heavy perspicillum seemed more than a spyglass. Galileo helped Cartophilus set up the tripod and to lift the fat tube, which looked to be made of something like pewter, but felt heavier than gold. When they had the device set on its stand and pointed toward Jupiter, which aiming it seemed to do on its own, Galileo swallowed hard, feeling again his dry mouth, his nameless apprehension. He sat on his stool, looked into the strangely luminous glass of the eyepiece. He fell up into it.

Around him lofted a transparent glow, like talcum in sunlight. What is it, he tried to say, and must have succeeded; the stranger replied in his crow's Latin, 'Around Jupiter hums a magnetic field so strong that people would die of it, if unprotected. It has to be held off by a similar field of our own creation, a counterforce. The glow marks an interference of the two forces.'

'I see,' Galileo murmured.

So he stood on the surface of Europa – again. Some memory of his previous visit had come back to him, though vaguely. The stars trembled overhead as if he were still looking at them through his occhialino, the bigger ones fulgurous, shedding flakes and threads of light into the blackness around them.

The surface of Europa, on the other hand, was exceptionally sharp and clear. The flat ice extended to the horizon that circled them so tightly, opaque white tinted the colour of Jupiter, and stained blue or ochre in some areas; sometimes pocked or chewed at the surface, sometimes deeply cracked in radial patterns; elsewhere smooth as glass. Everywhere it was littered with small rocks, and here and there stood a few house-sized boulders, pitted with holes and depressions. Most of the rocks were almost as black as the sky, but a few were metallic

87

grey, or red, the same shade as the red spot low on the banded immense surface of Jupiter. That awesome globe loomed directly overhead, huge in the starry night sky even though only half lit. That was the thing that was twenty-five or thirty times bigger which he had been trying to remember. Its dark half was very dark.

Possibly the tight horizon and the thin air gave the landscape its unreal clarity. The thin air was cool, the sun nowhere to be seen. The two men cast sharp shadows on the ice under them. Galileo, constantly troubled at home by fogged or ringed vision, stared around avidly. Here everyone had hawks' eyes.

'This is a hot spot, in local terms,' the stranger said in the breathy silence. To Galileo the ice looked everywhere the same, and cold. Their feet crunched as the stranger led him to one of the biggest boulders.

There proved to be a door in this rock, which was not a rock, but rather some kind of carriage or ship, roughly ovoid in shape, lying on the ice like a great black egg. Its surface was smooth, not rocky or metallic, but more like horn or ebony.

A door in this surface opened by sliding sideways in the wall, revealing a flight of low black steps. The stranger gestured to Galileo, indicating the entry.

'This is our vessel. We have learned that the Europans are going to stage an illegal incursion into the ocean under this ice. They have ignored our warnings, and the relevant authorities in the Jovian system have declined to interfere, so we are taking it on ourselves to stop them. We think any incursion will be potentially disastrous in ways these people haven't even considered. We want to intercept them if we can, and keep them from doing harm. And at the very least, see what they do down there. If what happens is as bad as I fear it could be, they will not tell the truth about it. So we must follow them in. With luck we will get down there first, and can stop them when they break through the layer of ice into the water below.'

'And you want me to go with you?' Galileo asked.

'Yes.' Ganymede hesitated, then said, 'You should know the nature of the threat.'

Then something caught his attention over Galileo's shoulder, and he looked startled; Galileo turned and saw a silver object on a tripod, like the perspicillum only bigger, coming down on a pillar of white fire, roaring faintly in the thin air.

The tall man put a hand to Galileo's shoulder. 'If there is danger, I will transport you back to your own time. The transition may be abrupt.'

A slit in the silver craft opened and a figure in white emerged.

'Do you know who this is?' Galileo asked.

'Yes, I think so. You met her before, when we spoke to the council.'

'Ah yes. Hera, she said. Jupiter's wife?'

'She thinks she's that big,' the stranger said sourly; then added under his breath, 'It's almost true.'

The woman was indeed large: tall, broad-shouldered, wide-hipped, thick-armed, deep-chested. She approached and stopped before them, looking down at the stranger with her ironic smile. 'Ganymede, I know you hate what they plan to do here,' she said. 'And yet here you are. What's going on? Are you planning to hurt them?'

The stranger, who did not look like Galileo's idea of Ganymede, faced her like an upright axe. 'You know what they'll say about this on Callisto if they hear about it. We hold the same view they do. The only difference is that we're willing to do something about it.'

'And so you bring this Galileo along with you?'

'He is the first scientist, he will be our witness to the council, and speak for us later.'

She did not think much of this, Galileo saw. 'You use him as a human shield, I think. While you have him with you, the Europans won't attack you.'

'They won't in any case.'

She shrugged. 'I want to be a witness too. I want to see what

89

happens, and I am your appointed mnemosyne, whether you acknowledge that or not. Let me join you, or my people will alert the Europans that you are here.'

Ganymede stepped to the side, gestured at the door of the ovoid vessel. 'Be my guest. I want everyone to see just how irresponsible their incursion is.'

Inside the vessel a few people huddled over banks of glass instruments and glowing squares of jewel colour. Their faces, lit from below by the glowing desk tops, looked monstrous. The livid glare of Jupiter seemed to leak out of their eyes.

Standing beside Galileo, Hera leaned over to speak in his ear; again her words came to him in a rustic Tuscan Italian, like something from Ruzante. 'You understand that they're using you?'

'Not necessarily.'

'Do you know where you are?'

'This is one of the four moons orbiting Jupiter. I named them myself; they are called the Medicean Stars.'

Her smile was wicked. 'That name didn't stick. It's only remembered now by historians, as a notorious example of science kissing the ass of power.'

Affronted, Galileo said, 'It was nothing of the sort!'

She laughed at him. 'Sorry, but from our perspective it's all too obvious. And always was, I'm sure. You failed to consider that major planetary bodies are not best named for one's political patrons.'

'What do you call them, then?'

'They are named Io, Europa, Ganymede and Callisto.'

'Collectively,' Ganymede interjected, 'they are called the Galilean moons.'

'Well!' Galileo said, taken aback. For a moment he was at a loss. Then he said, 'That's a good name, I must admit.' After a moment's confusion he added, 'Not greatly different than a name like Medici, if I am not mistaken—' with a bold look at Hera.

She laughed again. 'The discoverer of something is not the same as the discoverer's patron. His hoped-for patron, to be precise. Making the name a gross bit of flattery, a kind of bribe.'

'Well, I couldn't very well name them for myself,' Galileo pointed out. 'So I had to choose something useful, did I not?'

She shook her head, unconvinced. But she had stopped laughing at him.

When he saw a chance, Galileo drifted over to her so they could speak *sotto voce* again. 'You all speak as if I am someone from your past,' he noted. 'What do you mean?'

'Your time is earlier than ours.'

Galileo struggled to comprehend this; he had been presuming that the stranger's device had merely been transporting him across space. 'What time is it here, then? What year?'

'In your terms it is the year 3020.'

Galileo felt his mouth hanging open as he struggled to grasp this news. Transported not only to Europa, but to a time some fourteen hundred years after his own . . . Stunned, he said weakly, 'That explains many things I did not understand.'

Her wicked smile again.

'Of course it creates new mysteries as well,' he added.

'Indeed.' She was looking at him with an expression he couldn't read. She was not an angel, or an otherworldly creature, but a human like him. A very imposing woman.

There was a ping, a small jolt, and the room tilted to the side. Ganymede pointed to a white globe, lit from within, floating in the corner of the room. 'A globe of Europa,' he said to Galileo. He explained that its whites were faintly shaded to indicate the temperature of the surface; most of it was pale blue, crisscrossed by many faint green lines. Galileo crossed the room to look more closely at it, checking automatically for geometrical patterns in the surface craquelure. Triangles, parallelograms, spicules, radiola, pentagons . . . Where the lines intersected, the greens sometimes turned yellow, and in a few cases the yellow shifted to orange.

'The tides break the ice,' Ganymede explained, 'and convective upwellings fill some of the cracks in the ice, forming vertical zones like artesian wells, that can serve as channels down to the liquid ocean. On Ganymede we called them flues.'

'Tides?' Galileo asked. 'How can there be tides?'

All the Jovians stared at him. Hera shook her head briefly, as if the explanation would be beyond Galileo's understanding. Irritated, he looked to Ganymede, who shrugged uncomfortably.

'Gravity, you see . . . Perhaps we can discuss it another time. Because now we have begun our journey into the interior. We descend by melting the ice as we go, to clear the flue.'

The craft tilted first at one angle then another. A large rectangular patch on the chamber's wall was filled with glowing primary colours, as if a rainbow had been used for paint. Ganymede informed him that their vessel was represented by the black pendant in the middle of this rectangle, and flowing upward past it were ribbons of rainbow colour, orange strands closest to the black blob, yellow and green twining around them. Off to one side, a larger rectangle was apparently a window, giving them a view of what passed outside; this consisted of nothing but a field of the darkest blue imaginable, a blue so deep and pure that it captured Galileo's eye, and exhibited small reticulations and lighter gleams, revealing perhaps that it was an icy slush. It gave him much less information than the other rectangle, the brilliant colours indicating temperatures as he was informed they did.

Down, down, down some more. The blue outside the window flowed upward more swiftly, and darkened even more. The temperature 'picture' likewise flowed. Otherwise there was only the hum of the vessel's machines, the brush of its air. Once Galileo had dreamed of falling off a ship and sinking into the Adriatic. Now they were all dreaming together.

Ganymede hated the necessity of this dive, hated the very idea of an intrusion into the ocean under the ice, and it soon became clear that his crew shared his opinion. They eyed their pictures with grim expressions, and said little; Ganymede strode back and forth nervously behind them, consulting with them in turn.

On the rainbow panel a green potato-shaped patch moved upward; it looked like a boulder. Galileo asked about it.

'A meteorite,' Ganymede replied. 'Space is full of rocks. The shooting stars you see in your night sky are rocks, often as small as sand grains, burning very brightly.'

'Friction with air is enough to ignite rock?'

'They are moving really very fast. Here on Europa there is no atmosphere, however, so whatever it encounters crashes straight into the ice. It happens a lot, but impact craters in ice quickly deform and flow back toward flatness.'

'No atmosphere? What about the air we were breathing up there?'

'We live inside bubbles of air, held in place by forces or materials.'

Their vessel stopped in its descent; it was interesting to Galileo how clearly he could feel the halt, subtle though it was.

Ganymede said, 'Pauline, is everything going well?'

'All is well,' said a woman's voice, apparently from within the walls of the vessel.

'How soon will it be before we reach the ocean?'

'If we maintain this speed it will be thirty minutes.'

'Is the Ariadne thread unspooling cleanly?'

'Yes.'

Ganymede said to Galileo, 'The Ariadne thread is also a heating element, and will keep the central line of our flue liquid, to ease our return.'

They waited, absorbed in their thoughts. The light downward pull of Europa made the crew's movements around the bridge fluid and slow, like dance in a dream. Galileo found it hard to keep his balance, it was somewhat like floating in a river.

He drifted to Hera's side and said, 'All these machines have to work for us to stay alive.'

'Yes, that's right.'

'It seems risky.'

'It is. But because it is, we engineer for safety. Materials and power available are terrifically advanced compared to your time. And there is a principle called redundancy at the criticalities, do you know this term? Replacement systems are available in case of failures. Bad things still sometimes happen. But there you are. They do anywhere.'

'But on Earth,' Galileo objected, 'on Earth, in the open air, the things you make don't have to work for you to survive.'

'Don't they? Your clothing, your language, your weapons? They all have to work for you to stay alive, right? We are poor forked worms in this world. Only our technologies, and our teamwork, allow us to survive.'

Galileo pursed his lips. There might be some truth to what she said, but still he felt it obscured a real difference. 'Worm or not,' he said, and she was a rather magnificently shaped worm, he did not add, 'you could stay alive on Earth, by breathing, eating, and staying warm. Granted these take effort, but you could make the effort. You have tools to help you, but they don't have to remain unbroken for you to survive. A single man alone on an island could do it. There are no mechanical contrivances that surround you and protect you, like a fortress, that have to function successfully forever or else you very quickly die.'

She shook her head. 'It's like a sea voyage. You could not have your ship sink and survive.'

'But you people never land. You sail on forever.'

'Yes, that's true. But it's true for everyone, always.'

94

Galileo recalled standing in his garden at night, in the open air, under the stars. It was an experience this woman had never had. Possibly she could not imagine it. Possibly she had no idea what he was talking about. 'You don't know what it is to be free,' he said, surprised. 'You don't know what it is to stand free in the open air.'

She shook her head impatiently. 'Have it your way.'

'I will.'

Again her amused glance, as if she were looking down on a child. She said, 'You were famous for that, as I recall. Until . . .'

The voice Pauline interrupted to announce they were near the bottom of the ice layer, and were in what she called brash ice. They could hear floating chunks and clinkers striking the hull, a grinding noise full of scrapes and thuds.

Then they were moving freely, in water. Galileo had spent so much time on barges and ferries, and on a few well-remembered trips out into the Adriatic, that he recognized the feel in his feet. Such kinetic sensations were so slight as to disappear when one focused on them, but when focusing attention elsewhere, one became aware of the totality of the effect.

Ganymede said, 'Pauline, search for the Europans' flue, also any other vessels, of course. And give us an analysis of the water, please.'

Pauline reported the water was nearly pure, with trace amounts of salts, floating particulates, and dissolved gases. Some of the crew began tapping madly at glyphs on their desk-tops. Outside the window was omnipresent black. They might as well have been deep in the bowels of the Earth. Only one's sense of movement suggested they were in a liquid.

Thus it was a great surprise to see a brief flash of cobalt blue in the window, like the random blue spark one sometimes saw crossing the inside of the eyelid.

'What was that!' Galileo said.

'We call that Cherenkov radiation,' Ganymede said.

'Somebody's patron?' Galileo inquired, glancing at Hera.

'The discoverer of the phenomenon,' she said firmly.

Ganymede ignored their fencing. 'There are tiny particles called neutrinos, which pour through our manifold in great numbers but very seldom interact with anything. Once in a while one hits a proton, which is a small but substantial part of an atom – hits a proton in such a way that the proton releases a muon, which is a very small component of a proton. If that happens in an ocean like this, the muon will fly through the water in such a way as to spark a short trail of light in the blue wavelength. We will see a few per minute.'

Another little flare of blue appeared, again like the flaws that plagued Galileo's vision. 'Like shooting stars,' he noted.

'Yes. A very subtle fire.'

'A fire in water.'

'Well, a light, let us say. Though some fires will burn in water, of course.'

Galileo tried to imagine that. Of course there were different kinds of fire. Blue streaks in blackness . . . This dream was testing him in all sorts of ways: could he find a way to test it back? Maybe answer the basic question: was this really happening? He looked around to see if there was something small that he could take and conceal in his coat. Stealing ideas from dreams – perhaps it wasn't so unusual. Perhaps it was a fundamental mode of thought.

The next flick of blue light was followed by a blue ball, which rapidly expanded, then became a kind of diffuse polyhedron, shedding spicules and other radiola of blue light which then curved away from the polyhedron in spirals, some of them tight equable spirals, making cylindrical coils, others equiangular spirals, growing wildly outward in conic shapes. One of these flashed right by the window, and for a second or two their chamber pulsed sapphire.

Some of the crew cried out; then there was silence.

Galileo said, 'What was that?'

Ganymede appeared astonished; he stood pressed against the window, his blade of a nose touching it.

He straightened up, expression black, 'It's here. I knew it. The anomalies made it very clear, I've been saying so all along.' He turned to his crew. 'We shouldn't be here! Have the Europans shown up yet?'

'We haven't seen them,' one replied.

'Find their flue then! Get to it – we have to get to it before they do, to stop them!'

They turned back to their screens and their crowded desktops. After a time one said, 'We've found it. We can hear them within it. They're descending. We're closing on it – wait. There they are. Two of them, just leaving their flue.'

Ganymede hissed. 'Go!' he exclaimed. 'Ram them! Get under them and ram them from below! Full speed until you reach them, then get in position to shove them right back up the flue!' He looked stricken, grim beyond telling. 'We have to make them leave!'

'How can you do that?' Hera asked.

'We'll ram them until they turn back.'

'Are you going to warn them?'

'I don't want to break radio silence. Who knows what effect it might have on what's in here?'

'What about the sound of collisions? What about the sounds and the exhaust from your engines?'

'That's what I've been saying to them! None of us should be here!'

Another blue conic spiral flashed by them. Ganymede read the screens and the desks. 'That could be some kind of signal. Speech, or thought, in some language of light.'

'Who would it speak to?'

'The light may be secondary. Who knows who it talks to. I have my suspicions, but . . .'

'Try numbers,' Galileo suggested. 'Display a triangle, see if it knows the Pythagorean theorem.'

Ganymede shook his head, visibly trying to remain patient. 'That's what the Europans will do, I'm afraid. Reckless interventions like that. They have no idea what they may be getting into.'

97

'Is it some kind of fish?'

'Not a fish. But on the floor of the ocean are layers of something. Perhaps a slime that is organized into larger structures.'

'But how would a slime make light?'

Ganymede clutched his black hair in his hands. 'Light from slime is bioluminescence,' he said tightly. 'Slime from light is photosynthesis. Both are very common. They're like alchemical interactions.'

'But alchemy doesn't really work.'

'Sometimes it does. Be quiet now. We have to get the Europans out of here.'

On the screen that had held the rainbow images of the flue, there stood now an image all in greys, in which near-white shapes defined an object much like their own vessel, shifting against a rumpled grey field. Ganymede took over at one desk and began to tap gently on the array of tabs and knobs. A solid bump, and then the screen showed nothing but the ghostly image of another ship. 'Hold on,' Ganymede ordered grimly, and began tapping harder than ever. 'Pauline, keep the vectors such that we push it up into its flue.'

Then a loud bang and instant deceleration knocked them all forward and up into the air. When they fell back Galileo found himself in a heap of bodies in the corner, Hera under him. He got up and tried to give her a hand, but staggered back as the vessel tipped again.

The voice named Pauline said, 'They're in their flue now, but they can descend out of it again, of course.'

'Go after the other one anyway. Wait, while we're in contact with them, speak hull to hull and tell them to get back to the surface. Tell them if they don't we'll ram them hard enough to breach both ships. Tell them who we are and tell them I'll do it.'

Suddenly a storm of blue flashes exploded in the window, and all the screens lit up as if with torn rainbows. The visual chaos was split by black lightning that somehow was just as devastating to the eyes as white lightning. Cries of alarm filled the air. Then the vessel lurched down and began to spin. Everyone had to hold on to something to stay upright; Galileo clutched Hera by the elbow, as high as his shoulder, and she held him up with that same arm, while grasping a chair back with her other hand. One of the crew clutched her desk while pointing at her screen with the other hand. Ganymede moved like an acrobat across the bucking deck, inspecting one screen and then another. The officers shouted at him over a high ringing tone. On the screens Galileo caught sight of a swirl of a steep conic spiral rising from the depths, now revealed to be immense, a matter of many miles. The blue light flashed in their chamber again.

'It doesn't want us here,' Ganymede said. 'Pauline, open radio contact with those ships. Send this: *Get out! Get out! Get out!*'

A high moan lofted up Galileo's spine, leaving his short hairs as erect as a hedgehog's. The sound resembled wolves howling at the moon. Often Galileo had heard them in the distance, late at night, when all the rest of the world slept. But the sound filling him now was to wolves' howls as wolves' howls were to human speech, a sound so uncanny that actual wolves would surely have run away whimpering. Fear turned his bowels watery. He saw all the others in the craft were just as afraid. He clutched Hera's thick biceps, felt himself moaning involuntarily. It was too loud now for anyone to hear him; the superlupine howls became a keening shriek that seemed everywhere at once, both inside and outside him. The blue flashes were now inside the vessel, even inside his eyes, though they were squeezed shut.

'Go!' Hera shouted. Galileo wondered if anyone else could hear her. In any case the vessel was spiralling upward now, so forcefully that Galileo was knocked to his knees. Hera swung him up and around the way he would have swung a child, and plopped him into a chair; she staggered, almost landed on him, sat hard on the floor beside him. Black flashes still shot through them like lightning, through floor to ceiling, as if carrying them along in some stupendous explosion, aquatic but incorporeal, everything spiralling in a dizzying rise. It was like being in the grip of a living Archimedes' screw. Up and up again, until there was an enormous crash, casting everyone up onto the ceiling, after which they flailed awkwardly down and thumped to the floor. They had struck the shell of ice capping the ocean, Galileo presumed, and it seemed the vessel might have cracked and everyone would soon drown. Then Galileo felt shoved toward the floor, indicating a new acceleration, as when rocked back on a bolting horse. The vessel itself now creaked and squealed, while the eerie shriek was muffled. The chamber was still bathed in flickers of blue fire. Ganymede, propped on both arms before the biggest table of screens and instruments, conferred in sharp tones with crew members holding on beside him. It seemed they were still trying to steer the thing.

Up they tumbled, turning and spinning this way and that, pitching and yawing but always moving up.

Ganymede said loudly, 'Are the Europans ahead of us?'

'There's no sign of them.' Pauline's voice was small under the muffled shriek.

The shriek shot up the scale in a rising glissando, until it was no longer audible; but immediately a violent earache and headache assaulted Galileo. He shouted up at Ganymede, 'Won't we emerge too quickly, if we don't slow down?'

Ganymede glanced at him, started tapping again on one of the desks.

Then the black on the screens turned blue, an indigo that lightened abruptly, and they shot up in a violent turquoise acceleration. Galileo's head banged the floor of the vessel and he thrust an arm under Hera; the back of her head smacked his forearm, and it hurt, but she turned and saw he had saved her a knock.

On one screen splayed the starry black sky, under it the shattered white plain of Europa's surface.

'We're going to fall!'

But they didn't. The column of water under them had fountained out of its hole and then quickly frozen in place, so that it stood there as ice, supporting their vessel just as certain sandstone columns held up schist boulders in an area of the Alps. Icicles broke and clattered away from the vessel's sides, shattering on the low frozen waves now surrounding the column. Black sky; white ice, tinted the oranges of Jupiter; their vessel, like a roc's egg on a plinth.

'How will we get down?' Galileo inquired in the sudden silence. His ears buzzed and hurt, and he could see crew members holding their heads.

'Something will come to us,' said Ganymede.

Hera laughed just a touch wildly, detached Galileo's fingers from her arm. 'The Europans will come for us. The Council will come for us.'

'I don't care, if they get the others too.'

'The others may have died inside.'

'So be it. We'll tell the Council what we did, and tell them they should have done it.' He turned to one of his crew. 'Prepare the entangler to send Signor Galileo back.'

The crewman, one of the pilots, bustled out of the chamber through a low door. Ganymede turned to speak to another of them.

Hera leaned over and said quickly in Galileo's ear, 'They will give you an amnestic, and you won't remember any of this. Drink salt water the moment you wake. Do your alchemists have magnesium sulphate? Well, shit – you won't remember this either. Here –' she reached inside her tunic, pulled out a small tablet, gave it to him. 'This is better than nothing. Hide it on you, and when you see it again, eat it!' She glared at him, her nose inches from his, and pinched his arm hard. 'Eat this! Remember!'

'I'll try,' Galileo promised, slipping the pill in his sleeve and feeling his arm throb.

Ganymede towered over him. 'Come, signor. There is no time to lose, we will soon be apprehended. The other ships may not

101

have made it, in which case good riddance to them, but we will have a lot of explaining to do. Let me convey you back to your home.'

Galileo stood. As he passed Hera she pinched him again, this time on the butt. Eat the pill, he thought, ignoring her, and walked with Ganymede to the side of his thick perispicillum. Eat the pill.

'Here,' Ganymede said, and a mist from his hand hit Galileo's face.

Chapter Six A Statue Would Have Been Erected

These confused and intermittent mental struggles slip through one's fingers and escape by their subtleties and slitherings, not hesitating to produce a thousand chimeras and fantastic caprices little understood by themselves and not at all by their listeners. By these fancies the bewildered mind is bandied about from one phantasm to another, just as in a dream one passes from a palace to a ship and then to a grotto or beach, and finally, when one awakes and the dream vanishes (and for the most part all memory of it also), one finds that one has been idly sleeping and has passed the hours without profit of any sort.
— GALILEO, *letter to Cosimo, 1611*

And indeed he came out of this syncope as one wakes from a dream, agitated, gasping, struggling to remember as it squirted away; you could see it in his face. 'No,' he moaned, 'come back . . . don't forget . . .'

This time it was his newly hired housekeeper who discovered him: La Piera had arrived at last. 'Maestro!' she cried, leaning over to peer into his staring eye. 'Wake up!'

He groaned, looked at her without recognition. She gave him a hand, hauled him to his feet. Though a braccio shorter, she was about as heavy as he was.

'They told me you suffer from syncopes.'

'I was dreaming.'

'You were paralysed. I shouted, I pinched you, nothing. You were gone.'

'I *was* gone.' He shuddered like a horse. 'I had a dream, or something. A vision. But I can't remember it!'

'That's all right. You're better off without dreams.'

He regarded her curiously. 'Why do you say that?'

She shrugged her broad shoulders as she tugged his clothes into position, holding up a little pellet she pulled from his jacket and then pocketing it. 'My dreams are crazy, that's all. Burning things in the oven while all the fish on the table come to life and start biting me, or sliding out the door like eels. They're always the same. Rubbish I say! Life is crazy enough as it is.'

'Maybe so.'

Then Cartophilus hustled onto the altana and came up short at the sight of them. Galileo shuddered again, pointed a finger at him: 'You!' he exclaimed.

'Me,' the ancient one admitted cautiously. 'What is it, maestro? Why are you up?'

'You know why!' Galileo roared. Then, piteously: 'Don't you?'

'Not I,' Cartophilus said, shifty as always. 'I heard voices and came out to see what was up.'

'You let someone in. In the gate?'

'Not I, maestro. Did you fall into one of your syncopes again?'

'No.'

'Yes,' La Piera confirmed.

Galileo heaved a huge sigh. Clearly he could remember nothing, or next to nothing. He glanced up; Jupiter was nearly overhead. He was cold, he slapped his arms to warm himself. 'Were the wolves in the hills howling earlier?' he asked suddenly.

'Not that I heard.'

'I think they were.' He sat there thinking about it. 'To bed,' he muttered, and stood. 'I can't do it tonight.' He glanced up again, hesitated. 'Ah, damn.' He plopped down again on his stool. 'I have to check them, at least. What time is it? Midnight? Bring me some mulled wine. And stay out here with me.'

Salviati was out of town, and Galileo was therefore stuck in his rented house in Florence. He found himself in a strange mood, distracted and pensive. He made it known to Vinta, in the most obsequious and flowery language he could manage, which was saying a lot, that he wanted to go to Rome to promote his new discoveries – or, as he admitted in a meeting with the Grand Duke's secretary, to defend them. For there were a lot of serious people who simply didn't have spyglasses good enough to see the moons of Jupiter, and even well-meaning parties like the Jesuits, the best astronomers in Europe aside from Kepler, were having trouble making the observations. And in Tuscany a new thing had happened: a philosopher named Ludovico delle Colombe was circulating a manuscript that not only ridiculed the notion that the Earth might move, but displayed a long list of quotes from the Bible to back his argument that Galileo's idea was contrary to Scripture. These quotes included 'You fixed the earth on its foundation' (Psalm 104:5); 'God made the orb immobile' (1 Chronicles 16:30); 'He suspended the earth above nothingness, that is, above the centre' (Job 26:7); 'The heaviness of stone, the weight of sand' (Proverbs 27:3); 'Heaven is up, the earth is down' (Proverbs 30:3); 'The sun rises, and sets, and returns to its place, from which, reborn, it revolves through the meridian, and is curved toward the North' (Ecclesiastes 1:5); 'God made two lights, i. e. , a greater light and a smaller light, and the stars, to shine above the earth' (Genesis 1:17).

Galileo read a manuscript of this letter, given to him by Salviati to show him what was being circulated, and cursed at every sentence. 'The heaviness of stone! This is stupid!'

Who wants the human mind put to death? he wrote angrily to Salviati. *Who is going to claim that everything in the world which is observable and knowable has already been seen and discovered?*

People were afraid of change. They seized on Aristotle because he said that above the sky there was no change; thus, if you died and went there, you would not change either. He wrote to the astronomer Mark Welser, *I suspect that our wanting to measure the universe by our own little yardstick makes us fall into strange fantasies, and that our particular hatred of death makes us hate fragility. If that which we call corruption were annihilation, the Peripatetics would have some reason for being such staunch enemies of it. But if it is nothing else than a mutation, it does not merit so much hatred. I don't think anyone would complain about the corruption of the egg if what results from it is a chick.*

Change could be growth, in other words. It was intrinsic to life. And so these religious objections to the changes he saw in the sky were stupid. But they were also dangerous.

So he wrote weekly to Vinta, asking him to ask the big-hearted brilliant splendiferous grandissimo Grand Duke to send him to Rome, so he could explain his discoveries. Eventually Galileo convinced Vinta that a visit could do no harm, indeed could add to the lustre of his prince's reputation. The trip was therefore approved; but then Galileo fell ill again. For two months he suffered such headaches and fevers that there was no question of travel.

He recuperated at Salviati's villa. 'I'm embroiled in something strange,' he confided to his young friend from out of a fever. 'Lady Fortuna has grabbed me by the arm, she has tossed me over her shoulder. God knows where I'm headed.'

Salviati did not know what to make of this, but he was a good friend to have in a crisis. He held your hand, he looked at you and understood what you said; his liquid eyes and quick smile were the very picture of intelligent goodness. He laughed a lot, and he made Galileo laugh, and there was no one quicker to point out a bird or a cloud, or to propose a conundrum about negative

106

numbers or the like. A sweet soul, and smart. 'Maybe it's La Vicuna who has taken you by the hand, the muse of justice.'

'I wish it, but no,' Galileo said, looking inward. 'Lady Fortuna is the one deciding my fate. The capricious one. A big woman.'

'But you have always been *avventurato*.'

'But with luck of all kinds,' Galileo groused. 'Good luck and bad.'

'But the good has been so good, my friend. Think of your gifts, your genius. That too is Fortuna making her dispensations.'

'Maybe so. May it continue that way, then.'

Finally, impatient at the delay forced on him by his body, he wrote to Vinta asking if a ducal litter could be provided for his travel. By this time it was becoming clear that the *Sidereus Nuncius* had made Galileo famous all over Europe. In the courts lucky enough to have been sent one of Galileo's spyglasses, star parties were being held, from Bavaria and Bohemia to France and England. Vinta decided that Galileo's presence in Rome could only bring honour and prestige to the Medici: the use of the ducal litter was approved.

On 23rd March, 1611, Galileo left with his servants Cartophilus and Giuseppe, and a little group of the Grand Duke's horsemen. He carried with him a letter of introduction to Cardinal Maffeo Barberini, written by an old acquaintance of his, Michelangelo Buonarroti, nephew of Florence's most famous artist, who had died the day before Galileo was born, causing talk (by Galileo's father anyway) of a transmigration of souls.

The roads between Florence and Rome were as good as any in Italy, but they were still slow, even in the best stretches, which were much abbreviated by winter damage. In a litter the trip took six days. By day Galileo sat on pillows inside the carriage, enduring the jouncing of the iron-rimmed wooden wheels into potholes and over stones, also the steady grind over cobbles or beds of gravel. Sometimes he rode a horse to give his kidneys and back a rest, but this meant a different kind of hammering. He hated to travel. Rome was as far away from Florence as he had ever been, and his only previous trip had occurred twenty-four years earlier, before the terrible incident in the cellar at Costozza had wrecked his health.

The roadside inns they stopped in along the way – at San Casciano, Siena, San Quirico, Acquapendente, Viterbo, and Monterosi – offered beds that were battered and flea-ridden, in rooms crowded with other bodies all snoring and hacking at once. It was better to spend the night outside in his coat, under a cape and a blanket, watching the sky. Jupiter was high, and every night he could log the positions of the four Jovian moons early and late, looking for the moments when a moon slowed and reached the outer point of its orbit, or the moments when it touched the lambent side of Jupiter itself. He was intent on being the first to determine their exact orbital times, which Kepler had written would be hard to do. He felt a strong bond with the moons, as if being their discoverer he somehow possessed them. One night he heard wolves howling and the bond seemed stronger than ever, as if wolves came from Jupiter. The white disc in his glass seemed to quiver with life, and he felt full of a feeling he couldn't name.

So the damp spring nights would pass, and he would collapse into the litter as the Grand Duke's men prepared for departure, hoping for sleep through the jouncing day on the road. Many mornings he succeeded in this, and was insensible to some hours of travel. But both his night and day routines were hard on his back, and he arrived in Rome exhausted.

On Holy Tuesday the litter ground its way through the immense shabby outskirts of Rome. The broad road was flanked hard on each side by innumerable shacks made of sticks, as if built by magpies. Once inside the ancient wall, which was easy to miss,

Galileo's party clopped slowly through packed paved streets. Rome was as big as ten Florences, and the tightly packed buildings were often three and even four storeys tall, balconies overhanging the narrow streets . People lived their lives and dried their laundry on the balconies, commenting freely on the passersby below.

The tight streets opened up by the river, where there were flood fields and orchards. Further into the city they came to the Palazzo Firenze, which overlooked a small campo. This was where Galileo was to be hosted by Cosimo's ambassador to Rome, one Giovanni Niccolini, a lifelong diplomat near the end of a long career in the Medici service. This worthy appeared in the entryway of the palazzo and greeted Galileo rather coolly. Vinta had written Niccolini to say that Galileo would be accompanied by a single servant, and here were two, Cartophilus having insinuated himself at the last minute. Financial arrangements between the Grand Duke and his ambassador were meticulously kept, so perhaps it was not clear to Niccolini that he would be reimbursed for the keep of this extra servant. In any case, he was distinctly reserved as he led Galileo and his little retinue into a big suite of rooms at the back of the ground floor, looking onto the formal garden. This elaborate green space was dotted with ancient Roman statues whose marble faces had melted away. Something about the look of them caught Galileo's eye and disturbed him.

Once moved in, Galileo launched into a busy schedule of visits to dignitaries strategic to his purpose, one of the most important being the Jesuit Christopher Clavius at the College of Rome.

Clavius greeted him with the same words he had used twenty-four years before, when Galileo had been an unknown young mathematician and Clavius in his prime, known throughout Europe as 'the Euclid of the sixteenth century':

'Welcome to Rome, young signor! All praise to God and Archimedes!'

He was not much changed in appearance, despite all the years: a slight man with a puckered mouth and a kindly eye. He led Galileo into the Jesuit college's workshop, where together they inspected the spyglasses the monk mechanicals had constructed. The glasses looked like Galileo's, and were equivalent in power, although more marred by irregularities, as Galileo told the monks freely.

Christopher Grienberger and Odo Maelcote then joined them, and Clavius introduced his younger colleagues as the ones who had made the bulk of the observations; Clavius lamented his aged eyesight. 'But I have seen your so-called Medicean stars several times,' he added, 'and they are obviously orbiting Jupiter, just as you say.'

Galileo bowed deeply. There were people out there claiming the moons were just flaws in Galileo's glass; he had angrily offered ten thousand crowns to anyone who could make a glass that would show flaws around Jupiter but not around the other planets, and of course there were no takers, but still – not everyone believed. So this mattered. Seeing was believing, and Clavius had seen. As Galileo straightened up he said, 'God bless you, Father, I was quite sure that you would see them, they are so prominent, and you such an experienced astronomer. And I can tell you that on my journey to Rome I have made good progress in determining the period of orbit of all four of these new moons.'

Grienberger and Maelcote raised their eyebrows and exchanged glances. Clavius only smiled. 'I think here we are in rare agreement with Johannes Kepler, that establishing their periods of rotation will be very difficult.'

'But . . .' Galileo hesitated, then realized he had made a mistake, and dropped the matter with a wave of the hand. There was no point in making announcements in advance of results; indeed, since he was intent on being the first to make every discovery having to do with the new stars, he should not be inciting competitors to further effort. It was already startling enough to see that they had managed to manufacture spyglasses almost as strong as his own.

So he let the talk turn to the phases of Venus. The Jesuits also had seen these, and while he did not press the point that this was strong evidence in support of the Copernican view, he could see in their faces that the implications were already clear to them. And they did not deny the appearances. They believed in the glass. This was a most excellent sign, and as he considered the happy implications of a public acknowledgment that their observations agreed with his, Galileo recovered from his uneasiness at the power of their devices. These were the Pope's official astronomers, supporting his findings! So he spent the rest of the afternoon reminiscing with Clavius and laughing at his jokes.

Another important meeting for Galileo, though he did not know it, came on the Saturday before Easter, when he paid his respects to Cardinal Maffeo Barberini. They met in one of the outer offices of St Peter's, near the Vatican's river gate. Galileo examined the interior gardens of the place with a close eye; he had never been inside the sacred fortress before, and he was interested to observe the horticulture deployed inside. Purity had been emphasized over liveliness, he was not surprised to note: paths were gravelled, borders were lines of clean cobbles, long narrow lawns were trimmed as if by barbers. Massed roses and camellias were all either white or red. It was a little too much.

Barberini proved to be a man of the world, affable, quick, well-dressed in a cardinal's everyday finery; lithe and handsome, goateed, smooth-skinned, fulsome. His power made him as graceful as a dancer, as confident in his body as a minx or an otter. Galileo handed him the introductory letters from Michaelangelo's nephew and from Antonio de Medici, and Barberini put them aside after a glance and took Galileo by the hand and led him out into the courtyard, dispensing with all ceremony. 'Let's take our ease and talk.'

Galileo was his usual lively self, a happy Pulcinella with a genius for mathematics. In his interviews with nobles he was quick and funny, always chuckling in his baritone rumble, out to please. The Barberini were a powerful family, and he had heard that Maffeo was a virtuoso, with a great interest in intellectual and artistic matters. He hosted many evenings in which poetry and song and philosophical debates were featured entertainments, and he wrote poetry himself that he was said to be vain about. Galileo seemed to be assuming that this was therefore a prelate in the style of Sarpi, broad-minded and liberal. In any case he was perfectly at ease, and showed Barberini his occhialino inside and out.

'I wish I had been able to bring enough of them with me to leave one with you as a gift, Your Eminence, but I was only allowed a small trunk for baggage.'

Barberini nodded at this awkwardness. 'I understand,' he murmured as he looked through the glass. 'Seeing through yours is enough, for now, and more than enough. Although I do want one, it is true. It's simply amazing how much you can see.' He pulled back to look at Galileo. 'It's odd – you wouldn't think that more could be held there for the eye, in distant things, than we already see.'

'No, it's true. We must admit that our senses don't convey everything to us, not even in the sensible world.'

'Certainly not.'

They looked through it at the distant hills east of Rome, and the cardinal marveled and clapped him on the shoulder in the manner of any other man.

'You have given us new worlds,' he said.

'The seeing of them, anyway,' Galileo corrected him, to seem properly humble.

'And how do the Peripatetics take it? And the Jesuits?'

Galileo tipped his head side to side. 'They are none too pleased, Your Grace.'

Barberini laughed. He had been trained by the Jesuits, but he did not like them, Galileo saw; and so Galileo continued, 'There are some of them who refuse to look through the glass at all. One of them recently died, and as I said at the time, since he would not look at the stars through my glass, he could now inspect them from up close, on his way past them to Heaven!'

Barberini laughed uproariously. 'And Clavius, what does he say?'

'He admits the moons orbiting Jupiter are really there.'

'The Medici moons, you have called them?'

'Yes,' Galileo admitted, realizing for the first time how this could be another awkwardness. 'I expect to make many more discoveries in the heavens, and hope to honour those who have helped me accordingly.'

The little smile that twitched over the cardinal's face was not entirely friendly. 'And you think these Jovian moons show that the Earth goes around the sun in an analogous manner, as Copernicus claimed?'

'Well, it shows at least that moons go around planets, as our moon goes around the Earth. Better proof of the Copernican view, Your Grace, is how you can see the phases of Venus through the glass.' Galileo explained how in the Copernican understanding the phases of Venus had combined with its varying distance from Earth to make it give to the naked eye always the same brightness, which had argued against the idea it had phases, when one had no glass to see them; and how its position, always low in the sky in the mornings and evenings, combined with actual sighting of the phases through the glass confirmed the idea that Venus was orbiting the sun inside the Earth's own orbiting of it. The ideas were complicated to describe in words, and Galileo felt at ease enough to stand and take three citrons from a bowl, then place them and move them about on the table to illustrate the concepts, to Barberini's evident delight.

'And the Jesuits deny this!' the cardinal repeated when Galileo had completed a very convincing demonstration of the system.

113

'Well, no. They agree now that the phenomena at least are real.'

'But then saying that the explanation is not yet so clear. Yes, that makes sense. That sounds like them. And after all, I suppose God could have arranged it any way He wanted.'

'Of course, Your Grace.'

'And what does Bellarmino say?'

'I don't know, Your Grace.'

The cardinal's smile was even a little wicked in its foxiness. 'Perhaps we will find out.'

Then he spoke of Florence, of his love for the city and its nobility, which Galileo happily echoed. And when Barberini asked the usual question about favourite poets, Galileo declared, 'Oh, I prefer Ariosto to Tasso, as meat over candied fruit,' which made the cardinal laugh, as being the reverse of the usual characterization of the two; and thus the interview continued well to its conclusion and Galileo's obsequious withdrawal. And Cardinal Barberini must have enjoyed it, for that very afternoon he wrote to Buonarotti, Michelangelo's nephew, and to Antonio de Medici, to say he appreciated their recommendations of Florence's new court philosopher, and would be delighted to help him in any way he could.

A few days later Galileo was invited to a party organized by Giovanni Battista Deti, nephew of the late Pope Clement III, where he met four more cardinals, and listened to a talk given to the group by Giovanni Battista Strozzi. In the discussion afterward Galileo held his tongue, as he told all his correspondents later, feeling that as a newcomer this was the courteous thing to do. Staying silent was no doubt difficult for him, given his natural tendency towards continuous speech, and also given what could only be called his growing intimacy with the topic of Strozzi's talk, which was Pride. For the success of all these visits was clearly going to his head. Night after night he was joining evening meals, often at Cardinal Ottavio

Bandini's residence on the Quirinal, right next to the Pope's palace, and after the food and the musical entertainment standing up to become himself the featured entertainment, speaking and then showing the guests what could be seen of nearby landmarks through his glass. People never ceased to be amazed, and Galileo puffed up accordingly; back at the Palazzo Firenze after these events we could barely get him out of his jacket and boots.

One meeting had lasting consequences. It took place at the palazzo of Federico Cesi, the Marquis of Monticelli, the young man who had founded the Accademia dei Lincei, the Academy of the Lynxes, in which matters of mathematics and natural philosophy were regularly discussed. Cesi also used his fortune to gather in his palazzo an ever-growing collection of natural wonders. When Galileo arrived at his palazzo, Cesi took him on a tour of two rooms that were filled to overflowing with lodestones, chunks of coral, fossils, unicorn horns, griffins' eggs, coconuts, nautilus shells, sharks' teeth, jars containing monstrous births, carbuncles that glowed in the dark, turtle shells, a rhinoceros horn worked in gold, a bowl of lapis lazuli, dried crocodiles, model cannons, a collection of Roman coins, and a box of truly exquisite lapidary specimens.

Galileo inspected each of these objects with genuine curiosity. 'Marvellous,' he said as he looked in the hollow end of a unicorn's horn chased with gold. 'It must be as big as a horse.'

'It does seem so, doesn't it,' Cesi replied happily. 'But come look at my herbarium.'

Most of all, it turned out, Cesi was a botanist; he had hundreds of leaves and flowers arranged in big thick books, all dried and displayed with descriptions. He pointed out his favourites enthusiastically. Galileo watched him closely: he was young and handsome, very wealthy, fond of the company of men. And his admiration for Galileo was boundless. 'You are the one we've waited for,' he said as they closed the plant books. 'We've needed

115

an intellectual leader to blaze the path to the higher levels, and now that you're here, I'm sure it will happen.'

'Maybe so,' Galileo allowed. He liked the idea of the Lincean Academy very much. To get out from under the thumb of the universities and all their Peripatetics, to elevate mathematics and natural philosophy to the highest level of thought and inquiry; it was a great new thing, a way forward. A new kind of institution, and a potential ally too.

Later that day Cesi hosted a dinner to introduce Galileo to the rest of the Lynxes. The party took place on top of the Janiculum, the highest of the Roman hills, in the vineyard of Monsignor Malvasia. The Lincean membership and a dozen other like-minded gentlemen assembled while it was still day, for the views from the Janiculum over the city were unobstructed in all directions. Among the guests were the foreign Linceans Johann Faber and Johann Schreck from Germany, Jan Eck from Holland, and Giovanni Demisiani from Greece.

Galileo trained his glass first on the basilica of St John Lateran, across the Tiber at a distance of about three miles, adjusting it until the chiselled inscription was legible on the loggia over the side entrance. It had been placed there by Sixtus V in the first year of his pontificate:

Sixtus
Pontifex Maximus
anno primo

Everyone was startled, as usual. When they had all looked through the occhialino more than once, and read and re-read the distant inscription, several toasts were proposed and drunk down. The group grew raucous, even a little giddy; Cesi's musicians, sensing the spirit of the moment, played a fanfare on horns they pulled out from beneath their chairs. Galileo bowed, and while the brassy music played on, turned his glass on the residence of the Duke of Altemps, on a hill in the first rise of the Appenines, far to the east of them. When he had it fixed the Linceans again crowded round, taking turns counting the windows on the façade of the great villa, some fifteen miles away. This made people stark amazed, and the Janiculum rang with cheers.

Later that night, after a great deal of eating and drinking and talk, and a brief look at the moon, which was too full to see through the glass as other than a white blaze, Demisiani the Greek sat down by Galileo and leaned into him.

'You should name your device with a new Greek word,' he said, his saturnine face alive with the humour of his suggestion, or the fact that he was the one making it. 'You should call it a telescope.'

'Telescopio?' Galileo repeated.

'To see at a distance. *Tele scopio*, distance seeing. It's better than perspicillum, which means merely a lens after all, or visorio, which is only to say visual or optical. And occhialino is petty somehow, as if you wanted only to spy on someone, it's too small, too provincial, too Tuscan. The other languages will never use it, and will have to make up words of their own. But *telescope* all will understand and use together. As always with Greek!'

Galileo nodded. Certainly the best scientific names were always either Latin or Greek. Kepler had been calling it a perspicillum.

'The root words are very old and basic,' Demisiani said, 'and the compounding method as well.'

Galileo surged to his feet and raised his glass, waited for the group to notice and go quiet. 'Telescopio!' he bellowed, dragging out the syllables as if calling for Mazzoleni, as if announcing the name of a champion: the group cheered, and Galileo leaned over to give the grinning Greek a hug, filled with sudden glee: of course his invention was such a new thing in the world that it needed a new name! No mere occhialino this!

'TEL E SCOP IO!' Who knows how many of the surrounding hills of Rome heard the party shouting out the new word. Galileo alone could have been heard halfway to Salerno.

The very next day, word came: the Pope wanted to see him.

An audience with Pope Paul V. The routine at the Palazzo Firenze took on a slightly frenzied air. Sleep was difficult. Galileo didn't even try, but watched Jupiter and considered what was to come, and so slept eventually. He woke early, before sunrise, and took a slow dawn walk in the formal garden among the statues. He performed his ablutions, ate a small meal. Perhaps on this day it was even smaller than usual. Then Cartophilus and Giuseppe helped him dress in his best clothes, choosing the darker and more formal of his two dress jackets, which were getting a lot of wear on this visit.

Niccolini came by while he was completing his toilet, to discuss the audience, and to tell him all the latest from the *Avvisi*, Rome's broadsheet of rumour and gossip, concerning His Holiness's activities the previous week and what seemed to be on his mind. Like everyone else, Galileo already knew the Pope's background: he had been Cardinal Camillo Borghese, a heretofore obscure member of that most powerful and dangerous of families, a canon lawyer whose election as Pope was so unlooked-for that he himself considered it an intercession of the Holy Ghost, and all his subsequent pontifical actions therefore divinely intended. This included the hanging of one Piccinardi, who had been so remiss as to write (though not to have published) an unauthorized biography of Paul's predecessor, Clement VIII. That had set a tone that no one forgot.

Niccolini did not remind Galileo of that particular example of Paul's severity, but made the point in more roundabout ways. The pontiff, he warned, was rigid, headstrong, peremptory; in these difficult years of the Counter-Reformation, he brooked no deviation from the rules and tactics laid out by the Council of Trent half a century before. In short, a pope. 'He has

118

grown a bit fat with papal power, in the usual way,' Niccolini concluded.

The audience was held at the Villa Malvasia, where Galileo had been only the night before. This was the Pope's idea; he wanted to get away from the Vatican. Niccolini led Galileo into the villa's giant antechamber, and there introduced him to Paul V, using rather stiff and nervous phrases.

The Pope was indeed fat, an immense man, nearly spherical under his red robes, his neck fleshy and as thick as his head, his piggish eyes deep in thick folds of skin. He had a triangular goatee. Galileo knelt before him and kissed the offered ring, murmuring the prayer of obeisance Niccolini had taught him to use.

'Rise,' Paul said gruffly, interrupting him. 'Speak to us standing.'

This was a great honour. Holding his features steady, Galileo got to his feet with the least clumsiness he could manage, then bowed his head.

'Walk with us,' Paul said. 'We wish to take a turn in the garden.'

Galileo followed the Pope and walked with him, Niccolini and a clutch of papal assistants and servants trailing behind. They wandered through the hilltop's vineyard, already well known to Galileo, and as he grew used to the big man's blunt manner, and his slow gait, he grew more comfortable. He seemed to forget the stiletto sticking in and out of Paolo Sarpi's head, and spoke as if to God Himself. Mostly he talked about the joy of seeing new stars in the sky, and of the blessing it was to witness the new powers now given to man by God.

'Some speak of theological problems arising from the new discoveries,' Galileo said calmly, 'but really these problems are not possible, as creation is all one. God's world and God's word are necessarily the same, both being God's. Any apparent discrepancies are only a matter of human misunderstanding.'

'Of course,' Paul said shortly. He did not like theology. He waved these problems aside as if they were the bees humming in the vineyard. 'You have our support in this.'

After that Galileo spoke of other things, billowing on this pronouncement like a sail filled with the wind. He became less serious, more his usual courtier self. Then, after three quarters of an hour of this slow stroll through the vines, Paul glanced back at his secretaries and simply walked away, down to his litter at the front of the villa.

Startled by this abrupt departure, Galileo stood with his mouth hanging open, wondering if he had said something to offend. But Niccolini assured him that this was Paul's way, that given the frequency of his audiences, the time he saved by dispensing with the always-lengthy farewells added up to an hour or more a day. 'The amazing thing is that he stayed as long as he did. If he had not been truly interested he would have left much earlier.' In truth the audience had gone wonderfully well, and Galileo had been shown great favour by being commanded to walk with the Pope. It had been one of the friendliest audiences the ambassador had ever witnessed. A triumph for both Galileo and for Florence. Coming from Niccolini, who was suddenly enthusiastic, Galileo knew it must be so.

After that Galileo lost his head, everyone around him saw it. The endless parade of banquets at which he was the centre of all attention and praise; the rich food; the balthazars and fiascos of wine; the long nights, when despite all the revelry he would stay up afterward to get some more sightings of Jupiter and its moons, so that even in the midst of everything else he was homing in on good orbital times for I, II, III, and IV – and yet he still had to rise early on the mornings after to prepare for yet another feast: all these began to take their toll on him. The idea that he would keep his mouth shut during a banquet discussion, be it on pride or anything else, became laughable. He talked lots: he discoursed, he lectured, he conversed, he boasted. He had always known that he was smarter than other people, but in the years when that had not actually seemed to benefit him, he had

120

not been so impressed by it. Now, as he became ever more full of himself, he began to use his wit like a sword, or to be more accurate, given the rough *buffo* tenor of his humor, like a club. *Buffo* became *buffare* as he swelled up.

Speaking one night of the uneven surface of the moon, for instance, revealed so clearly by his telescope, he reminded everyone that this was a big problem for the poor Peripatetics, as the Aristotelian orthodoxy was that everything in the heavens was perfectly geometrical, and the moon therefore a perfect sphere. Even Father Clavius, he said, had ventured, and in print, that although the visible surface of the moon was uneven, this could be illusory, and all its mountains and plains could be encased in a clear crystal shell that constituted its perfect sphericality. Galileo's tone of voice expressed his incredulity at this opinion, and as the audience chuckled they also grew more attentive; this was treading a little close to the edge.

Cartophilus had joined some of the other servants in borrowing a pillow and a bottle of wine and lying out in the vineyard, outside the cast of the torchlight bathing the long banqueting table, there to watch and listen. The guests in their bejewelled finery were like a painting come to life and performing for them alone; but Cartophilus sat up and put the bottle down as Galileo began to poke fun at the famous old Jesuit:

'If everyone is allowed to imagine whatever they please, then of course someone can say that the moon is surrounded by a crystalline substance that is transparent and invisible! Who can deny it? I will grant it without objection, provided that with equal courtesy I be allowed to say that the crystal has on its outer surface a large number of huge mountains, thirty times as high as terrestrial ones, but invisible because they are diaphanous. Thus I can picture to myself another moon ten times as mountainous as I said in the first place!' The guests at the table laughed. 'The hypothesis is pretty,' Galileo went on, goaded by their amusement, 'but its only fault is that it is neither demonstrated nor demonstrable! Who does not see that this is a purely arbitrary fiction? Why, if you counted the Earth's atmosphere as a similar kind of clear shell, then the Earth too would be perfectly spherical!'

And of course they all laughed. Ha ha! Very funny! And it was. Galileo's signature mix of wit and sarcasm had been making people laugh for years. But Christopher Clavius had always been friendly to him; and more generally, it was never good to make fun of the Jesuits. Especially publicly, in Rome, and right before the Jesuits were to host a lavish feast at the College of Rome to celebrate your accomplishments. Yet here he was. Cartophilus could only groan and take another swig from his bottle: from the darkness of the vineyard, the sight of Galileo standing in the torchlight over the long table of seated revellers was the very image of Pride before its Fall.

But Galileo did not notice any danger. He ate, he talked, he boasted. He trained his telescope on the sun, using a method suggested by Castelli: the sun's light was directed through the tube onto a sheet of paper, where one could look at the big lit circle with no danger to the eyes. And immediately it became apparent to any viewer that the lit image of the sun was dotted by small indistinct dark patches. Over the course of days, these dark spots moved across the sun's face in a manner that suggested to Galileo that the sun too was rotating, at a speed that he calculated made its day about a month long. Rotating at about the same speed as the moon in its course around the Earth, therefore; and they were the same size in the sky. It was odd. He made sketches each day of the sun spots' patterns, and placed the sketches side by side to show the sequence of movement.

Galileo claimed this discovery of the sun's rotation for himself, though there were astronomers – Jesuits again – who had been tracking the sun spots for some time. He proclaimed his discovery far and wide, ignoring the fact that it was another inconvenient finding for the Peripatetics, also that it contradicted certain astronomical statements in the Bible. He didn't care; if he noticed such problems for his opponents, he would only make another sharp heavy joke about them.

For now, none of these indiscretions seemed to be having any bad effect. At the Jesuit banquet in his honour no one spoke of his jape at Clavius's expense, and Clavius's colleague, the Dutch astronomer Odo Maelcote, read a learned commentary on *Sidereus Nuncius* which confirmed every discovery Galileo had reported. It appeared he did not have to care.

Then the newly enthusiastic Niccolini was replaced as Cosimo's ambassador to Rome by Piero Guicciardini, who, finding Galileo at the height of his magniloquence, did not like him. And back home, Belisario Vinta was replaced as secretary to Cosimo by Curzio Picchena, who shared with Guicciardini a more jaundiced view of Galileo's loud advocacy of the Copernican position. They saw no reason the Medici should be drawn into such a potentially awkward controversy. But if Galileo noticed these new men and their attitude toward him, again he did not seem to care.

Meanwhile, Cardinal Bellarmino, Pope Paul's closest advisor, also a Jesuit, and the inquisitor who had handled the case of Giordano Bruno, initiated an investigation into Galileo's theories. This was probably on Paul's instruction, but the spies within the Vatican who had found out about it could not be sure of that. Bellarmino, they said, had looked through a Jesuit telescope himself; he had asked his Jesuit colleagues for an opinion; he had attended a meeting of the Holy Office of the Congregation, which subsequently began to look into the case. Bellarmino seemed to have been the one to order the investigation.

But no one told Galileo about this troubling development, being not quite sure what it meant. And because of his meeting with the Pope, and everything else that had happened, he was still full of himself, bumptious and grand. The visit to Rome was a triumph in every way, even if Guicciardini was now hinting that it might be best to leave while he was still being lionized. The ambassador stayed just on the right side of politeness about this, but if Galileo had sneaked into his office and looked at the letters on his desk, as proved fairly easy to do, he would have gained a truer sense of the ambassador's mind:

Galileo has little strength of judgement wherewith to control himself, so that he makes the climate of Rome extremely dangerous to himself, particularly in these times, when we have a Pope who hates geniuses.

Eventually Galileo took the ambassador's hint, or decided on his own, and announced he was returning to Florence. Cardinal Farnese hosted the farewell banquet in his honour, and accompanied him in his trip north as far as Caprarola, the country villa of the Farnese, where Galileo was invited to rest a night in luxury. Galileo carried with him a written report he had requested and received from Cardinal del Monte, addressed to Cosimo and Picchena. The Cardinal had finished his tribute with the words, *Were we still living under the ancient republic of Rome, I am certain that a statue would have been erected in his honour on the Capitol* – perhaps next to the statue of Marcus Aurelius – not a bad companion in fame. No wonder Galileo's head had been turned. The visit to Rome was a complete success, as far as he knew.

Things continued that way after he got back to Florence. He was feted in fine style by Cosimo and his court, and it was clear that Cosimo was extremely pleased with him; his Roman performance had made Cosimo's patronage look very discriminating indeed.

The Medici youth was no longer so young; he sat at the head of his table like a man used to command, and the boy Galileo remembered so well was no longer evident. He looked quite a bit the same, physically: slight, a bit pale, very like his father in his features, which was to say long-nosed and narrow headed, with

124

a noble forehead. Not a robust youth, but now much more sure of himself, as only made sense: he was a prince. And he like everyone else had read his Machiavelli. He had given hard commands, and the whole duchy had obeyed them.

'Maestro, you have set the Romans on their heels,' he said complacently, offering a toast to the room. 'To my old teacher, the wonder of the age!'

And the Florentines cheered even louder than the Romans had.

Soon after his return, Galileo got involved in a debate concerning hydrostatics: why did ice float? His opponent was his old foe Colombe, the malevolent shit who had tried to hang scriptural objections around his neck and thus cast him into hell. Galileo was anxious to stick the knives in this man while his Roman victories were fresh in everyone's mind, and went at the contest like a bull seeing red, yes. But then he was frustrated by Cosimo, who ordered him to debate with such insignificant enemies in writing only, speaking over such a gadfly's head to the world at large. Galileo did that, writing as usual at great length, but then Cosimo ordered him to debate the issue orally with a Bolognan professor named Pappazoni, whom Galileo had just helped to get his teaching position at Il Bo. This was like staking down a lamb to be killed and eaten by a lion, but Galileo and Pappazoni could only play their parts, and Galileo could not help enjoying it, as it was only a verbal killing after all.

Then Cardinal Maffeo Barberini came through Florence on his way to Bologna. Cardinal Gonzaga also happened to be in the city, and so Cosimo invited both of them to attend a repeat performance of Galileo's debate on floating bodies, to be held at a court dinner on 2nd October. Papazzoni again made a reluctant appearance, and after a feast and a concert, and much drinking, Galileo again slaughtered him to the roaring laughter of the audience. Then Cardinal Gonzaga stood and surprised everyone by supporting Papazzoni; but Barberini, smiling appreciatively, perhaps remembering their warm meeting back in the spring in Rome, took Galileo's side.

It was therefore another triumphant evening for Galileo. As he left the banquet, well after midnight, and long after the sacrifice of Pappazoni, Cardinal Barberini took him by the hand, hugged him, bade him farewell, and promised they would meet again.

The next morning, when Barberini was to leave for Bologna, Galileo did not show up to see him off, having been unexpectedly detained by an illness he had suffered in the night. From the road Barberini wrote a note to him:

I am very sorry that you were unable to see me before I left the city. It is not that I consider a sign of your friendship as necessary, for it is well known to me, but because you were ill. May God keep you not only because outstanding persons such as yourself deserve a long life of public service, but because of the particular affection that I have and always will have for you. I am happy to be able to say this, and to thank you for the time that you spent with me.

Your affectionate brother,
Cardinal Barberini

Your affectionate brother! Talk about friends in high places! To a certain extent it seemed he had a Roman patron now to add to his Florentine one.

All was triumph. Indeed it would be hard to imagine how things could have gone better in the previous two years for Galileo and his telescope: scientific standing, social standing, patronage in both Florence and Rome – all were at their peak, and Galileo stood slightly stunned on top of what had proved a double *anno mirabilis*.

But there were undercurrents and counterforces at work, even on that very morning when Galileo did not show up to see off Cardinal Barberini. Galileo had been ill, yes: because a syncope had struck him when he got home from the banquet the night before. Cartophilus had hopped down from the trap in front of their house in Florence, had stilled the horse, and opened the gate; and there in the little yard stood the stranger, his massive telescope already placed on its thick tripod.

In his crow's Latin the stranger said to Galileo, 'Are you ready?'

Chapter Seven The Other Galileo

You are given a light to know evil from good,
And free will, which, if it can endure
Without weakening after its first bout with fixed Heaven,

If it is believed in, will conquer all it meets later.
So if the present world strays from its course,
The cause is in you; look for it in yourself.
— DANTE, *Purgatorio, Canto XVI*

'Yes, I'm ready,' Galileo replied, his blood jolting through him so that his fingers throbbed. He was afraid!

But he was curious too. He said to the stranger, 'Let's go up to the altana.'

Cartophilus carried the massive telescope up the outside stairs, bent double under the load. 'Local gravity getting to you at last?' the stranger asked acerbically, in Latin.

'Someone has to carry the load,' Cartophilus muttered in Tuscan. 'Not everyone can be a virtuoso like you, signor, and fly off when the bad times come. Skip away like a fucking dilettante.'

The stranger ignored this. On the roof's little altana, with the telescope on its tripod, he put a fingertip to the eyepiece and swung it into Jovian alignment; it came to rest with a refinement that seemed all its own. Again Galileo felt the sensation that this had happened before.

And indeed the telescope was somehow already aligned. The stranger gestured at it. Galileo moved his stool next to the eyepiece of the glass and sat. He looked through it.

Jupiter was a big banded ball near the centre of the glass, strikingly handsome, colourful within its narrow range. There was a red spot in the middle of the southern hemisphere, curling in the oval shape of a standing eddy in a river. A Jovian Charybdis – and was he going there to meet his own Scylla? For a long time he looked at the great planet, so full and round and banded. It cast its influence over him in just the way an astrologer would have expected it to.

But nothing else happened. He sat back, looked at the stranger.

Who was frowning heavily. 'Let me check it.' He looked at the side of the telescope, straightened up, blinked several times. He looked over at Cartophilus, who shrugged.

'Not good,' Cartophilus said.

'Maybe it's Hera,' the stranger said darkly.

Cartophilus shrugged again. Clearly this was the stranger's problem.

They stood there in silence. It was a chill evening. Long minutes passed. Galileo bent down and looked through the lens again. Jupiter was still in the middle of it. He swallowed hard. This was stranger than dreaming. 'This is not just a telescopio,' he said, almost remembering now. Blue people, angels . . . 'It's something like a, a tele-avanzare. A teletrasporta.'

The stranger and Cartophilus looked at each other. Cartophilus said, 'The amygdala can never be fully suppressed. And why shouldn't he know?'

The stranger re-examined the boxy side of the device. Cartophilus sat down on the floor beside it, stoical.

'Ah. Try it again,' the stranger said, a new tone in his voice. 'Take another look.'

Galileo looked. Moon I was just separating from Jupiter on its west side. III and IV were out to the east. An hour must have passed since the two visitors had arrived.

Moon I cleared Jupiter, gleamed bright and steady in the black. Sometimes it seemed the brightest of the four. They fluctuated in that regard. I seemed to have a yellow tinge. It shimmered in the glass, and in the same moment Galileo saw that it was getting bigger and more distinct, and was mottled yellow, orange, and black – or so it seemed – because in that very same moment he saw that he was floating down onto it, dropping like a landing goose, at such the same angle as a goose that he extended his arms and lifted his feet forward to slow himself down.

The spheroid curve of Moon I soon revealed itself to be an awful landscape, very different to his vague memories of Moon II, which were of an icy purity: I was a waste of mounded yellow slag, all shot with craters and volcanoes. A world covered by Etnas. As he descended, the yellow differentiated into a hell's carnival of burnt sulphur tones, of umbers and siennas and burnt siennas, of topaz and tan and bronze and sunflower and brick and tar, also the blacks of charcoal and jet, also terracotta and blood red, and a sunset array of oranges, citron yellows, gilt, pewter – all piled on all, one colour pouring over the others and being covered itself in a great unholy slag heap. Dante would have approved it as the very image of his burning circles of Hell.

The overlayering of so many colours made it impossible to gauge the terrain. What he had thought was a giant crater popped up and reversed itself, revealed as the top of a viscous pile bigger than Etna, bigger than Sicily itself.

He floated down toward the peak of this broad mountain. On the rim of the crater in its summit was a flat spot, mostly occupied by a round yellow-columned temple, open to space in the Delphic style.

He drifted down onto the yellow floor of this temple, landing easily. A square box made of something like lead or pewter lay on the ground beside him. His body weighed very little, as if he were standing in water. Overhead Jupiter bulked hugely in the starry black, every band and convolute swirl palpable to the eye. At the sight of it Galileo quivered like a horse in shock and fear.

On the other side of the box stood a knot of some dozen people, all staring at him. The stranger was now standing behind him.

'What's this!' the stranger exclaimed angrily.

'You know what this is, Ganymede,' said a woman who emerged from the knot of people. Her voice, low and threatening, came to Galileo in language that was like a rustic old-fashioned Tuscan. She approached with a regal stride, and Galileo bowed without thinking to. She nodded his way, and said, 'Welcome to Io, you are our guest here. We have met before, although you may not remember it very well. My name is Hera. One moment please, while I deal with your travelling companion.'

She stopped before the stranger, Ganymede, and looked at him as if measuring how far he would fall when she knocked him down. She was taller than Galileo and looked immensely strong, in form like one of Michelangelo's men, her wide shoulders and muscular arms bursting from a pale yellow sleeveless blouse, made of something like silk. Pantaloons of the same material covered broad hips, thick long legs. She seemed both aged and young, female and male, in a mix that confused Galileo. Her gaze, as she looked from the stranger to Galileo and back again, was imperious, and he thought of the goddess Hera as described by Homer or Virgil.

'You stole our entangler,' Ganymede accused her, his voice coming to Galileo's ears in an odd Latin. The Jovians' mouths moved in ways that did not quite match what Galileo heard, and he supposed he was the beneficiary of invisible and very rapid translators. 'What are you trying to do, start a war?'

Hera glared at him. 'As if you haven't already started it! You attacked the Europans in their own ocean. Now the council's authority is shattered, the factions are at each other's throats.'

'That has nothing to do with me,' said Ganymede coldly.

131

As Galileo listened to them denounce each other, little flashes of imagery brought to him the extraordinary idea of a voyage down into the subglacial ocean of Europa. He wondered what had happened, and what the situation here was. Ganymede's indignation sounded suspiciously defensive to Galileo, and was causing the man to thrust his narrow jaw out to the side, making his face look like a bent plough blade. 'This is no joke! This is Galileo you're kidnapping!'

'You're the one who kidnapped him,' Hera replied. 'I am rescuing him from you. Really your fixation on this particular analepsis is getting to be too much. Galileo of all people is no one to trifle with, and yet you use him just to scare the council with your rashness.'

Ganymede put his hands to his jaw and straightened it with a visible effort, his face flushed a dark red. 'We'll talk about this later.'

'No doubt. But for now I want you to leave us alone. I am going to explain some things to our visitor here.'

'No!'

At this the people standing behind Hera moved forward en masse. They wore clothes similar to hers, and were similarly big and brawny, and moved in a way that reminded Galileo of Cosimo's armed retainers, the Swiss guards in particular, when they were muscling in to keep the peace or remove someone no longer in Cosimo's favour.

Hera nodded at them, and said to Ganymede, 'Stay here with my friends. You know Bia and Nike, if I am not mistaken.'

'I can't allow this!'

'It's not a question of what you allow or don't. You have no authority on Io. This is our world.'

'This is nobody's world! It's a world of exiles and renegades, as you well know, being chief among them. My own group has taken refuge here.'

Hera said, 'We let people live here who will, but we've been here the longest, and we decide what happens here.' She went to

Galileo's side, and her friends moved as a group to stand between the two of them and the stranger.

Hera said to Galileo. 'Welcome to Io. I was with you when they made their dive into the ocean of Europa. Do you remember that?'

'Not quite,' Galileo said uncertainly. Blue depths; a sound like a cry . . .

With a disgusted glance at Ganymede, she said, 'Ganymede's use of amnestics is crude, very much of a piece with the rest of his actions. I can perhaps return some of your memories to you later. But first I think it may be best to explain the situation to you a bit. Ganymede has not told you the full story. And some of what he's told you is not true.'

She picked up the pewter box from the ground, and held it in her arms as she led him away from the expostulating Ganymede and the group surrounding him. Despite Ganymede's objections, Galileo followed her. Galileo was interested to hear what she might say; and he already knew that she was going to get what she wanted no matter what. He had seen wilful women before.

She was at least a hand taller than he, maybe a head taller. Walking uncertainly at her side, bouncing up and down, he had to grasp her arm to keep from falling. He let go when his feet were under him, then almost fell and had to grab her again; after that he held onto her upper arm as if to the trunk of a grapevine. She did not seem to mind, and it helped him to keep up with her. After a while he found himself helplessly making various erotic calculations having to do with her obvious strength (the box she carried looked heavy), calculations that caused his eyes to widen and his heart to pound. It was a little hard to believe she was human.

'You are well named,' he murmured.

'Thank you,' she said. 'We name ourselves when we are young, at our rite of passage. That was a long time ago.'

When they reached the far side of the little temple she paused. He let go of her arm. From here they had a view down the shattered sulphurous side of the great volcano they stood on, a view immensely tall, and so broad in extent that he could see a distinct curvature to the horizon, and at least a dozen smaller volcanoes, some of them steaming, others blasting great white geysers into the black sky.

Hera waved at the awesome prospect in a proprietary way. 'This is Ra Patera, the biggest massif on Io. Io is what you call Moon One, the innermost of the big four. Ra Patera is far taller than the tallest mountains on Earth, bigger even than the biggest mountain on Mars. We are looking down the eastern flank toward Mazda Catena, that rupture crack in the side of the shield, down there steaming.' She pointed. 'Ra was the ancient Egyptian sun god, Mazda the Babylonian sun god.'

Galileo recalled the spotted surface of the sun as seen on the paper put under the telescope's eyepiece. 'It looks as if burnt by the sun, though we are so far from it. As hot as Hell.'

'It is hot. In many places if you walked on the surface you would sink right into the rock. But the heat comes from inside Io, not from the sun. The whole moon flexes in the tidal stresses between Jupiter and Europa.'

'Tides?' Galileo said, thinking he had misunderstood. 'But surely there are no oceans here.'

'By tides we mean the pull a body has on all the others around it. Every mass pulls everything else toward it, that's just the way it is. The bigger the mass, the bigger the pull. So, Jupiter pulls us one way, and the other moons pull other ways. Mostly Europa, being so close.' She grimaced expressively. 'We are caught between Jove and Europa. And all the pulls combine to warp Io continuously, first one way then another. We are therefore a hot world. Thirty times hotter than Earth, I have heard, and almost entirely molten, except for a very thin skin, and thicker islands of hardened magma like the one we stand on. The entire mass of Io has melted and been erupted onto its surface many times over.'

Galileo struggled to imagine a world regurgitating itself, molten rock flowing inside to outside, then sinking down to be melted and thrown up again.

'There isn't a single drop of water left,' Hera went on, 'nor any of the other light and volatile elements you are used to on Earth.'

'What is it made of, then?'

'Silicates, mostly. A kind of rock, mostly melted. And a lot of sulphur. That's the lightest element not to have been burnt off, and being the lightest, it tends not to sink but to froth on the surface, as you see.'

'Yes. It looks like burnt sulphur.' He had seen pots of the stuff, bubbling in an alembic. He sniffed but smelled nothing.

'Mostly sulphur, yes, or sulphur salts and sulphur oxides. Here we are near the triple point for sulphur, so it vaporizes when it erupts out of the interior, literally explodes on exposure to the vacuum. It can shoot out of a geyser and land more than fifty miles away.'

'I don't understand,' Galileo confessed.

135

'I know.' She gave him a glance. 'You are brave to admit it. Very few people really understand.'

'I've noticed that.'

'Yes. Well, I'm not the one to tell you the details of the physics or chemistry involved. But I can tell you more about what you have seen here, and the person who brought you here. And why he and his group are acting as they are.'

'I would appreciate that very much,' Galileo said politely. It was always good to have potential alternative sources of patronage; sometimes one could then balance them, or pit them against each other, or otherwise use them to create a differential advantage, a leverage. 'You said they brought me to Europa, and we descended into its ocean – it must be a very different world from here, I must say! – and they were hoping to stop others from descending, because that is a forbidden place. But something happened. Some kind of encounter. I almost remember; it was like a waking dream. I seem to recall we were somehow . . . hailed. By something living in the ocean. There was a noise, like wolves howling.'

'There was. Very good. Quite a noise it was. I'm not surprised you remember it, despite the amnestics they gave you. Abreactions fire across the blocked areas by way of similar memories, so being here helps you to recall your previous visits.'

'Visits?'

'What I am surprised at is that Ganymede took you along on that incursion. It may be that he did not know the timing of the Europans' descent, and had to include you in something that was not meant for you.'

'Ah.'

'I do know he's been telling you that his group has brought you to our time to advise them on a matter of fundamental importance.'

'It seemed unlikely,' Galileo said with an unconvincing show of modesty.

She smiled briefly. 'According to Ganymede, you are the first scientist, and therefore one of the most important people in

136

history. Nevertheless, to ask your advice was not his reason to bring you here.'

'But what was?'

She shrugged expressively, like a Tuscan. 'Possibly he felt your presence would help him defend his actions on Europa. No one else on the council wanted to take the responsibility of interfering with the Europans. Ganymede insisted that what they were proposing was a dangerous contamination of a crucial study zone, so that stopping them would be the best scientific practice, also the safest for humanity. He brought you forward in a prolepsis that he hoped would support that position.'

'Why should my presence matter?' Galileo wondered.

'I don't know,' she admitted, frowning as she looked at him. 'He's created so many more analepses than anyone else that it's hard to get a fix on what he is up to. I do wonder if he brings you here primarily to change you, to cause you to do what he wants you to do back in your time. Even with the amnestics blocking your conscious memory, you are still changed here. Then again, when he has you here he flaunts his rashness with the entangler, and thus hopes to scare the council. Or perhaps he thinks you bolster his authority, as you are the first scientist. The patron saint of scientists, you might say. Or of Ganymede's cult, anyway.'

'Archimedes was the first scientist, if you ask me.'

'Maybe so.' She frowned. 'There were analeptic intrusions around Archimedes as well, actually. But you are the first modern scientist, the great martyr to science, the one everyone knows and remembers.'

'People don't remember Archimedes?' Galileo asked incredulously, thinking: martyr?

She frowned. 'I'm sure historians do. In any case, you are right to question Ganymede's stated rationale. He may want your effect here in a prolepsis, or he may be shaping his analepsis by what he exposes you to here.'

Galileo mulled over the terms, which to him came from rhetoric. 'A backward displacement?'

'Yes.'

'What year is it here, then?'

'3020.'

'Thirty twenty? Three thousand years anno Domini?'

'Yes.'

Galileo swallowed involuntarily. For a while the cat had his tongue. 'That's a long time off,' he said at last, trying to be bold. 'Coming back to me is indeed an analepsis.' He recalled the stranger's face in the market, his news of the telescope. From Alta Europa, Ganymede had said that first time. 'How does that work? What does it mean?'

Again she frowned. 'You are in need of an education in physics, but I am not the one to give it to you. Besides, there is no time. My seizure of his entangler, and of you, will have diplomatic and maybe even direct force consequences, which may arrive soon. In the time we have, I want to talk to you about other things. Because now that they have made this analepsis into your time in Italy, it is likely to endure, and it will have effects on all the other temporalities entangled with it. Meaning all of them. Including your life, among other things. My feeling is that the more you know of the situation, the more you can resist the effects of Ganymede's intervention. Which makes it safer for us, as our time is then likelier to endure in substantially its current form.'

'You mean it might not?'

'That's why analepses are so dangerous. There are many temporal isotopes, of course, and they are all entangled, and braid together in ways that are impossible to comprehend, really, even if you are a mathematician specialized in temporal physics, to judge by what they say. What you need to know is that time is not simple or laminar, but a manifold of different potentialities that interpenetrate and influence each other. A common image is to think of it as a broad gravel riverbed with many braided channels, with the water running both upstream and downstream at once. The channels are temporal isotopes, and they

138

cross each other, shift and flow, become oxbowed or even dry up, or become deeper and straighter, and so on. This is just an image to help us understand. Others speak of a kelp forest in the ocean, floating this way and that. Any image is inadequate to the reality, which involves all ten dimensions, and is impossible for us to conceptualize. However, to the extent that we understand, we see that your moment represents a big confluence, or a bend, or what have you.'

'So – I am important?'

Her eyebrows shot up; she was amused at him. He recognized the glance, felt he had seen it before. She gestured at the hellish surface gleaming below them. 'Do you know how people came to be here?'

'Not at all!'

'Ultimately, we came here by conducting experiments and analysing their results using mathematics. That is an idea, or a method, if you like, that changed forever the course of human history. And you were the one who had this idea, or invented this method, decisively and publicly, explaining the process so that all could understand it. You are Il Saggiatore, the Experimentalist. The first scientist. And so therefore everywhere, but especially here in the Galilean moons, you are much revered.'

'The Galilean moons?'

'That's what we call the four big moons of Jupiter.'

'But I named them the Medicean Stars!'

She sighed. 'So you did, but as I said to you before, this has always been regarded as a notorious example of science kissing the ass of power. No one but you ever called them that, and since your time very few people have remained interested in the sordid details of your supplications to a potential patron.'

'I see.' He paused. 'Well, the Galileans is just as good a name, I suppose.'

'Yes.' She had several different looks of amusement, he was finding.

He considered all that she had said. 'Martyr?' he asked despite himself.

Now her look grew truly serious. She stared into his eyes, and he saw that her pupils were dilated, the oak brown of her irises a vivid ring between glossy blacks and whites. 'Yes. I suppose we call these moons the Galileans to memorialize what happened to you. No one has ever forgotten the price you paid for insisting on the reality of this world.'

Galileo, thoroughly spooked, blurted, 'What do you mean?' She said nothing.

Now a kind of dread began to fill his stomach. 'Do I want to know?'

'You do *not* want to know,' she said. 'But I've been thinking I'm going to tell you anyway.'

She surveyed him in what now struck him as a cold way. 'They are giving you amnestics before sending you back into your own time, while underneath that shaping what you learn here, trying to influence your actions at home in a certain direction. But I am thinking that I could give you an anamnestic to counteract their treatment, and teach you some other things, and if you therefore remember what you learn here, it might have a very good effect on your actions. It might change things, in your time and after. That could be dangerous. But then again, there is much since then that needs changing.'

She pointed at the pewter box she had taken from Ganymede, now lying on the polished yellow floor between them.

'What is that?' he quavered, feeling a squirt of fear slide through him.

'That's what the entangler really looks like. The other entangler, in Italy, is at the event I want to show you.' She took him by the shoulders and moved him next to it, and said coldly, like inflexible Atropos, the most terrible of the Fates, 'I'm going to put you back there.' And she crouched and touched a tab on the side of the box.

The pain was such that he would have screamed immediately, but an iron muzzle clamped an iron gag into his mouth. His tongue was nailed into his palate by a spike set in the gag. He worked desperately to swallow the blood pouring into his mouth fast enough not to choke on it. His heart was racing, and when he saw and comprehended where he was, it beat even harder. Surely it would burst with the strain.

The hooded brothers of the Company of Saint John the Beheaded, also known as the Company of Mercy and Pity, had just finished strapping the muzzle and gag onto his head. Now they lifted him up onto the back of a cart. They were outside the Castel Sant'Angelo, down on the banks of the Tiber. The horses in harness jerked forward under the lash of the whip, and he tried to hold his head upright to keep it from hitting the sides of the cart. The cartwheels ground over the paving stones at a walking pace. Dominican monks flanked the cart and led the way. These Dogs of God barked at him as they went, hectoring him to recant, to confess his sins, to go to God with a clean conscience. I confess! he wanted to say. I recant, no question about it. The streets were lined on both sides with a ragged crowd, many falling in behind as they passed, joining the procession into the city. In all the shouting there was no chance anyone would hear his moans. It was assumed that he was past speech, he could see that in their eyes, which were feasting on the sight of him, and needed no sound other than their own roar. He stopped trying to speak. Even to moan was to choke on blood, to drown on it. Perhaps he could choke on purpose at just the right time.

Slowly they crossed the city, from the great prison on the Tiber to the Campo dei Fiori, the Square of Flowers. Low dark clouds scudded overhead on a stiff wind. Priests in black prayed at him and tossed holy water on him, or thrust their crucifixes in his face.

He preferred the hooded and impassive Dominicans to these grotesque faces, twisted by hatred. No hatred like that of the ignorant for the learned; now he saw that even greater was the hatred of the damned for the martyr. They saw the end they knew would eventually engulf them for their sins. Today they rejoiced that it was happening to someone else, but they knew their time would come and would be eternal, and so their fear and hatred exploded out of them, putting the lie to their pretended joy.

In the Campo dei Fiori one of the black Dominicans intoned in his ear. The Pope had commanded that his punishment be inflicted with as great a clemency as possible, so there was to be no effusion of blood. How this squared with the blood pouring out of his mouth was a question he was never going to get to ask, for the priest was now explaining that this meant he was to be burned at the stake without first being eviscerated. Many hands lifted him off the cart. The low underside of the clouds was rippled like a windblown field of wheat. He was dragged by the heels over to the pyre, and there stripped naked, the penitent's white cloth thrown to the ground, although the iron muzzle was left on his head. His arms were pulled behind him around the thick post of the stake and tied tightly at wrist and elbow. Like everyone he had burned himself once or twice at stove or candle; it was hard to face the idea of his whole body immersed in that pain. Surely it would not last long. The crowd was roaring. He tried to choke on his blood, tried to hold his breath and faint. Around him the Dogs of God chanted their imprecations. He did not see who lit the stack of kindling under him. He smelled the smoke first, then felt fire on his toes. His feet tried to slide up the stake of their own accord, but his ankles were chained to a hole in the post. He had not noticed the chains before. In a few seconds the fire shot up and over his legs, became an agonizing burn all over them. His body tried to scream, and he choked on his own blood, began to drown, but did not faint. He smelled the roasting skin and meat of his own legs, a kitchen smell. Then there was nothing but the pain filling his skull and blinding him, red pain like a scream.

He cried out. His mouth was free, his tongue whole. He lay on a smooth stone floor. The pain was now only a ghost of the plenum it had been. An afterimage of it seemed to fill everything with a faint red haze.

He was back on the floor of the mountaintop temple, on Jupiter's moon Io. He lay on the polished rock with his head clutched in his hands, the meaty stench of his burning still in his lungs, on his whole tongue: only not. It was the ghost of the stench only, a memory; it was in his mind only. Surely it was a memory he would never escape, no matter how hard he tried. Every time he ate roast meat –

His palate was whole, and he swallowed nothing but his own snot and saliva, pouring down his throat like blood. He felt sick to his stomach. He had been weeping hard, and his body was covered with a cold sweat. He sat up, held his jaw in his hands. The taste of blood was gone; except in his mind.

The Ionian woman, Hera, stood over him, as tall and massive as Zeus's wife should be. She put out a hand, helped him to his feet; it must have been like pulling up a puppet that had had its strings cut. He almost tripped over the pewter box. She balanced him carefully, let him stand.

He wiped the tears from his face, glanced up at her full of shame and fear. She shrugged, uncomfortable and sympathetic. It was nothing to be ashamed of, the shrug seemed to say, not to like being burned at the stake. Also: not her fault. Only acquainting him with reality.

'But this is bad!' he said.

'Yes.'

'It cannot happen!'

'But it already has, as you will come to see.'

'But – you said there were different times, braided together?'

143

'Well, that's right. You are quick. But in almost all the potentialities, this is what happens.'

He swallowed hard. 'When?'

'You don't want to know.'

'I suppose not. Although, maybe . . .' He didn't know what he meant well enough to finish the sentence.

After a silence she said, 'You see now why you are revered.'

'I *don't* see why,' Galileo objected. 'Your Ganymede said it was because of my success! That it was because I invented the method of science, as a mathematical experimentalist!'

'Yes. And so he thinks we *need* you to succeed, you see. Or none of this will come to pass.'

'But surely that was not success!' A shudder rippled his muscles, as in frightened horses or dogs. 'That was no triumph, if I am not mistaken!'

She said carefully, 'In some people's eyes, your success includes your immolation. Ganymede and his followers are among them. They have a fixation on you and your work, on what it meant to the rest of history. From that point on, they say, science began to dominate, religion to recede. The secularization of the world began. That alone saves humanity from many centuries of darkness, in which science is perverted to the will of insane religions. So they think of you as the great martyr for science.'

'But why should science have to have a martyr?'

'That has been my point precisely.'

A wave of affection for this woman surged through Galileo. He took up her hand, feeling stabbed by hope: 'Can you help me, then? Help me to escape that fate?'

She looked down at the sulphurous world that lay shattered below them, thinking it over. She was pondering his fate, becoming like Atropos again. He watched her avidly; she was suddenly beautiful to him, and he remembered a line from Castiglione: *Beauty springs from God and is like a circle, the centre of which is goodness.*

'I think I can,' she said at last. He could not help kissing her hand. She looked at him speculatively. 'It is probably true that you have to achieve what you will achieve, for the main channel of history to be as it has been. And it's probably also true that that achievement is certain to get you in trouble with your theocracy.'

'I don't see why!' This was already such a grievance with Galileo that he almost shouted this. He wrenched it into a plea: 'There is no contradiction between science and scripture! And even if there were –' for their very presence under the giant banded ball of Jupiter seemed to suggest something beyond the Bible's purview, beyond what scripture would countenance – 'even if there were, as God made both nature and scripture, the problem would then be with the details of the scripture, or with our poor understanding of it. Because the two cannot disagree, as God made both, and He can't be logically inconsistent. And the Earth goes around the sun, with all the rest of the planets. Since that is true, there is nothing blasphemous in it.'

'No. Of course not. But that was never the issue.'

She stopped, thought, decided to continue: 'One question was, who gets to speak? Who has the authority to make statements about the ultimate nature of reality? This was what your church objected to – that you asserted that you had the right to make statements about fundamental things. Cosmology was a religious matter, do you see? This was what you were saying, under all your details, which as often as not were wrong, or at least unsupported – that you had a right to your own opinion about reality, and that you had the right to say it in public, and argue for it against the views of theocrats.'

'So I was a kind of protestant, you're saying,' Galileo concluded glumly. 'I might as well have gone north and become a Lutheran.'

'Maybe so.'

'And so . . . Well, in that case, I am doomed.'

'You are headed for trouble. That is certain. If you insist on asserting yourself in that way. Which is what you did, and which is precisely what made you a crucial figure in the human story.

145

So that it is indispensable for you to make that assertion, and thus to be the first modern scientist.'

'And so burned at the stake, like Bruno!'

'Yes. But . . . the burning at the stake part, I would argue, is not the important part of your story. What is important is not the punishment, but the assertion.'

'You are good to think so, Lady!' How he admired this woman's intelligence! He could have kissed her feet at that moment, as he already had her hand; in fact he barely restrained himself as the urge came to throw himself to the ground before her. 'And so, if . . . If . . .'

'If you could both make the assertion, and escape the consequences of it, somehow . . . Yes. It will be a close run thing, but I should think it would do. There are so many potentialities, after all. How the wave function collapses at any given moment is never completely determinative of what follows. There are inertias and instabilities, and many subsequent interventions. And if there are longer-term changes that follow, I think they could be good. The histories we have now are not such that a change in the centuries subsequent to yours would be such a bad idea. It might lessen the depth of the low point, and get us here with less suffering.'

'But it might change you out of existence?'

'But here we are,' she pointed out.

'But it might still happen?'

'Maybe. But how would that make our situation any different? We might always wink out of existence, at any time.'

Galileo shuddered at the thought. 'And so you will help me?'

She regarded him curiously. She seemed almost to hesitate. But then:

'Yes. I will. It will have to be done carefully, you understand. The change will have to be subtly done. And there will be people who will try to prevent any such change, Ganymede and others.'

'I understand.'

She looked up suddenly, scowled at what she saw. Galileo followed her gaze, saw the star-studded black sky and nothing more; except then he spotted a small cluster of moving lights, like fireflies. Reinforcements from Ganymede's people, perhaps.

Hera said, 'We should return you to Ganymede.'

'What should I say to him about this?'

She smiled, it seemed at his quickness to fall into conspiracy with her. 'Whatever you like,' she said. 'Here on Io you are free to speak your mind. You can tell him everything I told you, if you like.'

'Yes, of course. Thank you. But should I tell him of our plan?'

'What do you think?'

'I would rather not! If his faction believes I must be burned for history to turn out as they want it, then they might try to keep it that way, not so?'

'Exactly.'

'Then we must keep our project a secret!'

'Ha!' she said. 'I'm not good at keeping secrets. I speak my mind.'

'But you said you were going to help me!'

'I am going to help you. It's just that I may choose not to do it in secret.'

'Ah. Well, then . . .' Galileo was confused. 'They will send me back to my time?'

'Yes.'

'And give me a preparation to make me forget what happened here, you said.'

'Yes.'

'But you can give me something to counteract their preparation?'

Her eyebrows bunched together as she thought it over. She glanced at him sidelong. 'Yes,' she said, 'I can. For every amnestic there are anamnestics. Although I am not so sure you will like remembering this. I can try to modulate your short-term memory, so that you remember just the outlines of it, and the feeling. But as I don't know which amnestic they will be using, it will be tricky. I can try to counteract the whole class of drug I think they will use.' She spoke quietly into the back of her hand. 'My people will give me what I think you will need. You must expect some confusion to result, whether it works or not.'

'Just so I don't forget!'

'No. What I give you, you will take now, in advance of their application. Then hold your breath right before they send you back. He shoots a mist into your face at the last moment. If you are successful, the result should be that you remember all this fairly well. The anamnestics are quite effective, you will see. Hopefully not in a way that proves intolerable to you.'

'Good. And – will you bring me back here to you, at some point, if you can? I feel that if I am to succeed in my effort at home, I need to learn more.'

She laughed at that. 'This is what you are always saying, yes?'

'So you'll bring me back?'

'I'm not sure.'

'You'll try?'

'Maybe. Don't mention that to Ganymede. That should be *arrheton* – not to be spoken of.'

Then vessels like sealed boat hulls, standing on pillars of fire, descended around them. Hera took him by the arm and led him across the smooth yellow stone parquet of the round temple to where her people were holding the stranger and his small group. Ganymede's eyes were burning with such curiosity that Galileo had to look away for fear his new knowledge would squirt out of him by glance alone. Meanwhile Hera took his hand and palmed him a small pill. She leaned down to his face and gave him a kiss on the cheek. 'Swallow it now,' she murmured; he brought his hand up to his face as if to touch hers, and as she withdrew he tossed the pill in his mouth and swallowed it. It had a bitter taste, like unripe limes.

Hera had turned to the Ganymede and his newly arrived

supporters, who were looking angry. She gave the pewter box to Ganymede and announced, 'Here, you can have him. But let him go back where he belongs!'

'We would have long before, if it weren't for you,' Ganymede said furiously, and then Galileo was surrounded by the stranger's associates, and Ganymede was holding the box before him, and he held his breath tightly. But one of them noticed what he was doing and tapped him hard in the solar plexus, then waited for him to suck in his breath after the involuntary exhalation, then sprayed the mist in his face.

Chapter Eight Parry Riposte

To hope without hope, which would be wise, is impossible.
                    – MARCEL PROUST, *Les Plaisirs et les Jeurs*

No one understood why the maestro was so anxious and melancholy after that night when Cardinal Barberini came through. It was true he had eaten and drunk too much at the banquet, and had then slept badly and eventually fallen into one of his syncopes, and come out of it too ill to attend the farewell breakfast the next morning; but none of that was particularly unusual for him, and the extremely warm letter from the cardinal should have more than reassured him about missing the send-off breakfast. Really, his *anno mirabilis* had lasted for almost three years now and was still going strong. He should have been happy.

But he wasn't. His sleep was frequently broken by nightmares, and his days were irritating to him. 'Something bad is going to happen,' he kept saying, looking through his telescope at Jupiter like a soothsayer. 'Something monstrous wants to be born.'

One night he called Cartophilus to him. Staring at the old man over a cup of warmed milk brought to him to ward off the chill, he said suddenly, 'Where is your master?'

'You are my master, maestro.'

'You know who I mean!'

'. . . He's not here.'

Galileo contemplated him, frowning. Finally he said, 'When I want him again, can you call him here?'

After another pause the old man nodded.

'Be ready,' Galileo warned him.

The ancient one slunk away. He knew why Galileo was afraid better than Galileo himself. He bowed under the weight of it.

Galileo often wrote to Picchena asking for Cosimo's permission to go to Rome. By the middle of 1613, some reasons for these requests became more evident to those around him. His detractors had grown more vehement in direct proportion to his growing fame. A good deal of this Galileo had brought on himself. A lot of people hated him for what they called his arrogance.

To his household that wasn't quite right. They spent a fair amount of time discussing him, as one does any great power in one's life. 'He's very defensive,' La Piera would say. 'So defensive that he attacks people first in self-defence, and thus he becomes offensive.'

To the other servants it was simpler than that: he was Pulcinella. All over Italy the figure of Pulcinella had begun appearing in the festivals and buffa plays, a loud fool constantly lying, cheating, fornicating and thrashing people, in short, the very image of a certain kind of master, which every servant in the land recognized and laughed to see. Once, as Galileo was snoring in his chair while wearing a white shirt, someone had put a black cloth over his head and the typical costume was thereby hilariously complete, and they all tiptoed in to look and treasure this knowledge ever after: they worked for the greatest Pulcinella of all.

Now this ham-fisted tendency was catching up with him, his enemies becoming remarkably numerous. Colombe for one had never slackened in his assault. Previously this Bible-quoting malevolence could be ignored or used as a foil, as he had had no patrons. But now he was being used by figures much higher than him, who were interested in the success of his tactic of accusing Galileo of contradicting Scripture. Joshua, these figures were now murmuring into higher ears, had ordered the sun to come to a halt, not the Earth. It was as clear as could be. Surely the church had to respond . . . ? They could beat Galileo with this kind of stick forever, because no one outside the Church should have been talking about Scriptural interpretation at all.

Galileo ignored that and tried to respond directly to his assailants. He pointed out that God stopping the sun in the sky for Joshua would entail stopping the celestial vault and all the stars as well, as Ptolemy said they were all affixed to each other, whereas if Copernicus were right, then all God would have had to do to fix the sun in the midday sky would be to stop the Earth's rotation, a much easier task, as could be easily seen. That this was ingeniously argued did not keep it from being also ridiculous, so much so that some people took it to be a mockery of the very idea of Biblical explanations of the skies. It was hard to tell; a deadpan sarcasm was one arrow in Galileo's sling. But either way it would have been wiser not to venture into such territory at all.

But he persisted in doing so. He wrote a long 'Letter to the Grand Duchess Christina', explaining to her and to the letter's wider readership the principles he thought should rule science's relation to theology. *In discussion of physical questions we ought to begin not from the authority of scriptural passages, but from sense experiences and necessary demonstration. God is known first through Nature, and then by doctrine; by Nature in His works, and by doctrine in His revealed word.*

'And God would not lie to us!' This was what he said over and over, from the very first moment of the controversy. In the workshop at Via Vignali, he had shouted it while striking the anvil with a long pair of tongs. 'God would not lie to us!'

This was logically and perhaps even theologically sound, but it didn't matter. The attacks continued, and many of them sounded like the kind of thing that might be accompanied by a secret denunciation to the Holy Office of the Inquisition. There were rumours that had already happened.

Galileo kept defending himself, in print and in person, but he fell ill again, more and more often, with rheumatism, bleeding hernias, shaking spells, blinding headaches, insomnia, syncopes and catalepsies. Hypochondria. Bouts of irrational fear. Whenever he was healthy he begged Cosimo, through his secretary Curzio Picchena, to be allowed to go to Rome so that he could defend himself. He was still confident he could demonstrate the truth of the Copernican hypothesis to anyone he spoke to in person. Picchena was not the only one who doubted this. Winning all those banquet debates had apparently caused Galileo to think that argument was how things were settled in the world. Unfortunately this is never how it happens.

Galileo also was ignoring new complications that mattered. The general of the Jesuits, Claudio Aquaviva, had ordered his people to teach only the Aristotelian philosophy. Then also there was a doctored copy of Galileo's 'Letter to Castelli' being passed around Rome which made his positions sound even more radical than they were. This forgery had worked with all too many Dominicans: the Dogs of God now sniffed a bear.

Worst of all, it was said that Bellarmino had again ordered an investigation of the Copernican position as put forth by Galileo. This was a secret investigation, but everyone knew about it. A trial had therefore begun, a secret trial that was not actually secret. That was the Inquisition for you; rumours were part of their method, part of their terror. Sometimes they liked to apply pressures that might cause a panic mistake.

Galileo fell ill again, very conveniently. He took to his bed for most of the winter, miserable and sleepless. In Rome Cesi made inquiries on his behalf to Bellarmino himself, asking what His Eminence thought Galileo should do. Bellarmino told Cesi that Galileo should stick to mathematics, avoid any assertions about the nature of the world, and avoid in particular any Scriptural interpretations.

'Happy to do so!' Galileo shouted hoarsely from his bed, shaking Cesi's fisted letter at his servants. 'But how? How can I do that, when these ignorant vipers use Scripture to attack me? If I can't reply in kind then I can't defend myself!'

Which was of course the point. They had him. Being thus garroted in a double bind, naturally he choked on it. His stomach too went bad, and he could keep nothing down. He had to remain in his bed for most of a month. His fear and anger were palpable, a sweaty stink that filled his room. Broken crockery littered the floor, one had to step carefully to serve him, toe the shards aside and pretend everything was fine, even while dodging things thrown at one. The household knew things were not fine.

'I have to go to Rome,' he would say, repeating it like a rosary. 'I *have* to go to Rome. I *must* go.' At night, watching the moons of Jupiter, taking notes as he hummed one of his father's old tunes, falling asleep on his stool, he would murmur, 'Help me, help me, help me. Get me to Rome.'

Finally Cosimo approved the visit. He wrote to his Roman ambassador to say that Galileo was coming *to defend himself against the accusations of his rivals.* The ambassador was to provide Galileo with two rooms in the Villa Medici, *because he needs peace and quiet on account of his poor health.*

Guicciardini, never a friend, wrote back to Cosimo, *I do not know whether he has changed his theories or his disposition, but I know this: certain Dominican friars who play a major role in the Holy Office, and others, are ill disposed toward him. This is no place to come and argue about the Moon and, especially in these times, arrive with new ideas.*

And yet that's what he did. A ducal litter carried him south to Rome as before, and after the arduous week of the journey,

Federico Cesi accompanied him into the city, through the ever-more-crowded outskirts of the great city, to the Pincian Hill in the northeast quarter. The hill rose out of squalid warrens crawling with people, all the poor souls who had migrated to the City of God hoping for succour either mundane or supernatural. Now Galileo made one more.

The Villa Medici occupied the very top of the Pincian Hill, which was also known as the Hill of Gardens, and deservedly so, as the few villas on it stuck out like ships on a billowing wave of vineyards. The Medici villa was the vast white hulk at the top, with a tall and nearly blank stucco façade facing the city centre. Newer galleries extended away from the main building into the great gardens surrounding it, where one could wander among the hedges and the magnificent collection of antiquities that the family had bought from the Capranicas a generation before.

The ambassador, Piero Guicciardini, met Galileo on the broad front terrazzo of the villa. He was an elegant man with a finely trimmed black beard, rather cool in his welcome, and so Galileo was likewise. They got through the diplomatic necessities as quickly as possible, after which Guicciardini turned him over to his master of the house, Annibale Primi. Primi proved to be a cheerful man, a tall sanguine figure whose head was set a little before his body. He led Galileo and his servant to the 'two good rooms' Cosimo had ordered to be provided for him, and when Galileo had seen them, and arranged with Cartophilus their disposition, Primi led him outside and up to the high point of the garden, a man-made mound fifty feet tall.

'This mound is dirt piled onto the nympthaeum of the ancient Acilian gardens. It's just the extra height you need to get a view over the other hills, see? People often say it's the best vista in the whole city.'

The other six hills at their various distances blocked a complete bird's-eye view of Rome, but the prospect still gave them an almost overwhelming sense of the city's tumbling vastness, an entire province of rooftops, it seemed to Galileo, like a million inclined planes set up for some supremely complicated experiment, with the Tiber a tin gleam here and there in the smoky expanse. All the other big hills were likewise occupied by great villas, and so appeared as mostly green islands sticking up out of tile-clad waves, the vineyards and cypresses on them creating lines horizontal and vertical.

'This is great,' Galileo said, wandering inside the high point's circular wall as if on a Venetian altana. 'What a city this is. We'll have to bring up a telescope.'

'I would like that.' Primi pulled a big bottle of wine from his shoulderbag and held it up for Galileo's inspection, a grin on his face.

'Ah ha,' Galileo said, bowing slightly, 'a man after my own heart.'

'I assumed as much,' Primi said, 'given what people say about you. And here we are, after all – on top of the world. You might as well celebrate when you get to a place like this.'

'So true.'

The two men sat on the low wall ringing the summit of the mound, and Primi uncorked the fiasco of wine. He poured tin cups full, and they toasted the day and sat and talked while they drank. Primi was the son of an innkeeper and reminded Galileo of his artisans, a quick man who had seen a lot and knew how to do a lot of things. He told Galileo about the greenhouses and the new galleries, and then they sat and looked at the city and drank. There was a noise to the city as well as a smoke, a general grumbling hum. Galileo could see across the roofs to the Janiculum, where just four years before he had triumphantly talked to the Pope and displayed his telescope to all the Roman nobility. So much had changed. 'It's a hell of a town,' he said, gesturing at it helplessly. He could not keep the fear in him entirely at bay, but the wine did loosen the strain of it in a comforting way. He breathed in that bracing effect, straightened up: here he was, after all. At least now he could fight!

Primi rattled on about the villas on the other hilltops. In the smoky sunset the city turned umber and orange, like a thing of granite under a cloudless sky.

Primi was a very active master of the house; he even helped them each morning to choose what would be most appropriate to wear for whatever meetings Galileo had that day. He arranged for the traps and drivers, giving the drivers instructions to take particular ways to their destinations so that Galileo would see things in the city that Primi thought he should see.

So, out he would go, dressed in his finest tights and one of his best jackets. And the nobles and prelates would meet with him, but they were less enthusiastic than before. Meetings ended in an hour, other engagements were pled. Something was going on, which was of course the rumour of Bellarmino's interest. That was enough to put a chill on anyone.

In his bustle and bluster it was not easy to tell if Galileo noticed this, but it seemed certain he must have, and was just trying to pretend all was well. It was either that or else he was even more oblivious than anyone had hitherto suspected. But it seemed more likely that he knew. Every afternoon he would return and drag himself wearily out of the trap and into the villa, having spent the day proclaiming the same thing to everyone: 'I am a devout Catholic,' he would have said, his eye fixed intently on his listener. 'My work is to reconcile Copernicanism and the Holy Church, it is an attempt to *help* the Church, which otherwise will soon find itself contravening *obvious facts* of God's world, quite visible to all. That can't be good for Her! We have to help Her in this Her hour of need!'

And everyone would have listened to him thinking, Bellarmino. *Don't be where Bellarmino is looking* had been a saying in the city for over twenty years. After so much evasion, when he got back to the villa, and the ambassador would be nowhere to be seen, Annibale Primi's appearance in the big garden doorway, with a lumpy shoulderbag under his arm and a big grin on his face, would cause Galileo to bow gratefully, and after changing his clothes he would walk up the spiral gravel path to the top of the garden mound, and often stay out there until the stars were twinkling overhead, eating and drinking, and, after calling for his telescope, viewing the city and the stars. On many mornings after these dissolute nights he could barely move, and yet he had new appointments to keep that day. Sometimes we had to dress him like a scarecrow or a tailor's dummy.

Then off he would go again, slapping himself in the face and drinking cinnamon concoctions, making his rounds every day like a tinker or a mendicant, crisscrossing that immense smoky city of the world, meeting anyone who would give him an invitation, or receive one from Cesi. Sometimes he had little successes; a few new potential allies and supporters met with him at Cesi's palazzo, including a newly appointed cardinal, young Antonio Orsini, who was a Galilean and possibly an important ally. But mostly people kept their distance. *Don't be where Bellarmino is looking.*

Thus it was a shock but not really a surprise when one afternoon a papal messenger came to the Villa Medici with an order. Galileo was to meet with Cardinal Bellarmino in the Vatican, on the very next morning.

That night the mood in the villa was tense and foreboding. Galileo did not go up to the mound with Primi, but stayed in his rooms. Twice in the night he called for Cartophilus to fetch him refreshment: first mulled wine, then warmed milk. It did not appear to Cartophilus that he slept at all that night. And so of course Cartophilus slept very little either.

In the morning, two of Bellarmino's inquisitorial officers of arrest showed up at the villa to convey Galileo and his aged servant to Bellarmino's house, on the river side of the Vatican grounds. On the way there Galileo said nothing, though he seemed cheerful enough, face ruddy and eyes bright. Time at last for action, his manner seemed to say. He glanced up frequently at the sky, which was flecked by flat small grey clouds.

Once inside Bellarmino's antechamber, the two arresting officers made their bows to Galileo and left. Only servants then remained, standing against the wall, the cardinal's and Galileo's side by side.

Then the cardinal himself entered the room. Galileo went to one knee and found he was nevertheless still taller than the cardinal. Roberto Bellarmino was a very short man.

He was around seventy years old. His neat goatee was white, his hair a salted brown. Dressed in his cardinal's red, he made a handsome and impressive sight, despite his diminutive size, which made him resemble a clock statue come to life. He greeted Galileo in a quiet, urbane voice. 'Rise, great astronomer, and speak with me.'

By comparison Galileo and his rough baritone seemed large and loud and somehow rustic. 'Many thanks, Glorious Lord Eminence. I kiss your sandal.' He huffed as he got awkwardly to his feet, then looked down at the little man, one of the chief intellects of their time. Bellarmino regarded him with a quizzical smile, seemingly friendly. Of course he would be used to looking up at people.

Then there came a murmured interruption from one of the servants, and another inquisitor from the Holy Office entered the room. The servant announced: 'Commissary General of the Holy Office of the Inquisition Father Michelangelo Segizzi.' He was accompanied by a few members of his staff, all Dominicans, as well as two tall men who were not Dominicans and whom Segizzi did not bother to introduce.

'We are here to serve as notary to the meeting,' Segizzi declared in a hard voice, meeting Bellarmino's eye boldly. 'Thus there will be an official record for His Holiness to read.'

The little cardinal's face reddened a bit; they were in Bellarmino's own home, and if he had not expected these men to join the meeting, it was an impudent thing.

But he said nothing to Segizzi, except to invite him and all the rest of them into his study. The group filed through the tall door into a sunny room dominated by Bellarmino's big desk, located under the north window.

Bellarmino then ignored Segizzi, and said to Galileo in a calm and kindly voice, 'Signor, you must abandon the error of Copernicanism, if, indeed, you hold the opinion. It has been found by the Holy Office to be erroneous.'

Galileo had apparently been expecting something less drastic. He said nothing; he grew as pale as Bellarmino was flushed. It was as if they had traded complexions. Twice he started to speak, hesitated, stopped. Ordinarily his only response to opposition was to whip it into submission by way of relentless argument: he had no other response in him.

In the charged silence, Commissioner Segizzi lowered his head like a bull and began to read loudly from a written proclamation he held out before him: 'You, Galileo Galilei, are commanded and enjoined, in the name of His Holiness the Pope and the whole Congregation of the Holy Office, to relinquish altogether the said opinion that the sun is the centre of the world and at rest, and that the Earth moves. Nor are you ever henceforth to hold, teach, or defend it in any way, verbally or in writing. Otherwise proceedings will be taken against you by the Holy Office.'

Again Galileo had nothing to say. Cardinal Bellarmino, looking startled, even angry, glared at Segizzi as sharply as any ordinary man.

161

'You must acquiesce to this order,' Segizzi told Galileo. 'Otherwise there will be another meeting, and not here.'

There was a long silence. Finally: 'I acquiesce,' Galileo said tightly. 'I promise to obey the order.'

Bellarmino, distracted, still red faced, waved a hand and brought the meeting to an end without adding anything more. He looked at his hands on the desk, frowning slightly, glancing once at Segizzi, then at his desk again.

Thus concluded the first trial of Galileo.

'What was that all about?' Galileo said as they walked behind the Medici carriage sent to carry them back up to the villa. He had been too agitated to sit inside the thing.

It was a rhetorical question, as he was busy examining his memory to secure his sense of what had been said; but Cartophilus offered up tentatively, 'Cardinal Bellarmino did not seem to expect the Dominicans to join the meeting.'

'Really?' Galileo frowned.

'Really.'

'But what does that mean?'

'I don't know, maestro.' The ancient one shook his head, confused.

Late that night Cartophilus slipped out into the garden of the villa, through the orchard to the servant's gate where he met a friend of his named Giovanfrancesco Buonamici. He told him what had happened that day at the Vatican.

Buonamici was tall and as lithe as a weasel under a voluminous dark cape. He chewed a fingernail thoughtfully for a while. 'That could be bad,' he said. 'They could produce a witness now who would claim that he tried to talk about Copernicus after this warning, maybe use what he's been saying all this last month against him by post-dating it, or something like that. It could happen fast. I'll get word of this to the father; he will decide what we ought to do.'

'Yes, that's good. Because that was something strange today, I don't know what.'

'If anyone knows, he will.'

Galileo was very lucky, given the power of his enemies, and the situation facing him, and his own fecklessness, that he had allies and supporters working for him too, not only in public, as with Cesi's Lynxes, but behind the scenes – not just us, but the Venetians. Because Venice had the biggest spy network in Europe, with a particularly comprehensive contingent in Rome – most of it in the Vatican, of course, but penetrating also into the Roman courts, the courier services, the academies, the hostels, and the brothels. Not even the Vatican itself had as complete an understanding of Rome's tangled mazes of rumour and machination as the Venetian spy service did.

When Cartophilus next heard Buonamici's looping whistle, the following week, he took the slops down to the villa's compost heap and went on to the orchard gate to meet him. Buonamici led him down the hill into the dense tenements east of it, then into the yard of a small church, one of many mouldering away in the city serving a local neighbourhood in complete anonymity; and there Buonamici knocked at a battered side door. Old hens pecked listlessly in the adjacent garden of the resident priest. The door opened, and after a word from Buonamici a man emerged, entirely covered by a monk's habit and hood. He turned to Cartophilus, who was shocked to see it was the Great Servite himself: Father Paolo Sarpi.

Sarpi had been the secret general of Venice's spy service for many years, since before the current war of words and knives between Venice and Rome. He was the perfect man for the job, comprehensive in his knowledge of Europe, and imbued with great analytical powers, and a keen vigilance when it came to Rome. The fact that Pope Paul had once tried to kill him was of course a factor in this vigilance, but not the main factor. Rome was always a big problem for Venice, and mostly Paul's assault had only caused the venerable Servite to take Rome seriously as a danger. The vengeance most people would have sought, Sarpi transformed into a plan for a larger victory; not just Paul's downfall, but the permanent hamstringing of Rome's imperial efforts.

Now Sarpi stood there with them, right there in a city where he could have been taken up and tossed into Castel Sant'Angelo, after which disappearing forever was the good option.

'Should you be here, Fra Paolo?' Cartophilus could not help asking.

'Bless you, I am well hidden here. An old monk is invisible in this city, as everywhere. I actually once spent months tucked away in this very church, when my presence in Rome was useful. Now I felt the situation is such that I am needed here again, so.'

'It's that bad?' Cartophilus asked, wondering how much he knew.

'Word has come that there is a faction here that would like our astronomer to be silenced for good. That's a real danger. So, first I need to know all that you saw in the meeting with Bellarmino.'

He listened closely as Cartophilus recited what he recalled of the meeting. 'What about the men with Segizzi?' he asked. 'Tell me everything you remember of them.'

Cartophilus told him everything he could, humming unhappily as he tried to recall the scene to mind. As Sarpi listened he frowned, causing his scarred face to bunch on the left side. When Cartophilus finished, he stood there silently for a while.

'I think that was Badino Nores with Segizzi,' he said at last, 'and Agostino Mongardo, from Montepulciano. They are Borgia men, and so is Segizzi. So. I very much doubt they were supposed to be at that meeting. Which means Segizzi intruded on a private conference in Bellarmino's own house. That is something Bellarmino would not have tolerated if he didn't have to.'

'But he's the Lord Cardinal?'

'Yes, in theory he fears no one. But in fact, he can't afford to cross the Borgias. I've been hearing from people in the other parts of this puzzle, and it's all beginning to fit together. I think Segizzi's appearance was a surprise attack. Possibly the warning Segizzi made to Galileo was stronger than what either Bellarmino or Paul had intended. And of course it matters what documents have now been placed in Galileo's Vatican file to memorialize the meeting. They might declare that Galileo was warned even more explicitly than what really happened, for instance. Our Galileo would be thus doubly deceived, so to speak, as to what exactly the Pope has allowed or forbidden him to say.'

'Dangerous,' Buonamici said laconically.

'Indeed. Very dangerous, because even when he is fully on his guard, our impetuous one is not so good at holding his tongue.'

The two men nodded wordlessly; it was an understatement to say the least.

'So.' Sarpi shook his head. 'Let us set about learning more of what is happening, and then untying this knot around Galileo's neck if we can.' He smiled at the prospect, which rendered his face even more terrifying than his frown. 'No matter what we find, Cartophilus, I think it would help if you were to convey to Galileo that he should ask Bellarmino for a signed declaration, one which memorializes explicitly what Galileo is commanded to do and not to do. I think Bellarmino will accommodate him, because he is likely to see this as a way to pay the Borgia back for invading his home.'

Cartophilus nodded gloomily. 'I'll do it. I hope it will be enough.'

'It will be just one move in a chess game, of course. But we can only do what we can do, at this point and always.' And with his hideous smile the great Servite slipped back into the ramshackle little church, into one corner of the immense anonymity that was Rome.

Late that same night, the ancient one carried Galileo's warmed milk to his room, and when Galileo brought up the subject of Bellarmino and Segizzi's ominous and contradictory warnings, as he did every night, obsessively, Cartophilus took the opportunity to say hesitantly, 'Maestro, I've heard that what people are saying now is that you were forced to make a secret abjuration or something like that.'

'I've heard that too,' Galileo growled. 'People have been writing to ask me about it, even from Florence.'

Cartophilus nodded and stared at the floor. 'Maybe you should get whatever warning it really is from Bellarmino himself, in writing and signed by him, so that you have it specifically spelled out and in a document that you can show people later. In case there is ever a question about it.'

'Yes.' Galileo glared at him; he did not like the old one interfering like this, in ways that made him think about him. 'Good idea,' he said heavily.

'It's nothing, maestro.'

Galileo began the process of obtaining another audience with Bellarmino. This had to be done through Guicciardini, so it took persistence and a bit of begging. While Galileo went through that distasteful process he spent every evening out at banquets, but now he no longer made virtuoso recitals in defence of the Copernican view, being merely convivial instead. Naturally people noticed this change, and rumours about how severely he had been warned off by the Lord Cardinal proliferated. Galileo ignored all that and soldiered on. He discovered that Rome had many more than seven hills. It became more and more difficult to clean his jacket without revealing how old and shabby it was. Every night he ate too much, and drank too much wine. Even on the rare night that he stayed home at the Villa Medici, he could not calm himself without copious amounts of wine, and he almost always stayed up late with Annibale Primi on the hilltop, drinking to distract himself in the very face of the huge city and the power it wielded over everyone. On more than one such hopeless night we had to load him in a wheelbarrow and trundle him down the hill to his bed, dumping him onto it like a load of bricks, him all the while snarling and snoring and muttering about bad things sure to happen.

We went to work with Sarpi's Roman network, wandering the back alleys in the low foul neighbourhoods near the Tiber, knocking on doors or meeting people in taverns and the backs of little churches. We talked to gate-keepers, servants, foreign diplomats' aides, secretaries, lawyers, cooks, clerks, beggars. Some had secrets to sell, or knew of others who did. We paid certain publicans, go-betweens, a poor noble, a defrocked priest, several madams and prostitutes; we hired a few observant old street dwellers to keep an ear to certain doorways, and even employed a roof-crawling professional eavesdropper, a man smaller even than Bellarmino, who was willing to try to make his way to within hearing distance of certain rooms in the Vatican. One contact led to another in this vast net of humanity on the sly, leading us deeper and deeper into the parasitical tangle of the clerical bureaucracy. Rome was an infinite maze at this level, a warren of alleys and dirt-floored piazzas where one passed arcade after arcade with their shops open to the world, where the smells filling the air changed abruptly from baking bread to tanning leather to rotten meat to the stink of the urinals. It was hard to sort the true from the false, or the useful from the

167

harmful, and this was was where a big network like the Venetians' showed its worth. Almost certainly they had a better sense of the whole situation than any other group in Rome, even the factions inside the Vatican; but it nevertheless remained a stubbornly murky thing. Forces were swirling.

Buonamici appeared at the gate one day, and when Cartophilus got free they went down to the little church where Sarpi was hiding, and sat in the cool of the shade among the chickens. Some of the street tykes were having a water fight, squirting it at each other through reeds they had found.

The spymaster flicked seed husks at the skinny birds as he told the men part of what he had learned. 'A few weeks ago young Cardinal Orsini made an appeal on Galileo's behalf directly to Pope Paul. He explained Galileo's view of the thing, and declared there was no contradiction between that view and Scripture, but the Pope told him Galileo should give up his views. When Orsini tried to continue, Paul cut him off by saying the matter was being looked into.'

'That was Bellarmino,' Buonamici said.

'Yes. Paul instructed him to convoke a special congregation of the Holy Office, who were to be explicitly tasked to identify Galileo's opinion as erroneous and heretical. This congregation gathered just a few days later – six Dominicans, a Jesuit, and an Irish priest. They reported to the Pope that the idea that the sun was the centre of the universe was "foolish and absurd". *Stultam et absurdam.* Also formally heretical. The idea that the Earth moved was "erroneous in faith" and "contradicted the sense of Holy Scripture".'

Cartophilus put his head between his knees, feeling sick to his stomach. Even Buonamici, coolest of men, was looking a bit pale. 'Formally heretical, that's new, yes?' he said.

'Yes,' Sarpi said dryly. 'And so it was that Galileo was called into Bellarmino, so that the Lord Cardinal could order him to abandon the Copernican view. If he refused to do it, he was to be sent to Segizzi, who would order him formally to abjure his positions. If he refused that order, he was to be incarcerated until he agreed to obey it.'

'So Segizzi jumped the sequence.'

'Yes.'

'All of this,' Cartophilus pointed out gloomily, 'was caused by Galileo coming to Rome to argue his case. If he had not come, all this would not have happened.'

Sarpi shrugged, staring at Cartophilus curiously. 'But that isn't what happened. So we have to deal with this, now.'

'Yes, Father.'

'It's also apparently the case that Segizzi has put a document in Galileo's file that states his warning was comprehensive. Now it's in the hands of the clerks, and back in the boxes and shelves of the innermost offices. Out of reach of anyone who might want to change it.'

There was silence for a while, and the low cackle and hum of the city wafted into the church and over them. The tykes were shrieking.

'We still have some angles of attack available,' Sarpi reassured them. 'Galileo needs to talk to Bellarmino again, because Bellarmino is angry, and could be a big help. It's ironic but true. And I'm going to see if I can get our man an audience with Paul again. Of course I will have to use an intermediary; I can't ask him directly!' His laughing face was both ugly and beautiful.

At first after the interview with Bellarmino Galileo had told everyone about it, getting angrier every time. His friends in the city came by and tried to calm him down, but he became even more enraged when they did, and shouted so loudly that anyone on the Pincian Hill could hear him. Cesi came by, then Antonio Orsini, then Castelli; but he only got angrier.

Guicciardini dictated letters home to Picchena and Cosimo that could be heard during their composition, or read by anyone who cared to slip into his offices at night and dig into the courier's bags. One at this time said,

Galileo has relied more on his own counsel than on that of his friends. Cardinal del Monte and myself, and also several cardinals from the Holy Office, tried to persuade him to be quiet and not to go on irritating the issue. If he wanted to hold this Copernican opinion, he was told, let him hold it quietly and not spend so much effort in trying to make others share it. Everyone feared that his coming here might be prejudicial and dangerous and that, instead of justifying himself and triumphing over his enemies, he could end up with an affront. Now this has happened, but he only gets more hotly excited about these views of his, and he has an extremely passionate temper, with little patience and prudence to keep it in control. It is this irritability that makes the skies of Rome very dangerous for him. He is passionately involved in this quarrel, as if it were his own business, and he does not see what it could lead to; so that he will get himself into danger, together with anyone who seconds him. For he is vehement and is all fixed and impassioned, so that it is impossible, if you have him around, to escape from his hand. And this is a business which is not a joke but may become of great consequence.

That same day, 6th March, Galileo was writing his own report to Picchena, which was something he did on a weekly basis. He apologized for not having written the previous week, explaining that it was because nothing had happened.

A week later news came that the Congregation of the Index had ordered Copernicus's books be taken out of circulation, until corrections were added to them that made it clear his hypothesis was a mathematical convenience only, and not a statement of physical fact. The Copernican books of Diego de Zuñiga and Foscarini were prohibited outright.

Galileo, however, was not mentioned in this decree, nor was the word *heresy* used. Nor had he been ordered to appear before the public tribunal of the Inquisition. So his warning from Bellarmino and Segizzi remained a private matter. Bellarmino and Segizzi had told no one about it, and Galileo belatedly began to keep the details of that meeting to himself.

Nevertheless, all Rome was buzzing with the news. The outline of the story was all too clear: Galileo had come to Rome to campaign for the Copernican view, and in spite of this – indeed, because of this – his view had been declared formally false and contrary to Scripture. Many were pleased at this, and rumours that he had been admonished even more severely in private were widespread.

Now Galileo wrote to Picchena, *I can show that my behaviour in this affair has been such that a saint would not have handled it either with greater reverence or with greater zeal toward the Holy Church. My enemies have not been so fine, having used every machination, calumny and diabolical suggestion anyone could possibly imagine.*

That was a bit of an exaggeration, but typical of Galileo's bitter rants against his enemies.

Then, to everyone's surprise, Galileo managed to obtain another audience with the Pope himself. This was a real coup, and, given Paul's part in instigating the actions against the Copernican view, difficult to account for. Young Cardinal Antonio Orsini was said to have interceded on his behalf, although even this did not seem like it should have worked. Nevertheless, Tuesday 11th March of 1616 found them strolling in the Papal garden of the Vatican, just as they had in the vineyards of the Villa Malvasia in 1611.

They walked ahead of their retinue, but spoke freely enough that trailing servants could hear most of their conversation. Galileo complained freely about the malice of his persecutors.

He swore that he was as good a Catholic as anyone, that everything he had ever done or said was designed to help the Church avoid an unfortunate error that would later embarrass her.

Paul nodded as he spoke, and answered that he was well aware of Galileo's uprightness and sincerity.

Galileo bowed deeply, then hurried to catch up to the immensely rotund pontiff. 'Thank you, Sanctissimus, thank you ever so much, eternal thanks, but I find I am still somewhat anxious about the future, because of the fear of being pursued with implacable hate by my enemies.'

Paul cheered him up brusquely: 'You can put all care away, because you are held in such esteem by me, and the whole Congregation. They will not lightly lend their ears to calumnious reports. You can feel safe as long as I am alive.'

'Thank you, Holiest One,' Galileo said, seizing the pontiff abruptly by the hand and kissing his ring with many enthusiastic whiskery kisses. Paul endured this for a while with a noble look into the distance, and then indicated it was time to leave, and headed back toward his chambers like a great ship in a light wind, Galileo trailing him and expressing his thanks in the floweriest terms. Never had anyone heard Galileo speak with such obsequious gratitude, except perhaps those who had seen him in the Medici's presence in the early years of the century.

Galileo returned to the Hill of Gardens in infinitely better spirits. He renewed his efforts to be allowed to see Bellarmino a second time, which turned out to be a long campaign; but several weeks later, again to everyone's surprise, an audience there too was granted. One morning near the end of May he returned to the diminutive Lord Cardinal's house in the Vatican, and told him of the rumours being reported back to him from all over Italy, and how badly they were harming his reputation and his health. He didn't mention Segizzi's unexpected appearance during his last interview, but he did assure Bellarmino that he had said nothing about that meeting afterward to anyone (an incredible lie), adding that he was sure Bellarmino had been perfectly discreet as well. The implication was clear: Segizzi and his companions must therefore be responsible for the rumours.

Bellarmino's eye twinkled a little as he listened to all this. There was no doubt at all that he took the implication. He nodded, looking around his study as if he had lost something in it; perhaps remembering Segizzi's little invasion. Finally with a small smile he called in a secretary, and had him write out a certificate for Galileo that he dictated on the spot.

We, Roberto Cardinal Bellarmino, having heard that it is calumniously reported that Signor Galileo Galilei has in our hand abjured and has also been punished with salutary penance, and being requested to state the truth as to this, declare that the said Galileo has not abjured, either in our hand, or the hand of any other person here in Rome, or anywhere else, so far as we know, any opinion or doctrine held by him. Neither has any salutary penance been imposed on him; but that only the declaration made by the Holy Father and published by the Sacred Congregation of the Index was notified to him, which says that the doctrine attributed to Copernicus, that the Earth moves around the sun and that the sun is stationary in the centre of the world and does not move from east to west, is contrary to the Holy Scriptures, and therefore cannot be defended or held. In witness whereof we have written and subscribed the present document with our own hand this twenty-sixth day of May 1616.

Still smiling his small ironic smile, Bellarmino signed the document, and when it was sanded and dried, gave it to Galileo, nodding at it as if to indicate that this was the warning he had meant to convey all along: no holding of the opinion, or defending it – but no ban on discussing it. This document would always exist to make that clear.

* * *

Guicciardini made his semi-annual review of the Villa Medici's accounts and went through the roof. He dictated at the top of his lungs a letter to Piccena: *Strange and scandalous were the goings on in the garden during Galileo's long sojourn in the company and under the administration of Annibale Primi, who has been fired by the cardinal. Annibale says that he had huge expenses. In any case, anyone can see that they led a riotous life. The accounts are attached. I hope this will be enough to get your philosopher ordered home, so that he will end his campaign to castrate the friars.*

It was enough. The same courier brought back Cosimo's order to Galileo, which was to return to Florence immediately.

During the week of the journey back to Florence, Galileo spoke to no one about what had happened. He looked exhausted and pensive. At nights he got out his telescope again, and made his usual viewings of Jupiter. By day he brooded in silence. It was obvious to all of us that his effort had rebounded on him, that by coming to Rome to strengthen his position he had forced the issue in a way that blocked his work entirely, and indeed brought him very close to Inquisitorial danger. And by no means was that over. From the road he wrote bitterly to Sagredo: *Of all the hatreds, none is greater than that of ignorance for knowledge.*

No doubt it occurred to him often that if he had just stayed in Florence and continued his work without drawing any attention to it, the storm from the clerics might have blown over. Cesi might have been able to campaign gradually on his behalf in Rome, at the level of the cardinals and the College of Rome. It might have worked. Instead Galileo had in his usual pig-headed way decided to reason with the Pope, to bombard him so suasively that the ultimate arbiter of the situation would be convinced to support him. He couldn't imagine things turning out any other way.

Either that, or else, as some of us said when he was asleep, he had seen a danger and run straight at it, attacking it in the hope of killing it when it was young. It was quite possible he had made an accurate estimate of the danger, had calculated the odds and made his best attempt. But failed.

Chapter Nine Aurora

Then it seemed to me, that time is nothing else but protraction;
but of what, I know not; and I marvel, if it be not of the mind
itself?

— ST AUGUSTINE, *Confessions, Book XI*

On his uneasy journey back to Florence, Galileo wrote letters to
all his correspondents, explaining to them why his visit had been
such a success, even more so than in 1611. All of them had
already heard the story from faster sources, and so did not
believe his account, but many wrote back to him reassuringly; a
success, no doubt about it.

Every night he complained about the inn food, the fleabitten
beds, the creaky floors and the endless snoring of the other way-
farers (he himself was a prodigious snorer); so that rather than
retire he went out to sleep on the cushioned seat of his litter, or
on his telescope stool under a blanket.

One night, at the inn on the road below Montepulciano, he
could not sleep at all, and sat wrapped in his blanket by his telescope. He crouched to look through it at Jupiter, his own little
emblem and clock, and in so many ways the home of his troubles. At this moment it was near the zenith. He marked down the
positions of its moons in the chart in his workbook.

After staring at the little orrery of white points for a long time, he got up and went into the stables, where he knew Cartophilus preferred to sleep. He thumped him un-gently on the back.

'What?' the ancient one croaked.

'Bring me your master,' Galileo demanded fiercely.

'What, now?'

'Now.'

'Why now?'

Galileo seized the man by his scrawny throat. 'I want to talk to him. I have questions for him. Now.'

'Gah,' Cartophilus croaked. Galileo let go of him and he rubbed his neck, frowning resentfully. 'Whatever you say, maestro, your wish is my demand, as always, but I cannot produce him immediately.' He reached for a jug of water he kept by his bed at night, took a pull and offered it to Galileo, who waved it off. 'I will as soon as I can. It may take a day or two. It would be easiest back in Florence.'

'Quickly,' Galileo ordered. 'I'm sick of this. I have some questions.'

The old one gave him a brief glance and looked into his jug. 'This trip to Rome was perhaps in reference to him?'

'In a manner of speaking.' Galileo put his big right fist under the man's nose. 'You know more about it than I, I'm sure.'

Cartophilus shook his head unconvincingly.

Galileo *hmphed*. 'Of course not. Are you really the Wandering Jew?'

The old one waggled his head equivocally. 'The story isn't really right. Although I do feel cursed. And I'm old. And I have wandered.'

'And are you a Jew?'

'No.'

'Did you mock Christ as he carried the cross to Golgotha?'

'Definitely not. Huh! That's a story the gypsies used to tell. A band of them would come into a town, a couple of centuries ago, and explain that they had been made immortal penitents, because they had accidentally insulted Jesus. Practically every

177

town we told the story to opened their gates and treated us like royalty. After that it was a case of transference.'

'So the Wandering Jew came from Jupiter.'

The old man's eyebrows arced high on his forehead. He took another pull before replying. 'You remember something from your last syncope, I take it.'

Galileo growled. 'You know better than I.'

'I don't. But I could see that you wanted to get to Rome to defend yourself.'

'Yes.'

'But it didn't work as you had hoped.'

'No.'

Cartophilus hesitated a long time. Just as Galileo thought he had fallen back asleep, he ventured, 'Often it seems to me, that when one tries to do something based on . . . knowledge – or even let us say foreknowledge, or a premonition, what the Germans call *Schwanung* – that whatever you do, it . . . rebounds. Instead of forestalling it, or fulfilling it, your action has the effect of bringing about exactly the opposite of whatever you might have been trying for. A complementary action, so to speak.'

'You would know better than I, I'm sure.'

'I don't.'

Galileo lifted his fist again. 'Just get your master to me.'

'As soon as I can. In Florence. I promise you.'

Back in Florence, Galileo moved into a newly rented house in Bellosguardo, the Villa del Segui, a fine establishment overlooking Florence from a hill to the south of the river. He had a real home again, for the first time since Hostel Galilei in Padua. Here he was, back in his gardens, back in La Piera's care, back in the arms of his girls (or Virginia's anyway).

He was barely settled in when, in the garden one night to complete his ablutions, a movement against the stable wall caused him to flinch.

A black figure emerged from the murk, and he was about to cry out when he saw that it was the stranger. At the sight of that narrow face, the unganymedean face of Ganymede, he experienced a big if vague abreaction; all of the blurred uncertain memories of what had happened to him on the Jovian moons came back to him in force. The memories of his earlier night voyages were like dream memories, with certain moments sticking out more distinctly even than events of the present moment – in particular, in this case, the fire – but the rest fuzzy beyond what was usual for his memory, perhaps because of the dreamy content. They had done things to his mind, he knew that; the woman Hera had helped him to counteract one preparation with another, he recalled. So odd effects were not surprising. In any case now the earlier voyages had bloomed in him, and all from the sight of the stranger's hatchet face. Galileo's heart beat in his chest at the vivid memory of the fire, which had never really left him, in particular not the fear of it. 'I want to go back,' he demanded. 'I have questions to ask.'

'I know,' Ganymede said. 'There are questions for you there as well. I have taken steps to secure the device at the other end.'

Galileo snorted. 'You hope you have. But I want to see Hera in any case.'

Ganymede frowned. 'I don't think that's wise.'

'Wisdom has nothing to do with it.'

This time Ganymede merely twisted a knob on a pewter box he was carrying crooked in his elbow, and there they stood, inside one of the green-blue ice caves of Europa.

'Hey,' Galileo said, shocked. 'What happened to your teletrasporta?'

Ganymede tilted his head. 'All that was done to give you a way to comprehend what was happening. It was felt that if you were bilocated without some way to explain the prolepsis to yourself from within your own frame of reference, you might be excessively disoriented. Some feared you would experience a

179

mental breakdown, or otherwise fail to accept the reality of the prolepsis. Perhaps assume you were dreaming a dream. So we constructed a simulacrum of a translation that would make sense in local terms – in your case, a flight through space. We made the entangler look like something that could cast your vision to us. Then the experience of flight was given to you after you had already been bilocated.'

'You can do that?'

The stranger gave Galileo a pitying look. 'Simulated experiences can sometimes be distinguished from real ones, but in data-poor environments, like space, it's hard to do.'

Galileo gestured at the great ice cavern extending away from them in every direction, its aquamarine roof starred by cracks. 'If this cave were not real, how would I tell?'

Ganymede shrugged. 'Maybe you couldn't.'

'I thought not,' Galileo muttered. 'These are all dreamscapes.' He thought again of his immolation at the stake. More loudly: 'What keeps us warm?'

'Heat.'

'Bah. Where comes the heat, where comes the air?'

'There are engines creating them.'

'Engines?'

'Machines. Devices.'

'So illuminating!'

'Sorry. The details would mean nothing to you. Very few people here understand them. The heat and air are simple, in any case. It's protection from Jupiter's radiation that is difficult. That's why we stay below the surface most of the time when on Europa. One of the reasons they've gone mad, if you ask me. On Ganymede we were out under the sky. On Io we take advantage of the new bubble fields. But here they have their older structures for dealing with the problem.'

'Radiation? Isn't that another name for heat?'

'Well, but there are vibrations along a spectrum of sizes. What our eyes see are wavelengths of a certain size, but that band of the visible is just part of a range that extends far to either side. Shortest are gamma waves, then longer wavelengths range from braccia to the width of the universe, more or less.'

Galileo stared at him. 'And these other waves manifest as?'

'Heat, sometimes. Damage to flesh that can't be felt. I don't know exactly how to explain it to you.'

Galileo rolled his eyes. 'Take me to someone who can,' he demanded.

'We don't actually have time for that, sorry –'

'Take me to someone who knows! Because you are an idiot.'

Ganymede rolled his eyes. 'I forbear –'

'Take me!' Galileo shouted, and shoved the man hard in the chest. At home he would have beat him, so why not here? He wasn't convinced any of it was real. He kicked Ganymede in the shins, yelling fit to turn all the blues of the place red. 'Come on! Someone who knows something! Surely there must be *someone* who knows *something*!' He raised his big fist.

'Stop it,' Ganymede complained. He was wispy despite his height, and looked confused to be assaulted. 'Quit trying to bully me. We aren't in one of your downriver alleys here. People notice what you do, and conclude you aren't really civilized.'

'Me! It's you who are uncivilized. You don't know even the basics of how your machines work.'

'Spare me. No one knows all these things. Could you tell me how every machine of your time worked?'

'Yes, of course. Why not?'

Ganymede pursed his lips. 'Well, it is no longer possible.'

'I don't accept that. The principles at least must be clear, if you make the attempt to understand.'

'You'll see.' And he muttered to the side, as if to an invisible angel.

'Take me to someone who can answer my questions.'

'I'll take you.'

*   *   *

181

The gallery they were in was a kind of giant open ante-chamber to another under-ice city. Broad spaces extended so many miles away from them that in the distance the blue ceiling curved down and met the floor, cutting off any further sight. Picking out one particular bright silver building ahead of them, just where the ceiling appeared to meet the floor, Galileo found it took only about fifteen or twenty minutes to walk to it. A close horizon. The alleys and strada of this cold town were sometimes crowded with tall graceful people, moving as if in water; other times the streets were nearly empty. The people wore clothing like Ganymede's, simple but fine, pastel warm tones making them appear illuminated in the green light.

They continued beyond the silver building for about an hour, he reckoned, passing crowded plazas extending to left and right, some of them open to the black sky, most roofed by ice. As the hour passed he learned better how to walk in the light down-ward pull. This strange lightness was suggestive of all kinds of things, including the idea that weight was perhaps proportional to the size of the planet one stood on. Another sign that Europa must be fairly small.

'Who is it you are taking me to?' he said.

'To a person who may be able to answer your questions. Or maybe you would call it a machine.'

'A machine? So none of you know?'

'No no, this person is a kind of . . . composite. A person quite like you, in fact – a physicist and mathematician, quite famous.'

'Good,' Galileo said. 'I want some explanations.'

They came to a lake, and stepped down into a long low boat, like a gondola. When they were settled in its bow, a boatman cast off and they hummed slowly over clear blue water, leaving a wake that ran in a clean curl that was slower than it would have been on the lagoon. Greenish blues pulsed overhead and in waves around them, and Galileo could not tell how deep the lake might be, as the many subtle shades of creamy blue bobbed darker and lighter, but always opaque. Royal blue, sky blue, azure, turquoise, aquamarine, all these bounced against each other in long bands, and it also seemed that waves of cobalt were passing through the other blues, staining them as it pulsed by, as if they boated through the veins of a beating blue heart. The buildings behind the broad fondamenta to their left looked like clean blocks of ice, painted in pastels that held their colour manfully even in the omnipresent green-blue glow, contradicting what Galileo thought he knew of colour theory. The sight of one curving row of waterfront buildings reminded Galileo strongly of the Grand Canal, and he saw the city was a kind of Venice carved in ice. 'Why doesn't it melt?'

'It's all cladded. Sheathed in diamond, in fact.'

People promenaded on the fondamenta just as they would have at home. Some of them looked out on the water, but not at Ganymede and Galileo; theirs was only one watercraft among many. All the wakes on the water created a fine curvilinear slow-motion cross-chop. The ice ceiling overhead was thicker in some places than in others, judging by the differences in the green-blue. Pulses most definitely were running through it.

'What are those waves of colour running through the roof?' he asked.

'The other moons exert tidal forces against the tug of Jupiter proper. We shine a type of light through the ice to reveal the stresses in it, so we can see these tides' interactions.'

'How do you keep these canals and lakes liquid?'

'We heat them,' Ganymede said patiently. 'In places you will see steam. In other places we will break through a skim of ice as we progress along certain canals.'

'But you don't know how the water is heated, do you.'

'That is not one of the more difficult accomplishments of our technology, believe me.'

Their boat hummed up to a fondamenta made of something like black stone. As they climbed out of the boat Galileo asked,

'Where do you get rock?'

'From meteorites, called here dropstones. One or two big ones will supply enough material for an entire city, as it just supplements the local ice.'

'How many people live in this Venice of yours?'

'This is Rhadamanthys Linea. About a million people.'

'That many! And how many cities like this are there on Europa?'

'Maybe a hundred.'

'A hundred millions!'

'It's a big moon, as you know.'

Overhead the broad crossing arcs of cobalt and violet pulsed from before them to behind them. Galileo said, 'The patterns of light are so complicated, it seems there must be more than four influences.'

'All the Jovian moons pull a bit on the rest.'

'But are there more than four moons?'

'There are about ninety.'

'Ninety!'

'Most are very small. Some are out of the plane of the rest. In any case they all have a pull, no matter how slight, and with the ice overhead charged as the locals have charged it, every change in tug registers piezoelectrically.'

'Why do they charge it that way?'

Ganymede shrugged. 'They like the way it looks.'

They were now walking down a broad crowded street flanked by long low buildings. Low carts moved at a running pace, without anything pulling them. Before them a cluster of very tall angular buildings reached right up to the ice ceiling.

'It must be the Tower of Babel,' Galileo said.

'Well, there is a great deal of confusion inside it, to be sure. And people who want it to fall.'

Soon they reached these tall buildings, and outside one they entered a glass antechamber, which then rose on the outside wall so fast that Galileo's ears popped, surprising him. He always had a small earache in his right ear, and now it throbbed unhappily. So it seemed that in some sense his body was here too. 'If I am here, how am I also back in Italy, lost in one of my syncopes?'

'You are here in a complementary potentiality.'

The glass antechamber stopped and a door opened on its inner side. They stepped out on a smooth broad roof terrace the colour of malachite, just under the ice ceiling. Ganymede led Galileo to a small group of people congregated against a railing that overlooked the city. From here Galileo could see far down the canal; it developed a mirror surface in just the place a waterblink would have appeared on Earth, about halfway to the horizon. From there on it looked like a silver road through undulant blue buildings. Venice had looked just so on certain moony nights, and again Galileo wondered if he were dreaming.

Ganymede said, 'This is Galileo Galilei, the first scientist, here in a proleptic entanglement.'

'Ah yes,' said a tall old woman at the centre of the group. 'We heard you were coming. Welcome to Rhadamanthys.'

Though old she was still straight, and stood a head taller than Galileo. Pendulant silver earrings emerged directly from her ear holes and then curved and seemed to dive into her neck. He bowed to her briefly, looked to his guide, muttered, 'And where is the mathematician?'

Ganymede indicated the old woman. 'This is she. Aurora.'

Galileo tried to conceal his surprise. 'I thought you said it was a machine,' he said to cover himself.

'That's partly true,' the willowy crone said. 'I am interfaced to various artifactual entities.'

Galileo kept a straight face, although the idea struck him as monstrous, like jamming one of his military compasses through an ear into one's brain. And in fact there were those earrings.

'Come with me,' Aurora said, taking him by the arm and moving him down the altana railing a short distance. Low creaks and hums that seemed to come from the ceiling kept them from being able to hear the other conversations on the terrace.

185

'It's a pleasure to meet you,' the ancient woman said politely. She had a voice like Ganymede's, hoarse and croaky, and her Latin had the same odd accent. 'You are often called the first scientist.'

'That would be an honour, but I was not the first.'

'I agree with you. But you were the first mathematical experimentalist.'

'Was I?'

'So it seems from what we read in history, and see in the entanglements. One must always make assumptions, of course. And the past is always changing. But as far as we can tell, you tried only to assert what you could demonstrate and describe mathematically. This is science. Wasn't it you that said that? That the world is written in mathematics?'

'I like that,' Galileo admitted. 'If it's true.'

'It's partly true.' Although she looked troubled. 'Reality is mathematical, as long as you understand that uncertainty and contingency can be mathematically described, without them becoming any more certain.'

'Teach me,' Galileo said. 'Teach me how you breathe here, and what these tides of colour are, and – teach me everything. I want to know everything! Teach me everything you have learned since my time.'

She smiled, pleased by his effrontery. 'That would take a while.'

'I don't care!'

She glanced at him curiously. 'It would take years, even for one of your intelligence.'

'Can't you do it quickly? Give me the short version?'

'The short version doesn't give you real understanding. It's only a matter of metaphors, images that don't really convey the situation. The mathematics is what you want, and that took a great number of people many centuries to develop. Now no one learns more than a small percentage of what there is, and even that takes many years.'

'Maybe not for me!'

'Even for you.'

Galileo shook his head. 'I don't want to take years. I don't have years.'

Aurora seemed to consult the patterns of intersecting waves in their low ice sky. She said, 'There is a drug complex we can give you that would enable you to learn faster. A synaptic velocinestic, it is called, made of a particular mixture of brain chemicals. With the help of it one can accomplish a certain forcing. Networks bloom in the brain extremely rapidly. It's useful in certain situations.'

'An alchemical preparation?'

'Yes, if you like.'

'Is it safe?' Thinking of the half-crazed alchemists he had met, pursuing something like witchcraft in their foul workshops, poisoned by their own hand.

'Yes, we think so. It is mildly carcinogenic, but it won't kill you. Although some people have felt distressed afterward, I've heard. But I have taken it, and felt no such thing.'

This, from a machine mind: Galileo could not stop a snort from emerging, though he curbed his tongue. After considering it briefly, he said, 'Give me this preparation of yours. And then who will teach me the mathematics? You?'

She gave him an amused look. 'One of our machines.'

'Another machine?'

'It's a standard curriculum, designed for use with the velocinestic. It will be faster than I could be, and clearer too. I will oversee the process.'

'Do it then. I want to know!'

Her people gave him a tight-fitting helmet, made of a mesh of metals in a dense weave. They insisted he sit down, and got him settled into what looked like a small throne tilted onto its back.

Recumbent in it, he stared at the ice ceiling. It was pulsing rapidly in dense interference patterns, waves from three directions tossing off brief glints of sapphire iridescence. These triple peaks formed their own moving pattern, like sunlight on wind-blown water. Even if there had been just the four big moons, the Galilean moons (such a good name), their tugging would of course create a very complex pattern. He had been so sure that the tides on Earth were the result of the ocean sloshing around in its basins of stone, shifting as the Earth both rotated and flew around the sun, creating differential speeds. But here they said it was not true. In that case, what *caused* tides? The tug of celestial bodies – but that was astrology all over again. And yet they seemed to be saying it was so. Was astrology right, then, with its celestial influences and its action at a distance, action without any mechanical forces applied? He hated such non-explaining explanations!

And yet here they were. He looked at Aurora's assistants, hovering over the bank of machines against the wall. He hoped the treatment would work for him, that it would not kill or derange him.

They slipped their preparation into his blood using a hollow needle that they inserted painlessly into his skin, an ugly little experience. He held his breath as they did this, and when he finally exhaled and inhaled, the world ballooned. He saw immediately that he was thinking several trains of thought at once, and they all meshed in a contrapuntal fugue that his father would have very much enjoyed hearing, if it were music, which in a sense it seemed to be: a polyphonic singing of his ideas, each strand taking its part in the larger music. To a certain extent his thinking had always felt that way, with any number of accompaniments running under the aria of the voice of thought; now these descants were choral, and loud, while at the same time architectonically fitted to the melody. He could think six or ten thoughts at once, and at the same time think about his thinking, and contemplate the whole score.

There remained a main melody, or a path through a maze, a maze which was like the delta of the Po. He seemed to look down on it as he sang it. A great number of channels were weaving down a slightly tilted plain. Each channel was a mathematical speciality, some of them shallow and disappearing into the sand, but most making their loop and reconnecting to other flows. A few were the kind of deep channels that ships would use. Upstream they coalesced until there were fewer, scattered streams. Fewer tributaries rather than more, leading up in different directions to sources, often at springs. Water out of the rock.

This was, he saw, an image of mathematics in time. Or maybe it was all time, or humanity in time; but it was the mathematics that sprang out at him.

The fewer channels upstream, in the distant past, before his time, were where Aurora's tutorial now led him. Then he was flying over the time stream, or in it, sometimes returning upstream to view a contemporaneous discipline. Mainly he had a general sense of flying downstream, over or occasionally inside some eternal landscape, the nature of which could not be discerned. He inhabited an image he had heard some time before, of history as a river, in which people were water, eroding the banks and depositing soil elsewhere downstream, so that the banks slowly changed and the river ran otherwise than it had, without the water ever noticing the changed courses of the braiding stream.

He tried to turn all the mathematics into geometry, so that he could see it and thereby grasp it. It often worked. It was definitely true what Aurora had said about the preparation: he grasped things he saw the moment he saw them, aspects even leaped out to him in advance as implications, shooting out before him like arrows. He was both in and out at once, back and forth, up and down, ranging widely, flying in stoops and gyres, and always looking forward with an eagle's eye. The voice of the machine tutor was Aurora's own hoarse voice, and Aurora

189

herself flew beside him or in him, and sometimes she spoke too in her odd Latin, so that it seemed there were two of her talking. Sometimes Galileo asked questions and all three of them spoke at once and yet he could follow all three lines of thought, which merged in his mind into music, into a trio for lute and two squawky *fagatto*.

He was shown glimpses of people and places, but always the main thrust of the tutorial was mathematical. He recognized Euclid and Pythagoras, and for a short but incredibly packed moment he was actually with his hero Archimedes, still crucial to the story, hurrah! The Greek's entire life bloomed in him at once, an island or bubble in the flow of the stream, and for a moment he knew it completely – and thought he saw Ganymede too standing there, and the burning mirror – also the Roman soldier at the terrible end –

Startled, for this was not like the rest of the lesson, he jerked up in his flight, feeling like a crow frightened out of a tree. Then he recognized Regiomontanus, and all that that brilliant man had rescued from the Greeks by way of the Arab texts, and was distracted that way; then on to Harriot with his algebraic symbols, which Galileo had known would be useful the very first time Castelli showed them to him. Then Copernicus and his system, and Kepler and his polyhedraic formula for planetary distance, which Galileo had not thought was correct, and indeed it was not. His own sense that all things moved naturally in circles was also shattered, however, as he was introduced to inertia – but that idea had always been on the tip of his tongue, indeed he had said it in slightly different words, as he cried out when he saw it. And then to the law of gravity, Newton's equation for it causing him to soar up, startled; such a simple deep thing! He had seen the evidence for the laws of both inertia and gravity, he had used them in his parabolic description of falling bodies, but he had not understood what he had used, and now he floated above them, abashed, glowing before their utter simplicity – the force of gravity simply an inverse power law, easy as kiss your hand, and resulting in obvious solutions to things like Kepler's orbits, which Kepler had only groped his way to after years of observation and analysis. So planetary orbits were naturally ellipses, with the sun occupying the major focus, the other gravitational pulls together locating the minor focus. Of course! Too bad he had never read far enough in Kepler's crazy tomes to get to these observations, it might have alerted him to the absence of circularity in the heavens; though he might have concluded they were just circles distorted by something he didn't see. Certainly any idea one had in mind altered what one could see. And yet still, despite his ideas against it, here was attraction and influence at a distance again, without a mechanical force or cause! It was a mystery. It could not be the whole story, could it?

He was not aware he had asked this aloud, but heard Aurora reply: 'This is the question that keeps coming up, as you will see. You are by no means the first or the last to dislike what one of us called spooky action at a distance.'

'Well, of course. Who could like that?'

'And yet as you will also come to see, such action is simply everywhere. You will find that there are serious problems with any simple concept of distance. Eventually distance becomes as problematic as time.'

'I don't understand.'

But already she and her machine voice had flown off to analytic geometry, and then to a form of analysing motion called the calculus, which was just what he had always needed and never had. And it seemed to have appeared just after his time, worked out by people young when he was old: an irritating Frenchman called Descartes, a German named Leibniz, and the English maniac Newton again, who to Galileo's chagrin had distilled Galileo's dynamics in just the way Galileo had struggled to do all his life. So simple when you saw it!

'If I have seen less far than others,' Galileo complained in irritation to Aurora, 'it is because I was standing on the shoulders of dwarves.'

191

She laughed out loud. 'Don't say that to anyone else.'

They flew over and through number theory, theory of equations, probability theory – which was ever so useful, and instantaneously true to experience as well – it was the way of the world, no doubt about it, the way of the world mathematicized, oh how he could have used that! And how broadly it could be applied!

Quickly with these tools they flew into differential equations, and then to advances in number theory, and what he learned to call differential geometry. Indeed at times it seemed to him that geometry continued to underlay everything, no matter how elaborated and abstracted it became. Geometry converted to numbers, the numbers then mapped by further, more complex geometries; thus trigonometry, topology; and all along he could still draw lines and figures to map what he was learning, though sometimes they looked like snarls of wool.

When Aurora led him further on, and they flew into the non-Euclidean geometries, he laughed out loud. It was like pretending that the laws for perspectival drawing were a real world, so that parallel lines met at a hypothesized horizon, which was infinitely far away and yet susceptible to ordinary calculations. A very funny idea, and he laughed again at the pleasure of it.

When Aurora then told him that these impossible geometries often made a better match for the real world of invisible forces and fundamental particles than did Euclidean geometry and Newtonian (which was really to say Galilean) physics, he was amazed. 'What?' he cried, laughing again, but this time in astonishment; 'no parallel lines anywhere?'

'No. Only locally.'

It struck him as funny. That Euclidean geometry was a formal artifice only – it was profound, it overthrew everything. There was no underlying Euclidean grid to reality. And it was true that he himself had once said that no one could build a true plane of any great size, because of the curvature of the Earth. So he had had an intuition of this non-Euclidean world, he had *almost* seen it all on his own – as with everything else he had learned so far! Oh yes: he had been right; the universe was a wild place, but mathematical; and God was not just *a* mathematician, but a superhumanly complex mathematician, almost one might say perversely inventive, such that He was often contrary to human sense and reason. Although still rigorously logical! And so: integration theory, complex variables, topology, set theory, complex analysis, theory of infinite sets (in which there was a paradox called Galileo's Paradox which he didn't recall ever having proposed, so that he was distracted momentarily as he focused on it and tried quickly to learn what he would otherwise have to discover). Then came the mathematization of logic itself, finally and at last – though when he flew through it, he was surprised how limited its usefulness seemed to be. Indeed it mostly seemed to prove the impossibility of logical closure in any mathematics or logics, thus destroying both its parents at one blow, so to speak – a double parricide!

That was confusing enough, but then they flew on. And just as non-Euclidean geometry had made him laugh, quantum mechanics made him cry. He tumbled and fell rather than flew. The live hum of intelligence, even wisdom, that the velocinestic had filled him with, had also had in it a huge emotional component, he suddenly understood; these two aspects of understanding were all entangled with each other. Learning so much so fast, he had been filled with joy; now that ended so abruptly it was like smashing into a glass wall that he had not seen. It *hurt*. He cried out in startled pain, tumbled downward, shocked and dismayed.

He became light. He was a single minim of light and he flew through two parallel slits in a wall, and the interference pattern of his collision with the wall beyond showed beyond doubt he was a wave. Then he bounced both off and through a half-mirrored glass and it was obvious he was an incredibly tiny particle, one of a stream of minims moving one by one. Depending on what flight he was made to fly, he was either particle or wave, so that it seemed he had to be both at once, despite the contradictions involved in that, the impossibilities. Maybe thoughts were minims and emotions were waves, for he was stuffed to exploding with both at once, the emotions in their waves also a myriad of pricking jolts, little affectinos that flew in clouds of probabilities and struck like icy snow. It was true but impossible.

Before he could even try to puzzle this out, he found himself looking at one of these minims, like a chip of sunlight on water; but to see it that meant that a minim of light had hit that chip and bounced to his eye; and this minimal hit had knocked the observed minim off course, so he could not make a measurement of its speed by taking two looks at it, because each look cast it on a new course that wrecked the calculation. There was no way to determine both position and velocity of these minims, and it wasn't just a measurement problem either, a matter of knocking off course; the two aspects existed at cross purposes and cancelled each other out at the smallest level. The probability of a course was all there was, a wave function, and measurement itself set one possible version in place. These blurs were the minims; and everything in the world was made of them! Some kind of smears of probability, with mathematical functions describing them that often involved the square root of negative one, and other flagrant irrealities. The wind on a lake, the sun beating down on it, a flutter of light on the water, points piercing the eye.

Galileo flew into another tilted mirror, and both shot through it and bounced off it at the same time, either reintegrating or not on the far side, breaking up as he became whole – 'Wait!' he shouted in panic to Aurora. 'Help! Help me! This can't be right, it makes no sense! *Help!*'

Aurora's voice croaked in his ear, full of amusement. 'No one understands it in the way you mean. Please, relax. Fly on. Be not afraid. Bohr once said, if you are not shocked by quantum mechanics, you have not seen it properly. We have come to an aspect of the manifold of manifolds that cannot be understood by recourse to any images from the sensorium, nor by your beloved geometries. It is contradictory, counter to the senses. It has to remain at the level of the mathematical abstractions that we are moving among. But remember, it has been shown that you can use these quantum equations and get physical experimental results of extraordinary accuracy, in some cases as close as one in a trillion. In that sense the equations are very demonstrably true.'

'But what does that mean? I can't understand what I can't see!'

'Not so. You have been doing that quite frequently now. Rest easy. Later the whole of quantum mechanics will be placed in the context of the ten-dimensional manifold of manifolds, and there reconciled to gravity and to general relativity. Then, if you go that far, you will feel better about how it is that these equations can work, or be descriptive of a real world.'

'But the results are impossible!'

'Not at all. There are other dimensions folded into the ones our senses perceive, as I told you.'

'How can you be sure, if we can never perceive them?'

'It's a matter of tests pursued, just as you do it in your work. We have found ways to interrogate the qualities of these dimensions as they influence our sensorium. We see then that there must be other kinds of dimensions. For instance, when very small particles decay into two photons, these photons have a quantum property we call spin. The clockwise spin of one is matched by a counterclockwise spin of the same magnitude in the other one, so that when the spin values are added, they equal zero. Spin is a conserved quantity in this universe, like energy and momentum. Experiments show that before a spin is measured, there is an equal potential for it to be clockwise or counterclockwise, but as soon as the spin is measured it becomes one or the other. At that moment of measurement the complementary photon, no matter how far away, *must* have the opposite spin. The act of measurement of one thus determines the spin of both, even if the other photon is many light-years away. It changes faster than news of the measurement could have reached it moving at the speed of light, which is as fast as information moves in the dimensions we see. So how does the far photon know what to become? It only happens; and faster than light. This phenomenon was demonstrated in experiments on Earth, long ago. And yet nothing moves faster than the speed of light. Einstein was the one who called this seemingly faster-than-light effect "spooky action at a distance", but it is not that; rather, the distance we perceive is irrelevant to this quality we call spin, which is a feature of the universe that is nonlocal. Nonlocality means things happening together across distance as if the distance were not there, and we have found nonlocality to be fundamental and ubiquitous. In some dimensions, nonlocal entanglement is simply everywhere and everything, the main feature of that fabric of reality. The way space has distance and time has duration, other manifolds have entanglement.'

'My head hurts,' Galileo said. He flew after her toward a beam of violet light. 'Spin is something I understand,' he said. 'Go back to that.'

'This spin is not like your spin. There can be two axes of spin going at once in the same particle. In the particle called the baryon there is a spin such that it has to rotate 720 degrees before it returns to its original position.'

'My head really hurts,' Galileo confessed. 'Could it be the preparation?'

'No. It's the same for everyone who comes to this point. Reality is not a matter of our senses. It can't be visualized.'

'And so time?' Galileo said, thinking of his travels.

'Time in particular is impossible to properly perceive or conceptualize, and very much more complex than what we sense or measure as time. We keep mistaking our sense of time for time itself, but it isn't so. It isn't laminar. It bubbles and eddies, percolates and disappears, is whole but fractionated, exhibits both the wave-particle duality and nonlocal entanglement, and is always changing. The mathematical descriptions we have of it now test out in experiments, even to the point of us being able to manipulate entanglement interference, as you know very well because of your presence here. So we know the equations must be right even when we can't believe them, just as with quantum mechanics.'

'I don't know,' Galileo objected, growing more and more afraid. 'I don't think I can come to terms with this. I can't see it!'

'Perhaps not now. It's been enough for one lesson, or too much. And some people have arrived here who want to talk to you.'

He came out of the visionary flight as if out of a dream that did not slip away on waking. He found himself back on the roof terrace of the tower, dazed and raw in his feelings. Clarity and confusion, a beautiful impossibility . . . He helped Aurora's assistants remove the helmet from his head, then looked down at a glowing mirror in his hand, which was covered with his notes, his crabbed handwriting made big and crude by using his fingertip as the pen. A large diagram of the two-slit experiment filled the top of the pad, like a sigil reminding him that the world made no sense. He inspected the back of the mirror, which appeared to be made of something like horn or ebony.

He said, as if reaching for something to hold onto in a fall, 'So it is true, then, that God speaks in mathematics.'

Aurora replied, 'There is a relationship between observed phenomenon and mathematical formulations, sometimes simple, sometimes complex. Philosophers are still arguing about what that means, but most scientists accept that the manifold of manifolds is some kind of mathematical efflorescence.'

'I knew it! God is a mathematician.' Though mentally exhausted, and confused, there was a glow in Galileo that he recognized, a kind of humming in him, as if he were a bell that had been rung some time before. For a long time there, he had been ringing! Then maybe the bell had cracked. 'That was quite a lesson.'

'Yes. About four centuries traversed. That's a lot. But you have to remember that we only covered a small portion of the whole story, and much of what you learned today would in later lessons be overthrown, or superseded, or integrated into a larger understanding.'

'But that's bad!' Galileo exclaimed. 'Why then did you stop?'

'Because to go on would be too much. I trust we will continue later.'

'I hope so!'

'I don't see why not.'

'Can I call on you?'

'Yes.'

'And will you come when I call?'

She smiled. 'Yes.'

Galileo thought over what he had learned. It was impossible to grasp. In a different way than the experiences of his previous trips to Jupiter, it lay just a bit beyond his reach; he remembered it clearly, but he couldn't comprehend or apply it.

Aurora was looking down at the canal running up to their tower. Galileo, following her gaze, said, 'What about the thing that lives in the ocean below you?' he inquired. 'Have you tried giving these lessons to it? Have you learned its language, or even hailed it and gotten an answer?'

'We have communicated with it, yes. And the communication has been entirely mathematical, as you have guessed.'

'What other way would there be?'

'Exactly. So, we have found it is in agreement with us on the existence and value of *pi*. That was a first success, established with simple diagrams and a binary number code. Also, it appears able to pick out the first fifty prime numbers, and the usual sequences like the Fibonacci sequence — you may say that when it involves real numbers, or the simplest Euclidean geometry, we appear to be in substantial agreement with it.'

'But?'

'Well . . .' She hesitated. 'When we have been unable to formulate clear questions, the sentience does not seem to recognize what we are saying. Quantum mechanics, for instance, appears not to register with it.'

Galileo laughed. 'So it's like me!'

She regarded him without joining his laughter. He reconsidered.

He said, 'Is this why you agreed to teach me? Because you think I am as sequestered as this thing in its ocean, so that you can use me to get ideas to communicate with it better?'

'Well,' the old woman said, 'it's true that a different perspective on the problem might bring new insights. You are well remembered here on the Galilean moons, as you might well imagine. I believe Ganymede entangled you into this time for other reasons, but some here think you might bring a certain freshness to our local problem too. Others feel your context is just a handicap, and that you can be of no help. In any case, while it's possible the Europan sentience exists in a mathematical moment roughly corresponding to your own, I think it is more likely that it senses principally in different manifolds than we do. That may form the basis of the problem. Mathematicians with a philosophical bent are having a heated discussion of the ontological and epistemological questions brought up by the situation, as you can imagine.'

'It may think it is dealing with a simpler mentality than itself,' Galileo suggested ironically. 'Like you think you are doing with me.'

'It is capable of generating very complicated geometrical patterns,' she said, 'conveyed to us by sound arranged in a binary code. But there are gaps that suggest it lives in some of the other manifolds.'

Galileo didn't know what this meant. 'The creature must be blind, no? It was really dark in there.'

'It may sense parts of the spectrum not visible to us, that would serve as equivalents to our sight. We continue to work out codes of communication in which it sings to us information that we can display as visual patterns for our own comprehension. So in that sense you could say that it sees, I think. Indeed, when we sent to it a schematic of the gravitational patterns created by all the bodies in the Jovian system, it sent us corrections that demonstrate it knows very subtle aspects of gravitation, aspects like gravitons and gravitinos, which are apparent only when seen in the context of the full manifold of manifolds theory. For us, working with that model is only a recent development. So this is rather thought provoking.'

Then there was an eruption of shouting at the vertical antechamber. It proved to be Hera and a retinue of followers, bulling their way through Ganymede's crowd. Hera was in the lead, angry and unstoppable.

'Oh dear,' Aurora said. 'She appears unhappy.'

Galileo snorted. 'Is she ever otherwise?'

Aurora laughed. Hera approached and loomed over them, her white arms thick, bare, muscular, and tensed, as if she were only just restraining herself from thrashing them both, and Aurora's assistants as well.

'I hope you have not been disturbed by this wandering ghost?' she inquired of Aurora.

'Not at all,' Aurora replied, looking amused. 'It was our pleasure to converse with such a famous person.'

'Do you know that such conversations can be dangerous? That you may alter the manifold analeptically enough to change us all, perhaps right out of existence?'

'I don't think anything that happens to Galileo here could have that kind of impact,' Aurora said.

'You have no way of judging.'

'Measured inertias of temporal isotopies give me a grasp of the chances involved,' Aurora said, in a tone that suggested Hera could form no such grasp.

'Ganymede must think it works,' Hera replied, 'that's why he brought Galileo here in the first place.'

'Perhaps so. But I don't think what happens to Galileo here is properly located to make any such change. Besides, Galileo has always had a remarkably strong sense of proleptic intuition. Indeed, when judged by that rubric, of anticipating future developments, I've read commentaries that rate him as the third smartest physicist of all time.'

'Third,' Galileo scoffed. 'Who are these supposed other two?'

'The second was a man named Einstein, the first a woman named Bao.'

'A woman?' Galileo said.

Hera shot him a look so full of contempt and pity, disgust and embarrassment that Galileo cringed, unfortunately shifting his balance so that his feet shot out sideways on the slick floor and he crashed down. By chance he bounced off the floor right back onto his feet, where he could only blush and smooth down his jacket sleeves as if nothing had happened.

'Come with me,' Hera said to him peremptorily.

He followed her, greatly apprehensive, but aware that if he didn't cooperate she would drag him away. 'What is it?' he complained.

She glared at him. 'Leave us,' she ordered her retainers, 'and keep anyone else from following.'

She took him by the arm and pulled him with her as one would drag along a reluctant five year-old. Under her fingers a shock tingled up his arm and all along that side of his body, from his ear to his foot.

Ganymede then emerged from a knot of his retainers on the other side of the terrace and hurried over to them. Hera cursed under her breath and said to Galileo, 'Stay put.'

She went to Ganymede and confronted him, and they argued in undertones that Galileo could not hear. When Hera returned to his side, she wore a look of grim satisfaction. 'Come,' she said again, and pulled him across the terrace. 'He's not supposed to be on Europa at all, he can't stop us.'

They reached the railing of the terrace that overlooked a veritable maze of white rooftops intersected by canals.

'Do you not remember what I showed you last time you were here?' she demanded of him.

'Yes, I remember!'

'Why did you come here then?'

'I wanted some answers,' Galileo said mulishly. 'I told Ganymede to take me to someone who could give me answers, answers that *you* had not given me.'

She was not moved by this. 'You can tell him to give you anything you want, but that doesn't mean you'll get it. Understand me: he wants you to end in just the way I showed you ending. In the fire.'

'Yes yes, but look. I took the preparation you gave me last time, but they made me breathe the mist you warned me against. I remembered part of what you showed me – certainly the, the essentials. So I went back and did everything I could to make sure that that event could never come to pass. But it only made things worse! Now I have been forbidden even to mention the Copernican theory. And yet there it rests, at the base of everything else. It's God's truth, a rather elementary truth at that, and we have finally perceived it, and I can't say a word about it! If I say anything at all, that could be it. And I have enemies watching my every breath. I might as well cut my tongue out of my head!'

She shook her head. 'You can find ways to say what you want to say. Meanwhile, you have to consider what will happen if your understanding is brought up to our time, and then you return to your own time. If you try to counteract that, and take the strong amnestics and forget everything, you will forget the fate you are trying to avoid. You may walk into your fiery alternative unaware. If, on the other hand, you take anamnestics like those I gave you before, and preserve your memory of this visit, *you will know too much*. Your work will be skewed, and you may change things in ways that would be disastrous to your future, and ours too. You have put yourself on the horns of a dilemma.'

'Can't you give me a preparation that would keep some memories and suppress others?'

'It doesn't work that way.'

'It seemed that it did. In my last few years, I remembered this world, but it was only a very partial memory, like a dream. I remembered the fire, and you warning me.'

'Possibly so, but there is no way of controlling it so finely as to be sure. Memory is very diffuse in the brain, it relies on multiple systems in concert. It's quite a feat to manipulate it as much as we do. You can't take the chance of knocking out too much.'

Galileo threw up his hands. 'But I *want* to know things, I'm made to know things! And I don't see how knowing more can possibly harm me! If you are trying to help, as you say you are, then help! But don't help me by telling me to stay more ignorant, because I won't accept that. I'm sick of being told not to know things!'

She heaved a sigh, looking grim. 'Prolepses are awkward,' she said. 'I wish Ganymede had not done this to you. Now we need to make a plan. In your own time, you should certainly stop talking about the Copernican theory for a while. Bide your time and work on other things. It isn't as if you understand very much of basic physics, after all, as you now know all too well. You could focus on that. I tell you what – I'll give you an amnestic that will obscure short-term memory. It will allow you to retain what you remembered before this little tutorial, but make this trip's contents hard to recall. Hopefully that will serve to keep your part in the flow of events consistent.'

'I want to know,' Galileo said. 'I don't see how it can hurt.'

'You don't understand. Not us, not time, not yourself.'

Now Ganymede and his gang on the other side of the terrace were pushing Hera's people to the side, approaching Hera and Galileo in a swirl of tussling and curses. Hera put a forefinger under Galileo's nose.

'*I'm* the one helping you to avoid your fate,' she reminded him as she took a pewter box from one of her retainers. 'So listen to me. You can't be one thing here and another there. You need to knit your selves together. You either make yourself whole, or else die in the fire.'

Chapter Ten   The Celatone

Alas, what evil fate and malefic star has led you into this
dangerous and oppressive darkness, cruelly exposed you to
many a mortal anguish and destined you to die from the fierce
appetite and violent maw of this terrible dragon? Alas, what if
I am swallowed whole to rot inside its foul, filthy and fecal
entrails, to be afterwards ejected by an unthinkable exit? What
a strange and tragic death, what a poor way to end my life! But
here I am, feeling the beast at my back. Who has ever seen such
an atrocious and monstrous reversal of fortune?
    – FRANCESCO COLONNA, *The Strife of Love In a Dream*

Back from Rome, Galileo spent most of the year 1616 collapsed in
his bed, exhausted and sick of the world. All the usual distempers
made their appearance: rheumatism, back pains, dyspepsia, faint-
ing spells, syncopes, catarrhs, nightmares, night sweats, hernias,
haemorrhoids, bleeding from the skin and the nose. He suffered. 'If
it's not one thing it's another thing,' La Piera would say.

The cock's crow started each day, followed by groans almost
as loud from the master's bed. The servants understood these as
the histrionics of a humorous man in the clutches of his black
melancholy, but poor little Virginia was frightened by them. She
spent many a day running back and forth between the kitchen
and his bedroom, ostentatiously nursing him.

Of course his moods had always varied. He had looked into this matter of temperament, and come to believe that Galen was better on it than Aristotle, not a surprise. Galen was the first he knew of to describe the humours, one of the few aspects of ancient medical knowledge that would certainly endure, for one saw evidence of them everywhere, all persons stuck under the rule of one humour or other, or occasionally, as with Sarpi, in a balance of them that led to perfect equipoise. For himself, Galileo Galilei, it appeared he was dominated by each of the four at different times: sanguine when his work was going well, choleric when he was attacked or insulted; melancholy often, as when thinking of his debts, or sailing home at sunset, or insomniac in the hours before dawn; and under all the others phlegmatic, somehow, in that his typical response to all his other states was to shrug them off and mulishly get back to work. To work through everything: his incredible tenacity was ultimately phlegmatic, although sanguine as well, and subject to choler. Up and down, side to side, thus he careened through the tumble of days, moving from one humour to the next, fully inhabiting each in its turn, unable to predict when any of them would strike – even the midnight insomnias, which sometimes instead of black melancholic could be so pure and serene.

Over the years the household had learned to deal with these paradoxical rapid shifts. But this time was the worst ever.

The villa in Bellosguardo was at least a good place to be hypochondriacal. On its hill, with a good prospect down onto the city, one could sit and rest, and observe the valley of tile rooftops and the great Duomo that appeared to sail east in the midst of a fleet. Villa de Segui, the House of the Pursuit (or the Pursued). He had signed a five-year lease for a hundred scudi a year. La Piera ran the place and disposed of everything to her own satisfaction. She and the whole household enjoyed the not very draughty building, and its expansive grounds. It was a good house, and with it their livings were secure.

Giovanfrancesco Sagredo came over from Venice to visit his sick friend, and this got Galileo out of bed and out to show off his new gardens, which were extensive and not too overgrown. Sagredo walked beside him and commiserated with him about Bellarmino's prohibition, never once saying 'I told you so' about his Roman troubles, while also frequently congratulating him on the new house and grounds. Sagredo was a sanguine man, a rare combination of joy and wisdom. How he loved life. In the three years Galileo had taught him in Padua, Galileo had often taken the barge into Venice to stay with him at his pink palazzo, and come to love Francesco's calm enthusiasm for everything. He ate and drank with a will, swam in the Grand Canal, conducted experiments in magnetism and thermometry, tended his menagerie like the abbot of a monastery of beasts; and always carefree about the task of the moment.

'This is a beautiful place,' he said again. 'You can use the little barn as your workshop, and from there have a view onto the city! What a prospect. You can fly over the people whose lives you will be changing forever by the experiments you will make there.'

'I don't know,' Galileo groused, unwilling to be satisfied. Like a lot of melancholics, he could ape a sanguine manner in a sanguine person's company; but he trusted Francesco enough to reveal his true feelings. 'I have this awful feeling of being gagged. I shouldn't let it bother me, but it does.'

Afterward, recalling Galileo's moaning and groaning, Sagredo wrote to him: *Vivere et laeteri; Hoc est enim donum Dei. Live and enjoy; this is a gift from God.* Later he wrote again on the same theme: *Philosophize comfortably in your bed and leave the stars alone. Let fools be fools, let the ignorant plume themselves on their ignorance. Why should you court martyrdom for the sake of winning them from their folly? It is not given to everyone to be among the elect. I believe the universe was made for my service, not I for the universe. Live as I do and you will be happy.*

That was probably true; but Galileo couldn't do it. He needed to work, that was a big part of him. Without work he tended to go mad. But now the Copernican theory lay at the base of all he was interested in, and he was forbidden to discuss it. And Galileo had been Copernicanism's chief advocate, in Italy for sure, and really in Europe generally, Kepler being so betangled; so without him it wouldn't go anywhere. Everyone understood his silence on the matter to be the result of a specific warning to him, no matter what the written testimonial from Bellarmino said. It was not as if he could whip it out every time he met someone and say I was not really rebuked, see? And of course much of the tale-telling was happening behind his back anyway, as he well knew. Despite which he could not reply to them; there was a crowd of vigilant enemies all ready to leap on anything he might publish or write privately, or even speak aloud. For the spies were everywhere, and the air of Florence was thick with sacerdotal menace.

It was obvious to all that he was on a short leash. Nothing like this had ever happened to him before. In the past he had been made happy by opposition, for that meant opponents trampled in debate, gloriously thrashed by his deadly combination of reason and wit. Now that was gone. 'I am forbidden to pursue the truth!' he whined pompously to his friends and his household. 'Forbidden by vague, confused, and completely unnecessary strictures of a Church in which I am member in good standing, a true believer. And it isn't even the Church as represented by the Pope that is persecuting me, for he met with me and gave me his blessing, but rather a cabal of envious lying secret enemies, who have harmed the Church with their poison even more than they have harmed me! It makes me crazy! No hatred like that of ignorance for knowledge. Because ignorance could know too, if it wanted to, but it's too damned lazy!' He recited his entire rosary of resentment many times a day, until the household grew heartily sick of it, and of him. And he grew sick of himself. He wanted to work. He wrote to a correspondent, *Nature likes to work, generate,*

208

produce, and dissolve always and everywhere. These metamorphoses are her highest achievements. Who therefore wants to fix a limit for the human mind? Who wants to assert that everything which is knowable in the world is already known?

Eventually he got bored even with his anger, and turned his attention to other things. He went out into the gardens in the morning, always a sign of returning sanity. He wrote long letters through the afternoons. Only on the clearest nights did he gaze at the stars, as he had so religiously before the trip to Rome; and now when he did it seemed he was in the grip of a compulsion to punish himself, as the sights he saw through the telescope only caused him to moan and curse his fate. It was like pushing at a sore tooth with your tongue.

He would sit on his stool looking through his latest telescope, thinking through the night. Once it occurred to him that as there was no natural longitudinal equivalent of the equator, the Earth's zero meridian for longitude ought to be designated as running right through the place in the world most aware of the Earth as a planet, meaning his house, or even his telescope, or his mind. '*I* am the zero meridian of this world,' he muttered irritably. 'That's what makes these bastards so envious.'

By day he tried to focus on other matters. Letters came in from old students, suggesting questions and projects to pursue. As the months passed, he worked with varying low levels of enthusiasm on many things: magnetism; the condensation of water; luminous stones; the proper way to price a horse; the strength of materials, an old interest; and the probabilities involved in the casting of dice, a new interest. In this field the quickness of his intuition was startling, but he only scowled at Cartophilus after a day of working on the matter. 'An ugly feeling,' he said darkly, 'to already know what you know.' To this Cartophilus skulked away, and Galileo went back to work on probability, then on a new kind of post-digger. Anything but astronomy.

Mornings were best. He wandered his new gardens and the newly-planted orchard and vineyard like a retired professor, chatting with Virginia and giving her errands, like planting things or running fruit into the kitchen, or sitting beside him and weeding together. Livia would not come out of the house. Vincenzio too had come to live with them once La Piera had arrived, but he was an unsatisfactory boy, balky and lazy. The children's mother Marina was now out of their life; she had married a Paduan merchant named Bartoluzzi, to Galileo's great relief.

He had new problems to worry about. And he was once again becoming obsessed with money. He was always looking for ways to make more, as the income from Cosimo was a fixed sum of a thousand crowns per year, and once again his finances were skating the edge of debt. He mulled over new ways to make money. He sat at a big table under the arcade of the villa and answered correspondence, often complaining to old friends or students, or his fellow scholars in the Academy of Lynxes.

One afternoon a knock came at the gate, and who was ushered in but Marc'antonio Mazzoleni.

'Maestro,' Mazzoleni said, his raffish grin a little more gap-toothed, a little more crooked. 'I need a job.'

'So do I,' Galileo said. He regarded the old mechanician curiously. 'How have you been?'

Mazzoleni shrugged.

When Galileo had first hired him out of the Arsenale, Mazzoleni had been shockingly poor, a single bag containing his entire household. Galileo had had to buy clothes for his family, who turned up in tatters. What he had been up to since Galileo's move, Galileo had no idea; he had left Venice and Padua behind and never looked back. He had given up making his compasses, and Mazzoleni had never inquired about keeping that business going. Perhaps the old man had been grinding lenses in the manufactories. Anyway here he was, looking a little bit desperate.

'All right,' Galileo said. 'You're hired.'

210

That was a good day. Not long after, Galileo banged open the doors of the little unused barn next to the villa's stable, and declared it the new workshop. They patched the roof, a big work table was knocked together, other tables were made from planks and sawhorses, and the boxes filled with his workbooks and papers were brought out from the main house and arrayed on shelves, as before. Soon his sketches and calculations began to litter the table and the floor around it. The days began as of old:

'Mazz – o – len – iiiiiii!'

The maestro was back to work. Everyone in Bellosguardo sighed with relief.

As the Pope and his Inquisition had forbidden all discussion of the Copernican theory, naturally Galileo's first public act once he had gotten on his feet again was to announce to the world a way of using the moons of Jupiter to determine longitude. This stayed within the letter of the prohibition, while defiantly reminding people of his great telescopic discoveries. And it seemed like it could be a device of great practical application to navies and seafarers of all kinds. It also put to use the hundreds of nights he had spent looking at Jupiter and plotting its moons' orbits. With this dogged effort, extended over years, he had managed to time the orbits so precisely that he could construct tables that predicted their locations for many months into the future. With those tables he had therefore a kind of clock, visible from anywhere on Earth, as long as you had a good enough telescope. As with any clock you could trust to be accurate, you could tell how far away you were in longitude from Rome by the discrepancy between local time and the Roman times listed in the ephemerides he could write for the Jovian moons.

Mazzoleni's gap-toothed grin greeted the first explanation of this. 'I think I get it,' he said.

Galileo slapped him on the side of the head. 'Of course you get it – and if you can get it, anyone can!'

'True. Maybe make a demonstration with little balls, to make it easier to understand.'

'Bah.' Although that started him thinking about a kind of astrolabe.

The first potential customer to show interest in such a device was the military attaché of King Philip III of Spain. When he came over from Genoa, in the company of the Tuscan ambassador to Spain, Count Orso d'Elci, Galileo described the possibilities for such a device enthusiastically. Everyone nautical agreed that determining longitude was the most important outstanding problem in seafaring navigation, and if it were solved it would provide a service of inestimable value (although a fee could be named). Come to Genoa, the Spanish officer said in reply, and give my colleagues there a demonstration.

Galileo prepared for the meeting with his usual thoroughness. It was not unlike his demonstration of the telescope to the Venetian Senate. A bit more technical, he admitted to Mazzoleni. His artisan carefully did not point out that his experiences with the military compass had never supported his belief that a computing device could help make people more intelligent than they really were. Something in Mazzoleni's face must have conveyed the thought to the maestro, however, because he decided that two devices would be needed, one mainly to remind people of how the Jovian system worked, and what the tables were describing. Together they constructed in the new workshop a thing that he called a 'jovilabe', much like an astrolabe, the usefulness of which was long established. The new brass device was set on a handsome solid tripod: it held a ring set flat, marked by degrees around its edge, and connected by an elaborate armature to a smaller disc that moved through the signs of the zodiac and contained tables for each of Jupiter's moons. It was a beautiful thing, displaying all that he had learned in his observations of the Jovian system.

'But you still will need to be able to see Jupiter and his wives from a ship at sea,' Mazzoleni said. 'Bouncing on the billowing waves, dodging whales and enemy cannonballs and who knows what. Who's going to have their hands free to do the looking?'

'Good point.'

The solution to that problem was so complex that he went over to Pisa to get some technical advice from his old associates in its little Arsenale. But in the end, as so often in the past, most of his real help came from the ingenious Mazzoleni. Together they built Galileo's most complicated contraption to date, an object he called a 'celatone'. Every time Mazzoleni looked at it he cackled. It was a bronze and copper helmet, with several telescopes attached to it, each of which could be rotated on armatures until it was in front of the eyes of the person wearing the helmet, giving sharp views of sights at various distances. One looked where one wanted by turning one's head, and one's hands therefore remained free, to steer a ship or do anything else.

Galileo showed this beauty off to the court in Florence, and one of his old enemies there, Giovanni de Medici, was so impressed he declared it a more important invention than the telescope itself. It could be of crucial help in battles at sea, he declared.

With these new devices perfected, Galileo went to Genoa to speak to the Spanish officials. Whether he was aware that Pope Paul at that moment was trying more and more desperately to stay neutral in the growing crisis between Spain and France, no one could tell. Sometimes Galileo ignored things on purpose, other times he was simply oblivious.

He met with the officials in the great hall of the Genovan palazzo that the Spanish had rented, under north windows that provided excellent light. Galileo unrolled the large sheets of parchment on which he had drawn more of his characteristic diagrams, their elegant circles only slightly marred by malfunctions of his compass-quill, their converging lines drawn straight with the help of a rule or a plumb, the page inscribed everywhere with his neatest script, with all its incomprehensible abbreviations and capital letters. The Spanish officers crowded around the table.

'The principle is very simple,' Galileo began, always a bad sign. 'So far, one of the only reliable ways that people have had to determine longitude is to observe an eclipse of the moon predicted in an almanac. In most ephemerides the times listed in the tables are Roman times. One can then determine how far east or west of Rome one is, by seeing the difference in time between when the eclipse is predicted for the Roman sky, as opposed to when it is actually seen from one's ship at sea. The relationship is clear, the method simple – but unfortunately, eclipses of the moon are fairly rare. Nor is it easy to determine the precise minute when an eclipse has begun, or when it has completely ended. So this theoretically good method is rendered impractical.

'However!' he declared triumphantly, raising a finger. 'We have now, with the power of a good telescope, which I can manufacture and provide better than anyone, a newly discovered reality which includes several eclipses every night! These are, of course, the passing of the four moons of Jupiter behind their great planet, or into its shadow. Either the planet itself, or else its shadow behind it, cuts off our sight of the moons as sharply as snuffing a candle. And that moment can be very simply calculated in advance. It's completely simple if the moon goes behind Jupiter, and if it moves into Jupiter's shadow, that is almost as easy, as Jupiter's shadow always extends straight away from the sun in a cylinder behind Jupiter.'

The Spanish officers were beginning to glance at each other; and then, worse, not to glance at each other. Some perused the diagrams more closely, putting their faces close to the parchment, as if the secrets eluding them were to be spied deeper in the ink.

'And who would make these observations?' one asked.

'Any officer free to make them, using – the celatone!' Galileo replied, indicating the elaborated helmet. 'Indeed, whoever you have already designated as responsible for navigation could take this on, and they would be thankful for it. They would merely

have to consult my jovilabe and ephemerides, to find out when
that night's eclipse of one or more Jovian moons was to take
place, and then observe Jupiter at around that time. Mark the
very moment you see the predicted eclipse, and then check the
ephemerides and see how much difference there is between the
predicted time and the time you marked. Enter that figure into a
simple equation, for which I could provide complete tables, and
one would then know, to within a degree's precision of longitude, where on the Earth one was!'

His finger was pointed to the ceiling in his characteristic pro-
fessorial gesture. But looking around the table he saw that all the
Spanish officers were looking at him like haddock in a fish
market, eyes round and appalled.

'What if Jupiter were not in the sky?'

'Then it wouldn't work. But Jupiter is visible nine months of
every year.'

'What if it were a cloudy night.'

'Then it wouldn't work.'

They considered the diagrams, the jovilabe, the bizarre
telescope-studded celatone.

'How does it work again?'

The Spaniards didn't buy it. At one point Galileo even offered his own services, at two thousand crowns a year, only twice what the Medicis were paying him; but they didn't go for that either. Probably this was just as well, as he would not have sustained the travel. And the Pope would have been annoyed to have his effort to stay neutral compromised in such a way; he would have had to answer to the French for Galileo's move.

Nevertheless Galileo was cast down, and disgusted with the Spaniards. He fell ill again. He spent a lot of time in his garden. He shifted his interests elsewhere. He visited Sagredo in Venice, feasted as of old, got drunk as of old; but he was older too, and angrier, and he ate and drank more than he used to, if indeed that was possible.

Once one of these dyspeptic saturnalia made him violently ill. At first when he returned home, helped there by Sagredo, he seemed totally blocked inside; and then he spent all the next day in the jakes, moaning with the diarrhoea of what some of the household guessed was food poisoning. Late in the afternoon he began to shriek with pain and fear. Sagredo, who had stuck around to make sure he was all right, ran down to the jakes to check on him, and after a while he sent a messenger for Acquapendente. When the physician arrived Sagredo led him to the jakes, and Galileo groaned up to them, supine on the malodorous floor, both hands at his crotch: 'I can't believe it – it could only happen to me – I got the runs so bad I've shitted myself a second asshole.'

And he wasn't just repeating the old joke; right in the peritoneum, about halfway between his anus and his balls, the bottom of his guts actually had burst through all but the outermost layer of skin. Sagredo took a squinting glance and looked away, his mouth pursed tight. 'It kind of looks like you have four balls now,' he admitted.

Acquapendente deftly shoved the guts back into place, through the wall of muscles back into the abdomen. 'You'll have to stay lying down for a day or two, at the least.'

'A day or two! I'll never be able to stand again!'

'Don't despair. You've healed from worse things before.'

'Have I? Have I ever healed from anything, God damn it?'

In the end they got him back to the house on a shutter, and after that he had to be very careful in the jakes, with many a setback to his condition any time he had a more than usually difficult evacuation. After weeks of pain and fear, he devised and manufactured a mechanical restraint to hold his guts up and in – a kind of iron codpiece, or really something more like a woman's chastity belt, about which naturally everyone in the house joked, saying that he had finally found a method to check his sensual urges at last; but they spoke only behind his back and when he was well out of earshot, for he had no sense of humour about it at all. He groaned around the villa, limping badly, usually balanced on a staff, and unable to sit; he could only stand or lie down.

He was in that most irritable state when Archduke Leopold of the Tyrol came by the villa to talk to him. Galileo ordered a feast, and as it was a nice day, hosted the archduke out on the terazza next to the house. Galileo stood next to the archduke, leaning with both hands clasped on his staff. Leopold seemed more capable than the Spaniards of comprehending the jovilabe, but his dukedom was entirely landlocked, and there was no need for his military to be able to determine their longitude. The celatone he also found interesting – though really, as he said, for purposes of warfare, an ordinary spyglass would do the trick. Nevertheless he was engaged and engaging, the very model of what a modern prince could be, and Galileo was encouraged by his visit. 'God bless Your Magnificence,' he said on the Archduke's departure. 'I kiss your clothes with all due reverence, Your Comprehension.' He was encouraged again by a kind note Leopold sent later, thanking him for the meal and inquiring whether he would ever want to travel up the valley past Lake Como to the Tyrol.

Unfortunately, as Galileo and the rest of Tuscany learned only a month or two later, on the very day Leopold sent this inviting letter, some Protestant officers had thrown two Catholic officials out of the window of a high tower in Prague. This defenestration was a sign; the war was intensifying all over the continent, Spain and the Hapsburgs in Germany fighting Catholic France and its Protestant allies to the north. Few knew how bloody it was going to get, but everyone saw immediately it was dangerous for all concerned. Leopold of Tyrolia, stuck in the middle of it, with allies on both sides of the conflict, had no more time for philosophers and their ideas.

In Bellosguardo Galileo did not have to try as hard as he had in the city to avoid his unhappy mother. Giulia was living in a little house in the city he rented for her, just around the corner from where they had lived when he was a boy, and she was specifically not invited across the river and up to the new villa and its fine view. When Galileo saw her at all, she treated him the same as she always had, as if no time had passed; it was like a nightmare in which her scorn for Vincenzio and her harsh treatment of her children had merely shifted down a generation without her noticing the people had changed, so that she spoke as if Galileo were her husband and his children hers, her every utterance still a hellish mélange of reproach and insult. She had a curious manner of inflicting her excoriations as if making ordinary conversation, as if they were really just neutral remarks. It started the moment he entered her presence:

'Oh here you are. I'm surprised to see you in the middle of the day like this, but I suppose you don't have anything better to do.'

'No.'

'But of course you always were a lazy boy, and clearly it's just stayed that way all your life.'

'Sorry for being so lackadaisical as to come to visit you, Ma.'

'No you're not. Listen, that door at the back is still missing its bottom hinge, I don't know why you don't just tell him to fix it, although you've always been afraid of people, I don't know why, really there's no reason to be a kiss-ass like you've always been, why don't you just face up to him?'

Galileo had long since learned to ignore this kind of thing, but a man in front of his servants could only take so much, and sometimes he made ripostes to her attacks with all the pent-up resentment of his half century under her lash, and these led inevitably to fierce arguments, for she never backed down. These fights never gave him the least satisfaction, for though he could out-shout her now, he could never come away feeling triumphant or virtuous. When all was said and done, the old gorgon was unbeatable.

These days her main reproach, or at least her newest one, concerned his treatment of his three children. Though Giulia had disapproved of the liaison with Marina, she had also disapproved of Galileo terminating it. 'Now what will you do with those poor bastard girls?' she would demand, lancing him with her medusa eye. 'No one will marry them, and you couldn't afford the dowries even if they would.'

'So it's all right then,' Galileo would mutter through his teeth. He had made strenuous efforts to get the girls early into a convent, which would solve both their problems and his, and seemed the best solution all round. But entering a convent before the age of sixteen was against canonical law, and only at thirteen could one become even a novitiate. It happened all the time that girls were allowed in early anyway, but of course Galileo's application for a special dispensation had been denied, no doubt because the clergy of Florence disliked his insults to Colombe.

Eventually, however, the day came when the girls were grown up enough to be entered as novitiates. By then he had found them spots in a Clarite convent where the abbess was the sister of Belisario Vinta. Galileo still had some unfortunate memories

219

when it came to Vinta, but he had been the broker of Galileo's move into the Tuscan court, and they had ended up on friendly terms. So it was a real advantage to have the man's sister in charge of his girls, as she proved immediately by dispensing with the feast the girls were supposed to give and delegating that money instead to buying the habits the girls would need as nuns, thus saving Galileo a considerable sum.

So at first it looked like a wonderful thing, even if his mother lambasted him for it. 'You've condemned those poor sweet things to a lifetime of drudgery and starvation,' she declared, curling her upper lip and slapping the air in his direction with the back of her hand. 'You heartless pig. You're just like your father. I don't know why I should be surprised at that, but I am.'

Galileo turned his back on her and looked at the bright side. The girls would be respectable nuns and set for life. Their abbess was a friend and ally. It would take him about an hour to walk over the hills to the convent in Arcetri, and the same to ride a mule, as usually his hernia would force him to do; this he could manage at least once a week. It was good. They would be fine.

It was true that the Order of the Poor Clares was well named. Clare had been a student of Saint Francis of Assisi, and her declared intent had been to imitate Francis and own nothing on Earth. But when you had thirty women gathered in one house supposedly there to do the same thing, it was not practical. Many Clarite convents had been given some land by their nuns' families, but not San Matteo. Giulia brandished at her son a letter one of the Clares had written to another local girl seeking entry, which had somehow found its way into her gnarled hands. She held it up before her and read loudly, '"We dress in vile clothing, always go barefoot, get up in the middle of the night, sleep on hard boards, fast continually, and eat crass, poor, and Lenten food, and spend the major part of the day reciting the Divine Office and in long mental prayers. All of our recreation, pleasure, and happiness is to serve, love, and give pleasure to the beloved Lord, attempting to imitate his holy virtues, to mortify and vilify ourselves, to suffer contempt, hunger, thirst, heat, cold, and other inconveniences for His love." Sounds great, eh? Sounds like a lot of fun! What a life! Why don't you just kill them and be done with it!'

'Why don't you just steal the eyes out of my head,' Galileo replied, leaving her company without a good-bye.

Virginia understood her father's motives. She was a good girl. She took as her nun's name Maria Celeste, to honour her father's astronomical accomplishments, and she entered the convent without complaint, and only a few hours of tears. Livia, on the other hand, was three years younger, and had always gone her own way; she had inherited Marina's sharp tongue, and Giulia's black outlook. Always dour, when the time came for the move to San Matteo she had to be restrained by the servants, and finally taken over to the convent in a sealed litter, trussed like a pig. Released into San Matteo, she composed herself into a white-faced ball in the corner of their public room, trembling like a trapped hedgehog. Looking at Galileo's feet she announced with dignity, 'I will never speak to you again,' and then hid her face on her knees and went silent.

To a much greater extent than Galileo would have believed possible, she kept her vow.

With Virginia gone, the place was less lively; with Livia gone, less stormy. Vincenzio remained as uninspiring as ever. Galileo's spirits began to flag as it became clear to him that the celatone was even more of a failure than the compass had been. As it turned out, no one would ever buy a single one.

He began to fall ill again. Months passed in which he seldom left his bed, seldom even said a word, as if Livia had put a curse on him. Salviati asked Acquapendente to come over from Padua to have a look at him, to attempt a diagnosis, but he had little success.

'Your friend is very full of all the humours,' he told Salviati afterward. 'I have bled him a little, but he doesn't like that, and

221

sanguinity is not the problem anyway. He is melancholy again, and when a choleric shifts into melancholy, it tends to be a black melancholy. Such people often suffer greatly from exaggerated fears, and Galileo it seems to me now is almost in a state of omninoia.'

'It probably doesn't help that he has a lot of real enemies who are trying to do him harm,' Salviati said.

Indeed, published attacks on Galileo were appearing more and more frequently. He could not reply to any of them, and everyone knew it. Astronomical attacks from ambitious Jesuits were constant. Rumours that Galileo was making rash private rebuttals were everywhere; and it was quite true that his fellow Linceans wanted him to make such a reply. When Galileo read these well-meaning but ill-advised letters of encouragement he would howl on his bed. He drank more and more wine. When he was drunk enough he would often fall into a sweaty delirium. 'They want to burn me at the stake,' he would assure people with deadly seriousness, eyes locked on theirs. 'They literally want me burnt alive, like the heretic Bruno.'

Thus when three comets arrived in the skies at the same time, injecting triple the usual air of doom and controversy they brought into human affairs, Galileo was at first irritated, then, it seemed, terrified. He retreated to his bed again, and refused to answer any letters that brought up the subject, or to receive any callers. When absolutely pressed, he told people that he had been so sick that he had not been able to make any observations of the phenomena. Luckily the comets soon disappeared from the night skies, and though the controversies continued to swirl, including veiled or open attacks against Galileo's astronomy, and even his knowledge of basic optics, he resolutely refused to respond.

'They're out to get me,' he moaned to La Piera and the other servants, throwing letters and books across the room. 'There's no other explanation for arguments this stupid! They're trying to goad me into speaking out by writing this idiotic stuff, but I'm not fooled.' One book, by a Father Grassi, a Jesuit astronomer, caused him particularly sharp distress, as it accused him of incompetence, mendacity, an inability to comprehend the heavens, and a habit of contradicting the ban on Copernicus. It seemed certain that it would call the Dogs of God down onto him again.

One day he snapped. 'Get me Cartophilus,' he said to Guiseppe, voice grating. When the ancient servant arrived, Galileo closed the door of his room and took the old man by the arm.

'I need to go back up there,' he said. He had lost a lot of weight; his eyes were bloodshot, his hair greasy and lying in hanks on his head. 'I want you to get me to Hera, do you understand?'

'Maestro, you know I can't be sure now who's going to be at the other end of the thing,' Cartophilus warned him in a low voice.

'Get me back there anyway,' Galileo ordered, pinching the old one's upper arm like a crab. 'Hera will find me once I'm there, she always does.'

'I'll try, maestro. It always takes a little while, you know that.'

'Quickly this time. *Quickly*.'

One night soon thereafter, Cartophilus came to Galileo in his bedroom. 'Maestro,' he said in a low voice, 'it's ready for you.'

'What?'

'The entangler. Your teletrasporta.'

'Ah!' Galileo heaved himself to his feet. He looked shabby and thin. Cartophilus encouraged him to dress, to comb his hair. 'It's colder there, remember. You'll be meeting strangers, no doubt.'

At the edge of the garden he had set a couch with blankets on it. Beside the couch on the ground was a metal box. It looked like pewter.

'What, no stranger? No telescope?'

223

'No. I'm the one in charge of this device. He was always just your courier, or guide. He came to get you. But now he's in trouble on Callisto, as you'll find out. Apparently I'm sending you to Aurora, who has been given the care of his entangler. She has agreed to see you again.'

'Good.'

'I think Hera will not be pleased.'

'I don't care.'

'I know.' Cartophilus regarded him. 'I think you need to learn what Aurora has to teach. Remember.' And he tapped the side of the pewter box.

Chapter Eleven   The Structure of Time

Imagination creates events.
  – GIOVANFRANCESCO SAGREDO, *letter to Galileo, 1612*

He stood by the reclining chair he had taken his tutorial in, high in Rhadamanthys Linea, the Venice of Europa. Aurora was indeed there to greet him. 'You look unwell,' she said, staring at him curiously.

Galileo said, 'I am fine, lady, thank you. Please, may we continue your tutorial where we left off? I need to understand better how things work, in order to alter my life away from a bad result. You said when we parted that I was only at the beginning of your science. That there was some kind of reconciliation that would solve the paradoxes we were mired in. That I am mired in.'

Aurora smiled. She had in her gaze the glow that her name led Galileo to expect, even though she was obviously aged. 'There is a reconciliation,' she said. 'But it will require you to go much further than we did before. That session took you through four centuries, as I said. To get to the theory of the manifold of manifolds you must keep going for a thousand more years. And mathematical progress has often accelerated in that time. Indeed there is one century called the Accelerando.'

'I like those in music,' Galileo said, climbing into the tutorial chair. 'Was it then followed by a ritard?'

'Yes, it was.' She smiled as the Aurora of myth would have at old Tithonius. 'Maybe that's part of the definition of an accelerando.'

Warmed by her glance, anticipating with pleasure another flight with her into the future of mathematics, Galileo said, surprising them both, 'I never knew a woman mathematician.'

'No, I suppose you didn't. The power structure in your time was not good for women.'

'Power structure?'

'Patriarchy. A dominance system. A structure of feeling. We are cultural creatures, and what we think of as spontaneous and natural emotions are actually shaped in a culture-made system that changes over time, as in arranged marriages to romantic love, or vengeance to justice. There are of course enduring hormonal differences in brains, but they are minor. Any hormonal mix can result in someone good at maths. And everyone is a mathematician.'

'Maybe in your world,' Galileo said, remembering some of his more hopeless students with a little snort. 'But please, give me the preparation, and let's be on our way. And I think it might go better for me this time, if you were to help the machine more often than you did before.'

Aurora looked amused that he would presume she was at his service. But he was too desperate for knowledge to be too concerned about courtesy, and perhaps she could see that too. 'I'll listen in,' she said. 'If I feel I can help, I'll speak up.'

Her assistants brought the wiry helmet to him, and the alchemical preparation.

Humans sensed only a small part of reality. They were as worms in the earth, comfortable and warm. If God had not given them reason, they would not by their senses know even a minim of the whole.

As it was, however, by the cumulative work of thousands of people, humanity had slowly and painfully built a picture of the cosmos beyond what they could see; and then had found ways to use that knowledge, and move around in the cosmos.

Galileo flew again in the space of ideas, as if through patchy white clouds, following the construction of mathematics' monumental edifice step by step through the centuries. He was thankful for the velocinestic, because he needed to be quick to apprehend what the machine was saying, and what Aurora added to its speech. This heightened apprehension now took him speedily beyond thought as he was used to it, into some larger realm of understanding, full of feeling and movement, something like a bodily music. He did not just see or sing the music, but become it. Maths was his body. Words, symbols, and images all formed in the vague enormous clouds inside him, all moving in a continuous dance of equations and formulas, operations and algorithms, together melding into an ongoing polyphonic chorus. He was singing along and being sung. This meant taking certain things on faith, hoping that his performance of them indicated a subsequent firmer understanding would grow and hold. Here Aurora helped him to hew to the main line, reassuring him that he was proceeding just as all the rest of them had at one point or another, enduring confusions to follow a line through them. 'No one can know everything,' she said. Galileo found this hard to accept. But in order to keep flying he ignored the bitter taste of his ignorance, of his faith in things he had not mastered. There were more important matters at hand than his sense of complete understanding. Apparently no one got to have that but God.

And so he flew on, exfoliating into the new fields and methods, gauge theory, chromoelectrodynamics, symmetry and supersymmetry, multi-dimensional topology, manifolds, on and on it went, smaller and bigger, more complex and simpler – and after an extended protraction of his mind he found the long looked-for reconciliation of quantum mechanics and gravity physics. It came only very late in the story, when they got down into the very finest grain of things, regarding sizes that were so small that

Galileo marvelled there could be any knowledge of them whatsoever. But apparently there was.

As the generations of scientists had succeeded each other, each step of comprehension had served as scaffolding on which to stand and erect the next level. At every step of the way quantum mechanics had proved itself accurate and useful. And so one aspect of it, Pauli's exclusion principle, could be combined with the speed of light to establish minimum lengths and times: these were true minimums, because further division would break either the speed of light or the exclusion principle. The minimum width established by this principle turned out to be 10^{-34} of a meter; and travelling at the speed of light a photon would cross this distance in 10^{-43} of a second, a second being about the equivalent of a pulse, which Galileo measured as the speed of his calm heart beating. The ultimate minim of time, in other words, was a billionth of a billionth of a billionth of a billionth of a heartbeat, more or less. That was brief! The universe was very fine-grained indeed. Just thinking about it gave Galileo a shiver – it was stunning to feel in himself that fine grain, the dense texture of the glossy plenum – to sense in that density also God's sense of artistry, His meticulousness or *pulitezza*. His love of mathematics.

He flew on, doing his best to catch up to Aurora, who was continuing as if the minimum units were not stupendously, unimaginably small. She was used to the idea of them, and moving on to the question of how physicists had dealt with the idea that all space and time might be created out of the vibration of objects of the absolute minimum's size and duration. Their most powerful experimental machines would have to be ten to the twentieth times more powerful than they were to be able to investigate these minimal particles or events; in other words, an accelerator ring large enough to create the energies needed would have to be as big around as the galaxy. The particles they sought were so small that if one of them were expanded to the size of the Earth, to stay proportional the nucleus of an atom would have to be expanded to ten times the size of the universe.

Galileo laughed at this. He said, 'It's the end of physics then.'

For it meant that a stupendous abyss lay between humanity and the fundamental reality that would explain things at all the larger scales. They couldn't cross that abyss. Physics was therefore stumped.

And indeed, for a long time mathematical physics and cosmology skittered around and appeared to stall, as physicists struggled to concoct scaffolding that they could cast all the way across the abyss in a single throw, that would give them even questions to ask.

'To an extent we are still there,' Aurora said. 'But a mathematician named Bao made a bridge that seems to have held, and allowed us to build from it. Let's go there now.'

Before Bao's time, Galileo saw, which was precisely the beginning of the period known later as the Accelerando, the goal of physicists was to explain everything. He recognized that; it was the *reductio ad absurdum* of science: to know everything. The unspoken desire in that urge was the hope that, knowing everything, humanity would also know what to do. The blank that was their sense of purpose would perhaps also be filled.

But to know everything was asking too much. 'They want to be like God!' he said.

'Maybe God is only a prolepsis,' Aurora said. 'Our image of what we could be, imagined by contemplating our future.'

'Which would make it an analepsis, no?'

She laughed as they flew. 'You like paradoxes, but of course this one is just entanglement all over again. We are extensive in time. Fly on and you will see.'

So they flew. Progress in physics struggled on. Theories of what occurred at the minimum and in postulated extra dimensions were elaborated, considered, challenged, refined. Predictions were made that could sometimes be checked against observation, or involved findings just beyond the realm of current observation. Ideas thus drove technologies. Slowly progress was made. But the unbridgeable abyss made every theory speculative. The wind from Galileo's flight could have knocked down some of these houses of cards, and the collapsed theories he flew through had perhaps been knocked down in just that way, by the off-hand remark of some observer like Bao, surveying the whole landscape and taking a completely new line over it.

It wasn't until the twenty-eighth century that a theoretical structure finally held. It was a physics based on Bao's bridge to the minim, and on experiments spanning the solar system, controversial experiments that had entrained significant portions of the system's total potential energy. Bao's work had clarified the ten-dimensional manifold of manifolds theory that had been proposed since the time of Kaluza and Klein, and Bao's version had created many cosmological and subatomic questions and predictions which had given them experiments to try, observations to make, a sense that they were on the right track at last – and in some ways had been all along, each generation serving as scaffolding for the generations that followed, and the work continuing through collapses and reversals, almost one might say mindlessly: 'It's like watching ants building a mound,' Galileo observed as he flew through the elaborations. 'The mass just keeps grinding.'

'Yes, although it's a strange thing to say about a process that had taken so much brain power.'

'Tell me more about the ten dimensions,' Galileo requested. 'Something more than their maths. What do they mean? What *can* they mean?'

Aurora flew next to him, so closely that he felt they were intertwined. He dipped and turned, dropped or soared, stooped or gyred, always trying to stay next to her; and he found that she could make writing appear as clouds, or red ingots in the air before him. His body was a flock of bannering thoughts, flying around her in a dance. The landscape under them was a mountain range made of symbols and numbers piled one on the next, gnarled tectonically.

'Recall the Euclidean space that you know and sense,' she said, 'having the three dimensions of length, breadth, and height. With Newton we added a different kind of dimension, which is time –'

'But I did that!' Galileo objected again. 'Falling things accelerate as a square of the time passed! This I found out, and it meant time and space were bound together somehow.' Although, he recalled uneasily, the finding lay still unpublished, buried in his folios out in the workshop.

'All right, call it Galilean space,' Aurora said easily. 'Whatever you call it, these four dimensions were understood as if they were an absolute, an underlying invisible gridwork through which physical phenomena moved. That's when you have Laplace declaring that with a sufficient physics and data base you could predict the entire past and future of the universe just by entering the numbers for the current moment, and running them through the equations either forward or back, as in an astrolabe. It was a thought experiment only, because no one would ever have the data set to do it. But the implication was that God, or something like it, could do it.'

'Yes. I can see that.'

'It implied a pre-determined, clockwork universe that many found depressing to contemplate. We weren't really choosing to do anything.'

'Yes. But your quantum mechanics destroyed all that.'

'Precisely.'

'Or imprecisely.'

'Ha, yes. With relativity and quantum mechanics we began to understand that the four dimensions we sense are artifacts of our perception of dimensions far more numerous than we knew. We began to see things that made it clear four dimensions were not adequate to explain what was happening. Baryons rotated 720 degrees before returning to their starting positions. Particles and waves both were confirmed even though they contradicted each other as explanations, as far as our senses and reason were concerned. In some cases our observations seemed necessary to make things exist at all. And something otherwise undetectable was exerting very marked gravitational effects, that if caused by a mass would out-mass the visible matter of the universe ten to one. Then also there appeared to be a kind of reverse gravity effect as well, an inexplicable accelerating expansion of space. People spoke of dark matter and dark energy, but these were names only, names that left the mysteries untouched. What they were was better explained by the existence of extra dimensions, first suggested by Kaluza and Klein and then put to use by Bao.'

Galileo said, 'Explain them to me.'

He felt himself become equations in the clouds inside him. Formulas described the motions of the minims, vibrating at the Planck distance and duration, thus small and brief beyond telling, and vibrating in ten different dimensions, which combined into what Bao called manifolds, each with its own qualities and characteristic actions.

'Investigations have now found evidence for all ten dimensions,' Aurora said. 'Even confirmation. The best way to conceptualize some of the extra ones is to imagine them enfolded or implicate in the dimensions we sense.' A long flat red sheet appeared before him; it rolled lengthwise into a long thin tube. 'Seen in two dimensions this looks like a ribbon, but in three dimensions it's obviously a tube. It's like that all through the manifolds. Dark matter had to be very weakly interacting but at the same time registering gravitationally at ten times the mass of all visible matter. That was an odd combination, but Bao considered it as a dimension we were only seeing part of, a hyper-dimension or manifold that infolds our dimensions. That manifold happens to be contracting, you could say, which gives the effect in our sensible universe of the extra gravity we detect. So that's dimension four.'

'I thought you said time was the fourth dimension,' Galileo said.

'No. For one thing, what we call time turns out to be not a dimension but a manifold, a compound vector of three different dimensions. But put that aside for a second, and let's finish with the spatial manifold. Dimension four we still call dark matter, as a gesture to our first awareness of it.'

'Four,' Galileo repeated.

'Yes, and dimension five in some ways counterbalances the action of four, as it is the perceived accelerating expansion of spacetime. Aspects of this dimension were called dark energy.'

'Do these dimensions pass through each other then?'

'Do length and breadth and height pass through each other?'

'I don't know. Maybe they do.'

'Maybe the question as formulated does not have an answer, or maybe the answer is simply yes. Reality is composed of all the dimensions or manifolds, compounded or coexisting together in the same universe.'

'All right.'

'Now let us come to time. Mysterious from the start, it seems mostly absent from our perception, but crucial as well. Past, present, and future are the aspects of time commonly spoken of as perceived by us, but they and other phenomena are the result of sense impressions compiled by living in three different temporal dimensions, which together make the manifold, in the same way our impression of space is a manifold. All three temporal dimensions impact on us even though we mostly have a very strong sense of moving forward in a manifold, so that we can only remember the past, and only anticipate the future, both of which remain inaccessible to us in any sensory way. Our senses are stuck in the present, which appears to move in only one direction – into the future, which does not yet exist, leaving behind the past, which exists only in memory but not in reality.

'But that present moment: how long it is, of what does it consist? How can it be as short as a single Planck interval, ten to the minus forty-third of a second, while even the briefest of phenomena that we are aware of takes much longer to happen than that theoretical minim? What can the present be? Is it a succession of Planck intervals, a clutch of them, is it even real?'

'God knows,' Galileo said. 'I count it in heartbeats. The beat of the moment is my present, I pray.'

'That's a long durée, in effect. Well, look at Bao's temporal equations, and see how neatly every present that we sense, like your long durée of a heartbeat, gets explained.'

They flew into something like a cathedral, or an immense snowflake, made of intersecting numbers and figures: a lacing of equations, the details of which now completely escaped Galileo. He tried to hold to the architectural shapes they made, but he was no longer following the maths.

'Her equations postulate a temporal manifold made of three dimensions, so that what we sense as time passing, what we call time, is a compound with a vector made up of the three temporalities. We can see it here, in something like a Feynmann drawing for elementary particles. Indeed we can fly in the drawing, see? The first temporality moves very fast – at the speed of light, in fact. This explains the speed of light, which is simply the rate of movement in this dimension if you consider it as a space. We call that time therefore speed of light time, or c time, from the old notation for the speed of light.'

'How fast is that again?'

'Two hundred thousand miles a second.'

'That's fast.'

'Yes. That component of time is fast. Time flies! But the second temporal dimension is very slow, by comparison. It's so slow that most phenomena seem suspended within it, almost as if it were that absolute grid of Newtonian, I mean Galilean, space. We call this one lateral or eternal time, thus e time, and we have found it vibrates slowly back and forth, as if the universe itself were a single string or bubble, vibrating or breathing. There is a systolic-diastolic change as it vibrates, but the vibration is weakly interacting with us, and its amplitude appears to be small.'

'All things remain in God,' Galileo said, remembering a prayer he had once learned, when as a boy he had briefly attended the monastery school.

'Yes. Although it is still a temporality, a kind of time we are moving in. We vibrate back and forth in this time.'

'I think I see.'

'Then lastly,' she went on, 'the third temporal dimension we call antichronos, because it moves in the reverse direction to c time, while it also interacts with e time. The three temporalities flow through and resonate with each other, and they all pulse with vibrations of their own. We then experience the three as one, as a kind of fluctuating vector, with resonance effects when pulses from the three overlap in various ways. All those actions together create the perceived time of human consciousness. The present is a three-way interference pattern.'

'Like chips of sunlight on water. Lots of them at once, or almost at once.'

'Yes, potential moments, that wink into being when the three waves peak. The vector nature of the manifold also accounts for many of the temporal effects we experience, like entropy, action at a distance, temporal waves and their resonance and interference effects, and of course quantum entanglement and bilocation, which you yourself are experiencing because of the technology that was developed to move epileptically. In terms of what we sense, fluctuations in this manifold also account for most of our dreams, as well as less common sensations like involuntary memory, foresight, déjà vu, presque vu, jamais vu, nostalgia, precognition, Ruckgriffe, Schwanung, paralipomenon, mystical union with the eternal or the One, and so on.'

'I've felt so many of those,' Galileo said, buffeted as he flew by memories of his lost times, his secret times. 'In the sleepless hours of the night, lying in bed, I feel these phenomena often.'

'Yes, and sometimes in the broad light of day too! The compound nature of the manifold creates our perception of both transience and permanence, of being and becoming. They account for that paradoxical feeling I often notice, that any moment in my past happened just a short time ago and yet is separated from me by an immense gulf of time. Both are true; these are subconscious perceptions of a delaminated e time and c time.'

'And the sense of eternity that occasionally strikes? When you ring like a bell?'

'That would be a powerful isolated sense of e time, which does in fact vibrate in a bell-like way. Then in a different way, the sense of inexorable dissolution or breakdown we sometimes call entropy, also the feeling called nostalgia, these are the perception of antichronos passing backwards through c and e time. Indeed Bao's work leads to a mathematical description of entropy as a kind of friction between antichronos and c time running against the grain of each other, so to speak. By their interaction.'

'Things get ground up,' Galileo agreed. 'Our bodies. Our lives.'

'That's the effect of being in a manifold made of three different motions.'

'It's hard to see.'

'Of course. We mainly experience time as a unified vector, much as we experience space as a plenum made up of the three spatial macro-dimensions. You don't usually see the plenum as length, breadth, and height, you simply experience space. Time is similarly triune but whole.'

'Like tides in a river mouth,' Galileo ventured. One time as a boy he had watched the seaweed flow first one way, then the other. And at the moment the tide changed: 'Sometimes there is flow both ways, and the interference chop can be either obvious or subtle. And the water is always there.'

'There are interference patterns, yes. Other people talk about Penelope's Loom, and how we are all in our place of the tapestry busily embroidering it, and now the analepts are hopping back and re-embroidering certain parts. Anyway, time is not laminar.

It shifts and flows, breaks up and eddies, percolates and resonates.'

'And you have learned to travel on these currents.'

'Yes, a little bit. We learned to shape a charge to create an eddy of antichronos, and push something along in it, and when that eddy touches c time again a complementary potentiality is created. That was enough to do a limited sort of time travel. We could perform analepses at certain resonant entanglements in the manifold. But it required very large applications of energy to make the first shift of the transference devices back in time. The required energies were so large that we were only able to move a few entanglers to bilcated past potentialities. Black holes sucked down large fractions of the gas of the outer gas giants for each entangler sent back, and they had to be sent back to resonance points fairly distant in historical time. After they were in place they were used as portals for entanglements of consciousness. These entanglements require much smaller energies, being a sort of field of induced or potential dreaming. The entanglements create a complementary potential time with every analepsis and prolepsis, and for this reason and others, the entire process remained controversial throughout the time it was being actively pursued. Shifting ten or a dozen entanglers had required the complete sacrifice of the two outermost gas giants. That was felt to be enough, or too much. So really, this was mostly a technology of about a century ago, when analepts were going back frequently, and sometimes fighting over their changes, as Ganymede did more than anyone. It has all since been reconsidered. By no means everyone agrees it was a good idea.'

'I should think not,' Galileo said. 'Why did they do it at all?'

'Some wanted to retroject science analeptically into a time earlier than it had naturally appeared, in the hope of making human history a bit less dire.'

'Why bother, now that you are here?'

'The intervening years were more dire than you know. And we are not just here; we are there too. You are not really comprehending what I have told you. We are all connected and alive in the manifold of manifolds.'

Galileo shrugged. 'Things still seem to happen one after the next.'

She shook her head. 'In any case, what you see here is a damaged and traumatized humanity. It was felt for a while that work on the past could make that better. A kind of redemption.'

'I see, I think. But, speaking of what you have taught me – that's only eight dimensions, if I have not lost track. Five of space, and three of time.'

'Yes.'

'And the other two?'

'One is a truly implicate micro-dimension, inside all the rest. Each minim holds a universe in that dimension. Then all these and ours too exist inside a macro-manifold, you might call it. This infolds a multiplicity of universes, a kind of hyperspace of potentialities, well beyond human perception, although discoverable by observations of cosmically high energies, and of the background radiation. It's said that in this manifold there are as many existing or potential universes as there are atoms in this universe, and some say even many orders of magnitude more than that, like ten to the three thousandth power.'

'That's a lot,' Galileo said.

'Yes, but it is still not infinity.'

Galileo sighed. They were no longer flying, but in a room the size of a lecture hall in Padua. Aurora could point at one wall and mime writing, and equations appeared on the wall before them. She walked him through the mathematics of the tenth dimension, the manifold of manifolds, and Galileo, as he struggled to follow her, was comforted by the idea that even here her work was a kind of spatial geometry. Maybe that was for his sake. Things laid out in relationships, with proportions, just as always. And all fell into place. Everything could be explained: the bizarre paradoxes of quantum mechanics, the strange billowing of the universe out from a single point that had never been anywhere; all the laws of nature, all the forces and particles, all the constants, and all the various manifestations of time, of being and becoming, their suprachronological travel in time, the bizarre giant reality of universal entanglement. It was a whole, a quivering organism, and God was indeed a mathematician – a mathematician of such stupendous complexity, subtlety, and elegance, that the experience of contemplating Him was inhuman, beyond what any human feeling could encompass.

'My head hurts,' Galileo admitted.

'Let's go back,' Aurora said.

Then, as she was flying him back into the world, he experienced a moment of selfish curiosity. In his first tutorial, he recalled, he'd caught a glimpse of his hero Archimedes, as clearly as if he had been through the teletrasporta and seen the Greek face to face, or even lived his life. Someone had mentioned something about Ganymede visiting Archimedes before he visited Galileo; perhaps that explained it. Now, with Aurora absorbed in a private conversation with her assistants, Galileo murmured a request to the teaching machine to show him the historical background of the astronomer Galileo Galilei.

Immediately he was cast into a space like that which had surrounded Archimedes; not a moment but a life – his life. Instantly he was filled with his own life, in Florence, Pisa, Padua, then Bellosguardo, then a smaller house he didn't recognize, in a village. All of it filled him at once, fine-grained to the minute, and fearfully he cried out, 'Stop! Take it away!'

Aurora now stood before him, looking surprised. 'Why did you do that?'

'I wanted to know.'

'You thought you did. Now you will have to forget.'

'I hope I can! But I suppose you can give me an amnestic that will help me to deal with it?'

'No,' she said, looking at him curiously. 'I can't. That's Hera's kind of thing. You will have to cope with whatever you learned yourself.'

Galileo groaned. He struggled up from his big reclining chair, Aurora's helmet on his head. He felt drained, frightened. The sensation of immediate powerful apprehension was still with him, but it all had to do with his life now. His past – the present moment –

People were talking. Aurora and her assistants. For a time he lost the sense of it. Thoughts in language, like the voice speaking in him; they were such simple things, like the twittering of birds; pretty, even sometimes beautiful, but nowhere near as *expressive* as mathematics. He tried hard to remember, he tried hard to forget; some of it was there and some of it was gone, but not in the ways he would have hoped. Nothing to be done about it. The tutorial had happened in him, it had left marks; it would remain somewhere in him, in what they called *e* time, or in that evanescent present that always bloomed at the edge of *c*. Or headed back through antichronos to him, all the way back to the curious boy looking at the lamp swinging in the cathedral. Memory as a kind of precognition.

He regarded Aurora afresh. An ancient woman, who had, he now knew, a knowledge of mathematics, and of the physical universe, that far, far, *far* transcended his. That was rather amazing. He had never thought that any such person could exist.

'Do you believe in God?' he asked her.

'I don't think so. I'm not sure I grasp the concept.' She hesitated. 'Can we get something to eat? Are you hungry? Because I am.'

Just as in Venice, they made their ground on their rooftops. He sat by the railing and looked at this Venice under its pulsing green-blue sky. On the table between them were plates of small cubes and slices of a vegetable substance unknown to Galileo, the bits flavoured ginger or garlic or various peppery spices he was not familiar with, which made his tongue buzz and his nose run. The water was berry flavoured; he drank deeply, feeling suddenly very thirsty. He surveyed the dim turquoise and cobalt buildings beneath them. Europa was a world of ice, Io was a world of fire. Were Ganymede and Callisto then earth and air?

'Have you had more conversation with the thing under us?' he asked Aurora. 'You were telling me about it before. It seems to know gravity well, you said?'

'Yes.'

'What about the compound temporality, the vector of three times?'

'That's been hard to determine.'

'Show me the exchanges with it.'

Aurora smiled. 'It's been eleven years since the ice was broached and the sentience confirmed. Most of the interactions have come to dead ends. But here – an abstract of it can be found here.'

She indicated their table, and Galileo looked at it and saw long strings of mathematical symbols and graphically organized information. The tutorial pulsed in his head like a kind of headache. He tried to pilot that knowledge into this new problem.

'Interesting,' he said at last. 'What physically constitutes the sentience, do you know? Have you located the bodily source of its mind?'

'It fills the ocean below us, but is not the ocean. The things like fish that you yourself saw, I believe –'

241

'I saw spirals of blue light, more like eels than fish.'

'Yes, well, these came from parts of a larger whole. Like brain cells of a sentience distributed across the group. But still it does not appear to be consciousness as we would recognize it. There is a kind of absence in its cognition, having to do with self-awareness and other-awareness. An absence which makes some suspect that what we are conversing with is part of a larger whole.'

'But what?'

'We don't know. But there are people who want to find out.'

'Not all of you?'

'Oh no, not at all. There is a . . . disagreement. A very basic philosophical or religious disagreement. One might call it a dangerous disagreement.'

'Dangerous?' Galileo was apprehensive: 'I was hoping you were all past that kind of thing by now?'

She shook her head. 'We are human, and so we argue. And this is an argument that could lead to violence.'

Dissent among the Galileans. Well, he already knew that. Hera had kidnapped him, Ganymede had rammed his ship into the Europans; he should not be surprised. It was people changing their nature that would have been surprising. 'Actual violence?'

'People are much more likely to kill each other over ideas than over food,' she said. 'It's very clear in the historical record, a statistical fact.'

'Maybe,' Galileo ventured, 'when food is secure, the grasp for certainty moves elsewhere.'

'Certainty!' she scoffed. 'In the manifold of manifolds!' She laughed.

As if to illustrate her point, out of the glass antechamber appeared Hera herself, ivory-armed and magnificent. She was trailed by her Swiss guard equivalent, a dozen bruisers even bigger than she.

242

Now she approached him, shaking her head as if at a child who did not comprehend his transgression.

'You again!' he said sharply, angered by this look. 'What is it this time?'

Then a loud group of locals spilled out of the next ante-chamber over. Hera saw them and said, 'This rabble is trying to keep us from joining you, here in a public space. One moment –'

She and her gang ran at the Europans, and a brawl began. In Venice such a thing would have been dangerous, with knives pulled from sleeves; here it was just shoving and shouting, and the occasional flailing roundhouse. Hera shouted, 'You'll be charged with assault! I hope you'll get exile!'

'You're the one who made the assault,' one of them shouted, and appealed to Aurora: 'We did what we could. She stops at nothing.'

The mathematician regarded them without expression. 'I say let her speak.'

Hera returned to Galileo's side. 'Take the entangler,' she said to her people, gesturing at the pewter box. She said to Aurora, 'I'm the one who should have it, and you know it.' One of Hera's guards went to the box and picked it up. Then without warning Hera grabbed Galileo by the arm, lifted him off his feet and walked with him toward the glass closets, leaving a rearguard behind to protect her retreat.

'Kidnapping again?' Galileo inquired caustically, struggling to free himself from her grasp. It was galling that he could not even slow her down.

'The drugs Aurora gives you,' she said emphatically, 'and the lessons, they do more than teach you our maths. *They change you*. By the time you're done, you won't remember what I showed you before! Do you remember that? Do you remember how they burned you?'

'Of course I do! I'm not going to forget that! How could learning more mathematics cause anyone to forget that?'

'By changing you so that even if you do recall it, you lose your understanding of why it happened.'

'I never knew why it happened!' Galileo shouted, suddenly furious. He took a big swing at her which she easily avoided. 'I'm still trying to figure that out!' He swung again and caught her on the arm, but it was like hitting a tree. 'Everything I've done since you showed it to me only seems to bring it closer! I'm a wreck! I've been destroyed. And it can get worse. That's precisely one of the reasons I want to learn more!' And he yanked his arm free of her grasp.

She took it again, with a grip like an eagle's. 'You don't understand. Your fate doesn't have to do with the maths and the physical theories. It has to do with your situation at home, and with you yourself, your nature or your characteristic responses. The kind of conclusions you draw, and how you react in a crisis. *You are your own problem.*'

She pulled him into the glass closet and let him go. Glowering, she poked buttons on the panel next to the door. 'I guess I have to teach you that part, just as Aurora taught you physics.'

'But we were working here. They're making an attempt to contact the thing inside Europa, and I was helping them.'

'That's none of your business. And there are people who think they understand the thing already. Including Ganymede, in fact. He and his followers are the ones causing the problems.'

'How so?'

'They still consider the Europan thing a danger to us, a mortal danger.'

'But why? How could that be?'

'It doesn't matter.'

'Of course it matters!'

'Not to you it doesn't! What matters for you is doing what you did in your time without getting burnt for it. Do you want to be burned?'

'No! I just don't see how me knowing more can change that.'

She shook her head, red-cheeked and still breathing hard, looking down at him with a grim expression. As they left the moving closet, now on the ground, she said, 'You understand nothing. Especially your self. All that celebrated ceaseless activity of yours, performed in ignorance.'

'I know as much as any man! Indeed more than most. *You* know less than I about how the world works, even with fourteen centuries' advantage. You have nothing to teach me.'

'There is no hatred like that of ignorance for knowledge,' she quoted him sardonically. 'Especially self-knowledge. Do you want to be burned or not?'

'Not.'

'Come along then.' She made a brief gesture at a new group of her retainers, waiting beside a long low boat, like a gondola. From behind them the guard with the teletrasporta ran up and put it beside Hera.

'I need to join the grand council on Callisto,' Hera told Galileo as she gestured at the gondola. 'The transit will take several hours. You will come along, and we can talk. There are some things you need to see in your life.'

'Spare me,' he said.

She wheeled and glared at him, face inches from his. 'I will not spare you! I'll put you through your life as many times as it takes!'

'As it takes for what?'

'For you to get it right.'

This was sounding bad.

For what has one been except what one has felt, and how shall there be any recognition unless one feels it anew?
— GEORGES POULET

Her retainers helped him into the gondola. He sat next to the teletrasporta, Hera got in at the back, and after an acceleration so rapid the bow lifted out of the water, they threaded a course through slower boats and docked with a thump at a dead end in a side canal. Here another vertically sliding closet lifted them and the box right up to the ice ceiling and through it (brief burst of pure aquamarine) to the surface of Europa, under the huge sphere of Jupiter's garish banded yellows. Hera picked up the entangler and led Galileo to a craft shaped like a seed pod, no bigger than their gondola had been, but enclosed. She instructed him to strap himself into a large cushioned chair, snapping some of his restraints herself, then likewise strapped herself in. 'One moment,' she said brusquely, and then he was pressed down into his chair, and they were slightly vibrating; looking through a little window he saw they were rising into space.

'Where are we going?'

'To Callisto, as I said. I have to attend the council meeting concerning this Europan creature, so I don't really have time for you now, but when I heard what you were doing here it seemed all too possible you would wreck your life, and much that followed it as well. So right now it's war on multiple fronts.'

She tapped at her console for a while, and suddenly their ship disappeared, so that it looked as if they sat in chairs on a small floor that was free floating in space. They flew at great speed, judging by the shifting of Jupiter and the stars, although there was no other sensation of movement. Galileo, startled by the

246

view, observed the great gas giant with a new set of mathematical tools in his mind that allowed him to see the rich phyllotaxic folding of the convolutions at the band borders as illustrations of fluid dynamics in five dimensions at least, making the vast ball's surface more textured than ever.

Hera too stared at it; the view seemed to calm her. Her breathing slowed, her cheeks and upper arms grew less red. Galileo, watching her as well as the Jovian system and the stars, thought about what he had learned during the maths lesson.

He saw her fall asleep. She napped sitting up for quite a while. It was the first time Galileo had seen any of the Jovians asleep, and he watched her slack face with the same close attention he had given to the maths tutorial. It was a human face; as such, mesmerizing. For a while he too may have slept, because the next thing he knew she was tapping away at her console, and all the bands of the great planet had changed aspect. Its lit part was a crescent now, the terminator a clean curving line, the gibbous dark part very dark indeed. They were closer to it than Galileo could remember ever having been, so that it took up the space of perhaps a hundred Earthly moons, filling a big portion of the sky. The lit crescent, an astonishing arc of banded unctuous oranges, seemed to cut into the black sky from some more vivid universe.

'Are we nearing Callisto?' he asked, looking around in the black starry night. No moons were obvious to him.

'No,' she said. 'It's still out there a long way. A few hours.'

The crescent was becoming visibly more slender. They had to be moving at great speed.

'How is your ship invisible?'

'It's not. The walls can be made screens on which is projected the image of what you would see if you were looking out through the ship.'

Very great speed. The crescent became like an immense bow, about twice the size that Orion would need, narrow and richly colourful, laminated in the wrong direction, pulled back hard as if to let off a shot. It shrank toward darkness symmetrically from top and bottom. With a final blink it was gone. The sun was now completely eclipsed, and they were looking at the dark side of Jupiter. With none of the four Galileans in sight, it had to be that the dark side of the great planet was lit only by starlight, and perhaps Saturn if it were up there among the stars they could see. In any case it was a dim light, but not nothing, not blackness; he could still make out the latitudinal bands, even the taffeta folding of their borders. Now that the light was so subtle, he could see that the surface of the planet was not a solid liquid, like oil paint, but rather cloud tops of varying opacity or transparency, shaded a thousand different combinations of dim sulphur and orange, cream and brick. In places the surface was fluted like the underside of a cloud on certain windy days; elsewhere geysers spurted out into the space above the cloud tops, forming lines of puffs that paralleled the bands and were carried off east or west. He thought he could even see the movement of the clouds, the powerful winds of Jupiter.

Hera yawned. She had seen this marvel before. 'We have time to do some work on you and your Italian existence. We might as well use it.'

'I don't see why,' Galileo objected, feeling uneasy. 'You didn't want me learning more mathematics.'

She said, 'No, but now that you have, you should understand the context. You need to know your life. It doesn't go away, so you either understand it or remain disabled by forgetfulness and repression.'

'So you are Mnemosyne,' Galileo said. 'The muse of memory.'

'I was a mnemosyne.' She gave him a metallic helmet that resembled Aurora's, or even his own celatone. 'Here,' she said. 'Put this on.'

Tentatively he placed it on his head. 'What does this one do?'

'It helps you to return. Pay attention!'

And she tapped him on the head.

*　　*　　*

His mother was screaming at his father. Sunday morning, getting ready for church; a regular time for her to yell. Galileo was hiding his head under his Sunday shirt as he put it on. Not pulling it on, staying covered by it, apart.

'What do you mean *be quiet*? How can I *be quiet* when I have to go begging more credit from the landlord and the grocer and everyone? What would we do for a roof over our head if I didn't speak up and spend every day spinning and carding and sewing until I go blind, while you moon over your *lute*!'

'I make a living,' Vincenzio protested. His defence was weak with long use: 'I had an appointment at court, and may again soon. I teach classes, I have private students, commissions, articles, songs –'

'Songs! That's right! You play your lute and I pay the bills. I work so you can strum your lute in the yard and dream about being a courtier. You dream and we suffer for it. Five children going ragged in the street and you sit there playing your lute! *I hate the sound of it*!'

'It's my living! What, would you steal my living, would you steal my hands, my tongue?'

'A *living* you call this? *Oh sta cheto, soddomitaccio*!'

Vincenzio sighed. He turned helplessly to his wide-eyed children, watching this scene as always. 'Let's go,' he begged her. 'We'll be late for mass.'

In the church Galileo looked around. They did appear a bit shabbier than many of the others there. His uncle was a textile merchant, like so many in Florence, and provided his mother with piecework, and with his workers' mistakes. While the priest sang the parts of the service set to music, his mother shot his father a black look that Vincenzio tried to ignore. It was not infrequent that she would loudly whisper something poisonously obscene right in church.

One of the acolytes lit a lantern suspended from the rafters overhead, and when he was done the lantern was slightly swinging on its chain. Back and forth, back and forth. Watching it closely, it seemed to Galileo that no matter how big or small an arc the lantern swung through, it took the same amount of time to do it. As the swings grew shorter they seemed to slow down accordingly. He put his thumb to his other wrist, and pressed down on his pulse to count and see. Yes; no matter the size of the arc, the lantern took the same time to pass through it. That was interesting. There was a little ping in it that made him forget everything else.

He was in space, flying some distance from the dark banded ball that was the back side of Jupiter. He shuddered at the disorientation, knew where he was.

Hera had been studying her console, it appeared. Seeing his thoughts.

She said, 'Do you know what happens to a boy who sees his father consistently abused by his mother?'

Galileo could not help but laugh. 'Yes, I think I do.'

'I don't mean did you experience it. Obviously you did. I mean, did you ever consider what it did to you. How it impacted your later relations.'

'I don't know.' Galileo turned his head away from her. The helmet was heavy on his head, and pricked at several places on his scalp. 'Who can say? I never liked my mother, I know that. She was mean to all of us.'

'This has effects, of course. In a patriarchy, a woman dominating a man seems unnatural. A joke at best, at worst a crime. So, you disliked and feared your mother, and you lost respect for your father. You vowed it would never happen to you. You might even have wanted revenge. All the rest of your life was thereby affected. You were determined to be stronger than anyone. You were determined to stay clear of women, maybe hurt them if you could.'

'I had lots of women.'

'You had sex with lots of women. It's not what I'm talking about. Sex can be a hostile act. How many women did you have sex with?'

'Two hundred and forty-eight.'

'And so you were free of them, you thought, while still having heterosexual sex. It was a common behaviour, easy to see and understand. But the psychology of your time was even more primitive than your physics. Temperaments, the four humours –'

'Those are very evident,' Galileo objected. 'You see them in people.'

'You do. Were you often melancholy?'

'I had all the humours in full. Sometimes overfull. The balance sloshed around, depending on my circumstances. As a result I often slept poorly. Sometimes not at all. Loss of sleep was my main problem.'

'And sometimes you were melancholy.'

'Yes, sometimes. Black melancholy. My vital spirits are strong, and sometimes the humours are overproduced, and some get burnt and ascend to the brain in a vapour, rather than a liquid as they should. It's these catarrhs that lead to abnormal moods. Particularly burnt black bile, that's the catarrh that leads to a melancholy adust.'

'Yes.' She regarded him. 'But it had nothing to do with your mother.'

'No.'

'It had nothing to do with your fear of women.'

'Not at all! I loved women!'

'You had sex with women. It's not the same thing.'

'There was Marina,' Galileo said, then, hesitating: 'I loved Marina. At least at first.'

'Let's see about that. Let's see how it began, and how it ended.'

'No –'

But she touched the side of the helmet.

*   *   *

251

He was at Sagredo's palazzo on the Grand Canal, waiting for the party girls to show. Sagredo always invited some by. Galileo liked all the different girls. Their variety had become something he lusted after – how each was big or small, dark or light, bold or diffident – but mainly, just different. As difference was what he had, difference was what he liked; for when it came to sex, people learned to like what they had. He kept count of them in his head, and could remember them all. There were so many kinds of beauty. So now he listened to Valerio play the lute, full of Sagredo's wine and the food from the feast, and waited to see what the world would bring to him.

Under the arch of the main door stepped a girl with black hair. In the first seconds of her appearance in the brilliant candlelight Galileo fell under a compulsion.

At first she did not see him. She was laughing at something one of the other girls had said.

What Galileo looked for in female company, beyond sheer difference, was some kind of liveliness. He liked laughing. There were some who were in high spirits during the sexual act, who made it a kind of child's play, a dance that friends did that made them laugh as well as come – there was some *dash* to the act, so that the dust in the blood was sent flying, the lanterns sparked, the gilt flaked, the whole world shone as if wet.

Just so this girl seemed to his eye. She had that spark. Her features were not regular, her hair was black as a crow's, and she had the classic Venice girl's figure, fish fed and lush, long legged and strong. She laughed at her companion as Galileo crossed the room to get closer to her. She had thick eyebrows that almost met over her nose, and beneath them her eyes were a rich brown starred with black radial lines, like stones. Feline grace, high spirits, black hair: then also wide shoulders, a fine neck and collarbones, nice breasts, perfect brown skin, strong arms. Fluid in movement, dancing through the room.

He got in her orbit, among some of her friends that he knew from previous parties, and he was ready and waiting for their

252

jokes about the crazy professor. As he made his sallies against her friends, she saw his regard for her and smiled; then reversed the flow of her movement in the room, and before long was at his side, where they could talk under the noise of everyone else. Marina Gamba, she said. Daughter of a merchant who worked on the Riva de' Sette Martiri; a fish market owner, Galileo gathered. She had lots of sisters and brothers, and did not get along with her mother, and so lived with cousins near her parents, on the Calle Pedrocchi, and enjoyed her evenings out. Galileo knew the type perfectly well, fish market girl by day, party girl by night. No doubt illiterate, possibly unable even to add, although if she helped in the market she may have learned that. But she had a shy, sly sideways glance that suggested a wit sharp but not mean. All good. He wanted her.

By the time the party moved upstairs to the palazzo's altana she was behind him, shoving him up the stairs with friendly pokes to the butt, and at the turn in the stairs, where there was a long window embrasure overlooking the canal, he reached back and pulled her by the hand into it. They collided there in a quick groping embrace. She was as bold as one could want, and they never made it up the stairs, moving in stages out to the long gallery fronting the Grand Canal on the second floor, skipping along it to a somewhat private couch at its far end, a couch Galileo knew well, having used it for this purpose before. Possibly she had too. There they could lie together and kiss and fondle under their clothes, which came apart or down in just the right ways. The couch was not quite long enough, but its cushions could be thrown in the corner behind it, and they did that and rolled around on them in a wild tangle. She was good at that, and she laughed at his wild-eyed ardour.

So all was well and more than well, and he had her on his lap riding him naked and most rapturous, when he leaned back into one of Sagredo's big pillows and encountered one of the many creatures of the house, something small and furry with needlelike teeth, which had been stirred from its sleep and now bit him on the left ear and clamped down. He roared as quietly as he could, and tried to pull the thing off without losing his ear or the rhythm of the love-making with Marina, who it seemed to him had closed her eyes on his distress to focus on her pleasure, which looked to be in its final accelerando. From the corner of his left eye Galileo could not make out exactly what kind of creature it was, perhaps a weasel or fox or baby hedgehog, hopefully not just a rat, but no matter, he turned his head and buried the creature between Marina's breasts, which were flying up and down so dramatically that he hoped the creature would become interested and transfer its toothy grip. Feeling the creature, Marina opened her eyes and yelped, leaned far back, laughed and slapped at it, hitting his face instead; he grabbed a breast and pulled her back toward him, while with the other he pulled at the twitching body of the thing. All three of them rolled off the cushions onto the floor, but Marina kept the rhythm going and even redoubled the pace of it. They both came in the wildness of this, at which point Galileo shouted, 'Giovan! Cesco! Come save me from your damned menagerie!'

He managed to detach the animal by holding its snout shut. Feeling this it convulsed free and instantly disappeared, and the two lovers lay there in the bloody afterglow.

'Giovanni! Francesco! Never mind!'

They lay there. Briefly she licked his blood from his neck. She teased him about being the mad professor, in the same way they all did, but then, when they started to make love again, she added a joke about how he might be able use his military compass to calculate the most pleasurable angles their bodies together might form, which made him hoot with laughter.

'Well, why not?' she said, grinning. 'They say you have made it so complicated that anything can be calculated, *too* many things.'

'What do you mean *too* many?'

'That's what they say, that you larded it down like your big belly here. They say you made it so hard no one can even understand it –'

'What!'

'That's what they say! They say no one can even understand it, that you have to take a class at the university for a year to learn it, and even then you can't.'

'That's a lie! Who says these things!'

'Everyone, of course! They say it's so complicated that on a battlefield it would be faster to pace out the distances in question than to calculate them using your thing. They say that to use it you'd have to be smarter than Galileo himself, so it's totally useless!' And she hooted with laughter at his expression, which combined dismay with pride.

'Absurd!' Galileo protested, although it was pleasing to think that people were saying he was too smart for something, even if it was for being sensible. He was also charmed by her insolence, and her knowledge of him and his affairs, not to mention her breasts and her smiling look.

So they laughed as they made love, the finest combination of emotions possible. All without any talk of an arrangement: just laughter. That's the way it was with a certain kind of Venice girl. At one point, kissing her in the ear, Galileo thought, this is number two hundred and forty-eight, if you have not lost count. Maybe it was a good number to stop at.

At dawn they lay in the window embrasure, looking out at the slightly misting surface of the Grand Canal, calm as a mirror, only creased by the wake of a single gondola; the world turning pink overhead, still dusky blue underneath. In the dawn light she was ravishing, dishevelled, relaxed all through her body, which lay pressed against him like a cat's. Young but not too young. Twenty-one, she said when he asked. Certainly under twenty-five, anyway; and maybe as young as she said.

'I'm hungry,' she said. 'Are you?'

'Not yet.'

'You look like you should be hungry all the time,' nudging her hip against his belly. 'You're like a bear.'

'Are bears hungry all the time?'

'I think they must be.'

When they dressed and joined those coming downstairs to break their fast he shoved a little purse of scudi down the front of her blouse and kissed her briefly, saying 'A gift till I see you again,' one of his usual lines, and she said, 'Thanks, maestro,' with a little nudge of the hip and a toss of the head to indicate what fun she had had.

On the barge back to Padua, Sagredo and Mercuriale laughed at him, and Sagredo, who was coming out to stay at his place for a week, said, 'She's pretty.' Galileo shrugged them off. She was a Venice party girl, a loose woman, but in a Venetian way that was not so much prostitution as it was a kind of extension of Carnivale, and who could object to that. Next time he was in the city he would drop by her neighbourhood and look her up. That could be arranged to be sooner rather than later. He could go back in with Sagredo, who was looking amused, pleased at the world and its conjunctions. Always sensitive to looks, Galileo now recalled several Marina had given him in the night, from her first glance at him, to her amazed laughter at the little beast attacking them, to her parting look, sweet and knowing, smart and kind. Something happened inside him then, something new, unfamiliar, strange. Love fell on him like a wall. Sagredo laughed; he saw it happening.

Chapter Twelve Carnival On Callisto

I was attacked with violent fever attended by extreme cold; and taking to my bed, I made my mind up that I was sure to die. Nature in me was utterly debilitated and undone; I had not strength enough to fetch my breath back if it left me; and yet my brain remained as clear and strong as it had been before my illness. Nevertheless, although I kept my consciousness, a terrible old man used to come to my bedside, and make as though he would drag me by force into a huge boat he had with him. This made me call out, and Signor Giovanni Gaddi, who was present, said, 'The poor fellow is delirious, and has only a few hours to live.' His fellow, Mattio Franzesi, remarked: 'He has read Dante, and in the prostration of his sickness this apparition has appeared to him.'
— The Autobiography of Benevenuto Cellini

On the terrace in Bellosguardo, Galileo lay sprawled over the tiles. Cartophilus had shoved blankets under him, and laid blankets over him, but he still lay there awkwardly, seemingly paralysed, chest rising and falling in shallow irregular breaths. His feet and hands felt cold. La Piera came out with a jug of mulled wine.

'Can you get any of this in him?'

Cartophilus shook his head. 'We'll just have to wait.'

*　　*　　*

They floated among the stars, just Galileo and Hera, with dark Jupiter majestically scrolling beside them. Ahead of them a white half-moon, covered with a black craquelure, grew visibly larger. Galileo shook his head hard, shocked by such a vivid immersion in his seldom-remembered past. Marina . . .

'From that point on you saw her as often as you could?' Hera said, looking at the pad in her lap.

'That's right,' he said.

'You had an understanding.'

'Yes.'

'You were in love.'

'I suppose so.'

It wasn't a feeling he remembered very well. It hadn't lasted long. But now it was right there in him, hard to deny. 'Yes. But listen – you sent me back into my past, but –' He gestured at the teletrasporta, on the floor between them. 'Where was the one in Italy? Where was Cartophilus?'

She regarded him calmly. 'These experiences aren't like your fiery alternative, where the entangler was in fact on hand, and I sent you back into yourself at that time. With the mnemonic helmet here, I don't send you back into the past, but into your own mind. Everything that happens to us with a strong enough emotional charge is remembered in full. But that ability to record events turns out to be much stronger than our ability to recall them at will. Recollection is the weak link. So, I was a mnemosyne, yes. It's a kind of doctor for the mind. Perhaps also what your priests do in confession. A kind of therapist. With the help of the mnemonic helmet I can locate memories in your brain and cause them to abreact in you.'

'You caused me to remember?'

'Yes.'

He touched her celatone. 'All your machines . . . they make you into a sorceress.'

'Brain scanning and stimulation are not that hard. Let's go back to Marina. You spent ten years with her and had three children with her, but you never married her, and when you moved to Florence, you left her behind.'

'Yes.'

'Do you know why you did that?'

'We fought.'

'Do you know why you fought?'

'No.'

She was staring at him, and he looked away uncomfortably. He saw that one of the Jovian moons, either Ganymede or Callisto, was now a large half-moon. 'We arrive, it seems.'

'Yes, I have to attend to the ship. Then we'll continue. It's important. Your mind is parcellated into many little archipelagoes. It's partly you, partly the structure of feeling in your time. But you're going to have to put yourself together, like a puzzle, if you want to live. Which means you'll have to remember the pieces that matter.'

'How can I forget them?' Galileo complained. 'Why do you think I can't sleep at night?'

But now she was focused on piloting their craft toward the looming moon, running her forefingers over the pad in her lap. Again Galileo felt the pressure against him, pushing him into his chair. Ahead the moon grew even more quickly. To their right and behind them, space glowed and then seemed to split in a great arc, as if a red blade were slicing into the black firmament, a crescent thin as could be, but immense in circumference. The lit side of Jupiter was coming back into view. The crescent thickened quickly, revealing the latitudinal bands, which made it look like a piece of brocade. The whole great ball was shrinking perceptibly, although not as fast as the half-moon ahead of them was growing, which of course made sense in terms of perspective.

'This is Callisto?' His Moon IV had often seemed the brightest of the four.

'No, this is Ganymede. Our Ganymede's home world, as you might have guessed. He and his followers came from the big city there, before they were exiled.'

The moon Ganymede bloomed in front of them; they were going to pass over the sunlit half of it. 'That's the city there, in that crater.' She pointed. 'Memphis Facula. The dark area around it is called the Galileo Regio, I'm sure you'll be pleased to know.'

Galileo frowned at the jab, though in fact he was pleased. 'Will we stop there?'

'No, we're just passing by. We're using Ganymede for a redirect and some sling. See there, the big star out there? That's Callisto.'

They shot just over the surface of bright Ganymede. It was big and rocky, lined with an orthogonal crackle almost everywhere, also pockmarked with many round impact scars, like a smallpox survivor. There was an infinite litter of rocks and boulders scattered over the lined plains, which were in some places very dark, in other places a blasted brilliant white, though the landscape seemed basically level. Long strips of different kinds of terrain, lined or smooth or rocky, were laid beside and over each other like gallery carpets.

'The white areas are called palimpsests,' Hera said. 'Now we're over Osiris, that's the big crater with the white marks radiating from it. And now we're coming over Gilgamesh.'

'Why was Ganymede exiled from his world?' Galileo asked.

Her expression grew sad and forbidding. 'He is a charismatic, the leader of a sect with a lot of power on Ganymede. The sect did something forbidden by Ganymede's government. Strange to say, they made an incursion into the Ganymedean ocean. This is the biggest of the four moons, the biggest moon in the solar system, in fact, and it has the biggest ocean too, much bigger than Europa's. The ice layer here is thicker too. So – something happened down there. Ganymede was at that time *the* Ganymede, a kind of religious leader, so that made it especially shocking, that he would initiate such a transgression.'

'You don't know what happened?'

'No. I was assigned to be his mnemosyne, when he and his group were exiled to Io, but after a few sessions he refused to continue working with me, and the judgement has not been

260

enforced. He has to be careful around me because of that, and pretends even to accommodate me, as when I joined you during the trip into Europa's ocean. But in truth he keeps his distance.' She shook her head, watching the big moon gloomily as they angled swiftly away from it, then shot into the night toward Callisto. 'Maybe he got somebody killed down there, or encountered something like what we ran into inside Europa. Whatever it was that happened when he explored the ocean on Ganymede, he will stop at nothing, as you know, to prevent the Europans from doing the same.'

'So you think he found a creature in Ganymede's ocean?' Galileo was surprised, but then said, 'Given there is one inside Europa, it seems possible.'

'Yes, it does. But the government in Memphis Facula say there isn't anything down there. None of the Ganymede's people has ever said anything about their incursion, and he refused to work with me, as I said. He and his circle have moved to a more distant massif on Io.'

'Which is your world.'

'Yes. But it is the world of all exiles.'

'So you did not cure him.'

'No. In fact I may have made him worse. He hates me now.'

Again Galileo was surprised. 'I will never hate you,' he said, without intending to.

'Are you sure?' She glanced at him. 'You sound like you're on your way sometimes.'

'Not at all. To be helped is to offer a kind of love.'

She didn't agree. 'That feeling is often just the displacement we call transference. Which then leads to other reactions. In the end it's lucky if you're even civil afterward. That's not what mnemonic therapy is about.'

'I can't believe that.'

'Maybe it's just that I'm not a very good mnemosyne.'

'I can't believe that either. Maybe your clients aren't very good.' This made her laugh, briefly, but he persisted. 'Surely living out here must make you all a little bit mad? Never to sit in a garden, never to feel the sun on your neck? We were never born for this,' waving at the stars surrounding them. 'Or at least, it is only night here. Never to experience the day – you must all be at least a little bit insane.'

She pondered this. They flew through the stars and black space, Ganymede receding behind them, crescent Jupiter still bulking to one side, but shrinking – as small as Galileo had ever seen it, perhaps only ten times the size of his moon.

'Maybe so,' she said with a sigh. 'I've often thought that cultures can go insane in ways similar to an individual. That's obvious in the record. Presumably it's only an analogy, but the symptoms map pretty well. Paranoia, catatonia, suicidal or homicidal manias, or both at once – denial, post-trauma, anachronism – you see them all. History has been a bedlam, to tell the truth. Maybe we're now permanently post-traumatic, given all that has happened. Here in the Jovian moons, it has inspired us to hold hard to peaceful ways for a long time. But that may be ending.'

They flew on in silence. Galileo recalled the memory of his first night with Marina. He felt various pricks of remorse, even a faint flush of sexual afterglow. They had had fun, once upon a time.

He was also shocked at the powers Hera had at her command, and how she was willing to use them. That she with her celatone could read his mind; that he himself could be made to read it, in a way so vivid that it was like reliving time itself, like a return to the past . . . Well, these people could voyage among the planets, and back and forth in time; of course they would also have tried to dive into themselves, penetrating the vast ocean that lay under every skull. So they had developed the power to dive into consciousness itself. Aurora's tutorials had been another manifestation of that power, a different use of it.

It was a power that made Galileo more frightened of the Jovians than ever. Which didn't really make sense, he knew: remembering something vividly should not be more alarming than being transported across centuries. But one's mind was a private place. And possibly this was simply a cumulative feeling in him. They could do so much. And yet, with all that power, what were they in the end? Just people. Unless of course there were aspects to them he was not even seeing. What did Aurora's machine supplements really do to her mind, for instance? And was it possible she took infusions of the velocinestic all the time? What would happen if you did? Were there more things like that he hadn't even been told about?

Before him the round surface of Moon IV continued to grow, illuminated almost in full. Callisto, they had named it. Another lover of Zeus, later turned into a bear. Its surface was flat but shattered, somewhat like Europa's, but scattered dark and light regions reminded Galileo of Earth's moon.

Then he saw emerging over the horizon a truly enormous crater. 'What happened there?' he asked.

'Callisto ran into something big, as you see. A little moon or asteroid of some considerable size. It's been calculated that if it had been only ten percent bigger, it might have knocked Callisto to pieces.'

The giant crater was multi-ringed, the first time Galileo had seen such a thing. The many concentric rings looked like the waves on a pond after a stone has been tossed in. They covered about a third of the half of the moon he could see. He counted eight rings, as in an archery target. White lights spangled the tops and sides of most of the crater walls, and the lights on the fourth ring out were so thick they made it a ring of diamonds.

Hera said, 'The crater is called Valhalla, and the city is called the Fourth Ring of Valhalla. We'll land there.'

As they descended Galileo saw that each ring was a circular mountain range as high as the Alps, or the mountains of the moon.

'The Jovian council meets here, you said?'

'Yes, the Synoekismus. The amalgamation of several communities into one.' She frowned as she said it.

'What does it debate?'

'What to do about the thing inside Europa. Again. Ganymede claims to understand it better than the Europans who are studying it. They don't agree, naturally. They want to make another descent, but that is controversial elsewhere in the system, and Ganymede and his group are adamant against it. You have to understand, there is a lot of fear.'

'But why?'

'Why fear the other?' She laughed at him. 'Come listen to the meeting with me, and judge for yourself. That's what I allow you, that no one else here thinks you can handle.'

As her craft made its last descent, he marvelled at the concentric ranges of what must have been a truly stupendous impact. The surface must have melted into a sea of rock, and waves then surged away from the point of impact just as on any other pond – and then the whole thing had frozen in place, set in stone for the eons. Earth's moon had nothing like it, at least not on the side facing Earth. 'So they built their city in these rings?'

'Yes, they make for a good prospect,' she said. 'The planet is otherwise fairly flat, and people always appreciate a view. And it helps that most of it lies on the subJovian side. Most of the early settlements in the system were placed on the moons' subJovian sides, to be able to look at Jupiter, and to get its extra light.'

'It is somewhat dim out here.'

'I've read it's about thirteen hundred times more light than full moonlight on Earth. That's still thousands of times less than daylight on Earth, of course, but the human eye can see perfectly well by it. The pupil dilates and on we go. Still, the extra light and colour coming off Jupiter were appreciated by the first settlers. And really it's a mesmerizing thing to look at, as you know

now. So they built on the subJovian hemispheres. Then those who wanted to get away from the early centres migrated to the antiJovian sides of their moon, so each moon tends to have two antithetical cultures. All the subJovian sides resemble each other in certain respects, or so it's said, while the antiJovian settlements likewise seem to gather all those who oppose the first settlements. The Fourth Ring of Valhalla is special in that it is mostly subJovian, but it's so big that it straddles the terminator, and Jupiter stays permanently half-risen in the eastern sky. So, the Fourth Ring served as a meeting place of sorts, cosmopolitan and various, a kind of convivencia. Now it's the biggest city in the system. People from the other moons gather here. It has a culture very different from the rest of Callisto's cities. Most of those serve as the capital of little groups of settlements on the outer moons, or among the asteroids, or the outer solar system. They use the Fourth Ring as the meeting place.' Here she frowned in a way Galileo could not interpret. 'It all makes it a rather wild place.'

Hera's little craft and its cabin suddenly reappeared around them. Soon after that Galileo felt weight returning to him, and he was pressed down into his chair. One screen on the wall served as a kind of window, but nothing but a patch of black starry sky appeared in it.

Hera landed them. Their door slid open, and they descended onto a broad terrazzo, white against the black of Callisto's rock. They were on a flattened section of the spine of the Fourth Ring of Valhalla. Inlaid into the spine was a long curving building, perhaps even a continuous gallery city, arcing all the way around the Fourth Ring. Certainly it went for as far as Galileo could see before curving behind the Third Ring: at least thirty degrees of its circumference, he reckoned. The crater wall had in effect been excavated and replaced by the city itself, which poked up out of the black rock in repeated towers and crenellations.

Hera led him to a broad staircase that descended into the crater wall. The stairs looked like white marble, though the stone was smoother and whiter than marble, something like ivory; and all the steps moved downward together under them, so that they stood on one and descended anyway. They had a long way to go, so far that the people below were the size of bugs. The curving gallery was broad as well as tall, with clear walls on both sides. Through the glass curves to each side he could see the concentric escarpments of the third and fifth rings of Valhalla, the third considerably closer to them than the fifth, which only made sense, Galileo realized, if one visualized waves expanding

266

on a pond. Long stretches of both escarpments had been exca-vated and walled by glass, in the same manner as the fourth ring, if less comprehensively.

The people on the gallery floor were the size of cats before it became obvious that most of them were naked, except for the big masks that covered every head. Either that, or they were not human.

'Carnivale,' Hera explained, seeing his startled look. 'This crowd isn't usually in this part of the circumference.'

'Ah.'

'The grand council meets further along the arc. Their meeting is part of the larger festival.'

The stairs brought them to the gallery floor. The revellers indeed were wearing elaborate masks and nothing else. Human bodies, male and female, tall and full, white, pink, various shades of brown – but always topped by the heads of animals of one sort or another. Some of the animals were familiar to Galileo, others were fantastic creatures: big hairy heads with antlers, feathered human faces as broad as the shoulders that held them up, insectile wedges. More familiarly, he spotted fox heads, wolves, lions, leopards, rams, antelope; here was a heron; there the very disturbing sight of a monkey's head on a woman's body. There beyond her stood a medusa, making him shudder and look away. Then he saw a group of tall bodies that appeared to be headless, their furry faces looking out from their chests, as in the old tales of the Greeks. Those were strange enough to give Galileo pause; were their bodies also masks?

But taken all in all, it still was recognizably Carnivale. A lot of bare skin was part of the topsy-turvy of the festival, and he had often been disturbed or frightened by particularly skilful masks, encountered on bright piazzas or in shadowy canalsides. Here the exposure of flesh had been taken to its *reductio ad absurdum*. To Galileo this and the masks in combination were what made the sights more disturbing than erotic, no matter the helpless tendency of his eye to track the women in view.

267

A group of jackal-headed people confronted them, preventing their progress with a restless stationary dance. Jackals, ravens, an elephant, all pressing in and surrounding them aggressively. One of the ravens held out an eagle mask to Hera:

'You must join the revel,' the raven said. 'Pan rules here, and this is spring. Great Hera, here is your mask.'

Hera looked at Galileo. 'It will be easiest if we comply,' she said. 'The dionysiacs can get pretty annoying if you don't join their panic. Do you mind?'

'It's just Carnivale,' Galileo said roughly, feeling rattled.

Without further ado Hera pulled off her clothes, a kind of singlet it now appeared, coming off in a single piece, leaving her naked, magnificent, and oblivious of his discomfited gaze. Galileo turned aside and pulled down his homely pants and shirt, rags in this context, and then unbuckled his hernia truss, feeling like some kind of injured ape, hairy and small. After making a frank evaluation, Hera took his clothes and truss from him and held them with hers in one hand. One of the jackals handed him the head of a boar, its mouth open, its tusks pointing up murderously.

'A boar?' Galileo protested.

Hera stared at him with a truly raptor intensity. 'You are pig-headed,' she observed.

'I suppose,' Galileo said, thinking it over. 'Well, I may be a boar, but I am never boring.' He put it on. It fit on his shoulders very comfortably, and he could see out of its eyes quite well, and breathe through it. Indeed it was meshing with him in ways he couldn't even define at first, but then realized he was feeling its skin and hair, which was frightening. On the other hand, with it on he did not feel so exposed.

Hera's eagle head was just right for her, although her figure was too massive for flight, her body very womanly and yet also tall, and muscled like a wrestler's. A female torso that Michelangelo would have marvelled at. Indeed all the people in the gallery looked as if the great Buonarroti had carved them, creating a set of ideal figures in the style of his heroic males, then touching them to life, as his God had his Adam. Compared to them Galileo was indeed a boar, lumpy and hairy and low.

Hera took him by the arm and, holding their clothes and his truss in her other hand, guided him through the crowd of revellers. Galileo stared through the boar's eyelids, wondering if there were also lenses that sharpened his vision; wondering if he had been somehow transmogrified into the boar.

The air he breathed so easily was thin and fresh, perhaps a little bit intoxicating. He stared at the women's bodies, his eyes as helpless as iron filings near a lodestone; only after absorbing this sight repeatedly did he notice also the men and their demonstrative pricks, which were often circumcized, as if he walked among Jews and Mohammedans.

Animal heads spoke to them. People seemed to know Hera and to want to speak with her. She introduced Galileo as 'a friend', which they accepted without question, despite how odd he must have looked. They were all at ease, and included Galileo in their jokes, and laughed loudly. He began to relax, even to feel a little giddy and hilarious, so that he almost laughed too, but was afraid that if he did his guts would spill out and hang between his knees, a prospect that curbed his mirth very effectively. Despite this he was enjoying himself. Here Carnivale had been distilled to its essence, or expanded to its dream. Music filled the air, people sang in human words or in choruses of animal and bird cries; they ate and drank from high-piled tables, they danced – they even took part in a formal dance in which couples approached each other, touched genitals together briefly, as if in a greeting kiss, then moved on to another partner and repeated the gesture. Many of them had tied little ribbons or coloured threads in their pubic hair, the women doing so in ways that exposed the flesh underneath, their private parts looking like orchids or irises. Quite a few of the men strode around with vigorous erections, making flowers of a different sort, lilies or snapdragons, although really they looked more like the noses of attentive dogs. Indeed it was remarkable how much character was revealed by all these exposed organs, which appeared friendly or austere, withdrawn or outgoing, not as an aspect of male or female, but of individual anatomy and presentation. Some women clearly believed that their parts unadorned were attractive enough, a theory Galileo found he agreed with, no matter how much his eye was at first drawn to the variously bejewelled or threaded nests of hair framing startlingly revealed labia; while the men were both more obtrusive and less interesting to him, by the nature of his inclinations; and the ones with their sporty priapic erections looked after a time very suspicious, as if their owners had had recourse to some kind of effective aphrodisiac. Galileo did not like the obsequiousness of dogs either.

As he and Hera made their way through this dance, he frequently glanced sideways at her. Surely the mere fact of this carnival custom meant there still existed concepts of decorum that could be turned on their head; that was what Carnivale was for, a release of restraint, an overturning, a misrule, an upwelling of whatever was repressed by the everyday. But Hera appeared unabashed by her nakedness, or his, or anyone else's. She spoke with acquaintances, introduced Galileo to some but not to others, all with the same demeanour she usually exhibited, severe but attentive. That this could be seen even on an eagle's face was indicative of some quality in her nature. Behind her, outside the long curving windows that held them in their orbit, the third and fifth rings of Valhalla arced to the close horizons as if looking in at them. Taken all together it was a strange sight.

'Is there a Lent to follow this Carnivale?'

'Some period of penance, you mean? No, I don't think there is.'

Then as they continued their promenade among the perfect animal-headed humans, Galileo spotted a real tiger, which gave him a huge start. No one else was paying any particular attention to it, and the tiger did not seem to notice the humans. Soon after that Galileo spotted a trio of giant white-furred bears, awesome to witness; and then a troop of baboons. A stag, a wolverine . . . All the creatures were relaxed and oblivious, as if the people there were only another kind of animal in some peaceable kingdom, where all together went boldly on their way, and where humans, with their skin so luminous, their long muscles so smooth, the women's figures so curvy, constituted somehow a natural royalty, even in such a magnificent host of beasts. The women of this world, he noted, were not like those of his time, or the female figures in Greek and Roman statues; they were longer-limbed, broader-shouldered. Humanity itself had changed over the centuries. And why not? It was almost four thousand years since the Greeks; and they were walking on one of the moons of Jupiter.

As they continued their circumnavigation, he noticed that the air was turning blue around them, and it felt humid. 'Your head will allow you to breathe no matter the medium,' Hera told him. 'Be ready to swim.'

Then suddenly, without any wall or other transition he could see, they *were* swimming, and far underwater at that. All the people ahead of them were horizontal, floating or swimming like fish in the sea. Water seemed to have coalesced around him, covering his piggy mask and filling his nostrils, and in a panic he stroked wildly upward, hoping for a surface.

'I told you, you can breathe,' Hera said to him, her usual rustic Tuscan still clear in his ears. 'Your mask will help you. Just breathe, you'll be fine.'

Galileo tried to reply, but he was too frightened to unclench his teeth. Finally, desperate for air, he breathed in water; and did not drown. It was air in his lungs, it seemed. He tried again and it was so. He was breathing air.

Hera was laid out horizontally now, stroking forward and away from him. He struggled to follow her, but he had never learned to swim, and in the depths of the blue liquid filling the gallery he could only flail, all the while tightening his buttocks

271

so that his guts did not squirt out of his hernia. 'Help!' he called through clenched teeth.

Hera stroked back gracefully, still holding their wet clothes in one hand. She then showed him how to move his arms, first straight and together ahead of him, then pulling out and back, like a turtle. It worked pretty well. He followed her awkwardly, and could not help noting that when she kicked like a frog she briefly exposed her private parts in a startling way, like a mare pulsing in heat. He could not kick in the same way without spilling his guts.

Around him to left and right were not only swimming people in their masks, fur or feathers flowing wetly, but also some kind of rounded black bird that flicked by at great speed. Also a giant truncated fish, like a head without its body; and then dolphins, sinuous and supremely graceful; and something grey and rounded like a fat woman; and then a whole pod of enormous whales, black and smooth, their long flippers paddling lazily. From nearby their eyes were as big as dinner plates, and seemed to regard the scene around them with intelligent curiosity. Soon after Galileo noticed them, a sound vibrated in his ear, a rising glissando that shot up and out of his range of hearing, then tore back down into it and dropped to a basso profundo so deep that his stomach vibrated uncomfortably. The low vibration was like the sound of the floor of the universe, buzzing its continuo under all.

With an effort he caught up to Hera's side. 'That's the same cry we heard inside Europa,' he managed to say. Even talking did not seem to drown him. He breathed a few more times, tried it again. 'Don't you think?'

She tipped her head toward the whales. 'Those are humpback whales,' she said. 'They're famous for their songs, which sometimes take them hours to sing. They can repeat them almost sound for sound. And it's a strange thing, but their songs have been getting lower in tone ever since humans began recording them. No one knows why that is.'

'Could they be, I don't know – in communication with the thing inside Europa?'

'Who knows? Everything is entangled, they say. What does your physics lesson from Aurora tell you?' And with a sharp pull she swam on.

He followed her, dodging the whales as best he could, watching the aquatic dance of the animals and the animal-headed humans, growing confident in his breathing, he began to enjoy himself. He was struck by the beauty of all the ways creatures moved – all except for him, he had to admit. Even birds knew how to swim, indeed he saw that it was more natural to them than it was to people.

After a while Hera turned to him and said, 'We'll be crossing back into air soon, take care.'

Which was all well and good but what kind of care he was to take was completely unknown to Galileo, and in a moment he found himself falling, spilling and sliding onto the wet floor of the gallery, gasping for air like a beached fish. Hera had landed on her feet, and was drying herself off before a blast of air, holding up their clothes before her. Galileo stood beside her and felt his body dry likewise in the hot wind pouring over them. Already he was somewhat habituated to her eagle head and statuesque white body. They were what they were. She was good to look at though. In her presence it was hard to imagine what else you might look at instead of her.

A person approached them with the grace of a dancer, smaller-breasted than most of the women, with indeterminate genitals, the mask a head of a buzzard, wrinkled and droop-mouthed. Involuntarily Galileo drew back, and the buzzard laughed, a high giggle.

'Is this the Galileo?' it asked Hera, in what Galileo heard as Latin.

'I am Galileo,' Galileo answered sharply. 'I can speak for myself.'

'So you can! You must be very proud!'

Galileo glanced down at its odd pudenda, painted magenta as if with lipstick. 'And so must you,' he replied.

The buzzard ignored this. 'What do *you* think is inside the ocean on Europa?'

'I don't know,' he said. Something in the way Hera stood beside him confirmed his first impression not to trust this person. *Never trust a buzzard*: it seemed simple enough, although it could also be said a buzzard was always quite forthright in its way. 'Come hear what the others are saying about it!' it said now. 'You really must!'

'We are on our way there,' Hera told it. 'Come along,' Hera said to Galileo, taking him by the arm and walking away. Behind them he could just hear the vulture hermaphrodite say, 'I must say, if that's the smartest person of his time, it's no wonder they're in such trouble.'

'They?' a voice replied. Galileo turned; it was Ganymede, taking a lion mask off of his narrow head and shaking his black hair. His body was long and willowy, very white. Beyond him Galileo caught sight of a group of jackal-headed people skewering one of the real animals, some kind of an ox, with long spears – quickly he looked away, shocked at the vivid red of blood.

They came to a reddish semi-transparent wall, which made Galileo fear they might pass through it and then float in fire, and be able to breathe it too; he didn't think he could handle that. They had passed under an arch in the red wall. Hera handed Galileo his clothes and truss, perfectly dry and ready to wear. Her singlet she shook out and put one leg into; quickly she was dressed and had taken off her eagle mask. Galileo did likewise, buckling on his truss with a sigh. Others around them were arriving in the chamber and dressing, pulling off their masks, shaking out their hair. Galileo took off his boar mask and regarded its piggy face, then put it with the rest on a long table piled high with them – an awful sight, as if the jackals had boarded Noah's ark and decapitated every living thing.

In the next chamber of the gallery, which ran again unbroken as far as they could see, people were standing in groups of five or six. After their traverse of the carnival gallery, Galileo found all the exposed faces a little shocking; the reversal reversed had created its characteristic moment of estrangement, when normality was for a moment bizarre. It seemed to him then that if the goal was not to be too sexual, it would be more appropriate to conceal faces than bodies. These living souls with their foreheads, cheeks, eyebrows, hair, chins, *mouths*, were both much weirder than genitals and ever so much more expressive, more suggestive, more *revealing*. He glanced shyly at Hera, and she noticed his glance, and looked back at him curiously, wondering what he meant, and their gazes met for a second – and there she was: there they were. To look someone eye to eye, my Lord what a shock! Eyes were indeed windows, as the Greeks had said; and mouths, my oh my, mouths that smiled, frowned, pursed, *spoke*. To share a gaze was a kind of intercourse. Maybe new souls were generated not with the fuck but the look. Indeed he had to look away from Hera to avoid feeling overwhelmed, to avoid making something new right then and there.

They passed under another archway into a segment of the gallery that was occupied entirely by Galileos. There were perhaps a hundred of them. Galileo stopped in his tracks at the sight.

'Oh, sorry,' Hera said, seizing his hand and dragging him onward. 'This is just a game people play, a kind of Carnival party group, which comes from living on the Galilean moons, I'm sure. No one will know you are the real item.'

The host of costumed Galileos was variously dressed in clothing more or less appropriate to his time, at least when seen from a distance; up close he could see how strange all the fabrics and cuts were, ridiculous clothing really. Their heads and bodies were all possible versions of his type, from men who looked just like the image he saw in the mirror all the way to grotesque parodies of his form; even women dressed as him and sporting false beards. All of the beards were grey: 'Why do they all look so old?' Galileo complained.

'I suppose it's because there is a famous portrait of you,' she said. 'At the stake, as a matter of fact. Looking up at the stars. Most people think of that one when they think of you.'

'Horrible,' Galileo said. Indeed there were some of them that were particularly unsettling – like him but not, distorted somehow, as in the little images of him seen in the outside curves of spoons, or in certain nightmares – these were by far the most shocking to see. He tried to express this response to Hera, and she nodded without surprise.

'You have quickly discovered the uncanny valley,' she told him. 'It was found long ago, when they were first developing machine intelligence, that people were willing to accept speech from crude boxes, and even from metal people, but that if you tried to create perfect simulacra of people, it could not be done well enough to fool the eye, and these were the speakers who were profoundly disturbing to people. Identity or difference were both acceptable, but between them lay an uncanny valley, where the partial resemblance creates a discord.'

'Please remove me from this uncanny valley,' Galileo begged her, averting his eyes. Some of these pseudo-Galileos were truly creepy, ugly to him in a sickening way. He looked down as she led him on through the next archway.

'You see why we have continued to contain our machine intelligences in boxes and desks and secretaries and the like,' she said as they left. 'No one could stand the simulacra. Sometimes I think this practice deceives us in a different way, because we can't imagine that mere boxes can have become as intelligent as they obviously have. So we fail to notice how powerful they have become, probably in many ways much more intelligent than we

276

are. Almost all our technologies, including the most bizarre ones in terms of impacts on us, have at this point mostly been invented by machines.'

'I wondered about that,' Galileo said. 'So, your world makes no sense to you.'

'Well, the world hasn't made sense since 1927. That hasn't kept us from carrying on as if we understood it.'

'Yes, I can see that,' Galileo said, curbing an urge to look over his shoulder, thinking of Lot's wife. 'Well, whatever it takes not to end up feeling like I did in there,' gesturing behind them. 'That was truly awful.'

'I thought you would have enjoyed it,' she said. 'Surely it was one of your dreams, to be one of the most famous people in history?'

Galileo shrugged. 'It only proves that when all your dreams come true you realize that you were an idiot to have such dreams.'

She laughed, and led him under another archway into a new room: here finally they had arrived at the meeting of the grand council of Jovian moons, the Synoekismus. It consisted of representatives from all the settlements in the Jovian system, Hera told him, and therefore theoretically numbered in the hundreds. There were about a hundred people on hand here, Galileo reckoned. Behind them he saw Ganymede entering the room as well, with a group of ten or twelve of his own followers.

The Fourth Ring of Valhalla was in this part of its arc higher than the Third and Fifth Rings, and out the clear side walls of the high gallery they could see far in all directions. Inward, buildings erupted from the Third Ring like great fangs and molars; through them Galileo caught glimpses of the Second Ring, which appeared also to support buildings. Outward, the Fifth and Sixth rings were lower and further away, and the fifth range of hills was less excavated and occupied, it seemed, although gleaming incurves of window indicated that galleries existed in that range too.

This arc of the long gallery was mostly empty, but at its far end some rows of chairs had been arranged, all facing a dais. The order that the furniture implied was obviously not regarded as binding by the people in attendance, however, as they circulated in a manner similar to that of the festival back along the arc, or to that of any court, for that matter; everyone mingling and talking, until someone called out, 'Come to order, please!' Eventually everyone had come together in two loud groups before the dais. The view out the glass walls, with their concentric ranges and the banded crescent spearing the night, was forgotten.

People in both of the two groups began shouting across a divide created by a clutch of very tall women, apparently guards charged with keeping order. A few furious men approached these guards to yell their insults even more vehemently at the other side, but no one made any serious attempt to get through the line and assault their antagonists. To Galileo it looked like a kind of masque, not dissimilar to certain after-dinner debates he had taken part in, although more immediately raucous.

And then, as sometimes happened at home, what began as a formal dispute fell over some unseen cliff into genuine anger. Perhaps, Galileo thought, these Jovians, these tall beautiful folk, deprived of the anchor of earth and wind and sunlight, were more choleric than people on Earth – the reverse of what he had at first assumed about them, given their angelic appearance. They shouted, faces red – Galileo caught brief snatches of Latin, and even Tuscan, but the translator in his ear was not coping with the crosstalk, and so to him it was mostly babble. What was it that mattered so much to them that they became this furious, pampered as they were? Well, perhaps the pampering explained it; perhaps they were possessed by the same things that possessed the Italian nobility of his time – honour, pride of place, patronage or the loss of patronage. Power. Maybe even when all people were fed and clothed these concerns with hierarchy and power never went away, so that people were always angry.

Galileo told Hera about the translation difficulty. She led him down the room to where he could hear better, and the cacophony resolved into the strange Latin Galileo had first heard from the mouth of Ganymede, in Venice so long ago.

And in fact it was Ganymede himself now speaking, standing in the middle of his crowd of supporters, tall and beaky and as angry as ever. His crow-black hair stood up, and his saturnine blade of a face had turned bright red with his expostulation.

'You don't know what you're talking about,' he said in a grating, disgusted voice. 'You don't have the imagination to picture the consequences. We've done a full analysis, there's more to it than the contact the Europans made during their incursion.' He spoke now to a group dressed in pale blue, possibly the Europan legation. 'You've touched the whisker of the beast,' Ganymede told them, 'and now you think you know the whole thing. But you don't. I've told you privately the danger, and I don't want to speak of it in public, because that would only add to it. But it is very real.'

A white-haired woman waved him away. 'You have to forgive us if we proceed as if what happens in a manifold detected only by you is not sufficient grounds for changing our actions.'

'No,' Ganymede said grimly. 'This is different. You ignore the potential effects of an interaction. That's what people like you always do. You hide your eyes and never learn, and claim new things will bring new things, and are always surprised when events fit the patterns we're made from. You never see the danger and you never count the risk. What if you turn out to be wrong? You can never imagine that, you are so full of yourself, so convinced you are *tabula rasa*. Now, this time, in this encounter – of humanity with a sentience that can't be grasped, let us say – no specific human good can come of it. But the harm could kill the species. So it makes sense to beware! For the risk is absolute. You're behaving like those men who set off the first atomic bomb, wondering as they did so if the explosion might not ignite the entire atmosphere of the Earth. Or the ones who started up a particle collider unsure whether a black

279

hole would be generated that would suck the Earth into it. Like them, you'd risk all – for nothing!' Suddenly he was shouting: 'We won't let you take the risk!'

'I don't see how your position is anything other than cowardice,' the white-haired woman said. 'It's simply fear of the future itself.'

Ganymede started to speak but stopped himself, eyes bulging out. With an expression of extreme disgust he gestured wildly to his supporters, and led the way as they all stormed out of the chamber, some shouting final curses as they left.

'Could you not execute a prolepsis,' Galileo asked Hera in a low voice, 'and see if his fears are confirmed?'

'No,' Hera said. 'In theory prolepsis is possible, but the energy required is more than we can muster. Sending the entanglers back analeptically cost us entire planets, and prolepsis apparently requires far more energy than that.'

'I see. So – do you think Ganymede is right to be so afraid?'

'I don't know. His is one of several competing efforts to understand what is going on inside Europa, and the physicists I've talked to say his group has been doing very advanced studies. Even exiled to Io, they have made progress others haven't, some say. And they are claiming something more than Europa is involved.'

'So there are different schools of understanding? Different factions?'

'There are always factions.'

Galileo nodded; it was certainly true in Italy.

'So,' Hera continued, 'I don't know. I was working with Ganymede, and fighting with him, as you have seen. And there are precedents to support what he is saying. Within human society, people have generally not reacted well to encounters with higher civilizations. Collapses have occurred. This could be worse still.'

Galileo shrugged. 'I don't see why it should matter.'

'That we might find out we are like bacteria on the floor of a world of gods?'

'When has it ever been different?'

She laughed at this. He glanced over and saw she was looking at him with a new surmise, as if at someone who was more interesting than she had thought. About time, as far as he was concerned.

'I suppose you yourself can serve as an example of a robust response to an encounter with a more advanced civilization,' she said with a little smile.

'I don't see why,' he said. 'I'm not sure I have done that.'

She laughed again, and led him to another moving staircase, which carried them up its long incline, through the gallery's ceiling and on to the spine of the Fourth Ring. There her space boat stood waiting for them, apparently having been moved for her convenience. Or perhaps it was another craft just like hers. In any case there were attendants on hand to welcome them into it and see them on their way.

Above them a fiery blaze of light hurt his eyes. It looked like one of the Jovians' spacecraft was shooting up into the black starry sky, headed toward Jupiter.

Hera's look turned grim again. 'That was Ganymede,' she said, gesturing upward. 'He and his people are off to make more trouble. We'll have to deal with him. There aren't any police forces or weapons any more in the Jovian system, as a matter of principle. So situations like this are hard to deal with. But something has to be done. He means to stop the Europans. He thinks he's right. There's no one more dangerous than an idealist who thinks he's right.'

'Sometimes I think I'm right,' Galileo said.

'Yes, I've noticed that.'

'And sometimes I am right. If you roll a ball off the edge of a table it falls in a half parabola. In that I'm right.'

'And in that,' she muttered, 'you too are dangerous.'

She led him into her spacecraft. They were going to follow Ganymede back to Io, she said, where apparently he was headed. The idea was to stop him from leading his followers into anything rash. She appeared to be willing to coerce the Ganymedeans in this regard, with the help of her fellow Ionians. She spent the first hour of their flight talking over the matter with various voices that spoke from the pad on her lap.

Somewhere in that hour Galileo fell asleep. How long he slept he was not sure; when he woke, she was asleep herself, her eyes darting about in tandem under closed lids. After that a long time passed, during which he found a little closet with a hollow chair into which he could attempt his difficult ablutions. In the midst of his effort warm water filled the chamber up to his waist, where it became warmer and rumbled with vibrations that were apparently in phase with his peristalsis, as his excrement seemed to be as it were drawn out of him. After that the water drew off and he was dried in a swirl of hot air, as clean as if he had bathed.

'Jesus,' he said. He opened the door and looked out at Hera, who was now awake. 'You people don't even shit naturally! Your shitting is midwifed by automatons!'

'What's wrong with that?' she asked.

Galileo had to think that one over, and so did not answer. She passed him on the way into the little closet herself, and when she came back out, she shared with him a small meal that consisted of something like a compressed bread, sweet and substantial, and plain water.

'You were dreaming as you slept,' Galileo noted.

'Yes.' She frowned, thinking about it.

'Are dreams also entanglements?' Galileo asked, thinking about Aurora's lessons.

'Yes, of course,' she replied. 'Consciousness is always entangled, but when we are awake our present moment overwhelms all that. When you're asleep then all the entangled moments become more obvious.'

'And you are entangled with?'

'Well, with other moments of your life, earlier or later. And with other people's lives too. Different times, different minds, different phase patterns. All expressed rather weakly in the brain's chemistry, and so perceived surreally in sleep's lack of sensory input.'

'Dreams are dreamlike,' Galileo agreed. 'And what were you dreaming of now?'

'It was something about when my family first moved to Io, when I was a girl. Only in the dream Io was already occupied by animals that we killed for food. I suppose that was day residue from our panic spring. Recent experiences get infolded in dreams, sometimes, and mix with the entangled times from elsewhere.'

'I see. So, you moved to Io as a girl?'

'Yes, my mother was exiled from Callisto for fighting. The bubble technology that allows us to live on Io had just recently been developed, and people convicted of major crimes were being sent there. My father and I went with her, in one of the first groups there. I liked to greet the new arrivals.'

'And so you became a mnemosyne,' Galileo suggested. 'You learned to like taking in damaged people, and healing them.'

'Maybe. Are we really so simple?'

'I think maybe so.'

She shook her head. 'People did enjoy seeing me welcome them, I think.'

After that she sat there, fidgeting unhappily. Jupiter was growing bigger again; it appeared they would pass before the sunward side this time. Galileo asked what he thought was an innocent question about the time needed for the voyage from Callisto to Io; she snapped back at him that it was different for every trip, which was not really answering. A few moments later,

283

glaring at him, she said, 'We'll be there soon. Still, we might as well continue your education in yourself. We're all going to need it in the end.'

'I prefer my own self-knowledge,' Galileo insisted. 'You can give up on your girlish ambition to rescue people.'

She glared at him. 'Do you want to live?'

'I do, yes.'

'Then put this on.' Roughly she placed her celatone on his head, and he did not flinch away.

'Do you know what you're sending me back to?' he asked.

'Not precisely. But different areas of the brain hold characteristic kinds of experience, located by the emotion that was the fixative. I'm going to look at nodes in the areas associated with embarrassment.'

'No,' Galileo groaned, and flinched as she touched the helmet.

His horrible mother ran into his terrible mistress there in the house on Via Vignali, and before Galileo even knew the old gorgon was visiting the two women were screaming at each other in the kitchen. This was not unusual, and Galileo trotted in from the workshop cursing at the distraction but not overly concerned, only to find them in a real fight, scratching and pulling hair, kicking and punching, Marina even landing one of her big roundhouse swings to the head, a blow Galileo had felt on his own ear many times. All this with the children and servants watching, happily scandalized, squealing and shouting. Galileo leaped into the fray, ears burning, supremely angry with both of them, and was rougher than he might have been as he grabbed Marina and hauled her back, so rough that his mother paused in her shrieking to berate him for his rudeness, while also seizing the chance to assault Marina yet again, so that he had to stop her too; and then there he was, trapped between the two of them in front of all the world and God, holding onto them by their hair, extended at his arms' length from each other as they screamed and swung. Galileo was forced to ponder a little what might be his least undignified mode of escape. Luckily he had a jacket on so that his arms were not getting scratched by their furious mauling.

'You whore!'

'You bitch!'

'Be *quiet*,' he begged them, not wanting the household to notice how accurate both women were in their insults. It was almost funny, but he had long ago lost his ability to be amused by either of them; aside from their nasty tempers, the debt burden they represented to him was enormous. Maybe if he suddenly released them both they would collide headfirst and kill each other. Two debts retired with a single collision! It was an elegant solution. Marina was the lighter of the two and would rebound further, as he knew well from experiments with balls tied to strings, not to mention their own fights –

'Enough!' he commanded imperiously. 'Leave this shit to the Pulcinella shows. If you don't stop I'll call the night watch and have you both thrown out of here!'

They were weeping with fury and the pain of being held back by their hair. Their eyes were pulled up so far they looked like Chinese people. When they didn't expect it he let them go and faced his mother, his shoulder blocking any attack from Marina at his back. 'Go home,' he instructed her wearily. 'Come back later.'

'I won't leave! And I won't come back!'

But finally she left, shouting down horrible curses on them all, and there was nothing Galileo could do but to deploy his usual defence, turning his back to her and waiting till she was gone.

Marina was more conciliatory; still angry of course, but also embarrassed. 'I had to defend myself.'

'She's almost sixty for God's sake.'

'So what? She's crazy and you know it.'

But then she desisted. She needed his money for her place around the corner, and so she left the room without further

285

excoriations. Galileo stumped back out to the workshop and stood there, staring sightlessly at the complete *cipollata* that was his life.

– which abruptly became black space, the stars, the great swirling banded yellow globe. Hera sitting across from him, watching his face attentively. She took her celatone from his head, which took a great weight off his shoulders.

'Well?' she said.

'I pulled them apart. I kept them from fighting.'

'And why were they fighting? Why were they angry?'

'They were angry people. Choleric. They had so much yellow bile in them that if you pinched them your fingers would turn yellow.'

'Nonsense,' Hera said. 'You know better than that. They were people just like you. Except that their minds were crimped, every day of their lives. Women in a patriarchy, what a fate. You know what I would have done if I were them? I would have killed you. I would have poisoned you or cut your throat with a kitchen knife.'

'Well.' Galileo regarded her uneasily; she towered over him, and her massive upper arms were like carved ivory. 'You said that a time's structure of feeling has a lot to do with how we are. Maybe you would have felt differently.'

'All humans have an equal amount of pride,' she said, 'no matter how much it gets crushed or battered.'

'I don't know if that's true. Isn't pride part of a structure of feeling?'

'No. It's part of the integrity of the organism, the urge to life. A cellular thing, no doubt.'

'Cellular maybe. But people are all different.'

'Not in that.' She looked down at the screen in the pad on her lap. 'There's another trauma node near that one. This area of your amygdala is crowded.'

286

'But we seem to be approaching Io,' he pointed out hopefully.

Hera looked up. 'True,' she said. She patted him on the arm, as if to indicate that she still liked him despite his primitive circumstances and instincts. She even pointed out to him various features of her home moon as it grew to a fiery spotted yellow ball, floating before the great sunlit side of Jupiter. Both spheres were florid arrays, but their colours were different in tone, and mixed very differently over their surfaces, as Jupiter was all pastel bands, its viscous eddies embroidering every border with gorgeous convolutions, like the side of a cut cabbage; while Io on the other hand was an intensely sulphurous yellow ball, spotted by random spatter marks of black or white or red, and with a broad orange ring around a whitish mound, which Hera said was the volcano massif called Pele Ra. She pointed out to him the shadow of Io on Jupiter's face, so round and black it looked unnatural, like a beauty spot pasted on.

As they approached this hellish little ball that was her home town, a blue aura began flickering around them. 'What's that?' Galileo asked.

'We are getting closer to Jupiter, which generates immensely powerful magnetic and radiation fields. We have to create fields to counteract them, or else we would quickly die. Moving at speed causes the two fields to interact, creating the aura you see.'

Galileo nodded carefully. Because of his mathematics tutorial from Aurora, he was pretty sure he understood the phenomenon better than Hera did. Probably it was best not to point this fact out, but her lack of awareness of it irked him. 'Like ball lightning,' he said.

'To an extent.'

'Like the sparks you can make if you rub two pieces of amber together.'

She gave him a look. 'Quit it.'

*   *   *

They flew close over the surface of the tortured moon, past the volcanic continent Ra Patera, where she had taken him during his previous visit. There were red rings around several of the volcanoes; Hera explained these were their plume deposits. 'There are about four hundred active volcanoes.' Once past Ra they continued their descent over slaggy plains that were the basic Ionian colour, a burnt sulphur, greened in some places like old bronze, and pimpled everywhere by volcanoes. Some of these were tall cones, others long cracks; some white as snow, others black as pitch. There was no correlation between morphology and colour, so that it was impossible to grasp the lay of the land. An occasional impact crater added to the topographic confusion, until in many areas Galileo found it hard to determine up from down in the landscape. The different minerals the volcanoes cast out, Hera told him, in plumes or rivers of different heights and viscosities, accounted for their disorienting and hideous variety. Most of the moon's surface was too hot and viscous to build on, she told him, or even to walk over. 'In lots of places if you tried to walk you would sink right into the ground.' Only the high massifs of dormant giant volcanoes stood far enough above the magmatic heat to cool down, serving as rock islands in an ocean of crusted lava.

They came over the antiJovian side of the moon and Hera manoeuvred her craft downward, slowing it until she could drop them vertically into the middle of a small but deep crater, filled with a lake of liquid orange lava. As they drifted down to the level of the crater's rim, Galileo had a closer view over the surface of the moon beyond the crater, lumpy beyond belief. The resemblance of the landscape to his concept of hell was amazing. He remembered now; this was the landscape in which he had seen his fiery alternative. Yellow plumes of sulphur fountained high out of bubbling orange cracks and arced up against the black starry sky, falling in slow sheets of spume away from the upright columns. He had heard that the inner crater of Etna was like this one, its floor a fiery orange lava lake, crusting over with black excrescences that folded under in steaming noxious vapours. In the *Inferno* Virgil had guided Dante into Hell by way of Etna, using caves and tunnels unfilled with lava. Now his own amazing Virgil was leading him down onto the real thing. Their little craft, transparent to them, held them hovering over the burning lake.

'What will you do here?' he asked.

'I'm hiding, waiting for my friends from Ra. We've decided to arrest Ganymede and his supporters. Their base is on Loki Patera, and it's not going to be easy to make our approach without them seeing us and taking flight.'

'You need to surprise them.'

'Yes.'

'Because you intend to imprison them?'

'Well, at least to keep them on Io. Disable their ability to leave. Because of the threats Ganymede made, the Synoekismus has authorized us to take such an action. In fact they demanded we do it. Since the Ganymedeans have set up a base on Io, the council can pretend they're our problem. Leave us to figure out how to do it. It's causing a bit of a tactical disagreement right now among my cohort.'

'This Loki Patera, is it an active volcano, with a lake of molten rock in its crater?'

'Yes indeed. It's one of the biggest calderas of all, and these days it's sending up quite a sulphur plume.'

'And the interior of Io, you said it's melted through and through?'

'Yes, that's basically right. The pressure makes the core a kind of solid, of course.'

'So chambers of liquid rock link up below the surface, or pool together?'

'I think so. I'm not sure how completely the interior is understood.'

'Or explored?'

'What do you mean?'

'These craft of yours are self-contained, right? They withstand the vacuum of space, as we see, and the ocean of Europa. Is the lava of Io any different, I mean in a way that matters to your ship?'

'It's hotter!'

'Does that matter, though? Wouldn't your craft withstand the heat, and the pressure?'

'I don't know.'

'You could ask your machine pilot, it would know. And it has systems of reckoning to locate itself in space, isn't that right?'

'If I understand you correctly, yes.' She was now tapping madly at her pad, head tilted to listen to something Galileo couldn't hear.

'So,' he continued, 'nothing would prevent us from sinking down into the lava chambers below some volcano near Loki, and traversing the channels down there until you could come up out of the erupting crater of Loki, thus surprising Ganymede in his refuge?'

Hera laughed shortly, with a look at him that seemed to contain a new surmise. 'Those maths lessons have made you ingenious!'

'I was always ingenious,' he said, irritated.

'No doubt. But in this case, I'm not sure it would work.'

'Your mechanical pilot will be able to calculate these things, I am sure.'

She smiled. 'I thought you didn't like how dependent we are on our machines.'

'But you are whether I like it or not. And no matter where you go. And so, as you said, you have made them strong. Maybe strong enough for the inside of Io.'

'Maybe.'

She tapped away, while also talking to interlocutors elsewhere. A voice murmured in a language Galileo did not recognize.

Eventually she barked a short laugh. She piloted the craft down onto the burning lake, landing with a final little tilt back, like a goose or a swan.

'So I was right? The ship won't burn?'

'Yes. No.'

She tapped on her pad, which reminded him of a spinet's keyboard. Their craft sank into the lake of fire. Having been a space craft and a submarine craft, it was now a sublithic craft, a sub-sulphurine craft.

'The heat is apparently not as extreme as it looks,' Hera said, as if reassuring Galileo. 'Molten sulphurs aren't as hot as the basalt further down. The craft has found that compared to Jupiter's radiation, the protections required are not significant.' She shook her head. 'You have to understand, people only began inhabiting Io when I was young. Before that the counter-fields weren't good enough. So the idea of going inside the moon hasn't really occurred to anyone. Although apparently robotic research craft have already been down here, mapping Io's internal flow patterns. So we'll use what they found.'

'Can you make this whole room like a window again?'

'If you like!'

Again she shook her head, trying to look amused. Suddenly he saw; she thought he was too ignorant to be afraid, while she, knowing more, was rattled by their situation. Making it look as if they were inside a clear bubble in the sulphur magma would not help her nerves. The Ionians were afraid of Io; no doubt with good reason. But he was pretty sure he remembered enough of Aurora's lessons to judge their safety better than Hera could. At their levels of material and field strength, melted rock was not a difficult habitat.

She changed the walls of their chamber into a continuous screen, and now they seemed to float like a soap bubble in a liquid mix of yellow, orange, and red, the false colours arranged to indicate heat in a way immediately comprehensible. Patches of bright red flowed by their bubble's ovoid space, darkening the angriest oranges, which shaded into the most violent of yellows. In theory it should not have been any more alarming to descend through molten rock than through frozen ice. But in fact it was.

'We will follow channels to the underside of Loki, where we will get shot out of one of the sulphur plumes, is that correct?'

'Yes.'

'And then?'

'We will disable their power plant. That will force them to use their ships to power their settlement. Their ships will thus have to stay on Io.'

'You plan to disable their power plant? That's all?'

She appeared to think he was being sarcastic: 'They'll be all right. Their ships will serve as emergency power. All will be well with them, but the ships will be confined to their base.'

'Couldn't you disable their ships directly?'

The light surrounding them shifted all over the fiery portion of the spectrum, washing Hera's face in colour and making it appear as if she were in turn scowling, grimacing, frowning, glaring.

'You don't understand,' she said at last. 'Not all their ships will be in their settlement at any one time, and I want to create a situation where the ones on hand have to stay put.'

'But the ones at large will still be at large.'

'We think most will be on hand. And Ganymede is there.'

Their craft shuddered underfoot, canted to the side. The flowing ribbons of colour on the screen had the look of a current, in which their craft struggled to make its way upstream; but the feeling of motion, which came entirely from tiny shifts underfoot, was now a confused juddering that did not add up to a coherent picture of progress in any given direction. He guessed that first they had been falling toward the centre of the moon, but were now bumping liquidly along, making way against resistance. Then it seemed they were rising like a bubble in water, shimmying from side to side as differential resistances caused little horizontal slips. He put his hand to his chair, feeling unsettled almost to the point of nausea.

292

'Up?' he asked.

'Up. And I've got some of my cohort meeting us inside here. We'll all come up together.'

Galileo held on. 'Won't they notice us?'

'They'll be assuming any approach will be visible,' Hera said. 'And some of our colleagues are making an approach from space, to serve as decoys. There are no weapons per se in the Jovian system, as I said, but of course various lasers and explosives can be adapted to the task. We'll hope that doesn't go too badly for our decoys, and jump them from behind. This will be the first time anyone has ever been attacked from out of the plume of a volcano.' She laughed.

Then he was shoved down at the floor, and understood that they were accelerating upward. The flows around them stabilized to pure yellow, like being inside a marigold, and he supposed that this meant they were now moving with the current they were in, but that the magma itself was accelerating in its channel as it approached its release into space.

The pressure down became stronger. For a moment his body felt some bone-deep familiarity, and he realized they were in exactly the pull of the Earth, and he feeling his true weight. But quickly he became heavier still, so much so that he let his head rest back in his chair, to keep from hurting his neck. Hera shifted the walls back in place and the colours of the flow around them returned to the screens, while other screens filled with rapidly changing columns of numbers; but none gave him a sense of what was going on. He said, 'Can you not display some sort of map that tells us where we are?'

'Oh sorry. Of course.'

She tapped her console, and the screen in front of Galileo suddenly became like a cabinet holding a little Io. A green thread running from its interior to its surface pulsed brightly from within a tangle of orange intestines. Then the screen changed again, and he was looking at a cross-section of the moon which cut the chimney of their volcanic channel, and the widening at its throat. Mid-throat a small cluster of bright green dots rose swiftly. 'Your colleagues have joined us?'

'Some of them.'

Then the downward pressure ceased, and he even felt that he might float up and away from his chair, as when they were between moons. A push from below returned, very slight; then nothing; then a slight pressure from above. Hera tapped quickly, and suddenly the walls of the craft became invisible again, giving them a view as if they flew freely in space. They were vaulting upward, already many miles above Io, arcing away from Loki Patera over the tawny fluxions of the surface, and the sulphur mist surrounding them was dotted with the silvery ovoid carapaces of the other ships in Hera's fleet. They were all floating down like spores after a mushroom explodes.

The fleet stayed in the drift of sulphur slurry, arranging itself as it fell until it was a phalanx, dropping in synchrony within one particular plume of the sulphur. Then in the final drop to the marigold slag on the lower flank of Loki, the whole fleet shot sideways out of the sulphur rain with startling rapidity, and in several heartbeats landed on the perimeter of a small cluster of buildings, apparently Ganymede's Ionian base. Some of the craft blazed fire as they were touching down, striking buildings in the base and causing brief explosions that seemed as tiny as sparks against the backdrop of the stupendous plume of the volcano.

Galileo was watching all this so intently that he was shocked when a jarring halt to their descent smashed him into his chair.

'We're down,' Hera said. 'Come on.'

'Where to?' he said as he clambered up.

'Their power plant. That's always the real seat of government.'

The grimness with which she said this gave Galileo the impression she had learned this truth in some personally disastrous way. But there was no time to inquire. She stuffed the pewter box of the teletrasporta into a satchel-like compartment on the back of her spacesuit, and then they had the suits on and moved into the craft's anteroom, putting on their space helmets, which reminded Galileo briefly of her memory celatone; then they were out onto the blasted yellow of the Ionian mountain side.

Outside the craft standing on the ground, Galileo looked around. Yellow sleet drifted down onto the slag a few miles away, splashing like rain when it struck. Out of this bizarre fountain shot twenty more sleek oval silver things, rocketing sideways with a dreamy speed. One of these craft tried to land right in the gap between two big low buildings of the settlement; a gate shut on it, and the craft buckled as it was caught. Hera shouted at the sight.

'All crews make straight for the power unit and turn their power *off*!' Hera snapped viciously, reminding Galileo of his mother. Uneasily he understood her as a general conducting a siege; no military officer he had ever met gave him the frisson of fear that he felt now as he regarded her. Imagine Giulia a general! The carnage would have been universal.

'Come on,' she snarled over her shoulder, and started running over the rugged plain toward the base. It had a kind of outer rock wall, it seemed, or was simply built on a broad low plateau. Galileo followed her toward it, struggling to keep up with her. She was big, and fleet of foot in a way he could not emulate, given the light pull of this moon, which caused him to launch up and forward with every stride, landing fearfully but again lightly, so that he could leap forward from one unsteady jaunt to the next, keeping his eye on Hera mid-leap, as it seemed to help his balance.

The slaggy plain of the volcano's side was bigger than it looked. Silver craft still fell like stars out of the black sky. Behind them the towering yellow plume of the volcano rained down, plashing onto its previous spew. Figures in helmets, looking like white statues of the Swiss Guard, emerged from the gates of the settlement, pointing at them. Red afterimages suddenly crisscrossed Galileo's vision, without him having seen anything to stimulate them in the first place. Hera stopped and held out a hand indicating he should stop too. In the general hissing silence which was perhaps the rolling impact of the nearby plume striking him through his feet, he could not hear her voice. He could see that she was talking to him and that she thought he could hear her, but something must have gone wrong with his helmet, because there was no sound but the background hiss.

Abruptly she was off again. Galileo hurried after her, fearful of losing her and therefore his way.

They were approaching the village of silver buildings from an unexpected angle, it seemed, for the defenders were all focused on an attack from the other direction. Hera simply leaped forward onto two of these people, flying twenty or thirty feet before smashing into them like something thrown by a trebuchet. Down they went, while she bounced up and with a ferocious punch to the gut levelled another of them. Galileo followed her as fast as he could, but now she was really off, and no matter how hard he tried he could not keep up. He kept bounding off into space, and as he passed through a gate in a wall between two big buildings he crashed into an arch topping the gate, landing hard on his back and driving the wind out of him, and his guts out of his hernia too. He staggered back to his feet, stuck his fingers between his legs and shoved the truss up so that his guts would go back into his torso. After that he gave up on normal locomotion, instead making clumsy painful leaps forward, like a toad or a grasshopper, gasping all the while. It was truly painful between his legs, but he was moving, and Hera was not far ahead of him when she finally came to a halt. He was mid-leap when he saw her stop and look to her left, and though he tried to twist in mid-air to dodge her, that of course didn't work, and he bowled right into her back. It was like running into a wall, slightly padded; even as he was falling to the ground he was recalling the feel of the contact, the rocky substance of her ribs, the hard muscles of her bottom, with a layer of softness over the brick; then he crashed down on his back and lay stunned at her heels, with his guts once again bulging out of his peritoneum. She had been knocked two or three steps forward by his impact, and in that moment a flash between them blasted him into a red blindness. Blinking through tears and the red bloom of bouncing afterimages, he saw her barking out orders without regard for him, as if he were her dog and had banged into the back of her knees while she was busy doing something.

By the time Galileo had shoved his guts back in and regained his feet, the local situation seemed to have come into compliance with her wishes. Defenders of the city lay twitching on the ground, looking like fish in the boxes at a market.

She grabbed Galileo by the arm, and he indicated that he couldn't hear what she was saying. She reached up and twisted at the outside of his helmet, under his right ear.

'Stand still,' she snapped.

'I'm trying!' he said. 'At least I can hear you now!'

He shrugged free of her hold, which reminded him too much of his mother: the old witch had had just such a clawlike grip. He swayed upright and held himself steady with a desperate effort of his whole body, glaring hotly at her. She was looking right back at him, both their faces behind clear faceplates that glowed with red numbers and diagrams in the corners, making it a literally red look that arced between them. The skin around her eyes crinkled; she was, for some reason, laughing at him.

'Your clumsiness saved my ass,' she said.

Galileo supposed she meant the flash that had blinded him. 'I like your ass,' he said without thinking.

Her eyebrows rose. But she was still amused.

She returned to the business at hand. Her commands were still abrupt, but her tone was not so urgent. The situation was apparently in hand. The power station was occupied, she told him, the Ganymedean village therefore in their hands.

Then, listening to voices Galileo did not hear, her expression again blackened. She cursed and gave a quick series of orders almost under her breath.

'We didn't shut them down fast enough,' she said grimly to Galileo. 'Ganymede and his closest followers escaped. Six craft. Some of them are returning to attack us, presumably so that he can get clean away. We have to get back to the ship.'

'Lead on,' Galileo said.

Outside the settlement, the black starry sky looked down on the scene, still eerily silent. The yellow plume to the east looked taller than a summer thunderhead. Even when an explosion flashed white and demolished one of the buildings behind them, there were no sounds, only a trembling underfoot. Galileo heard nothing but his own gasps, which seemed to come from outside his helmet, as if the cosmos itself were short of breath, and scared.

On the run back to her craft, the ground under his feet began to become sticky. It became like running on a viscous mud.

'Shit,' Hera said. 'Apparently they set off some underground explosions just now. Big ones. One of my people say it's the Swiss defence. The whole base will sink into the ground. A magma chamber has been breached, and it's heating the ground in this area from below.'

'The ground is melting?'

'Yes. We have to hurry.'

'I'm trying.'

But they began to sink further into the ground as they stepped on it, as if they traversed yellow mud that grew deeper and softer. Very sticky mud too. Hera's craft was now visible on the horizon, but they could no longer run. They had to pull up hard at the end of each step to free their feet from the viscous surface, then step forward and sink back into it again. First they were sinking in to their boot tops, then their ankles. Then their shins. The yellow ground, looking granular and knobby with rubble, was quivering and quaking, pulsing under them like a live thing. Soon they were struggling forward knee deep in it. Knee deep, in the melting surface of Io!

'We keep sinking further in,' Galileo pointed out.

'Just keep walking!'

'I am, of course, but you see how it is.'

'Shove your legs forward hard at first, then they'll move easier after that.'

Now they were struggling through viscous rock that reached to the tops of their knees.

'Will our suits melt?'

'No. But we do need to stay above the surface.'

'Obviously.'

She wasn't listening to him. They were wading forward through the molten surface now, thigh deep and working hard. Her craft was still a long way off.

Finally she stopped and pulled something out of her suit.

'Here,' she said, looking around and conferring in a low voice with her colleagues. 'I've got a sheet here I can sit on, that will keep me afloat long enough for my friends to get here and pick me up. But I don't know if it will hold both of us up long enough, so I'm going to use the entangler to send you back to your time.'

'But what about you!'

'I'll use the sheet and float by myself, like I said. We're not that much denser than the sulphur.'

'Are you sure?' Galileo exclaimed, wondering if she were preparing to die.

'I'm sure.' She cast a thin silver sheet out over the lava, and they crawled onto it, rolling quickly to the middle to keep the edge of the sheet from shoving too far down into the melting rock. They huddled together in the centre of the sheet, and Galileo could see that the friction of the sheet spread over the rock would hold them up, for a while anyway.

'Get in the field of the entangler,' she said as she pulled the box from the pack on the back of her spacesuit. She patted the sheet before her.

They sat cross-legged, knees touching, sinking rather slowly into the sheet. She placed the flat square box between them and tapped at its surface. Finally she looked up, and they regarded each other face to face through their faceplates.

'Maybe you should come back with me,' Galileo said.

'I need to stay here. I've got to deal with all this. The situation is completely fucked up, as you see.'

'You're sure you'll be all right?'

'Yes. My people are on their way. They'll be a while, but they'll get here in time, if you aren't weighing me down. Now get ready to go back. I don't have any amnestics with me, so you will remember all this. It will be strange. It could be bad, but –' She shrugged. There was no alternative.

'You'll bring me back when you can?'

Again a brief moment, a shared look –

'Yes,' she said. 'Now,' tapping the teletrasporta, 'go.'

Chapter Thirteen   Always Already

We aren't even here but in a real here
Elsewhere – a long way off. Not a place
To go but where we are: there.
Here is there. This is not a real world.
                                        – WILLIAM BRONK

Laid out in the garden shivering, Galileo looked around himself.
There he was, looking around himself. It was just before sunrise,
at Bellosguardo. In the dawn light the citrons on their branches
glowed like little Ios.

Cartophilus was sitting on the ground beside him, wrapped in
a blanket. He had thrown another one over Galileo's supine
form. Galileo croaked at him and Cartophilus gave him a cup of
watered-down wine. Galileo sat up and drank it, gestured for
more. Cartophilus refilled the cup from a jug.

Galileo drank again. He blinked, looking around him, sniff-
ing, then crumbling a clod of dirt in his hand. He regarded the
citron bush curiously, leaning toward the big terra cotta pot containing it.

'How long was I gone?'
'All night.'
'That's all?'
'Did it feel longer?'

'Yes.'

Cartophilus shrugged. 'You were gone longer than usual.'

Galileo was staring at him.

Cartophilus sighed. 'She didn't give you the amnestic.'

'No. They were too busy fighting. I left Hera on Io, sinking into lava! Do you know her?'

'I know her.'

'Good. I want to go back and help. Can you send me back now?'

'Not now, maestro. You need to eat, and get some rest.'

Galileo considered it. 'I suppose I need to give her time to get out of that fix, anyway. If she can. But soon.'

Cartophilus nodded.

Galileo poked him with a finger. 'This stranger of yours, the Ganymede – did you know he is a kind of Savaranola? That his cult is reviled by the rest of the Jovians, and that now they are fighting?'

'Yes, I'm aware of that.' Cartophilus gestured at the teletrasporta. 'I can see here what happens to you there, if I stay in the complementary field. As for Ganymede, I am not one of his people any more. I just tend the device. I stay with it. Things around Jupiter are always changing. The people in power aren't the same. Their attitude toward entanglement is not the same.'

'How long have you been keeping this end of the teletrasporta?'

'Too long.'

'How long?' Galileo insisted.

Cartophilus waggled his hand. 'Let's not talk about it now, maestro. I've been up all night, I'm tired.'

Galileo yawned hugely. 'Me too. I'm thrashed. Help me up. But later we are going to talk.'

'I'm sure.'

* * *

303

That winter Galileo's illnesses struck him worse than ever, and he stayed in bed for months, often writhing and moaning. Sometimes he shouted furiously, others he shuddered epileptically, or spoke in Latin as if in conversation with someone invisible, sounding engaged and curious, surprised, humble, even supplicatory – all tones his voice never contained when he spoke to the living, when he was always so peremptory and sure.

'He speaks with the angels,' the servant Salvadore ventured. The boy was often too frightened to go into his room. Guiseppe thought it was funny.

'He just doesn't want to work,' La Piera muttered. She would barge in on him no matter his state, and demand that he eat, that he drink tea, that he lay off the wine. When he was conscious of her presence he would curse her, his voice hoarse and dry. 'You sound just like my mother. My mother in the disgusting form of a cook shaped like a cannonball.'

'Now who sounds like your mother. Drink something or die whining.'

'Fuck off. Leave me. Leave the drink and go. I had a real life once! I got to speak with real people! Now here I am, trapped with a bunch of pigs.'

Some days he sat upright in bed and wrote feverishly, page after page. The things he said and wrote got stranger and stranger. In a letter to the Grand Duchess Christina he changed the subject abruptly and wrote, *The open book of heaven contains such profound mysteries and such sublime concepts that the labour and studies of hundreds of the sharpest minds, in uninterrupted investigation for thousands of years, have not yet completely fathomed them. This idea haunts me.*

Another time he got up from bed, where he had been only semi-conscious, and went to his table saying 'Pardon me, I need to get this down,' in a soothing voice none of us had ever heard before, and wrote a new page in a letter to a correspondent named Dini, a page that read like the Kepler he had always laughed at: *I have already discovered a constant generation on*

the solar body of dark substances, which appear to the eye as
very black spots which then later are subsumed and dissolved;
and I have discussed how they could perhaps be regarded as part
of the nourishment (or perhaps its excrements) that some
ancient philosophers thought the Sun needed for its sustenance.
By constantly observing these dark substances, I have demon-
strated how the solar body necessarily turns on itself, and I have
also speculated how reasonable it is to believe that the motion of
the planets around the Sun depends on such a motion –

After which he had returned to his bed and fallen comatose again. And there it was, in writing, him saying to a stranger that the sun was a living creature, eating and shitting, slinging the planets around itself by its rotation, like bangles extending from a top. Was this heresy, was it insanity? Could he not help himself? He had to know it was dangerous to commit such thoughts to print after Bellarmino's warning, but he seemed helpless to stop himself, under the spell of a compulsion no one could comprehend. He only slept a few hours every night, and babbled in his sleep.

He pulled himself out of bed one morning and went out to collar Cartophilus. Rough hands at the ancient one's neck: 'Get out your teletrasporta, old man. I need to get back up there to Hera. Now.'

Cartophilus had no choice but to obey, but he didn't like it. 'This is a bad idea, maestro. You need to have the other end ready to receive you.'

'Do it anyway. Something's wrong. Maybe up there too, but definitely here. Something's wrong in my mind.'

Cartophilus went to the closet where he slept and came back with the small but heavy pewter box that had replaced the stranger's telescope some years before. He worked at its knobs for a time, muttering unhappily. 'Get next to it,' he said.

Galileo sat next to the box, swallowing involuntarily. Where would she be now? What if the teletrasporta was at the bottom of a lake of liquid rock?

Nothing happened. 'Come on,' Galileo said.

'I'm trying.' Cartophilus shook his head. 'There's no response. I wonder if she disabled the other resonance box.'

'I wonder if it sank into the lava,' Galileo said. 'And her too.' He shuddered. 'I need to go back! There's something wrong here.'

'What do you mean?'

'I . . . When I was there last, I got a mathematics tutorial from Aurora, do you know her? No? A wonderful mathematician, and she and her machines were teaching me. They immerse you in the mathematics itself, it's like flying. You have done it?'

Cartophilus shook his head.

'Well, you should. But I saw they had immersions that teach you about the mathematicians of the past, so that for instance you could find yourself in the world of Archimedes, and Euclid, and Archytas, as in a dream but still conscious, and there was one for me. And so I took that immersion. I was just curious to see what they would say about me. But it wasn't what I thought. It was more than a biography. You lived it, but all at once too. I saw my life! They had recorded it!'

Cartophilus sighed. 'I know. I saw it too. When they first made the entanglers they did a lot of things, for years and years. Event engineering, mnemostics, all that. It took a while before people turned against them.'

'Well, I can see why they did.' Another shudder. 'I saw too much. It wasn't just learning a – a bad fate, off in the distance. It was everything.'

'Why didn't you stop it?'

'I did! But not before I saw too much. Now I know what will happen. I mean, day by day. I'm sure I know all of it, but I can't quite bring it to mind until it happens. But it bulks there behind every moment, every thought.' His grip on Cartophilus's arm was like an iron clamp. 'While I was up there it didn't seem to matter. Now it does.'

'Do something different,' Cartophilus suggested.

He almost lost his arm for it, Galileo clutched him so. 'I've tried,' Galileo moaned, 'but it doesn't work. The different thing is what I already did. I follow myself as if from a couple of steps behind. It's horrible.'

'Like a Rückgriffe?'

'What's that?'

'That's German for something like "retroceptions".'

Galileo shook his head. 'It's more like foresight.'

'Syndetos means bound together, so an asyndeton is when the connections between things goes away. The French call that jamais vu.'

'No. I am all too connected.'

'Déjà vu, then. The French have a whole system. Already seen.'

'Yes. That would be one way to say it. Although it isn't seeing so much as feeling. *Already felt*. Always already. Here – try Hera again. Get me there.'

Cartophilus attended to his device. 'There's still no response,' he said after a while. 'She may be busy with other matters. Let's try it again later, maestro. You're killing my arm.'

Galileo let him go, slumped down beside him, bereft. 'Damn. I hope she's all right.' He heaved a big sigh. 'This will kill me faster than anything.'

We all have seven secret lives. The life of excretion; the world of inappropriate sexual fantasies; our real hopes; our terror of death; our experience of shame; the world of pain; and our dreams. No one else ever knows these lives. Consciousness is solitary. Each person lives in that bubble universe that rests under the skull, alone.

Galileo struggled on with his new sickness, his ability that was a disability, alone.

*   *   *

Some of his friends were like La Piera, and wondered if his illnesses were not perhaps a little too convenient. For the fact was, in the first months of 1619 more comets had appeared in the night skies, alarming everyone. For a while no one spoke of anything else, and the unearthly phenomena filled all the horoscopes and the pages of the *Avvisi*. Of course all the astronomers and philosophers had to weigh in with an opinion on these new apparitions, and naturally, as before, everyone waited to hear what the notorious astronomer of the Medicis would say about them.

But the Dominicans were watching, the Jesuits were listening; everything he wrote or said would eventually get reported to the Holy Office of the Index, and to the Holy Congregation. As with the comets that had shown up a few years previously, it was not obvious if or how they might fit into either the Ptolemaic or Copernican cosmologies; but they were undeniably in the sky. How convenient, then (everyone said), that Galileo was so sick he could not even go out on his terrace in the evening and take a look! Galileo, the greatest astronomer in the world! What a chicken!

Silence from Bellosguardo.

Life limped along, day after tumbled day. Galileo had never looked so ill before. 'Everything has already happened,' he would complain, surveying his visitors as if they were all new acquaintances. 'Everything is happening for the second time. Or perhaps for the millionth time, or simply infinitely.' Or he would insist, even to strangers: 'I am out of phase. I am living in the wrong potential time. She sent me back to the wrong self. It's an interference pattern, the one where the two equal waves cancel each other out! That's what's happening to me! I'm not really here.'

A letter was going to come from Maria Celeste. It came, and as he had always done, he took out the little stiletto he used as a letter-opener and watched himself cut the wax of the seal neatly away. He had unfolded it in just the way he unfolded it, and he read what he had read. *Of the candied citron which you ordered, I have only been able to make a small quantity. I feared the citrons were too shrivelled for preserving, and so it has proved. I send two baked pears for these days of vigil.* He tasted the fruit he had been going to taste, and it tasted the way it was going to taste when he tasted it. It had an underlying bitterness, as with all his life. But she was also going to have put a rose and two baked pears in the basket, as he saw when he saw them. *But as the greatest treat of all I send you a rose, which ought to please you extremely, seeing what a rarity it is at this season.* Indeed the time was out of joint, things blooming out of season. Really there was nothing but asynchronous anachronism. Time was a manifold full of exclusions and resurrections, fragments and the spaces between fragments, eclipses and epilepsies, isotopies all superposed on each other and interweaving in an anarchic vibrating tapestry, and since to relive it at one point was not to relive it at another, the whole was unreadable, permanently beyond the mind. The present was a laminate event, and obviously the isotopies could detach from each other, slightly or greatly. He was caught in a mere splinter of the whole, no matter how entangled with the rest of it. Caught in what his poor brilliant daughter called *the darkness of this short winter of our mortal life*, the words of her letter jumping off the page, the phrase something he had always read, like a prayer said every night of his life. Each moment reiterated. The brevity and darkness of the winter of our mortal life.

He followed himself out into the garden. The world became as it was as it was. The day would be what it had always been. Sun struck the back of his neck. The great Saint Augustine had also felt this pseudo-iterative feeling, he would notice in his desperate reading. Had the deepest of all the Christian philosophers also encountered the stranger? No one else Galileo knew had ever written about time the way Augustine did: *Which way soever then this secret fore-perceiving of things to come, be; that only can be seen, which is. But what now is, is not future, but present. When then things to come are said to be seen, it is not themselves, which as yet are not (that is, which are to be), it is rather their causes perchance or their signs that are seen, which already are. Therefore they are not future but present to those who now see that from which the future, being fore-conceived in the mind, is foretold. Which fore-conceptions again now are; and those who foretell those things, do behold the conceptions present before them.*

That was right there in *The Confessions*, Book XI. Augustine made no conclusions in the long feverish chapter that held his meditation on time, but only confessed to his own confusion. Of course he was confused; and so was Galileo. These thoughts had always been there, and now he read them just after they generated themselves spontaneously in his head. It gave him a headache to read like that.

But in the garden he would sit still, and think. It was possible, there, to collapse all the potentialities to a single present. This moment had a long duration. Such a blessing; he could feel it in his body, in the sun and air and earth sustaining him. Blue sky overhead – it was the part of the rainbow that was always visible, stretching all the way across the dome of sky. Sitting there he knew he would go back inside and eat, and try to write to Castelli. He was going to shit without shitting his guts out his second asshole. It was going to hurt. He would be standing at the edge of his field at sunset, watching the last light burnish the tops of the ripe barley, praying for the consolation of the sky. There was nothing for it but to pace through just behind or ahead of the spooling present that was never there, caught in the nonexistent interval between the nonexistent past and the nonexistent future. He would precede and follow his own footsteps. It would happen later, as he had already seen. It had already happened, as he would see later.

*   *   *

Finally, one spring morning just after sunrise, Galileo roared furiously from his bedroom. What inspired his defiance of the pseudo-iterative no one knew, and to him it was still just a matter of obeying the compulsion of the now; but after the trembling happy boys had helped him to dress, cringing at his every move, each of which looked like the start of a blow, which they would have welcomed to see even as they dodged, he hobbled out to the narrow terrace that overlooked Florence in the valley below them to the north. Down there the Duomo stood above the sea of tile rooftops like something from a different world, bigger and more geometrical. Like a little moon come down to earth, or like the nubilous clouds rafting over it.

Over his shoulder he growled to La Piera, 'Bring me breakfast. Then have the boys move my desk out here. No doubt I have letters to catch up on. I'll just have to follow myself out there and work through it. Hopefully it will feel like being a scribe making copies. Someone else can do the thinking.'

Everyone in Bellosguardo ignored his grousing, pleased by his actions. The maestro had returned to life – surly life, it was true, ill-tempered, whining life – but better than the miserable limbo of the winter. He would spend much of the next few weeks writing fifteen or twenty letters a day; it always happened that way when he snapped out of a funk. He was sick so often that even his recovery period was a ritual they all knew.

'Send me Cartophilus,' he said to La Piera, when she brought out food and wine at the end of a long day of scribbling and cursing.

When he had finished eating, staring at each biscuit and capon leg as if it were entirely new to him, the ancient servant stood before him.

Galileo surveyed him wearily. 'Tell me more about déjà vu.'

'There isn't much to say. It's a French term, obviously. The French language has always been very analytical and precise about mental states. Déjà vu is the feeling something has happened before. Presque vu is the feeling that you almost understand something, usually something important, but you don't quite.'

311

'I feel that all the time.'

'But mystically, I mean. A really big spiritual tip of the tongue moment.'

'Pretty often, even so. I feel like that pretty often.'

'And then jamais vu is a sudden loss of comprehension of anything, even just the ordinary day.'

'I've felt that too,' Galileo said thoughtfully. 'I've felt all of those.'

'Yes. We all do. When some French were assembling an encyclopedia of paranormal experiences, they decided to leave déjà vu out, because it was so common it could not be considered paranormal.'

'That's for sure. Right now I am stuck in it all the time.'

Cartophilus nodded. 'Why didn't she give you the amnestics when she returned you?'

'There wasn't time! I barely got out of there alive. I told you, I need to go back. Hera's in trouble. They all are. They need an outside force to arbitrate.'

'I can't do it without them doing their part at their end. You know.'

'I don't know. I want you to get me back. I can't stand this, it's like torture. It will kill me.'

'Soon,' the old man said. 'Not right now. I'll ask again, but there hasn't been a response. It may be some while. But that won't matter in the end, if you see what I mean.'

Galileo glared at him. 'I don't, actually.'

Cartophilus picked up an emptied platter. 'You will, maestro. You will or you won't, but nothing to be done about it now.' And he slunk away in his usual craven manner.

The latest letter from Maria Celeste had come. He will open it.

You having let the days go by, Sire, without coming to visit us, is enough to provoke some fear in me that the great love you have always shown us may be diminishing somewhat. I am

312

inclined to believe that you keep putting off the visit because of the little satisfaction you derive from coming here, not only because the two of us, in what I suppose I would call our ineptitude, simply do not know how to show you a better time, but also because the other nuns, for other reasons, cannot keep you sufficiently amused –

'Get some food on the mule,' Galileo had snapped at the boys. 'Be ready in an hour. Go.'

Galileo had long since beaten a path of his own over the hilltops between Bellosguardo and the convent of San Matteo in Arcetri. Every time he walked or rode over, he took a basket of the food he grew at Bellosguardo. For the sake of the nuns he had shifted the focus of his gardening to staple crops, so on this morning the mule was loaded down with bags of beans, lentils, wheat, and garbanzos; also zucchini, and the first of the gourds. He will add a bouquet of lupines he found in bloom around the borders of the piazza. Already it was well into spring; he had missed a lot of the year.

This morning was one he had very definitely lived before: the mule, the hills, the boys ahead, Cartophilus behind, all under whatever sky the day might bring. Today it would be high clouds like carded wool. The previous fall he and Maria Celeste had begun collaborating on jellies and candied fruits, so that both establishments might have some variety and pleasure in their diet; hanging from the mule also was a bag of citrons, lemons, and oranges. They still looked like little Ios to him.

On the way Cartophilus would keep well behind, and it was too nice a morning for Galileo to want to talk to him anyway. They would be arriving at San Matteo just after midday. Convent rules forbade outsiders to go into most of the buildings, and the nuns were forbidden from going outside; supposedly they were required to have a screen to be set between them and any visitors. But over the years the screen had slowly shrunk to

313

a waist-high barrier, and finally been dispensed with altogether, so that Galileo and his daughter could embrace, and then sit side by side in the doorway looking out at the lane, Maria Celeste holding him by the hand.

These days she was even thinner than she had been as a girl, but she was still bright and outgoing, and obviously attached to her father, who served as a kind of patron saint for her. Livia, now Suor Arcangela, on the other hand, was more withdrawn and sullen than ever, and never came out of the dormitory to see Galileo. From reports it appeared she was uninterested in anything but food, which was a bad sole interest for a Clare to have.

Maria Celeste, whom he persisted in thinking of as Virginia, today would be overjoyed to see him again. She would inquire repeatedly about his health, and seem surprised when he did not want to discuss it. He would see that this was one of the only subjects of conversation in the convent, perhaps the principal one. How they felt; how they were too hot or too cold; and always, how they were hungry. He would have to bring bigger baskets of food. He had given up trying to slip his daughters gifts he could not give to the other nuns; Maria Celeste felt it was wrong. So if he wanted to help her and Arcangela, he would have to help all of them. But that he couldn't afford.

They had talked as they ate a dinner together with the abbess; then it was time to go, if they were to get back to Bellosguardo in the light.

On the mule on the way back he would be silent, as usual. He had the grim look he always had when thinking about family or money; perhaps the two simply went together. His annual retainer from the Medicis was a thousand crowns, more than the Grand Duke paid anyone except his secretary and his generals; and yet still it wasn't enough. His expenses continued to mount. And much of it had to do with family. He supported the old gargoyle, of course. His sister Livia, who had left the convent she had entered in order to get married, had been unable to keep her odious husband Landucci from abandoning her. This after he had sued Galileo for non-payment of what was really Galileo's brother's part of her dowry. Livia had come to Galileo for shelter, then died while he was in Rome; died of a broken heart, the servants said. Now Galileo had the care of her children. And Landucci was suing yet again for non-payment of Michelangelo's portion of the dowry – talk about déjà vu – even though he had left the marriage and the abandoned wife was dead. Meanwhile Galileo's invertebrate brother had sent his own wife and seven kids to Galileo while he stayed in Munich and continued trying to make a living as a musician. That was family.

So even though Galileo was no longer teaching, and took in no student boarders, the household in Bellosguardo consisted of about the same number of people it had had in Padua, where people had often called the big house on Via Vignali the Hostel Galileo. Roughly forty people – he didn't even bother to keep count any more. La Piera kept the house accounts, and very capably. She always gave him the bad news with a straight face. They were running at a loss. Galileo had *definitely* lived these things before. And no one had ever bought a celatone, or ever would; and the ones he had given away, in hope of creating orders, had been expensive to manufacture.

A bad time came to Tuscany, years of plague, years of death. Sagredo asked him to think about a telescope for looking at things close up, to see more clearly objects like paintings and Cellini's medallions, and Galileo and Mazzoleni worked up a thick rectangular lens, convex on both sides, which worked admirably, and which gave Galileo ideas for a compound lens system that might work even better; but then word came that Sagredo had died, with no warning and very little illness. The shock of it was like a sword thrust to Galileo's heart; his knees buckled when he heard it. Giovanfrancesco, his big brother, gone.

Then his mother Giulia died: September, 1620. After eighty-two years of making everyone in her life miserable. Galileo made all the arrangements for the funeral, he emptied and sold her house, he dispersed the money to his sisters and his hapless brother, all without a word or a sign, staring grimly at the walls as the furniture and goods left the place, revealing it to be pitifully small. For a long time it had been a comfort to him to realize that his mother was insane, and had been for the entirety of his life. But not now. *She was angry. She was a person just like you, just as smart as you. She wanted what anyone would want. Everyone is equally proud.* In one of her cabinets at the bottom of a mass of papers he found two glass lenses, one concave and one convex.

Then Cardinal Bellarmino died, leaving no one alive who knew exactly what had passed between him and Galileo in the crucial meetings of 1616.

Then Grand Duke Cosimo died, after many years of illness: Galileo's patron, gone at age thirty. This was the kind of disaster his Venetian friends had warned him against, when he had opted for Florence's patronage over Venice's employment.

But Cosimo's heir, Fernandino II, only ten years old, was put under the joint regency of his mother, the Archduchess Maria Maddelena, and his grandmother, the Grand Duchess Christina. In Christina Galileo still had his patron, which was a very lucky thing. She took up his offer to tutor the new prince as he once had his father, and on they went, Galileo and his Medicean stars. This particular arrangement did not lead to much time with the boy, and when Galileo did meet with him he found it a very melancholy thing – instructing and entertaining a sweet little boy of ten, who so resembled his father at the same age that it was uncanny to experience, like living a loop in time – another way his life was repeating itself, although he himself grew older at every repetition. A particularly dark kind of déjà vu. He walked in his own footsteps.

Then Marina died. When the maestro got the news from Padua, he sat out on the terrace of Bellosguardo all night long, a fiasco of wine at his side. The telescope was set up, but he did not look through it.

More than once that night he recalled the time the two women had fought so furiously, and he had stood there holding them apart. How these things stick in the mind. *Everyone is equally proud*. Now when he relived that scene he held them apart with his heart full of an anguished affection. They had been strong people. Lady Fortuna had seized him from both sides and kicked him through the world! He had been crucified between two harpies. He could even for once see the comedy of that ridiculous scene. No doubt the servants had laughed about it for years afterward. Now he laughed himself, full of remorse and love.

Then Pope Paul V died. The cardinals gathered in Rome, and could not agree on a successor; in the end they elected an obvious place-holder, Alessandro Ludovisi, an old man who chose the name Gregory XV. No one had any expectations of him, but as soon as he was invested he named two Lynceans to secretarial posts, an excellent sign, possibly a portent of things to come. Certainly Cesi was pleased. But for the most part everyone waited for the next puff of white smoke to tell them who would really shape the next period in their lives.

Meanwhile Galileo continued to work desultorily, in a daze of regretful expectation. He took on various studies: what could be seen through a microscope; magnetism again; the strength of materials again; even, since he had Mazzoleni there, a return to some of his old work on the inclined planes, trying to recapture that magic. He wrote letters to his ex-students, and looked for new ways to supplement his income. Every week, sometimes more often, he visited his daughters at San Matteo, riding the old mule over the track he had beaten into the hills. They were suffering there; he always came home distressed at their threadbare hunger. 'In this world a vow of poverty is going too far!' he would complain to La Piera. 'They would be poor even if they took a vow to prosper! Make up another basket for them and send it with the boys.' He had changed his gardening practices even more drastically, and the new crops made it more a farm than ever; he grew beans, garbanzos, lentils, and wheat, and in a big oven, built under Mazzoleni's supervision, they were now baking bread, and cooking big pots of soup and casseroles to strap to the mule and take over to the sisters. Also sacks and bushels of uncooked beans and grain. Still, there was no way he could grow enough to feed all thirty of the sisters of San Matteo. They were the thinnest group of nuns he had ever seen, although all nuns were thin. And Maria Celeste the thinnest of them all.

He gave no lectures to the Florentine court. He wrote no books. He contrived no tests or demonstrations. He did not even want to go to Venice for Carnivale; he claimed now that he had never liked Carnivale, which was odd, because everyone could remember how much he had enjoyed it in the old days, how much he had loved any party or festival. Some in the house joked that now he understood it marked the beginning of Lent, which he had definitely never liked; others said it was because it reminded him too much of his iron truss. In any case, now he looked confused, even alarmed, whenever Carnivale was mentioned.

One night, unable to sleep, he sat out on the piazza looking through a telescope at Saturn. Jupiter was not in the sky. Saturn seemed to be some kind of triple star, oddly wide and shimmering, not with fulgurous rays but with bulbous articulations that made it look like a head with ears. He had seen that first in 1612, then watched the ears go away over the years, and Saturn become a sphere like Jupiter; now the ears had reappeared, and he could write to Castelli that he should expect to see them in full in 1626. They were not there yet, but on the way. It was an odd thing.

But the heaviness in Galileo did not allow him to vibrate to this sight in his usual way, much less to ring. It had been many years since he had rung like a bell at the discovery of some new thing. And really, the objects seen through the telescope had been disenchanted for him by all that he had seen in his proleptic visitations

318

to Jupiter. People would inhabit the stars and yet remain as petty and stupid and contentious as ever – all the vices fully active, in fact, still writhing as lustily as ever in their vicious ways. It was horrible.

He would pick up his lute and pluck a tune of his father's that he called 'Desolation'. His father, so quiet and withdrawn. Well, imagine what it must have been like, living with Giulia all those years. No matter how valid the causes, she had not been sane. Later the mnemosynes would help the insane, and people's characters in general would be smoothed by society as if on a lathe, but in his time they were hacked out by chisels and hatchets, and crazy people were really crazy. If you lived with one you had to withdraw somehow. But no one could disappear. Some parts remained in the world. And so this tune, the saddest he had ever heard. His old man, sitting there at the table looking down as the old rolling pin pounded him. Sometimes Vincenzio would try to argue with her, first reasonably, then snapping and shouting like she did, but always at half speed compared to her. His thought was adagio, while her thought and tongue were always presto agitato. Not that he had been unintelligent, rather the reverse; he had been a fine musician and composer, and he had written books about the theories and philosophy of music that were still admired all over Italy for their profounod thoughts; and yet in his own kitchen the nightly debates revealed him most cruelly to be only the second smartest person in the house – and really, after Galileo reached about the age of five, the third. It must have been disheartening. And so he had died. Without your heart you died. This late tune of his was a kind of last confession, a shriving, a testament. A remaining thought of his, still alive in this world.

In the shadows under the arcade there was a movement. Somebody up and about, skulking.

'Cartophilus!'

'Maestro.'

'Come here.'

The ancient one shuffled out. 'What can I get you, maestro?'

'Answers, Cartophilus. Sit down beside me. Why are you up so late?'

'Had to pee. Is that the answer you wanted?'

Galileo's low 'Huh huh huh huh,' like the huffing of a boar. 'No,' he said. 'Sit down.' He handed the old man the jug of wine. 'Drink.'

Cartophilus had already been drinking, as became clear when he abruptly collapsed on one of Galileo's big pillows, groaning as he folded into a tailor's position. He rolled the jug over his bent elbow and took a long pull.

'How old are you, Cartophilus?'

Another groan. 'How can I tell, maestro? You know how it is.'

'How many years have you been alive, that's all.'

'Something like four hundred.'

Galileo whistled low. 'That's old.'

Cartophilus nodded. 'Don't I know it.' He drank again.

'How old do you people live to?'

'It isn't certain, as far as I know. I think the oldest people are about six or seven hundred. But they're still going.'

'And how long have you been here in Europe, with the tele-trasporta?'

'Since 1409.'

'That long!' Galileo stared at him. 'Where was it that you appeared? Did you come with the first arrival of the thing? And how did it get here, when it was not here to bring it?'

The old man put up a hand. 'Do you know about the gypsies?'

'Of course. They are supposed to be wandering Egyptians, as you are supposed to be the wandering Jew. They come into towns and steal things.'

'Exactly. Except really they came from India, by way of Persia. The Zott, the tsigani, the zegeuner, the Romani, et cetera. Anyway, we pretended to be a tribe of them, in Hungary in 1409. We were the ones who started what the gypsies call *o xonxano baro*, the great trick. In those days there was a different attitude toward penitents. We found we could go from town to town and say that we were nobles of lesser Egypt who had briefly fallen into paganism and then reconverted to Christianity, and as a penance we were to be homeless wanderers and beg strangers for help. We might even say we had accidentally offended Christ himself and so were forced to wander forever after, asking for alms, and that worked just as well. We also had a letter of recommendation from Sigismund, King of the Romans, asking people to take us in and treat us kindly. Thus the Romani. And we could tell fortunes with startling accuracy, as you might imagine. So the tricks worked everywhere we went. We could say anything. Sometimes we told them that we had been ordered to wander for seven years, and during those years we were allowed to thieve without being liable to punishment for it. Even that worked. People were credulous.' He laughed a mirthless laugh.

'And you had the teletrasporta with you the whole time?'

'Yes. Ganymede was with us as well, visiting off and on. He had tried all this before, you see. He made an earlier analeptic introjection, trying to get the ancient Greeks to develop science to the point of igniting a technological revolution very much earlier in the human story.'

'Ah ha!' Galileo said. 'Archimedes.'

'Yes, that's right. He even showed him a laser –'

'– the mirror that could burn things at a distance!'

'Yes, that's right. But it didn't work. The analepsis, I mean. It was too anachronistic, there was no way to build the culture around the knowledge. Ganymede found out that the manifold is not so easily changed – to the despair of some of us, and the great relief of others, as you might imagine.'

'I should think so! What if he had changed you all right out of existence? You might have disappeared on the spot!'

'Well, maybe so. But how would that be any different from the way it is now? People disappear all the time.'

'Hmm,' Galileo said.

'Anyway, judging by a kind of tautology, since we existed, we didn't think it could happen. And the manifold of manifolds doesn't really work like that. I am not competent to speak to the physics involved, but I think I catch a glimpse of it in the analogy of the river mouth, with braiding channels, each one of which is a kind of reality, or a potentiality.'

'That's the one Aurora told me about.'

'It's a common image. You have your three or four or ten billion currents running concurrently, and tides running back upstream, and the riverbeds themselves all shifting in the force of the various flows. Anastomosing. Some water goes upstream, some downstream, the banks get eroded, there's cross-chop on the surface, and so on. Some streambeds go dry and get ox-bowed, while new ones are carved.'

'Like at the mouth of the Po.'

'I'm sure. So, Ganymede thought he could kick a riverbank so hard that the subsequent erosion would carve an entirely new river downstream, if you see what I mean. But it isn't like that. There's a bigger topography somehow. And a single kick . . .'

He took another drink of wine, wiped his mouth. 'In any case, it didn't work. Archimedes – he got killed. And all that was lost. Even that device, that teletrasporta, to use your word for it.'

'Please do. It's better than entangler – I mean, everything is already entangled, so that's not what the device is doing.'

Cartophilus actually smiled at this. 'You may be right. Whatever you call it, there's one of them on the bottom of the Aegean somewhere. It's likely to last a long time, too. It was disguised to look like an Olympic calendar, but that won't be enough to explain it if it's ever found.'

'How did Ganymede get back to Jupiter?'

'He returned at the last moment before his ship sank. Determined to try again. He's a stubborn man, and the nature of analepsis makes it possible to try over and over. He decided he needed more time to prepare, to help on the scene. He read intensively in the historical record, and visited various resonant times, and decided you were his best chance to make a significant change in the disaster centuries that follow you. But he wanted to visit Copernicus too, and Kepler.'

'So you came back as gypsies.'

'Exactly. With a different teletrasporta, probably the last one. I doubt they will send back any more.'

'That's what Hera said, but why not?'

'Well, results have been uncertain, or bad. And there are philosophical objections to that kind of tampering. We are all entangled always, as you said, but introjections are a kind of assault on another part of time, according to some people. It's been controversial from the start. Also, the energy requirements to actually move a device in the antichronos dimension are prohibitive.' He shook his head. 'You wouldn't believe it.'

'I might. I had quite a tutorial last time I was up there.'

'Well, you know how Jupiter is a gas giant, and Saturn is another, also Uranus and Neptune and Hades. Five gas giants.'

'Yes?'

'Well, before the analepses that sent back the devices, there were seven gas giants. Cronus and Nyx were further out, so far out that their gravitational effect on the other planets was not crucial to the inner orbits. People argued against destroying them, but the interventionists did it anyway. They needed the power. Ganymede was part of that too. Black holes were created that sucked gas in, and the collapse energy was used to push everything in a small field antichronologically. After a device was back here, it was possible to shift consciousness back and forth with hardly any energy expended. It's more a case of just stepping into the complementary field.'

'And how many teletrasportas were sent back?'

'Something like six or seven.'

'And so you came back with this one, to be a gypsy.'

'Yes.' Cartophilus heaved a big drunken sigh. 'I thought I could do some good. I was an idiot.'

323

'Don't you ever want to go back?' Galileo asked. 'Couldn't you go back?'

'I don't know. Even Ganymede has gone back for good, have you noticed? He's done what he wanted to do here. Or decided the situation at home is so important he needs to be there. There's only a few of us left here. It's hard to stay here.' He stopped speaking for a while, took another slug. 'I don't know,' he muttered finally. 'Cartophilus can always leave if he wants to.'

'Cartophilus? You speak of someone else?'

The ancient one gestured weakly. 'Cartophilus is just a . . . performance. No one is really there. One tries not to be there.'

Galileo, startled, looked at him closely. 'But what sadness this sounds like! What guilt!'

'Yes. A crime.'

'Well,' Galileo said. 'Still, it must be in the past. Now is now.'

'But the crime goes on. All he can do now is . . . deal with it.'

Galileo's eyes narrowed. 'Do you know what happens to me? Are you trying to make it happen? Have you already made it happen?'

The old man raised his hand like a beggar warding off a blow. 'I'm not trying anything, maestro. Truly. I'm just here. I don't know what I should do. Do you?'

'No.'

'Does anybody?'

All Galileo's friends, and the Linceans especially, wanted him to reply to the attacks that had been made on him in the work on the comets published under the name Sarsi, which he knew was a pseudonym for the Jesuit Orazio Grassi. Galileo had avoided writing this response for a long time, feeling there was nothing to be gained by it, and much to be lost. Even now he was unwilling to venture it, and complaining about the situation. But with Paul V gone, and Bellarmino also gone, Galileo's friends in Rome were convinced that a new opportunity lay before them.

And Galileo was their Achilles in the ongoing war with the Jesuits.

Mostly Galileo ignored these pleas for action, but a letter from Virginio Cesarini, a young aristocrat he had met in Rome at the Academy of Lynxes, caused him to laugh, then groan: *Knowing you has marvellously inflamed in me a desire to know something.* This was the laugh. *What happened to me in listening to you was what happens to men bitten by little animals, who do not yet feel the pain in the act of being stung, and only after the puncture become aware of the damage received.* This was the groan. 'Now I'm a wasp,' Galileo groused. 'I'm the mosquito of philosophy.'

I saw after your discourse that I have a somewhat philosophical mind.

The strange thing was, he did. Typically people were quite wrong when they felt they were philosophical, as one of the chief features of incompetence was an inability to see it in oneself; but Cesarini turned out to be quite a brilliant youth, sickly but serious, melancholy but intelligent. And so, if he too was writing to ask Galileo to write about the comets, adding his aristocratic position and wealth to the influence of Cesi, Galileo's best advocate in Rome . . .

'God damn it.'

Mazzoleni regarded him with his cracked grin. He had heard all about it, a thousand times or more. 'Why not just do it, boss?'

Galileo heaved a sigh. 'I'm under a prohibition, Mazzo. Besides, I'm sick of it. All these questions from the nobility, they never stop, but to them it's just a game. It's banquet entertainment, you understand? Why do things float or sink? What are tides? What are sunspots? How should I know! These are impossible questions! And when you try to answer them you can't help but run afoul of fucking Aristotle, and thus the Jesuits and the rest of the dogs. And yet really we don't know enough to say one way or the other. You know what it's like – we can barely figure out how fast a ball rolls down a table! So answering these silly people's questions just gets me in trouble.'

'But you have to do it.'

Galileo gave him a sharp look. 'It's my job, you mean, as court philosopher.'

'Yes. Isn't that right?'

'I suppose it is.'

'You thought when you stopped teaching in Padua, you would be able to do anything you wanted.'

'I suppose so.'

'No one gets that, maestro.'

Another sharp look. 'You impertinent old fool. I'll send you back to the Arsenale.'

'I wish.'

'Go away or I beat you. In fact, go get me Guiducci and Arrighetti. I'll beat them.'

These two young men, private students he had taken on as a favour to Grand Duchess Christina, joined him in the workshop where his crew had made the celatones. He showed the two youths his old folios, filled with the notes and theorems from all his work on motion in Padua. 'I want you to make fair copies of these,' he told them. 'We worked fast back then, and we didn't have much paper. See, there are often several propositions per page, and on both sides. What I want you to do is move each proposition or set of calculations onto a single sheet, using one side only. If you have any questions as to what's what, ask me. When you're done then maybe we can make some progress on all this.'

At the same time as all this, however, despite his fears and premonitions, his near certainty that it was a bad idea, he watched himself begin to write a treatise on the controversy concerning the comets.

Now the truth was, as he would explain in conversation when friends visited Bellosguardo, he really had been sick, and had only observed the comets when they were visible once or twice, out of curiosity. So he did not know what they were, and probably would not have known even if he had observed them more.

326

He could only offer suppositions based on what he had heard. So on the one hand as he wrote he questioned the whole basis of the phenomenon, and wondered if a comet was merely sunlight on a disturbance in the upper atmosphere, like a night rainbow; and then also he suggested, with his usual edge, that whatever it was, it surely did not fit any of Aristotle's celestial categories. Along the way he could make fun of 'Sarsi's' lame logic, for Grassi had made some real howlers attempting to explain what he had no grounds for understanding. And so, as Galileo sat on his high chair before his desk, writing in the shade on the terrace in the mornings, he would add observations and arguments that made for a defence of his method of observation and experiment, of mathematical explanations. Of avoiding the why of things, and concentrating first on the what and the how. Mornings spent writing about these matters were a good distraction from everything else, and the pages piled one on the next. Sometimes it was nice to just be following yourself through the motions of the day. It certainly made writing easier.

In Sarsi I seem to discern the firm belief that in philosophizing one must support oneself upon the opinion of some famous author, as if our minds remain sterile and barren unless wedded to the reasoning of some other person. Possibly he thinks that philosophy is a book of fiction by some writer, like The Iliad *or* Orlando Furioso, *productions in which the least important thing is whether what is written there is true. Well, Sarsi, that is not how matters stand. Philosophy is written in this grand book, the universe, which stands continually open to our gaze. But it cannot be understood unless one first learns to comprehend the language and recognize the letters in which it is composed. It is written in the language of mathematics, and its characters are triangles, circles, and other geometric figures, without which it is completely impossible to understand a single word of it. Without these, one wanders in a dark labyrinth.*

While with these concepts, on the other hand – Galileo thought but did not write, looking at his words and feeling the bulk of futurity in him – with these concepts, the universe is blasted by a light, as if a great flash has exploded in your eyes. Everything is clear, all too clear, to the point of transparency; and one walks as if in a world of glass, seeing too far, running into things not quite noticed, the present moment just one abstraction among a host of others. Hera was right; no one should know more than his moment can hold. The future inside you pushes for its release, and the pain of living with that canker is like no other pain.

There was no recourse but to try to forget. He became expert at forgetting. As part of the work of that forgetting, he wrote. To write was to live in the moment, and say what one could there, put it down and forget it, letting the rest fall away.

Once again he told the story of how he had first learned of the telescope. *In Venice, where I happened to be at the time, news arrived that a Fleming had presented to Count Maurice a glass by means of which distant objects might be seen as distinctly as if they were nearby. That was all.*

Well, not exactly; not at all, in fact. But he felt defensive about it. Someday people would know. But there was nothing for it, so he returned to the demolishing of the malevolent 'Sarsi':

There is no doubt whatsoever that by introducing irregular lines Sarsi may save not only the appearance being discussed, but any other. Lines are called regular when, having a fixed and definite description, they can be defined and can have their properties listed and demonstrated. Thus the spiral, or the ellipse. Irregular lines then are those which have no determinacy whatever, but are indefinite and casual and hence undefinable; no property of such lines can be demonstrated, and in a word, nothing can be known about them. Hence to say, 'Such events take place thanks to an irregular path' is the same as to say, 'I do not know why they occur.' The introduction of such supposed explanations is in no way superior to the 'sympathy', 'antipathy', 'occult properties', 'influences', and other terms employed by some philosophers as a cloak for the correct reply, which would be: 'I don't know.' That reply is as much more tolerable than the others, as candid honesty is more beautiful than deceitful duplicity. I don't know!

But long experience has taught me this about the status of mankind with regard to matters requiring thought: the less people know and understand about them, the more positively they attempt to argue concerning them; while on the other hand, to know and understand a multitude of things renders men cautious in passing judgement upon anything new.

While he was at work on this new treatise, Pope Gregory died, as expected; Galileo was not unlike many others in feeling this was foreordained and unsurprising, as if it had already happened. And over a long malarial summer, the convocation of cardinals would decide on the new Pope.

But this time they couldn't do it. They appeared to be truly deadlocked; weeks passed, the manoeuvring between the great families was intense but stalemated, the rumours in Rome and all over Italy flew like clouds of flies. It went on so long that six of the eldest cardinals died of exhaustion. Only late in August did the white puff of smoke emerge from the chimney in the Vatican.

The announcement was brought up to Bellosguardo in person by the Medici's secretary Curzio Picchena. Emerging from his coach onto the terrace resplendent in his best finery, his arms outspread, a big smile lighting his face, 'Barberini!' he exclaimed. 'Maffeo Barberini!'

For once Galileo Galilei was speechless. His jaw dropped, his hand clapped over his open mouth; he glanced wild-eyed at Cartophilus, then threw his arms wide and howled. He hugged La Piera, who had come out with the other servants to see what was going on, and then called the whole household to join the impromptu celebration. He fell to his knees, crossed himself, looked at the sky, dashed tears from his eyes.

Finally he rose and took Picchena by both hands.

'Barberini? Are you sure? Can it be true? Gracious Grandissimo Cardinal Maffeo Barbarini?'

'The very same.'

It was astonishing. The new pope – that very cardinal who had written a poem in honour of Galileo's astronomical discoveries of 1612; who had argued on Galileo's side in the debate with Colombe over floating bodies; who had conspicuously stayed away from the proceedings of 1615 which had put Copernicus on the Index; above all, who had written Galileo a letter signed 'Your Brother.' Urbane, worldly, intellectual, literary, liberal, handsome, young – he was only fifty-three, too young for a pope really, as Rome relied on a frequent turnover of popes – which was one reason no one had expected this outcome – but still, there it was. Pope Urban VIII, he had named himself.

Weak with amazement, with enormous, dizzying relief, Galileo called for wine. 'Break open a new cask!' Geppo brought him a chair to sit on. 'We have to celebrate!' But he was almost too weak to do so.

That night he woke Cartophilus and dragged him out to the telescope.

'What's going on?' he demanded. 'This is new, this didn't happen before!'

'What do you mean?'

'You know – everything that has been happening this year, I've felt it as if it had already happened. It's been hell. But this, Barberini become pope – it's new! I had no premonition.'

'That's strange,' Cartophilus said, thinking it over.

'What does it mean?'

Cartophilus shrugged. He met Galileo's gaze. 'I don't know, maestro. I'm here with you, remember?'

'But did you not know what happened, before you came back as a gypsy? Don't you remember this or not remember this?'

330

'I don't remember if I remember right or not, anymore. It's been too long.'

Galileo growled, raised his hand to cuff the man. 'You lie.'

'Not at all, maestro! Don't hit me! I just don't know. It's been too long.'

'But you came to me with the Ganymede, you stay with me and watch me, you don't go back to Jupiter – and you say you don't know?' He bunched his fist.

'I stay here because I have nowhere else. Cartophilus has to play his part. And now I'm used to it. I like it. It's home. The sun, the wind, the trees and birds – you know. This is a real place. You can sit in the dirt. You yourself have noticed how *removed* they are up there. I don't think I can go back to that.'

They stared at each other in the darkness. Galileo let his arm fall.

Everything was changed. The Linceans were overjoyed at the opportunity that this new Pope represented, what they called a *mirabile congiunture*. They begged Galileo to finish his treatise, which he was now calling *Il Saggiatore*. It was the word used to describe those who weighed gold and other valuables – *The Assayer* – but Galileo meant more than that by it, hoping to suggest the kind of weighing done by those who put all nature on the balance, like Archimedes: *The Experimenter*, one might say, or *The Scientist*.

But the Assayer too, sure: in this case he was weighing Sarsi's Jesuitical arguments, and finding them wanting. Knowing Pope Urban VIII would be one of the readers of his book – its ultimate reader, its recipient, one might say – he began to write in a more literary and playful style, pastiching the Pope's own liberal writing. He considered what he loved in Ariosto, and took pains to do similar things. He had long since understood that all these debates were a kind of theatre, after all.

If Sarsi wants me to believe with Suidas that the Babylonians cooked their eggs by whirling them around in slings, I will do it;

331

but I must add that the cause of this cooking of the eggs was very different from what he suggests. To discover the true cause I reason as follows: 'If we do not achieve an effect which others formerly achieved, then it must be that in our operations we lack something that was part of their success. And if there is just one single thing we lack, then that alone can be the true cause. Now we do not lack eggs, nor slings, nor sturdy fellows to whirl them; yet our eggs do not cook, but merely cool down faster if they happen to be hot. And since nothing is lacking to us except being Babylonians, then being Babylonians is the cause of the hardening of the eggs, and not friction of the air.' And this is what I wished to discover. Is it possible that Sarsi has never observed the coolness produced on his face by the continual rush of air when he is riding post? If he has, then how can he prefer to believe things related by other men as having happened two thousand years ago in Babylon, rather than present events which he himself experiences?

Sarsi says he does not wish to be numbered among those who affront the sages by disbelieving or contradicting them. I say I do not wish to be counted as an ignoramus and an ingrate toward Nature and toward God; for if they have given me my senses and my reason, why should I defer such great gifts to the errors of some mere man? Why should I believe blindly and stupidly what I wish to believe, and subject the freedom of my intellect to someone else who is just as liable to error as I am?

Finally Sarsi is reduced to saying with Aristotle that if the air ever happened to be abundantly filled with warm exhalations in the presence of various other requisites, then leaden balls would melt in the air when shot from muskets or thrown by slings. This must have been the state of the air when the Babylonians were cooking their eggs. At such times things must go very pleasantly for people who are being shot at.

Ha ha! The Linceans laughed; they loved passages like this when Galileo sent them along for revision and approval. This was the first time Galileo had ever submitted drafts of a book to a committee of fellow philosophers, and though he found it frustrating, it was interesting as well. It was going to be a statement with the imprimatur of the Academy of Lynxes, and with that it would enter the Roman intellectual wars, where the new was now battering the old into the ground. Cesi begged him to finish the book, and then come to Rome and rout the Jesuits utterly. Cesi would publish it in the name of the Linceans, and had already had the title page altered so that the book would now be dedicated to Urban VIII.

Good surprises kept happening: Cesarini was made an official member of the Academy of the Lynxes, and four days later the new Pope made him a cardinal. So a Lincean was now a cardinal! And the Pope also appointed his own nephew Francesco to be a cardinal, that very same Francesco whom Galileo had just helped to obtain a teaching position at the university in Padua!

Galileo began to believe Cesi: this was indeed a *mirabile congiunture*. It might even be possible to get Copernicus taken off the list. So he wrote more of his treatise every day. He sent letters to Cesi and the other Linceans, promising to finish the revisions they had suggested to him. Cesi had the publication scheduled in Rome. He urgently wanted Galileo to come to the capital. Galileo wanted it too. He made the request to Picchena to be allowed to go, and after some hesitations, Picchena and the Medici lady regents agreed to the plan. Preparations for another trip to Rome were made, and the book was almost finished.

Near the end of *Il Saggiatore*, the first book Galileo had published since the ban of 1615, he dispensed with the sarcastic attacks on Sarsi, and made some philosophical points that were new. These would come back to haunt him later:

I must consider what it is that we call heat, as I suspect that people in general have a concept of this which is very far from the truth. For they believe that heat is a real phenomenon, or property, or quality, which actually resides in the material by which we feel ourselves warmed. Now I say that whenever I conceive any material or corporeal substance, I immediately feel the need to think of it as bounded, and as having this or that shape, as being large or small in relation to other things, and in some specific place at any given time; as being in motion or at rest; as touching or not touching some other body; and as being one in number, or few, or many. From these conditions I cannot separate such a substance by any stretch of my imagination. But that it must be white or red, bitter or sweet, noisy or silent, and of sweet or foul odour, my mind does not feel compelled to bring in as necessary qualities. Without the senses as our guides, reason or imagination unaided would probably never arrive at qualities like these. Hence I think that tastes, odours, colours, and so on are no more than mere names so far as the object in which we place them is concerned, and that they reside only in the consciousness. Hence if the living creature were removed, all these qualities would be wiped away and annihilated.

Very deep stuff, and strangely, even suspiciously ahead of its time. But Galileo knew perfectly well that he was describing his state of mind *before* Aurora's tutorials; that was something he wanted to do here, just to clarify his thoughts in their evolution. He wrote as he had always written. That it was also true that what he was calling effects of consciousness extended beyond heat and tickling and taste and colours, to fundamental qualities like number, boundedness, motion or rest, location or time – that was something he knew but still could not feel. It remained a conundrum to him, part of the feeling of anachronism always disorienting him.

That these sentences of *Il Saggiatore* could be construed as denying the reality of the transubstantiation of the bread and wine into Christ's body and blood, during the sacrament of communion – that they were, in other words, according to the Council of Trent and the doctrinal law of the Holy Church, heretical statements – did not occur to Galileo, nor to any of his friends and associates.

But it did to some of his enemies.

*　　*　　*

In the midst of all this excitement, the weekly letter would arrive from Maria Celeste: *As I have no bedroom of my own, Sister Diamanta kindly allows me to share hers, depriving herself of the company of her own sister for my sake. But the room is so bitterly cold, that with my head in the state it is in these days, I do not know how I will be able to stand it there, unless you can help me by lending me a set of those white bed-hangings which you will not want now. I should be glad to know if you could do me this service. Moreover, I beg you to be so kind as to send me that book of yours which has just been published, so that I can read it, as I have a great desire to see what you have said.*

These few cakes I send are some I made a few days ago, intending to give them to you when you came to bid us adieu. Sister Arcangela is still purging herself, and is much tried by her remedies, especially the two cauteries on her thighs. I am not well myself, but being so accustomed to ill health, I do not make much of it, seeing too that it is the Lord's will to send continual little trials like this. I thank Him for everything, and pray that He will give you the highest and best felicity. To close I send you loving greetings from me and from Suor

> *Arcangela.*
> *Sire's Most Affectionate Daughter,*
> *S. M. Celeste*
> *You can send us any collars that want getting up.*

Galileo heaved heavy sighs and had blankets sent over to the convent, and with them a letter asking Maria Celeste if there was anything else he could do. He was sure to go to Rome sometime soon to meet with the new Pope, he told her; he could ask the Sanctissimus for something for the convent, perhaps some land to generate income; perhaps a direct endowment, or some simpler form of alms; what did she think the nuns would like most?

Maria Celeste wrote back to say that alms would be very well, but what they needed most was a decent priest.

335

Galileo cursed when he read this. 'Another priest! They need food!'

Her letter went on to explain: *Since our convent finds itself in poverty, as you know, Sire, it cannot satisfy the confessors when they leave by giving them their salary before they go: I happen to know that three of those who were here are owed quite a large sum of money, and they use this debt as occasion to come here often to dine with us, and to fraternize with several of the nuns; and, what is worse, they then carry us in their mouths, spreading rumours and gossiping about us wherever they go, to the point where our convent is considered the concubine of the whole Casentino region, whence come these confessors of ours, more suited to hunting rabbits than guiding souls.*

Galileo couldn't be sure if she knew what hunting rabbits meant in Tuscan slang, or if she actually meant hunting rabbits; but he suspected the former, and laughed, both shocked and pleased at her sophistication.

And believe me, Sire, if I wanted to tell you all the blunders committed by the one we have with us now, I would never come to the bottom of the list, because they are as numerous as they are incredible.

She was so smart. Surely she was her father's daughter; for the acorn never fell far from the tree (except when it did, as with his son). Indeed it sometimes seemed to Galileo that Maria Celeste was the only sane and competent nun in the entire convent, carrying the other thirty on her slim shoulders, every day and every night: supervising the cooking, nursing their ills, making their preparations, writing their letters. Keeping her sister out of the wine cellar, which apparently was a new problem to add to all Arcangela's others. Maria Celeste's letters to Galileo were almost always written in the seventh or eighth hour of the day, which began at sunset, meaning she was only getting a couple of hours of sleep before the bell rang for compline, and their pre-dawn prayers would begin. The relentless routine was beginning to tell on her; she had no meat on her bones, there were always dark rings under her eyes, and she complained of stomach trouble; she was losing her teeth; all this and more, and she was just twenty-three years old. He feared for her.

And yet still her letters came, each one exhibiting intense care to make it shapely on the page, utilizing her characteristic clear hand with its big loops, and the flowing proud signature at the bottom.

But so often filled with trouble. One morning Galileo watched himself opening a letter from her and felt himself full of a sudden dread, and started to read, then shouted with alarm. 'Oh *no*! No! Jesus Christ! Pierrrrrrr-a! Find Cartophilus and tell him to get Cremonini ready. Their mother abbess has gone mad.'

This worthy was no longer Vinta's sister but another woman, small, dark, and intense. 'She's slashed herself thirteen times with a kitchen knife,' Galileo told La Piera as he pulled on his boots. 'These people are not competent to live!' he exclaimed bitterly.

La Piera hustled off with a shrug; convents were like that, the shrug said. But she was angry too. 'I'll come along,' she said as she reappeared.

On the way over the hills to San Matteo, it was easy to feel that all this had happened before, because it had. His feet had made the very track through the grass that they now followed. It all just kept happening. Sky as grey as rain.

Over at San Matteo they found things even worse than Maria Celeste had reported, which was not unusual, but this time far beyond anything previous. Not just the mother abbess but also Arcangela had lost her mind, and on the very same night. Arcangela had apparently heard the abbess screaming in her suicidal hysteria, and in response had begun banging her head against the wall of her room. She had done that until she fell insensible. Now she was conscious, but refusing to speak even to her own sister, who clung to Galileo's arm red-eyed with fear and grief. All around her was nothing but weeping and lamentation, as all the sisters demanded her attention at once.

337

Seeing it Galileo lost his temper and said to them loudly, 'It's like a hen house with a fox inside it, except there's no fox, so you should all shut up! What kind of Christians are you anyway?'

This last sentiment started Maria Celeste crying too, and Galileo enfolded her in his arms. They looked like a bear holding a scarecrow pulled from its pole. She wept on his broad chest, into his beard. 'What happened?' he asked again helplessly. 'Why?'

She composed herself, and led him back to the dispensary as she told him the story. The mother abbess had been more and more anxious, upset about problems that she would not confess to anyone. At the same time, Suor Arcangela had stopped speaking entirely. The latter had happened before, of course, and although it was a cause for concern there was nothing they could do about it, as they knew from long experience. 'So we were limping along the best we could, when last night the full moon brought on a lunacy in the mother abbess. She was heard crying out, and when we went to her chambers to see what was wrong, we found her slashing her arms with one of the kitchen knives, and moaning. In the uproar we didn't hear Arcangela yelling in her room,' – a private room that Galileo had paid for, to keep her out of the dormitory at night, where she had trouble sleeping, and disrupted the others as well. 'When we finally heard Arcangela, I was the first one there, and I found her – pounding her forehead – hard! – against the wall! The bricks had cut her and she was bleeding. It was a cut on the forehead, you know how those bleed. Her face was covered with it. And she still wouldn't speak. It took four of us to get her to stop beating her brains out, and now she is restrained on her bed. She's just begun to talk again. But all she does is beg to be let free.'

'You poor girl.' Galileo followed the shivering Maria Celeste to his younger daughter's room.

Arcangela saw him in the doorway and turned her battered head away. She was tied to the mattress with innumerable strips of cloth.

Then: 'Please,' she begged the wall. 'Let me go.'

'But how can we,' Galileo asked her, 'when you harm yourself like this? What would you have us do?'

She would not answer him.

After sunset, in the last hour of light, they headed back to Bellosguardo. It was clear to all of them that no matter Maria Celeste's courage and ability, they had left behind a convent in desperate disarray. On the trail over the hills, Galileo was full of heavy sighs. That night he sat at the table before his roast capon and bottle of wine, and barely ate. La Piera moved around with as little noise as possible.

'Fetch Cartophilus to me,' Galileo said at last.

A few minutes later the old man stood before him in the lantern light. Clearly he had been asleep.

'What can I do, maestro?'

'You know what you can do.' With a look as black as any of Arcangela's. The family resemblance in that moment was startling.

Cartophilus knew when Galileo could not be denied. He ducked his head and nodded as he left the room.

That night when Galileo was out on the terrace, looking stubbornly through his telescope at his little Jovian clock in the sky, Cartophilus emerged from the workshop, carrying the pewter box under one arm.

'You'll send me to Hera?' Galileo said.

Cartophilus nodded. 'I'm pretty sure she still has the other end of it.'

When Cartophilus had prepared the box, Galileo stood next to it. He looked up at Jupiter, so bright up there near the zenith. Suddenly it bloomed.

Chapter Fourteen Fear of the Other

In order to produce a significant shift in the collective psyche, it would require a great many more people than are at present able to integrate their animality into their conscious mind. At present, powerful women who reject the Eve complex, and males who are ridding themselves of misogyny, tend to trigger or inflame the misogyny of those caught in the Thanatos complex. There is simply not a powerful enough female or feminine object of the ego ideal to pull women away from the patriarchal archetypal structures that maintain misogyny, let alone pull men away. The next movement in the evolution of the collective psyche has to be a spiral return to the archetypal mother.

         – J. C. Smith, *Psychoanalytic Roots of Patriarchy*

Black space, the dense spangle of stars; the great bulk of Jupiter, almost entirely sunlit, surreally present to the eye, crawling phyllotaxically with its hundreds of colours and thousands of convolutions –

He was sitting in his chair in Hera's little space boat, which was again rendered transparent, a kind of Plato's cave through which the cosmos poured in. Below and behind them the virulent ball that was Io jumped out of the starry blackness.

'You're back,' she noted. Her teletrasporta lay on the floor beside his chair. 'Good.'

'Where are you going?' he asked.

'To Europa, of course.' She looked at him. 'We're still trying to keep Ganymede and his people away from there.'

'You got off the melting land, I see.'

'Yes, I was picked up by my people pretty soon after you left. Good that you did leave, though. It was touch and go.'

'How long ago was that?'

'I don't know, a few hours maybe.'

'Pah!' Galileo blew out through his lips. 'Pah.'

'What?'

'For me that was a few years ago.'

She laughed. 'Proof again that time is not a steady progression, that it fluctuates and eddies, and we are in different channels. I hope you have been well?'

'Not at all!'

'How so?'

'I was sick. And I remembered what was happening here, and also what will happen to me there. It was all in me at once. Not only what you showed me, the fire I mean, but also, I have to confess – I used Aurora's tutorial to take a look at my life, the last time I was with her. To see the science. I didn't know it would be so – comprehensive. It wasn't just someone's account. I was *there*. Only it was all at once.'

'Ah.'

'Since then I seem to be dislocated somehow. Not in the moment, but a bit behind it, or before. I knew what was going to happen. Not really, but it felt like it. It was bad. Unsustainable. Can you – can you help me with that, Lady?'

'Maybe.'

He shuddered, remembering, then brightened: 'On the other hand, there's a new Pope, a man who has been like a patron to me. I think I can get him to lift the ban on discussing Copernicus. I think it's even possible to persuade him to approve the Copernican view, to make it the Church's understanding, so that the Church itself will support it! And then I'll be safe.'

341

She stared at him, shaking her head. 'You still don't get it.'

'Things at home aren't so good,' Galileo went on, ignoring her. 'But maybe His Holiness can help there too.'

She sighed. 'What do you mean?'

'Well – my daughters are in a convent. But their order is too poor. A lot of them are sick, and some have gone mad. I'm hoping I can get this new pope to grant them some land. Because it's bad for my daughters.'

'You are the one who put them in their situation, right?'

'Yes yes.' Then, trying to distract her: 'What will you do when we get to Europa?'

She saw through him. 'Distract me or not, you are still stuck in a situation you don't understand.'

There was nothing he could say to that. 'I don't see that I'm much different than you,' he parried lamely.

She brushed that aside. 'It has always been the same pope in charge when you are condemned to be burnt at the stake.'

This startled Galileo. 'Of course,' he temporized. 'But, if I could convince him to support the Copernican view, then surely . . .'

She only stared at him.

'I think it can work,' Galileo ventured. Then: 'You said you would help.'

She only shook her head.

They seemed to float without moving. The great banded giant stood off to one side, impossible to believe. The whorls and eddies within each tawny band moved, slightly but visibly, and the imbricating borders where band met band moved even faster, their viscous colours crawling over each other like snakes. Hera's transparent bubble of a craft only just shifted over this massive spectacle, such that its terminator, that smooth border of sunlight and shadow, rolled westward at a speed they barely could see. By close attention one could spot the progressive illumination of new embroideries in the bands.

But all these stately contradances were as motions in some syrupy dream, and Galileo could see that Hera was impatient for action. She tapped at her console in her usual way, had several fraught conversations with absent colleagues he could not hear; then she fell silent, brooding over problems Galileo was not privy to.

'How long till we get there?' he asked.

'Hours. Europa is on the other side of Jupiter right now, unfortunately.'

'I see.'

Time passed; seconds, minutes: it became tangible, like something you could hold in your hands, or weigh on a scale. Protraction.

Finally she sighed. 'Put the mnemonic back on,' she said. 'We might as well keep working. I can perhaps also block some of your memories from the life lesson you so rashly entered. So there are things you need to forget, and things you need to remember. Because you are still misunderstanding your situation at home.'

Galileo regarded her memory celatone uneasily. Mostly he feared what another immersion would reveal to him; but there was an awful fascination in it too. That the mind held within it such vivid scraps of the past – there was a majesty to that, full of pain and remorse – and a desire, despite all, for all the lost time somehow to come back. I want my life back! I want life back. And then also, to lay down so many memories so fully in the mind, and yet be unable ever to call them back – what were they, to be so oddly made? What could God have been thinking?

'Where will you send me?' he asked apprehensively. 'What knowledge will you flay me with this time?'

'I don't know. There's so much to choose from, maybe we'll just go spelunking. Your brain is full of trauma nodes.' She scanned her console screen, now apparently displaying maps of his brain, there visible to his sidelong glance in virulent pulsing rainbows. 'Maybe we should continue with your relations with the women in your life.'

'No!'

'But yes. You don't want to be one of those supposed scientific geniuses who is also in his home life a jerk and a fool. There are more than enough of those already. It would be a shame if the first scientist were to be also the first of that crowd of assholes.'

This was interesting news, but also offensive. 'I did my duty,' Galileo objected. 'I took care of my family, I supported my sisters and my brother and their families, and my mother and my children, all the servants, all the artisans, all the students and hangers-on – the whole damned menagerie! I worked like a donkey! I wasted my life paying for my wastrel family!'

'Please. Self-pity is simply the reverse side of bravado, and just as unconvincing. That's something you never seemed to learn. You lived a life of privilege that you took for granted. You started with a little bit of privilege and leveraged it upward, that's all.'

'I worked like a donkey!'

'Not really. There *were* people who worked like donkeys, literally, in that they were porters and carried burdens for their living, but you weren't one of them. Let's see what your own mind tells you about that.'

Roughly she put the helmet on his head, and he did not really resist her. Where in his lost life would he return to?

With an odd look, perhaps of pity, almost of affection, a kind of indulgent *amorevolezza* that was very affecting to see in someone so *amorevole*, so lovely, she reached out to touch him on the side of the head.

It was mid-summer, very hot and humid, and the Count da Trento had invited Galileo's colleague Bedini to his villa in Costozza, in the hills above Vincenza. Galileo, recently arrived in Padua with the entirety of his worldly possessions in a single trunk, had been introduced to everyone by Pinelli, over wine in Pinelli's library of eighty thousand volumes. Bedini and Pintard were two of these new friends, and now, courtesy of Bedini's noble friend, they were off to the hills together.

At the Villa Costozza they joined their convivial host and did just what they would have done at home, eating and drinking, talking and laughing, while the Count opened bigger and bigger bottles of wine, until they were hoisting fiascos and balthazars and small casks, and had eaten most of three geese, along with condiments, fruits, cheeses, and a great number of pies; and all on a day so hot that even here in the hills they were sweating greasily.

Finally the Count was overcome, and staggered off to vomit like a Roman. The young professors groaned at the prospect, feeling stronger than that. It seemed if they jumped in one of the villa's fountains or pools they could immerse themselves to cool their stomachs and slow their bile. When he returned, the Count shook his head groggily as they proposed this. 'I have something even better,' he said, and led them to a back room on the ground floor, where the villa had been dug into the hillside. In this room the plaster wall did not meet the marble floor, and out of the black gap between wall and floor flowed a cold humid breeze, making the whole room as cool as an ice pantry. 'It's always like this,' the count mumbled, still gasping a little from his vomiting. 'There's a little spring somewhere down there. Please, be my guest. On days like this I simply lie on the floor. See, here are some pillows. I would join you, but I fear I must retire again,' and he stumbled off.

Laughing at him, the three drunk young men pulled off their clothes, groaning and joking and elbowing each other, and arranged the pillows as bedding and fell on them with happy moans and snorts. And there in the cool relief, after sliding right onto the marble and oohing and aahing like pigs in mud, all three of them fell asleep.

Galileo was hauled out of an ugly red dream by the Count and his servants. 'Signor Galilei! Domino Galilei, please, please! Wake up!'

'Qua – ? Qua – ?'

His mouth would not form words. He could not focus his eyes. They were dragging him by the arms over the rough floor, and he felt his butt scraping over flagstones as from a great distance, while hearing someone else's groans. He wanted to speak but couldn't. The groans were his. Looking up as if from the bottom of a well, he felt a nausea so deep that it seemed if he vomited he would throw up his bones. Someone nearby was groaning in a truly heart-rending way. Ah – he himself again. It was frigidly cold . . .

When he came to again, the anxious Count and his retainers surrounded him as if looking down into his grave. 'Signor, it's good to have you back,' the Count said solemnly. 'Something made you three very sick. I have no idea what it could have been. The air out of the hill is usually very fresh, and all the food and wine was checked, and seemed fine to the servants. I don't know what could have happened! I'm so sorry!'

'Bedini?' Galileo said. 'Pintard?'

'Bedini has died. I'm so sorry to tell you. It's really a mystery. Pintard is in a state like yours. He has roused a couple of times, but is now fallen into a catalepsy again. We are keeping him warm and dripping some spirits into his mouth, as we did with you.'

Galileo could only gag. He too could have died. Death, the fundamental nausea; he felt the horror of it, then the terror.

Hera's big white face. She stared into his eyes. 'You could have died right there.'

'I almost did. I was never right again.'

'Yes. Almost died of an excess of privilege.'

'Of poisoned air!'

'The poisoned air of a rich man's villa. You ate yourself sick, you drank yourself into a stupor. And it wasn't the first time, or even the hundredth. While your women drudged and starved. Had the babies and raised the children and did all the real work, the work that's work. The woman you had children with, she

346

didn't even know how to read, isn't that what you said? Didn't know how to add or subtract? What kind of a life is that?'

'I don't know.'

'You did know.'

She reached out. Touched him on the forehead.

When Marina told him she was pregnant, part of him was pleased; he was thirty-six years old, and had been with two hundred and forty-eight women, if his count was right, and none had ever reported to him that he had gotten her pregnant. Of course they had their ways, and some of the regulars made you hood the rooster, but still he had had reason to wonder if he were sterile. It could make sense that he was like a mule, in that his father had mated with some kind of gorgon. Not that the lack of children bothered him, given the women and children already underfoot everywhere in his household, screeching for his attention. But it was nice to know one was normal, like any other healthy animal or plant. In his garden everything flourished, and so he should too in his way.

But it was a bit of an embarrassment as well. Here he was angling to become the tutor of the little Medici, one of his best chances of improving his patronage and getting back to Florence, and yet nothing had proceeded there yet, and it was not going to be any kind of help if people said Oh Galilei, he got his Venice girl pregnant, a fishmarket puttella, a Carnivale puttana who can't even read. Her fine qualities would only make them nod their heads knowingly and conclude Galileo had lost his head, that his cock led his fate, that he was not really a courtier, that he was a bit of a drunken obnoxious fool. And of course his enemies said that every time his name came up. It was not that hard of a case to make.

All this passed through his mind in less than a second. He sat her down on the edge of the Grand Canal, on the steps of the Riva Sette Martiri, and said, 'I'll care for the child, and for you too, of course. La Collina will be made the godmother, and Mazzoleni the godfather, and I'll set you all up in a house near mine in Padua. You'll move there.'

'Ah yeah.'

Her mouth had turned down into a bitter cast that he had never seen before. It had a swoop like a gull's wing. He was leaving her, so she was leaving him – this was what her look said.

She sat there holding her belly. She was (he suddenly saw) starting to show. A bit pale and sweaty, perhaps with morning sickness. She nodded, looking down at the trash floating on the canal, thinking her own thoughts. She gave him another sidelong look, sharp as glass under a fingernail.

Then she looked away, roused herself. She was realistic, a smart girl. She knew how things went. That he was going to support her and the child was perhaps even as much as she had been hoping for. Although one always hopes for more than one hopes for, as he well knew. And they had been in love. So he felt a little flash of vertigo as he watched her slip away. Things would never be the same, he could see that already. But there was no other choice for him. He had to get patronage, he had to work. So this was the way it had to be. He would have to cheer her up.

But that look. In his voluminous Catalogue of Bad Looks, this one was perhaps the worst. A whole life ended there.

'It all could have been different,' Hera said. Black space, her white face, bilious Jupiter crawling above them. The stars.

'I know,' Galileo said, subdued. Marina was dead now, a ghost from his past; and yet there she had sat, on the fondamente in his mind, as vivid as Hera herself. The two were not that dissimilar in some ways.

'You made your children illegitimate. The son without prospects, the girls unable to marry.'

'I knew I could put the girls in a convent. They're better off there.'

She merely looked at him.

'All right then,' Galileo said, 'send me back earlier than that! You want me to change the, the *fire* – let me change this too!'

'I don't think so.'

'Because you need my science! You don't want me to go back and change my life in a way that will damage my work! You see? I had to do it!'

'You could have done both.'

He held his head in his hands, felt the celatone on him like a condemned man's hood. 'So what's the point? Why do you torture me like this?'

'You need to understand.'

He snorted. 'You mean I need to have my nose rubbed in my mistakes. I lived with a prostitute, it wrecked everything. You make me feel like shit! How does that help me?'

Relentless as Atropos, she said, 'Look again. You have to keep looking. This is the essence of Mnemosyne's physic. In the nothingness which extends behind you, the blackness that you call the past, there are certain luminous points, isolated and discrete. Fragments of your former life that have survived the loss of the rest. Behind you then is not blackness, but a starlit blackness, constellated into a meaning. Without that constellation there is no chance of a meaningful reality in your present. The living force of those small fires you are discovering make you whatever you are, they constitute a sort of continuous creation of yourself, of the being you are by way of the being you have been. Those crucial moments, unachieved in their time, are entangled with the present always, and when you remember them, they give birth to something that is then achieved, that is your only reality. So look now. Look at your work. First – hmmm – let us look at it in the light of your relations with Marina.'

She touched his head.

*　　*　　*

349

Belasario Vinta came to him and asked him to do a horoscope for the Grand Duke Ferdinando, who was sick. Galileo was both pleased and nervous. The gratuity would come in handy, and the Medicis were his best chance for patronage; Grand Duchess Christina was already almost in hand, having asked him to teach mathematics to her son Cosimo, Ferdinando's heir. Galileo was not surprised when Vinta told him she was also the source of this new request. She was frightened.

Galileo had studied astrology, and it was precisely this that made him uneasy. Vinta stood there regarding him, waiting for his response.

'Of course,' he said. It wasn't a request one could refuse, as they both knew. 'Tell His Serenity the *meraviglioso* that I am most deeply honoured, *obbligatissimo*, and that I will attend to the matter directly. And give him my best wishes concerning his health. Has he considered consulting Acquapendente? I have been cured many times by that great doctor.'

'The Grand Duke has his own doctors, but thank you. How soon can he expect your horoscope?'

'Oh, let us say a week, or perhaps ten days –' As it was not the kind of thing that should be performed too quickly. 'But in any case, as fast as I can.'

When Vinta was gone, without discussing remuneration at all, Galileo sat down heavily on a bench in his workshop.

It was a system that could be defended, if you granted its premises. Which were probably true. Every event was the effect of some prior cause, everything moved in a woven tangle of cause and effect, which included of course the stars and planets. But unweaving the tangle was very difficult; in that sense astrology was a doomed project, or at least quite radically premature, no matter its antiquity. But he could not say that to the Medici. And one could at least calculate the positions of the planets at the time of the subject's birth. Do what everyone else did.

He groaned and called out for a new folio, quills, ink, a dusty old ephemerides. Vinta had left a big packet of papers containing the Grand Duke's birth information.

For a long time he stared at all these things. He had paid sixty lire each for birth charts for the girls when they were born. He had only passed on one for Vincenzio because by then he could not afford it. He pulled the relevant tomes from the dusty top shelf on the back wall of the workshop. The basic text was Ptolemy himself: just as his *Almagest* covered all Greek astronomy, his *Tetrabiblios* described all their astrology. His description of celestial influences was derived from a mix of philosophers, Zeno, Pythagoras, Plato, Aristotle, Plotinus . . . Archimedes made no appearance. There was no way to apply to this problem the mechanics of Galileo's hero.

In the more typical Greek way, Ptolemy and most of his sources saw the *idios cosmos* in the *koinos kosmos*, and vice versa; they spiritualized matter, materialized spirit. Fine; no doubt true; but the action at a distance! The unsupported assertions! Galileo cursed aloud as he read. The *Tetrabiblios* was simply an endless string of assertions. To use that as a basis for genethlialogy, the construction of individual horoscopes . . .

Well, Kepler had done it, and was still doing it. His Latin was so weird (if the problem did not reside in Kepler's thinking itself), that Galileo was not sure what his books said; he had only paged around in them trying to find things he could understand. The astrological sections were worst of all in that regard. There Kepler was even more confusing than Ptolemy.

For one thing, Kepler called himself a Copernican, and Galileo tended to agree with him on that; but astrology was Ptolemaic. Perhaps Kepler's incomprehensibility had to do with his attempt to make his astrology as Copernican as his astronomy, to save the appearances there as well as in the sky. St Augustine had reconciled astrology with Christianity; perhaps Kepler felt he could reconcile it with Copernicanism.

But there wasn't the time to work through Kepler to find out. He had to set all the foundational issues aside and focus on

Ferdinando. His chart marked the locations of all the planets at his birth moment, either square, oppositional, sextile, or in conjunction. Jupiter had been in the strong ascendant at his birth, Venus in conjunction. Consult the *Tetrabiblios* for the main significations for these luminaries. For Jupiter these were expansion, increase, honour, advancement, enjoyment of patronage, financial gain, joy, charitable instincts, travel, legal matters, religion, and philosophy. All these qualities suggested that Galileo himself must be a Jovian, but he knew already that Jupiter was not his Great Benefic, but rather Mercury. The slippery go-between; it didn't seem right. Possibly he needed to make for himself a prosthaphaeresis, which was that correction necessary to find the 'true' place of a planet, as opposed to its apparent or 'mean' place.

But Ferdinando seemed to have been born under a good description. Good, good, and more good. Of course almost everywhere in the sky was good. Clearly, no matter which benefic was in the ascendant, astrology focused on what good could be found in it. Ptolemy himself had noted this in the introduction to the *Tetrabiblios* – *one looks to the stars for the good that can be seen*, he had written – which was very convenient. Jupiter was definitely good. Enjoyment of patronage? Financial gain? Who wouldn't want to be born under Jupiter!

He shrugged away his unruly thoughts and worked through the querents, the aspects and ceremonies, the conjunctions retrograde and indulgent, the oppositions and squares, houses and cusps, sextiles and tines. He applied the simpleton mathematics, so basic that he wondered if he could perhaps construct an astrological compass like his military one – or if perhaps his military compass already had the capacity to calculate horoscopes! He would have shared this joke with Marina had she been there. One more thing it could do.

It took two days to complete the work. Happily the horoscope genuinely predicted for Ferdinando long life and good health – both much in the ascendant, in fact, because of the current position of Jupiter in the zodiac. His death was most likely to fall twenty-two years in the future, at a square conjunction of quick Mercury and dour Saturn – not that ordinary horoscopes traditionally sought out such information, but Galileo had run the calculations through to their end, just out of curiosity. Astrology, he understood as he did this, was an articulated structure of hope. One never looked for ends of lives, even though the calculations could be made.

He wrote it all up, not including the end calculations of course, and had the finished drawings done by Arighetti. He took the handsome foursquare charts and a fair copy of his calculations to the palace, and gave them in person to Vinta, who unceremoniously broke the seal on the leather case, which Mazzoleni had embossed with a gilt version of the Medici arms. Quickly he read the main page, nodding as he did so.

'Jove, Venus and the Sun, all in the ascendant. Good. His Highness and the Grand Duchess will be very pleased, I am sure.' A sudden piercing glance: 'You're sure about this?'

'The signs are very strong. His subjects can rejoice to know that their most benevolent Grand Duke is favoured by Fortune and the stars.'

Vinta said, 'God be thanked. For he complains of a gnawing inside him.'

Galileo nodded; he too was afflicted with such pains. He went home with the gift of a gold cup that could be sold for a decent sum to the goldsmiths.

Twenty-two days later, Ferndinando died.

When Galileo heard the news, his face burned. He cursed the servants scurrying away from his heavy hand. He stormed out of the house and wandered the streets of Padua, glumly imagining the next time he saw Vinta. For a moment he was even afraid; perhaps he would be blamed!

But given this world, in which all prediction eventually proved wrong, in which death touched down any time, anywhere, such blame was unlikely. There was no reason to be more than embarrassed. He sent a long letter of condolences to the Grand Duchess

Christina, and to Cosimo, with also a cover note of bafflement to Vinta, one which even delicately suggested the possibility of poison as an explanation for the discrepancy between Fernandino's stars and his actual fate. The celestial influence, he wrote, had somehow been overruled by a mundane cause.

And in the hubbub of the succession, no one actually seemed to remember Galileo's most inaccurate horoscope. It was the kind of thing people forgot to remember. And it was also true that he had tutored the new Grand Duke, Cosimo II, as a boy. The prospects for patronage were probably enhanced.

Still, the moment he had imagined finally came: Galileo visited the court in Florence to pay his respects, and was welcomed into the room by Vinta. Galileo entered already talking, 'So sorry to hear of the Grand Duke's unexpected and untimely death,' he began, but Vinta dismissed these sentiments with a flick of the hand – and with it a look of contempt, and even of a kind of unctuous complicity, as if Vinta was now in on a secret truth, which was that all Galileo's mathematics were as fraudulent as astrology.

That look cut Galileo's mind. It never left him, he could always see it, and it always brought the same hot flush of shame and defilement. He tried to banish the memory of it, but sometimes he even dreamed it: it jumped out of other faces and stabbed him. One of the Bad Looks of his life, for sure; one of the ever-growing collection of terrible looks that haunted him in the sleepless hours.

No one else remembered the horoscope at all, as far as he could tell. Even if they proved right no one remembered them. People were so scared.

It did not follow, of course, that because one horoscope was wrong, all astrology was wrong; nor that if astrology were wrong, all Ptolemy was wrong; nor that if all Ptolemy were wrong, all Aristotle was wrong; nor even that if Aristotle was wrong, Copernicus was therefore right. Those were bad syllogisms; and even good syllogisms were not for Galileo conclusive.

But that look.

After that he tried to restrict himself to making only those assertions he could demonstrate the truth of. He tried not to speak of causes. Probably the Copernican explanation was correct, but he would not speak of it. He could not see the proof for it. Kepler obviously believed it, but Kepler was crazy. Although even Kepler had said it: *astrology is the prostitution of mathematics.*

The look always remained in him, leaving his mind scarred like poor Fra Paolo's face. In the pursuit of patronage, he had prostituted his mathematics.

'So you knew you were a hypocrite,' Hera said to him. Under the ghastly yellow light of Jupiter her broad face before him was as big and cruel as one of the Fates. Mnemosyne had metamorphosed, as she so often did, into dire Atropos, chopping into his brain with her scissors, a pair of scissors injected from the inside of the helmet on his head, scissors made of mirrors that reflected back broken images of his staring face, his misspent life. He shut his eyes, but Mnemosyne lived there too, on the inside of his eyelids.

'You refused to marry the woman who was the mother of your three children,' she said, 'precisely because she was like you, in that she had sold access to herself to better her position. It was the same thing you did with the horoscope, and so you knew you were wrong about her. But by then it was too late.'

'I wasn't wrong!' Galileo said. 'And it wasn't just that. We didn't get along. Even so I kept her in a house and took care of her and the kids. I found her a husband.'

She stared at his face for a while. The Atropos mask dropped from her own. She said, 'Do you know what you did that really mattered to you, and that still really matters to us now?'

'No!'

'Look.' And she touched him.

* * *

355

Mazzoleni had planed the edge of a long board of fine-grained hardwood, then cut a smooth groove in it, so that they had as perfect a Euclidean plane and line as they could make in this world. He pegged this board into a big L-shaped framework of boards with holes drilled into them at different heights, so the plane's inclination could be adjusted at will. The balls to be rolled down the plane were iron musket balls, ground and polished and dropped time after time through circular holes just big enough to fit them, until Galileo was convinced they were as close to geometrical spheres as humans could achieve. When they were done they had a really interesting apparatus.

After that they spent hours and hours, day after day, in the workshop running tests of different kinds. Balls that were dropped through the air fell faster than Galileo and Mazzoleni could time them, so now they tilted their plane sufficiently to slow balls in their descent. By altering the angle of inclination in a regular way, and comparing times of descent for the same balls over and over again, Galileo came to see that the tilt of the plane made a proportional ratio with the speed of the descents, a relationship so clear that he could conclude that balls in free fall would accelerate in the same proportion, as an end case; so the inclined plane was teaching them things about free fall as well.

Even given this gift of stretched time, their clocks were not good enough. Galileo muttered about a pendulum clock, remembering the observation of periodicity that had come to him when he was a boy; but he had not figured out how to keep the pendulum swinging without disturbing it, and meanwhile the balls were ready to roll.

Finally it came to him, right out there in the workshop staring at the inclined plane apparatus. 'Maz-zo-len-iiiiiii!'

'Maestro?'

'We will weigh time.'

Mazzoleni laughed. 'Maestro, you're funny.'

'No, it's perfect. We can weigh time easier than we can mark its passing, in fact we can weigh differences very closely! Ha ha!'

He did his little jig and kick, a sign that he was feeling the rung-bell feeling, which he described as being like sexual afterglow, only better.

'It's just what Archimedes would have done. It's like his weighing density, more or less. Here's how we'll do it. We'll make a kind of clypsedra. When the balls drop, have a mechanism also open the stopper on a jug of water.'

Mazzoleni frowned. 'How about just put your thumb on the stopper and do it yourself when you see the ball start,' he suggested. 'Your eye would be more accurate than any gate I can make. Water is slippery stuff.'

'All right, that's fine. That being the case, I'll also stop the water by eye and by thumb. The water that has been released will have run into a flask. We can then weigh the water to within a featherweight! A featherweight of time, in this case, because the weights will always be proportional to the times we were letting the water flow. We'll be accurate to the speed of our eyes and thumbs, which means a tenth of a pulse, or even better!'

'Good idea.'

Mazzoleni's gap-toothed grin: this was the sigil and emblem of the rung-bell feeling. When his bell was rung, he was always seeing Mazzoleni's battered face. The face of God in an old man's face. It made Galileo laugh.

So they weighed time, and continued the work of investigating falling bodies. He tried all kinds of different things. He dropped balls down one inclined plane and watched them roll up another, and found that no matter how the two planes were inclined inward to each other, the balls always rolled back up to the same height they had been dropped from. Preservation of momentum: this fit well with Galileo's earlier studies of balance and leverage. It also shattered the Aristotelian notion that things wanted to be one place or another, but by now he was far beyond mere refutation of Aristotle. A ball returned to the height it was dropped from, no matter the shape of the V: so what happened if they set the second plane horizontally? The ball would roll forever, it seemed, neither accelerating nor decelerating, except that the resistance of wood and the air itself finally stopped it. If not for friction, in other words, it would roll forever. So it seemed; though that was rather amazing. Of course any supposedly perfect plane set on Earth was actually covering a part of a large sphere, so that one might say the tendency of things to move in circles, as the stars did, was an appearance saved even here. But in principle, on a true plane, motion would continue. Motion continued until something stopped it. *Once something started to move, it would continue moving until something changed it.*

Again, this was contra Aristotle. More importantly, it was interesting in its own right.

There was so much that was interesting in what they could see with this apparatus. They started dropping balls freely and letting them hit an inclined plane, then a horizontal plane. Other times they sent balls rolling off the end of a horizontal plane, and watched them fall in a quick curve to a bed of sand they had set on the floor, so the balls would leave a mark that could be measured precisely. Very interesting! Different distances, angles, therefore speeds; and all of them timed proportionally, by the weight of water. These various set-ups divided motion into parts of different kinds, when before motion had been all mixed together in nature, and thus difficult to study. He had been working on these problems for almost twenty years, and never had he been able to articulate differences like he could now. By manipulating the variables one could measure different things, and establish that there were relations – just as one would have expected, but could never before create and measure. Relations of past speed, present speed, future speed.

And so now they were sure, at last, after twenty years of various formulations that had not worked, that *the downward acceleration of a ball increased as the square of the time elapsed in its fall*. It was as simple as that.

Galileo showed the equations to Mazzoleni: 'See? See? Acceleration is a very simple ratio! Why should it be true? Why? God made it that, that's why! God likes mathematical ratios. He must, He must! He puts them there for all to see!'

'For you to see, maestro. Has anyone else ever seen this?'

'Of course not. Archimedes would have seen it, if he had had such a fine apparatus. But no. I am the first in the world to see it.'

The gap-toothed grin. When God created the cosmos, He had had just that grin. He had put it on Mazzoleni to show Galileo how He had felt.

Combined results began to accrue. When a rolling ball fell off a horizontal plane into the air, the curve of its fall was a mix of two motions, first, the uniform speed of the horizontal motion, which did not diminish just because the ball left the table top, and second, the accelerating speed of its vertical fall, which was *precisely the same as if it were falling without any horizontal motion*, something they established by repeated testing. So the horizontal speed was uniform, while the downward speed was increasing as the square of the time elapsed, as already demonstrated. And the combination of those two was, by definition, a half of a parabola. One could therefore describe the motion with a simple parabolic equation.

He stood looking at these equations he had written down, and at the numbers and sketched diagrams on the pages before it. His one hundred and sixteenth work folio was almost completely filled.

'MAZZ-O-LEN-IIIIIIIIII!'

The simian face of the ancient one. 'Something good?'

'PAR-A-BO-LAAAAAA! Let me show you. This is something even you can understand.'

But first he had to dance around the table, out into the garden and back again, feeling bell-struck. All the world struck, all the world ringing, ringing inside him. *Gong! Gong! Gong!*

*   *   *

359

Black space; Hera's face.

'So. Can you see why what you did then is still remembered by us?'

Galileo found the answer was already in his mind. 'You could seek the mathematics inside nature, and find it.'

'Yes. This is what you loved. This is what gave you joy.'

She sat back, watching him closely. 'The apparatus,' she went on, 'allowed you to create events that in nature were compound, but now were teased apart. You had independent variables under your control. Each experiment was unique, but when the variables were the same, the results were the same. It was as if you were enacting the calculus in advance of the mathematics of the calculus – doing calculus as if it were geometry, or even mobile sculpture.

'And these events you staged; if anyone else were to stage them in the same way, they could not help but get the same results you did. You could take the various descriptions of motion that were competing in your time, and put them to the test, and the event itself would determine, in a way everyone could replicate, which of the explanations matched the results. Then, with your mathematical description in hand, you could predict what would happen in new situations. When you were right, this was something no one could ever revise. If we were to do it here and now, it would be just the same.'

'Well, but there is no pull downward here.'

'You know what I mean.'

'Yes yes. It was a way of seeing the truth.'

'Not so fast. It was an accurate description of events at that scale. It was an abstraction with a concrete referent, which meant that no one could logically deny it. If someone were to assert that there was a different description for motion, then you could put it to the test, and show that they were wrong and you were right. You could in fact withdraw, and let motion speak for itself. Motion then speaks, and your rivals in explanation are silenced, without you having to say a word.'

360

'I liked that,' Galileo admitted. 'I liked that very much.'

'Everyone does. And so we still speak of Galilean motion. We still have inclined planes in physics classrooms.'

'I like that too.'

'It was your chief joy.'

'Well, maybe,' Galileo temporized, thinking of all the other things he had enjoyed. He realized that he had loved his life.

'No – it was your chief joy, as revealed by your own mind. Remember that the mnemonic is a brain scanner that locates your most powerful memories by identifying and stimulating the largest coordinating clusters in the amygdala. The strongest memories make the biggest clumps, and they are always entrained with the strongest emotions, in particular the strongest pleasures and the strongest pains. The emotional component is determinative for intensity and permanence of memory. Thus, sexual release can be memorable or forgettable, depending on if it is attached to more complex feelings. To joy, for instance – that feeling you describe as being rung by a bell. And then physical pain, all your many ailments, most of which originated with the poisoned cellar that killed your weaker companions; pain leaves a mark, especially at first, when accompanied by dismay and fear. But much more powerful is shame, perhaps the strongest of the negative emotions. Although fear, humiliation – well. The point is, we have very emotional memories. So, I have just been visiting your strongest memories, that's all. This is what we find among the most pleasurable of your memories.'

'Not the telescope?'

'No, of course not! That's just the thing that Ganymede gave you! And by so doing he bent your whole life in a new direction, until what you were martyred for and remembered for was a drama that overshadowed your real contribution, which was the inclined plane work. Your telescopic discoveries were just what anybody would see when they look through such a glass. And your astronomical theories were usually wrong.'

'What do you mean?' Galileo demanded.

'Your explanation of the comets? Your theory of the tides?'

'Well, but that isn't fair,' Galileo objected. 'The real explanation for the tides is ridiculous. That the Earth's water moves because space itself is bending – it's inexcusable.'

'And yet real.'

Gallileo sighed. 'Maybe we need to be able to forget more than we need to remember,' he said, thinking of what she had said about emotions. About shame, and his catalogue of bad looks.

'You need to remember what helps you, and forget things that don't help you. But you have not achieved that. Few people have, I have found.'

'You did this to many people, I take it.'

'It was my work.' She shook her head unhappily. 'It's what I did, before this thing in Europa drew us all down into its maelstrom.'

'Is the creature really such a problem?'

She looked grim. 'The debate over what to do about it is the problem. We are the problem. But the problem is tearing us apart.'

'As bad as that?'

She gave him one of her sharp looks. 'You know better than most how people can fight over an idea.'

'Indeed. That's what Aurora said too.'

'Fights over ideas are the most vicious of all. If it were merely food, or water, or shelter, we would work something out. But in the realm of ideas one can become *idealistic*. The results can be deadly. The Thirty Years' War, isn't that what they called the religious war that Europe was fighting during your time?'

'Thirty years?' Galileo exclaimed, dismayed.

'So I seem to remember. And here, now, it may be happening again.'

*   *   *

For a while they flew to Europa in silence, both of them locked in their thoughts. By now the equivalence of change of speed and the physical sensation of weight was firmly established in Galileo's body and mind, so when he felt pressed back into his chair he came out of his reverie.

'You're speeding up?'

'Yes.' Hera was grim again. 'Apparently Ganymede and his group are already there. Four ships in a tight orbit, just over the ice they say. There's no good way to stop them now.'

Ahead of them bulked the white ball of Europa. Hera muttered viciously in a language he did not know, tapping hard at her control pad. 'Come on!' she complained.

You must be patient, Galileo prevented himself from saying. Instead he asked, 'Why does Ganymede want me to be burnt at the stake? What difference would it make? Aren't there so many potentialities that they all happen or not, cancel each other out or not, so that any one doesn't matter?'

She looked at him with the expression he had seen before that he could not decipher: pity? Affection? 'All the temporal isotopes have effects downstream. Think again of the braided channels of a river. Say you kick the bank of one stream so hard it crumbles, and the stream wears away the bank until it breaks into a nearby channel, and they both become so strong together that they cut a straighter line, take water from some channels, reroute others . . . Well, so, Ganymede thinks you are at a crucial point, a big bend. He's been obsessed with changing that bend for a long time. He keeps going back to it, I think. And I wonder if he doesn't want the change he causes to be so profound it alters things even in our time too. I wouldn't be surprised.'

'But say I am burned – what's different?'

'Maybe the more accurate question would be, what would be different if you weren't burned.' She glanced at him, sensing his shudder. 'After you, there is a deep divide between science and religion. A war of two cultures, two worldviews. And with you

363

burned at the stake for stating an obvious physical fact, religion is thereafter discredited, even disgraced. The intellectual innovators of the world are secularized, science rises to dominate human culture, religion is seen as an archaic power system, like astrology, and it fades away.'

'But that's not good,' Galileo said. 'That would be bad, in fact. Why would anyone want that? That's no different than these bastard priests who are attacking me!'

She regarded him carefully. 'Interesting to see again the structure of feeling you grew up in. To us it seems clear that your religion was a kind of mass delusion, serving the powerful by justifying their hierarchy.'

Galileo shook his head. 'The world is sacred. God made it all, as an expression of mathematical playfulness, perhaps, but however that may be, He did it.' She shrugged at this and he went on: 'Besides, how can you say that science dominating civilization is such a good thing? You told me that your histories have been nightmares, that most cultures in most times, including your own, have been to one degree or other insane? Where's the great advantage in that?'

'The question,' she said carefully, 'is whether the alternatives are not even worse.'

This was sobering. Galileo thought it over. 'Do you have a tutorial for the history of human affairs between my time and yours, like the one Aurora had for mathematics?'

'Of course,' Hera said, still brooding. 'There are many. They describe different potentialities, or attempt to show the whole wave function. But there's no time for that now. We're approaching Europa.'

And in fact Europa stood directly before them, growing rapidly larger, blossoming like a white rose, its surface crackled like the ice on the Arno just before it broke up in the spring.

It was striking how for the longest time in their flights, their objectives remained at the same small size, only growing incrementally, and then in a final rush bloomed to the size of an entire world.

Now Hera was cursing again.

'What's wrong?' he asked.

'They're landing,' she said, and pointed. 'Just over the north pole.'

Galileo did not have a sense of orientation to apply to this. 'You can see them?'

'Yes! There!' She pointed, and Galileo saw a cluster of tiny stars, very close to Europa's white surface, swirling down toward it. 'They're landing, and the Europans are trying to stop them, but . . .'

'They don't have cannons to fire at them?'

'Weapons have been forbidden, as I told you, but there are things that can be used as weapons, of course. Power systems, construction tools, field generators.' She shook her head as she watched her screen and listened to her interlocutors. 'Hurry, hurry! I wish they would generate a small black hole in their midst and suck them out of existence!' She cursed in the language that didn't get translated.

A streak of brilliant white light shot down out of the quartet of firefly ships onto the surface of Europa, and she stopped in her tirade.

'What was that?' Galileo said.

'I don't know. Possibly one of their ships flew right into the moon, like a meteorite. I don't know how that could have happened though. The pilot systems shouldn't have allowed it . . .'

'What?'

She hissed. 'Whatever hit the surface just exploded again. Maybe its reactor. There's an electromagnetic pulse that has registered that is – ah! See that bright white spot?' She tapped away quickly and then began cursing again. 'A lot of them are in trouble now, on both sides. Hold on,' she ordered. 'I'm taking us down fast.'

Their ship tilted forward, rocketed down toward the shattered icescape. Only in the last seconds before they would have impacted like a meteor did the invisible ship tilt and shudder and roar, throwing Galileo against his restraints.

They thumped down on the tawny ice. Hera began rattling out a long list of instructions to the ship and the various machine intelligences among its crew.

'Shouldn't you get the rest of your grand council involved in this?' Galileo asked.

'Yes.' She gave him a look. 'But we'll meet with the Europan council for now.'

'Oh I see. Very good.'

'Very bad. We've failed to stop Ganymede. I don't know what he's done, but that was a big explosion. Possibly one of their ship engines.'

She had landed them very close to an entry ramp into Rhadamanthys, the under-ice Venice. They walked down a broad white entrance, through a diaphanous barrier, into a broad ice gallery, where the pulsing blues interlocked in their patterns overhead. Soon they reached the edge of the canal they had taken before, and beside it, a sunken amphitheatre where a small crowd of people gathered. This too looked familiar, and though he couldn't recall the specifics of any previous incident, he assumed there had been one, there on the far side of some amnestic he had ingested. Already seen . . .

'You have to give me something so I don't remember so much of my life,' he reminded her.

'I tried a few things with the mnemonic, while you were remembering. I hope certain parts will be occluded for you now.'

People in the crowd saw them as they descended the stairs. Some threw up their hands as if to say What next! or What have you done! But Galileo saw that was a pretence; he saw that they were afraid. Some were chewing on knuckles; others were

366

weeping without knowing it. Even in the ubiquitous green-blue light of the vast articulated cavern, most of them were white-faced with fear.

Watching Hera confer with them, Galileo heard snatches of a debate over who had the right to land or to forbid landing on Europa. He wandered down to the floating transparent globe which modelled the icy moon. The dark grey rocky core of the globe was surrounded by a transparent blue gel representing the ocean, all of which was held in a thin white shell that tinted the ocean below it to a pastel shade somewhat like the Earth's sky. The outer shell was scored by faint lines representing the crack systems on the surface, a crystalline craquelure.

Inside this globe the creature of the ocean was not rendered visible, although Galileo thought that tiny fluctuations in the blueness of the blue light might be intended to represent some manifestation of it. Down there under their feet – a mile down, a hundred miles down . . . He wanted to talk to Aurora, to see if anything new had come of the mathematical conversation with the sentience. The listening devices they had emplaced in the ocean were connected to sound repeaters within this floating globe, he assumed, as emanating from it he could hear, at a much reduced volume, the uncanny singing he remembered so well. The lowest sounds appeared to match the little shifts in blueness of the model's ocean; he wondered if the colour changes marked the spatial origin of the sounds.

One of the locals was complaining to Hera, 'You were supposed to keep him sequestered on Io!'

'We tried,' she countered, 'unlike you. Where were you? It might have helped to have some numbers there, if you really wanted a quarantine.'

The argument persisted, grew louder –

Then the blue in the floating globe turned white at a point under the surface, near the upper part of it. That would be its north pole, no doubt. The blossom of incandescence propagated away from it in waves; they struck the solid mass of the core and rebounded back toward the surface. Threads of white light coursed through the interior like lightning.

Then there was a tremble underfoot, and the ice around them groaned, sounding much like the creature within had sounded during their incursion. Perhaps the sentience had learned to sing by mimicking the natural creaks of its moon's ice.

Then the sounds coming from the globe changed. The clustering glissandos coalesced to a single dissonant chord; the pitch dropped abruptly, down to a *basso profundo* so profound that Galileo heard it more in the gut than the ear. It *groaned*. As the awful sound lifted back into the range of the audible, it seemed to lift Galileo's body with it, chelating him with a thousand claw tips, so that his skin crawled and the hair rose on his forearms and the back of his neck. He recalled the cries that had driven them up through the ice shell of the moon to the safety of the surface. That, however, had been an angry sound, like the roar of a lion. This one was pain and confusion. Then in a brief crescendo that spiked into his head just above his eyes, it changed to raw fear. This lasted only a moment, thank God, for everything it felt Galileo felt; but it seemed the machine transferring the sound had damped the volume, reducing it to a lunatic whimper. That hurt in a different way, the sound of it too high, and somehow broken. The anguish pierced him right to the heart, he felt it fully himself, anguish like something he somehow recognized . . .

Galileo found he had his nose to the floating globe, that he was embracing it and whimpering himself, muttering desolately, 'No, no, no, no, no.' The pain in him was unbearable, like the stab of a cry of grief.

'Has it been wounded?' he asked, wiping his face as Hera approached. 'Has it changed?'

'Yes.' Her expression was grim. 'As you can hear. Aurora tells me its messages have gone away.'

'Is she here in this quarter of the city? Can you take me to her?'

Hera nodded. 'She'll send an avatar.'

The people standing in the amphitheatre looked crushed, heartbroken. Clearly the painful sounds affected everyone the same. Aurora herself suddenly appeared before them, also stricken, her nose to a screen before her as she tapped at the buttons on her table, muttering to herself, or to the alien beneath them.

'What's happened?' Galileo exclaimed to her.

'Here – ohhh –'

'What?'

'Can't you see? Look there!' Tapping at the screen at her hands, without ever moving her face. It looked like she wanted to dive through the screen. She held onto her desk's edge as if to the railing of a ship. She moaned, oblivious of those around her.

'Its articulation is bad, the signals off sequence,' she whispered. 'The equations are wrong. It's as if it's been drugged, or . . .'

'Or injured,' Galileo said. 'Damaged.'

'Yes. It must be. The explosion included a big electromagnetic pulse, very powerful, especially in the area just under the blast, of course. What did they do? Why did they do it?'

Galileo turned away. He had met a man once who had been struck on the left side of the head by a falling hoist beam in the Venetian Arsenale; the beam had sheered off, this was one of the incidents that had made him interested in strength of materials. The man had recovered in most senses, and been able to speak; but his speech was slurred, and he stuttered, babbled, forgot himself, repeated himself; and all with a huge grin, rendered horrible by his babble.

Behind them the Europans' argument had become ferocious, several people shouting at once. Galileo saw again that through the centuries people had never grown less emotional. Hera was shouting: 'I'm going to kill them. The first mind we have ever encountered, and they attacked it!'

Chirrups and oscillating moans now came from the globe. The faces of the Europan councillors blanched or reddened according to their humours. Too many people were shouting at once; in the cacophony nothing could be distinguished.

Then the gallery turned purple. The transparent aquamarine tones, so green in their blue, all shifted through aquamarine to a dusky purple.

Everyone stopped talking and stared around. Hera's gaze fixed on Galileo: 'What's this?' she said.

A part of him warmed to see that out of all of them she had asked him, but the cold dread in his heart was not touched. 'Let's go outside and see,' he suggested, gesturing at their ceiling, which now pulsed through various shades of grape. He took her by the hand, pulled her toward the broad opening that led up to the surface.

In Europa's light pull she was quickly moving faster than he could go. After a moment they ran side by side; then she took his hand again and pulled him along, and he could do nothing but focus on keeping his feet. She dragged him along as his mother had once dragged him out of church, after he had started to laugh at the sight of a swinging lamp. They burst through the diaphanous air barrier and ran up the broad ramp, out from under its ceiling and into the black night of the world. Overhead hung giant gibbous Jupiter –

But it was not the Jupiter he had grown used to during their flights among the Galileans. The Great Red Spot had been joined by scores more red spots, spinning in every band, from pole to pole. Most of the spots were horizontally linked, like bloodstones in necklaces. It was as if the planet had caught a pox, each of the new spots a livid brick red oval, spinning slowly but distinctly, squiggling like wet paint. Some spots straddled bands, and threw their convoluted boundaries into wild spurts and splashes of ruddy colour. The dominant colour of the stupendous planet had shifted from yellow to a plague of various reds. The light in the city below had therefore shifted from greens to purples.

Hera, head canted back, staggered and cried out at the sight. She grasped his shoulder to keep on her feet.

'What is it?' she cried.

'It's Jupiter,' Galileo said stupidly, but then clarified what he meant: 'It's Jupiter itself, thinking. Like the thing underneath us, you see? The bands and the swirls have always been its thoughts. Now it's angry. Or grieving.'

'But why?'

'Because!' Galileo glanced at her in surprise; she was staring wildly at him. 'Because we killed its daughter,' he suggested.

Chapter Fifteen   The Two Worlds

The die is cast, and I am writing the book to be read either now or by posterity, it matters not. It can wait a century for a reader, as God himself has waited six thousand years for a witness.
— JOHANNES KEPLER, *Harmonies of the World*

He woke so stiff he could not move, feeling the pressure of full bowel and full bladder, which seemed to be in competition with each other to shove their way out of his second asshole. He was in his bed. Cartophilus was staring him in the face with his peculiar look, either knowing or intensely curious, it was impossible for Galileo to say.

'What?' Galileo croaked.

'You've been entangled, maestro.'

'Yes.' He thought about it while he made the effort to roll into a sitting position. 'You know what happens to me when I'm gone, isn't that right, Cartophilus?'

'Yes. I see it here.' He gestured at his device.

'So you saw?'

Cartophilus nodded unhappily. 'It keeps getting worse. That must have been quite a noise. All of you were groaning and weeping near the end. It got so bad I decided to bring you back. I hope I was right.'

'I don't know.' Galileo tried to hold on to what had happened. Life seen by lightning bolts – 'I'll have to go back, I think.'

Then La Piera swept in with a basket of bread and citrons, followed by Guiseppe and Salvadore, who carried between them a pot of hot mulled wine flavoured with grenadine. They in turn were followed by kitchen girls carrying bowls and cups and plates and implements, and flowers in vases. By way of several slow and articulated movements, groaning at each, Galileo stood. He stared at the faces surrounding him as if he had never seen them before. The syncope this time, La Piera told him, had lasted two days. He had to be starving.

'First help me out to the jakes,' he ordered the boys. 'I need to make room for food first. God help me not to shit my guts out.'

In the days that followed he was very subdued. 'Things aren't clear,' he complained to Cartophilus. 'I remember it only in bits and pieces. I think Hera must have done something to my mind. I can't make it hold together.'

But he wrote one last passage to add to *Il Saggiatore* before sending it off for publication in Rome. The added passage was a curious thing, unlike anything he had written before:

Once upon a time, in a very lonely place, there lived a man endowed by nature with extraordinary curiosity and a very penetrating mind. For a pastime he raised birds, whose songs he much enjoyed; and he observed with great admiration the happy method by which they could transform at will the very air they breathed into a variety of sweet songs.

One night this man chanced to hear a delicate song close to his house, and being unable to connect it with anything but some small bird, he set out to capture it. When he arrived at a road he found a shepherd boy who was blowing into a kind of hollow stick while moving his fingers about the wood, thus drawing from it a variety of notes similar to those of a bird, though by

373

quite a different method. Puzzled, but impelled by his natural curiosity, he gave the boy a calf in exchange for this flute and returned to solitude.

The very next day he happened to pass by a small hut within which he heard similar tones; and in order to see whether this was a flute or a bird he went inside. There he found a boy who was holding a bow in his right hand and sawing upon some fibres stretched over a hollowed piece of wood such that he drew from this a variety of notes, and most melodious ones too, without any blowing. Now you who participate in this man's thoughts and share his curiosity may judge of his astonishment. Yet finding himself now to have two unanticipated ways of producing notes and melodies, he began to perceive that still others might exist.

His amazement was increased when upon entering a temple he heard a sound, and upon looking behind the gate discovered that it came from the hinges as he opened it. Another time, led by curiosity, he entered an inn expecting to see someone lightly bowing the strings of a violin, and instead saw a man rubbing his fingertip around the rim of a goblet and drawing forth a pleasant tone from that. Then he observed that wasps, mosquitoes, and flies do not form single notes by breathing, as did the birds, but produce their steady sounds by swift beating of their wings. And as his wonder grew, his conviction proportionately diminished that he understood how sounds were produced.

Well, after this man had come to believe that no more ways of forming tones could possibly exist, when he believed that he had seen everything, he suddenly found himself plunged deeper than ever into ignorance and bafflement. For having captured in his hands a cicada, he failed to diminish its strident noise either by closing its mouth or stopping its wings; yet he could not see it move the scales that covered its body, or any other part of it. At last he lifted up the armor of its chest and there he saw some thin hard ligaments beneath; thinking the sound might come from their vibration, he decided to break

374

them in order to silence it. But nothing happened until his needle drove too deep, and transfixing the creature, he took away its life with its voice, so that he was still unable to determine whether the song had originated in those ligaments. And by this experience his knowledge was reduced to complete ignorance, so that when asked how sounds were created, he answered trembling that although he knew a few ways, he was sure that many more existed which were not only unknown but unimaginable.

I could illustrate with many more examples Nature's bounty in producing her effects, as she employs means we could never think of without our senses and our experiences to teach us – and sometimes even these are insufficient to remedy our lack of understanding. The difficulty of comprehending how the cicada forms its song, even when we have it singing to us right in our hands, ought to be more than enough reason for us to decline to state how comets are formed or anything else.

When Cesi read this addition to the new book he was puzzled, and wrote back to ask what it meant. Was it a way of saying that Copernicanism might not be the correct explanation for the movement of the planets after all – the cicada's song representing therefore something like the music of the spheres?

Galileo wrote back tersely. *I know certain things which have been observed by no one but myself. From them, within the limits of my human wisdom, the correctness of the Copernican system seems incontrovertible.*

Maffeo Barberini becoming pope had been a miracle; him making his nephew Francesco into a cardinal just three days after Francesco had joined the Lyncean Academy was another miracle. The year before Galileo had helped Francesco to get his doctorate from the University of Pisa, for which favour his uncle the new Pope had sent Galileo a gracious letter of thanks. Now Francesco was one of Urban's closest advisors and confidantes.

Then another of Galileo's disciples, and one of his most enthusiastic supporters, a young man named Giovanni Ciampoli, was appointed to the powerful position of Papal secretary. This almost defied belief, given Ciampoli's grandiloquent self-importance relative to his actual accomplishments and station. He was a rooster, in fact, and yet now he was gatekeeper to the Pope and in his company every day, advising, conversing, even reading aloud to him as he ate his meals. Ciampoli read *Il Saggiatore* to him, in fact, and afterward wrote to Galileo and the Lynxes to say that Urban had often laughed out loud as he listened to it.

And not just the Pope was reading *Il Saggiatore*, it seemed, but everyone in Rome – the literati, the virtuosi, the philosophers, the Jesuits, and everyone else with an interest in intellectual matters. It was the book of the hour; it had completely transcended the original question of the comets, or any of the individual scientific controversies Galileo had gotten embroiled in. It was a rock that people were using to shatter the heavy somnolent resentful conformity of the Pauline years. Someone had spoken freely at last, and in the vernacular, about all the new things being discovered. High Barberinian culture was born, emerging like an Athena. Galileo was no longer alone, or part of a faction, but the leader of a movement. With Urban VIII on the Throne of Peter, anything was possible.

Again, however, Galileo's trip to Rome was delayed by illnesses, not all of them his own. Urban VIII was so exhausted by his intense campaign for the papacy that he retired into the Vatican for over two months. By the time he was well enough to receive supplicants and visitors, and Galileo had recovered from his own ailments enough to travel, it was the spring of 1624.

But finally the time came. On his last day at Bellosguardo, Galileo rode his mule over to San Matteo to say good-bye to Maria Celeste.

She knew perfectly well why he had to go. She felt that this new pontiff was a direct answer to her prayers, an intercession from God in their favour; she was the one who had first called it a 'miraculous conjunction', giving Galileo both the idea and the phrase. In her letters to him she had revealed her ignorance of courtly protocol by expressing the hope that he would write Urban VIII to congratulate him on his ascension, not understanding that one at Galileo's level could not address directly someone so much higher, but must express thanks and best wishes through an intermediary; which Galileo had of course done, using for the purpose Cardinal Francesco Barberini, as he had explained to her in his return letter.

Now Maria Celeste clung to him in her usual way, trying not to cry. Just in the way that she held him he could feel that no one had ever loved him so intensely.

'Are you sure I can't ask His Holiness to give you all some property?' he said, trying to distract her.

But Maria Celeste said, 'What we need is better spiritual guidance! These so-called priests they have inflicted on us, well – if we could only have a decent priest, a real priest.'

'Yes yes,' Galileo said. 'But not perhaps some land that you could rent? Or an annuity?'

Maria Celeste frowned her quick frown. This was not the kind of thing one asked the Pope for, her look said. 'I'll ask the abbess,' she temporized.

Back at Bellosguardo, making his final preparations, a letter from her was brought to him by the convent's servant Geppo. Please ask Urban for a real priest, it reiterated. *Someone educated, and at least somewhat pure of spirit.*

Galileo cursed as he read this. There on the page lay his daughter's beautiful Italian script, the big loops inclining in perfect diagonals to the northeast and northwest, if it had been a map; a true work of art, as always, written by candle in the middle of the night, after the day's chores were finally done and she had some time to herself. In so many of these beautiful letters she excused herself for falling asleep as she wrote, and it often took several nights for her to compose one. She apologized also for mentioning the most pressing physical need of the moment, for begging a blanket, or his oldest hen to thicken their broth. And yet now she asked him to ask the new Pope for a better spiritual advisor.

'I see the way it is,' he said gloomily as he stared through her letter. 'In order to be a Poor Clare and yet not go mad, you have to believe it all, utterly and to the depths of your soul. Otherwise despair would drown you.'

As it had Arcangela, and several other of the sisters, including the poor abbess. Maybe you could even say that most of them were sunk into despair, weighed down by hunger and cold and illness, while Maria Celeste buoyed herself with her belief, and held the rest of them up with her otherworldly goodness. Galileo muttered sulphurously as he considered his two daughters, stuck in the same situation and thereby illustrating a truly Aristotelian either-or in their response to it. Neither was quite sane; but Maria Celeste was beautiful. A saint.

Later, in Rome, when he made the request she had asked for, he also asked for a sinecure for his son Vincenzio, combined with a papal indulgence that would legitimize his birth. This too was granted, the sinecure giving the youth sixty crowns a year; but since it came with the requirement that he perform some religious exercises, he refused to accept it. At this news Galileo threw up his hands. 'I've done my duty by these people!' he roared. 'They won't get another scudi from me, not another quattrini. Family, what a fraud! Blood is no thicker than water, as you see when you cut yourself.'

'When it congeals it gets thicker,' Cartophilus pointed out.

'Yes, and when it dries it sticks to you. And so family is the scab on a wound. I'm sick of it! I renounce them all!'

Cartophilus ignored this, knowing it was just talk. And by then there were more pressing problems.

*   *   *

378

Unfortunately the Grand Duchess Christina was not convinced of the necessity of this journey to Rome, and did not want to pay for it. The new Medici ambassador to Rome, a Francesco Niccolini, cousin to the previous ambassador but one, was informed in a letter from the young Grand Duke Ferdinando II that Galileo was not invited to stay at the embassy or at the Villa Medici. So Galileo had to make arrangements to stay with his ex-student Mario Guidicci, who lived near the church of Santa Maria Maddalena.

This was the first sign that the *mirabile congiunture* was not quite as miraculous as it had seemed – or that it was already disjuncting, in the way of many a spectacular but brief astrological conjunction.

The second sign of disjunction was far worse. He was still on his way to Rome, resting at Cesi's villa in Acquasparta, when the news came that Virgilio Cesarini, that brilliant and melancholy young cardinal, had died.

This was a real blow, for Cesarini had been perhaps the leading figure in all the competing intellectual circles of the city – known to everyone, high up in the Vatican, and at the same time very much a Lynx, a true Galilean. No one had expected his death, despite his slight frame; but these things happened.

His vacant position at the Holy Office was soon given to the enormously fat Fra Niccolo Riccardi, a priest who seemed sympathetic to the Lynxes, and who loved Galileo's new book, but who was also anxious to please everybody. He would be little help to them.

Conjunctions and disjunctions; there was nothing for it but to get to Rome as soon as possible, and do what he could. So it was back into the litter to endure again the jounce and squeak of the ruined springtime roads.

On the day of his arrival in the sprawling smoky city, Galileo stayed up late with his host Guidicci, and was brought up to date on the situation. As Galileo had seen in the tight crowded streets, the capital of the world was in a state of high excitement because of the new order of things. For the first time in decades a pope with ambition was on the throne of Peter, calling for new building projects, clearing whole quarters of the city, staging gigantic festivals for the populace, and encouraging literary societies and new organizations like the Linceans. No one remembered a time quite like it; it was not just the Lynxes who had felt the miraculous. To have the Borgias out of power (and the Medicis), all replaced by a vigorous, curious intellectual – it was springtime for everyone.

The next morning, therefore, Galileo's hopes were high as he went to the Vatican to pay his respects. The familiar buildings and gardens had been recently washed; they looked bigger and more imposing, the gardens more luxuriant and beautiful. Giovanni Ciampoli, beaming happily, led him through the papal foyer and the salons to the inner garden, now bursting with flowers. There, taking a walk with his brother Cardinal Antonio Barberini, was the new Pope, God's envoy on earth.

In the first second of the audience Galileo saw that Maffeo Barberini was a changed man. It was not just the white robes, the surplice, the red vestment over his shoulders framing his elegant goateed head, the ermine-lined red cap; nor the deferent retainers on all sides, and the Vatican itself; although all these things were of course new. It was the look in his eye. Gone was the gleam of mischief Galileo remembered so well, and the look of open admiration for Galileo's achievements, and the desire to be admired in return. All gone. Urban VIII was not present in the same way. His skin was smooth and pink, his domed forehead and long nose shiny. His eyes, round rather than oval, were now like watchful dark pebbles, alert even though his gaze angled away from Galileo's as if looking at something else. He expected obedience, even obeisance, and already he was used to getting it; he was not even suspicious that he might not get it.

And of course Galileo gave it in full, kneeling and bowing to kiss the sandalled feet, which were perfectly clean and white.

'Rise, my Galileo. Speak to us standing upright.'

As he did so Galileo bit his tongue, checking the congratulations he had prepared. There was no question now of suggesting there had been anything won, or that the matter could have turned out any other way; one had to act as if things had always been like this. Referring to the past would have been a faux pas, even an impertinence. Silently Galileo kissed the big ring on the pontiff's offered hand. Urban let Ciampoli speak for him, only nodding to indicate his approval of what was said, and occasionally murmuring things Galileo could barely hear. One curious glance was sharp, then he returned to the contemplation of some inner landscape. Even for Galileo, his favoured scientist, he could not be bothered to be entirely present. It was as if the carapace of power he now wore was so heavy that he needed to attend to it always, and so thick that he did not believe anyone could penetrate it. Now he lived alone, at all times and in all places. Even his brother Antonio watched him as if observing a new acquaintance.

Ciampoli, always one of Galileo's most peculiar and unhelpful advocates, a man boundless in enthusiasm but shaky in everything else, now spoke eagerly of Galileo's accomplishments, in ways that pitched them too high, that caused Urban's gaze at the flowers to sharpen again for a second as he tilted his head to listen. Barberini knew Galileo's story already, and clearly this was not the moment to rehearse it. Why Ciampoli had been named Urban's secretary was beyond Galileo to tell.

Soon Urban lifted a hand, and Ciampoli saw, well after Galileo, that the interview was over. Nervously Ciampoli thanked Galileo for coming, speaking for Urban just as he had a moment before been speaking for Galileo. He was enunciating both halves of the conversation! Then he led Galileo away. No more than five minutes had passed.

Out in the vast antechamber Ciampoli repeated what he had written already in his letters, that he had been reading *Il*

Saggiatore aloud to the Pope during meals, and that Urban had laughed and called for more. 'I am sure you are now free to write anything you want, about astronomy or anything else.'

But Ciampoli was a fool. He had speculated aloud that he was Virgil reincarnated, or perhaps Ovid. He wrote verses making fun of Urban behind Urban's back, then distributed these verses to friends like Cesi and Galileo and others, as if the poems would not then eventually circulate and land in the hands of his enemies – and more importantly, in the hands of Galileo's enemies.

So now Galileo merely murmured sounds of agreement, deeply irritated and uneasy. That his audience with Urban had gone less well than the ones he had had with Paul! It was startling, disturbing – hard to believe.

Thinking it over intensively in the days that followed, it finally occurred to him that old friends and favoured ones were precisely the people that a new pope had to put in their place, which was at the same distance as everyone else: below. A very great distance below.

Clearly he would need another meeting with Urban, without Ciampoli there to get in the way. But how to get that was not obvious. Possibly no one ever met privately with this pope.

The next morning he visited Cardinal Francesco Barberini at the Villa Barberini, overlooking the brown Tiber. They sat in the little courtyard just inside the wall of the grounds.

Between Francesco and Galileo it could be honestly said that at this point Galileo had helped Francesco more than Francesco had helped him. Francesco seemed perfectly willing to acknowledge this; he was gracious, he was grateful, he was without the slightest tinge of that resentment that gratitude so often contains. It was a truly enjoyable meeting rather than the pretence of one, full of laughter and shared memories. Francesco was taller than Urban and more handsome, sanguine and affable, with a big head like a Roman statue's. His cardinal's robes and regalia had been made in Paris, where he had lived for several years. That he had been one of the least effective diplomats in Vatican history was not so widely known.

He sounded encouraging when Galileo gingerly brought up the subject of Copernicanism. 'My uncle once told me,' he said, 'that if it had been up to him in 1616, you would not have been forbidden to write on this subject. That was Paul's issue, or Bellarmino's.'

Galileo nodded thoughtfully. 'That seems right,' he said as he unpacked a microscope he had brought with him to show people, a kind of telescope of the small, which gave observers new and astounding views of the unsuspected detail and articulation of all the smallest things, including flies and moths, and now, because a trio of bees formed the Barberini family emblem, bees.

Francesco looked into the eyepiece and grinned. 'The sting is like a little sword! And those eyes!' He held Galileo by the shoulder. 'You always have something new. His Holiness my uncle likes that. You should show it to him.'

'I will if I can. Maybe you can help me?'

But before he next met with the Pope, Galileo gave the device to Cardinal Frederick Eutel von Zollern, perhaps in the hope of gaining more support from Catholics north of the Alps. No one could be sure, as this was a meeting Galileo attended by himself. And he was saying very little about his plans; he was preoccupied, even worried. The first meeting with Urban had thrown him off his stride. He complained of the endless procession of meetings and banquets, and wrote back to Florence that being a courtier was a young man's business.

Indeed, in his monomaniacal focus on his own affairs, he did not even seem to notice the matter that was consuming everyone else in Rome at this time, which was the war between Catholic France and Catholic Spain. This conflict was beginning to engulf all of Europe, with no end in sight. The Barberini were closely associated with the French court, as Francesco's history made clear; but France recently had developed Protestant allies. Their foes the Spanish Hapsburgs still controlled both Naples and several duchies in northern Italy, squeezing Rome between them. They had immediate power in Rome as well, being the church's principal financial support. So despite his French sympathies, Urban could not openly oppose the Spaniards. In theory he could as Pope tell all the Catholic crowns what to do, but in practice that hadn't been true for centuries, if it ever had been, and now the two Catholic countries ignored him as they fought – or worse, threatened him for not supporting their side. Despite his wealth and the authority of St Peter, in his foreign relations Urban was finding he had to walk a line even finer than the one on which Paul had balanced: a kind of thread across the abyss, with war waiting below.

After about a month in Rome, Father Riccardi, whom Philip III of Spain had long ago nicknamed Father Monster, agreed to a meeting with Galileo to discuss the question of Holy Office censorship and the ban of 1616. This meeting was crucial to Galileo's hopes, so he was pleased when it was scheduled.

But in the meeting itself Riccardi was very clear and unequivocal. His views were only Urban's here, Riccardi said; and the Pope wanted Copernicanism to remain theory only, with never a suggestion that it had any basis in physical fact. 'I myself am sure that angels move all the heavenly bodies,' Riccardi added at the end of this warning. 'Who else could do it, seeing that these things are in the heavens?'

Galileo nodded unhappily.

'Don't concern yourself too much,' Riccardi advised. 'We judge that Copernicanism is merely rash, rather than perverse or heretical. But the fact of the matter is, this is no time to be rash.'

'Do you think it's possible that the Pope could say that the theory is permissible to be discussed as a hypothetical mathematical construct only, *ex suppositione?*'

'Perhaps. I will ask him about that.'

* * *

Galileo settled in to Guidicci's house in Rome. He had begun to understand that his visit needed to be a campaign. Weeks passed, then months. Urban agreed to see him several times, although they were for the most part very formal and brief occasions, and in the company of others. At no time did Urban meet his eye.

Only during his final audience did the matter of Copernicus come up, and even then, only accidentally. Ciampoli was the one who raised the subject, seizing a lull in the conversation to remark, 'Signor Galilei's fable concerning the cicada was both witty and profound, wasn't it? I recall you said it was your favourite part when I read it to you.'

Galileo, his face reddening, watched the Pope closely. Urban continued to contemplate a bed of flowers, apparently still thinking of other things. Even in the months of Galileo's stay the hard shell of papal power had thickened on him. His eyes were glazed; sometimes in this audience he stared at Galileo as if trying to remember who he was.

But now he said, 'Yes,' firmly, as if waking up. He shifted his absent gaze to Galileo, looked him straight in the eye for a second, then looked at the flowers again. 'Yes – it seemed to refer to what we have spoken of before. A parable of God's omnipotence, which is sometimes overlooked in philosophical discussions, it seems to us, although we see the power everywhere. As we are sure you will agree.'

'Of course, Holiest Holiness.' Galileo gestured helplessly at the garden. 'Everything illustrates that.'

'Yes. And because God is omnipotent, there is no way for mankind to be sure of the physical cause of anything whatsoever. Isn't that right.'

'Yes . . .' But Galileo's head tilted to the side, despite his efforts to stay motionless and deferent. 'Although one has to remember that God created logic, too. And it is clear He is logical.'

'But He is not *confined* by logic, because He is omnipotent. So, whether a physical explanation is logical or not, whether it

385

conserves the appearances poorly or adequately, or even with perfect precision, all that makes no difference when it comes to determining that explanation's actual truth in the physical world. Because if God had wanted to do it otherwise, He could have. If He wanted to do it one way while making it look like another way, He could do that too.'

'I cannot imagine that God would want to deceive his –'

'Not deceive! God does not deceive. That would be as if to say God lied. It is men who deceive themselves, by thinking they can understand God's work by their own reasoning.' Another round-eyed quick look, sharp and dangerous. 'If God had wanted to construct a world that looked like it ran one way, when actually it ran another way, even a supposedly impossible way, then that is perfectly within His abilities. And we have no way to judge His intentions or desires. For any mere mortal to assert otherwise would be an attempted restriction on God's omnipotence. So any time we assert that a phenomenon has only a single cause, we offend Him. As your curious and beautiful fable makes so eloquently clear.'

'Yes,' Galileo said, thinking hard. Again he thought, but could not say, *But why would God lie to us?* And so he had to think of something else. 'We see through a glass darkly,' he admitted.

'Exactly.'

'And so, but this line of argument suggests that anything can be supposed?' Galileo dared to ask. 'Theories, or simply patterns seen, and only expressed *ex suppositione*?'

'I am sure you will always, in all your studies and writing, continue to make our argument for omnipotence. This is the work God has sent you to do. When you make this ultimate point clear, then all your philosophy is blessed. There is no contradiction to our teaching.'

'Yes, Sanctissimus.'

Escorting Galileo out of the Vatican after the audience, Ciampoli was ecstatic. 'That was His Holiness telling you to

386

proceed! He said that if you included his argument then you can discuss any given theory you like! He has given you permission to write about Copernicus, do you see?'

'Yes,' Galileo said shortly. He himself could not be sure what Urban had meant. Barberini had changed.

But in the days that followed, when telling Cesi about it, Galileo said it this way: 'What he gave me was a dispensation to discuss these matters *ex suppositione*.'

That was what he wanted it to be. But it was not a dispensation. It was the *angelica dottrina*, Urban VIII's contribution to natural philosophy. Whether Galileo understood that was not clear.

Even with his telescope the lynx-eyed astrologer cannot look into the inner thoughts of the mind.

– FRA ORAZIO GRASSI

So Galileo returned to Florence willing to believe that Urban had given him permission to describe the Copernican explanation as a theoretical construct, a mathematical abstraction which could account for the observed planetary motions. A supposition. And if he made the supposition convincing enough, the Pope might then give it his approval, as he had the various arguments in *Il Saggiatore*. And then all would be well.

And so, over the next several years, he wrote his *Dialogue Concerning the Two World Systems*, which was known around the house as the *Dialogo*. He wrote it in fits and starts, between interruptions required by the Grand Duke, or by his family situation, or by illnesses; but always one way or another he kept at it, as if under some kind of compulsion.

In those years, the first question every day was whether Galileo would be well enough to get up. Every time he was ill it could be just a *febbre efimera*, a one-day fever, or on the other hand something that would fell him for a month or two. Everyone feared his illnesses as being little catastrophes in the household's routine; but of course the plague also was abroad, and so his complaints could always be the harbinger of something much worse. One day one of the workshop's glassblowers died of plague, which gave them all a terrible fright. Galileo closed the workshop, so the artisans had nothing to do; they shifted out to the fields, the barn and granary, the vineyard and cellar. Bellosguardo now served as farm to the convent of San Matteo, and that took a lot of work. And it was true that out in the open air, the plague seemed less of a danger. Out under the sky, tall clouds billowing over the green hills: it looked safer.

Some could not shake the plague fear, however. Galileo's son Vincenzio and his new wife Sestilia, a wonderful woman, moved away from Florence for a time, leaving their infant behind in the care of La Piera and a wet nurse. Why they left the babe no one could understand, and everyone assumed it was yet more of Vincenzio's spineless ditherings. No one could figure out why Sestilia Bocchineri had married him. There was a lot of gossip about it; Galileo's household at this time numbered about fifty people, including still the family of his brother Michelangelo, who played on in Munich. Views on the explanation for Sestilia were split between the notion that Galileo had found her in Venice and paid her to marry his son, or that God had noted Galileo's uncharacteristic visit to the house of the Virgin Mary in Loreto, the month before Sestilia had appeared in their lives, and had therefore rewarded his devotion. This sacred home of the Virgin Mary, Casa Santa, had landed in Loreto during the Crusades, after flying across the Mediterranean from the Holy Land to escape destruction at the hands of the Saracens. Galileo on his return from his pilgrimage had been heard to remark that the place had a pretty good foundation, all things considered, but God could have ignored that impertinence and blessed his family anyway. There had to be some explanation for a girl as good as Sestilia going for a sponge like Vincenzio.

Every morning, rain or shine, was punctuated by the awful sounds of the maestro waking up. He would groan no matter how he felt, then curse, then shout for breakfast, for wine, for help getting out of bed: 'Come here!' he would bark. 'I need to hit somebody.' After drinking several cups of tea or watered wine, he would get up and dress, go out and limp around his garden, inspecting the many varieties of citrons he had planted in big terracotta pots, on the way down to the jakes to relieve himself. On his way back up he would limp, moaning again, and often stop in the bean and wheat fields, fingering the stalks and leaves.

When he returned to the house they could tell whether he was feeling in good health that day or not. If he was, then all was well. The house would begin to buzz with the work of the day. If he wasn't he would crawl back into his bed and cry hoarsely for La Piera, the only one who could deal with him in these crises. 'Pee! – air! – aaaaah!' Then a gloom would settle on the place as we prepared to wait out another period of illness. There were so many of them.

But if things were well with him, he would go to a big marble-topped table that he had had set up under the arches at the front of the villa, in the shade and the cool, out of the rain but in the clean air, and the light that he required. He sat before it in a chair with cushioning contoured to support his hernia, which allowed him to take off his iron truss. His Padua notebooks and the fair copies made by Guidicci and Arrighetti lay stacked on the desk according to a system that the servants all had to respect unfailingly or else they would be kicked and struck and horribly cursed. As the morning progressed he paged through these volumes thoughtfully, studying them as if they had been written by someone else; and then, leaving one or two of them open, he would take up blank sheets of parchment, his quill and inkpot, and begin to write. He would only write for an hour, two at the most, either chuckling or swearing under his breath, or heaving great sighs; or reading sentences aloud, amending them, trying different versions, writing drafts on blank loose sheets or the backs of notebook pages that had not been filled. Later he would transcribe what he liked onto new blank pages, and when they were full, file them with the other finished pages in a particular pigeonhole of a cabinet set on the desk. Sometimes when finishing for the day he would shuffle the pages to make the stack of them appear higher. Some days he wrote a page or two, other days twenty or thirty.

390

Then with a final loud groan he would stand, stretching like a cat, and call for wine. He drank cups off in a couple of swallows, then strapped on his truss and took another walk in his fields. If it was late enough for good shade, he would sit on a stool and move down the rows of vegetables, pulling out weeds with the stab of a little trowel. He took great satisfaction in killing weeds, filling bushels with them for the compost heap down by the jakes. Sometimes he would hurry back up to the villa to write down something good that had occurred to him in the garden, orating the idea so as not to forget it. 'Oh, the inexpressible baseness of abject minds!' he would shout as he limped up the hill. 'To make themselves slaves willingly! To call themselves convinced by arguments that are so *powerful* that they can't even tell what they mean! What is this but to make an oracle out of a log of wood, and run to it for answers! To fear it! To fear a book! A hunk of wood!'

Another time, limping hastily uphill: 'For every effect in nature some idiot says he has a complete understanding! This vain presumption, of understanding everything, can have no other basis than *never understanding anything*. For anyone who had experienced *just once* the understanding of *one single thing*, thus truly tasting how knowledge is accomplished, would then recognize that of the infinity of other truths, he understands *nothing*.' Shouting this at the top of his lungs, down at Florence, out at the world. Writing it down as he pronounced it again at the top of his lungs. Back and forth, from desk to garden to desk.

In the late afternoon, if it was nice, he would usually stay in the arcade until sundown, writing faster than ever, or reading in his notebooks as he drank more wine. He would watch the sunset, for those few moments seeming at ease. He would sketch the clouds if there were any. The blue of the sky was something he never tired of. 'It's just as beautiful as the colours of a rainbow,' he would insist. 'Indeed, I say the sky itself is the eighth colour of the rainbow, spread over the whole sky for us, all the time.'

On many afternoons a letter would arrive from Maria Celeste. These he always opened and read immediately, frowning with worry as he began, but often enough then smiling, even bursting into laughter. He loved these letters and the candied fruit that sometimes accompanied them, tucked in a basket that he would return to her filled with food. Often he sat down and wrote his reply on the spot, eating candies as he wrote, then calling for La Piera to prepare the basket for return that same day.

He liked to write, it appeared; and when he was writing, life at Bellosguardo was good. There were hours when he would just sit there contentedly, staring at nothing, *grattare il corpo* as the saying goes, scratching his belly in the sun: very rare for Galileo. He withdrew from the world at large, and ignored even matters he should have attended to. He neglected his court duties, and paid no attention to the larger European situation, or indeed anything outside the villa other than his scientific correspondence, which was always voluminous. The household was happy.

But ignoring the European situation was a mistake. And he should have been paying more attention to what people were learning about Pope Urban VIII as the months and years passed. For people in Rome were telling stories. It was said, for instance, that Galileo had again been denounced to the Inquisition. The denunciation was anonymous, but was said to have been made by one of his enemies among the Jesuits, perhaps even Grassi, whom he had made such fun of in *Il Saggiatore*. Because Grassi had hidden behind a pseudonym, Galileo had been free to stick his supposedly unknown opponent mercilessly. Sarsi's subsequent rebuttals had been just as sharp; he had referred to *Il Saggiatore* as *L'Assagiatore*, The Wine-taster, which everyone laughed at, except Galileo.

But that was just a joke. A denunciation to the Holy Office of the Congregation was a very different thing. One rumour said that the denunciation had nothing to do with the banned

Copernican world system, but rather with something about the atomistic views of the Greeks. Bruno had spoken for atomism; the war with the Protestant countries in northern Europe was supposedly being fought over atomism, because of what it implied about transubstantiation. So it was potentially more dangerous even than discussing the two world systems, and yet Galileo was unaware that it even constituted a problem.

Then there were other, more public signs of trouble. Urban was beginning to flex his papal muscles, taking on with gusto the traditional task of rebuilding Rome. He decided to build an arch over the altar in St Peter's, under which only he could conduct services; and since beams long enough to span the altar were no longer available on the deforested slopes of the Appenines, his builders raided the Pantheon and took most of its beams away, almost wrecking the ancient building. 'What the barbarians failed to do, the Barberini finished off,' people said of this vandalism. Slogans like this were only the surface of a growing undercurrent of dislike for the new Pope. 'On ascension, the bees turned to horseflies,' people were saying. The *Avvisi* began to print rhymed attacks on the Pope, and alarming horoscopes that predicted his imminent death. Urban had a now rather old-fashioned obsession with astrology, and these scurrilous dark horoscopes disturbed him so much that he made it a capital crime to predict a pope's death. After that no more were published, but the word was out, the feeling was abroad. Popes were appointed in old age for a reason; good or bad, they did not last long, and the frequent succession of doddering elders kept churning the pots of patronage. But Urban was hale in his fifties, and full of nervous choleric energy.

His ambitions and problems of course ranged far beyond Rome. He continued to favour the French over the Spanish in their war, and so came to fear Spanish spies in the Vatican; and rightfully so, as there were many of them. He had not been pleased, people said, to learn of Galileo's attempt to sell the celatone and jovilabe to the Spanish military. And when he was not pleased it could go very badly. Once someone sneezed during a service he was conducting in St Peter's, and afterward he decreed that anyone taking snuff in church would be excommunicated. Even more of an eye-opener was his decision to have Archbishop Mark Anthony de Dominis burned at the stake for heresy. De Dominis had already been dead for three months when this happened, having expired in the Castel Sant'Angelo after an interrogation by the Inquisition, but no matter: on the feast day of Doubting St Thomas, the body was exhumed and taken to Campo dei Fiori and burned at the stake, its ashes then thrown in the Tiber. The offence that had outraged the pontiff to such a degree involved speaking about precisely this matter of atomism and transubstantiation for which Galileo had been secretly denounced.

Well, a heretic was a heretic, and anything could happen to them. Servants all across Italy were much more shocked by a new story that spread with the speed of amazement: Urban, oppressed by all his worries, had been having trouble sleeping at night, and it seemed to him that it was the chirping and singing of the birds in the Vatican gardens that was keeping him awake, and so he ordered them all killed. 'He ordered his gardeners to kill every bird in the Vatican!' people said. 'All the birds killed, so he can sleep better in the morning!' This was the man Galileo was trying to reason with.

Often as he wrote he sighed. So many had died. His parents and Marina, Sarpi and Sagredo and Salviati, Cesarini and Cosimo ... The world of his youth, and of the years in Padua, seemed to have disappeared into the darkness of a previous epoch. He had lived on into a more troubled time. When he was sick it often seemed to the household that it was sorrow that kept him in bed more than any pains of the flesh.

To comfort himself for two of these losses, Galileo structured his new treatise as a series of dialogues between Filipo Salviati, Giavanfrancesco Sagredo, and a third character named Simplicio. Salviati would express the views that Galileo himself was trying to teach, although Salviati also referred from time to time to an 'Academician' which the context made clear was Galileo himself. Sagredo, the man Galileo had eulogized as 'my idol', was then the voice of an intelligent courtier of the time, curious and open-minded, willing to be educated by Salviati's explanations. This was so much the way they had been in real life – not just patrons to Galileo, but friends, teachers, brothers – like the elder brothers he had never had, and had so much enjoyed having. There had to be someone you could boast to who would enjoy hearing it, who would be proud to hear it from you; and wiser heads who would look after you too. He wrote with his heart full and his throat tight:

Now, since bitter death has deprived Venice and Florence of those two great luminaries in the noon of their years, I have resolved to make their fame live on in these pages, so far as my poor abilities will permit, by introducing them as interlocutors in the present argument. May it please those two great souls, forever cherished in my heart, to accept this public monument of my eternal love. And may the memory of their eloquence assist me in delivering to posterity the promised reflections.

The character Simplicio, on the other hand, was indeed a

simpleton, as the name suggested, although there had been a Roman philosopher with such a name centuries before. But his meaning was obvious: he stood for all the enemies Galileo had sparred with over the years, the whole crowd mashed together, not only the many who had denounced him openly but also the many more who had spoken in private, or in lectures or sermons all over Italy. Simplicio's lame arguments would illustrate every one of the logical errors and deliberate misunderstandings, the exaggerations and false syllogisms and irrelevancies, the sheer stubborn stupidity, which Galileo had faced over the years. Often he laughed aloud as he wrote, not his low 'huh huh huh huh' of true amusement, but the single bark of his sarcastic laugh. 'Ha! I've heard you say that very thing!'

The book was structured as four days of dialogue between the three men, gathered to talk at Sagredo's palazzo in Venice, that pink ark where Galileo had spent so many magnificent hilarious nights. The first day's discussion concerned his astronomical discoveries, including many new observations about the moon that he had made since publishing the *Sidereus Nuncius*. Along the way he interspersed jokes, wordplay, odd little observations that were mysterious even to him:

From the oldest records we have it that formerly, at the Straits of Gibraltar, Abila and Calpe were joined together with some lesser mountains which held the ocean in check; but these mountains being separated by some cause, the opening admitted the sea, which flooded in so as to form the Mediterranean. Consider the immensity of this . . .

Well, yes; but this event had happened a million years before, and the 'oldest records' he spoke of did not exist. How did Galileo know about it? He himself was not completely sure. His old dreams haunted him; he remembered them in fluctuating detail, sometimes even dreaming he was out in space again. He knew for sure he had unfinished business there; but he was less and less sure what it was. He knew that his mind had been tampered with, and more than once overwhelmed.

396

Thus he had his Sagredo ask, when they were discussing the telescope,

Will the new observations and discoveries made with this admirable instrument never cease?

And his Salviati answered,

If its progress follows the course of other great inventions, one may hope that in time things will be seen which we cannot even imagine at present.

Indeed.

Later in that First Day he wrote,

But we are not keeping track of the flight of time . . . a person's memory becomes so confused with such a multitude of things.

So true. Later still he wrote,

But surpassing all stupendous inventions, what sublimity of mind was his who dreamed of finding means to communicate his deepest thoughts to any other person, though distant by mighty intervals of place and time! Of talking with those who are in India; of speaking to those who are not yet born, and will not be born for a thousand or even ten thousand years . . .

What sublimity of mind, indeed! People really had no idea. He revised the passage so that it seemed to refer to language and to writing; but for him it also referred to something both more immediate and more mysterious. To speak with people who would not be born for a thousand years . . .

The Second Day of his dialogues concerned the movement of the Earth; the evidence for it, and the explanations for why it was not immediately evident to those standing on the Earth's moving surface. This required a detailed description of some parts of his motion studies, and Galileo could not help having Salviati say about this,

How many propositions I have noted in Aristotle (meaning always his science) that are not only wrong, but wrong in such a way that their diametrical opposites are true.

397

Ha! But Simplicio was a stubborn character, in the book as in the world. Sagredo tried to explain to him the concepts of relative motion. He tried everything: he used for an example the effect of back spin on tennis balls; he even proposed a clever thought experiment concerning shooting crossbow bolts from a moving carriage, forward and back, to see if the bolts flew further or shorter distances if shot in the direction of the carriage's movement or against it. He pointed out, almost kindly, after the failure of one such Socratic lesson, that Simplicio could not seem to free his mind from his preconceptions enough to perform a thought experiment. None of this made any difference to Simplicio, and the Second Day came to an end without him being illuminated by any new understanding.

The Third Day was then a technical discussion of the astronomical issues, which Galileo augmented with many small geometrical drawings, to make clearer his meaning concerning the Earth's movement. Some of Tycho Brahe's data were included, and a dense discussion of all Galileo's telescopic work: the attempt to find parallax, the phases of Venus, the odd motions of Mars, the difficulty of seeing Mercury. It turned out to be the longest dialogue of the four, and inevitably, it seemed, the least entertaining.

The Fourth Day was a revision of Galileo's earlier treatise on tides and how they provided clear evidence of the Earth's rotation. This meant that the final fifty pages of his masterpiece were devoted to a false argument. Galileo was obscurely aware of this, but he wrote the chapter anyway, following the plan he had set down years before – because, among other reasons, it seemed to him that his Jovian understanding of the cause of tides was too weird to be true, as well as impossible to describe. 'I don't like this,' he grumbled to Cartophilus one night. 'It's giving me that feeling again. I'm just doing what I always have done.'

'So change it then, maestro.'

'The changes too have already happened,' Galileo growled. 'Fate changes, not us.' And dipped his pen and forged on. It was the book of his life; he had to finish it in style. But would it be enough to convince Urban VIII to its views?

By now Galileo over the course of his life had accrued three kinds of enemies. First came the Dominicans, the Dogs of God (cani Domini), who since Trent had been using the Inquisition to smash all challenges to orthodoxy. Then there were the secular Aristotelians, all the professors and philosophers and laymen who stood by the Peripatetic philosophy. Lastly and most recently, for they had supported Galileo during his first visits to Rome, the Jesuits too had turned on him, perhaps because of his attack on Sarsi; no one was quite sure about that, but enemies they now were. It was getting to be quite a crowd. His character Simplicio would be certain to offend scores, even hundreds of men. Galileo was perhaps being ironical when he had Simplicio say late in the Second Day, *The further this goes on, the more confused I become,* and Sagredo then replies, *This is a sign that the arguments are beginning to change your mind.*

Or perhaps it was a sign that Galileo still had not learned that arguments never change anyone's mind.

One day, returning from the convent of San Matteo alone, his mule Cremonini shied away from a startled rabbit and threw the inattentive Galileo to the ground. Galileo was too sore to remount, and had to limp all the way home.

'We're too far away,' he declared when he got there. 'We need to move closer to San Matteo.' He had said this often before, but now he meant it.

No one at Bellosguardo was pleased. Arcetri, where San Matteo was located, was a village in the hills west of the city. It was not as easy to get to Florence from there as it was from Bellosguardo. And Bellosguardo was such a big place that any villa in Arcetri would be smaller, and so would not require as large a staff.

Still, this became a new project for Galileo. The *Dialogo* was nearing completion, so he could give the matter some attention, when he was not working on the problem of publication. Then also Maria Celeste was happy to help organize a house hunt in Arcetri. Indeed she was so good at it, so industrious and resourceful, that Galileo began to wish aloud that she could arrange for his book's publication as well. And then Vincenzo and his sweet wife Sestilia returned to Bellosguardo, and the hunt for a new house became something they all did together, a kind of family outing, a pleasure for all.

Things might have gone equally well in regard to publishing the *Dialogo,* except Federico Cesi died. Another great young Roman Galilean dead in his meridian, long before his time; it was a pattern of bad luck that almost looked providential, or diabolical, and some of us worried about that.

This time it was a disaster for Galileo beyond what he realized. Cesi was the only patron who might have been powerful enough to publish the *Dialogo* without trouble. And with him gone, his Lyncean Academy immediately collapsed too. Only now did it become obvious that it had been his private club all along.

His loss meant Galileo had to seek a publisher in Florence, which meant obtaining formal approval from the censor there as well as from Father Monster in Rome. And in Florence, the prospect that publication would cause political trouble was upsetting the Medicis. Young Ferdinando had by now come into full possession of his crown, and he was concerned to consolidate his power. The last thing he wanted was for his father's old court astronomer to be causing trouble with the Inquisition. So there were Florentine factions to add to the Roman ones opposed to publication. Indeed, with the single faction that had been in favour of the book now defunct, only an irregular band of Galileans scattered all over Italy were left to hope for its success.

By 1629 the book's situation had become so complicated that Galileo decided another trip to Rome was in order, to make sure his permission to publish was secure. He went in 1630, at great trouble and expense, and against the will of the Medicis.

As with all the previous times he had been in Rome, everything there seemed to have changed. It was as if each time he visited it was the Rome of a slightly different universe.

This time Urban agreed to meet with him only once, and that only after a great diplomatic effort by ambassador Niccolini, who made this effort on his own, apparently because of his liking for Galileo.

Once again Galileo woke in the Medicis' Roman embassy, and carefully dressed in his threadbare finest, remembering all the times this had happened before. He was conveyed down to the Vatican in an embassy litter, mentally rehearsing his points, and so intensely curious as to what he would find that he saw nothing of the narrow alleys and broad strada of the endless hilly city.

This time Urban was calmly formal. Lacking an invitation to rise, Galileo remained on his knees and spoke from there.

Urban's carapace of power was now reinforced by a solid layer of flesh. He was more voluble than before; he spoke of his garden, his Florentine relatives, the poor state of the roads. He made it clear that he did not want the subject of astronomy to arise – not yet, anyway. He left it unclear if he were ever going to want it to arise. Galileo felt his knees begin to splinter under him as he made his part of the conversation; from this perspective he saw a different man. It was not just that Barberini's face had thickened, his jaw gone more massive, his small eyes smaller, his skin more coarse and pale; it was not even that his goatee had been coloured a brown that did not quite match the hair on his head. He looked down at Galileo as if from an enormous distance, of course, but also as if he knew things about Galileo that he thought Galileo should know but didn't. As was indeed the case, because of the secret denunciation of *Il Saggiatore*. Spies had recently passed along word that Urban had had the charge investigated; but no one had heard the result. Occasionally there were times when the Vatican was like a black box with no lid, and this was one of them.

The silence on that topic made it seem possible that Urban had set the matter aside, at least for now. And there were developing aspects of the larger situation in Europe that oddly protected Galileo from Urban. Prosecuting his previously favoured scientist for heresy would not help Urban in his struggles with the Spanish, but merely be taken by them as a sign of weakness, a baring of the throat. Urban did not want that at all.

His look now suggested that he had not forgotten the denunciation, that he knew he could use it if he wanted to. But Galileo did not know enough to read the look. He had his eye on one thing only, and seizing the thorny opportunity, he felt a quiet moment come on them and asked, 'Your Holiness, I wonder if you will bless me with your opinion of my book on the world systems, which I have continued to write, and am ready to submit to Fra Riccardi for approval?'

Urban's brow furrowed and his look darkened. 'If our Commissioner is to approve it, why do you ask us? Do you think we would countermand our own appointment to the Holy Office of the Congregation?'

'Not at all, Your Holiness, it's just that your word is all in all to me.'

'You have made it clear in your book that God can do anything He pleases, correct?'

'Very much so, Holiness. That is the book's point.'

At the back of the Vatican garden, Cartophilus trembled to hear this. It was impossible to tell from the look on Galileo's face whether he knew he was lying or not.

For a long time Urban too regarded him closely. The kneeling old astronomer looked like a dressed barrel topped by an upraised head, his bearded red face open and sincere. Finally the Pope nodded, a single slow, deep nod, a blessing in itself. 'You may proceed with our blessing, Signor Galileo Galilei.'

These words surprised several of the people who heard it. The sound of the sentence hung in the air. Hope itself seemed to hoist Galileo back to his feet, as if he were a much younger man than the one who had kneeled.

Francesco Niccolini provided him a room in Ferdinando's Roman embassy, so that for the next two months Galileo could be comfortable as he went out every day to do his best to align the rest of the forces in Rome in the way Cesi would have. Urban's private approval had been given, but clearly there was more diplomatic work to be done to secure the project. And yet Galileo had never been a great diplomat. All his life he had flattered his superiors excessively while also presuming to know much more than they did. This was not a good combination, and worse yet, he was still quick with the cutting sarcastic rejoinder if anyone disagreed with him. Thus it was no coincidence that after five visits he had more enemies in Rome than friends. And with rumours of his purpose in the capital widespread, there were many now out to subvert him if they could.

They were effective. At the end of the two months he had managed only to secure a partial permission to publish from Riccardi, conditional on Riccardi's approval of the full text, which would come only after revision of any areas deemed problematic.

In truth, given the overall situation, he could have expected little more. The words of Urban were the ones he had wanted to hear most, anyway.

So he returned to Florence. He was beginning to hate these trips to Rome, and yet of course they had all been spring picnics compared to the one left to come.

*   *   *

While he was gone, Maria Celeste found a suitable villa for rent in Arcetri, called *Il Gioello*, the Jewel. The rent was only thirty-five scudi a year, much less than Bellosguardo's hundred, because it was so much smaller, and in a less convenient location. But Galileo declared that despite the diminution in size he would keep the entire staff, so everyone was happy. They left Bellosguardo, where they had lived together for fourteen years, without a backward glance.

Galileo was particularly happy with the new house. From his bedroom window on the second floor he could look down the lane and see the corner of the convent of San Matteo. He could visit every day, and he did. The house rules there had relaxed to the point where he was free to enter the central hall, and to help the women with their domestic repairs. He did carpentry, he fixed their clock. He wrote them little plays to perform, and even music to sing; once he intertwined all his favourites among his father's melodies into one polyphonic chorus, which brought tears to his eyes to hear. He played the lute for them.

Maria Celeste was in her own personal paradise. Arcangela, on the other hand, still would not speak to him. In fact she had stopped speaking entirely; also bathing and combing her hair. She had the look of a madwoman, which was only appropriate; she was a madwoman. They had to keep her away from the wine cellar, even the kitchen. Maria Celeste fed her by hand. If she hadn't, her sister would have starved. But she did.

Stuffed into Galileo's new house were his sister's family, his brother's family, Vincenzio and Sestilia and child, the servants, and a number of artisans, including Mazzoleni and his family, now jammed into a shed off the larger shed they had converted into a new workshop. Despite La Piera's best efforts in the kitchen, it was chaos every day. Galileo ignored all that and persisted in getting the *Dialogo* published, now by a new publisher in Florence, which meant he could work directly with the printers in their shop. It proceeded very slowly, but eventually it was time to submit it to Riccardi and get his approval, if he could.

At this point Galileo had obtained permission to publish from the Medicis' bishop's vicar, from the Florentine Inquisitor, and from the Grand Duke's censor. Riccardi had read some chapters and discussed their contents with Urban, he said; but now he told Galileo that he would need to read the whole manuscript in its final form. That was bad enough, but also the plague had again forced a quarantine on everything moving up and down the peninsula, and a bulky manuscript was unlikely to make it all the way to Rome. Galileo offered to send the preface and conclusion, which was where the potential problems were dealt with, he said, while the main text of the book could be reviewed and reported on by someone in Florence chosen by Riccardi. Riccardi agreed to this, and his designated reviewer, Fra Giacinto Stefani, read the main text with minute attention to detail, and was won over to the book's views in the process. Meanwhile Riccardi was slow at getting to the preface and conclusion; when he finally did, he changed nothing to speak of, but merely ordered that Galileo add a last paragraph, like a chord at the end of a coda, or an Amen, which would make it clear that the book's speculations were not physical arguments about the real world but mathematical concepts used to help predictions and the like. The *angelica dottrina* would be thereby affirmed.

Galileo wrote it out thusly, as the final argument of the book, which he put into the mouth of Simplicio:

I admit that your thoughts seem to me more ingenious than many others I have heard. I do not therefore consider them true and conclusive; indeed, keeping always before my mind's eye a most solid doctrine that I once heard from a most eminent and learned person, and before which one must fall silent, I know that if asked whether God in His infinite power and wisdom could have conferred upon the watery element its observed reciprocating motion using some other means than moving its containing vessels, *both of you would reply that He could have, and He would have known how to do this in many ways which are unthinkable to our minds. From this I conclude that, this being so, it would be excessive boldness for anyone to limit and restrict the Divine power and wisdom to some particular fancy of his own.*

To which Galileo had Salviati reply: *An admirable and angelic doctrine, and well in accord with another one, also Divine, which, while it grants to us the right to argue about the constitution of the universe (perhaps in order that the working of the human mind shall not be curtailed or made lazy), adds that we cannot discover the work of His Hands. Let us, then, exercise these activities permitted to us and ordained by God, that we may recognize and thereby so much the more admire His greatness.*

Which was very nicely expressed, Galileo thought, both to affirm Urban's *angelica dottrina* and at the same time assert the freedom Galileo had been given to discuss things *ex suppositione.*

Riccardi approved the book without having read the whole of the finished version. With an endless number of small problems and delays, the publisher in Florence began the work of printing a thousand copies.

With the *Dialogo* finished and published, he was happy to see an invitation to a banquet come from the Grand Duchess Christina. She had not been sending these to him as often as before, and when they had come Galileo had been too harried to be pleased. Now he was happy to accept and attend.

In the antechamber to the great dining salon of the Medici palazzo, Galileo made his way through the crowd of courtiers to the drinks table and was given a tall gold goblet filled with new wine. He greeted Picchena and all the rest of his acquaintances at the court, and was circulating and talking with them when the Grand Duchess Christina, as distinguished and regal as ever, called him over to the open French doors leading out to the terrace and formal garden. 'Signor Galileo, please come here, I want you to meet a new friend of mine.'

The friend was Hera.

Galileo clapped both hands to his chest; hopefully this resembled his usual flamboyant court mannerisms enough that it did not look too bizarre, because he was helpless to stop himself – he simply had to press down on his pounding heart, to keep it from breaking his ribs and flying free of him. It was definitely her, right out of his dreams: a woman quite tall but otherwise ordinary enough, her muscles concealed by her clothes, fair-haired, fine featured, well dressed in the style of the court – looking rather stout in such raiment. She had the same intelligent look in her eye as always, now curious to see his reaction to her presence, both concerned and amused, a very familiar look.

'Well met, my lady,' he managed to croak as he took up and kissed her offered hand. It felt chill.

'It's my honour,' she said. 'I read your *Sidereus Nuncius* when I was young, and thought it very interesting.'

407

Here in Italy she called herself Countess Alessandra Bocchineri Buonamici. She was Sestilia Galilei's long-lost older sister, she said, and the diplomat Giovanfrancesco Buonamici's wife. Here she spoke Tuscan with all the fluency of a Florentine, her voice richer and more vibrant than the internal translator's had been. Galileo mouthed some typical phrases of courtly small talk, feeling Christina's eye on them. Knowing his confusion, Alessandra did most of the talking. He learned that she spoke French and Latin, and played the spinet, and wrote poems, and corresponded with her friends in Paris and London. Count Buonamici was her third husband, she informed him; the first two had died when she was quite a bit younger. He could only nod; it was a common story; the plague in the last decade had killed half the people of Milan, and almost as many everywhere else. People died here. But not on Jupiter –

'I will seat you two next to each other at the banquet,' Christina declared, happy to see them hitting it off.

'Many thanks, Your Beautiful Highness,' Galileo said, and bowed.

When Christina had left them alone in the doorway, Galileo swallowed hard and said, 'You remind me of someone?'

Her oak-coloured eyes crinkled at the corners. 'I should think so,' she said. 'Perhaps you can escort me out to the terrace. I would like to take the air before we eat.'

'Of course.' Galileo felt a strange kind of pleasure growing in him, fearful but romantic, uncanny but familiar. To *know* she was real – it made him shudder.

Out on the terrace there were some other couples, and the two of them talked in distracted semi-coherence about Florence and Venice, Tasso and Ariosto. He spoke for Ariosto's warmth while she defended Tasso's depth, and neither were surprised to find they came down on opposite sides of the question. Her husband had just been assigned to a posting in Germany, she said; she would have to leave quite soon.

'I understand,' he said uncertainly.

408

She asked about his work, and Galileo described the problems he was having with the publication of his book.

'Perhaps you could delay publication?' she asked. 'Just by a year or two, until things calm down?'

'No,' Galileo said. 'The printing has already begun. And I have to publish. The sooner the better, as far as I'm concerned. I've already waited fourteen years, or even forty.'

'Yes,' she said. 'And yet.'

A crease appeared between her eyebrows as she considered him. She took his hand and led him around a corner of the palazzo, to a long bench against the wall in the dark. She asked him to sit down, and then reached out and touched him.

Chapter Sixteen The Look

I do not wish, Your Excellency, to engulf myself inadvertently in a boundless sea from which I might never get back to port, nor in trying to solve one difficulty do I wish to give rise to a hundred more, as I fear may have already happened in sailing but this little way from shore.

— GALILEO, *The Assayer*

He stood on the fractured ice, under the livid gas giant. Hera stood beside him, looking uncharacteristically abashed. 'Sorry to intrude like that,' she said, 'but you went away without warning.'

'Cartophilus took me away. He said it looked like I was in distress.'

'We all were,' she said. 'We still are.' She gestured up at writhing Jupiter. 'I need your help.'

'Good,' he said. 'Because I need yours.'

The gas giant was still roiling in the sky, great red spots all over it, many of them swirling into each other and casting off convoluted squiggling ribbons.

Hera said, 'Aurora's people have captured Ganymede and his group. She's getting messages from Jupiter itself, she says, and because of them, she wants to take Ganymede physically up there, to Jupiter.'

'*To* Jupiter? But why?'

'That's what I want your help to find out. At this point you appear to have a better understanding with Aurora than anyone else,' shooting a sharp glance at him. 'All she'll say to me is that we need to hurry if we want to be part of it. I thought you would want to be here, and as you had disappeared, I went to see.'

'I'm glad you did. It was good to see you there.' This was true beyond what he could explain, even to himself.

She nodded and led him to her ship, which was where they had left it, on the ice outside the gate of Rhadamanthyus. He climbed up after her and strapped himself into his chair. This place was like a room in his mind now, a closet where many memories from his past were housed, along with the conversations with Hera. Here he had seen the dark side of Jupiter, and its new crescent slicing into the starry black.

She tapped at her pad and said, 'It seems you were right about the breakout of storms. Jupiter, or whatever lives in Jupiter, is upset. Aurora says we need to let it know that the attack on Europa was an aberration in us, a criminal act that we abhor. She says we must go there to make that clear. It's responding to her now, and she says it appears to want to contact the mind of the one responsible for the . . .'

'For the damage,' Galileo suggested.

'Yes.' She shuddered, tapped on her pad, and the ship rose until they were pressed back hard into their chairs. 'I guess it can do what it wants with him.'

'It might kill him.'

'So be it.'

'It might kill all of us.'

'I know. I can send you back if you want.' She gestured at the box of her teletrasporta, there between them on the floor of the cabin.

'Not yet.'

On the window screen he could see that other ships were also rising over the now ruddy curve of Europa, silver pips surrounding them above and below. Hera spoke at speed to her unseen interlocutors. He saw a new icy crater wall that looked as though it were blanketed by diamond dust; this was where Ganymede's ship had crashed landed, presumably. All the ships were staying well away from the hole, which still spewed a faint talcum into space, not at speed, as with the sulphur geysers of Io, but as if the planet were breathing out frost on a cold morning. Hopefully it was not its last breath.

Galileo was thrown forward against his restraints by an abrupt deceleration. Their viewscreen showed that they had been docked by another ship so alike in appearance that it seemed to be the image of theirs in a mirror. Hera was both talking and tapping at her pad. Galileo felt or heard the antechamber doors opening and shutting. The other ship pulled away.

'To Jupiter,' Hera said.

A sharp acceleration up. On the screen Jupiter lay ahead of them, spotted like a pox victim. Poor young Ferdinando had looked like that in 1626. The rest of their little fleet was nowhere to be seen. After a period of silent flight, heading up to the hectic sphere, now more awesome than ever, Galileo said, 'Can you give me the tutorial that tells me what happened between my time and yours? Something compressed? Because I think I need to know.'

'Yes.' She handed him her celatone. 'It will go fast. It will be a sum over histories, as it is called, showing you many potentialities at once, in the braided stream format. It will anastomose in you as a synaptic bloom. Those can be confusing, and give you a headache.'

Galileo put the heavy helmet on his skull. Marina's face – the old dragon – a ball falling through space in a swift curve –

Then there it was. Voices speaking in Latin overlapped in his head, as if several Plutarchs spoke at the same time; but mostly it was an instantaneous flood of images. Galileo was on the Earth and even in it. He was everywhere. He looked, he listened, but more than anything else he felt the ferocious tempests in Europe after his time, felt how the early advances in maths and physics that he had learned from Aurora, so beautiful and inspiring, were somehow intertwined and complicit with a continuous tale of war and spoilation. It didn't have to be that way, and there were fragile strands in which it seemed not to have happened, but the main broad channel of history was filled with blood. Humanity's increasing power over nature meant more powerful weapons, of course, along with more powerful medicines. Populations bloomed, the whole world was explored and settled, the primitive peoples killed off, those less primitive enslaved or conquered and turned into client states of the European powers. Even Italy coalesced into a single state, as Machiavelli had so much desired, although late in the imperial moment and at a point where their only colony was poor Abyssinia. But none of that mattered; all over the world newly growing populations were at each other's throats, fighting, killing, dying. In the nineteenth and twentieth centuries the world was carved up entirely into industrial empires; people were enslaved in factories and cities. Galileo felt their lives: not one in ten of them even tended a garden. 'They live like ants,' he groaned.

In the next period the wars between empires grew massive, every part of civilization so mechanized, cruel and powerful, that a point came where entire nations of people were gathered up and fed into roaring furnaces and destroyed. Billions died. Sickened, appalled, Galileo watched on with a shrunken heart as all nature was then in effect fed to the furnaces to feed a rapacious humanity that quickly rebounded from the deaths and became superabundant again, like an infestation of maggots, a sporulating mass of suffering beasts. In such conditions war and pestilence were constant, no matter the progress in mathematics and technology. Total war was more the rule than the exception; army against army was rare. Marking all the potentialities and mocking all their potential, innumerable natural and human catastrophes broke out all

413

across the time streams, until in Galileo's mind the Earth appeared not unlike the maelstrom-strewn face of Jupiter, a planet red with blood. It came to the point where it was an open question how much of humanity could survive; and all this in a supposedly scientific world, with continual advances in their technologies and their potential physical control over nature. It was horrifying to witness; it was as if a cosmic race between creation and destruction had both sides succeeding at once and accelerating all the while, creating in their conjunction something unexpected and monstrous.

Galileo moaned as he experienced all this, as it blossomed all at once and entire in his memory, something he always seemed to have known. The inherent anger, the depth of hatred, the potential for evil; he had always known, always seen it. At any point the monsters could break out. Again he saw that he was being shown not just one single history but a superimposition of many of them, following the same meta-pattern but all collapsing into chaos to one degree or another, so that he was being flooded with many bad potentialities at once. Some were bad, others were horrific, a few were stark apocalyptic.

He saw further, saw then that the centuries after those were always a miserable desperate struggle, in which a much reduced and demoralized humanity tried to get by in the wreckage of the world. Having ruined so much, being so many fewer, and yet also becoming quickly more powerful, also more chastened and realistic, people began patching things up. Some recoveries went better than others. Nature itself was robust, and its harrowed surviving forms proliferated as always. For humanity it was slower and less steady. So much had been lost; Galileo felt in his stomach the iron ball of despair that had dragged down every single version of these generations' efforts. Shattered, traumatized, frightened, they did what they could. Science itself proved as robust as any other living survivor, as tough as some jungle vine spreading through the tropics. A new paradigm, born of exhaustion as much as hope, led them into an array of emergency landscape restorations. Centuries of various duration told of a dogged and heroic effort to rebuild some minimal scaffolding for the future. It was all done for the future. A human civilization now aware of the dangers that the extinction of any species posed for all of them, did what it could to restore the natural fauna and flora of the Earth, and the underlying chemistry of the ocean and air, so badly poisoned. Here they were aided by the fecundity of life, its resilience; and in this time science finally was directed entirely at the problem of restitution, and put foremost in humanity's judgement of its efforts. Now it seemed that there was a strong channel in these braiding streams that ran clear toward something healthy. In these worlds some of the huge menageries of extinct species were returned, reconstituted or engineered from what germs and seeds remained of them.

After that he saw the slow restoration of Earth, and even the return of humans to space. They had been there briefly before, in the midst of the wars, when it had meant little or nothing; now their launch into the solar system was a burst toward fresh starts, as all kinds of groups went out to begin anew on Mars, in the asteroids, around Jupiter and Saturn and Mercury. This was their Accelerando, bursting away from Earth like a seed pod, people and potentialities everywhere expanding outward in what looked like Fibonacci spirals. By this time all the histories looked much alike. Tiny moons were made into little worlds, the big planets altered toward something like gardened new Earths. As their powers grew, ventures were made into new dimensions, only partly understood, which then led them to the control of truly vast new sources of energy.

The two outermost gas giants were destroyed to power thrusts into the entangled manifolds, including the technology that allowed analeptic introjections, the shift of consciousness and effective action backward in time. The idea to try changing some of their pasts, it seemed to Galileo, was born out of the trauma of the nightmare humankind had earlier unleashed on itself and the world. The hope was for restitution: if the past could be changed, it was possible that an amount of suffering and extinction beyond all telling might be averted, and humanity spared the cataclysm of its earlier self. Not only restitution, then, but redemption. But even that was very much in doubt.

Galileo came to in Hera's little ship. They were a finger or two closer to Jupiter, it seemed. He wiped the tears from his eyes and rubbed his face hard, feeling much as he had after the vision of his fiery alternative. The whole world put to the stake. It seemed he could taste the ashes in his mouth.

'The overall course of events,' he said to Hera, trying to hold his voice steady, 'reminds me of one of my old experiments, where I placed two inclined planes in the shape of a V. However low the ball dropped, it rose back up to that same level. After all the years, and with all your powers, you've only just managed to get back up to the level where you started to fall.'

'Where *we* started to fall,' Hera corrected him grimly. 'It's all one manifold, remember? It's all happening perpetually.'

This Galileo still could not grasp in his feelings, however, no matter how much he understood the mathematics involved; which was more than she did, probably. But she seemed to accept the paradoxical wholeness and multiple flows of time and history. She accepted the nonlocality, the fractured interweaving of potentialities, collapsing in and out of being in a continuous dance of past and future, a complex vector of c time and e time and antichronos, moments of being flickering in the triple wave.

'No wonder Ganymede tried to change things,' he said.

'Yes.' She nodded, grimacing. 'But he may have tried too hard, and made things worse. In a way that you must be very familiar with.'

*   *   *

There was a light clang from below them. A small group of people in silver spacesuits entered Hera's command room, carrying someone who was in a suit like theirs but which was rigid, it appeared, so that they carried its occupant by the elbows. Behind the faceplate of the rigid suit's helmet, Ganymede's sweaty hatchet face glared out at them. His spittle dotted the inner surface of his faceplate, and he was still talking, though they could hear nothing of what he said.

His captors took off their helmets. One of them was Aurora, her face flushed, so that she looked younger to Galileo than she had on Europa, perhaps forty or fifty; a woman in her prime, mature and alive. Galileo was surprised to see such a transformation, and wondered if she came from some different temporal isotope, an oxbow in which she was literally younger. But she appeared to recognize him, and in fact came over and gave him a brief hug. Like all the rest of them, she was considerably taller than he was.

'You,' Hera said to the imprisoned Ganymede. 'Be prepared to face the Jovian, if you can. We're taking you to it.'

Ganymede spoke again, but made not a sound. Hera slapped his chest and suddenly he could be heard:

'– think it will notice our presence?'

'It already has. Be ready to explain yourself.'

Ganymede was strapped into one of the chairs behind Galileo's, his suit still rigid, his helmet left on his head.

There was a silence; no one knew what to say. Hera made the craft transparent again, and they flew toward Jupiter fully exposed to the sight of its awful metamorphosis.

The gas giant now occupied about a third of the black sky; it was so massive it was beginning to look like a plane rather than a sphere – a world they were falling onto – a god they now confronted, like mosquitoes hovering before a poxy moon face. The myriad new vortices had disrupted the huge surface so thoroughly that the heretofore obvious latitudinal bands were getting hard to make out. The once-beautiful planet had become a great plain of boils, a choleric ocean of maelstroms.

'Where will you go?' Galileo asked Hera.

She shrugged and looked over at Aurora, who was staring at Jupiter as if in a trance. They all watched her as she regarded it.

Finally Aurora said, 'Head into the Great Red Spot.'

Hera said, 'Can you still tell which one it is?'

'Yes.'

As before in his transits with Hera, the ship's progress appeared slow.

'We look like a sperm headed for the egg,' Aurora said at one point. 'I wonder if we will be fertile? And what might be born of it?'

'Are you in communication with Jupiter itself?' Galileo asked her.

'Yes, or what lives in it. But only in the same way we were in communication with the Europan sentience. The exchange is mathematical, and seems to indicate our interlocutor exists in other manifolds, so this is a somewhat weak interaction for it. For those reasons, or others, we are having trouble establishing any system to convey meaning.'

'How did you know it wanted us to come up to it?'

'A kind of geometrical schematic. And then there were changes in Ganymede's ships that allowed us to capture them. We are being drawn there by logical inference, you might say. A tractor beam of logical inferences.'

Galileo said to her, 'Can you give me some more of the learning drug that you gave me during the tutorials?'

She nodded, never taking her eyes from Jupiter. 'I was thinking the same thing myself. Do you think it's wise?'

'Why not,' Galileo said. Anything to get the taste of your ashes out of my mouth, he didn't say. She handed him a tiny pill, which he swallowed dry. He wondered what effect it would have on her, augmented in her mentation as she already was by her machine earrings. He realized he had no idea what might be going on in her head, what kind of creature she was; and she was their leader now.

Time passed. A protraction of mind. Galileo's thoughts began to race and bloom, sing in their polyphonic fugue. He watched the godlike planet with its storm-racked surface slowly fill their entire sky. Space was now a black velvet ring bordering an immense mottled red plane. When Galileo looked behind his chair, he saw that the black was a dome, starry as before; but everything was now obscured by a flickering indigo mist, as if they flew within a giant spark.

They homed in on one of the biggest of the many red spots. The original, apparently. From where they were now, the texture of the Great Red Spot was much more articulated, revealing that it was not flat but rather an immense broad dome raised up from the surface of the planet, marked by finer and finer turbulences. Smaller swirls were still visible outside the great red one, some spinning clockwise like it and raised up like boils, others spinning counterclockwise and forming depressions like whirlpools. All these phenomena seemed to Galileo to be elaborations of the simplest forms: they were circles spun hard, until under the impetus of irregularities and each other they became elliptical shapes, spitting out colourful streamers at their edges. These shot away in parabolic paths, slowed in the resistance of gas clouds of umber and sulphur, then spiralled up into new red circles of their own. The characteristic eddying repeated across all the scales visible: the surface of the planet was a riot of spinning ellipses.

Hera was absorbed in a conversation with Aurora. Galileo got up and went over to Ganymede, looked into his helmet. Ganymede recognized him and looked startled at his presence.

'You have misunderstood why things went awry,' Galileo said to him. 'Science needed more religion, not less. And religion needed more science. The two needed to become one. Science is a form of devotion, a kind of worship. You made a fundamental mistake, both in my time and your own.'

419

Ganymede tried to shake his head within the immobilized helmet, squashing first one narrow cheek then the other against it. His blade of a nose slightly tilted to his left, Galileo saw. 'We each must play our part,' Ganymede said, the hoarse woodwind sound of his voice coming from the side of his helmet. 'You have to understand that. You think you know enough to judge me, but you don't. If only you knew. I know you have been listening to Hera, that you take her view of things. But she has a perspective no broader than yours. Understand me: I come from a future time, as far from hers as hers is from you. I've seen what happens if we do not play our parts. I wish I could show you the future that lies in wait if we interact with the gas giant and its children. It leads to extinction. I've seen it, I come from the end times. We know how to avoid it. I'm doing what has to be done. *And you must do the same.*'

His eyes bugged out, they seemed the only part of his face fully free to move. They were little twinned worlds of their own, unmatched by anything else in their intensity. He continued:

'The nonlocal entanglement of the manifold is total, everything part of everything else. It's all still happening, all still becoming. Each significant historical action collapses a wave function of potentialities, and alters the temporal vector. If you play your part, that of the first scientist martyred by religion, the impetus toward more scientific futures is profound. No matter what happens after that, the worst is only so dire. We arrive at this moment you now visit in your prolepsis – problematic, yes, but in recovery from the bad years, which are less bad than in the other flow of potentialities. And when you are brought here to this time, as I have done, we escape the worst consequences of the encounter with the alien mind.'

Aurora and Hera came over and now listened to him too. He said to Aurora, 'Have you shown him what happens in the interval between his time and yours? Or did you just give him the mathematics?'

'It was a maths tutorial,' Aurora said dryly.

420

Behind his facemask Ganymede was sweating. He glared at her: 'Why not give him the historical context? How does your mathematics matter, without that?'

Aurora said, 'Mathematics was what humanity managed to do despite the disasters. Of course it matters. It was the only achievement that was real.'

'He needs to know the price that was paid.'

'He knows,' Hera said. 'He experienced an overview just before you joined us.'

Ganymede, his gaze transfixing Galileo, said, 'You know?'

'Yes,' Galileo confirmed. 'I saw. It was a long descent, a desperate recovery. In short, for the most part, a nightmare.'

'Yes! Precisely! But look: if you don't play your part and become the scientist martyred for telling the truth, then the religions persist in their primitive insanities, and the wars go on for many centuries longer. *Many* centuries! Those were the bad potentialities you saw, the worst ones. The exterminations and counter-exterminations proliferate and extend, until billions and billions of people have died. That's just how it is. The tide turns at your bend in the river. The precise initial conditions of the birth of science are simply that important to the human story. They are crucial. One start leads to struggle and then harmony, the other to catastrophe. So compared to that, what's a few minutes in the fire? You only remain conscious for a minute or two! In fact we could visit you beforehand and give you an anaesthetic. You could experience it as if from the outside. And with those few moments give science the moral high ground for all time.'

'I don't see why,' Galileo protested. That his death could be good for humanity – it didn't make sense. Surely the reverse should be true.

'It doesn't matter whether you see why,' Ganymede insisted. 'This is no theory or prediction, it is an analepsis! *I'm telling you what my time has seen*. We've seen it, we know what can be changed and what can't, and your condemnation is determinative. Without it, religious wars continue for centuries longer than with it, all across the field of potentialities. I know Hera has been telling you otherwise, telling you it doesn't matter, telling you that you can avoid it. But you can't. For the sake of the billions, for the sake of all the extinct species, you have to do it.'

'No,' Galileo said.

'But the billions!'

'I don't care. I refuse.'

But he was uneasy. Ganymede's eyes were almost bursting from his head in their desperation, they seemed almost to press against the glass of his facemask. If he had seen some pattern, some bifurcation in the possibilities . . .

Galileo said, 'Aurora?'

'Aurora!' cried Ganymede. 'You have to tell him!'

'Be quiet,' Galileo warned him, 'or I will have Hera shut you up.'

Then he led Aurora to the farthest part of the cabin, behind Ganymede. Hera came along with them.

'Please, lady,' he said to Aurora. 'Can you tell me if what he says is true? Can it matter so much, what I do?'

Aurora said, 'It matters what all of us do. The manifold of manifolds is a complex of potentialities, each one implicate in all the others. They co-exist, they come in and out of existence complementarily, there are sums over history and wave function collapses, eddies and oxbows. As you have seen.'

'So things can change. I mean, by way of your analepses, using the entangler.'

'Yes.'

'And so Ganymede? When he said he came from your future – that he has seen the times to come beyond yours – is he telling the truth?'

Hera answered that: 'We don't know. He's been saying that for a long time. But there's a lot of confusion around his cult on Ganymede. He led them into Ganymede's ocean, before they started objecting to the Europans going into theirs. No one is sure what that means. And we see no other signs of analepsis from out of our future. We only know he is a charismatic to his group, and they do what he says. He has made many analepses, more than anyone else, we think, and each one collapses a wave function and creates a new stream, and influences all the rest. Some people have been trying to stop him. And that process, that struggle, has led us all here.'

They were closing on Jupiter's cloudy surface, which looked now like the side of an entirely different kind of universe, space itself everywhere dense with colour flowing. It was time for Ganymede to face his judgement; time for all of them to face the Other.

Galileo who has entered the aetherial spaces, cast light on
unknown stars, and plunged into the inner recesses of the
planets –
                – URBAN VIII, *letter to Grand Duke Ferdinando II*
                                    (written by Ciampoli)

The Great Red Spot was revealed more clearly than ever as a kind of thunderhead top rising out of the surface of the great planet, as big perhaps as the whole Earth, now palpably down below them, so that they looked past their feet at it. Their ship descended until the turbulent brick-coloured clouds of the overturned bowl's top were just under them. The sky above was tinted indigo, the stars barely visible. No part of Jupiter beyond the red storm was visible to them.

The clouds below them were not a uniform red, but rather shifting woven banners of salmon, brick, sand, copper, citron. There was no sign of anything aware of their presence. The little voice of Ganymede nattered on from his helmet, complaining still that he had been kidnapped, that approaching Jupiter was a fatal error, a stupid gesture likely to fry them all in radiation if it did not bring down death by ontological exposure, and so on. More than once Hera reached to him and turned down the volume coming from his helmet, but she never silenced him entirely.

The ship touched the clouds of the Great Red Spot.

'What now?' demanded the little voice of Ganymede.

Hera was studying her screens.

'Down,' she said.

*   *   *

They felt a little rocking side to side, front to back. Like being in a boat in a tidal race.

'Down again.'

It got darker. The light became like that of certain smoky sunsets, dull yellows shading to the orange nearest brown, streaked with swirls of bronze, or an occasional patch of bright spun gold. There were no patterns Galileo could discern, though he stared into the murk wondering if something might emerge. Everywhere there were ripples, including a cobalt pattern like the ripples of a damasked blade. This S folding was also a spirality, ruled by the Fibonnaci series but made dynamic and strange by compression and torque, a chaotic mass of tightly curving lines.

Then he saw more shapes in the warp of colour. Spicules that were like thorn balls, usually triradiate in form; various calymma, looking like masses of vesicles whipped into a stiff froth; also bubbles, free or suspended within cubes or tetrahedrons. Banners spiralled in all kinds of ways: in the spiral of Archimedes in which each unit or gnomon added was the same, making coiled cylinders like springs that rolled in the flow; also equiangular spirals, each gnomon bigger in a geometric progression, thus conical, nautiloid. Seeing them, Galileo tried to say to Aurora, Had the force of gravity varied as the cube rather than the square of the distance, the planets would have shot away, as their orbits would have become equiangular spirals. Then: see how the pattern breaks sequence there; it would need to be described by a new equation.

Aurora replied in his head, This is an organism. This is a mind, thinking. Its body is a swirling mass of gas clouds, elements intermixing. It's not like us. At least not superficially. It's some kind of whole. But so are we. To think that a body must be a colony, a mosaic of individual and separable characteristics – I could never believe there was more than a very small element of truth to that. We are nonlocal, we are all of a piece. Only a symmetry can beget asymmetry.

Galileo didn't know what to say to that. He understood that even his very eyesight was cognition, that he was seeing what the great planet's clouds displayed to them through his own experiences, with Aurora's tutorials as a light overlay. The patterns he saw now were riverine, they reminded him of the image of the temporal vector the Jovians used so frequently, anastomosing streambeds released in three mutually contradictory directions and moving in all of them, so that there were loops and eddies, oxbows and lost channels, and always a main channel snaking through, anastomosing perpetually in ever more complex ways. This was how beings moved in time.

'It seems dangerous to go so deep,' he noted after a while. 'Are you sure you will be able to get out again?'

'We're here on sufferance,' Hera said. She too was staring at the cloudscape, but her mouth was still set in the scowl it had held ever since the moment she had learned Ganymede and his group had escaped from their Ionian compound. Possibly she was not seeing the changes in the patterns.

They continued to descend, deep into the clouds of Jupiter. There were hundreds of miles to go below them before the clouds would condense to something resembling a surface, a sludge of gas compressed to liquid. They wouldn't be going there; the gravitational pull there was 240 times Earth's, and though the ship might be able to escape from that, they would not. Galileo already felt heavier even than he did at home, even after the most shameless feasting.

Hera went to Ganymede, turned up the volume of his suit's transference of his voice. She questioned him not in her guise as Mnemosyne, but as dread Atropos, inevitable and inflexible: 'Why did you do it?'

'You wouldn't understand.'

'I want to know what you were thinking. And so does Jupiter.'

Galileo saw that she thought the planet might be listening, or reading their minds. If not, then it was for them alone. Atropos was putting Ganymede on trial.

426

But Ganymede only shrugged. 'You don't want to know, not really. You think you understand the world, you have your words and your categories and equations, and you think they have some correspondence with reality that you can trust. The idea that we are living in a bigger space than that doesn't really penetrate you, or isn't taken seriously if it does. And yet there stands Galileo Galilei, proof that we live in a nonlocal manifold, in clouds of potentiality. This is reality, we can't escape it. Consciousness is part of how it gets created.'

'I know that,' Hera said sharply. 'I act on the basis of that knowledge. But you have been trying to collapse the wave function differently, not just with Galileo here, but in your assault on the Europan. You would change huge realms of possibility. I'm asking you why.'

'There are possibilities we should forestall if we can. They entail too much pain, they might even lead to the extinction of the species. If a certain kind of despair took root in us, then the end would be in us already. Whether we committed suicide or not, we would be dead.'

'This is always true,' Galileo interjected. 'Despair is always there *in potentia*, an abyss under us. It takes courage to live. People with courage can stand all the reality there is.'

Ganymede tried to look toward Galileo, eyes bulging. 'It would be good if that were true,' he said, 'but it isn't. A weight can come that crushes life. You don't know that yet, but you will learn it.'

This he said with such certainty that Galileo shuddered, as if the cold draught of some bad futurity had just wafted through him and chilled him to the bone.

'The primitives on Earth in your own time show what happens when more advanced powers descend on them,' Ganymede said. 'When they learn how far beyond them in power and understanding the invaders are, the primitives always, always, always fall into despair. They will be crushed by awareness of your superiority, and they will die. Most of them will die within a few years

427

of encountering you. Some will see you, understand what you mean, and die on purpose within a few days.'

'This is a paralogism,' Galileo said. 'A false argument, based on syllogisms that have no real connection. And even good analogies are never proofs. These primitive people were looking at other people. The discrepancy in human fortune is what crushed them. If they were to encounter angels, or God, they would not react the same.'

The man shook his head. 'It is the awareness of superiority that does it.'

'We know God is superior.'

'God is only an idea you have, a kind of proleptic leap toward some future vision of humanity. It's not a reality you face. Even so, the craven, abject cruelty of your time might be explainable as an artifact of your imagined superior being in the sky. You think there is a god and so you act like one to those supposedly below you. But if a god were to manifest itself in reality, you would be crushed like any primitive tribe.'

'Even if that were all true, which I do not grant,' Hera said, 'why assume anything about the creature in Europa?'

'I make no assumptions. I'm quite sure of the nature of what we've encountered. The mathematics we've used to communicate with it spoke the situation clearly. There is a being inside Jupiter. This being, as you perhaps have deduced by the mathematics expressed in the changes in the planetary surface, is a much greater being than the one living in Europa. And the Jovian mind is in full contact with a congeries of other minds, minds so vast we cannot remotely grasp any ideas of them, but only sense their presence. If humanity at large becomes aware of this realm of greater minds, beside which all human history is a fleck of foam on a sand grain, despair will quickly spread. It will be the end of humanity.'

'I don't see why,' Galileo said.

'Because we don't have the strength to withstand such knowledge! You have no idea!'

428

'Of course I do.'

'We will be revealed to be pitifully stupid.'

'When has it ever been otherwise? We are as the fleas on fleas, compared to God and his angels. We have always known this.'

'No. The ideas of your time are merely delusions, protecting you from the knowledge of death. In your structure of feeling you don't have to face reality. It's reality that crushes you.'

'You're still trying to save the appearances,' Galileo said, suddenly understanding. 'You're trying to save the appearance that humans are at the centre of things, just like the poor friars.'

'No. Listen, you've already felt what it would be like. Remember what it felt like when you heard the cry of the Europan, during our dive and then after it was hurt? How you couldn't bear to hear it? That's what it would be like, but all the time. That was the agony you were feeling. No human can bear it.'

Galileo remembered the overwhelming cry, felt the bulk of the manifold mathematics in his head. He hesitated. Who could say what the nonlocality of all things, the wholeness of the manifold of manifolds, really meant to humanity, locked as it was in its single manifold, its three spatial dimensions and its relentlessly unidirectional Time, in which everything was always becoming something else. Who could say? The end of reality? Extinction of the species? Maybe Ganymede knew things they didn't. Maybe he was only speaking the truths no one else would say.

Then there was a shudder in their ship, and the sensation of falling fast, so fast they almost lifted off the floor. The smoky light darkened, then brightened. They appeared to have entered a thin spot in the clouds, the gases over them transparent, then lightening to a glare. Something was changing –

In the infinity of worlds and heavens
There is so much radiance the light bedazzles.
One sees myriad faces in the sublime breathing air.
  – TORQUATO TASSO, *'The Seven Days of Creation'*

The looping glissandos first heard in the Europan ocean filled his mind. Long ups, steep downs, even wild excursions sideways, it seemed, in tone and in texture, or some realm of sound he had never known. The howl of the wolves in the hills at night, the sound of the whales in the aquarium gallery on Callisto; the only sob he had ever heard from his father, choked and desperate, one time as he rushed from the house into the street. There was an ear in his mind, cringing at sounds that only he heard.

The clouds grew diffuse and created in their midst an enormous spherical transparent space. They floated now in a bubble as big as a world, as big as Earth. There in the middle of the space with them hung a little Europa, vivid and solid against the distant clouds. It looked to be several hours of travel away from them; he had seen it look that way on one of his transits with Hera. Underneath it the clouds coalesced to a version of one segment of the banded monster itself. One could see past the bands, deep into it. Ropes of smoke emerged from the upper clouds, coalescing into imago versions of the other moons; the clouds outside the transparent sphere went dark, it seemed disappearing in a universal night; then sparks appeared in the blackness, stabilizing after a while to the constellations he was familiar with. There to the east tilted fulgurous Orion. The stars seemed to be staring down at the Jovian system from outside it, as in the model of concentric shells.

430

Galileo was still perfectly aware that they had descended into the vast cloudbanks of Jupiter, and that now they must be moving with the clouds at enormous speed, the speed of cannonballs shot from cannons. But as he had argued in the *Dialogo*, once you were moving with a system you could not feel that movement. What he saw now appeared still, and was an imago or emblem, presumably created for them by the mind within the planet. Jove was speaking to them, in other words, in images it thought they would comprehend. Like God's light striking stained glass; and indeed Jove's emblematic stars shed rays of fulgor that were like shards of crystal, and the black of its rendered space was in some places obsidian, in others velvet; and the four moons were like round chips of semi-precious stone, topaz and turquoise, jade and malachite. It was stained glass expanded into three dimensions.

Then the Europan imago pulsed and became semi-transparent, which made visible within it clouds of tiny spinning lights, like a glass jar filled with fireflies. The moon Ganymede also clarified to transparency, and it too had fireflies in it. Galileo wondered again what Ganymede had found in Ganymede to frighten him so, to put him under such a compulsion to stop the Europans' descent into Europa. Had he already hurt one child of Jove, or been hurt by it? Had he seen the connection to Jupiter and beyond, seen a Jovian doom that would fall on them all?

Part of the lapidary imago of Jupiter in turn became transparent, revealing within it many darting flocks of lights, flocks infinitely more various and layered than Europa's or Ganymede's. The points of light inside the giant were as numerous as all the stars in the rest of the sky. Their swirling filled the great sphere so completely that its outer surface was visible as an interweaving of horizontal currents of light, banded in ways similar to the gas clouds they usually saw.

Aurora's voice was somewhere in him, whispering to itself, about belts and zones, the meaningful patterns in the south equatorial belt plumes, the inexplicable way that alternating latitude bands of wind could hold firm in both directions over years and even centuries. So strange, Aurora said, to think that one could have said, I live on Jupiter at forty degrees north, therefore I will have winds of two hundred miles an hour from the east, as I did yesterday, and a thousand years ago. And this all a matter of gas clouds. It never seemed right. It makes sense that it was organized, that it was mentation.

But there were storms too, Galileo said to her in his mind. And pulsing spurts, and festoons and barges, and all the other patterned movements we saw.

Yes, she said, and spontaneous storms, and changes in colour that were not tied to changes in wind speeds, and fractal borders, bounded infinities scrolling inside each other. We are looking at a mind thinking. A mind feeling.

The woodwind glissando of the whale's cry.

Then time seemed to shatter, and the whale's eerie cry rasped through him in reverse, setting his nerves all ashudder. He heard a hundred whale songs offset each from the next, forward in time, backward, sideways. He was floating out into the other unperceivable spatial dimensions, becoming larger as he also subtilized and made inward spiral turns into himself. An abrupt inflation, as if he were three seconds into his own new universe –

The light-fizzing imago of Jupiter had shrunk to the size of a pearl, its satellites like pinheads.

'Look,' Hera said aloud. 'The solar system. The galaxy. We move out logarithmically.'

A swirl of stars lay in a spiral swath before them. There was a polyphonic singing, mostly lower than he could usually hear, but he heard now many octaves lower than he was used to. The Milky Way was now granulated star by star, like a fling of crystal sand across the black. Millions of white dots, foam racing up a beach in moonlight – a broken wave of stars, tossed on the beach of the cosmos. Expanding further into both the big and the small, Galileo saw with utmost atomic clarity that each star was its own flock of bright swirling points, pulsing inside its burning sphere.

Wherever Galileo directed his attention, the stars in that field resolved into clouds of minute firefly lights, spinning in complex patterns. Together they sailed majestically in a galactic weave that also seemed to pulse and blink. He was in all ten dimensions now, in the manifold of manifolds, as he always had been; but now he sensed all of them at once, and yet could still make a clear gestalt of the whole. The pulsing lights were the thoughts of thinking beings, and together they made a larger mind, the great chain of being scaling up to the cosmos itself. A living cosmos, singing something in concert. The wolf's howl in the night.

As Galileo regarded what he could only think was the mind of God, he lost all sense of his three-dimensional space and felt himself spinning and spiralling in the manifold of manifolds, spanning all times. Every fire from the tiniest chip of firefly light to the blazing pebbles of the galaxies bloomed a trail and arced forward, so that he saw lines rather than points, and felt rather than saw a dense latticework into which he too was woven, like a cosmic chrysanthemum of white lines filling a blackness felt rather than seen, heard in a song beyond hearing. Still watching the lines, he felt and heard the ways in which the ten dimensions warped, stretched, bowed and shrunk, the whole breathing in and out and also almost holding still, all at once. His sight was whole, his touch-immersion whole, his hearing whole, while also coextensive with the ten dimensions. The manifold of manifolds moved, breathed, sideways or at an angle to time, singing a fugue with parts out of different dimensions. All the temporal isotopes were flickering in and out of their braids of potentiality, blooming and collapsing, systole and diastole. At the merging with this he rose into an existential sublime, a true ecstasy or exstasis blooming in his consciousness, and the familiar ringing, always before so faint, was now all in all, the culmination of the fugue. All things remain in God, he said, but no one heard. He understood then the solitary nature of transcendence, since wholeness was one. He was entirely alone and by himself, he realized: the manifold of manifolds was another one of the secret lives. It was some kind of moving eternity, encompassing an infinity of universes. Everything was always changing, always: so it was change itself that was eternal. Eternity too had a history, eternity too evolved, strove to change and even to improve, in some sense beyond human comprehension – in growth, complexification, metamorphosis. In any case, eternal change. A ten-dimensional organism, pulsing with granular light like the finest snow, everywhere entangled, all points discrete like the points in Euclid's definition and yet also part of a whole plenum, flowing in curves, in glissandi still audible in him, a majestic dense chorus of whales and wolves and heartbroken souls, louder and louder, a kind of red loon's cry –

Galileo found himself sitting on the floor. Hera was still standing, although she was holding onto her chair like a sailor holding a plank after the ship has gone down. The terror in her eyes was new to Galileo, he was shocked to see it. He felt that he could not speak, that a spike had stabbed up through his tongue, or worse, speared down through his skull and pricked just that part of the mind that initiated speech. There was a roaring in his ears. He looked at her console screen, trying to think, trying to remember. What had happened? He held on to her thick leg like a child clutching its mother.

Spun gold went white. Shapes coalesced in the unspeakable glare: eyes, tumbling bodies, whole worlds or something more. Spinning whorls of stars, fireworks in his head, pain in every nerve at once – or had it been joy? Exstasis. Rushing up, out, in. Into a centre that was a pinprick of the most fulgurous black, piercing his eye, mind, and soul, sucking him into it. Then a syncope; all was still, cold, dead. Was that how it had ended? What came before was a blur, a dizzy feeling. There had been an awesome roar of the sublime; within it, the tiny ringing of a bell. He had been the bell. Then something had pricked, like a pin through a castle wall, and no more Galileo. A syncope came like sleep, like blessed sleep.

Then Galileo was gone again, but a consciousness remained, cosmic and manifold. The sun was a star, the stars all suns. Each held a mind that was as vast and bright as the sun in the noonday sky. You could not look at it, but saw only its light on paper. A kind of angel – or the being, ever so much greater than an angel, that the idea of an angel had been invented to suggest. The sky was filled with trillions of such minds, and clusters of them swirled in whirlpools of their own weight, were drawn down into themselves continuously. At their centres they compressed

435

to nothing, and their substance was sucked away, into other universes in other dimensions. They were all entangled throughout the manifolds. Present, past, future, eternity, all become one and then transmuted elsewhen. Which meant . . .

A wolf's mournful howl, a whale's eerie glissando. Time splintered and Galileo was back again in the midst of it. An eddy in time; Jupiter reiterating a point, in a loop of grief, an ecstasy, another entangled moment. Which meant . . .

He stopped trying to understand. This took an immense effort, it was utterly contrary to him, the hardest thing he had ever done. The work of Oelilag: give up trying. Folding inside out. Just exist, he commanded himself, just see. But it was too big to see, too bright, it blinded him to try. A whirlpool of infinite minds, an infinity of whirlpools. One could not compare infinities, he felt that clearly. There were an infinite number of starry whirlpools, and in each, an infinite number of minds. Kepler had suggested this was the case, Bruno had claimed it outright. Bruno had died for saying it. Galileo did not want to die. The world was too astonishing to die for saying something, no matter what it was.

Although it was also true that there was a sort of universal syncope, in which death did not obtain. It was not heaven, but ecstasy, *ex stasis*, out of one's tiny individual body into the universal body, the manifold of manifolds. All the possibilities came true. All things remained in God – he sang this phrase, held to it in his mind. It became all he had to hold on to, his floating plank in the tossing sea of stars. All things remain in God.

And yet decisions are made, the wave functions collapse. Consciousness and the manifold are entangled. There was a voice, like a pin through a castle wall. Release me, oh Jove.

Then another return to the consciousness of being Galileo. He struggled in his head, completely exhausted, thinking, Hello! I'm here! Let me go! Where are you? Who are you?

It was his faithful dog, nuzzling his face.

No, it was Hera. She held his face in her big hands.

'What happened?' Galileo croaked. Something filled him, an ocean of clouds inside his chest, stuffing him with a feeling he did not recognize, a feeling that made him want to weep, for what he did not know; and yet he was too confused even for tears. But it had to do with her presence. If he had gone through this without her, if she hadn't been there at his side, it would have been insupportable. It was too much to bear alone.

'I don't know,' she said, looking him in the eye. There was a tenderness in her look, an *amorevolezza*, as Maria Celeste was always putting it, that he had not known existed in her. Perhaps she had been going through something similar in the period of exstasis, no doubt she had. We all go through the same things! Her face was streaked with tears. She leaned in toward him until their faces were aligned nose to nose; the tips of their noses touched as if kissing, their eyes were as mirrors to the complementary other, her irises a deep living field of flecks and streaks, like rounds of polished jasper or the insides of two flowers, the black holes of her pupils lightly pulsing in and out, reminding him of something just seen in his recent shattering. Her eyes floated in toward his until they were as big as the surface of Jupiter, filled with warmth, their affection coursing into him. Then her eyes simply moved into his eyes, they merged as if touching in a mirror, two as one. Jove will be jealous, Galileo tried to say, but her eyes stopped him, and he yielded to her, falling up as in the nights of his youth, into the wild girls of Venice. Her fractured stone irises bloomed like emblems of his feelings. This was the entangled cosmos they always inhabited, but now felt. *Amorevolezza, eros, agape* – one made love the way one pronounced a word, the way one made a sentence. He had never made love with someone he knew to be his equal, someone as strong and as full and as smart as him, and that thought pierced him, swept him away on such a wave of grief and love that he might have felt fear, if it were not for her eyes, telling him all was perfectly well. Their eyes merged entirely and he saw what she saw, and felt their extasis as a tall thick chord, a harmonic. The mother goddess inside him.

All these things happen in the mind. Imagination creates events. What matters is something that happens in the mind.

They sat on the floor of her little spaceship, confused. A conjunction of spirits. It was all meant to be something that equals did together. Remembering this, Galileo found he was weeping again. When he blinked tears detached from his face and floated down like little moons of Jupiter. Lazily Hera stuck her tongue out and licked one into her mouth. No wonder he had been so lusty in his wasted youth, no wonder he had jumped at the idea of a Marina quick and true. No wonder his mother had been so angry. Everything in his life had been based on a misunderstanding, a base fear, a refusal to see the other, similar in its cowardice and malignity to the absurd misreadings that his enemies had applied to his theories. Men in his time had been furiously afraid of whatever was other; and thought women were other; and thought it adequate justification of their fear to invoke the dead past, the authority of all the stupid popes. As if might made right. But it wasn't so. He wept with regret for his wasted life and world and time. What a crazy thing to be human.

They sat side by side on the floor, arm touching arm, leg touching leg. She was bigger than he was, even around the torso, though he was a barrel-chested and pot-bellied man. He was completely relaxed. He could feel she was too. They were entangled. This was only a moment, it would pass: a fragment of time to which clung a fragment of space, in which two minds joined and were whole.

We all have our seven secret lives. Transcendence is solitary, daily life is solitary. Consciousness is solitary. And yet sometimes

438

we sit together with a friend, and the secret lives don't matter, they're even part of it, and a dual world is created, a shared reality. Then we are entangled and one, transitory but imperishable.

The light in the cabin grew. They were no longer alone; they became aware of Aurora, of Ganymede locked in his spacesuit, of the crew of the ship, all scattered on the floor of the cabin like ninepins, stirring now like the dead come to life. Outside their transparent cocoon, their little platform in space, Galileo saw that they had emerged from the upper clouds of Jupiter, and were shooting up into space like a hummingbird. They were just over the dome of the Great Red Spot; it spun up under them at great speed as they rose, the bevelled ruddy bands tumbling over themselves, brick on orange on umber on tan on sienna on yellow on bronze on copper on white on mud on hazel on gold on cinnabar on cinnamon, on and on and on, round and round and round. A thought, or a dance, or a life.

Hera stood up and walked to her chair, as free in her movements as a dancer. Galileo watched her transfixed: she was big and muscular, her female curves parabolic volumes in space, an ultimate reality. Everything he had thought he had known was wrong, and as when it happened to him in the workshop, that realization made him happy. The proof of his wrongness stood there before him, tapping at her keyboards – the goddess animal that humans could be. In his time such a person wasn't even possible. Force constrained by pale freckled skin. Dark auburn hair suffused with black, wild from her head like Medusa's snakes. All this talk of gods: he saw that it really had been a prolepsis all along, that they had dreamed of human potential and spoken of it as if already achieved in the sky. The gods were future humans imagined, the gods were our children. 'Ahh,' he said.

She glanced over her shoulder, smiled a tiny smile. She saw him.

Then she saw Ganymede, and her look turned serious. 'We need to talk to Ganymede.'

'Yes.' He considered it, looked at the locked spacesuit.

'I wonder what he saw in there.'

'Me too.' She walked over to Galileo, he took her in like a drink of cold water, tears starting again in his eyes, obscuring the sight of her, and he blinked and smiled helplessly as the tears spilled down his cheeks into his beard. There was nothing left to hide at this point, he was what he was, and felt content. She extended a hand to help him up, he took it and rose. Possibly the high point of all his lives was now come to an end. Even so he was content. All things remain.

'I know what his punishment should be,' Galileo said.

She shook her head. 'Later,' she said. 'That's our business. You have your own trial to deal with.' And she pushed a tab on the pewter box next to him.

Chapter Seventeen   The Trial

'I want what Fate wants,' said Jove.
— GIORDANO BRUNO, *The Expulsion of the*
Triumphant Beast

The Holy Office of the Index's ban on Galileo's *Dialogo*, and the papal order commanding him to present himself to the Holy Office in Rome for examination in the month of October 1632, came as great shocks to Galileo. His book had been approved by all the relevant authorities, and its very title announced its impartiality:

DIALOGUE

Of

Galileo Galilei, Lyncean

Outstanding Mathematician

Of the University of Pisa

And Philosopher and Chief Mathematician

Of the Most Serene

GRAND DUKE OF TUSCANY

Where, in the course of four days, are discussed

The Two

CHIEF SYSTEMS OF THE WORLD,

PTOLEMAIC AND COPERNICAN

Propounding inconclusively the philosophical and
natural reasons
As much for one side as for the other.
Florence: Giovan Battista Landini, MDCXXXII
With the permission of the authorities

He found out by way of a letter from the Grand Duke's new secretary, Cioli, sent to him at Arcetri by a single courier. *You are hereby commanded by the Holy Congregation of the Church to account for your book in person in Rome. The book itself is banned.* Just as flat as that. No one wanted to know him now. Despite all the warning signs and struggles and premonitions, he still couldn't believe it.

If he had known more of what was going on in Rome, however, he would not have been so surprised. The Grand Duke's ambassador to the pontiff, still Francesco Niccolini, could have explained a great deal to him, being caught in the thick of it. The situation far transcended Galileo's philosophical speculations, which no one but Galileo considered of paramount importance. Gustavus Adolphus, the Swedish king, and previously an ally of Rome, was now leading his Protestant army south through Germany, chopping Catholics down. The Spanish were furious, and were of the opinion that Urban was to blame because he had started his papacy over-tolerant of Protestants and all kinds of other heterodoxies. Now they wanted to see the harsh suppressions they felt were necessary to keep Catholicism together.

The Jesuits were also angry; their widespread order was the one most harmed by the Protestant inundation of northern Europe. In the Jesuit Good Friday oration in St Peter's Cathedral, Father Orazio Grassi himself, Galileo's old opponent Sarsi, delivered a spine-chilling sermon warning against any further papal weakness, with Urban sitting right there red-faced in his papal box. Such a public reproach of a sitting pope, for negligence in the care of the embattled Church, had not been seen in living memory. As Grassi spoke the congregation fell so silent that they could hear the unkillable pigeons cooing from their nests at the top of the dome.

That was one bad moment among many others. Urban was a superstitious man, and Vesuvius had recently erupted after a hundred and thirty years of complete calm, blanketing the countryside near Naples with a wall of lava that people likened to the Protestant armies. A bad sign, for sure; and the stars themselves all portended catastrophe. Urban's ban on the publication of horoscopes predicting his death was of course still in force, but more general predictions of disaster could not be stopped, and were the order of the day.

The Thursday convocations of the cardinals became more and more tense. Several were the scene of bitter recriminations between Urban and his chief enemy, the hugely corpulent Cardinal Gasparo Borgia, who served as the Spanish king's ambassador to the pontificate. The power of Spain was such that the Borgia was almost as influential in Rome as Urban, and every Thursday he stood up and with open contempt accused Urban of being excessively tolerant of heretical activities.

This simmering cauldron had finally boiled over on 8th March, 1632. Word quickly got around that at a meeting of the cardinals, the Borgia had stepped up onto a little block of a dais and with his massive bulk thus elevated had announced in a bellow that he was going to read a formal document, 'a matter of the greatest interest for religion and the faith.' Copies of the document had been made for distribution by his supporters, and so everyone could read for themselves afterward what he had said, and marvel at its boldness: it was an astonishingly virulent denunciation of all Urban's policies, labelling in particular Urban's earlier alliance with Gustavus as heretical.

Instantly red-faced, for he was thin-skinned in body as well as soul, Urban had tried to shout Borgia down, screaming

'Stop this!' and 'Shut up!' and the like. But the Borgia had ignored him and continued to read, bellowing louder than ever. The effrontery of this flagrant insubordination shocked everyone there. Urban's supporters all cried out and surged toward Borgia in a mass to drag him down and stop him. But the Borgia had been prepared for this, and around him the cardinals of his faction stood like a bodyguard – Ludovisi, Colonna, Spinola, Doria, Sandoval, Ubaldini, Ablornoz, all facing down the press of Barberini men, while Borgia continued his denunciation in tones that could be heard over everything. People were amazed to tell how Cardinal Antonio Barberini, Urban's brother, had then hurtled over the Spanish crowd with a great roar, fists and elbows flying, breaking through them to snatch Borgia by the robe and drag him off his dais. Suddenly all the cardinals were in a pile on the ground punching and kicking like two drunken gangs, Colonna flailing at Antonio Barberini until he tore him away from the Borgia, who stood as if to continue proclaiming. Urban was seen to take a step toward Borgia, fist raised, before remembering his station and screaming for his Swiss guards.

The Swiss in their steel vests and red sleeves restored order with upright pikes, insinuating themselves between Colonna and Antonio Barberini and all the other elderly combatants, who were madly shouting and spitting, their red robes and red faces separated by the red-sleeved peace-makers, all liberally dashed with blood from cracked lips and pates. A red scene. The Borgia's men gave out printed copies of his denunciation as they marched out of the room in a mass. Urban had been able to do nothing after that but stand on the confiscated dais and insist on his prerogatives, but at that point his heavy-breathing supporters scarcely even heard him.

It was as close to an open revolt against a pope as could be imagined.

*   *   *

News of the fistfight of the cardinals quickly spread. Niccolini, writing to the Florentine court about it, predicted that loud accusations of heresy would now become the Spanish party's chief instrument of political pressure on the Curia. Urban was without a doubt cast on the defensive; extremists on the Spanish side, including Cardinal Ludovisi, were already threatening to begin the formalities of a papal deposition. The riot in the consistory had shown very clearly that Urban could count only on his own family for real support. Happily he had already appointed lots of Barberinis to the Vatican, so that he could now strike back at the Spanish party in various ways. As a first move he expelled Ludovico Ludovisi from Rome.

Borgia himself, however, as ambassador of the Spanish king, and simply as a Borgia, could not be touched. Most of the observers in Rome felt that until Urban could somehow bring Borgia down, or outlive him, he could only play the game Borgia had called; he had to show his leadership by crusading against heresy. Which meant that in some senses Borgia and the Spanish had already won. High Barberinian culture was gone, the *mirabile congiunture* a thing of the past.

So the ban on Galileo's *Dialogo* was just one part of this turn in the Italian political landscape. Once the book was out there, almost all of Galileo's enemies complained to the Holy Office about its publication, and the hunt was therefore on. Riccardi was in a panic, as he could not deny that he had approved it. He wanted to do whatever would placate Urban in the matter and make it go away. And so late in the summer of 1632 the book was banned, and Galileo ordered to come to Rome to explain himself.

Such a command was already a judgement, as Galileo well knew. It was not like an ordinary trial; the Holy Office of the Congregation made its judgements in advance, in secret, and then called you in to tell you what your punishment would be.

Galileo tried everything he could think of to avoid going to Rome. Grand Duke Ferdinando II and his court at first helped him in this effort, as both intermediary and advocate, for they too stood to lose if their court philosopher and mathematician were put on trial for heresy. They asked the Pope on his behalf if he could submit to examination by written questions from his home in Arcetri, his health being so poor.

The answer came back from Rome: no.

They wrote to ask if he could be interrogated by the Florentine office of the Inquisition.

The answer came back again: no. He must appear in Rome.

He took to his bed, and wrote to explain that at his advanced age of seventy (he was sixty-seven), his health was too poor to allow him to travel.

After a month, a Florentine official of the Inquisition visited him at home to see just how sick he was. Galileo received him from bed, moaning, hectic, and bleary-eyed. It looked like an act, although in fact the household had all seen him look just like that hundreds of times. He held out to the church official a note from his three doctors, to be read and then conveyed to Rome:

We find that his pulse intermits every three or four beats. The patient has frequent attacks of giddiness, hypochondriacal melancholy, weakness of stomach, insomnia, and flying pains about the body. We have also observed a serious hernia with rupture of the peritoneum. All these symptoms, with the least aggravation, might become dangerous to life.

This letter and the cleric's report were sent to Rome. The Pope received them angrily, and had word sent back; Galileo must either come to Rome voluntarily or be brought there in chains.

This was too much papal heat for Grand Duke Ferdinando to withstand. He was only twenty, and Urban had already taken the duchy of Urbino away from him by force, replacing the rightful Medici heir with one of his own people. Ferdinando was intimidated, people said. Whatever the reason, he chose to do nothing more to defend Galileo. In truth it was not a good time to oppose the pope. There had never been a good time for that, of course, but now less than ever, or so Ferdinando's new secretary Cioli and his men explained to Galileo, there in the courtyard of *Il Gioello*, as they assured him that he would have the Grand Duke's full support, that they were going to convey him to Rome in a fine litter, and that he would be put up there as a guest of the Grand Duke, as he had not been during certain previous visits, so he could live in comfort there at the Villa Medici, and so on. It would be fine. The ambassador Francesco Niccolini was a most canny diplomat, who would help him in every way possible. There was no escaping it, they concluded. He must go.

As this news sank in, Galileo's face displayed a most curious mix of surprise, dismay, and something like resignation. He knew this moment. His trial had come.

Before his departure for Rome, Galileo went to see Maria Celeste and Arcangela one last time. Arcangela would not speak, of course, and glared at the walls triumphantly, as if she had prayed for this judgement and was happy it had arrived at last. Galileo couldn't converse with Maria Celeste properly until he had had Arcangela escorted out of the room.

Then they sat in the sunlight coming in the window, holding hands. Maria Celeste survived by belief, he knew; the Church was all to her, and she revered her father as much as she did by making him a saint in her holy pantheon. Now that was all crossed up by this awesome order from the Pope, and she wept in short stifled sobs, as if she were being torn in two but trying to hide the fact out of politeness. Her wretched gasping was a sound that recurred to Galileo often in the sleepless months to come. In that moment, however, he had his own torn feelings, his own fears to preoccupy him; he was contracting into himself, and did not have the usual amount of attention to give to her. All that fall he had been calm, one might even have said serene.

Cartophilus knew something unusual had happened in his last syncope; but Galileo wasn't saying anything, so there had been no way for others to tell. He had seemed to have faith that things would turn out well. Now his look was darker. He patted her head and left for Rome.

It was a hard winter journey, that January of 1633. It was his sixth trip to Rome: again everything the same but everything different. This time the world gone dark, and made all of mud. Plague was abroad, and a half quarantine held him in Acquapendente for twenty days, living on nothing but bread, wine, and eggs. He was in no hurry to get to Rome, but there was too much time to think, to worry, to regret. How he longed then for the tumble of ordinary days.

In Rome, meanwhile, Niccolini requested an audience with the Pope to deliver the Grand Duke's protest concerning the make-up of the commission of clerics that had been convened to judge Galileo's book. This was as close as the Grand Duke could come to protesting the judgement itself, and although it was not likely to be successful, Niccolini could use the meeting to try to find out what was behind the reversed approval of Galileo's book, and the sudden call for him to come to Rome. Hopefully a clearer understanding of the cause would help in preparing Galileo's defence.

The meeting was not a success. Back at the Villa Medici, Niccolini wrote a detailed account of it for the young Grand Duke and his new secretary Cioli. It had taken place, he wrote,

in a very emotional atmosphere. I too am beginning to believe, as your Most Illustrious Lordship well expresses it, that the sky is about to fall. While we were discussing the delicate subject of the Holy Office, His Holiness exploded into great anger, and suddenly told me that our Galilei had dared enter where he should not have, into the most serious and dangerous subjects which could be stirred up at this time.

This was strange, because the Pope had personally, and more than once in the last few years, assured Galileo that he could write about the Copernican system of the world. As Niccolini in fact had reminded him:

I replied that Signor Galilei had not published without the approval of his ministers, and for that purpose I myself had obtained and sent the prefaces to Florence.

He answered, with the same outburst of rage, that he had been deceived by Galileo and Ciampoli.

And he went on, Niccolini said, to list in quite knowledgeable detail the ways Galileo had promised an acceptable text and not delivered it, and also the ways Ciampoli and Riccardi had likewise promised to make sure it was so; and all of it traduced by the text itself, and by the lies told by everyone involved.

Niccolini had been forced to take this at face value, although it did not make sense to him, given the many assurances Galileo had made in the book that all his theorizing was only *ex suppositione*. But Niccolini did not know about the anonymous denunciation of *The Assayer*, accusing Galileo of denying the doctrine of transubstantiation. Because of that he continued to press the Copernican matter, as being the ostensible cause of the ban and arrest:

I interjected that I knew His Holiness had appointed a Commission for the purpose of investigating Signor Galileo's book, and that, because it might have members who hate Signor Galilei (as it does), I humbly begged His Holiness to agree to give him the opportunity to justify himself. Then His Holiness answered that in these matters of the Holy Office, the procedure was simply to arrive at a censure and then call the defendant to recant.

But Niccolini had persisted in Galileo's defence: 'Does it thus not seem to Your Holiness that Galileo should know in advance the difficulties and the objections that brought forth the censure, and what the Holy Office is worried about?'

Urban, red-faced, had replied violently, 'We say to your Lordship that the Holy Office does not do these things and does not proceed this way, that these things are never given in advance to anyone. Such is not the custom. Besides he knows very well where the difficulties lie, if he wants to know them, since we have discussed them with him and he had heard them from ourselves.'

450

Niccolini had tried reminding the Pope, 'Please I beg you to consider that the book is dedicated to the Grand Duke of Tuscany.'

Urban snapped at that, 'We have prohibited work dedicated to our self! In such matters, involving great harm to religion, indeed the worst ever conceived, His Highness the Grand Duke too should contribute to preventing it, being a Christian prince! He should too be careful not to get involved, because he would not come out of it honourably.'

Niccolini held firm: 'I am sure I will receive orders to trouble your Holiness again, and I will do it, but I do not believe Your Holiness would bring about the prohibition of the already approved book without at least hearing Signor Galilei first.'

Urban replied darkly, 'This is the least ill that can be done to him. He should take care not to be summoned by the Holy Office. We appointed a Commission of theologians and other persons versed in various sciences, who are weighing every minutia, word for word, since one is dealing with the most perverse subject one could ever come across. Write to your prince to say the doctrine in question is extremely perverse, and that His Highness should therefore go slow. And we now impose on you the knowledge that this is secret information we are telling you, which you can share with your prince but which he too must then keep secret. We have used every civility with Signor Galilei, we explained to him what we know to be true, and we have not sent the case to the Congregation of the Holy Inquisition, as would be normal, but rather to a special commission newly created. We have used better manners with Galileo than he has used with us, for we have been deceived!'

Thus I had an unpleasant meeting, Niccolini concluded with a shudder, having written down the conversation in full, *and I feel the Pope could not have a worse disposition toward our poor Signor Galilei. I believe it is necessary to take this business without violence, and to deal with the ministers and with the*

Lord Cardinal Barberini rather than with the Pope himself, for when His Holiness gets something into his head, that is the end of the matter, especially if one is opposing, threatening, or defying him, since then he hardens and shows no respect to anyone. The best course is to temporize and try to move him by persistent, skilful, and quiet diplomacy.

Which is what Niccolini had done through the rest of that fall and winter. From Riccardi he received assurances that all would probably be well; but Riccardi gave him a warning too, which Niccolini passed on to his superiors:

However, above all he says, with the usual confidentiality and secrecy, that in the files of the Holy Office they have found something which alone is sufficient to ruin Signor Galilei completely.

This was in fact Segizzi's record of Bellarmino's 1616 prohibition, as Riccardi eventually explained to Niccolini. The hidden card had come out of its hole in the Vatican.

But certain spies added to this information that the anonymous denunciation of *Il Saggiatore* made in 1624 had also been located. So Galileo was in trouble on two fronts, only one of them counteracted by Sarpi's defensive schemes.

Niccolini's own sources only told him of something mysterious without specifying it, and in a subsequent audience with the Pope, he confirmed the suspicion he had expressed to the Grand Duke and Cioli, that something odd was going on here that they didn't understand. In this audience the Pope told Niccolini, as the ambassador reported, *to warn the Grand Duke not to let Signor Galilei spread troublesome and dangerous opinions under the pretext of running a certain school for young people, because he had 'heard something' (I know not what).* There were forces swirling around Rome, descending on this trial.

The Villa Medici was much the same as it had been eighteen years before: a big blocky white building, surrounded by extensive formal gardens that were full of old Roman statues, slowly melting into smooth marble plinths. The ambassador Francesco Niccolini welcomed Galileo into the place with the greatest of solicitude, in marked contrast to the greetings Galileo had received on previous visits. Each time he came to Rome his standing was inexplicably different to before. A dreamlike place; and this time a nightmare. But in this nightmare, incongruously, thankfully, there emerged this friendly and generous face.

'I am here to help you in any way I can,' Niccolini said, and Galileo could see in his face that it would be true.

'Where do such good people come from?' Galileo asked Cartophilus that afternoon, as the ancient servant unpacked his bags. Their rooms had east-facing windows this time, and a high ceiling; they were beautiful.

'The Niccolini have always been a force in Florence,' Cartophilus said blandly into the big wardrobe where he was hanging Galileo's shirts.

Galileo blew air between his lips rudely. 'This is no ordinary Niccolini.'

Ordinary or not, he was a generous host and a fine advocate. He arranged meeting after meeting with the crucial cardinals, and joined many of the meetings to ask for the cardinals' help. He worked around all the edges; and at the centre he asked for yet another audience with Urban for himself, to arrange if possible for lenient and swift treatment of the old astronomer, stressing Galileo's official capacity at the Tuscan Court, and his advanced age.

However, as Niccolini described it in his letter to Cioli in Florence, the Pope was unmoved by these appeals.

He replied to me that Signor Galilei will be examined in due course, but there is an argument which no one has ever been able to answer: that is, God is omnipotent and can do anything; and since he is omnipotent, why do we want to bind him? I said that I was not competent to discuss these subjects, but I had heard Signor Galilei himself say that first, he did not hold the opinion of the earth's motion as true, and then that since God could make the world in innumerable ways, one could not deny, after all, that He might have made it this way. However, the Pope got upset at that, and told me that one must not impose necessity on the blessed God. Seeing that he was losing his temper, I did not want to continue discussing what I did not understand, and thus displease him to the detriment of Signor Galilei. So I said that, in short, Galileo was here to obey and to retract everything for which he could be blamed in regard to religion; then, in order not to arouse suspicion that I too might offend the Holy Office, I changed the subject.

Before the papal audience was over, Niccolini requested that Galileo be allowed to stay at the Villa Medici even during his trial; but the Pope denied the request, saying he would be given good rooms at the Holy Office, inside the Vatican.

When I got home I did not tell Galileo about the plan to move him to the Holy Office during the trial as I was sure this would worry him a great deal and would make him restless until that time, especially since it is not known yet when they will want him.

I do not like His Holiness's attitude, which is not at all mollified.

Galileo was then left to fret in the Villa Medici and its gardens for over two months. Nothing to do but sit in the formal gardens and watch the shadows move on the sundials; and think; and endure.

On 9th April, 1633, his old student Cardinal Francesco Barberini appeared at the Villa Medici to break the long silence. He warned Niccolini that the trial would begin soon, and that Galileo would indeed be ordered to stay at Holy Office during it.

Niccolini wrote to Cioli:

However, I could hide neither the ill health of this good old man, who for two whole nights had constantly moaned and screamed on account of his arthritic pains, nor his advanced age, nor the hardship he would suffer as a result.

Niccolini therefore persisted with Urban:

... this morning I spoke to His Holiness about it, who said he was sorry that Signor Galilei had involved himself in this subject, which he considers to be very serious and of great consequence for religion.

Nevertheless, Signor Galilei tries to defend his opinions very strongly; but I exhorted him, in the interest of a quick resolution, not to bother maintaining them, and to submit to what he sees they want him to hold or believe about any detail of the Earth's motion. He was extremely distressed by this, and, as far as I am concerned, since yesterday he looks so depressed that I fear greatly for his life.

This whole house is extremely fond of him and feels unspeakably sorry about it.

Spies and rumour-mongers were spreading every kind of story explaining the situation, but it still was not clear to those in Galileo's camp what was going on in the Vatican, or why. But understanding or not, the day came: the trial began. On 12th April, 1633, at ten in the morning, Galileo was escorted into the Vatican through the Arch of Bells to the palace of the Holy Office, a domed building on the south side of St Peter's Cathedral. Swiss guards led the little contingent of inquisitors and the accused man down the halls to a small room, its walls white plaster and decorated only by a single large crucifix. A large desk occupied the centre of the room; the inquisitors stood behind it, the accused before it, and a Dominican nun serving as recording scribe sat at a tall writing desk to the side. Servants stood in waiting in the hall outside, silent and unnoticed.

The chief inquisitor was Cardinal Vincenzo Maculano di Firenzuola, a thin Dominican about the same height as Galileo. His ascetic life had left the skin of his face so wrinkled, and his eyes so sunken, that he appeared almost older than the aged astronomer, though he was only forty-five. His nose was large, his mouth small.

As the trial began his gaze was sharp, although his mouth had a relaxed and even a friendly set to it. 'Time for a deposition,' he said gently.

Summoned, there appeared personally in Rome at the palace of the Holy Office, in the usual quarters of the Reverend Father Commissary, in the presence of the Reverend Father Fra Vincenzo Maculano of Firenzuola, Commissary General, and of his assistant Reverend Father Carlo Sinceri, Prosecutor of the Holy Office, etc.

Galileo, son of the late Vincenzio Galilei, Florentine, seventy years old, who, having taken a formal oath to tell the truth, was asked by the Fathers the following:

He was asked: By what means and how long ago did he come to Rome.
Answer: I arrived in Rome the first Sunday of Lent, and I came in a litter.

Cardinal Maculano's questions were asked, and recorded by the nun, in Latin, while Galileo's answers were made and recorded in Italian. At the first sound of Galileo's Tuscan vernacular, Maculano looked up from the desk, surprised; but after a moment's hesitation he did not stop the answer, or request that Galileo make his replies in Latin. He only spoke his next question in Latin again:

'Did you come of your own accord, or were you called, or were you ordered by someone to come to Rome, and if so, by whom?'

Galileo answered as seriously as if this were the crux of the matter: 'In Florence the Father Inquisitor ordered me to come to Rome to present myself to the Holy Office, this being an injunction by the officials of the Holy Office.'

'Do you know, or can you guess, the reason why you were ordered to come to Rome?'

Galileo said, 'I imagine that the reason why I have been ordered to present myself to the Holy Office in Rome is to account for my recently printed book. I imagine this because of the injunction to the printer and to myself, a few days before I was ordered to come to Rome, not to issue any more of these books, and similarly because the printer was ordered by the Father Inquisitor to send the original manuscript of my book to the Holy Office in Rome.'

Maculano nodded at this. 'Please explain the character of the book on account of which you think you were ordered to come to Rome.'

'It is a book written in dialogue form, and it treats of the constitution of the world – that is, of the two chief systems. Also the arrangements of the heavens and the elements.'

'If you were shown the said book, would you be prepared to identify it as yours?'

'I hope so,' Galileo said. 'I hope that if the book is shown to me I would recognize it.'

Maculano glanced up sharply at him. Was this sarcasm? A feeble attempt at a joke? The accused man's flat tone and innocent expression did not allow an interpretation. He was intent, on point; this was clearly serious business to him, as well it should be; his gaze was transfixed on the face of Maculano. If there was a part inside him struggling against a sharp rejoinder or sarcastic put-down, it was still bottled in him, and escaping perhaps only in quick uncontrollable squirts, odd statements that were all that remained of a lifelong habit of skewering opponents in debate.

This opponent was too dangerous to be touched. Maculano let a few more moments go by. Was he appreciating Galileo's irony, or silently warning him against it? It was just as impossible for Galileo to tell what Maculano was thinking, as it had been for Maculano to determine what Galileo had meant. Impassively they stared at each other. Suddenly those of us watching had it brought home to us what the trial was going to

457

be like; it was rhetoric as chess, but with an executioner standing behind the man playing the black pieces. Galileo was one of the smartest scientists ever to live, but chess is not science; and this was not exactly chess.

And who was the man playing white? Who was this tall emaciated Maculano from Firenzuola? A Dominican from Pavia, a functionary of the Holy Office, a mediocrity unnoticed by anyone until this moment. Once again a new player had stepped out of the shadows, confounding any sense that the cast of characters was fixed in number, or fully known to anybody involved. Or complete.

Having been shown one of his books, he said:

'I know this book very well; it is one of those printed in Florence; and I acknowledge it as mine and written by me.'

This was said with no inflection at all; but the inspection of the book had been rather drawn out, as if to match Maculano's delay, perhaps thus to toss Maculano's silent warning back in his face.

Maculano, seeing this, again waited longer than seemed necessary. Finally he said, with a little press of deliberation or emphasis, as if warning Galileo yet again:

'Do you likewise acknowledge each and every thing contained in the said book as yours?'

Now Galileo replied quickly, almost impatiently: 'I know this book shown to me, for it is one of those printed at Florence. I acknowledge all it contains as having been written by me.'

'When and where did you compose this book, and how long did it take you?'

'In regard to the place,' Galileo said, 'I composed it in Florence, beginning ten or twelve years ago. It must have taken me seven or eight years, but not continuously.'

'Were you in Rome any other times, especially in the year 1616, and for what occasion?'

'I was in Rome in the year 1616,' Galileo confirmed, as if answering a real question; it had been a very famous visit. He listed all his subsequent visits to Rome as well, explaining that the last was to get permission in person to publish the *Dialogo*. He went on to explain that the visit in 1616 was made of his own accord, because 'having heard objections to Nicolaus Copernicus's opinion on the Earth's motion, in order to be sure of holding only holy and Catholic opinions, I came to hear what was proper to hold in regard to this topic.'

'Did you come of your own accord, or were you summoned, and what was the reason you were summoned?'

'In 1616 I came of my own accord, without being summoned, for the reason I mentioned,' Galileo said firmly, as if correcting a student's wrong answer in a class. Maculano nodded, and Galileo went on: 'I discussed this matter with some cardinals who oversaw the Holy Office at that time, especially with Cardinals Bellarmino, Aracoeli, San Eusebio, Bonsi, and d'Ascoli.'

'And what specifically did you discuss with the above-mentioned cardinals?'

Galileo took a deep breath. 'They wanted to be informed about Copernicus's doctrine, his book being very difficult to understand for those who are not professional mathematicians and astronomers. In particular they wanted to understand the arrangement of the heavenly spheres according to Copernicus's hypothesis, how he places the sun at the centre of the planets' orbits, how around the sun he places next the orbit of Mercury, around the latter that of Venus, then the moon around the Earth, and around this Mars, Jupiter and Saturn. And in regard to motion, he makes the sun stationary at the centre and the Earth turn on itself and around the sun, that is, on itself with the diurnal motion, and around the sun with the annual motion.'

Maculano watched Galileo very closely, as the old man said all this as calmly as could be. 'What then was decided about this matter?'

'It was decided by the Holy Congregation that this opinion, taken absolutely, is repugnant to Holy Scripture and is to be admitted only *ex suppositione*,' Galileo using the Latin phrase here, as the term had a precise theological and legal meaning. Then he added, 'In the way that Copernicus himself takes it.'

This was the first of Galileo's lies under oath. Copernicus had made it quite clear in several places in his books that he regarded his explanation of planetary movement to be both mathematically expedient and also literally true in the physical world. Galileo knew this. Very possibly Maculano knew it also.

If so, Maculano brushed it aside. He said slowly, 'And what did the Most Eminent Bellarmino tell you about this decision? Did he say anything else about the matter, and if so, what?'

Galileo replied firmly, 'Lord Cardinal Bellarmino told me that Copernicus's opinion could be held *ex suppositione*, as Copernicus himself had held it. His Eminence knew that I held it *ex suppositione*, namely in the way that Copernicus held it.'

Three times the lie, like Peter denying Christ. Now Maculano was frowning heavily. But Galileo forged on. He quoted from the letter Bellarmino had written to the Carmelite Father Foscarini, after the meetings of 1616 had ended; Galileo had brought a copy of this letter with him, and now he pulled it from his small stack of documents and read from it: 'It seems to me that Your Paternity and Signor Galileo are proceeding prudently by limiting yourselves to speaking *ex suppositione* and not absolutely.'

Maculano shrugged this off. 'What was decided and then made known to you precisely, in the month of February 1616?'

Galileo answered readily: 'In the month of February 1616, Lord Cardinal Bellarmino told me that since Copernicus's opinion, taken absolutely, was contrary to Holy Scripture, it could be neither held nor defended, but it could be taken and used *ex suppositione*. In conformity with this I keep a certificate by Lord Cardinal Bellarmino himself, dated the 26th of May 1616, in which he says that Copernicus's opinion cannot be held or defended, being against Holy Scripture. I present a copy of this certificate.'

With that he showed Maculano a sheet of paper with twelve lines of writing on it. 'I have the original of this certificate with me in Rome,' he added, 'and it is written all in the hand of the above-mentioned Lord Cardinal Bellarmino.'

Maculano took the copy and entered it as evidence in the case, marking it Exhibit B. His face was impassive; one could not tell if this letter's existence was news to him or not. Certainly a signed certificate from Bellarmino allowing Galileo to discuss Copernicanism *ex suppositione* would seem to constitute unassailable evidence that if Galileo had written something hypothetical about Copernicus, the Church had allowed him to write it; which would mean that the accusation that had brought him here was incorrect. Which would make the Holy Office guilty of a mistake – or even of a malicious unfounded attack.

But Maculano did not look disturbed. He asked Galileo how he had been warned by Bellarmino, and if there had been anyone else there to witness it; Galileo described the conversation in Bellarmino's chambers, and explained that Commissioner Segizzi and some other Dominicans had been there.

Maculano said, 'If I read to you a transcript of what you were ordered, would you remember it?'

'I do not recall that I was told anything else,' Galileo said, with just a trace of uneasiness at this persistence. 'Nor can I know whether I shall remember what was then told me, even if it is read to me.'

Maculano then handed him a paper which he said was the actual text of the injunction given to him by Bellarmino. 'You see,' he said while Galileo was quickly reading it, 'that this injunction, which was given to you in the presence of witnesses, states that you cannot in any way whatever hold, defend, or teach the said opinion. Do you remember how and by whom you were so ordered?'

Galileo's ruddy complexion had gone pale. He had never seen this document before, and had not known of its existence. Supposedly a record of the warning given in the meeting, it prohibited him from even teaching Copernicus, either orally or in

461

writing. The ban on teaching or discussing was not in Bellarmino's certificate to Galileo.

This new injunction was not actually signed by Bellarmino, however; nor by anyone else. Galileo noted this, and saw also that it had been written on the back side of another document. This, together with the lack of any signature, made him suspicious. Segizzi must have added it to the file without Bellarmino's knowledge. Or possibly it was even a forgery, written later, on the back of a document with a date from that time, and added to the file to give weight to any later case against him. It could have been written the previous week.

Galileo looked quizzically at both sides of the document, turning it back and forth rather ostentatiously. He began his reply very slowly, as if working his way around the edges of a trap. For the first time his answers included some admissions of uncertainty. That he could speak at all after such a shock was yet another testament to his quickness of mind.

'I do not recall that the injunction was given to me any other way than orally by Lord Cardinal Bellarmino. I do remember that the injunction was that I could not hold or defend . . . and maybe even that I could not teach. I do not recall, further, that there was the phrase "in any way whatever", but maybe there was. In fact, I did not think about it or keep it in mind, having received a few months thereafter Lord Cardinal Bellarmino's certificate dated 26th of May, which I have presented, and in which is explained the order given to me not to hold or defend the said opinion. Regarding the other two phrases in the said injunction now produced, namely not to teach and in any way whatever, I did not retain them in my memory, I think because they are not contained in the said certificate, which I relied upon and kept as a reminder.'

It was the best he could do, and it was a pretty good defence at that: he had a signed injunction, after all, while the Inquisition did not. He pursed his lips and stared back at Maculano, still a bit pale, and with a sheen of sweat now on his forehead.

Probably it had not occurred to him until that moment that they might forge evidence to get him.

Maculano let the moment hang, then he said, 'After the issuing of the said injunction,' gesturing at his document, not Galileo's, 'did you obtain any permission to write the book identified by yourself, which you later sent to the printer?'

'After the above-mentioned injunction,' Galileo said, gesturing at his own certificate, not Maculano's, 'I did not seek permission to write the above-mentioned book, which I have identified, because I did not think that by writing this book I was contradicting at all the injunction given me not to hold, defend or teach the said opinion, as after all I was refuting it.'

Maculano had been looking down at the injunction – now his head shot up. Staring incredulously at Galileo, he started to speak, paused, put a forefinger to his lips. He returned his gaze to the papers on the table, stared at them for a long time. He picked up the pages covered by his notes.

Finally he looked up again. His expression now was hard to read, as he seemed both pleased and upset that Galileo had been so bold or so foolish as to utter a bald-faced lie while under oath before the Holy Office of the Inquisition. Up until this point Galileo had been saying that his book described the Copernican view suppositionally, as one of two equally possible explanations. That was already questionable. Now he was claiming that he had actually been refuting Copernicus's view! In the *Dialogo*, a book containing hundreds of pages of gentle criticism and sharp scorn aimed at poor Simplicio! It was so untenable a point that it could be taken as insulting. The book itself would easily serve as proof of the lie, and so . . . Possibly Maculano's anger was not only at being insulted, but at the way Galileo had put both of them in a very tricky situation, having said such a dangerous thing. He stared at Galileo for a long time, long enough for Galileo also to grasp the possible repercussions of his rash answer.

Finally Maculano spoke. He backtracked, as if to give Galileo another chance to avoid such a spectacular error. 'Did you

463

obtain permission for printing the same book, and if so by whom, and for you or for someone else?'

Galileo, buying time in order to rethink the matter, launched into a long, detailed, and impressively coherent description of the complicated interactions he had had with Riccardi and the Holy Office in Florence. The book had been approved by all of them. To that he added a detailed account of the convoluted chain of events by which the book had finally been printed in Florence rather than Rome, blaming this shift on the advent of the plague, rather than on Cesi's death. This was a very little lie, compared to the other one, and perhaps not important; although it was true that since Cesi's death the Linceans had fallen far out of favour with the Jesuits, so that here and now it was perhaps better not to mention him.

After perhaps ten minutes of steadily explaining his actions over the last couple of years, really a testament to his powers of mind, as he had to be thinking hard about other things, Galileo finished. 'The printer in Florence printed it observing strictly every order given by the Father Master of the Sacred Palace.'

Maculano nodded. Implacable, he returned to his question a third time:

'When you asked the above mentioned master of the Sacred Palace for permission to print the above mentioned book, did you reveal to the same Most Reverend Father Master the injunction previously given to you concerning the directive of the Holy Congregation, just mentioned?'

Now Galileo, his eyes bulging slightly, swallowed, and then spoke slowly. 'When I asked him for permission to print the book, I did not say anything to the Father Master of the Sacred Palace about the above-mentioned injunction, because I did not judge it necessary – having no scruples, since with the said book I had neither held nor defended the opinion of the Earth's motion and the sun's stability. On the contrary, in the said book I show the contrary of Copernicus's opinion, and show that Copernicus's reasons are invalid and inconclusive.'

He was sticking with the lie.

The room was silent. For a moment they all seemed frozen.

Maculano put down his notes and the copy of the injunction. He looked over at Father Sinceri; at Galileo again; his silence grew longer and longer; his face reddened. Galileo held his ground and did not look away, or blink, or spread his hands – he did not make any move at all, but his face was pale. For what seemed an endless moment everyone was still, as if they had all together fallen into one of Galileo's syncopes.

'No,' Maculano said. He gestured to the nun.

With this the deposition ended, and Signor Galilei was assigned a room in the dormitory of the officials, located in the Palace of the Holy Office, in lieu of prison, with the injunction not to leave it without special permission, under penalty to be decided by the Holy Congregation; and he was ordered to sign below and was sworn to silence.

I, Galileo Galilei, have testified as above.

His handwriting was very shaky. By the time he had finished scratching out the letters of the sentence, Maculano had left the room.

For Galileo to assert under the stricture of an oath both legal and sacred, that in his *Dialogo* he had been trying to refute Copernicus's world system, was astonishing to everyone who heard about it. Maculano had not been expecting it; no one could have, it went so against the grain of the evidence in hand, there on almost every page.

What did Galileo expect them to do? Accept a blatant lie? Did he think they could not tell it was a lie, or would not say it was if they knew it? Or did he think that the existence of a few feeble disclaimers in his final pages would obscure the work of the previous three hundred? Could anyone be that stupid?

No. No one could be so stupid as to miss the point of the *Dialogo*. Galileo had been very deliberate when he wrote it; as in all of his writing, he had worked hard to achieve clarity and to be persuasive, to win the debates with his philosophical foes by means of impeccable logic and telling examples. All his gifts as a writer had been put to use, and in Tuscan Italian at that, so anyone could read it and not just scholars versed in Latin. Everyone could see that the book's purpose was clear.

The special commission of three clerics that Urban had convened to report on the book was now called on, and they were unanimous in judging it to be a piece of advocacy for Copernicanism, not that it took Jesuitical expertise to do so. The first commissioner, Oreggi, made his evaluation in a single paragraph, concluding *the opinion is held and defended which teaches that the earth moves and the sun stands still, as one gathers from the whole thrust of the work.*

The second commissioner, Melchior Inchofer, was a livid choleric second-rater of a priest, pulled out of the inner depths of the Holy Office of the Index specifically for this job. His report on Galileo's book was a vituperation that filled seven dense pages, complaining bitterly that Galileo was *vehemently suspected of firmly adhering to this opinion of Copernicus's, and indeed that he holds it. He ridiculed those who are strongly committed to the common scriptural interpretation of the sun's motion as if they were small-minded, unable to penetrate the depth of the issue, half-witted, and almost idiotic. If he did not firmly adhere to the view of the earth's motion as if he believed it true, he would not have fought so vigorously in its favour; nor would he have regarded so despicably those who believe the opposite, as if he thought them not to be numbered among human beings. He does not regard as human those who hold the earth's immobility.*

This last statement referred to one of Galileo's jokes, a passage in the book where he said some of the anti-Copernican arguments were not worthy of man's definition as *homo sapiens: 'rational animals',* he wrote, *here has only the genus*

466

(animals) but lacks the species ('rational'). Inchofer did not appreciate the joke.

The third commissioner's report, by one Zaccaria Pasqualigo, was less angry than Inchofer's, but even more detailed, and ultimately the most devastating. It described the *Dialogo* argument by argument, pointing out errors in fact and logic, the best of which was *He tries to show that, given the earth's immobility and the sun's motion along the ecliptic, the apparent motion of sun spots cannot be saved. This argument is based on a premise about what de facto exists and infers a conclusion about what de facto may exist –*

– in other words, a tautology! What joy for a theologian to identify a tautology in Galileo's supposedly superior reasoning!

So these three commissioners' reports lay there on the desks of the Vatican officials like coffin nails, along with the nun scribe's transcript of the first deposition. Galileo versus Orregi, Inchofer and Pasqualigo. Galileo versus the evidence of his own book. An assertion under oath that black was white. It was so blatant it could even be taken as insolence, as contempt of the court. He wasn't stupid, he must be enacting some kind of a plan – but what? And what should the Inquisition do in response?

Day after day passed in which nothing seemed to happen, while behind the scenes the machinations of the Holy Office gnawed at the situation with a grinding that was almost audible throughout the city. The accused was under arrest in the Vatican, and going nowhere. Only his single servant was allowed him. The more time that passed, the more nervous he might become concerning his supremely risky tactic, whatever it was.

During these suspended days, which slowly turned into weeks, Niccolini reported what he could to Cioli and Grand Duke Ferdinando. He had inquired of Maculano's secretary what could be expected next. Maculano's secretary had replied that the matter was being considered by His Holiness the Pope, but that Galileo was being treated *in extraordinary and agreeable ways*, being held in the Vatican as opposed to Castel Sant'Angelo, where those on trial before the Inquisition were usually held. *They even allow his servant to wait on him, to sleep there, and what is more, to come and go as he pleases, and they allow my own servants to bring him food in his room. But Signor Galilei must have been enjoined from discussing or disclosing the contents of the cross-examination, since he did not want to say anything to us, not even whether he can or cannot speak.*

More time passed. It resembled an impasse. By ordering Galileo to come to Rome and face trial, Urban had already committed the Church to rendering a judgement against him; this was understood by all, including Galileo. That was why he had tried so hard to dodge the summons. Now that he was here, some kind of judgement was going to be rendered. It was not possible to find that the Church had made a mistake and Galileo therefore innocent of all wrongdoing. Yet that was what he was claiming had happened.

Did he not realize he could make things tremendously worse?

The Church had all the time in the world. Archbishop di Dominis had been held for three years, before dying after an interrogation. Giardano Bruno had been held for eight years.

Galileo's room was in one of the little Vatican dormitories used by priests working in the Holy Office. The dormitory had been evacuated for the period of his confinement; Galileo had the entire draughty hall to himself. His servant Cartophilus was on hand, but none of his Roman friends and acquaintances were allowed to call, and none of the Vatican's clerics visited him either. It was very close to solitary confinement.

The quarters themselves were adequate, but the hours stretched out and grew long. Again Galileo had time to think –

too much time, which of course was the point. He began to lose his appetite, and as a result his digestion and excretion. His sleep was disrupted. He was always prone to insomnia, and it often hit him in times of crisis. Now, in the depths of the chill spring night, Cartophilus would be called in to him, asked to bring a basin of warm water, or a loaf of bread. In the candlelight Galileo's bloodshot eyes stared out as from a deep cave. Once Cartophilus came back from the little brazier he kept outside the entryway, balancing a basin of steaming water, only to find the old astronomer frozen in something like one of his syncopes. 'What's this?' the servant said wearily.

But it was only an ordinary trance or dream, the old man asleep on his feet. He whimpered once or twice as Cartophilus helped him out of his paralysis and put his hands in the warm water.

In this suspended manner sixteen long days passed, during which nothing whatsoever happened, as far as anyone outside Maculano's office could tell. Of course the spies were everywhere, but they were now hearing almost nothing, and what they heard was contradictory. Galileo frequently urged Cartophilus to find out more, and the ancient one had been trying, but his opportunities from inside the Vatican were limited. Galileo's nerves had begun to fray by the third or fourth day of his confinement; by the end of the second week he was a wreck.

'You have to sleep, maestro,' Cartophilus suggested for the thousandth time.

'I have the certificate from Bellarmino himself, signed by him, forbidding me from holding the belief but not from discussing it *ex suppositione*.'

'Yes you do.' This had been said at least a thousand times.

'Their own supposed injunction wasn't signed by anyone. It was written on the back of some other document, a letter with a

1616 date on it. I'm sure it's a forgery. They pulled out something from the files from that year and wrote it up, probably this winter, to frame me, because they have nothing.'

Cartophilus said, 'It must have been a shock when you saw it.'

'It was! I couldn't believe my eyes. Everything became obvious the moment I saw it. Their plan, I mean.'

'And so you decided to deny everything. You claimed that your book refutes Copernicus.'

Galileo frowned. He knew perfectly well that the claim was absurd and unsupportable. Possibly it had been a panic response to Maculano's sudden deployment of the forged injunction. Possibly it was a move that he now regretted. Sixteen days was a long time.

Cartophilus persisted. 'Didn't Ambassador Niccolini advise you to go along with them, to say whatever they wanted? To allow them to slap you on the ear and let you go?'

Galileo growled.

Cartophilus observed him wrestling with all this. 'You know they cannot admit the accusation was wrong.'

Another growl, his bear's growl.

'Perhaps you could write to the Pope's nephew,' the old one suggested. 'Didn't you help him to get his doctorate, and his position in Padua?'

'I did,' Galileo said grimly. After a time he said, 'Bring me paper and ink. Lots of paper.' Even at the best of times Galileo's letters could be very long. This one would be thick, but not as thick as some; Cardinal Francesco Barberini was already familiar with the situation.

As Niccolini had reported to Florence, servants from the Villa Medici were allowed to cross town and bring Galileo his meals every day; and so it was no great difficulty to get messages back and forth. Word finally came by way of this conduit, conveying Cardinal Francesco Barberini's reply to Galileo's appeal for help. His Holiness was still too angry about the matter to be approached, Francesco let it be known. A way would have to be found within the normal procedures of the Holy Office. Given Galileo's stated position, impossible to believe, and an affront to the process, it would be difficult. Happily, given all this, a letter from Maculano to Francesco had recently arrived, which made it clear that Maculano too was trying to broker a solution. A manuscript copy of the letter itself was enclosed, under the cloth lining a basket with bread in it:

I reported to the Most Eminent Lords of the Holy Congregation, and then they considered various difficulties in regard to the manner of continuing the case and leading it to a conclusion; for in his deposition Galileo denied what can be clearly seen in the book he wrote, so that if he were to continue in his negative stance it would become necessary to use greater rigour in the administration of justice, and less regard for all the ramifications of this business.

Meaning if they had to torture him to obtain a confession, not only would it be bad for him, but as he was one of the most famous people in Europe, and had been so for twenty years, it would be bad for the Church. More important still, it would be bad for Urban. Urban had favoured Galileo as something like his personal scientist for many years. If Galileo's punishment was harsh, it would be obvious to all that Urban had been made to sacrifice one of his people to satisfy the Borgia, and this would weaken him further in his struggle against the Spanish. In his own interest, Urban could not be forced into harming Galileo too much – not even by Galileo himself, in the form of his most egregious lie under oath before the Holy Office.

Was this Galileo's point? Could he have risked so much to force the realization of this truth on Urban? Was this what he had been hoping for? If so, it was one hell of a gambit.

Finally I proposed a plan, Maculano continued, *namely that the Holy Congregation grant me the authority to deal extrajudicially with Galileo, in order to make him understand his error*

471

and, once having recognized it, to bring him to confess it. The proposal seemed at first too bold, and there did not seem to be much hope of accomplishing this goal as long as one followed the road of trying to convince him with reasons; however, after I mentioned the basis on which I proposed this –

Maculano did not identify this 'basis' in the letter, although it was easy to assume that he meant the threat of torture; but he might have had something else in mind. In any case he concluded his letter to Cardinal Barberini: *They gave me the authority.*

This time it was truly a private interview. No scribe was on hand, no transcript recorded, no witnesses of any kind. Only Maculano and Galileo, in a small office of the dormitory next to the Holy Office; though if one were at hand in the servant's closet, the ability to hear what was going on in the little inner room had long since been established.

Galileo was eager to talk. His voice was louder than Maculano's, his tone animated, inquisitive, intense. He wanted to know what had been going on, he wanted to know where he stood, he wanted to know why Maculano was visiting him; and all at once.

Maculano sounded conciliatory. He told Galileo that he was there to discuss the next stage of the trial with him, to make sure that Galileo knew where he stood, so that no further problems would accidentally arise as a result of any misunderstandings.

'I appreciate your courtesy,' Galileo said. After a pause, he said, 'My student and friend, Fra Benedetto Castelli, conveyed to me that he earlier met and spoke with you about these matters.'

'Yes.'

'He said that you were a good and devout man.'

'I am glad he thought so. I hope it is true.'

'He also wrote that he had spoken to you about my book, and that he had spoken as vehemently as he knew how against any persecution of my book, and in favour of the Copernican view, and that you had said to him that you agreed with him – that you too believed the Copernican explanation.'

'That is neither here nor there,' Maculano said calmly. 'I am not before you as Father Vincenzo Maculano da Firenzuola, Dominican. I am before you as Commissary General of the Holy Office of the Inquisition. As such, I need you to understand what is required of you for a successful completion of your trial.'

After a pause, Galileo said, 'Tell me then.'

'Privately, then – just between you and me, as men talking over a matter of mutual interest – you made a mistake at the end of your first deposition, by speaking of what you did or did not intend to say with your book. Understand me: if you focus your answers on your intentions, you put yourself more and more in the hands of your enemies. *I* am not your enemy; but you have enemies. And for reasons of state, they must be satisfied – or better, they must be put off in a way that is not too unsatisfactory to them. A judgement of some kind is going to be rendered against you. If it is a matter of the intention of your book, it will be very easy to convict you of heresy.'

He let that statement hang there for a while.

'If, on the other hand, it is merely a matter of you forgetting to obey in every respect the injunction levied against you in 1616 – if you confess to that error, then this is not such a serious thing.'

'But I have the certificate from Bellarmino himself!' Galileo protested.

'There is the other injunction.'

'Nothing of that was ever said to me at the time!'

'That's not what the other injunction says.'

'I never saw that injunction! It isn't signed by me or by Cardinal Bellarmino!'

'Nevertheless. It exists.'

A long silence.

'Remember,' Maculano said unctuously, 'there has to be something. If the trial moves to the matter of your intentions concerning your book, the decision of the special commission that investigated it is unanimous and overwhelming; you advocated for the Copernican view, not just *ex suppositione*, but factually and in earnest. You don't want to try to contest that.'

No reply from Galileo.

'And listen further,' Maculano said with a sharper tone. 'Listen closely. Even if the licence you received to publish your book, and the disclaiming sentences you added to the first and

474

last pages, were to prevail in our judgement, this might not save you. It might only shift the inquiry into even more dangerous areas.'

'What do you mean?' Galileo exclaimed. 'How so?'

'Remember what I said; something must be found. You say there was no second injunction, you say your book was licensed and included the proper disclaimer. Maybe so. But what then? For something must be found.'

No reply from Galileo.

'Well, then,' Maculano said, 'something will be found. For there are other problematic areas in your work. There are some, for instance, who insist that the theory of atomism that you advocated in your book *Il Saggiatore* constitutes a direct contradiction of the doctrine of the transubstantiation as defined by the Council of Trent. This is a very serious heresy, as of course you know.'

'But that has nothing to do with this!'

Maculano let a silence go on for a while. 'Something must be found,' he repeated gently. 'So you cannot say that. Everything is germane to this case. It is a question of your beliefs, your intentions, your promises, your actions. Your whole life.'

Silence.

'That being the case, the best possible outcome is to stay focused on the procedural issue that you seem to have tripped over, having to do with the injunction of 1616. That you may have inadvertently forgotten an order, and created a misunderstanding concerning the theory of Copernicanism, is, in other words, the least bad of your alternatives.'

'I obeyed the injunction given to me.'

'No. Don't keep saying that. Recall that if you continue to insist on that point, things get worse. The examinations of the Holy Office include methods that I would not want to see used in your case. These examinations always yield the answers they desire, and then it is a matter of throwing yourself on the mercy of the Holy Office. That could be lifetime imprisonment in the

Castel Sant'Angelo. It has often happened. Or, it could be worse yet. That would be a disaster for all concerned, wouldn't it.'

'Yes.'

'So, if you were to plead forgetfulness, and perhaps a lapse of judgement – too much pride, or complacency, or carelessness – whatever venial sin you choose – then this would be a basis to go forward. Your punishment could be to recite the seven penitential Psalms weekly for some years, or something like that.'

'But I got the licence to publish! I discussed the situation with His Holiness himself!'

'That defence only constitutes yet another attack on the Church.'

It was getting repetitive now, as in one of those end games in chess where the stronger side has to slowly and patiently nudge the opponent's king into a spot where it has no more options.

'But, remember what my Salviati says at the end of Book Four, in the book's penultimate scene –'

'No. I need to keep reminding you, this is not a good avenue for you to pursue. The book has been read with the closest attention to logic, reason, rhetoric, mathematics, and incidentals, by learned scholars and judges, and their reports have been unanimous in asserting you made a case for the Copernican view. You cannot add a few words to the end of such an argument and hope to change the effect of the whole. Especially not since most of your ameliorative equivocations are put in the mouth of a character named Simplicio, an Aristotelian who has been shown to be foolishly wrong everywhere else in the book. Indeed a kind of dunderhead, a simpleton in fact as well as name! Urban's words, his doctrine, put into this person's mouth! It will not do. Your own book, as written, makes things so very clear. You are a good Catholic, and yet you have disobeyed an injunction from the Holy Office, as judged by officials of that Holy Office. This could lead to a disastrous consequence. As I hope you know.'

'I know.'

'Do you? Do you understand me?'

'I understand.'

'And so? What then do you intend to do about it?'

'I don't know! I don't know! You tell me what I should do!'

There was a long silence. Who sighed it was hard to tell. Both men were breathing heavily, as if they had been tossing each other around like wrestlers.

'Tell me, then. Tell me what I should do.'

Checkmate.

To His Eminence Cardinal Francesco Barberini:

Yesterday afternoon I had a discussion with Galileo, and, after exchanging innumerable arguments, by the grace of the Lord I accomplished my purpose: I made him grasp his error, so that he clearly recognized that he had erred and gone too far in his book; he expressed everything with heartfelt words, as if he were relieved by the knowledge of his error; and he was ready for a judicial confession. However, he asked me for a little time to think about the way to render his confession honest.

I have not communicated this to anyone else, but I felt obliged to inform Your Eminence immediately, for I hope His Holiness and Your Eminence will be satisfied that in this manner the case has been brought to a point where it may be settled without difficulty. The Tribunal will maintain its reputation; the culprit can be treated with kindness; and, whatever the final outcome, he will know the favour done to him, with all the consequent gratitude one wants in this. I am thinking of examining him today to obtain the said confession; after obtaining it, I hope the only thing left for me will be to question him about his intention and allow him to present a defence. With this done, he could be granted imprisonment in his own house, as hinted to me by Your Eminence, to whom I now offer my most humble reverence,

Your Eminence's most humble and most obedient servant

Fra. Vinc. Maculano da Firenzuola

Confession of sin; examination concerning intentions; the guilty party's defence of his actions; the pronouncement of punishment. These were the formalized steps taken in heresy trials; they all had to be taken.

That night in the empty dormitory, Galileo groaned, shouted, whimpered, cursed. When Cartophilus went to his little room and asked if there was anything he could do, Galileo threw a cup at him.

Later in the night, however, the moans grew to shrieks, and Cartophilus hustled to the old man's room, alarmed. The maestro did not answer either calls or knocks on his door, but instead went suddenly silent.

Cartophilus forced the door open, entered into the dark room holding a candle before him.

Galileo pounced on him, held him fast. The candle fell and went out. In the dark the old astronomer growled, 'Send me to Hera.'

Cartophilus did it. He made the entanglement, then got the old man slumped onto his bed, half on the floor, almost as if praying. A foam of spittle drooled from Galileo's open mouth, and his open eyes stared fixed at nothingness. Another syncope to be endured; Cartophilus shook his head, muttered under his breath.

He pulled a blanket over the inert body. He closed the door, went back and sat on the bed by Galileo's side, checked the old man's pulse, which was slow and steady. He gazed into the little screen on the side of the box. There was no way to know how long he would be gone.

'I know what his punishment should be,' Galileo said to Hera again.

Ganymede appeared to have been struck dumb by the encounter with Jupiter. He stared out of his facemask and would not speak – would not or could not. Possibly the Jovian mind had inflicted some damage on him. The look in his eye suggested to Galileo that he was angry or shocked – or perhaps furiously insane. Something bad. And he would not give them the satisfaction of knowing his thoughts. Although it was not clear what satisfaction they could have. Galileo himself was baffled, and Hera appeared unhappy with the experience she had forced Ganymede to submit to.

But now Galileo thought he knew.

That there was a mind in Jupiter greater than the mind in Europa, and connected to vast minds elsewhere, was what Ganymede had been hinting all along, and finally admitted. He had learned of it somehow, either in his early incursions into the oceans of Ganymede, or during his existence in some future time; no way to tell. Although Galileo wanted Hera to look into his past using her memory celatone, if she could. But however he learned it, he had been aware of the Jovian mind, and so his mad look could now be saying *I told you so*. Or perhaps he was simply overwhelmed. Galileo did not fully understand himself what he had seen in Jupiter. The cosmos, alive with thought, yes; but he could not recapture the huge feelings that had overwhelmed him on experiencing this reality. Something big had happened in him, but it was all confused now, obscured by the merging with Hera afterward, by his return to Italy. It was not something he was going to be able to understand.

Ganymede stared at them.

Galileo said, 'You wounded Europa, child of Jupiter, deliberately. You tried to kill it. To think that the first otherwordly creature encountered by humanity should be attacked and injured by us is beyond deplorable.' Suddenly he thought of all the bad faith, the backstabbing, the hatred of the ignorant for all that was new, and he stuck his face nearly onto the prisoner's faceplate and bellowed, 'It's a crime for ever!'

Ganymede's eyes flinched. Possibly it was just a reflex, for no sign of remorse appeared in his stony expression. To emphasize his point Galileo struck the side of the man's helmet, sending him flying. From the floor Ganymede looked up at an angle to see Galileo. Galileo took a step toward him, suddenly furious. 'You lie and you cheat and you stab in the back! All you cowards are alike. You try to kill anything you find different, because it frightens you!'

Suddenly Ganymede spoke. 'I raised you up from nothing,' he said, his voice like bronze. 'You were a second-rate maths teacher in a second-rate life. I made you Galileo.'

'*I* made me Galileo,' Galileo said. 'You only fucked me up. You're trying to get me killed. You should have left me alone.'

'I wish I had.'

'Jupiter has spoken to us . . .' Hera said.

Galileo nodded, returned to the point. 'The Jovian mind knows now who the criminal is. It also knows we are not all as depraved and murderous a species as it might have suspected. It might even know that some of us tried to prevent your rash act.'

Ganymede glowered from the floor. Hera saw this expression, so full of hate, and said to him, 'You attacked the alien because of what we might have learned from it. You judged humanity to be cowardly, and so you acted like a coward.'

The prisoner only grimaced.

Hera said, 'We'll take you back to Europa, and turn you over to the people there. They can decide how to deal with you. Although I don't know what they can do that would be appropriate.'

'Restitution,' Galileo said.

They all looked at him.

'He wanted restitution, and now he will get it.' He looked to Aurora. 'You told me what you can do across the temporal manifolds, and what you can't do. You described the energy costs. If you had enough energy at your disposal, could you not effect changes nearer to you than the resonance entanglement with my time?'

'What do you mean?'

'Some of you have gone back and interfered with me, so that what happens to me is different than what would have happened if you hadn't visited me. So why couldn't you change this awful deed your Ganymede has committed? Why couldn't you send him back to a time before he did it, and then prevent him from doing it?'

Aurora said, 'Entanglement is easiest at the triple interferences in the wave patterns in the temporal manifold. Inside the first positive interference it takes very much more energy to establish an entanglement. It would take a truly stupendous amount of energy to move an entangler to a time so close to ours.'

Galileo pondered the maths she had taught him, swimming hazily in his memory. Overlapping concentric waves on a pond . . . 'But it's not impossible,' he concluded. 'Send him back even to before he entered Ganymede's ocean, before his exile, and stop him there. That you could do, yes? It would only be a matter of the amount of energy brought to bear?'

She considered it, perhaps venturing into her machine augmentations to do so. 'Yes, but the energy might be impossible to marshal.'

'Use the gas of an outer gas giant, as you did when you sent back the first teletrasportas.'

'What if those gas giants are all alive, like Jupiter?'

'The vision it just gave us indicated they are not. There are three giants left outside Saturn, didn't you say?'

'Yes. Uranus, Neptune, Hades.'

'Any one of them would provide enough power for a short analepsis into Ganymede's past,' Galileo said.

'Possibly.'

Galileo turned to Hera. He pointed at Ganymede. 'Send him back,' he said. 'Send him back, and make him change what he did before.'

'It might kill him.'

'Even so.'

'It might change things such that all this voyage goes away,' she said, looking at Aurora. 'All that we have done since his attack could be lost.'

'It's lost anyway,' Galileo pointed out. 'Everything is always changing.'

She shook her head. 'In the *e* time –'

'But even there. Alas.'

They shared a gaze.

'Remember for me,' Galileo said.

'And you for me,' she replied. She gave him the smallest of smiles, looking him in the eye. Galileo saw it and said to himself, *remember*.

He glanced at Ganymede, but Ganymede was staring up at the ceiling of the ship's cabin, or through it to infinity. Whether he was looking for atonement or just another chance to do the job, Galileo couldn't tell. Real hopes are one of the seven secret lives.

Chapter Eighteen   Vehement Suspicion

You see then how treacherous time subdues us, how we are all subject to mutation. And that which most afflicts us among so many things is that we have neither certainty nor any hope at all of reassuming that same being in which we once found ourselves. We depart, and do not return the same; and since we have no recollection of what we were before we were in this being, so we cannot have an indication of that which we shall be afterward.
– GIARDANO BRUNO, The Expulsion of the Triumphant Beast

Galileo woke with a start, and Cartophilus put a hand to his arm.

'You're in the Vatican. Remember?'

'I remember,' Galileo croaked, looking around.

'Are you all right?'

'Yes.' Galileo stared at him. 'I want justice.'

Cartophilus frowned. 'Everyone does, maestro. But there may be more important things to want right now. Like your life.'

Galileo growled at him.

Cartophilus shrugged. 'Just the way it is, maestro. Here. Drink this wine.'

*   *   *

483

Eighteen days after his first deposition, and two days after his private conversation with Maculano, Galileo asked to speak to the Commissary General again. He was brought before his examiners, there in the same room where the first deposition had taken place.

When they were all in their assigned places, Maculano said in his sonorous Latin,

'Please state whatever you wish to say.'

Galileo read aloud from a page of writing he held in his hand, enunciating clearly his Tuscan Italian. 'For several days I have been thinking continuously and intensively about the interrogation I underwent on the sixteenth of this month, and in particular about the question of whether sixteen years ago I had been prohibited, by order of the Holy Office, from holding, defending, and teaching in any way whatever the opinion, then condemned, of the Earth's motion and sun's stability. It dawned on me to reread my printed *Dialogo*, which over the last three years I had not even looked at.'

This was impossible to believe, given the job it had been to print it; but onward –

'I wanted to check very carefully whether, against my best intentions, through an oversight, I might have written not only something enabling readers or superiors to infer a defect of disobedience on my part, but also other details through which one might think of me as a transgressor of the order of the Holy Church. Being at liberty, through the generous approval of superiors, to send one of my servants for errands, I managed to get a copy of my book, and I started to read it with the greatest concentration and to examine it in the most detailed manner. Not having seen it for so long, I found it almost a new book by another author. Now, I freely confess that it appeared to me in several places to be written in such a way that a reader not aware of my intention might have had reason to form the opinion that the arguments for the false side, which I intended to confute, were so stated as to be capable of convincing

484

because of their strength, rather than being easy to answer. In particular, two arguments, one based on sunspots and the other on the tides, are presented favourably to the reader as being strong and powerful, more than would seem proper for someone who deemed them to be inconclusive and wanted to confute them, as indeed I inwardly and truly did, and do, hold them to be inconclusive and refutable. As an excuse for myself, for having fallen into an error so foreign to my intention, I did it because I was not completely satisfied with saying that when one presents arguments for the opposite side with the intention of confuting them, they must be explained in the fairest way and not be made out of straw to the disadvantage of the opponent. Being dissatisfied with this excuse, as I said, I resorted to that of the natural gratification everyone feels for his own subtleties and for showing himself to be cleverer than the average man, by finding ingenious and apparently correct considerations of probability even in favour of false propositions. Nevertheless – even though, to use Cicero's words, "I am more desirous of glory than is suitable" – if I had to write out the same arguments now, there is no doubt I would weaken them in such a way that they could not appear to exhibit a force which they really and essentially lack. My error then was, and I confess it, one of vain ambition, pure ignorance, and inadvertence.

'This is as much as I need to say on this occasion, and it occurred to me as I reread my book.'

He looked up at Maculano and nodded, and Maculano again gestured to the nun. In a moment the transcript was ready for his signature, boldly and clearly executed:

I, Galileo Galilei, have testified as above.

When he was done with that, after swearing him again to secrecy, Maculano concluded the hearing.

Galileo was free to leave the chamber, and did. But all of a sudden he rushed back in, looking stricken. Everyone there was startled to see him reappear. Pop-eyed, his voice far humbler than it had been at any time so far, he asked Maculano if he could add something to his deposition.

Maculano, taken aback, could only agree. Galileo then spoke *extempore*, almost faster than the scribe could write:

'And for greater confirmation that I neither did hold nor do hold as true the condemned opinion of the Earth's motion and sun's stability, if, as I desire, I am granted the possibility and the time to prove it more clearly, I am ready to do so. The occasion for it is readily available since in the book already published the speakers agree that after a certain time they should meet again to discuss various physical problems other than the subject already dealt with. Hence, with this pretext to add one or two other Days, I promise to reconsider the arguments already presented in favour of the said false and condemned opinion and to confute them in the most effective way that the blessed God will enable me. So I beg this Holy Tribunal to cooperate with me in this good resolution, by granting me the permission to put it into practice.'

If granted, this would of course imply that the *Dialogo* were to be taken off the prohibited list. It looked like he had come back in on an impulse, to beg for the book's life, even though the changes he proposed would make it into one gigantic mass of incoherent contradiction.

He stood there red-faced, drawn up, shoulders back, staring at Maculano.

Maculano nodded impassively, instructed the scribe to show Galileo the revised deposition. After reading it, Galileo again signed.

I, Galileo Galilei, affirm the above.

So, Galileo had kept his part of the deal. Confession in return for a reprimand. He had confessed to vainglorious ambition, which had led him to break the rule of an injunction from 1616 that he had never seen – that in fact he suspected had been forged, either back at the time or recently. He had given Maculano what Maculano had asked for. Now he had to wait for Maculano to do his part.

At first things looked promising. Niccolini's weekly letter to Cioli reported that Maculano had spoken to Cardinal Francesco Barberini, and after that conversation, on the cardinal's own authority, the Sanctissimus being away at Castel Gondolfo, Francesco Barberini had ordered that Galileo be allowed to move back to the Villa Medici to await the next stage of the proceedings, *so that he can recover from the discomforts and his usual indispositions, which keep him in constant torment.*

At the Villa Medici, Niccolini wrote in his next letter, *he seems to have regained his good health.* He was allowed to walk in the extensive gardens daily, even to help with the weeding if he wanted to. He looked hungrily over the wall at the gardens of the Trinita church, and on his behalf Niccolini asked Maculano to ask Cardinal Barberini if Galileo could extend his walks there. This too was allowed. Galileo's own letters home, to Maria Celeste and various associates, though silent on the trial, as they had to be, were optimistic. The letters to close colleagues indicated that he expected the *Dialogo* to survive the trial, revised but with the prohibition lifted.

After reading one of his letters to her, Maria Celeste wrote back the next day,

The joy that your last dear letter brought to me, and the having to read it over and over to the nuns, who made quite a jubilee on hearing its contents, put me into such an excited state that I was seized by a terrible headache that lasted from the fourteenth hour of the morning on into the night, something truly outside my usual experience. I do not say this to reproach you, but to show how I take to heart all your concerns. And though I am not more strongly affected by what happens to you than a daughter ought to be, yet I dare to say that the love and reverence I bear my dearest lord and father does surpass by a

good deal that of the generality of daughters. And I know that
in like manner he excels most parents in his love of me, his
daughter: and that is all I have to say.

Actually she had much more to say, as she wrote almost daily; and he wrote her back at least weekly, and often more frequently, depending on how he was feeling. She gave him news of the convent and of his own household at *Il Gioello*: the fate of the crops and the wine production, the behaviour of the donkey, the affairs of the servants; her shock that her brother Vincenzio had not written to Galileo even once; and so on. Always there was encouragement for him, and reassurance that he was blessed by God, and lucky to be who he was. Galileo snatched these letters when they arrived and stopped whatever else he was doing, and read them like a man in a desert drinking a long draught of water. Sometimes he shook his head at their contents, with a sad or cynical smile. He kept them in a neat stack, in a basket on a night table by his bed.

During these days of waiting for a judgement, Grand Duke Ferdinando had Cioli write to Niccolini to say that the time during which the Grand Duke was willing to pay for Galileo's lodging had come to an end, and that Galileo should now pay for his own upkeep. Niccolini let nothing of this particular slight be heard by Galileo himself, though it did get around the villa. Not that it took this news to make Galileo aware of the weak support he was getting from home. He was already aware of it; he would never forget it, or forgive it.

For now, he enjoyed the friendship and support of Niccolini and his wife, the wonderful Caterina Riccardi. Indeed all the staff of the Villa Medici seemed both proud of him and fond of him – like all the other Galilean households, in other words, except that this one was not also afraid of him.

Niccolini wrote sharply back to Florence:

In regard to what Your Most Illustrious Lordship tells me, namely that his Highness does not intend to pay for his expenses here beyond the first month, I can reply that I am not about to discuss this matter with him while he is my guest. I would rather assume the burden myself. The expenses will not exceed 14 or 15 scudi a month, including everything; thus, if he were to stay here six months, they would add up to 90 or 100 scudi between him and his servant.

'A trifling amount for a Grand Duke to be stingy about,' he said aloud but did not add.

Galileo's third deposition was to be a formality only, completing the steps every trial for heresy had to go through: confession, defence, abjuration. This was both confession and defence, and what Galileo must confess to and what he could say in his own defence had both already been worked out in the private meeting with Maculano.

When the time came for it – the tenth of May, a month after the first deposition, and three months after his arrival in Rome – Galileo was returned to the Vatican with the document he had carefully written out, copying it over five times before getting it to his own satisfaction.

The white examination room with its crucifix was as before, the occupants likewise.

Maculano began by explaining to Galileo that he had eight days in which to present his defence, if he wanted it.

Having heard this formality, Galileo nodded and said, 'I understand what Your Paternity has told me. In reply I say that I do want to present something in my defence, namely in order to show the sincerity and purity of my intention, not at all to excuse my having transgressed in some ways, as I have already said. I present the following statement, together with a certificate by the late Most Eminent Cardinal Bellarmino, written with his own hand by the Lord Cardinal himself, of which I earlier presented a copy by my hand.'

So he persisted with the signed document from Bellarmino's own hand, which he had done well to ask for, as it was serving as the crucial counterweight to the forged injunction that had been sprung on him during his first deposition. Thus Sarpi's actions in 1616 now helped him at last.

'For the rest,' Galileo concluded, 'I rely in every way on the usual mercy and clemency of this Tribunal.'

After signing his name, he was sent back to the house of the above mentioned Ambassador of the Most Serene Grand Duke, under the conditions already communicated to him.

The written defence Galileo had handed to the Commissary focused mostly on the question of why he had not informed Riccardi that he was writing a book that included discussion of the Copernican view. He explained that this was because in his first deposition he had not been asked about it, and now he wanted to do that, *to prove the absolute purity of my mind, always opposed to using simulation and deceit in any of my actions.* Which was almost true.

He described the history of the letter he had obtained from Bellarmino, and the reason for its existence: that he had requested it, in order to have an explicit guidance for future action. He went on to claim that what it said in print, frequently consulted by him over the years, had no doubt allowed him to forget any supplementary prohibitions that had only been spoken, if they had been, at one of the many meetings Galileo had initiated in 1616. The new and more extensive prohibitions *which I hear are contained in the injunction given to me and recorded, that is, 'teaching' and 'in any way whatever', struck me as very new and unheard. I do not think I should be mistrusted about the fact that in the course of fourteen or sixteen years I lost any memory of them, especially since I had no need to give the matter any thought, having such a valid reminder in writing.*

'Very new and unheard,' he insisted.

He also reminded the commission that he had handed the manuscript of his book over to the censors of the Inquisition and gotten it approved. Therefore, *I think I can firmly hope that the idea of my having knowingly and willingly disobeyed the orders given me will not be believed by the Most Eminent and Most Prudent Lord judges.*

Most Prudent, he reminded them.

Then he ended his written defence with the following:

Finally, I am left with asking you to consider the pitiable state of ill health to which I am reduced, due to ten months of constant mental distress, and the discomforts of a long and tiresome journey in the most awful season and at the age of seventy. I feel I have lost the greater part of the years that my previous state of health promised me. I am encouraged to do this by the faith I have in the clemency and kindness of heart of the Most Eminent Lordships, my judges; and I hope that if their sense of justice perceives anything lacking among so many ailments as adequate punishment for my crimes, they will, I beg them, condone it out of regard for my declining old age, which I humbly also ask them to consider. Equally, I want them to consider my honour and reputation against the slanders of those who hate me, and I hope that when the latter insist on disparaging my reputation, the Most Eminent Lordships will take it as evidence why it became necessary for me to obtain from the Most Eminent Lord Cardinal Bellarmino the certificate attached herewith.

Despite the pathos of old age stuff, it was on the whole a robust, one might even say defiant, defence. All he had confessed to *was the vain ambition and satisfaction of appearing clever beyond the average popular writers.* To the attentive eye it even seemed he had obliquely alluded to the possibly fraudulent nature of some of the evidence brought against him.

Perhaps it was this defiance that did it; perhaps it was something else. In any case, for whatever reason, the trial did not proceed. A judgement did not arrive.

Weeks passed, and more weeks. No word came from the Holy Office of the Inquisition. Galileo spent his days walking the paths of the Villa Medici gardens, in its layout so much like the legal maze in which he now found himself.

It was late spring by now, and everything was bursting with new life. The white clouds pouring in from the Mediterranean dropped rain. At the Vatican the Inquisition was presumably preparing its final report to Pope Urban; or perhaps they were done, and waiting for the Sanctissimus to return from Castel Gondolfo. Around the city, so full of agents and observers, any judgement on Galileo seemed possible.

Meanwhile here he stood, in a big green garden. The vegetable plots, located out against the back wall, helped feed the villa's big household, which numbered over a hundred. Galileo strolled down and sat on a stool in the rows of tomato plants, weeding. When hands are dirty the soul is clean. There was nothing he could do but wait. His rheumatism bothered him, his hernia. At night, his insomnia. He had not even brought a telescope with him. Occasionally, despite the garden, he would be overcome with melancholy, or fear, even terror. The sleepless nights and the days after were especially hard. All day in the garden was sometimes scarcely enough to pull him out of his black apprehension.

May ran out of days. Then in early June, the Pope returned to his residence in the Vatican.

Niccolini met with him as soon as permitted, and asked for a speedy end to the trial, and for a merciful judgement. Urban explained he had been merciful already, but that the judgement had to be a condemnation. He promised it would come soon.

'There is no way of avoiding some personal punishment,' he told Niccolini brusquely.

Niccolini came home worried. Something had changed, he could tell. Things no longer seemed to be going so well.

He wrote to Cioli, *So far to Signor Galileo I have only mentioned the imminent conclusion of the trial and the prohibition of the book. However, I told him nothing about the personal punishment, in order not to afflict him by telling him everything at once; furthermore, His Holiness ordered me not to tell him in order not to torment him yet, and because things will perhaps change through deliberations. Thus I also think it proper that no one there at your end inform him of anything.*

Then, halfway through June, word came: he was to prepare for a fourth deposition.

This was a surprise, a new and unwelcome development, in that it extended beyond the proscribed form for a heresy trial; also beyond the deal that Maculano had outlined in their private meeting. It seemed something had gone awry. Everyone in the villa could feel it.

That night, when all the people of the Villa Medici were asleep, Cartophilus slipped out the back gate, and made his way toward the Vatican.

The streets of Rome were never entirely empty, even between midnight and dawn. People and animals made their solitary ways. Partly this was frightening, as the possibility of footpads or assassins was all too real; partly it was reassuring, as most of those out were simply doing the night business of the city, like removing the offal and dung, or bringing in the food and supplies for the day to come. It was possible to follow carts, drays, mule trains, donkeys that were apparently working on their own recognizance, and by doing so, and staying at the verge of the illumination coming from various scattered torchlights, move unseen and unmolested. The wild cats of the streets were doing the same thing, picking their way from scent to scent, and one had to avoid kicking them as one darted from one shadow to the next.

In the flickering shadows down near the Vatican's river gate, Cartophilus met with his friend Giovanfrancesco Buonamici, who was now sometimes acting as a bodyguard for Cardinal Francesco Barberini.

'Something's changed,' Buonamici said.

'Yes,' Cartophilus replied shortly. 'But what?'

'I don't know.'

'Where is it coming from? The Jesuits?'

'Of course. But it's more than them. The *chiusura d'istruzione* has been sent up to the Congregation and to His Holiness, and the thing is, it wasn't written by Maculano. It was written by the assistant, Sinceri.'

'Oh no.'

'Oh yes. And none of the depositions or supporting documents were sent up with it. Only a little stiletto in prose from "the magnificent Carlo Sinceri, Doctor of both laws, Proctor Fiscal of this Holy Office", as he styled himself in his signature.' Buonamici snorted and spat on the ground beside him.

'And what did he report?' Cartophilus said, mouth tight.

'It was all the same old shit, all the way back to Lorini and Colombe. How he said the Bible is full of falsehoods, and God is an accident who laughs and weeps, and the saints' miracles didn't happen, and so on.'

'But that isn't even what the trial has been about!'

'Of course not. As to that, it puts all the prohibitions in the injunction they forged as being in his certificate from Bellarmino, so the distinction he was trying to make there has been destroyed.'

'Jesus. So – the whole Sarpi defence is knocked aside just like that.'

'Yes. They're going for heresy.'

Cartophilus thought it over. 'And Sinceri sent it up where?'

'To Monsignor Paolo Bebei, of Orvieto. He's just replaced Monsignor Boccabella as the Assessor of the Holy Office. Boccabella who was friendly to us.'

'So, yet another change, then. I mean, we already knew about Sinceri.'

'Yes. But I thought he wouldn't matter. Obviously I was wrong.'

'So they have the Assessor, and Sinceri. And they've stacked the Congregation. And the Pope is only hearing what the Congregation tells him. And he's still angry.'

'As usual. He'd be out of his mind right now anyway. There was another bad horoscope published in the *Avvisi*, and now he's having all his food tested. He's perfectly primed, what can I say'

Cartophilus nodded. For a long time he stared at the paving stones, thinking things over.

'What are we going to do?' Buonamici asked.

Cartophilus shrugged. 'Let's see what happens in this fourth deposition. I don't think there's any way we can avoid that one anyway. Depending on how it goes, we'll see. We may have to intervene.'

'If we can!'

'If we can. We've got Cardinal Bentivoglio in place, and Gherardini. They should be able to help, if we need it. All right. Keep your ear cocked and find out what you can. Let's be in touch right after the fourth deposition is over.'

And he slipped back into the unquiet Roman night.

On Midsummer's Day of 1633, six weeks after his third deposition, Galileo was summoned back to the Vatican to submit to a fourth one.

Called personally to the hall of Congregations in the palace of the Holy Office in Rome, fully in the presence of the Reverend Father Commissary General of the Holy Office, assisted by the Reverend Father Prosecutor, etc.

Galileo Galilei, Florentine, mentioned previously, having sworn an oath to tell the truth, was asked by the Fathers the following:

Maculano said, 'Do you have anything to say?'

Galileo, sticking to Italian and holding to an impassive manner that hid his irritation and fear, said, 'I have nothing to say.'

There was a long silence. Maculano spent the time looking down at his notes on the table. Finally he said, very slowly, as if reading, 'Do you hold, or have you held, and for how long, that the sun is the centre of the world and the Earth is not the centre of the world, but moves also with diurnal motion?'

Galileo too hesitated before speaking. This was a new line of attack, a *direttissima*, when supposedly they already had a deal.

Finally he replied, 'A long time ago – that is, before the decision of the Holy Congregation of the Index, and before I was issued that injunction, I was undecided, and regarded the two opinions, those of Ptolemy and Copernicus, as disputable, because either the one or the other could be true in nature. But after the above-mentioned decision, assured by the prudence of the authorities, all my uncertainty stopped, and I held, as I still hold, as very true and undoubted Ptolemy's opinion, namely the stability of the Earth and the motion of the sun.'

Once again, a very questionable assertion under oath.

Maculano tapped the fat copy of the *Dialogo* on the table for emphasis. 'You are presumed to have held the said Copernican opinion *after* that time, from the manner and procedure in which the said opinion is discussed and defended in this book you published *after* that time, indeed from the very fact that you wrote and published the said book. Therefore you are asked to freely tell the truth whether you hold or have held that opinion.'

Therefore you are asked. Maculano seemed to be distancing himself from these questions – as well he might, considering how they broke the deal he had made. These were not his questions; he had had these questions pressed on him from somewhere above. Galileo could either take comfort from that realization or be newly afraid, depending on which aspect of it he considered. Meanwhile he had to answer very, very carefully.

'In regard to my writing of the *Dialogo* already published, I did not do so because I held Copernicus's opinion to be true,' he said steadily. 'Instead, deeming only to be doing a beneficial service, I explained the physical and astronomical reasons that can be advanced for one side and for the other; I tried to show that none of these, neither those in favour of this opinion or that, have the strength of a conclusive proof, and that therefore to proceed with certainty one would have to resort to the determination of more subtle doctrines. As one can see in many places in the *Dialogo*.'

This was not actually true, but what else could he say? His ruddy complex had turned beet red, and he stared at Maculano as if to burn holes in him.

Maculano, however, now kept his eye on his notes. The trial had gone over his head.

Galileo saw this, and went on: 'So for my part, I conclude,' as if studying it objectively from the outside, 'that I do not hold, and after the determination of the authorities I have not held, the condemned opinion.'

Maculano paused, then read on from the sheet he held as if he had not heard Galileo's response.

'From the book itself, and the reasons advanced for the affirmative side, namely that the Earth moves and the sun is motionless, you are presumed, as it was stated, that you hold Copernicus's opinion, or at least that you held it at the time you wrote. Therefore you are now told, that unless you decide to proffer the truth, one would have recourse to the remedies of the law and to appropriate steps against you.'

The instruments of torture were laid out on a table against the side wall of the room. All this was according to the strict laws governing the Inquisition; first the warnings, then the display of the instruments of torture; only after that, if the accused persisted in obstructing the judgement, the use of the instruments. As the chapter of the Inquisitor's manual entitled, 'On the Manner of Interrogating Culprits by Torture' put it: *The culprit having denied the crimes with which he has been charged, and the latter not having been fully proved, in order to learn the truth it is necessary to proceed against him by means of a rigorous examination; in fact, the function of torture is to make up for the shortcomings of witnesses, when they cannot adduce a conclusive proof against the culprit.*

As, for instance, now. But Galileo could not admit to more than he already had admitted to, without putting himself in extreme danger of admitting to heresy. His back was already to the wall.

Also, unfortunately, he was getting more and more angry at Maculano, and at those above Maculano who had ordered this move; you could see it in the way the back of his neck went dark red, and in the set of his shoulders. Anyone who had ever worked for him would have exited the room immediately.

He spoke tightly, grimly, the words chopped each from the next: 'I do not hold this opinion of Copernicus, and I have not held it after being ordered by injunction to abandon it. For the rest, here I am in your hands; do as you please.'

'Tell the truth!' Maculano ordered. 'Otherwise we will have recourse to torture!'

Galileo, with no idea of what the Pope might want him to confess, drew himself up. 'I am here to submit, but I have not held this opinion after the determination was made, as I said.'

Silence in the room.

And since nothing else could be done for the execution of the decision, after he signed he was sent to his place.

'The execution of the decision'. Which decision must ultimately have been Urban's – to haul him in for this added interrogation and confession. But what had been decided beyond that, no one beside Urban seemed to know.

Galileo was again confined to the rooms of the Dominican dormitory where he had been held during the time of his first three depositions. This was a bad sign, retrograde and ominous. There was no way to tell what would happen next, or when. Whatever deal or understanding there had been was obviously gone.

He sat on his bed, staring at the wall, eating a bit of his supper, drinking his cup of wine thoughtfully. He lay down late in the night, and only after he fell asleep did he moan and groan; although it has to be said that he often moaned and groaned while he slept, no matter the circumstances. His sleep was not comfortable to him. But his insomnia was even worse.

The Congregation of the Holy Office was composed of ten cardinals, and since the Borgia was one of them, it was not a sure thing that Urban's will would determine their judgement. Borgia wanted Urban brought down so badly that the possibility of Urban being poisoned was on quite a few minds, most of all

Urban's. It was entirely conceivable that faced by this bitter animosity Urban might cast Galileo into the fire, to clear the area around him so that he could fight on without liabilities.

Buonamici had access to the Vatican at night, because of his job with Cardinal Barberini. Inside the walls of the holy fortress, it was possible for him to disguise himself as a Dominican, and thus make his way everywhere in the silent grounds, including through the hallways to Galileo's room. From there, he could lead Cartophilus out and behind Saint Peter's, where they could skulk in the shadows and visit any chamber they chose, if care was taken.

'They're still in the Sele of the Congregation talking it over,' Buonamici said to Cartophilus in a low voice. 'It's gotten pretty vicious. The cardinals who are implacable are the Jesuits. Scaglia, Genetti, Gessi, and Verospi. They're all Romans, and they don't like Florentines.'

'And the Borgia?'

'He's their leader, of course. But he's gone to the Villa Belvedere to get some sleep.'

'Can any of the Jesuits be turned?'

'No, I don't think so. They can only be opposed by the cardinals on our side. My master Barberini, of course – he's really furious, because his solution to the problem has been overthrown, so that he will look to the Grand Duke like a liar. Then Zacchia, I'm sure he will refuse to sign anything he doesn't agree with. Bentivoglio also – and as he is the general, he could probably force a compromise sentence, because if he refused to sign, it would look too bad to go forward. It would look like Urban was forcing it, which could only mean that he had caved to the Borgia. So Urban doesn't want that. He wants it to look like he has come in all merciful at the last moment. And Bentivoglio could make the implacables accept a compromise, I think. Of course it would be much, much more certain if the Borgia were absent for the rest of the debate. That would probably do more than anything else we could manage. That, and provide the substance of a compromise to Bentivoglio, something for him to work with.'

'See to that part, then. I'll be back in at dawn.'

The Villa Belvedere was an enormous complicated pile, anchoring one corner of the Vatican's outer wall. There were the usual night watchmen at its gates and doors, of course; but none were stationed around the back of the villa, which stood as a four-storey cliff overlooking the outer wall, fortresslike in its vertical mass.

But in the dark it was easy enough to jump from a tree to the outer wall, then crawl over a branch to the building itself, and there inch along the narrow ledge left by the stonemasons on the wall of the villa. There it was possible to use expanders in the vertical cracks between the huge blocks of sandstone that formed the villa, and ascend the blank side of it.

The window casements high on the wall were enormous, and made it possible to sit outside the windows, which were closed against mosquitoes and the mephitic vapours of early summer. In some comfort, catching one's breath, a person could work a flat knife between the window frames and push up the latch holding the windows closed. And then slip inside.

Where it was dark as a cave. In the infrared, shapes were red-black in the blackred. Possible then to make one's way to the fourth floor, where a sleeping pair of bodyguards lay across the doorway of the Borgia's bedroom. Very gently mist the men with a soporific, and step over them; unbolt the inside bolt on the door by the use of a magnet; enter the room. Information provided by household members, which had included this bedroom's location, also described the cardinal's daily habits, which included a cup of wine mixed with citron water to break his fast and start each new day on a right note. More substantive fare would soon follow. So: mist the face on the boulderlike head sticking out of the blankets. Small injection. Lift the jug by the bed to estimate the volume of liquid, unstopper a vial of a more powerful kind of soporific, touched with an amnestic, both of them tasteless and colourless. Leave a drop at the bottom of the cup next to the jug as well, just in case a new jug was called for. Make sure not to underdose; the massive lump snoring under the blankets was a constant reminder what a heavy man Gasparo Borgia was. Then retreat, rebolt the door, retrace steps, climb out the window and downclimb the wall, the most difficult part of the whole operation, tough on old joints; and away.

There was already a Roman expression for this kind of turning of a method onto its usual perpetrators; it was called *to poison the Borgias.*

Galileo was escorted to the convent of Minerva by a little phalanx of Dominicans who showed up at his dormitory. The black and white Dogs of God looked as grim as executioners. Before leaving his chamber, they gave him the white robe of the penitent to put on over his own clothing. Nothing of his own could appear outside the robe, they said; and he had to be bareheaded.

So it was time for the sentence.

They surrounded him wordlessly then, and led him on the short walk to the room of judgement. Inside that room it was much more crowded than during any of the depositions; most of the Holy Congregation was there to witness the ruling. Pope Urban VIII was not present, of course.

Maculano read the judgement:

We:

Gasparo Borgia, with the title of the Holy Cross in Jerusalem;
Fra Felice Centini, with the title of Santa Anastasia, called d'Ascoli;

Guido Bentivoglio, with the title of Santa Maria del Popolo;
Fra Desiderio Scaglia, with the title of San Carlo, called di Cremona;

Fra Antonio Barberini, called di Sant'Onofrio;
Laudivio Zacchia, with the title of San Petro in Vincoli, called di San Sisto;

Berlinghiero Gessi, with the title of Sant'Agostino;
Fabrizio Verospi, with the title of San Lorenzo in Panisperna, of the order of priests;

Francesco Barberini, with the title of San Lorenzo in Damaso; and

Marzio Ginetti, with the title of Santa Maria Nuova, of the order of deacons;

By the Grace of God, the Cardinals of the Holy Roman Church, and especially commissioned by the Holy Apostolic See as Inquisitors-General against heretical depravity in all of Christendom:

Whereas you, Galileo, son of the late Vincenzio Galilei were denounced to this Holy Office in 1615 for holding as true the false doctrine that the sun is centre of the world and motionless and the Earth moves with diurnal motion;

And whereas this Holy Tribunal wanted to remedy the disorder and the harm which derived from this doctrine, the Assessor Theologians assessed the two propositions of the sun's stability and the Earth's motion as follows:

That the sun is centre of the world and motionless is a proposition which is philosophically absurd and false, and formally heretical, for being explicitly contrary to Holy Scripture;

That the Earth is neither the centre of the world nor motionless but moves with diurnal motion is philosophically equally absurd and false, and theologically at least erroneous in the faith.

Whereas, however, we wanted to treat you with benignity at that time . . .

Maculano, reading the judgement aloud, went on to describe how Paul V had used Bellarmino's injunction to warn him, also to issue a decree against the publishing of any books about the matter. Then:

And whereas a book has appeared here lately, the title being Dialogo *by Galileo Galilei on the two Chief World Systems, Ptolemaic and Copernican, the said book was diligently examined and found to violate explicitly the above-mentioned injunction given to you; for in this book you have defended the said opinion already condemned, although you try by means of various subterfuges to give the impression of leaving it undecided and labelled as probable; this is still a very serious error, since there is no way an opinion declared and defined contrary to divine Scripture may be probable.*

Therefore, by our order you were summoned to this Holy Office.

The judgement went on to describe the process of the trial in some detail, ending with a sharp dismissal of all Galileo's arguments, including the worth of the signed certificate from Bellarmino that Galileo had brought with him:

the said certificate you produced in your defence aggravates your case further since, while it says that the said opinion is contrary to Holy Scripture, yet you dared to treat of it, defend it, and show it as probable; nor are you helped by the licence you artfully and cunningly extorted, since you did not mention the injunction you were under.

Because we did not think you had said the whole truth about your intention, we deemed it necessary to proceed against you by a rigorous examination. Here you answered in a Catholic manner, though without adequate defence to the above-mentioned matters confessed by you and deduced against you about your intention. Therefore, having solemnly considered the merits of your case, together with the above-mentioned confessions and excuses and with any other reasonable matter worth considering, we have come to the final sentence against you:

We say, pronounce, sentence, and declare that you, the above-mentioned Galileo, because of the things deduced in the trial and confessed by you, have rendered yourself according to this Holy Office vehemently suspected of heresy.

This was a technical term, a specific category. The categories ranged from slight suspicion of heresy, to vehement suspicion of heresy, to violent suspicion of heresy, to heresy, to heresiarchy, which meant not only being a heretic but inciting others to heresy as well.

Maculano, having paused briefly for Galileo and everyone else to take in the relevant phrase, continued:

Therefore you have incurred all the censures and penalties imposed by the sacred canons against such delinquents. We are willing to absolve you from them provided that first, with a sincere heart and unfeigned faith, in front of us you abjure, curse, and detest the above mentioned errors and heresies, in the manner and form we will prescribe to you.

Furthermore, so that the serious and pernicious error and transgression you have committed does not remain completely unpunished, and so that you will be more cautious in the future and an example for others to abstain from similar crimes, we order that the book Dialogo *by Galileo Galilei, Lincei, be prohibited by public edict.*

We condemn you to formal imprisonment in this Holy Office at our pleasure. As a salutary penance we impose on you to recite the seven penitential Psalms once a week for the next three years. And we reserve the authority to moderate or change, wholly or in part, the above-mentioned penalties and penances.

This we say, pronounce, sentence, declare, order, and reserve by this or any other better manner or form that we reasonably can or shall think of.

So we the undersigned Cardinals pronounce:

Felice Cardinal d'Ascoli
Guido Cardinal Bentivoglio
Fra Desiderio Cardinal di Cremona
Fra Antonio Cardinal di Sant'Onofrio
Berlinghiero Cardinal Gessi
Frabrizio Cardinal Verospi
Marzio Cardinal Ginetti

The missing signatures, therefore, were from Francesco Barberini, Laudivio Zacchi, and Gasparo Borgia.

A compromise had prevailed.

* * *

The white-robed old man was then handed his abjuration, to be read aloud in the formal ceremony ending the trial. It was as formulaic as any mass or other sacrament, but Galileo first read over it silently, very intent on it, turning the pages as he went. His face was pale, so that in his white robe, and with his previously reddish hair all mixed now with white and grey, and gaunter than he had ever been, he looked like a ghost of himself. It was a cloudy day outside, and the massed candles and light from the clerestory windows still left the room slightly in gloom, so that he stood out.

While he read, Cartophilus was standing outside the open door with the other servants, shaking Buonamici by the hand and breathing deeply for the first time in months, maybe years. Confinement, book banned, et cetera: success.

But then Galileo suddenly gestured to Maculano. Cartophilus sucked down a breath sharply and held it, as Galileo began to tap hard at one of the pages of his abjuration. 'What is he doing?' Cartophilus whispered in agony to Buonamici.

'I don't know!' Buonamici whispered back.

Galileo spoke loudly enough that all the cardinals in attendance could hear him, indeed everyone in the room and in the hall outside; his voice had a hoarse ragged edge, and his lips were white under his moustache.

'I will abjure my error willingly, but there are two things in this document that *I will not say*, no matter what you do to me.'

Dead silence. Out in the hall Cartophilus was now clutching Buonamici's arm in both hands, whispering, 'No, no, why, why? Say whatever they want, for Christ's sake!'

'It's all right,' Buonamici whispered, trying to calm him. 'The Pope only wants him humiliated, not burned.'

'The Pope may not be able to stop it!'

They held each other as inside the room Galileo showed the relevant page to Maculano, poking at the objectionable phrases. 'I will *not* say I am not a good Catholic, for I am one and I intend to stay one, despite all that my enemies can say and do. Secondly, I will not say that I have ever deceived anybody in this affair, especially in the publishing of my book, which I submitted in full candour to ecclesiastical censure, and had it printed after legally obtaining a licence for it. I'll build the pyre and put the candle to it myself if anyone can show otherwise.'

Maculano, taken aback at the penitent's sudden ferocity, looked to the cardinals. He took the abjuration over to them, pointed out the passages Galileo had objected to. Out in the hallway Cartophilus was hissing with dismay, almost hopping up and down, and Buonamici had stopped trying to reassure him and was peering anxiously through the doorway at the cardinals.

Bentivoglio was whispering to the others. Finally he nodded to Maculano, who took the document to the scribe and had her mark two passages for deletion. While she did so, Maculano faced Galileo with a stern eye that seemed also to contain a gleam of approbation. 'Agreed,' he said.

'Good,' Galileo said, but not thank you. Tears suddenly poured from his eyes down his cheeks into his beard, and he wiped them away before taking the revised document from the Commissary General. 'Give me a moment to compose myself,' he said. He looked over the document again while he wiped his face clear and whispered a prayer. He pulled a small necklace crucifix out from under his white robe to kiss and then replace it. After that he nodded to Maculano and walked to the centre of the room, before the table where the pad for kneeling had been placed. He crossed himself, handed the abjuration to Maculano, kneeled on the pad, adjusted his penitential robe, took the document from Maculano. He held it in his left hand, put his right hand on the Bible that stood on a waist-high stand before him. When he spoke his voice was clear and penetrating, but flat and void of all expression.

'I, Galileo, son of the late Vincenzio Galilei of Florence, seventy years of age, arraigned personally for judgement, kneeling before you Most Eminent and Most Reverend Cardinal Inquisitors-General against heretical depravity in all of Christendom, having before my eyes and touching with my hands the Holy Gospels, swear that I have always believed, I believe now, and with God's help I will believe in the future all that the Holy Catholic and Apostolic Church holds, preaches, and teaches.

'However, whereas, after having been judicially instructed by the Holy Office to abandon completely the false opinion that the sun is the centre of the world and does not move and the Earth is not the centre of the world and moves, and not to hold, defend, or teach this false doctrine in any way whatever, orally or in writing; and after having been notified that this doctrine is contrary to Holy Scripture; I wrote and published a book in which I treat of this already condemned doctrine and adduce very effective reasons in its favour, without refuting them in any way; therefore, I have been judged vehemently suspected of heresy, namely of having held and believed that the sun is in the centre of the world and motionless, and the Earth is not the centre and moves.

'Therefore, desiring to remove from the minds of Your Eminences and every faithful Christian this vehement suspicion, rightly conceived against me, with a sincere heart and unfeigned faith I abjure, curse, and detest the above-mentioned errors and heresies, and in general each and every other error, heresy, and sect contrary to the Holy Church; and I swear that in the future I will never again say or assert, orally or in writing, anything which might cause a similar suspicion about me; on the contrary, if I should come to know any heretic or anyone suspected of heresy, I will denounce him to this Holy Office.

'I, the above-mentioned Galileo Galilei, have abjured, sworn, promised, and obliged myself as above; and in witness of the truth I have signed with my own hand the present document of abjuration and have recited it word for word in Rome, at the convent of the Minerva, this twenty-second day of June 1633.

'I, Galileo Galilei, have abjured as above, by my own hand.'

And he took the pen from Maculano and carefully signed the bottom of the document.

*   *   *

In the hall outside, Cartophilus collapsed into Buonamici's arms. Buonamici stood stalwart and held the old man to his chest, whispering to him, 'The wound was small, if we consider the force behind the dart.'

Cartophilus could only clutch his mouth and nod. It had been a close run thing. He could feel the younger man's heart pounding hard; he too had been shaken. We had seen what could happen. We had seen too much.

At the Villa Medici that night, Ambassador Niccolini wrote to Cioli in Florence to give him the news of the trial's conclusion. *It is a fearful thing to have to do with the Inquisition*, he concluded. *The poor man has come back more dead than alive.*

Chapter Nineteen   *Eppur Si Muove*

Ancora imparo. I'm still learning.
– MICHELANGELO, *age 87*

Confined again to the Villa Medici, Galileo spent his days smouldering with rage and despair. He did not seem to appreciate that he had escaped a dire fate. He was too bitterly angry for that to matter. He spoke only in low outbursts to himself: 'Fake documents – broken promises – betrayal. Liar. Liar! Who could imagine a man breaking his word when he didn't have to? But that's just what he did.'

He spent his waking hours in the villa's big kitchen, eating compulsively. His moaning by day came mostly from the jakes. While in the hands of the Inquisition he had been unable either to eat or shit. Now he made up for lost time at both ends. Occasionally he would afterward limp around the formal garden, looking at plants as if trying to remember what they were. Everyone who approached him heard the same thing. 'That lying bastard has eaten my life. From now on when people think of me, they'll think of his trial of me. It's the ultimate power.'

'Ultimate,' Cartophilus would scoff under his breath.

'Shut up,' Galileo would growl, showing Cartophilus the back of his hand and stumping away.

This was all bad enough, although predictable. But at night it was much worse. In the late hours, on his bed half asleep and half

511

awake, he would roll in agitation, groan, moan, even shout; even shriek in agony. No one in that wing of the villa could sleep well in those pathetic hours, and Niccolini and his wife Caterina were beside themselves. The ambassador ignored the usual niceties of protocol, and returned to the Vatican repeatedly to beg some relief for the astronomer. Caterina rallied the servants and the villa's priest to hold midnight masses, with lots of chanting and singing, the music echoing down the dark halls from the chapel to the east wing. Sometimes it seemed to help him.

Word of Galileo's nocturnal fits got around, of course, and a couple of weeks after the abjuration, Cardinal Francesco Barberini worked on his uncle in private. The Sanctissimus finally agreed to shift Galileo's house arrest to the palazzo of Archbishop Ascanio Piccolomini, in Siena. Piccolomini, another ex-student of Galileo's, had requested it, and Urban agreed to the plan, perhaps hoping to remove Galileo and his histrionics from the rumour mill of Rome, to get rid of him at last.

It was 2nd July of 1633 when Galileo left Rome for the last time, in a closed ecclesiastical carriage. In Viterbo, just outside the capital, he yelled for the carriage to stop, got out, gestured rudely back at the city, spat at it, and then walked for four or five miles down the road before he would agree to get back in.

In Siena, however, his night terrors only got worse. He seemed to have lost the ability to sleep, except in snatches near dawn. Red-eyed, he would stare up at his caretakers and rehearse all the crimes committed against him, and then rail against all his enemies, a list that now ran well into the scores, so that if he described them all individually and in order of their appearance, as he sometimes did, it could take him close to an hour to run through them. He used set phrases that he always repeated, like Homeric epithets. The lying horsefly. The blind astronomer. The backstabber. That fucking pigeon. The deal breaker. Eventually his rants would exhaust him to incoherency and these epithets would be the only words left that anyone could understand, after which he would fall into bouts of piteous moaning, sharp thin cries, even short high screams, as if he were being murdered.

Everyone rushed to him at those times, and tried to comfort him and get him back into bed. Sometimes he didn't even recognize us, but reacted as if we were jailers, beating at our arms and kicking our shins. There was something upsetting enough about these panics that for a while we would all fall headlong into his nightmare, whatever it was.

But Archbishop Ascanio Piccolomini was a persistent man. He was almost as short as Bellarmino had been, and indeed he resembled what Bellarmino must have looked like in his forties, with the same neat handsome triangular head, sharpened to a point by a trim goatee. This graceful intellectual had never forgotten his childhood lessons with the maestro, when he had been lucky enough to be designated one of young Cosimo's friends. When teaching Cosimo, Galileo had tried to be as Aristotle to Alexander, authoritative yet charming, entertaining, instructive, transformational – the perfect pedagogue. Piccolomini had been immersed in the bath of that performance, and it was indeed a baptism to a different life, for from that time on the young aristocrat had explored mathematics and engineering with a passion, and taken a lively interest in everything; in short he had been a better pupil than Cosimo, and become a true Galilean. It was a real shock for him to witness the broken old man wandering like a lunatic through his palazzo. His hope had been to provide a sanctuary for the scientist, something very like the Lincean Academy, but with the added comfort of being located inside the Church, thus implying that Galileo's sentence was not a unanimous judgement, and definitely not an excommunication, no matter what people said. Now that Piccolomini saw how distressed the old man was, he realized it was going to be a more complicated process of recovery than he had imagined. Every night the spell of insomniac horrors returned. At times Galileo seemed to have lost his wits entirely, even by day.

One morning, after a particularly gruelling night, the arch-bishop drew Galileo's old servant aside. 'Good man, do you think we should restrain him? Should we tie him to his bed to keep him from doing himself a hurt? These fits that come on him are so violent, it seems they could lead to a fatal fall.'

Cartophilus bowed. 'Oh, Your Eminence, thank you, of course you are right. Although, possibly, I wonder if he may now be past the, the . . .'

'Past the worst of it?'

'I don't know. But it's always one thing at a time with him, Your Serenity.'

'Yes? Oh, yes. Well, I have been trying to give him something else to think about. But maybe it should be more direct.'

'A fine idea, Your Grace.'

The archbishop's grin was like a schoolboy's. 'I've got just the man in mind.'

'Not an astronomer, I trust.'

Piccolomini laughed and gave the old servant a touch to the head that was half blessing, half schoolboy tap. And in the days following he invited several of the local natural philoso-phers of Siena to come to the palazzo and speak with Galileo. He asked them to initiate discussions about the strength of materials, magnetism, and similarly earthbound topics. They did that, keeping resolutely away from the old man's sore point, even to the point of spending much time looking through a microscope at the spectacular articulations of moths and fleas.

And while in these men's company, it was true that Galileo seemed calmer. He attended to whatever they brought up, clearly relieved at the distraction. And the men were happy to be in his presence. They saw that the moment had finally arrived when one could safely condescend to Galileo. There was a real benevolence in the air as they enjoyed this new pleasure, some-thing like sharing the room with a caged tiger.

But then the nights would come, and sleep would not. Wine

did nothing to put him out, nor warm milk neither. Half-crazed he would prowl and howl down the cold moonlit galleries, staring out windows, seemingly confused by the striped duomo of Siena's cathedral, looming over all the tilted planes of tile. By morning he would have collapsed somewhere, staring red-eyed at nothing, his voice and mind shattered. It seemed incredible that he could face the day to follow in anything like a coherent form, the night having exhausted rather than refreshed him. And indeed by day there were dark hollows in his face, and his politeness to guests was a brittle thing. One afternoon a Father Pelagi joined the group to give a presentation on whether whirlpools created vortices of attraction or repulsion, and Galileo sat by the window with his arms crossed over his barrel chest, glowering as he listened to this priest's unexpected mish-mash of Aristotle and scripture. At the assertion that a floating body would sink if the material's buoyancy was not enough to keep it on the surface, he snorted and said, 'I see your whirlpool has pulled in even your argument, it runs in such circles!'

'What do you mean?' Pelagi snapped.

'I *mean*,' Galileo said, 'you make a circular argument. You are saying things float because they want to float. These are not whirlpools, but tautologies.'

'How dare you,' the priest retorted. 'You who have been reproved by the Holy Office!'

'So?' Galileo said. 'The Earth still moves, and you're still a fool!' And he leaped to his feet and jumped on the man and started beating him. The others had to haul him off and then get between them. After some shouting and scuffling Pelagi was ejected, indeed nearly defenestrated. Piccolomini announced that he was banished from the palazzo for the rest of Galileo's stay. On the other hand it had been good to see the old warrior so feisty again, and everyone hoped it might be a sign of recovery.

But that night the howls from Galileo's room were more anguished than ever. The moon happened to be full, giving his performance the true lunatic brio. For those who had to endure it, it was like when a baby is crying; an hour seems a year, a night all eternity.

Then the next day some real problems also arrived to disturb him, in news conveyed by one of Maria Celeste's letters: Galileo's friends Gino Bocchineri and Niccolo Aggiunti had come to San Matteo to ask her for the keys to his house and desk, so that they could enter and remove certain papers. *It was during the time we suspected you to be in the greatest danger; they went to your house and did what had to be done, seeming to me at the time well conceived and essential, to avoid some worse disaster that might yet befall you, wherefore I knew not how to refuse them the keys and the freedom to do what they intended, seeing their tremendous zeal in serving your interests.*

This action had come on Galileo's instruction, as he informed Maria Celeste later; he had sent a letter to his friends (ex-students again) requesting their help. So he must have been afraid that the case against him was not yet over. And he was probably right to think that some of the things he had written down through the years might prove dangerous. Copernicanism, atomism, the sun a live creature, something like a god – he had written a lot of things that could worry him now.

Even with those papers in the house spirited away, there were still reasons to fear. It was becoming obvious to us that Urban was still very angry at Galileo. It was possible Urban felt now that Galileo had been let off too lightly – that in order to show resistance to the Borgia, he had not inflicted as much pain on Galileo as he really wanted to. Luxurious house arrest in an admiring archbishop's palazzo was not much of a punishment for vehement suspicion of heresy. For now, Urban was taking out his anger elsewhere; the news coming to Siena made it clear that all those who had helped Galileo were being punished for it. Riccardi's prevaricating did not save him; he was dismissed as Master of the Sacred Palace. The inquisitor in Florence who had approved the publication was reprimanded. Castelli had fled from Rome to avoid notice. Ciampoli was ordered to leave

Rome, and for life, Urban told everyone. He was going to be a parish priest in one of the miserable villages of Umbria for the rest of his days.

And these were by no means the strictest punishments Urban was ordering, for he was in a truly foul mood. A bishop and two priests accused of conducting black masses to call down his death were tied together to the stake and burned in the Campo di Fiore. People said these unknown miscreants had served Urban as replacements for Galileo, who had somehow slipped away – at least so far. The story was not necessarily over. For the Pope was clearly no longer quite sane. So there were real reasons for fear; and at night the fears took over, each one a blacker dark night of the soul.

Piccolomini, at a loss, consulted Cartophilus again. After that he went out to the cathedral's workshop and asked the artisans what they were working on. From them he learned of a problem they were having in the city foundry, where they were trying to cast a replacement for the cathedral's largest bell. The casting mould for the new bell was made of two immense blocks of clay, with the outer mould turned upside down and held in position by a framework of heavy beams, and the inner mould, a massive solid plug with its outside carved to the shape of the inside of the bell, suspended from a lattice of cross beams in a position very close to the curved clay of the outer shell. The empty space between the two moulds was the shape of the bell. This was the usual method, and all seemed well with it, but when they poured in the molten metal, it ran to the bottom of the open space and pooled there, shoving up the inner mould even though the massive block of clay weighed much more than the poured metal did. No one could understand it.

Piccolomini, walking around the great wooden armature holding the cast, smiled. 'This is good,' he said. 'This is just what we need.'

He went to Galileo and described what had happened, and Galileo sat and thought about it for a while. For a time it looked

517

as though he had forgotten the matter and slipped into sleep, which even by itself would have been a benefit; then he stirred. He took up a big sheet of paper and his quill and inkpot, and drew a side elevation of the problem to illustrate his points to the archbishop. 'I discovered this when I was working on the floating bodies problem. What I found was that a very small weight of liquid can lift a much greater solid weight, if the liquid is trapped in a curve below the weight, as here.'

'But why?'

'Let's not ask why,' Galileo requested.

For Piccolomini this brought back memories of his boyhood lessons, and of poor Cosimo, long since dead. 'And how then did you deal with it, maestro?'

Galileo insisted on demonstrating the truth of his old finding with a model before proceeding any further. He made use of the glass urinal in his room for the model's bottom mould, and the cathedral artisans made a wooden inner mould to fit it, filling the wood with shot to make it heavy. Then it was placed in the urinal such that, as Piccolomini said, 'You couldn't fit a piaster between them.' After that Galileo had a flask of quicksilver brought in, and he poured it in the gap between the glass and wood; and though the weight of the quicksilver was less than a twentieth that of the shot-filled wooden form, the form rose up a finger or two higher than it had been. Almost all the quicksilver pooled at the bottom of the urinal.

'Even Mercury's silver urine gives wings to things,' Galileo joked, head cocked to the side.

Piccolomini laughed obligingly. 'A very clear demonstration,' he said happily. 'But then, this being the case, strange though it seems, what should we do about casting our bell?'

Galileo shoved down on the wooden mould with his hand. 'The inner mould, heavy or not, has to be fixed in place like the outer one. To prevent it rising you will need to bolt it to a pavement below. Use the heaviest beams and bolts, and all should be well.'

So they did as he had recommended, and the bell was cast successfully. Regarding the bright new thing when it emerged from its massive mould, for a moment Galileo appeared content.

But that night he howled more painfully than ever.

Cartophilus got up and found him collapsed over a railing, in the stairwell of the bell tower overlooking the piazza where the famous horse race was soon to be run. He was barking into the dark space of the stairwell, then groaning in a kind of harmony as the echoes bounced up and down it. He had been weeping so hard he could barely see; the light of the ancient servant's candle lantern seemed to hurt his eyes.

'You must not have had your glass of milk before bed,' Cartophilus said, sitting down heavily beside him. 'I told you never to neglect that.'

'Shut up,' Galileo moaned piteously. 'Talking of milk when they've thrown me in hell.'

'It could be worse,' Cartophilus pointed out.

Silence.

Then Galileo growled. It was his wounded bear growl, and the old servant, surprised to hear it, could not help but smile. Once in the Bellosguardo years the two of them had witnessed a bear-baiting in Florence, and late in the fight the baiters had poked the bloodied bear in the back, to get it to come out of its corner and fight the dogs, and it had briefly glanced up over its shoulder at its tormentors and growled – a low sound, bitter and resigned, that stood the hair upright on the necks of everyone who heard it. On the way home Galileo had imitated the sound over and over. 'That's me,' he told Cartophilus when he got it to his satisfaction. 'That's my growl. Because they've got me cornered, and they'll make me fight.'

Now, these many years later, the same sound vibrated out of his hulk and filled the stairwell. 'Errrrrrrrrrrrrrrr . . .' By his glance at Cartophilus, the old servant knew Galileo was reminding him of that moment in Florence, his recognition of the ursine fate awaiting him.

'Yes yes,' Cartophilus murmured, as he tugged the old man back toward his room. 'But it could be worse, that's all I'm saying. You need to remember that. You need to pick yourself up somehow and carry on.'

Galileo clutched him by the arm. 'Send me back,' he demanded hoarsely. 'One more time. Send me to Hera.'

'All right,' Cartophilus said after a pause. 'If you want. Let's go.' And later that night the old man fell into one of his syncopes.

Hera approached him wearing white. They were back at her Ionian temple, high above the sulphurous landscape of her volcano moon. Galileo's heart leaped to see her, he extended his arms; but she stopped short of them, looking down at him with her amused expression. His heart knocked inside him like a child trying to escape.

'So,' she said, 'you escaped your fiery alternative.'

'I did,' he said. 'I did that time, anyway.' A flash of anger shocked him: 'I never deserved it!'

'No.'

'And you – you're still here!'

'I'm still here. Of course.'

'But what about that Galileo who burned, Lady? You sent me back to the fire, and it had already happened to me, even though when you sent me back I was younger than that.'

She shook her head. 'You still don't understand. All the potentialities are entangled. They are all vibrating in and out of each other, all the time. In the *e* time they resonate. We saw that for a time, when we were in Jupiter. I did anyway.'

'I did too.'

'So there you have it.'

Galileo threw up his hands. 'So what did Ganymede think he was doing, then? Why did he want me to burn?'

She led him to a bench and they sat on it side by side, overlooking the slaggy downslope of the yellow mountain. She took

521

his hand. 'Ganymede has an idea about time that he insists on even now. Whether he comes from our future or not is unclear. I took your suggestion and had a look at him with the mnemonic, and I think it may be true. I don't recognize much that I saw from his childhood. The Ganymede period, however, was clear. It was as I suspected. He made an incursion into the Ganymedean ocean with a small group of supporters, and there he learned of the Jovian mind and the minds beyond. How he learned so much more than the Europans I don't know, and maybe that's another confirmation that he came back to us from a future time. But at that point he silenced the creature in Ganymede with an explosion, and began making analepses using one of the entanglers, focusing on the beginning of science. He sees that start and the encounter with the alien consciousness as parts of a single whole, a situation that he has been trying for centuries to alter in both our times. These he believes are crux points in the organism, sensitivities where small changes can have big effects. I think his working theory is that the more scientific culture becomes in your time, the better chance it will have to survive first contact with an alien consciousness in ours. Anyway, what is certain is that he has made more analepses than anyone else. His brain is simply stuffed with these events, which are often traumas to him. He must think they help. He must think that since each one collapses the wave function of potentialities, it changes the sum over histories and therefore the main flow of events. So he made scores of bilocations, hundreds of them. It's like he's kicking the bank of the stream over and over again, trying to carve a new channel.'

'And has he succeeded?' Galileo asked. 'And – are the years that follow really worse if I am spared? Have billions really died because of it?'

'Not necessarily.' She took his hand in hers. 'There are more than two alternatives here, as everywhere. Every analepsis creates a new one, so there is a sense in which we can't be sure what Ganymede has done, because we can't see it. There are times where you are martyred. But we know there is also a stream of potentialities in which you succeeded in convincing the Pope to your point of view, and the Church then took science under its wing and blessed it, even made it a tool of the church.'

'There is such a time?' Galileo asked, amazed.

'Yes.'

'Why didn't you tell me?'

'I didn't want you to know. I thought if you knew, you would try for that outcome no matter what.'

'Well of course! I did anyway!'

'I know. But I didn't want you to have any extra encouragement. Because that's the potentiality cluster with the worst outcomes of all.'

'No!'

'Yes. When you succeed in a reconciliation, and religion dominates science in its earliest phase, you get the deepest and most violent low points in the subsequent histories. This is what Ganymede saw, and this is what he has insisted ever since. When you are burned and become a martyr to science, science more quickly dominates religion, and the subsequent low point is much reduced. It's bad, but not as bad. This is what Ganymede insisted on.'

Galileo thought it over, confused by this newly proliferating vision of the past. 'And so,' he said, 'what happened after this time, then? This one I am in now?'

'This time is an alternative, as they all are in their time. But this is what you and I, and everyone else in our strand, managed together. An analeptic introjection that made a big change.'

'And is it better?'

She looked him in the eye, smiled very slightly. 'I think so.'

Again Galileo considered it. 'What happens to the me who burned, then? What happens to that Galileo now?'

She said slowly, explaining again, 'All the potentialities exist. When an analepsis creates a new temporal isotope, it co-exists with the others, all of them entangled. All together they make up the manifold, which shifts under the impact of the new potential, and changes, but continues too. Whether we can oxbow a channel and cause it to disappear entirely is an open question. Conceivable in theory, something people claim to have seen, but in practice hard to do. As you might know better than I, I suppose, because of your sessions with Aurora.'

Galileo shook his head doubtfully. 'So there is still a world in which Galileo is burned as a heretic.'

'Yes.'

'But no!' Galileo said, rising from the bench to his feet. 'I refuse to accept that! I am the sum of all possible Galileos, and all I ever did was say what I saw. None of us should burn for that!'

She regarded him. 'It has already happened. What would you do?'

He considered; then said, 'Your teletrasporta: I must beg you the use of it. The other box must be there in Rome on that day, I know that already.'

She stood herself and looked down on him, her gaze serious. 'You could die there. Both of you.'

'I don't care,' he said. 'All of us are one. I can feel it – they're in my mind. In my mind I'm burning at the stake. You have the means for a return. So I have to do this.'

Smoke had filled his lungs and was choking him by the time the fire reached his feet. Pain stuffed his consciousness, blasted it until there was nothing but it, and he almost swooned; if he could hold his breath he would faint, but he couldn't. His feet were catching fire.

Then through the smoke he saw the mass of distended faces break apart at the impact of a man on horseback riding through, his charge smashing people aside so that their roar panicked to a scream. The ring of Dominicans guarding the pyre bunched to repel this helmeted invader, but they all knew what happened when a horse struck men on foot, and before it reached them they broke and ran. The horse reared and twisted before the fire, disappeared behind Galileo. There was a slashing at the chains holding him that made their iron instantly hotter; then he was grabbed around the waist by the horseman, yanked up onto the bucking horse and thrown before the saddle. His ankles were apparently still chained to the stake, so that his feet twisted almost out of their sockets, but then they came free, and he bounced like a long sack on the horse's flexing shoulders. Everything around him jumbled into a slurry of curses and screams, a horse's twisting flank and a sword flashing in smoke. His rescuer roared louder than all of them together as he mastered the horse and charged away; he caught a glimpse of a bearded lower face under the helmet, square mouth red with fury. As he lost consciousness he thought, at least I died dreaming that I saved myself.

And came to in Count da Trento's cellar in Costozza, moaning. He hurt all over. His companions were still on the stone floor.

'Signor Galilei! Domino Galilei, please, please! Wake up!'

'Qua – ? Qua – ?'

His mouth would not form words. He could not focus his eyes. They were dragging him by the arms over the rough floor, and he felt his butt scraping over the flagstones as from a great distance, while hearing someone else's groans, muffled as if through a wall. He wanted to speak but couldn't. The groans were his.

Hera's voice, then, in his ear, as he looked down the blasted mountainside of Io, clutching her arm, laid out on the bench.

'You died on the floor of the cellar, that first time, along with your two companions. Now we'll take the dead body from there

525

and put it back on the stake, to fill your absence in the fiery alternative. Here in Costozza, the rescued one will survive his trauma, and live on. But understand: there will always be this little whirlpool in you, between the worlds.'

'So I live it all again?'

'Yes.'

Galileo groaned. 'Do I have to know it?' he asked. 'Can you let me forget?'

'Yes, of course. But it will be in you anyway. The potentiality is always there. And sometimes therefore you will remember it, despite the amnestics. Because memory is deep, and always entangled, and while you live, it lives.'

'That's fine, as long as I don't remember it.'

'Yes. But even when you don't, you do. It lies below your feelings.'

'And the others? The other Galileos, in the other potentialities?'

'Please understand. They are always there. There are so many.'

'Will they end? Will it ever end?'

'End? Do things end?'

Galileo groaned again. 'So,' he said, 'even if I saved myself an infinite number of times, there would still be an infinite number of me that I hadn't saved. I will live through them again and again. Make the same discoveries and the same mistakes. Suffer the same deaths.'

'Yes. And sometimes you'll know that. Sometimes you'll feel it. This is your paradox of the infinities within infinities, which you will have discovered by feeling it in yourself. You live in Galileo's paradox. You'll hold your wife and mother apart as they try to kill each other, and it will strike you as horrible, then ridiculous, then beautiful. Something to love. This is the gift of the paradox, the gift of memory's spiral return.'

'Always in me. Even if I forget.'

'Yes.'

'Then let me forget. Give me the amnestic.'

'Is that what you want? It will mean losing your conscious memory of a lot of this that you have seen out here.' Gesturing at Io's slaggy grandeur, and at Jupiter's enormity. And at herself.

'But not really,' Galileo said, 'as you have just told me. It will still be in me. So, yes. I have to. I can't stand to know about the others. I would have to keep going back and trying to change things, like Ganymede. I can't face that. But I can't face the bad alternatives either – all the deaths, all the burning. It isn't right. So – so I need to forget, to go on.'

'As you wish.'

She gave him a pill. He swallowed it. She had slipped another one in the mouth of the Galileo there on the floor of the poisonous cellar, he was sure; a Galileo who would therefore live again through all that followed that moment, in ignorance, just as he had already; or at least until the stranger arrived. When it would all begin again.

'So I didn't really do anything by rescuing him,' he said. 'I didn't change anything.'

'We made this eddy in time,' she said gently, and touched him.

In Siena, when he came out of his syncope, he was shaking and white-faced. He stared up at Cartophilus, clutching him by the arm.

'I had a dream,' he gasped, confused. Trying to hold onto it: 'I was stuck!' He stared up at Cartophilus as if from out of a deep well. From the bottom of that depth he said, 'I am the sum of all possible Galileos.'

'No doubt of that,' the old servant said. 'Here, maestro, drink a bit of this mulled wine. That was a hard one, I could tell.'

Galileo gulped down the wine. Then he fell asleep, and when he came to, he had forgotten that he had even experienced a syncope that night.

He was left with a very strange feeling, however. In his weekly letter to Maria Celeste he tried to describe it: *I am caught in the loops of these events, and thus crossed out of the book of the living.*

She replied in her usual encouraging way: *I take endless pleasure in hearing how ardently the Monsignor Archbishop perseveres in loving you and favouring you. Nor do I suspect in the slightest that you are crossed out, as you say,* de libro vivendum. *No one is a prophet in his own country.*

Galileo shook his head as he read this. 'No one is a prophet anywhere,' he said, looking out his window to the north, toward San Matteo. 'And thank God for that. To see the future would be a most horrible curse, I am quite sure. Let me be not a prophet in my own country, but a scientist. I only want to be a scientist.'

But that was no longer possible. All that life was gone. He sat in the gardens in Siena now, but did not see anything. Piccolomini tried to interest him in more problems of motion and strength, but even those old friends did little to rouse him. He sat waiting for his mail. If Maria Celeste's letters didn't arrive when he expected them, he would cry. Some days he could barely be persuaded out of bed.

Around that same time, some of the Venetian spies reported that Piccolomini had been anonymously denounced to the Pope. It was all still happening. The letter received at the Vatican said:

The archbishop has been telling many people that Galileo was unjustly sentenced by this Holy Congregation, that he is the first man in the world, that he will live forever in his writings, even if they are prohibited, and that he is followed by all the best modern minds. And since such seeds sown by a prelate might bear pernicious fruit, I hereby report them.

The identity of this Siena informer was never found out, although the priest Pelagi would have been a good guess. In any case, the campaign against Galileo clearly had not ended. Cartophilus, hearing of this secret denunciation when Buonamici came up from Rome to tell him about it, went that evening to Archbishop Piccolomini, and asked him in a shy way if the time might have come when Galileo could hope to be remanded to Arcetri. Piccolomini thought it might indeed be possible, and he took the old servant's hint that it could be a case of getting the old man home before he died. And Buonamici made sure that same night to convey his news of the secret denunciation to the archbishop's confessor, so that soon afterward Piccolomini would know of that danger too.

So he began to campaign for Galileo's return to Arcetri. This was the start of October, 1633. He pretended not to know he himself had been denounced, of course, and intimated, in letters to people outside the Vatican who would take the idea into the fortress, that confining Galileo to house arrest in Arcetri would be a more severe punishment than his relatively luxurious and public situation in the archbishop's palazzo in Siena.

When Urban heard it put this way, people said, he agreed to the plan. In early December a papal order came to Siena: Galileo was to be removed to Arcetri, there to be confined to house arrest.

Piccolomini himself took this news to Galileo, beaming with pleasure for his old teacher, whom he feared had gone a long way toward permanently losing his mind. A reunion with his girls would surely help. 'Teacher, the news has come from Rome, the Sanctissimus has blessed you with permission to return to your home and family, God be praised.'

Galileo was truly startled. He sat down on his bed and wept, then stood and embraced Piccolomini. 'You saved me,' he said. 'Now you are one of my angels. I have so many of them.'

He did indeed. So many, stepping onto the stage from nowhere: the people who helped him, the crowd who tried to do him harm. Any event in history that gets more crowded the longer you look at it – that's a sign. Sign of a contested moment, a crux that will never stop changing under your gaze. The gaze itself entangles you, and you too are one of the changes in that moment.

On the day of his departure from Siena, a strong wind poured over them from the hills to the west, tossing the last leaves on the trees in a wild flight. Galileo was hugged by several well-wishers, and when he finally embraced the little archbishop he lifted him up. When he set him down and stepped back, wiping his eyes and shaking his head, Piccolomini held him by the arm to help him up into the carriage. Galileo's grey hair and beard streamed in the wind, as did the banners over the palace, and the clouds. Birds wheeled overhead. Galileo stopped to look around, gestured at the spectacle, stomped on the ground. 'It still moves!' he said. '*Eppur si muove!*'

Later Piccolomini told the story of Galileo's parting remark to his brother, Ottavio Piccolomini; who, later still, when living in Spain, commissioned the painter Murillo to paint a painting to commemorate his brother's tale. Murillo depicted the scene as taking place before the Inquisition itself, Galileo pointing at the wall over the congregation, where fiery letters spelled out *Eppur si muove*. In this way, and by word of mouth, the story was passed on. At some point the painting's story became the one people told, and later still it must have been regarded as too blasphemous to show, and its canvas was folded and reframed so that the inscribed wall was hidden from view. It only came back to light when the painting was cleaned, many years later. But all the while people kept telling the tale, of Galileo's sidelong defiance of his persecutors, his muttered riposte to the ages. It was true even though it wasn't.

The carriage only took two days to bring Galileo to Arcetri and the gates of *Il Gioello*. All the household was standing there to greet him, with Geppo jumping in front and La Piera standing impassively at the rear. He had been gone eleven months.

He levered himself out of the carriage, stood with the help of a hand on Geppo's shoulder, groaned as he straightened up. 'Take me to San Matteo,' he said.

If anyone is to be loved, he must love and be lovable.
— BALDASSARE CASTIGLIONE, *The Book of the Courtier*

It was a shock to see how much thinner Maria Celeste had become in his absence. She had driven herself hard those eleven months, running the convent and also helping to take care of *Il Gioello*. Geppo had fallen ill, and afterward suffered a truly noxious skin rash; Maria Celeste had cured it with a salve of her own devise. She had authorized for La Piera the extra spending needed to get through a three-month flour shortage, and late in that bad time had instructed the housekeeper to shut down the house's oven and get their bread from the convent, setting the price at eight quattrini a loaf. She never ate unless everyone else had.

As a result of all this she was skinnier than ever. No doubt her incessant worry about Galileo had also had its effect. She had tried to help him with his trial, which from her position was a little futile, but she had written repeatedly to Caterina Niccolini, asking her to petition a particular sister-in-law of the Pope to intercede with him. Pursuing these chains of female influence, which were everywhere even though invisible to the men and to the history books, may or may not have helped his cause; it was even possible this had been the crucial intervention, and Caterina the architect of the strategy that got Galileo out of Rome alive. But there was no way to tell from outside that network. In one of her last letters to him before his return, Maria Celeste had mentioned her efforts, saying of them, *I know, as I freely admit to you, that these are poorly drawn plans, yet still I would not rule out the possibility that the prayers of a pious daughter could outweigh even the protection of great personages.*

She went on to address another matter brought up in his last letter, one of his feeble attempts at a joke in such dismal circumstances: *Now, thinking this over, as I said, when your letter came telling me that one of the reasons why I desired your return was that I wanted a present you had for me, oh then I can tell you I did get angry! But such an anger as King David speaks of in the psalm, Irascimini et nolite peccare – be angry, but do not sin. For it seemed to me that you thought I wanted to see the present more than to see you; which is as far from my thoughts as darkness is from light. Perhaps I did not quite understand your letter, and I try to keep quiet with that thought. But if indeed you meant that, I do not know what I should say or do. Do see if you cannot come back to your tower, which cannot bear to remain so desolate any longer! And now it is time to think about the wine casks as well. La Piera beg to be remembered to you, and says that if her wish to see you and your wish to return were put in the scales, her scale would go down to the ground and yours up to the ceiling.*

So the women in his life had joked with him, teased him back when he teased them, sent their love in the rough *buffa* style that he liked best, Maria Celeste's burst of temper like something out of Marina herself, back in the day. Question my love and I'll beat the shit out of you! This *amoravolezza* had given him heart in a bad time.

Now, as he stood there before her in the convent, she collapsed in his arms and wept. Even Arcangela, looking down to the side, sidled up and touched him briefly on the arm. Galileo touched her back, on the shoulder, gently, then seized up Maria Celeste and lifted her in a hug, kissed away her tears of joy. She was like a bird in his hands, he too wept to feel her lightness. 'My little Virginia,' he said into her ribs, shocked and afraid.

*   *   *

In the weeks following his homecoming, he devoted himself to the sisters at the convent. Arcangela reverted to her usual distance; she looked away whenever he spoke to her. She too was more gaunt and angular than ever. Uneasily Galileo tried yet again to befriend her, this time with bits of candied fruit, in the way you would tame a crow; and she would duck her head and snatch the food and drift away.

Meanwhile Maria Celeste talked incessantly, as if to make up for lost time; and though Galileo knew that time lost could never be regained, he indulged her happily. It was good to be home again, and responsible for real things, for physical objects, not only for the ovens and chimneys and windows and roofs of his own house, but also for the ramshackle convent of the Clares, which at this point was nearing a material collapse to match the mental collapse long since suffered. San Matteo was a wreck.

So he spent many days inside the place, the old prohibition against men's presence a thing of the past. He measured beams for the servants to cut, and augured in the peg holes and hammered in the pegs himself. What joy to pop a dovetail into place like a key in a lock. Theorems you could hit with a hammer. With materials less prone to rot he could have made a roof that would hold off rain for a thousand years. But lead was expensive, and cedar too; pine shakes would have to do.

There weren't so many chores to accomplish in his garden. It had been tended closely by La Piera, as being one of the things that kept them alive. Now there was little to do except decide on which varieties of cedros and lemons to put in the broken wine casks that had been cut in half for use as tubs.

Then San Matteo came into an agricultural inheritance. 'First your prayer was answered and then mine!' Galileo said to Maria Celeste. The elder brother of Suor Clarice Burci had left the sisters a farm at Ambrogiana worth five thousand scudi. Maria Celeste estimated it would yield them annually two hundred and ninety bushels of wheat, fifty barrels of wine, and seventy sacks of millet. 'It was my prayer too, believe me,' she replied with a dark expression. 'My ten thousand prayers.' Burci had attached a farm crew to the bequest, as well as an obligation to the nuns to say a mass for him every day for the next four hundred years, and to absolve him three times a year for the next two hundred years. That was fine, but the land had been neglected and was now nearly wild, crew or no.

It was something he could do, and he threw himself into it. To be able to get one's hands on a problem and strangle it was a very satisfying thing. Clever engineering could do a lot; once he was pacing the floor of the dining hall, considering a difficult problem in counterbalancing, and a nun got in his way and he explained to her very firmly that she shouldn't do that, that he was fixing the roof, and afterward she told all the other nuns, 'He fixes things by thinking about them!' Indeed yes, and when he was done thinking about the new farm the nuns would have reliable sustenance at last. It was what he had been hoping for in 1624. He should not have asked Maria Celeste about it, he realized now, but merely requested the land grant he had been thinking of.

Now they had it, and he stumped across the neglected winter field, under low pewter skies, bark-ringing the mid-sized trees already overgrowing the pasture, then cutting down the smaller ones with hard awkward swipes of his ax, swinging as if taking off the heads of certain Dominicans, Jesuits, Benedictines, and professors. He was an executioner of trees; at age seventy, and despite his truss, he could still strike harder than most of the boys, and his shout on impact was the loudest by far. It was very satisfying. He would bring this farm into production and give them a sustenance. 'Things occur in their own time,' he said.

He wished he could help Maria Celeste in the same kind of way. She had pulled her teeth out as they rotted, and now had nearly none, but was at least free from infections of the jaw. But the lack of teeth could not be good for her digestion. He contrived some rending devices for mashing meats, scavenging bits of an old framework of one of the inclined planes with a bitter smile. There was more than one way to chew on reality.

The workshop was much reduced, it was only a small room stuffed with tools and machinery and beams and metal rods and slats. Mazzoleni was ancient and shrivelled and slept most of the time, even though he was in fact four years younger than Galileo himself. Of course Galileo was beyond ancient at this point. But Mazzoleni had perhaps been a bit baked in the head by his many hours in the Venetian sun, and next to the fumes of furnaces. His brains had dried out a little, though he still had his cracked cheery grin, the sight of which now sent a stab through Galileo, who recalled so clearly what it used to mean.

So, he did what he could to help Maria Celeste to eat, and worked on the convent, and their farm, and the garden of *Il Gioello*. When he was tired of the garden he went to the workshop and paged through his dusty old folios, making lists of propositions for the book he was now thinking of writing.

This was another good idea that Piccolomini had been inspired to recommend to Galileo: to go through his old experiments and write a book that had nothing to do with Copernicus or the heavens, a book that instead gave to the world what he had learned about local motion, and the strength of materials. He had started one dialogue while still in Siena, using Salviati, Sagredo and Simplicio as his speaking characters again, in an obvious act of defiance, even insolence, as he himself recognized with some pleasure. He could decide to keep the names or not, if it ever came to the point of publishing. He would never be allowed to publish anything anyway, at least in Italy, or anywhere the Pope held sway. But there were Protestant acquaintances who might be interested. In any case that was not the point. So sometimes he worked on adding new pages to the dialogue.

But the main project was Maria Celeste. He had seen a lot of women's bodies in his younger days, and like everyone else, he had seen a lot of people sicken and die. And so each day he walked down the lane that was the main street of Arcetri to the convent, and met her at the gate and kissed her cheeks and lifted her up, as if weighing her, as she once observed – and it was true;

and each day therefore his stomach clenched, and he thought about the food on hand that could be made attractive that day. Of course for the most part he needed to be providing for all the nuns equally, so it had to be a matter of some bulk, usually something that could be made into a thirty-bowl soup. These soups were often pretty thin gruel, and they usually poured their wine in to give it a little more body. Maria Celeste complained of a cold stomach, and he could well believe it, as she had no fat on her. And so soups were always good. Galileo had suffered so much disease in his life that he knew all the signs of it, and knew what they meant; and so, watching her, although he threw himself into every day, he too always suffered a bit of a cold stomach, chilled by the fear in him. Even the sun beating on him in the garden could not warm that part. In her letters during his time away, she had written of her fear that she would not live long enough to see him return, and she was not the type to exaggerate fears, or even to speak of them. So it had been a true feeling. He knew how that felt, to sense that the end could be near; he had felt it himself more than once, and it was unmistakable. It marked you. And in her closeness to him she had not hesitated to write to him and let him know what she was feeling.

Well, this was life. You never really escape this fear. Once long before he had written, *Men are forced into their strange fancies by attempting to measure the whole universe by means of their tiny scale. Our deep hatred of death need not make fragility such a bad thing. Why should we want to become less mutable? We should thereby suffer the fate caused by the medusa's head, being converted to marble and losing our senses and the qualities which could not exist in us without bodily changes, and the fact that we are always becoming something new and strange.*

Easy to say, when you're healthy. But healthy or not, it was still true.

As the days passed, he got used to her new gauntness, it was just the way she looked. She was as rapid and talkative as ever, like some finch turned into a woman, always babbling on about anything and everything, much as she had in her letters, but now it was music too; as if her letters had been only sheet music, written so that he could imagine her saying it all in his head, but only in the same way he could hear his father's old melodies by looking at the sheet music he had left behind. Being in the presence of the musician herself, as she sang the music of her thoughts aloud in the air, was an entirely different thing. He soaked it up like sunlight, like church music; it was Kepler's ridiculous music of the spheres, immanent in the world. Her brown eyes burned like Marina's had. Her skin tone was a little hectic, the cold stomach notwithstanding. She acted hot. There were a lot of ways in which she resembled Marina.

In the tumble of days he watched her flitting around the convent, talking all the while. 'The cedros aren't dry enough to candy yet, and one of them has mould so I'm afraid if it rains we'll lose them all, and there's thirty scudi lost to the carpenter who tried to fix the door, father you will look at that door's lower hinge won't you? Look at it. I said your penitential psalms for you, by the way, so you don't have to think of that. Suor Francesca please, don't peel those here it will only make more work for Suor Luisa later, move over here if you would, that's right, you're a good soul, come with me father, let's sit in the garden and pick the lemons while it's still cool –' and out there, while they picked, under a blue sky and tall puffy white clouds, she would enumerate every quattrini then available to them, this time in the hope of calculating if they had enough to make a first payment on two dozen blankets.

She effervesced. She could not keep up with the pace of her thoughts. It was a wonder that her letters managed to hold their chain of thought together as well as they did, the act of writing being so much slower than the speed of her thinking. When Galileo found his own thoughts racing ahead of him like that, he tended to focus on individual words, fingering them like pebbles to slow himself down; but she did not. She had perhaps inherited some of Galileo's mental habits, along with her mother's imperious will; and all of that power had to be vented into the battered confines of San Matteo. It made him think of Ariosto's stanzas about the princess confined to a walnut shell and yet holding court there just as always. You could not help but love such a gift for sizing one's ambition in accordance to a real situation. He had never been able to do that.

Once, he stopped work on the gears and pulleys of their balky old clock to sketch out a possible plan for a pendulum-based clock, which would rely on a spring pushing at the very top of the swing to keep it going, a fine idea it seemed on first inspection; the potential force that was forged into a spring, making it a kind of weight always pushing sideways, would be all you would need for a clock that might run for years. When Maria Celeste came in he told her the idea and she laughed to see his face. She looked over his shoulder and asked about the column of numbers he had written beside one sketch of his plan, and he tried to tell her what he had been thinking about. She nodded her comprehension, and so he went on, and eventually came to his rule of falling bodies, and she looked startled at the very idea that there was a ratio of distance to time, in a way that brought a tear to his eye.

'*Yes*,' he confirmed to her. 'The world works by mathematical rules. This is *much* more amazing than people usually seem to realize. Consider it – numbers are ideas, they are qualities in our minds that we abstract by looking at the world. So we see that we have two hands, and that there are two sheep in the meadow, but we never see a two anywhere. It's not a thing but an idea, and therefore intangible. Like souls in this world. And then we teach each other some games we can play with these ideas – we see how you can add them together and get resulting numbers, as if adding sheep to the meadow. We see for instance that any number can be added to itself by its own number of selves, two twos, four fours, we call them squares because they can be put into squared patterns with the same number of sheep on each side, and we see how larger numbers multiplied by themselves grow larger than the previous number very quickly, and that this rapid growth also happens in a proportion. An interesting idea. It makes a nice pattern in the mind or on the page. Then we look at the world around us. We drop a ball and watch it fall to the ground. It seems to be speeding up as it falls, the eye tells us that much, and so we measure the falls in various ways, and lo and behold, we find that all things fall at the same speed, and that the distance that something falls increases by the square of the increase in the *time* of the fall – this quite precisely! – and despite the fact that time and distance seem to be such very different things! Why should it be so? Why should the ratio be so simple and neat? Why should the two be related at all? All we can say is, they are. Things fall by rules, acting the same always, and the rules are simple, or then later, not so simple. But the world moves by mathematical laws! The world is proportionate to itself across things as disparate as time and distance! How can it be?'

'It can only be because God made the world that way.'

'Yes. God makes the world using mathematics, and he has given us minds that can see it. We can discover the laws He used! It is a *most beautiful thing* to witness and understand! It's prayer. It's more than prayer, it's a sacrament, a kind of communion. An apprehension – an epiphany – it's *seeing God*, while still in this body and in this world! How blessed we are, to be able to experience God like that! Who would not devote their time to understanding more, to seeing deeper into God's manner of thinking about these things?'

'Not I,' she said, looking at him fondly.

And then to feel God's goodness in the sun on his back, in the garden. He had a little rolling seat he could move about between the row of plants, with a groove in it for the bottom of his truss. His knees and back got some relief as he sat on the cart and leaned down and pulled out weeds, feeling the dirt in his fingers and the sun on his back. It was feeling the touch of God in the world, just as determining the proportion in nature was seeing the mind of God. He could not help wishing that Maria Celeste would be allowed to come up the lane to *Il Gioello*, to help La Piera around the house, and sit with him in his garden as he sat with her at the convent. He would have to try to arrange that. The new abbess could probably be convinced. Ah the blessed tumble of days.

But he was right to be afraid. Well, we always are. One day, a few months after his return, some tainted meat gave her the runs, and she had not enough flesh to hold water or give her extra strength when she needed it. The dysentery quickly wrung her dry, twisting her insides so that she writhed with the pain of it, having already evacuated everything in her. She became parched and began to pass blood, and the various other internal liquids and viscosities that line the gut, and after that there was nothing to do but to sit by her on her bed and call for the other nuns to lift her up if she needed relief, retiring so as not to offend her modesty, returning as soon as he could to wipe her brow and give her citrons to suck on, and then to sit and see how much broth she could hold down, urging sips on her every time he could get her attention. In her fever she became delirious, and her lips cracked. Her body gave up squirming and she lay there breathing shallowly, not even sweating, her pulse faint, and by the fifth day, erratic.

Galileo sat there beside her and stared at the wall. Sarpi was dead, Sagredo was dead, Salviati was dead, Cesi was dead, Marina was dead, his sisters, his parents. The list went on. Cosimo, Cesarini. The Bible spoke of three score and ten, but so few got that, so few. It was a fallen world.

Hours passed pulse by pulse, breath by breath. Hours like weeks, days like months. There aren't enough things to think about during time like that.

At the end of the fifth day he hauled himself to his feet and went outside to talk things over with the doctor who visited the convent, a man he had learned to trust more than most doctors.

Now the man wiped his sweating pate and squinted with the distress of his news. 'It's gone too far,' he said. He clutched Galileo's arm as if it were his own daughter he was talking about. 'She can't come back when she's this dried out.'

'How long?' Galileo said.

'A day, or less.'

'I'll come back as soon as I get some things. See that she receives the sacrament.'

'She already has. I'll walk you up to your place.'

He dragged himself up the village lane, already so familiar that it seemed the only lane he had ever known. At *Il Gioello* they found the gateway occupied by a little group of clerics from Florence, led by the local vicar of the Inquisition.

'What do you want?' Galileo demanded roughly.

The vicar drew himself up to indicate the importance of his pronouncement. 'His Holiness the Pope forbids you to continue to petition the Holy Office in Florence for freedom of movement, or else you may be removed to your prison at the Holy Office in Rome.'

Galileo stared at him. Geppo and La Piera watched in horror from the yard; surely the maestro was about to erupt in one of his black furies, he would beat these prelates and then where would they be.

Finally Galileo said, 'I have been trying to get permission to go into Florence to see my doctors.'

'You are forbidden to try.'

Galileo waved a hand and went inside without a word. We watched as the clerics conferred, red-faced, and then departed.

That night Galileo returned to the convent and sat by Maria Celeste, holding her cold hand. She was unconscious and barely breathing. For a while Arcangela came by and cried with her face in her apron and the crook of her elbow. She even smashed her face against Galileo's side and cried, without once looking at him. In the tenth hour of the night, after the bell for second matins, Maria Celeste died.

Thirty-three years old. The same age as Christ. A bride of Christ, his little saint, Santa Maria Celeste, now celestial indeed. If he had not made her a nun, if he had found her a husband and a dowry. The poor Clares were too poor, they died of their vow. She could have been raising his grandchildren and running *Il Gioello*, the saint of the jewel.

2nd April, 1634.

Silence descended on the sleepless household. This silence was in such contrast to the howls and shrieks that always emerged from Galileo whenever he was sick or miserable, that no one in the household who heard it could believe it. Now they understood that those earlier histrionics had been like the roaring of a lion with a thorn in its foot, the roar of someone intent that no one should sleep when he could not. Nothing like that now. No sound from his closed room. It was acutely painful to the household to hear that silence, it rang in their ears like a blackness in the heart of everything. Please groan, they said to themselves, please shriek, please shout at the sky and curse the Pope and even God, please beat us to within an inch of our lives, please, anything but this silence, which was so unbearable that they went into his room and served him impassively and then went outside and put their arms to the wall and sobbed; and in the soundless nights they huddled in the kitchen or curled on their beds, helplessly listening; and even I myself, ancient beyond all feeling and sanity, sick of everything in this world, even I wept. It would have been better for him if he had died in the fire.

Chapter Twenty The Dream

A man riding high on Fortune's wheel
Cannot tell who really loves him
For his friends true and false stand side by side
And show him equal devotion.
But should he fall upon hard times
His crowd of flatterers will slip away.
Only the ones who love from the heart
Will stand by him when he is dead to the world.
    —LUDOVICO ARIOSTO, *Orlando Furioso*

A long time passed and did not pass in that house of grief. The old man lay around in his bed, unable either to sleep or to wake. When he did manage to fall asleep he slept as if dead, and resisted being roused. Then, if La Piera managed to wake him, he dragged himself out to his couch on the patio and lay there. He could not be convinced to eat. Sometimes he would pass through the kitchen and take a loaf of bread with him out to the garden, where he sat on the ground and tore the bread with his teeth and chewed grimly. When he was done he sometimes started to weed under the vegetables, but he pulled his starts as often as his weeds, eyes blinded by tears. His right eye was going bad in any case. Sometimes he gave up and lay on the ground. At his desk he only shuffled his papers around, staring through them.

Eventually he wrote some letters, answered some of the sympathy notes. His writing had become his talking now, and maybe it was easier to talk to strangers. To a French correspondent he barely knew he wrote: *Here I live on in a silence, frequently paying visits to the neighbouring convent, where I had two daughters who were nuns and whom I dearly loved, but the eldest in particular, who was a woman of exquisite mind and singular goodness, and very fond of me. She had suffered much from ill health during my absence, and had not paid enough attention to herself. At length dysentery came on, and she died after six days' illness, leaving me shattered and unable to speak. And by a sinister coincidence, on returning home from the convent, in company with the doctor who had just told me her condition was hopeless and that she would not survive the next day, as indeed came to pass, I found the Inquisitor's Vicar here, who informed me of a mandate from the Holy Office in Rome that I must desist from asking for grace or they would take me back to the actual prison of the Holy Office. From which I can infer that my present confinement is to be ended only by that other one which is common to all, most narrow, and enduring forever.*

To another distant acquaintance he wrote, *I feel immense sadness and melancholy, together with extreme loss of appetite. Perpetual sleeplessness makes me afraid. I am hateful to myself, and continually hear my beloved daughter calling to me.*

La Piera kept the household going through the long silence. She dropped his food before him with the same absent methodical air she had when she chopped the heads off the chickens. Galileo ate as if he were dead. He too had heard the silence, which came out of an abyssal blackness. He knew now that all the wailing after his trial had been at nothing. To be distressed at the judgement of other men, over nothing more than an idea; it was absurd. Well, grief too was an idea. And as you got older, your grief grew in you. Probably there was an equation for this change in grief, a rate of acceleration. Like a dropped rock. You collect all your selves together just in time to smash to the ground, and so it all goes to waste. The dust devil falls to the ground, its whirlpool of wind gone. The atoms, the affectinos of that particular field dispersed. If anything is conserved, he thought as he sat in the garden, looking at the signs of spring in all the plants, it must be in the generations that follow. Something that could be put to use. This was all that would remain in time.

One afternoon he walked down to the convent and found Suor Arcangela. She was startled to see him and turned her face away.

'Sit down,' he said. 'I've brought some candied citron.' And he sat on a bench in the sun. She would not speak, but the citron slices were hard to resist. Eventually she sat on the far end of the bench. She took the slices and ate them, all the while looking the other way. After a while she curled on the bench like a cat, her back to him, but in such a way that the back of her head just touched the side of his leg. It seemed she fell asleep.

Galileo sat there looking at the strawberry plants at his feet. The new leaves came out of the ground neatly folded. Any new leaf was a remarkable thing when considered closely. The little plant emerged from brown mud that was granulated and unpromising. Wet dirt, nothing more. And yet there were the new leaves. Earth, water, air, the subtle fire of sunlight, driving the life into everything. Something in the mix of these, and something beyond them . . . For a long time he sat there staring, feeling on the edge of understanding, of seeing things clearly. The feeling swelled in him as he realized that it was an emotion he felt all the time, that his entire life had been one protracted case of presque vu. Almost seen! Almost understood! The blue sky quivered with this feeling.

On his way home he stopped to see the abbess. Recently Arcangela had been leaving the convent and wandering Arcetri and the country lanes around the village, until someone noticed and she had to be retrieved. Now Galileo said to the abbess, 'Just let her go if she goes. She'll always come back in time for supper. If she doesn't I'll send one of the boys out to get her.'

Then, because he was old, because he had lost everything and all the people he loved most had died, because life had no meaning and there was nothing left to do to fill his preposthumous hours, he occupied his time writing up his results from the experiments he and Mazzoleni had performed in Padua, forty years before.

To get him started, we put his old folios out on the table under the arcade, as if taking them out there to be dusted. Sometimes he would turn the pages, and then with a heavy sigh he would take up a pen and jot down some notes, or transcribe some conversation going on in his head. It was only a way to pass the time before death took him; at least at first.

Then somehow it got its hooks into him, and made him sweat and grunt in the old way. Work, work, work; the work of thinking, the work of understanding something that had never been understood before; this was the hardest work in the world. And he liked that. He needed that. Arcangela still would not speak to him, even though she sometimes wandered up to the house, skulking around the gate like a stray dog. The Lady Alessandra was still in Germany, and his letters to her could only be so long, especially when so much that he wanted to say to her could not be written down, but only translated into comments on gardening and the weather. After the mornings when he wrote those letters, the hours hung heavy on him. And yet the book of his life was still there to be written. So, hey to.

Almost all of the material had been in his mind, or at least in his notes, since before 1609, when the arrival of the telescope had upended his life. He had noted and sketched the various raw propositions during the intense collaboration with Mazzoleni in the Padua workshop, thinking at the time that he would write them up formally in book form during the following school year. Now it was thirty years since he had stopped, and some of the notes had been transcribed by Guiducci and Arighetti, but most of the notebooks he had not even opened again since that time. Some pages he even had serious trouble understanding. It was like reading the handwriting of another man; and he supposed that was actually the case, because now he was only revising the work of an entirely different Galileo, a younger and more nimble mind. What if all those past selves don't count, he thought as he looked at the notebooks, no matter how much they wrote down? What if the person you are now is really the only person that matters? Because that's how it is.

So he worked, and lost himself in geometries. The horrible year 1634 passed. A whole crop grew in the fields, there was weed after weed to kill, and after a while he grew unable to recognize his grief as something discrete; it was now simply the world, the way things were.

Pages piled up. He kept using the format of dialogues between Salviati, Sagredo, and Simplicio. This little defiance was a good sign, we all thought; using those names had not been forbidden, the dialogue form had not been forbidden, and yet they would remind everyone of the book that had been forbidden. Of course it was likely they would ban this one before it was ever published. The *Dialogo* and the *Discorsi* – two very dangerous books, being so real.

He found it interesting to read over his old notes and diagrams. As he did so he could not help but recall also all the other things that had happened in Padua when he had been writing these pages. Eighteen long years of teaching mathematics to the students at Il Bo and living in the house on Via Vignoli – lecturing, tutoring, working on the military compass, inventing new devices, trying to determine various qualities and properties in the workshop demonstrations. Here was a page on the weight of air as compared to water, for instance. Then also taking the barge out to Venice, to eat and drink and talk with his friends, and play with the two hundred and forty-eight girls, and later to see Marina. It was all a jumble, like a kind of carnival inside him, and he could not in fact associate any given experiment with any given year, it was all as one and of a piece: Padua. It was strange how that time felt like it had happened just yesterday, and yet also was separated from him by an abyss of a million years – yet another example of time's odd doubled aspect. Strange also that he had fought with such fury to escape that life, when it had turned out to be precisely the happiest time he would ever have! How could he have been so stupid? How could he not have known what he had? There was a deep stupidity in ambition, a blindness in it, the way it was so serious, so unplayful; it failed to value the moment, and so failed to recognize happiness, even though that was the most important consideration of all. It failed to value more than anything else the ringing feeling that had come over him, as when he saw a proof, or on that first night with Marina, or sometimes on the dawn barges back over the lagoon to terra ferma. These were the moments that mattered.

'Mazzoleni, I am stupid.'

'I don't know, maestro,' the old one objected. 'Where does that leave the rest of us?'

'Ha ha.'

Eventually, these moments he was trapped in now would also meld together and become all of a piece: the mornings splayed in the garden, the afternoons working on the new dialogues; the grief for Maria Celeste, infusing everything with its black light. Arcangela turning her head away when he visited, the look that was not a look, and thus worse than any look, which at the very least was a contact. His sister-in-law, Anna Chiara Galilei, moving into *Il Gioello* with three daughters and her youngest son Michelangelo, then all five of them promptly dying of the plague. More black light piercing all; all part of the one thing of this particular time.

People continued to write to him, and one day that fall, he got up one morning and stacked up all their letters and started writing back. He answered questions, and inquired about other people's physical or mathematical investigations, and told people about the new dialogues he had begun. It was of course unlikely he could ever have these dialogues published. That he was using the same three characters only increased the difficulty. So when a correspondent he had never met, Elia Diodati, wrote from Holland offering to help with the publication of a new book, Galileo quickly agreed.

At first this seemed like a good thing; but we noticed that Galileo soon began to create more requirements for the book, so that it appeared he would never be able to finish it. It became obvious he didn't want to finish it, that that for him would be like finishing his life. He was trying to fit in everything he had ever learned, or even thought to be possible – everything but the cosmological matters he was forbidden to discuss. Those in any case remained speculative matters, mysterious no matter how hard one tried to see into them – as was made clear by the confounding information coming in from correspondents about tide times in the Atlantic, which made his theory of how tides were formed seem clearly wrong, as he had to admit in his replies.

Whereas on the other hand, with these simple propositions about motion, force, friction and strength, he could stick to only those assertions that he had demonstrated by experiment. After all the guesses about comets and stars and sunspots, about buoyancy and magnetism and all the fascinating mysteries he did not have any basis for comprehending, that were in the end the equivalent of astrology, it was a tremendous pleasure to write down only what he had seen and tested. 'This is the book I should have written all along,' he said one day as he finished writing. 'This and only this. I should have avoided words and stuck to equations, like Euclid.'

Let AC be the inclined plane and AB the perpendicular, each having the same vertical height above the horizontal, namely, BA; then I say, the time of the descent along the plane AC bears a ratio to the time of fall along the perpendicular AB, which is the same as the ratio of the length AC to AB.

Space and time, in a relation. So satisfying! A little bell rings!

In the new book's first day of dialogue, there in the pink ark of Sagredo's palazzo on the Grand Canal in his mind, he had Salviati, Sagredo and Simplicio discuss the following subjects: ratios of size to strength in machines; the strength of braided rope; a method for separating the action of the vacuum from other causes; the breaking point of a column of water, which was always eighteen cubits; the role of fire in liquifying hot metals; the paradox of an infinite within an infinite; the geometry of shrinking surfaces; an experiment that might determine the speed of light; problems and theorems in projective geometry; questions of buoyancy and the speed of falling objects; the question of why water beads up on some surfaces; what terminal velocity is, and air resistance, as well as water resistance and the resistance of a vacuum; results of attempts to weigh air, to find out the ratio of the weight of water to air (which was forty to one, not Aristotle's ten to one); results from the experiments on inclined planes to measure the speed of falling objects; designs for pendulums made of different materials; questions of percussion and impact; and lastly, a long discussion of harmonies and dissonances in music, explained as functions of proportion in vibrations of a pendulum string, with speculations as to why such strong emotions could be created by such sounds.

On the second day, the three characters discussed the equilibrium and balance of beams, the longitudinal and latitudinal strength of beams, strength as a function of size, and strength as a function of shape.

On the third day, they discussed questions of motion, both local and uniform; questions of speed and distance; naturally accelerated motions, in which everything was said about gravity but the word itself; inclined plane experiments to test motion; pendulum experiments for same; and various inclined plane theorems of equal speeds, with comparisons to vertical fall.

On the fourth day the three discussed the motion of projectiles, as being a combination of uniform and naturally accelerated motion, thus leading to the theorem of the semi-parabola, with a lot of tables recording information from experiments to support these assertions, and to let the objects speak for themselves.

Early in the dialogue of the first day, Salviati said something that startled Galileo when he read it later:

And here I must relate a circumstance which is worthy of your attention, as indeed are all events which happen contrary to expectation – especially when a precautionary measure turns out to be a cause of disaster.

That was 1616, he suddenly saw; his precautionary measure had led to disaster. But how could you tell until after the fact? And so didn't you have to try? You did. You could only try. You learn things that make you try.

He had done what he could with what he had. As he wrote on, thinking about this, he had Salviati defend his practice:

Our Academician has thought much upon this subject, and according to his custom has demonstrated everything by geometrical methods, so that one might fairly call what he does a new science.

'Has demonstrated everything by geometrical methods!' Galileo said, reading it with a shake of the head. 'Ha. If only you could. That would be a new science indeed.'

As the book continued to pile up, page after page, he kept writing down things that surprised him later, things he didn't know that he knew:

The attributes 'equal', 'greater', and 'less' are not applicable to infinite quantities.

Amazing the force which results from adding together an immense number of small forces. There can be no doubt that any resistance, so long as it is not infinite, may be overcome by a multitude of minute forces.

553

Infinity and indivisibility are in their very nature incompre-
hensible to us; imagine then what they are when combined. Yet
that is our world.

Any velocity once imparted to a moving body will be rigidly
maintained as long as the external causes of acceleration or
retardation are removed . . . motion along a horizontal plane is
perpetual; for if the velocity be uniform, it cannot be diminished
or slackened, much less destroyed.

A body which descends along any inclined plane and contin-
ues its motion along a plane inclined upwards, will, on account
of the momentum acquired, ascend to an equal height above the
horizontal; and this is true whether the inclinations of the two
planes are the same or different.

At times when he wrote it seemed as if Salviati and Sagredo
were still alive somewhere and talking to him from that place,
their minds as lively as ever. Sometimes he put into the book
actual things he had heard them say in life, as when he included
one of Salviati's many fine off-hand remarks:

I shall attempt to remove, or at least diminish, one improba-
bility by introducing a similar or greater one, just as sometimes
a wonder is diminished by a miracle.

A wonder diminished by a miracle. That had happened to him
fairly often, it seemed. He had lived in a miracle.
At times these voices from the page said things with a mysterious power to move him:
Please observe, gentlemen, how facts which at first seem
improbable will, even on scant explanation, drop the cloak which
has hidden them and stand forth in naked and simple beauty.

He had seen that, he felt; seen the cloak drop, and beauty stand
forth. An image evoked by the phrase pushed at the back of his

eyes, naked and simple, not seen but almost seen. A beauty like Marina, but taller.

Later a strange sensation struck him again, very powerfully, when he read over a passage in which Salviati and Sagredo began talking about musical strings vibrating either in time or out of time, *sproporzionatamente*, and Salviati suggested that within those interference patterns, every wave held secret lives. As he read over the passage, Galileo did not quite remember writing it:

A string which has been struck begins to vibrate and contin-ues the motion as long as one hears the sound (risonanza); these ripples expand far into space, and set into vibration not only strings, but also any other body which happens to have the same period as the plucked string. The undulations of the medium are widely dispersed about the sounding body, as shown by the fact that a glass of water may be made to emit a tone merely by the friction of the fingertip upon the rim of the glass; for in this water is produced a series of regular waves. Would it not be a fine thing if one had the ability to produce waves which would persist for a long while, even months and years – even centuries?

Sagredo: Such an invention would, I assure you, command my admiration.

Salviati: The device is one which I hit upon by accident; my part consists merely in the observation of it, and in the appreci-ation of its value as a confirmation of something which I plunged into quite deeply.

Wave interference. The long reach across time. Something which I plunged into quite deeply. A secret at the heart of time, deep inside him . . . he could not quite say it. So much was always almost seen, at the tip of the tongue. Had it ever been any different? Or was it only that now he was noticing it more?

He could only keep writing.

*   *   *

This *Discorsi*, then, was to him something living and breathing. It was not the kind of book one wanted to finish. Best for it to go on and on, page after page, forever. He understood now those obsessed alchemists who wrote right into the grave, never even attempting publication.

Finally Diodati persuaded him to declare the book done by suggesting that it was not really done at all, but only being published in pieces, with these four parts being only the first of many to follow. This was brilliant; Diodati got a book to publish, while at the same time Galileo could still write, still live.

So the book was published. Galileo's suggested title was *Dialogues of Galileo Galilei, Containing Two Entire Sciences, All New and Demonstrated from their First Principles and Elements, so that, in the Manner of other Mathematical Elements, Roads are Opened to Vast Fields, with Reasonings and Mathematical Demonstrations Filled with Infinite Admirable Conclusions, from which Far More Remains to be Seen in the World Than has been Seen Up to the Present Time.*

Diodati titled it *Discourse on Two New Sciences*. The *Discorsi*, we all called it. Its four days of dialogue were to be followed by fifth and sixth days, the preface announced, and so on after those, perpetually.

Galileo distributed a few copies of the book to certain friends and ex-students for their commentary. The note to his friends in Rome apologized for the book's contents: *I find how much old age lessens the vividness and speed of my thinking, as now I struggle to understand quite a lot of things I discovered and proved when I was younger.*

His friends in Rome read this and laughed. 'He's slowing down!' they told each other, leafing through the book. 'Only three hundred and thirty-seven pages this time, I see.' 'Every page stuffed with ideas, I see, many new to the world.' 'And not a few difficult to understand!' 'Oh, yes,' they said to each other. 'It's a real falling off.' And they all cackled helplessly.

With the *Discorsi* sent off to Holland, he fell back into melancholia. This was not helped by the fact that his right eye, which had spent so many hours jammed against the eyepiece of a telescope, had begun to fail him. By day he ran tests on the eye as if it were one of his telescopes, taking notes on its reduced field, perspicacity, and sensitivity to light. By night he moaned.

One morning he got up saying that if he went blind he would never be able to see Maria Celeste's handwriting ever again, never read her thoughts there expressed so clearly that it was as if reading her mind; and he took the basket holding the letters from the side of his bed and began to read through them, holding the pages close to his face, breathing in the scent of them as he read. The big diagonal loops of her handwriting brought all their banter back to him, the years when together they had run both San Matteo and Bellosguardo, keeping accounts and managing both field and household. They brought back also the way she had encouraged him during the trial, even though she had been terrified.

He came on the one that told the story of the time he had sent over to her a basket of game birds, to sweeten the last meals of another young nun, who had wasted away and was dying despite Maria Celeste's ministrations. She wrote back to him, *I received the pannier containing the twelve thrushes: the additional four, which would have completed the number you state in your letter, Sire, must have been liberated by some charming little kitten who thought of tasting them ahead of us, because they were not there, and the cloth cover had a large hole in it. So, as the thrushes arrived a little the worse for wear, it was necessary to cook them in a stew, so that I stood over them all day, and for once I truly surrendered myself to gluttony.*

For once. Surrendering to a stew of birds chewed up by a cat. Galileo put the letters back in their basket.

After some weeks of blackness, I asked if he had heard anything lately from the Lady Alessandra Buonamici, in Germany with her husband. 'No,' he said shortly, but later that day he called for some paper. He wrote her a long letter, and after that, he got into the habit of it. Because of the distance between them, he could say things he wouldn't have said to the people around him; and say other things also without any danger that anything was expected to come of it. So then, often, after his morning in the garden, he sat in the shade of the arcade and wrote a note to her, bundling five or six into a package, and keeping others to himself.

On that first day, in his mind he wrote, How I loved you, dearest lady. You fill my mind to such an extent that it seems you are here with me. You are so beautiful here in my garden, I must say. I am sure it is even more true in Mainz. I wish you were here instead, though I feel the vibration of your presence even over that distance, for I am tuned to the same harmonic. Maybe there is a world in which you did not go to Germany, a world in which things happened differently, so that I could pass more time with you. Not only could have spent time with you, but have; not only have, but am, in some other part of this very moment. That's the part of the moment I like best. Meanwhile, however, I live on in this world in which I am imprisoned, in which you are in Germany, or somewhere else, and so I must speak to you in my mind only, and here on the page capture just the smallest fraction of the thoughts I have spoken to you in that empty room.

In the last year of his sight, he often sat out in the garden at night on his reclined divan, looking at the moon and what he could see of the stars. He noticed for the first time that although the moon always showed the same face to Earth, it was not exactly the same face; there were small shifts, as if the man in the moon were looking in a mirror and inspecting his face from different angles – which is how Galileo put it when he wrote about the discovery to his friends – first tipping his head down, then up, then left, then right. This might be part of how the moon had its effect on the tides; for his theory, that they were caused not by the moon but by the Earth's rotation and its movement around the sun, had turned out to be not just heretical, but wrong. The moon seemed to be involved after all; or at least things were happening to both moon and tides in concert. Possibly this shifting face had something to do with it. So hard to tell; but when he understood the reality of this little libration, which no watcher of the moon no matter how vigilant had ever observed in the history of mankind, the little bell inside him rang again.

That bobbing face of the man in the moon was his last observation; soon after that his left eye went too, and then that kind of thing was over. A combination of infections and cataracts had blinded him. Only a short time after that, the Vatican sent word that he was allowed to move temporarily into Florence to be seen to by doctors. But it was doubtful they could have done anything, even if they had seen him before.

With his world gone dark, he had to dictate his letters, which continued to go out into the world as before. A young student named Vincenzio Viviani, only seventeen years old, was invited to move into the house as an assistant. He joined us and proved to be a serious young man, intelligent and helpful, very intent on his duties. Galileo spent many an hour talking through his correspondence, and Viviani wrote it all down.

In a letter to Diodati Galileo said, *This universe, which I with my astonishing observations and clear demonstrations enlarged a hundred, nay, a thousandfold beyond the limits commonly seen by wise men of all centuries past, is now for me so diminished and reduced as to have shrunk to the meagre confines of my own body.*

*　　*　　*

When he said gloomy things like this around the household, I would say to him, 'It could be worse.'

'Worse?' he would snap. 'Nothing could be worse! It would have been better to have been burned at the stake by that liar who went back on his word!'

'I don't think so, maestro. You wouldn't have liked the fire.'

'At least it would have been fast. This falling apart, one piece at a time – if only I would trip on a stair and hit my head and be gone. So leave me! Leave me or I'll kick you. I know where you are.'

He could tell many weeds by feel, and so continued to sit in the garden in the mornings, even when he did nothing but listen to the birds and feel the sun on his face. He got out his lute, had it repaired and restrung, and started playing it again. As the calluses on his fingers thickened he played it more and more, repeating the songs he knew, and humming or mumbling in a hoarse baritone the words to some of them. He often played a little suite of his father's compositions, and musical settings for Ariosto and Tasso, and long wandering melodies of his own devise. La Piera ran the house along with Geppo and the other longtime servants; Viviani served as Galileo's secretary and amanuensis; I continued on as his personal servant; a new student, Torricelli, moved in to take mathematics lessons. Things continued in their new way.

And then Alessandra Buonamici came back. She showed up in the spring of 1640, announcing that her husband's diplomatic assignment had unexpectedly brought him back to Florence. She stood there in his room; she touched him on the arm, let him touch her on the face. 'Yes, I'm here,' she said.

Again Galileo was saved by a stranger appearing at a crux in his life. This time it was Alessandra, nearly forty now, she said, childless, tall and rotund. She came to visit almost every day, accompanied only by a servant or two. She brought with her gifts for him that he could feel or eat: rolls of yarn, different fabrics of linen, dried fruits, scraps of blacksmith metal, polygons made of woodblock, chunks of coral. He would sit forward in his chair and rub swatches between his fingers and against his cheek, or stack cubes, and tell her about cohesion and the strength of wood.

I long to talk to you, he wrote when she could not come. *It is so rare to find women who can speak so sensibly as you.*

She replied even more boldly: *I have been trying to find the way to come there and stay for a day of conversation with you, without creating scandal.* She suggested fantasy plans, things that could never happen but which she knew would please him to imagine; that they might go boating on the Arno, that she might slip a small carriage into Arcetri to spirit him away to Prato for several days together, and so on. *Patience!* she wrote.

I have never doubted your affection for me, he wrote back, *certain that you, in this short time which I may have left, know how much affection flows in me for you.* He invited her to come with her husband and stay for four days. Somehow this never happened.

Life at *Il Gioello* contracted in on itself, orchestrated by La Piera and performed by the entire household, with the youth Viviani almost always at the maestro's side, to the point where Galileo sometimes ordered him to go away. Many days he only wanted to lie on the divan in the shade, or sprawl in the dirt of the garden, tugging up weeds. You could see that grovelling in the soil, embracing it, was a comfort to him.

But he was famous all over Europe, because of his books, and the trial; and foreign travellers often inquired if they could come to visit him. He always agreed to these requests, which flattered his vanity, and also broke the daily routine and helped pass the time. He only requested that the visitors be discreet, and generally they were, at least beforehand; after they left, they often wanted to tell the world the story of their visit. That was gratifying. He was still a figure on the great stage of Europe – an old lion, defanged and blind, but a lion still. To the Protestants he was yet another image of the corruption of the Roman Catholic Church, which was not a role that he liked to play; he felt he was a victim not of the Church but of corruption within the Church, as he tried to make clear if he got the chance. *I do not hope for any relief*, he wrote to a supporter named Peiresc, *and that is because I have committed no crime. I might hope for a pardon if I had erred. With the guilty a prince can show forbearance, but against one wrongfully sentenced when he is innocent, it is expedient to uphold rigour, so as to put up a show of strict lawfulness.* This was like something out of Machiavelli, a writer Galileo knew well. Galileo had met his prince too, and suffered the consequent tortures just as Machiavelli had.

Apparently a translated edition of the *Dialogo* had been published in England; he had had no idea, until Englishmen began to appear at his gate. One of the first of them, a Thomas Hobbes, told him of the translated edition and then wanted to talk philosophy, and get Galileo to say things he didn't want to say. Because they conversed in Latin (and the English way of pronouncing Latin was very strange, like something he seemed to recall), he was able to bend the talk to topics he was comfortable discussing. Thus Hobbes went away without any denunciations or blasphemies to quote.

A younger pair of Englishmen were more congenial, at least at first. They were travelling around Europe together: a Thomas

Hedtke and one John Milton. Hedtke was the more pleasant of the two, but Milton did most of the talking, for along with excellent Latin he spoke a mangled but comprehensible version of Tuscan Italian, a very unusual ability for a foreigner. He talked a lot; he did not appear to have heard that proverb for travellers in foreign lands, that one should proceed with '*i pensieri stretti e il viso sciolto*,' closed thoughts and an open face. He declared that he was good with languages, and knew how to speak Spanish, French, Tuscan, Latin, and Greek. And he had a thousand questions, most of them leading questions, intended to make the Pope look bad, and also the Jesuits, for whom he seemed to harbour a particular dislike, which was funny given how jesuitical he was.

'Do you not agree that the judgement rendered against you was an attempt to assert that the Roman Church has the authority to say what you can think and what you can't think?'

'Not so much what you can think, as what you can say.'

'Precisely! They claim the right to decide who gets to speak!'

'Yes. But every society has such rules.'

This silenced the young man for a time. He was sitting on a stool drawn up next to Galileo's divan. Hedtke had gone out to the garden with Galileo's old student Carlo Dati, who had brought the two Englishmen to Arcetri; now Milton crouched by his side, asking questions. Were the Medicis tyrants, were they poisoners, did they believe what Machiavelli taught? Did Galileo believe what Machiavelli taught? Did Galileo know who was the greatest Italian poet after the incomparable Dante? Because Milton did – it was Tasso! Did Galileo know what huge benefits were conferred by chastity?

'I haven't been noticing those,' Galileo muttered.

'And even more so, the benefits conferred by that sage and serious doctrine, virginity?'

Galileo was at a loss for words. He saw again that there were men who were both highly intelligent and deeply stupid. He had been that way himself for much of his life, and so now he was a bit more tolerant than he would have been in years past. He kept steering the conversation back to Dante, for lack of a better subject. He did not want to hear any more about the vast superiority of the reformed protestant faith, which was the youth's favourite topic. So he talked about Dante and what made him so great. 'Anyone can make hell interesting,' he said. 'It's purgatory that matters.'

Milton laughed at this. 'But there is no such thing as purgatory!'

'Yours is a hard creed. You Protestants are not quite human, it seems to me.'

'You still undertake to defend the Church of Rome?'

'Yes.'

The young man could not agree with this, as he explained again at length. Galileo tried to divert him by saying that he had studied as a youth to be a monk, but then had noticed a lamp in the cathedral swinging overhead after being lit by an acolyte, and by timing the period of the swings with his pulse, had confirmed that no matter how widely the lamp swung in its pendular motion, it always took the same amount of time to cross the arc. 'As I saw the truth of the situation, I rang like a struck bell.'

'This was God, telling you to leave the Church of Rome.'

'I don't think so.'

Galileo drank more wine, and felt the old sadness sweep through him like any other pendulum, steady in its cosmic beat. He grew sleepy. Like a garden-variety fool, the priggish young virtuoso was overstaying his welcome. Galileo stopped listening to him, drifted off into a light sleep. He came to at something the youth said about blindness being a judgement on him.

'The blind still see inside,' he said. 'And those who see are sometimes the blindest of all.'

'Not if they shield themselves by their own prayers, made direct to God.'

'But prayers are not always answered.'

'They are if you have prayed for the right thing.'

564

Galileo couldn't stifle a laugh. 'I suppose that's true,' he said. 'I want what Jove wants.'

There were no words that would reach the youth. You could never teach other people anything that mattered. The important things they had to learn for themselves, almost always by making mistakes, so that the lessons arrived too late to help. Experience was in that sense useless. It was precisely what could not be passed along in a lesson or an equation.

The young foreigner sat there nattering on in his bizarre Italian. For a while Galileo dozed off, and dreamed of plunging through space. When he woke again the youth had gone silent, and Galileo was not even sure he was still in the room. 'Pride leads to a fall,' he murmured, 'you should remember that. I know, I was proud. But I fell. My mother stole my eyes. And the favourite has to fall, in the end, to make room for more. The fall is our life, our flight. If I could say it properly, you would understand. You would. Because I had such dreams. I had such a daughter.'

But the disagreeable youth apparently had already slipped away.

So Galileo fell back asleep. When he woke again, the house was silent around him, but he could feel that someone stood in his doorway. The person stepped toward him furtively, and he knew it was not the Englishman. He patted the divan. She lay down beside him, the back of her head against his knee, wordless and unforgiving. They lay there like that for a long time.

Eventually he fell asleep again, and while asleep he had a dream. He dreamed he was in church, worshipping with his family and friends. Around him stood Sarpi and Sagredo and Salviati, and Cesi and Castelli and Piccolomini, and Alessandra and Viviani and Mazzoleni; and at the back, Cartophilus and La Piera. At his side stood Maria Celeste. Near the altar he saw that Marina and Maculano were conferring over something, as

Maculano prepared the service. Overhead swung the lamp he had seen as a boy, still making its pendulum, and now there was a little spring at the point of attachment which at every swing gave the pendulum cord a little extra push near the fulcrum, so that the lamp would pendulum forever, forming a clock keeping God's own time. That spring device was a good idea.

The altar in this church was a big pair of his inclined planes, and all of them together under Maculano's direction ran the experiments on falling bodies, moving the beautifully finished frames this way and that, setting balls free, timing their falls by way of water running into chalices. Marina let the balls drop, Mazzoleni grinned his gap-toothed grin, and everyone sang the hymn 'All Things Move By God'. Fra Sarpi spread his arms and said, 'These ripples expand far into space, and set into vibration not only strings, but also any other body which happens to have the same period,' and Sagredo said, 'Sometimes a wonder is obscured by a miracle.' Then they moved two planes into a V shape and placed a little ivory curve at the bottom to connect them, so that the ball would shift smoothly from down to up. At the top of the second plane Mazzoleni placed the workshop bell on its side. The Lady Alessandra, her head touching the vault of the dome, reached down and released a ball from the top of the first plane: a steep drop, a long decelerating rise, and then the ball hit the edge of the bell. And Galileo heard the bell ring over all the worlds.

Then he fell sick again. He had gone to bed ill so many times before that it took a while to understand that this time was different. His kidneys hurt, his urine was cloudy. The doctors were called, but there was nothing they could do. His kidneys were failing. They forbade him wine, but La Piera slipped him a cup or two at night anyway.

When it got really bad, such that he resumed his moaning as he never had since Maria Celeste's death, we sent a letter out, and Lady Alessandra showed up unannounced. She sat by his bed and washed his face with a cloth dipped in cold water. Sometimes he would hand her the basket, and she would read Maria Celeste's letters aloud to him. Somehow all the news of food shortages and pulled teeth and catarrhs and madness were gone, leaving only the shared recipes, the devotional prayers, the snippy comments about her brother, the expressions of love, of *amorevolezza*. Alessandra's reading voice was calm and distant. She spoke of other things, and made dry little jokes, and Momus, the god of laughter, briefly touched down.

'You remind me of someone,' Galileo said. 'I wish I could remember.'

'We are all everyone. And we all remember everything.'

On her way out she looked at me and shook her head. 'I have to go,' she said. 'I can't do this any more. Not when he could be fixed in a day.'

She didn't come the next day, sending a letter instead. Viviani read it to Galileo, and he heard it silently. He dictated his reply.

Your letter found me in bed gravely indisposed. Many, many thanks for the courtesy which you have always shown to me, and for your condolences which visit me now in my misery and my misfortune.

That was his last letter. A few days later he fell unconscious.

That night the wolves out on the hills howled, and he struggled on his bed such that it seemed to us that he heard them calling. At dawn he died.

The household wandered around in the raw morning light. Of course it was true that we had just lost our employer, and this was no small part of our despair; Sestilia notwithstanding, Vincenzio could be counted on for nothing. But it was more than that: it was also immediately obvious that with the maestro gone the world would never again be so interesting. We had lost our hero, our genius, our own Pulcinella.

It was La Piera who pushed us through the awful duties of that day and those that followed. 'Come on, get on with it,' she would say. 'We are all souls, remember? We exist in each other. To get him back you just have to think of what he would do, what he would say.'

'Ha,' Mazzoleni said mournfully. 'Good luck with that!'

Ferdinando II approved Viviani's plan for a grand memorial to Galileo, which would have included public funeral orations and the construction of a marble mausoleum; but Pope Urban VIII denied permission for either. Fernandino submitted to this denial, and so Galileo's body was buried privately, in the novice's chapel of the Franciscan church of Santa Croce, in a chapel room under the campanile. This impromptu crypt was almost an unmarked grave.

But Pope Urban was sixty-four, while Vincenzio Viviani was only nineteen. When Urban died, in 1644 (at quarter after eleven one morning, and it was said that by noon his statues in Rome had all been pulled down and pulverized by angry mobs), Viviani had fifty-five more years of life to live, and every day of those years he devoted to the memory of the maestro. He paid for the design of a monument, to be located in San Croce across from the tomb of the great Michelangelo; their tombs would then make a matched pair, Art and Science together holding up the church. While he worked to get this monument approved and built, Viviani spent many years collecting all of Galileo's papers that he could find; and somewhere along the way he began writing a biography.

Once while he was at work on this project he found me in Arcetri and enlisted my help. 'What can you tell me about Signor Galileo, Cartophilus?'

'Nothing, Signor Viviani.'

'Come on, nothing? You must know something we don't know.'

'He had a hernia. And he had trouble sleeping.'

'All right, shut up then. But help me now to make a search of San Matteo.'

'How can we do that?'

It turned out he had a certificate from the local priest allowing us into the convent. He was hoping to find Galileo's letters to Maria Celeste, to add them to the immense collection of papers and notebooks and volumes that now filled an entire room of his house. So far Galileo's letters to his daughter had not been found, although they had to have numbered at least as many as the ones she had sent to him, a pile which Viviani possessed, still in their basket. Knowing Galileo's prolixity, and whom he had been writing to, this correspondence presumably formed a unique look into his thinking, and also a considerable physical mass, difficult to conceal, and now, for Viviani, of consuming interest.

But we couldn't find them. Whether the nuns had burned them for fear of harbouring some kind of heresy, which seemed the most likely of various bad explanations, or they had simply been thrown out or used to start kitchen fires, no one could say. They could not be found.

More years passed, and Viviani wrote his biography of the maestro in the most devoted, hagiographic terms possible. He got it published, but he could see that the big tomb he wanted was not going to get built in his lifetime. The Medici had lost their nerve, if they had ever had any in this matter, and Rome was implacable.

Finally, when Viviani was getting to be an old man himself, he had a plaque cast and affixed to the entryway to the little room where Galileo was buried in San Croce. He wrote into his will a request that he be buried in that same room. Then he took the front door off of his house, and turned the front façade of the building into a kind of archway. We helped him with the plastering of this façade, as Salvadore and Geppo had become bricklayers, and when that was done we cemented a bust of Galileo over the open doorway. This improvised memorial arch stood forlornly on the street of a shabby residential district of Florence, looking like the occasional architectural oddity you see in modest neighbourhoods when a homeowner has lost his mind with pride of ownership. Viviani was a bit like those people, in fact, but he was such a serious man, so devoted to all the good causes of the city, and always writing to scientists all over Europe, that it was hard to joke with him about it. We plastered long marble panels vertically into each side of the arch, and on these Viviani listed Galileo's accomplishments, painting the words on the marble very carefully as guides for me to chip away at with a chisel.

While we worked, he and I sometimes talked about the maestro and what was going on with his reputation. Viviani expressed great disdain for the Frenchman Descartes, who had been too chicken to publish anything controversial after Galileo's condemnation, but who had recently distributed a long critique of the maestro's *Discorsi* in which he listed no less than forty supposed mistakes, all but two of which were actually his own mistakes, Viviani judged, with Galileo in the right of it. I had to laugh when Viviani said that one of the things Descartes had got right was to scoff at Galileo for believing in the story of the burning mirrors of Archimedes.

Viviani, still offended by Descartes' impertinence, only shook his head at my pained laughter. Geppo and Salvadore tried to ignore his seriousness and distract him with teasing remarks about how funny his house was going to look after all this work, and how cold the entryway was going to be without a door, but he only stepped back to look at it again, and sighed. 'Someone's got to do it,' he said. 'Hopefully my nephews will pick up the torch.' He had never married or had children, and now he shook his head. 'I'm not sure about them, but I hope someone will do it.'

His had been a strange life, it occurred to me. To meet the maestro, blind and old, when you were seventeen; work with him till he died, when you were nineteen; then for the rest of your life, work for him still. I stopped my chipping and put a hand to his shoulder. 'Many will do it, Signor. You've made a good start. Saving his papers was huge. No one could have done that but you. You've been a faithful student, a real Galilean.'

So I thought, at that point. But the border between devotion and madness is so narrow. Several years later he came around to the little warren of low houses tucked behind San Matteo, and there he found me again, as ancient as ever, but no more so. It was impossible to tell how old I was. After a while it just seems like forever.

Viviani, on the other hand, was aging fast. It's hard to watch such mayfly lives. The end of the seventeenth century was near.

'Come help me,' he said now, face racked with urgency, but also with that high mystic serenity that people sometimes fall into when they begin a pilgrimage to a place where they believe everything can change.

I could have begged off then, but I didn't. He might have tried to haul me along with him bodily. Anyway it was a look that couldn't be denied, even after all these years. I followed him down to the back of San Matteo where their own little mausoleum was dug into the earth, crowded with dark holes to each side, like a giant honeycomb. It was dusk of the first night of carnival, and everyone in the village had gone down to Florence to see the parades and the fireworks. Everyone except for Geppo and Salvadore, it turned out, and also the short round crone who now swept the floors at San Croce: La Piera. Viviani had stayed in touch with her, as had I.

And he knew just which hole Maria Celeste's coffin was in. We heaved up on the end of it and tugged it back a little, by the light of a single candle lantern. The coffin weighed just the same as it would have if it were empty, but in that narrow passage we had a bad angle on it.

'Signor Viviani,' I said. 'This isn't a good idea.'

'Pull!'

So I kept pulling with them, until we had it out and turned so we could carry it out of the mausoleum. I held the bottom of it, Viviani led the way, Salvadore and Geppo took the sides. La Piera carried the lantern. We walked across the convent yard to a small donkey cart outside the gate, which had in it already some mason's tools and some dry mortar sand and a few buckets. We lifted up the coffin and placed it beside the sand, then covered it with a tarp.

Viviani took the donkey's rope and led us down the lane of Arcetri to the big road from the western hills, where we joined all the late traffic into the city. We looked like four poor servants, following our master and his donkey. Carnival revellers hooted and shouted as they rushed past us.

Down into Florence and its noise we trudged, across to San Croce, then we carried the coffin down the stairs into the novice's chapel. Inside the small room under the campanile, the brick tomb stood dark and dusty. Viviani took a sledge from Geppo and smashed it down on the top of the tomb.

'This is a terrible idea,' I said, looking down the stone passageway to the open door to the street. 'Someone will see us.'

'No one cares,' he said bitterly. 'No one will notice.'

'No one at all!' I said. 'Not even Galileo! He is dead, Signor.'

'He will see it from heaven.'

'In heaven they don't think about us. They're done with us, and happy to be so.'

He shrugged. 'You can't be sure.'

We pulled Galileo's heavy coffin out of its opened tomb, a much tougher job than moving his daughter. Following Viviani's directions, we then placed down in the tomb Maria Celeste's coffin, so pitifully light. It was like burying a cat. Salvadore and Geppo wedged a few crossbeams into the bricks over her coffin for support; then we replaced Galileo's coffin, right there on top of hers, as if to shield her from the sky.

The old boys brought a bucket of plaster down from their cart, and replaced the bricks at the top of the tomb one by one, plastering them into place over another set of bracing crossbeams.

There were noises in the street outside, and for a while we all froze in fear.

'This is so pointless,' I complained. 'The maestro is dead and gone. We could get in such trouble, and he'll never even know about it.'

'He would like it if he knew,' Viviani said.

*You, Occasion, walk ahead, precede my footsteps, open thousands
and thousands of different paths to me. Go irresolutely, unrecog-
nized and hidden, because I do not want my coming to be too easily
foreseen. Slap the faces of all seers, prophets, diviners, fortune-
tellers, and prognosticators. In one moment and simultaneously,
we go and come, rise and sit, stay and move. Let us then flow from
all, through all, in all, to all, here with gods, there with heroes, here
with people, there with beasts.*

— GIORDANO BRUNO, *The Expulsion of the
Triumphant Beast*

He would like it if he knew.

Maybe this is as good a way to put it as any. Just do what the
maestro would like. Viviani, who believed that the soul of the
dying Michelangelo had flown into baby Galileo at the moment
of his birth, the two having happened at nearly the same hour,
followed that principle all his life. He died a few years after our
carnival night, and he was buried next to Galileo, as he had
requested, without anyone noticing that the scientist's tomb had
been rebricked. By the time his nephew's heirs finally succeeded
in getting the approval of a pope – Clement XII, a Florentine –
for the construction of the elaborate tomb that Viviani had
advocated, it was 1737. When that tomb's construction was finished, they moved the coffins, and were surprised to find three
together in Galileo's little tomb. It was pretty obvious then what
had happened; and all three of the coffins were placed in the new
monument, right across the nave from Michelangelo's. Art and
Science, buried side by side! With a student and a poor Clare
included, wisping through the world unnoticed. From Galileo's
body they took a vertebra, a tooth, and three detached fingers,

574

for use as relics. The remainder of the three bodies are still there: Galileo, Maria Celeste, Vincenzio Viviani.

The rest of us moved on: forwards, backwards, sideways. I went to Holland, then England, then France, where I have been most of the time since. I've tended the entangler, and kept in touch with La Piera and Buonamici and Sestilia. The wars have been almost continuous. Huygens was a good man, Leibniz too. All in all we helped several people. All over Europe Galileo's ideas were taken up by the philosophers, and his methods by the scientists. Nevertheless very little scientific progress has been made, or progress of any kind, to be frank. And yet I notice no one is coming back in the entangler any more. Sometimes Hera checks in, but she doesn't tell me much, and it's painful to report to her what I've seen. The suffering is if anything getting worse, as populations rebound from the Black Death but epidemics remain virulent and unchecked. And people keep killing each other.

Somehow in all this protraction of years, watching all the lives rush by, Galileo keeps coming back to me. If La Piera was right, and we are alive when people are thinking about us, then Galileo is definitely still alive, coming back in us as I suppose he keeps coming back to that poisoned cellar floor: unkillable, boastful, sarcastic, self-regarding – all the obvious flaws, sure.

The good that he fought for is not so easy to express. But put it this way: he believed in reality. He believed in paying attention to it, and in learning what he could of it, and then saying what he had learned, even insisting on it. Then in trying to apply that knowledge to make things better, if he could. Put it this way: he believed in science.

But listen to me, because I saw it myself: science began as a Poor Clare. Science was broke and so it got bought. Science was scared and so did what it was told. It designed the gun and gave the gun to power, and power then held the gun to science's head and told it to make some more. How smart was that? Now science is in the position of having to invent a secret disabler of guns, and then start the whole process over. It's not clear it can work. Because all scientists are Galileos, poor, scared, gun to our head. Power lies elsewhere. If we can shift that power . . . that's the if. If we can shift history into a new channel, and avoid the nightmare centuries. If we can keep the promise of science, a promise hard to keep.

In fact, so far, so bad. When I made my first analepsis, so long ago that I shudder to think of it, history was little more than a long descent toward extinction, a matter of ever more devastating wars and genocides, famines and epidemics – growing immiseration for the bulk of humanity and the rest of life on Earth. When I taught young children history, and saw the look on their faces when they understood, I was ashamed.

So I left all that, left Ganymede to go with Ganymede. I joined his attempt to make a retrojection that would shove the nightmare a different way. If people would only understand earlier, we thought, that science is a religion, the most ethical religion, the most devoted and worshipful religion . . . Clearly I was wrong even to try. It isn't really possible. The paradoxes and entangled potentialities are the least of the problems. Worse by far is the enormous inertia of human weakness, greed, fear – all the sheer bloody mass of us. It's been a nightmare. I joined the nightmare, I helped to dream it. We went back that first time and interfered with Archimedes, we taught him things that got him killed; I got him killed. I could have saved him if I'd been fast enough, but I wasn't. I was too scared. I watched the soldier spear him, paralysed by fear. So I went back again with Ganymede, thinking I could make up for that – then, when I saw Ganymede doing his best to get Galileo burned at the stake, I started trying to make up for that too, trying to undo it, to stop it. Even though everything that happens happens. All at cross purposes. So many mistakes, so much misery. And yet here I am still. Why do I stay, why? It's not as if I've helped in any noticeable way. So far it seems I've mostly done harm. I stay for the sunlight, I suppose, for the wind and the rain and for Italy. But mostly I stay because I don't know what else to do.

And in fact I've stayed too long. The revolution has overtaken everything, Lavoisier was just guillotined yesterday, and I'm in a cell of the Bastille waiting my turn, which I think comes tomorrow. Sitting on stone in the dark, hearing the voices outside, I recall the poem that Machiavelli wrote after he was released from the prison where they tortured him, the place that taught him the lessons about power he tried so hard to pass on to the rest of us:

> *What disturbed me most*
> *Was that close to dawn while sleeping*
> *I heard chanting: 'per voi s'ora.'*

For you we are praying. I hope so. La Piera has the entangler, which would otherwise have been taken from me. Whether she and Buonamici and Sestilia will be able to meet me outside with it and help me out, I can't be sure. This may be it. One last night. I find it hard to believe, which no doubt explains my stoic lack of fear. If it happens it happens; I'm tired of the tumbrel of days. And if this turns out to be the end, in these last hours I'll be thinking hard. Imagination creates events, and by dawn I intend to have lived ten thousand years. Then my part of the tapestry will loop back in, the threads spreading out through the rest of the pattern.

And I'll be done with this story, which I tried so hard to stay out of. Some of it I saw, some of it Hera told me, some of it I made up – that's fine, that's the way it always is – some of it you made up too. Reality is always partly a creation of the observing consciousness. So I've said what I like; and I knew him well enough to think I got it mostly right. I know he was like us, always looking out for himself; and unlike us, in that he acted, while we often lack the courage to act. I wrote this for Hera, but no matter what time you are in when you read it, I'm sure that the history

577

you tell yourself is still a tale of mangled potentiality, of un-necessary misery. That's just the way it is. In all times people are greatly lacking in courage.

But sometimes they aren't. Sometimes they keep trying. This too is history. We are all history – the hopes of people in the past, the past of some future people – known to them, judged by them, changed by them as they use us. So the story keeps chan-ging, all of it. This too I've seen, and so I persist. I hope without hope. At some point the inclined plane can bottom out and the ball begin to rise. That's what science is trying to do. So far it hasn't worked, the story has been ugly, stupid, shameful, sure; but that can change. It can always change. Because understand: once I saw Galileo burned at the stake; then I saw him squeak his way clear. You have to imagine how that feels. It makes you have to try.

And so when sometimes you feel strange, when a pang tugs you or it seems like the moment has already happened – or when you look up in the sky and are surprised by the sight of bright Jupiter between clouds, and everything suddenly seems stuffed with a vast significance – consider that some other person some-where is entangled with you in time, and is trying to give some push to the situation, some little help to make things better. Then put your shoulder to whatever wheel you have at hand, what-ever moment you're in, and push too! Push like Galileo pushed! And together we may crab sideways toward the good.

Acknowledgements

But truly to find a way to adapt physical, metaphysical, and theological senses to words that may have been but a simple fantasy, not to say a chimera of your spokesman, redoubles in me my marvel at minds so acute and speculative.

— GALILEO, *letter to Liceti, 1640*

Thanks for help with this to:
Terry Bisson, Roland Boer, Linda Burbank, Sam Burbank, Joy Chamberlain, Joe Dumit, Dana Gioia, Jane Johnson, Chris McKay, Colin Milburn, Lisa Nowell, Katharine Park, David Robinson, Don Robinson, Carter Scholz, Ralph Vicinanza, and Joëlle Wintrebert.

A special thanks to Mario Biagioli.

Author's Note

*My book sprang wholly from the application of a special
sense, very difficult to describe. It is perhaps like a telescope
pointed at time.*

— MARCEL PROUST

The italicized passages in this novel are mostly from Galileo's
writing or that of his contemporaries, with a few visitors
from other times. I made some changes in these texts, and
many elisions that I did not mark, but I was always relying
on the translators who translated the source material from
Italian or Latin or French into English. In particular I would
like to acknowledge and thank Mary Allan-Olney, Mario
Biagioli, Henry Crew and Alfonso deSalvio, Giorgio de
Santillana, Stillman Drake, John Joseph Fahie, Ludovico
Geymonat, Maurice A. Finocchiaro, Pietro Redondi, James
Reston, Jr, Rinaldina Russell, Dava Sobel, and Albert van
Helden.

Despite the work of these translators and many more, not
all of Galileo's writing has yet been translated into English.
This is a real shame, not only for novelists writing novels
about him, but for anyone who doesn't speak Italian but does
speak English, and wants to learn more about the history of
science, or one of its greatest characters. His complete works
were first edited by Antonio Favaro at the turn of the last

century, then recently revised and updated by a communal effort. Surely some English-language history of science programme, or Italian department, or university press, could perform the great service of publishing a complete English translation of the *Opere*. The project could even be done as a wiki, in a communal online effort. I hope it happens. It would be good to read more of Galileo's words – even after this moment, when with the writing of this sentence he slips back into the pages. Good-bye maestro! Thank you!

Printed by RR Donnelley at Glasgow, UK